MW01469731

SCHOLARSHIP ALMANAC

7th Edition

THOMSON
PETERSON'S

Australia • Canada • Mexico • Singapore • Spain • United Kingdom • United States

About The Thomson Corporation and Peterson's

The Thomson Corporation, with 2002 revenues of US$7.8 billion, is a global leader in providing integrated information solutions to business and professional customers. The Corporation's common shares are listed on the Toronto and New York stock exchanges (TSX: TOC; NYSE: TOC). Its learning businesses and brands serve the needs of individuals, learning institutions, corporations, and government agencies with products and services for both traditional and distributed learning. Peterson's (www.petersons.com) is a leading provider of education information and advice, with books and online resources focusing on education search, test preparation, and financial aid. Its Web site offers searchable databases and interactive tools for contacting educational institutions, online practice tests and instruction, and planning tools for securing financial aid. Peterson's serves 110 million education consumers annually.

For more information, contact Peterson's, 2000 Lenox Drive, Lawrenceville, NJ 08648; 800-338-3282; or find us on the World Wide Web at www.petersons.com/about.

ISSN 0894-9336
ISBN 0-76891238-5

Printed in Canada

10 9 8 7 6 5 4 3 2 1   05 04 03

Seventh Edition

CONTENTS

Contents

Introduction

The news media seem to constantly remind us that a college education is expensive. It certainly appears to be beyond the means of many Americans. The sticker price for four years at state-supported colleges can be more than $40,000, and private colleges and universities could cost more than $100,000. And these costs continue to spiral upward!

But there is good news. The system operates to provide the needed money so that most families and students are able to afford a college education while making only a reasonable financial sacrifice. Although most families will have to plan on bearing the primary burden of college costs, almost all colleges truly want to admit students regardless of a family's ability to pay. Colleges will try to find various forms of student financial aid to make up enough of the difference between what a family can afford and what an education will cost so all admitted students will be able to enroll in the college that best fits their requirements.

First in any family's consideration is the large amount of federal government money available to students and parents in the form of scholarships, work-study salaries, and low-interest loans. Second, colleges themselves have increased their own student aid efforts, and many colleges also have ways to assist families who are not eligible for need-based assistance. These include an increasing number of merit scholarships as well as direct student loans and jobs and various forms of parental loans. Third, private sources of aid, including civic organizations, labor and trade groups, religious and ethnic groups, and associations provide billions of dollars in scholarship aid each year.

The college financial aid system is complex. It demands study, planning, calculation, flexibility, filling out forms, and meeting deadlines. However, for most people it can produce positive results. Because this may be the first guide to student financial aid that you buy, we have provided a quick review of the elements of this system in our three introductory chapters.

Most of the rest of this book is about the third stream of student financial aid—the $2-$3 billion made available annually by sources outside the colleges and college-channeled federal aid. Parents and students planning for college need to keep in mind that despite the immense size of this third stream and the tremendous help it can provide, it is a fraction of the $62 billion that comes from colleges and college-administered federal sources. If you find that you want a more complete explanation of the system, including details about the student financial aid programs offered by individual colleges, we recommend that you look at Peterson's *College Money Handbook,* which is available in bookstores, libraries, and guidance offices everywhere.

The System and How It Works: The ABCs of Paying for College

How Can You Pay for College?

There are four basic sources of funds you can use to pay for college:

1. Family resources, including income, savings, and borrowing
2. A student's contribution from savings, loans, and jobs
3. Need-based scholarships or grants
4. Aid that is based on factors other than financial need

Loans are borrowed money that must be repaid (either after graduation or while attending college); the amount you have to pay back is the total you have borrowed plus interest.

Scholarships and grants are outright gifts and do not have to be repaid.

A student's contribution (other than a loan) usually takes the form of student employment, or work-study, which is a job arranged for a student during the academic year.

Colleges are the primary contact point for most student financial aid. The college's financial aid office, using information submitted by you on the Free Application for Federal Student Aid (FAFSA), constructs an aid "package" that is awarded after the family contribution has been determined. In most cases, this package consists of a combination of grants, scholarships, loans, and work-study.

ESTIMATING COLLEGE COSTS

The starting point for organizing a plan to pay for your college education is to make a good estimate of the yearly cost. You can use the College Cost Worksheet on the next page to do this. Most colleges publish annual tuition and room and board charges in their catalogs and often include an estimate of how much a student can expect to spend for books and incidentals. Any college should be able to provide you with figures for the current year's tuition and mandatory fee charges, as well as estimates for room and board and other expenses.

Peterson's publishes a number of comprehensive guides, including Peterson's *Four-Year Colleges,* Peterson's *Two-Year Colleges*, and Peterson's *College Money Handbook*, that are one-stop resources for college cost information. You can find these in bookstores, libraries, and high school guidance offices.

To estimate your college costs for 2004–05, use 2003–04 tuition and fees and room and board figures, and inflate the numbers by 5 percent (or, if it is available, use the college's estimate for 2004–05 expenses). Add $750 for books and $1300 for personal expenses. If you will commute from your home, use $2000 instead of the college's given room and board charges and $900 for transportation. Finally, estimate the cost of two round trips if your home is more than a few hundred miles from the college. Add the items to calculate the total budget. You should now have a reasonably good estimate of college costs for 2004–05. (To determine the costs for later years, add 5 percent per year for a fairly accurate estimate.)

The next step is to evaluate whether or not you are likely to qualify for financial aid based on need. This step is critical, since more than 90 percent of the yearly total of $74.4 billion in student aid is awarded only after a determination is made that the family lacks sufficient financial resources to pay the full cost of college on its own. To judge your chance of receiving need-based aid, it is necessary to estimate an Expected Family Contribution (EFC) according to a government formula known as the Federal Methodology (FM). You can do so by referring to the Expected Family Contribution Table.

College Cost Worksheet

	College 1	College 2	College 3	Commuter College
Tuition and Fees	_____	_____	_____	_____
Room and Board	_____	_____	_____	$2000
Books	$ 750	$ 750	$ 750	$ 750
Personal Expenses	$1300	$1300	$1300	$1300
Travel	_____	_____	_____	$ 900
Total Budget	=====	=====	=====	=====

How Aid Matches Need

	COLLEGE X	COLLEGE Y
Cost of Attendance	$10,000	$24,000
− Expected Family Contribution	− 5500	− 5500
= Financial Need	$ 4500	$18,500
Financial Need	$ 4500	$18,500
− Grant Aid Awarded	− 675	−14,575
− Campus Job (Work-Study) Awarded	− 1400	− 1300
− Student Loan Awarded	− 2425	− 2625
= Unmet Need	0	0

Expected Family Contribution Table

Consult the following expected family contribution table using estimated 2003 income and likely asset holdings as of December 31, 2003. First, locate the approximate parental contribution in the table. If more than one family member will be in college at least half-time during 2004-05, divide the parental contribution by the number in college. If your child has savings, add 35 percent of that amount. If your child earned in excess of $2300 in 2003, include 50 percent of the amount over $2300 in the income figure. To see whether or not you might qualify for need-based aid, subtract the family contribution from each college's budget. If the family contribution is only a few thousand dollars over the budget, it is still worthwhile to apply for aid since this procedure is only intended to give you a preliminary estimate of college costs and your family contribution.

Table Used to Approximate Expected Family Contribution for 2004–05

		INCOME BEFORE TAXES								
ASSETS	FAMILY SIZE	$ 20,000	30,000	40,000	50,000	60,000	70,000	80,000	90,000	100,000
$ 20,000										
	3	$ 0	950	2,550	4,500	7,300	10,100	12,800	18,300	21,300
	4	0	160	1,750	3,450	5,800	8,600	11,350	16,800	19,800
	5	0	0	1,000	2,600	4,600	7,200	10,000	15,400	18,500
	6	0	0	200	1,800	3,500	5,700	8,400	13,800	16,900
$ 30,000										
	3	$ 0	950	2,550	4,500	7,300	10,100	12,800	18,300	21,300
	4	0	160	1,750	3,450	5,800	8,600	11,350	16,800	19,800
	5	0	0	1,000	2,600	4,600	7,200	10,000	15,400	18,500
	6	0	0	200	1,800	3,500	5,700	8,400	13,800	16,900
$ 40,000										
	3	$ 0	950	2,550	4,500	7,300	10,100	12,800	18,300	21,300
	4	0	160	1,750	3,450	5,800	8,600	11,350	16,800	19,800
	5	0	0	1,000	2,600	4,600	7,200	10,000	15,400	18,500
	6	0	0	200	1,800	3,500	5,700	8,400	13,800	16,900
$ 50,000										
	3	$ 0	950	2,550	4,800	7,700	10,500	13,300	18,700	21,800
	4	0	160	1,750	3,700	6,200	9,000	11,800	17,200	20,300
	5	0	0	1,000	2,800	4,900	7,600	10,400	15,800	18,900
	6	0	0	200	2,000	3,800	6,100	8,800	14,200	17,300
$ 60,000										
	3	$ 0	950	2,550	5,200	8,300	11,100	13,800	19,300	22,300
	4	0	160	1,750	4,100	6,700	9,600	12,400	17,800	20,900
	5	0	0	1,000	3,100	5,400	8,200	11,000	16,400	19,500
	6	0	0	200	2,300	4,100	6,600	9,400	14,800	17,900
$ 80,000										
	3	$ 0	950	2,550	6,200	9,400	12,200	15,000	20,400	23,500
	4	0	160	1,750	4,800	7,800	10,700	13,500	18,900	22,000
	5	0	0	1,000	3,800	6,300	9,300	12,100	17,500	20,600
	6	0	0	200	2,800	4,900	7,700	10,500	15,900	19,000

	ASSETS	$ 20,000	30,000	40,000	50,000	60,000	70,000	80,000	90,000	100,000
										INCOME BEFORE TAXES
	$100,000									
FAMILY SIZE	3	$ 0	950	2,550	7,200	10,500	13,300	16,100	21,500	24,600
	4	0	160	1,750	5,700	9,000	11,800	14,600	20,000	23,100
	5	0	0	1,000	4,500	7,400	10,500	13,200	18,600	21,700
	6	0	0	200	3,400	5,800	8,800	11,600	17,000	20,100
	$120,000									
FAMILY SIZE	3	$ 0	950	2,550	8,300	11,600	14,400	17,200	22,600	25,700
	4	0	160	1,750	6,700	10,100	12,900	15,700	21,100	24,200
	5	0	0	1,000	5,400	8,500	11,600	14,300	19,800	22,800
	6	0	0	200	4,100	6,800	10,000	12,800	18,200	21,300
	$140,000									
FAMILY SIZE	3	$ 0	950	2,550	9,500	12,800	15,600	18,400	23,800	26,800
	4	0	160	1,750	7,800	11,200	14,100	16,900	22,300	25,400
	5	0	0	1,000	6,300	9,700	12,700	15,500	20,900	24,000
	6	0	0	200	4,900	7,900	11,100	13,900	19,300	22,400

SCHOLARSHIPS

What Are Scholarships? What Importance Should You Give Them?

The word "scholarship" can cause confusion. Precise usage limits the use of scholarship to "free money" given to students to help cover educational costs. However, many people, including college financial aid officials and program sponsors, use the word generically to refer to all forms of student gift aid, including fellowships and grants, especially if a program covers both undergraduate and graduate levels of study. In the profiles of scholarship programs in this book, we use whatever term the sponsor uses.

However, so that you are aware of the differences in meaning when you encounter the terms, here are further definitions:

- *Scholarships:* Undergraduate gift aid that is used to pay educational costs.

- *Need-Based Scholarships:* Gift aid based on demonstrated need. Need, as defined by colleges and the federal government, is the difference between the cost of attending a college and the EFC, which is determined by a federal and/or institutional formula.

- *Merit-Based Scholarships:* Financial aid based on criteria other than financial need, including academic major, career goals, grades, test scores, athletic ability, hobbies, talents, place of residence or birth, ethnic identity, religious affiliation, your own or your parents' military or public safety service, disability, union membership, employment history, community service, or club affiliations. The preponderance of scholarship programs described in this book are merit based, although many also use need to set the size of the award.

- *Grants:* Graduate or postdoctoral awards to support specific research or other projects. Grants cover expenses directly related to carrying out the proposed research (e.g., materials, interview costs, or computer time). Sometimes a grant includes allowances for travel and living expenses incurred while conducting research away from the home institution. Usually, living expenses at the home university are not covered. (NOTE: The word grant is also used to refer to undergraduate gift aid, for example, the Federal Pell Grant.)

- *Fellowships:* Graduate- and postgraduate-level awards to individuals to cover their living expenses while they take advanced courses, carry out research, or work on a project. Some fellowships include a tuition waiver.

- *Prizes:* Money given in recognition of an outstanding achievement. Prizes often are awarded to winners of competitions.

- *Internships:* A defined period of time working in the intern's field of interest with and under the supervision of the professional staff of a host organization. Often the intern works part-time or during the summer. Some internships offer stipends in the form of an hourly wage or fixed allowance.

- *Assistantships:* Graduate-level awards, usually waiving all or some tuition, plus an allowance for living expenses. In return, the recipient works at teaching or research facilities. Teaching assistants teach in their field of study. Research assistants often work on projects related to their dissertation or thesis.

- *Work-Study:* When capitalized, Work-Study refers to a federally supported program that provides students with part-time employment during the school year. The federal government pays part of the student's salary. Employers are usually college departments. Local agencies also can participate in the program. Eligibility for Federal Work-Study is based on demonstrated need. Work-study (not capitalized) is used to describe any student job in an aid package.

Sources of financial aid include private agencies, foundations, corporations, clubs, fraternal and service organizations, civic associations, unions, and religious groups. These sponsors provide grants, scholarships, and low-interest loans. Some employers also provide tuition reimbursement benefits for employees and their dependents.

It is always worthwhile to look into scholarships that can be found beyond the college financial aid office's network. For a family that does not qualify for need-based aid, these "outside" scholarships and merit scholarships available from colleges are the only form of gift aid available. No matter what your situation regarding need-based aid, scholarships from noninstitutional sources (those not administered by colleges or the U.S. Department of Education) are almost always useful. Be aware that the amounts received from "outside" scholarships to pay tuition and expenses may be deducted from the amount of aid offered in your college financial aid package. An "outside" scholarship may prove most useful in reducing the loan and work-study components of the college-offered package.

Use the following checklist when investigating merit scholarships:

- Take advantage of any scholarships for which you are automatically eligible based on employer benefits, military service, association or church membership, other affiliations, or student or parent attributes (ethnic background, nationality, etc.). Company or union tuition remissions are the most common examples of these awards.

- Look for other awards for which you might be eligible based on the characteristics and affiliations indicated above, but where there is a selection process and an application required. Peterson's *Scholarship Almanac* provides information about the largest scholarship programs, but there are thousands of smaller programs that may be right for you. Scholarship directories, such as Peterson's *Scholarships, Grants & Prizes*, which details more than 3,000 scholarship programs, are useful resources.

- See if your state has a merit scholarship program. Also, check to see if the state scholarships are "portable," meaning they can be used in other states or must be used at in-state institutions.

- Look into national scholarship competitions. High school guidance counselors usually know about these scholarships. Examples of these awards are the National Merit Scholarship, Coca-Cola Scholarship, Aid Association for Lutherans, Intel Science Talent Search, and the U.S. Senate Youth Program.

- ROTC (Reserve Officers' Training Corps) scholarships are offered by the Army, Navy, Marines, and Air Force. A full ROTC scholarship covers all tuition, fees, and textbook costs. Acceptance of an ROTC scholarship entails a commitment to take military science courses and to serve as an officer in the sponsoring branch of the service. Competition is heavy, and preference may be given to students in certain fields of study, such as engineering science. Application procedures vary by service. Contact an armed services recruiter or your high school guidance counselor for further information.

- Investigate community scholarships. High school guidance counselors usually have a list of these awards, and announcements are published in the town newspaper. Most common are awards given by service organizations such as the American Legion, Rotary International, and the local women's club.

- If you are strong academically (for example, a National Merit Commended Scholar or better), or very talented in fields such as athletics or performing/creative arts, you may want to consider colleges that offer their own merit awards to gifted students they wish to enroll.

Federal Scholarship Programs

The federal government is the single largest source of financial aid for students, accounting for about $62 billion available annually. At the present time there are two federal grant programs—the Federal Pell Grant and the Federal Supplemental Educational Opportunity Grant (FSEOG); three loan programs—the Federal Perkins Loan, the Direct Loan, and the Stafford Loan; and a job program that helps colleges provide jobs for students—Federal Work-Study (FWS).

The application and need evaluation process is controlled by Congress and the U.S. Department of Education. The application is the Free Application for Federal Student Aid (FAFSA). In addition, nearly every state that offers student assistance uses the federal government's system to award its own aid. By completing the FAFSA, you automatically apply for state aid. However, you should check with your state Higher Education agency or high school guidance counselor for any other forms that may be required in addition to the FAFSA. (NOTE: In addition to the FAFSA, some colleges also ask the family to complete the PROFILE® application.)

The FAFSA is your "passport" to receiving your share of the billions of dollars awarded annually in need-based aid. If the college cost worksheet shows that you might qualify for aid, pick up a FAFSA from your high school guidance office after mid-November. The form will ask for your current year's financial data, and it should be filed after January 1, in time to meet the earliest college or state scholarship deadline. Online application can be made by accessing the FAFSA Web site at www.fafsa.ed.gov/. Both the student and at least one parent should apply for a federal PIN number at http://www.pin.ed.gov. The PIN serves as your electronic signature when applying for aid on the Web. Within two to four weeks after you submit the form, you will receive a summary of the FAFSA information, which is called the Student Aid Report (SAR). The SAR will give you your EFC and also allow you to make corrections to the data you submitted.

Federal Pell Grant

The Federal Pell Grant is the largest grant program: more than 4.3 million students receive awards annually. This grant is intended to be the starting point of assistance for lower-income families. Eligibility for a Federal Pell Grant depends on your EFC. The amount you receive will depend on your EFC and the cost of education at the college you will attend. The highest award depends on how much the program is funded. The maximum for the 2002–03 school year ranged from $400 to $4000. The maximum for 2003–04 is $4050.

To give you some idea of your possible eligibility for a Federal Pell Grant, the following table may be helpful. The amounts shown are based on a family size of 4, with 1 in college, no emergency expenses, no contribution from student income or assets, and college costs of at least $4000 per year.

Table Used to Estimate Federal Pell Grants for 2003–04

Adjusted Gross Income	Family Assets							
	$50,000	$55,000	$60,000	$65,000	$70,000	$75,000	$80,000	$85,000
$ 5000	$4000	$4000	$4000	$4000	$4000	$4000	$4000	$4000
$10,000	4000	4000	4000	4000	4000	4000	4000	4000
$15,000	4000	4000	4000	4000	4000	3950	3750	3650
$20,000	3650	3450	3250	3150	3050	2950	2850	2750
$25,000	2750	2550	2450	2350	2150	2050	1950	1750
$30,000	1750	1650	1550	1450	1350	1250	950	650
$35,000	1250	1150	950	750	450	400	—	—

Note: Based on family of four, one child enrolled in college, oldest parent age 41.

Federal Supplemental Educational Opportunity Grant (FSEOG)

As its name implies, the Federal Supplemental Educational Opportunity Grant provides additional need-based federal grant money to supplement the Federal Pell Grant. Each participating college is given funds to award to especially needy students. The maximum award is $4000 per year, but the amount you receive depends on the college's policy, the availability of FSEOG funds, the total cost of education, and the amount of other aid awarded.

Federal Financial Aid Programs

Name of Program	Type of Program	Maximum Award Per Year
Federal Pell Grant	Need-based grant	$4000
Federal Supplemental Educational Opportunity Grant	Need-based grant	$4000
Federal Work-Study	Need-based part-time job	no maximum
Federal Perkins Loan	Need-based loan	$4000
Subsidized Stafford Direct Loan	Need-based student loan	$2625 (first year)
Unsubsidized Stafford Direct Loan	Non-need-based student loan	$2625 (first year, dependent student)
PLUS Loan	Non-need-based parent loan	Up to the cost of education

Note: Both Direct and Stafford Loans have higher maximums after the freshman year. Students who meet the federal qualifications for independent status are eligible for increased loan limits in these programs.

College-Based Gift Aid

Next to the federal government, colleges provide the largest amount of financial aid to students. In addition, they control most of the money channeled to students from the federal government.

College need-based scholarships frequently are figured into students' financial aid packages. Most colleges award both need- and merit-based scholarships, although a small number of colleges (most notably the Ivy League) offer only need-based scholarships. Colleges may offer merit-based scholarships to freshmen with specific academic strengths, talents in the creative or performing arts, special achievements or activities, and a wide variety of particular circumstances. Some of these circumstances are parents in specific professions; residents of particular geographic areas; spouses, children, and siblings of other students; and students with disabilities.

A college's financial aid office can inform you about the need-based scholarships available from that college. Usually, the admissions office is the primary source to get information about any merit-based scholarships the college offers. Some colleges have information about their scholarships on their Web sites. Peterson's *College Money Handbook* is a one-stop reference guide to the financial aid programs at more than 2,100 four-year colleges and universities. You may notice that private colleges usually have larger financial aid programs, but public colleges are usually less expensive, especially for in-state students.

Colleges have different requirements regarding necessary financial aid application forms. Be prepared to check early with the colleges you are interested in about which forms they need. All colleges require the FAFSA for students applying for federal aid. The other most commonly required form is PROFILE®, the College Scholarship Service's financial aid form. To see if the college you are applying to requires PROFILE®, read the financial aid section of the admission material.

Athletic Scholarships

Some scholarships for athletic ability or participation are available from various noninstitutional sources, but the great preponderance comes directly from the colleges themselves. Athletic scholarships may be the most widely used single category of merit scholarship, and certainly they are the most widely known and sought by students. Athletic scholarships are controlled by the coaches in the athletic department of a college.

Most financial aid provided on the basis of athletic ability or achievement is in the form of scholarship aid. Loans for athletic participation are uncommon. Some coaches may describe the aid that they are offering to athletes as scholarships, when the aid really is in the form of a loan. If you believe that you are being offered a scholarship (that is money *given* to you based on need or athletic ability), insist that it be confirmed in writing and that it is not a loan or "indebtedness." Remember, scholarship money is *given* to you, while loans must be repaid. Be sure you are clear about which type of aid a coach may be offering.

Athletes who are good enough even to consider competing at the collegiate level frequently dream of being awarded an athletic scholarship, whether or not their family can afford to pay for their education. Potential college athletes want to be "on scholarship" because it is a reward, an honor, a status symbol. An athletic scholarship is a reward for your hard work and success in high school or junior college. It is a status symbol because it tells other students that the college wants and needs you at least as much as you want to attend the college.

Many students struggle to pay for their years in college, while the athlete with a full scholarship (tuition, room, board, a book allowance) cashes in just for being an athlete. This may give you high status in the minds of many students, but it has a downside in two ways. First, athletic scholarships sometimes generate resentment and jealousy among other students. Where money is available to "buy" athletes, there is a temptation to bring in star athletes who might not meet the same academic standards that others must meet. Nonathlete students may resent the "free ride" that athletes get, while they have to work, save their money, deplete their savings and other assets, go begging to their parents, fill out numerous forms, wait in long financial aid lines, and hunt for money to make ends meet in college.

A second problem for scholarship athletes is that coaches often demand a tight reign over the athletes to whom they have given money. Many coaches believe they have a right to control their investment. As a scholarship athlete, you run the risk of being treated as an employee with much of your life being governed by your coach. Athletes who have scholarships might lose their place on the team if they displease the coach or if they do not perform up to the coach's expectations. If you need that money to continue in college, having it taken away could be devastating. You might not have even chosen that school if not for the scholarship. But even if you do not absolutely need the money to pay for your education, losing the scholarship could mean a struggle to find new sources of money, often after the financial aid application season has passed and the available funds have been awarded to other students.

According to current national athletic association guidelines and practices, athletic scholarships are given on a one-year, renewable basis. While your coach may have "sold" you on his or her college with the promise of having your entire education paid by an athletic scholarship, the money and free tuition could disappear at the end of any year, leaving you to search for some other way to pay for the rest of your education. Worse, if you then want to transfer to another college, you lose a season of eligibility for athletics. The chances of getting another athletic scholarship elsewhere are much less if the coach at your new school will not be able to use your talents until the following year.

So, if you are eligible to be a scholarship athlete, the primary question you must decide is whether you want *and* need an athletic scholarship or whether you just want one. The status and honor that may come with an athletic scholarship can be enjoyable, but is it worth the cost? While some coaches feel more of a commitment to athletes who are their "employees," other coaches will appreciate it if you get funds for college in some other way, freeing up a scholarship for them to offer to another athlete.

In any case, the availability of an athletic scholarship should not be your primary reason for selecting one college over another. There are too many nonathletic sources of financial aid available for you to let the offer of an athletic scholarship determine which school you attend.

Who Gets Scholarship Offers?

Most athletic scholarships at schools with top-level teams are reserved for the best high school and junior college athletes, the ones who have established a reputation in their sport. Especially in football and men's basketball, college coaches do much of their hunting for talent with the help of computer-based scouting services, which keep records of the statistics of the nation's best prospects. Athletes at that level—"blue-chip" prospects—do not have to search for athletic scholarships; recruiters come knocking at *their* door (sometimes knocking *down* the door). Occasionally an unrecruited athlete in those sports (a "walk-on") may be given a partial or full scholarship after proving him- or herself under fire.

Virtually all NCAA Division I schools (except for the Ivy League and Patriot League colleges) offer athletic scholarships, and in most sports the coach does his or her own scouting rather than using computerized scouting services. The same is true at Division II schools, a lower level of athletic competition. These schools are allowed fewer scholarships, and many of these cover only part of the educational costs. Division III NCAA schools—the lowest level—are not allowed to offer scholarships directly for athletic talent, yet most of them still scout high school and junior college prospects.

NCAA colleges may compete at a particular level in one sport and at another level in other sports. For example, a school with a

Division II basketball team (athletic scholarships allowed) may field a Division III soccer team (no athletic scholarships). While this may be confusing, you only need to be concerned about the level at which they field a team in *your* sport.

Many colleges affiliated with the NAIA (National Association for Intercollegiate Athletics) also offer scholarships. These schools are among the smaller and lesser known, so they generally do not have as much money to put into athletic scholarships. A number of junior colleges, or community colleges, also offer athletic scholarships. As at NCAA Division II schools, NAIA and junior college scholarships are more likely to be partial (i.e., quarter, half, or tuition-only) rather than "full rides."

Athletic scholarships for women have increased tremendously in recent years. In large part, this is a result of Title IX (part of a federal law called the Education Amendments of 1972). Within this law, colleges must provide athletic scholarship aid to female and male athletes in proportion to their enrollment. Also, all resources, support, and opportunities to compete in athletics must be shared equitably by men and women. Title IX was reinforced in 1997 by a Supreme Court ruling in a case filed by women student-athletes against Brown University.

Despite these advances, the opportunities women have for obtaining athletic scholarships at some schools still may lag behind the financial aid offered to men. Once you are in college and can see what types and amounts of aid are available to female athletes as compared to male athletes, you will be in a better position to determine whether female athletes are being discriminated against at that school. Contact the campus affirmative action office and ask its staff to look into the situation if you think that female athletes are not getting their fair share. You may be considered a troublemaker by some people in the athletic department, but you deserve what the law allows and should be allowed to stand up for your rights.

How to Generate an Offer

While colleges at all levels of athletic competition scout and recruit athletes, those at levels *below* Division I of the NCAA are more likely to consider information submitted by an individual student seeking an athletic scholarship. The amount of scholarship money available each year in any given sport varies greatly, and even if recruiters have not been knocking down your door, you still may have the chance to get a scholarship offer if you follow the approach described below:

1. Draw up a preliminary list of colleges that meet the criteria that are important to you, such as location, size, overall cost, type of academic environment, availability of particular academic programs or majors, and sports opportunities. (You should check on whether the school has a junior varsity team in case you do not make the varsity your first year.)

2. Find out the name of the head coach in your sport at the colleges on your list. Starting with the top contenders on your preliminary list (three to six colleges), write a letter to the head coach at each school. In the letter describe several important reasons why you want to attend his or her college. Explain that you are interested in competing on the team and that you would like to know what sources of financial aid are available for athletes. Don't be shy about telling the coach of your athletic strengths, including statistics (true ones!), that might generate the coach's interest in you. Include copies of newspaper write-ups and action photos, if you have them. A videotape of you in competition can also help in selling yourself to the coach. That is what you are really doing, *selling yourself.* There is absolutely no shame in that. In fact, it is good practice for when you graduate and have to sell an employer on your qualifications and accomplishments.

3. If you do not receive encouragement from the first group of head coaches you write to, work down your list of college choices. There are no guarantees, but using this process certainly is more likely to result in finding athletic-related financial aid than doing nothing.

4. Ask your current or former coach to write a letter on your behalf to specific coaches on your list. A letter to a specific, named coach carries more weight than a generic letter to any coach (i.e., "Dear Coach"). The letter of recommendation should stress how much of an asset you have been to your team and would be on that coach's team. Letters from two coaches are better than one, three are better than two, etc.

Seldom will a coach offer financial aid to an athlete sight unseen. Since most coaches operate with a tight recruiting budget, you may have to pay your own travel expenses to see a coach who shows some interest. If you are then offered financial aid—full or partial scholarship, loans, work-study, or some combination—your efforts have paid off *and* that coach knows you as more than just another "wanna-be." He or she knows that you are hungry to compete on that team and that you are an aggressive seeker of success, a trait all coaches want in their athletes. But beware when a coach promises financial aid in the future, if things work out. The coach may come through for you, but do not bank on such promises because they are "written on air."

Even if, after all that effort, you receive no athletics-related financial aid, you are likely to be in a better position to be accepted by the school and to be considered for other types of aid not directly tied to athletics. Students who have special talents—i.e., those who are "well-rounded" and take the initiative to make these talents known—are often more desired by schools than those who present only academic credentials. If you get only a partial athletic scholarship or none at all—like the majority of college athletes—you may be eligible for financial aid based on need.

Great athletes and good ones are sometimes tempted to accept—or even to ask for—money or other financial benefits beyond the amount for which the rules allow. It is not worth whatever "extra" you might get, since there are penalties and other liabilities. For example, in 1997, the University of Massachusetts men's basketball team forfeited its "Final Four" standing (achieved a few years before) and had to return $151,000 because one of its players took money that he should not have. Why compromise friendships, your teammates' goals, your own ethics, possibly your athletic career, and even your chance at the aid you deserve by trying to take more than you should?

State and Local Scholarships

Each state government has established one or more financial aid programs for qualified students. Usually, only legal residents of the state are eligible to benefit from such programs. However, some are available to out-of-state students attending colleges within the state. In addition to residential status, other qualifications frequently exist. States may also offer internship or work-study programs, graduate fellowships and grants, or low-interest loans in addition to grant and forgivable loan programs.

If you are interested in learning more about state-sponsored programs, the state higher education office should be able to provide information. Information brochures and application forms for state scholarship programs are usually available in your high school guidance office or from a college financial aid office in your state.

Increasingly, state government agencies are putting state scholarship information on their Web sites. The financial aid page of state-administered college or university sites frequently has a list of state-sponsored scholarships and financial aid programs. You can access college and university Web sites easily through Peterson's Education Center (www.petersons.com).

Businesses, community service clubs, and local organizations often sponsor scholarship programs for residents of a specific town or county. These can be attractive to a scholarship seeker because the odds of winning can be higher than they would be for scholarships that draw from a wider pool of applicants. However, because the information network at the local level is spotty, it is often difficult to find information about their existence. Some of the best sources of information about these local programs are high school guidance offices, community college financial aid offices, high school district administrative offices, and public libraries. In addition, you may want to check with the local offices of organizations that traditionally sponsor scholarships, such as the International Kiwanis Club, the Benevolent and Protective Order of Elks, the Lions Club International, or the National Association of American Business Clubs (AMBUCS).

Private Aid

Billions of dollars are given every year by private donors to students and their families to help with the expenses of a college education. Last year, noninstitutional and nongovernment sponsors gave more than $3 billion in financial aid to help undergraduate students pay for college costs.

Foundations, fraternal and ethnic organizations, community service clubs, churches and religious groups, philanthropies, companies and industry groups, labor unions and public employees' associations, veterans' groups, and trusts and bequests all make up a large network of possible sources.

It is always worthwhile for any prospective student to look into these scholarships, but they are especially important to students who do not qualify for need-based financial aid, to students and families who wish to supplement the aid being given by governmental or university sources, and to students who possess special abilities, achievements, or personal qualifications (e.g., memberships in church or civic organizations, specific ethnic backgrounds, parents who served in the armed forces, etc.) that fit the criteria of one or more of the various private scholarship sponsors.

Some factors that can affect eligibility for these awards, such as ethnic heritage and parental status, are beyond a student's control. Other criteria, such as academic, scientific, technological, athletic, artistic, or creative merit, are not easily or quickly met unless one has previously committed himself or herself to a particular endeavor. However, eligibility for many programs is within your control, especially if you plan ahead. For example, you can start or keep up current membership in a church or civic organization, participate in volunteer service efforts, or pursue an interest, from amateur radio to golf to raising animals to writing and more. Any of these actions might give you an edge for a particular scholarship or grant.

The eligibility criteria for private scholarships, grants, and prizes are a real mosaic; they vary widely and include financial need as well as personal characteristics and merit. The number and amounts of the awards available from individual sponsors can vary each year depending upon the number of grantees, fund contributions, and other factors. However, practically anyone can find awards to fit his or her individual circumstances.

Peterson's *Scholarship Almanac* was created to provide students and their families access to the biggest and most lucrative private financial aid programs. In this publication you will find detailed information about the top 500 scholarship/grant programs and prize sources. Peterson's *Scholarships, Grants & Prizes* is a comprehensive guide to the more than 3,000 scholarship/grant programs and prize sources that will provide more than 1.6 million financial awards to undergraduates in the 2004–05 school year.

SOURCES OF COLLEGE FINANCING OTHER THAN SCHOLARSHIPS

Financing strategies are important because the high cost of a college education today often requires families, whether or not they receive aid, to think about stretching the payment for college beyond the four-year period of enrollment. For high-cost colleges it is not unreasonable to think about a 10-4-10 plan: ten years of saving; four years of paying college bills out of current income, savings, and borrowing; and ten years to repay a parental loan.

Family Savings

Although saving for college is always a good idea, many families are unclear about its advantages. Families do not save for two reasons. First, after expenses have been covered, many families do not have much money to set aside. An affordable but regular savings plan through a payroll deduction is usually the answer to the problem of spending your entire paycheck every month.

The second reason that saving for college is not a high priority is the belief that the financial aid system penalizes a family by lowering aid eligibility. The Federal Methodology determination is very kind to savers. In fact, savings are ignored completely for families that earn less than $50,000 and who are eligible to file a short form federal tax return (1040A or EZ). Savings in the form of home equity and retirement plans are excluded from the calculation. And even when savings are counted, a maximum of 5.6 percent of the total is expected each year. In other words, if a family has $40,000 in savings after an asset protection allowance is considered, the contribution is no greater than $2240, an amount very close to the yearly interest that is accumulated. Therefore, it is possible for a family to meet its savings contribution without depleting the face value of its investments.

A sensible savings plan is important because of the financial advantage of saving compared to borrowing. The amount of money students borrow for college is now greater than the amount they receive in grants and scholarships. With loans becoming so widespread, savings should be carefully considered as an alternative to borrowing. Your incentive for saving is that a dollar saved is a dollar not borrowed.

Several state governments are enacting new programs to help families save for college education. There are two basic categories of these programs. Under a prepaid or guaranteed tuition program, in exchange for early tuition purchase (usually in installments), a tuition rate is locked in at the plan's participating colleges or universities, almost always public institutions. In a college savings plan trust program, participants save money in a special college savings account on behalf of a prospective student. These accounts usually have a guaranteed minimum return and offer favorable treatment for state and federal taxes. In many cases, the interest earned in these programs will result in no tax liability. You should check with your state's higher education agency for more details.

Work-Study and Jobs

Federal Work-Study (FWS)

The Federal Work-Study program provides jobs for students who need financial aid to pay for their educational expenses. Funds from the federal government and the college (or the employer) pay the salary. The student works on an hourly basis on or off campus and must be paid at least the federal minimum wage. Students may earn only up to the amount awarded, which depends on the calculated financial need and the total amount of money available to the college.

Many colleges, after assigning jobs to students who qualify for Federal Work-Study (FWS), offer other part-time positions to nonqualifying students from regular college funds. In fact, at many colleges, the ratio is about 50-50, meaning half are employed under the FWS program while the other half are paid directly by the college. Students who qualify for FWS are usually assigned jobs through the student employment office. Other students should contact the Career Planning Office, or check with individual offices and departments for possible openings. In addition, there are usually off-campus employment opportunities available to everyone.

AmeriCorps

AmeriCorps is a national umbrella group of service programs for a limited number of students. Participants work in a public or private nonprofit agency providing service to the community in one of four priority areas: education, human services, the environment, and public safety. In exchange, they earn a stipend of $7400 to $14,800 a year for living expenses and up to $4725 for two years to apply toward college expenses. Students can work either before, during, or after they go to college and can use the funds to either pay current educational expenses or repay federal student loans. Speak to a college financial aid officer for more details about this program and any other new initiatives available to students.

Cooperative Education Programs

Co-op programs, also known as cooperative education, are special programs usually administered at the departmental level. A formal arrangement with off-campus employers allows students to combine work and study, either at the same time or in alternating terms. Generally, these programs begin at the end of the sophomore year and add a year or a semester to the length of the degree program. Co-op programs enable students to earn regular marketplace wages while gaining experience, often specifically related to the field they are studying. The National Commission for Cooperative Education, 360 Huntington Avenue, Boston, Massachusetts 02115-5096, 617-373-3770, is a central source of information about these programs.

Loans

In addition to scholarships and work-study, there are loan opportunities available for all students. The federal loan programs are called the Stafford and Direct. Student and parent loans are provided by both programs. Some of the organizations that sponsor scholarships, such as the Air Force Aid Society, also provide loans.

For those students who demonstrate need, the interest on the loans is paid by the federal government during the time the student is in school. If you do not demonstrate financial need, or your need has been met with other forms of aid, you can apply for the unsubsidized Stafford or Direct Loan. Unsubsidized loans begin to accrue interest as soon as the money is received.

Federal Perkins Loan

This loan is a low-interest (5 percent) loan for students with exceptional financial need. Federal Perkins Loans are made through the college's financial aid office with the college as the lender. Students may borrow a maximum of $4000 per year for up to five years of undergraduate study. They may take up to ten years to repay the loan, beginning nine months after they graduate, leave school, or drop below half-time status. No interest accrues while they are in school and, under certain conditions (e.g., they teach in low-income areas, work in law enforcement, are full-time nurses or medical technicians, serve as Peace Corps or VISTA volunteers, etc.), some or all of the loan can be canceled or payments deferred.

Stafford and Direct Loans

Stafford and Direct Loans have the same interest rates, loan maximums, deferments, and cancellation benefits. A Stafford Loan may be borrowed from a commercial lender such as a bank or credit union. A Direct Loan is borrowed directly from the U.S. Department of Education. Once you have decided on the college you plan to attend, the financial aid office will inform you of the program it participates in and advise you on all application procedures.

The interest rate varies annually up to a maximum of 8.25 percent. If you qualify for a need-based subsidized Stafford Loan, the interest is paid by the federal government while you are enrolled in college. There is also an unsubsidized Stafford Loan that is not based on need, for which you are eligible regardless of your family income.

The maximum amount dependent students may borrow in any one year is $2625 for freshmen, $3500 for sophomores, and $5500 for juniors and seniors, with a maximum of $23,000 for the total undergraduate program. The maximum amount independent students can borrow is $6625 for freshmen (of which no more than $2625 can be subsidized), $7500 for sophomores (of which no more than $3500 can be subsidized), and $10,500 for juniors and seniors (of which no more than $5500 can be subsidized). Borrowers must pay a fee of up to 4 percent of the loan, which is deducted from the loan proceeds.

To apply for a Stafford Loan, you must first complete a FAFSA to determine eligibility for a subsidized loan followed by a separate loan application that is submitted to a lender. The financial aid office can help in selecting a lender, or you can contact your state department of higher education to find a participating lender. The lender will send a promissory note indicating that you have agreed to repay the loan. The proceeds of the loan, less the origination fee, will be sent to your college to be either credited to your account or released to you. Longer term repayment plans may be available depending on your overall debt level, income, and other factors.

If you qualify for a subsidized Stafford Loan, you do not have to pay interest while in school. For an unsubsidized Stafford Loan, you will be responsible for paying the interest from the time the loan is established. However, some lenders will permit borrowers to delay making payments and will add the interest to the loan. Once the repayment period starts, borrowers of both subsidized and unsubsidized Stafford Loans will have to pay a combination of interest and principal monthly for up to ten years.

PLUS Loans

PLUS is for parents of dependent students to help families who may not have the cash available to pay their share of the charges. There is no needs test to qualify. The loan has a variable interest rate that cannot exceed 9 percent. There is no yearly limit; you can borrow up to the cost of your education less other financial aid received. Repayment begins sixty days after the money is advanced. A fee of up to 4 percent of the loan is subtracted from the proceeds. Parent borrowers must generally have a good credit record to qualify. Parents are urged to contact the financial aid office to determine if the PLUS program is the best source of alternative loan funds. Many schools have arranged other private loan programs that may offer better loan terms. Some programs administered by the state higher education agency may have parental loan programs with better terms and conditions.

Famous Scholarship Programs

The two most famous and prestigious scholarship programs are the Fulbright and Rhodes scholarships. Here is a quick overview of the programs.

The Fulbright Scholarship Program

The Fulbright Scholarship Program is the U.S. government's premier scholarship program available for international study. The Fulbright Program sponsors study, research, or teaching by American graduate scholars and artists in more than 100 host countries and by graduate-level students, teachers, or researchers from more than 125 countries at U.S. universities. In its fifty-seven years of operation, the Fulbright program has sponsored nearly 200,000 scholars. The program was established in 1946 to foster mutual understanding through educational and cultural exchanges of persons, knowledge, and skills between the United States and other countries. It is named for Senator J. William Fulbright, who sponsored the legislation in the United States Senate as a step toward constructing alternatives to armed conflict. The program's primary source of funding is the United States Information Agency (USIA).

The U.S. Student Program is designed to give recent baccalaureate-level graduates, master's and doctoral candidates, and beginning professionals and artists an opportunity for personal development and international experience. Recipients plan their own programs. Projects may include course-related work, library or field research, classes in music or art, research projects in the sciences or social sciences, or various hybrid projects. The Fulbright Scholar Program is designed to provide senior teachers and professionals the opportunity to conduct research, teach, or study abroad and to make a major contribution to global understanding.

There are five basic types of Fulbright grants open to U.S. citizens:

- *Fulbright Full Grants:* Provide round-trip transportation; language or orientation courses; tuition, in some cases; book and research allowances; maintenance for the academic year, based on living costs in the host country; and supplemental health and accident insurance. Fulbright Full Grants are payable in local currency or U.S. dollars, depending on the country of assignment.

- *Fulbright Travel Grants:* Available only to Germany, Hungary, Italy, or Korea. They are available to supplement a student's own funds or an award from a non-Fulbright source that does not provide funds for travel or to supplement study. Travel grants provide round-trip transportation to the country where the student will pursue studies for an academic year, supplemental health and accident insurance, and the cost of an orientation course abroad, if applicable.
- *Foreign and Private Grants:* Offered by international governments, universities, and private donors in specific host countries. The benefits and special requirements of the grants are determined by the sponsoring agency. If the awards do not cover the entire expense of international study, candidates are expected to cover the additional costs from their own funds, although some international grants may be supplemented by Fulbright travel grants.
- *Teaching Opportunities:* Belgium/Luxembourg, France, Germany, Hungary, Korea, Taiwan, and Turkey offer assistantships for teaching English in secondary schools, middle schools, or higher educational institutions.
- *Fulbright Scholar Program:* Offers grants for college and university faculty and administrators, professionals (lawyers, government officials, journalists, research scientists, and others), artists, and independent scholars to conduct research, teach, or study abroad.

Fulbright recipients are selected on the basis of their academic or professional record, language preparation, the feasibility of the proposed project, and personal qualifications. The decision-making procedure involves review of the application by three groups: a National Screening Committee (NSC) of the Institute for International Education that consists of specialists in various fields and area studies, the supervising agency (the USIS post at the American Embassy or a special binational Fulbright Commission in the host country), and the J. William Fulbright Foreign Scholarship Board.

An application form is available from the Fulbright Program Advisor at the graduate's campus or from the Institute of International Education, 809 United Nations Plaza, New York, NY 10017-3580. Applications should be submitted between May 1 and mid-October. Check with the Fulbright Program Advisor or the Institute of International Education for the specific year's deadline.

The Rhodes Scholarship

Cecil Rhodes, a remarkable public figure of late Victorian Britain, made a fortune in diamond mining in South Africa and forcefully advocated a single world international government. On his death in 1902 at the age of 49, he left his fortune to Oxford University to establish the Rhodes scholarship program. The aim of the Rhodes scholarship is to bring from throughout the world young men and women of proven intellectual and academic achievement, integrity of character, interest in and respect for their fellow beings, the ability to lead, and the energy to use their talents to make an effective contribution to the world around them.

Because of a long history of prominent individuals who have been Rhodes scholars and the extreme selectivity of the award, the Rhodes scholarship is regarded in academe as an extremely high honor. Colleges and universities take great pride in their students who go on to win Rhodes scholarships and view the cultivation of a Rhodes scholar to be a great status symbol.

The Rhodes scholarship provides payment of all tuition and related fees in any field of study at Oxford plus a stipend for living expenses. The Rhodes trustees assist successful applicants with their travel expenses to and from Oxford.

Appointment to a Rhodes scholarship is made for two years with a possible third year if the scholar's plan of study and record at Oxford warrant extension of the award. An American Rhodes scholar with a degree from an approved American university or college is entitled to Senior Status. Subject to the consent of their college, Senior Status entitles students to read for the Oxford B.A. in any of the Final Honour Schools. If qualified by previous training and with the consent of their colleges and relevant faculty, Rhodes scholars may be admitted to read for a higher degree.

Candidates must be citizens, between the ages of 18 and 23 as of October 1 of the year of their application, and have sufficient credits to ensure completion of a bachelor's degree before the October 1 following application. Selection is made on four criteria: scholarship, character, leadership, and physical vigor. Participation in varsity sports is a usual way to demonstrate physical vigor, but it is not essential if applicants are able to demonstrate physical vigor in other ways.

Each of the world's nations is assigned a number of Rhodes scholarship slots that they may fill each year. The United States of America selects 32 Rhodes scholars annually. Applications are made through the Office of the Institutional Representative for the Rhodes scholarships at the candidate's college or university. A campus committee evaluates applicants and sends the evaluations to a state Committee of Selection. In each state a Committee of Selection may nominate 2 or 3 applicants to appear before the District Committee (the U.S. is organized into eight districts of six or seven states each). The Rhodes trustees will pay round-trip transportation of applicants nominated by State Committees to the place of the District Committee meeting. Applicants must pay their own lodging, food, and other expenses when appearing before State Committees. The names of scholarship winners are announced at the close of the District Committee meetings in December.

After selection of the scholars, the Rhodes scholarship authorities in Oxford seek places for them in Oxford colleges, following the electees' preferences, if possible. Because the colleges make their own admissions, there is no guarantee of a place. Two samples of written work, approximately 2,000 words each, are required for college placement. The award of the scholarship is not confirmed by the Rhodes Trustees until the scholar-elect has been accepted for admission by a college. Rhodes scholars are expected to be full-time students at Oxford for the duration of their degree programs. Scholars-elect enter Oxford University in October following their election. Deferment of the scholarship is not allowed except for medical internships.

Prospective applicants should study the academic system of Oxford University to determine if their plan of study is one that is feasible at Oxford. The best sources of information are the current issues of the *University of Oxford Undergraduate Prospectus* and *Graduate Studies Prospectus*, published by the Oxford University Press and available in the offices of Institutional Representatives for the Rhodes scholarships in colleges and universities. In addition, the *Oxford University Examination Decrees* is available for a charge from the Oxford University Press Bookshop, 116 High Street, Oxford OX1 4BZ, England. Copies of a brochure, *Oxford and the Rhodes Scholarships*, giving information about the scholarships and life and study at Oxford, may be obtained from Institutional Representatives at each campus as well as from the Office of the American Secretary. Students who wish further information or have difficulty in obtaining application forms should write to: Office of the American Secretary, The Rhodes Scholarship Trust, PO Box 7490, McLean, Virginia 22106-7490.

Where Can You Find Help?

THE COLLEGE FINANCIAL AID OFFICE

The cost of education at a private college likely will fall in the range of $12,000 to $35,000 annually for tuition, room, and board. Public college education is about half this amount. Your actual cost, though, depends upon your financial aid award. No matter what your family's income level or your academic record, you are likely to be eligible for some form of financial aid. Whether through scholarships, awards, grants, loans, or student employment, most colleges endeavor to provide financial assistance to admitted freshmen that will enable these students to enroll at their institution. That's why it is important to look beyond the "sticker price" of attending the college of your choice and apply for financial aid before ruling out a college based on cost.

Most financial aid is based on financial need. However, whether you demonstrate 100 percent financial need or hardly any, you can look to the financial aid office of the college that has accepted you to work with you to create a financial aid package that addresses your unique situation and makes your college education an investment that you can afford. The primary purpose of the college student financial aid office is to remove financial barriers to student enrollment and ensure that any qualified student can obtain sufficient resources to attend their college. The essential job of the financial aid administrator is to help students who would otherwise be unable to attend their college seek, obtain, and make the best use of all financial resources available.

The financial aid office in any college will guide you to the financial aid options available from a variety of sources—state and federal government programs, friends of the college, alumni, and the college itself. The actual amount of a financial aid package is determined not only from the evaluation of your personal financial situation but also by the unique financial resources, policies, and practices of each institution.

Financial aid packages vary significantly from school to school. Moreover, the amount of aid available from each college can fluctuate widely from year to year, depending on the number of applicants, the amount of need to be met, and the financial resources and policies of the college.

After you have narrowed down the colleges in which you are interested based on academic and personal criteria, we recommend that you contact the college's financial aid office. Here are just a few questions you might want to ask the financial aid officers at the colleges you are seriously considering:

- What are the types and sources of aid provided to freshmen at this school?
- What factors do the college consider in determining whether a financial aid applicant is qualified for its need-based aid programs?
- How does the college determine the combination of types of aid that make up an individual's package?
- How are non-need awards treated—as a part of the aid package or as a part of the parental/family contribution?
- Does this school "guarantee" financial aid and, if so, how is its policy implemented? Guaranteed aid means that, by policy, 100 percent of need is met for all students judged to have need. Implementation determines how need is met and varies widely from school to school. For example, grade point average may determine the proportioning of scholarship, loan, and work-study aid. Rules for freshmen may be different from those for upperclass students.
- To what degree is the admission process "need-blind"? Need-blind means that admission decisions are made without regard to the student's need for financial aid.
- What are the norms and practices for upperclass student aid? A college might offer a wonderful package for the freshman year, then leave you relatively on your own to fund the remaining three years. Or the school may provide a higher proportion of scholarship money for freshmen, then rebalance its aid packages to contain more self-help aid (loans and work-study) in upperclass years. There is an assumption that, all other factors being equal, students who have settled into the pattern of college time management can handle more work-study hours than freshmen. Grade point average, tuition increases, changes in parental financial circumstances, and other factors may also affect the redistribution. If you feel your financial situation warrants additional review, the financial aid office is always willing to work with you to help you find solutions to financing your education.

THE HIGH SCHOOL GUIDANCE OFFICE

The high school guidance office is often the first source of information that students and parents have to learn about their college options, including financing. High school guidance counselors, among other responsibilities, work to educate students and their parents about college options and the college admission and financial assistance process. They counsel individual students about their postsecondary career and educational choices.

Many guidance offices are well equipped for this task, with libraries of college catalogs, college guides, interactive career or college selection software. Many high school students have access to a first-rate college and career information center and a counselor who has great knowledge about specific colleges, college selection, admissions processes, and student financial aid options and can work with students as they make the transition from high school to postsecondary education. Thousands of high schools are fortunate to have this type of resource.

Resources devoted to college advisement vary tremendously from district to district. Guidance counselors sometimes have an overwhelming number of students to counsel and urgent responsibilities in other areas that can demand a greater share of their time, energy, and expertise. They often cannot find the time to provide personalized consultation to individual students about their college options. It is always necessary for parents to assess the situation at their children's particular high school. If college counseling resources at your high school are limited, it may be necessary to fill in, either by yourself or, if you can afford it, with an independent college advisement counselor.

With respect to financial aid, any high school guidance office should be able to provide you with the current FAFSA, forms for state-sponsored financial aid programs, and information about locally sponsored scholarship programs.

College fairs are a worthwhile resource available to many parents and students. There are college fairs sponsored by school districts as well as a program of National College Fairs sponsored by the National Association for College Admission Counseling (NACAC). These usually offer exhibits and presentations by individual colleges and universities. Students and parents are able to meet with admissions representatives of different colleges; view their information presentations; take home a range of informative brochures, periodicals, and other products; and attend information sessions on college admissions and financing. Many high schools allow time off during the school day for students to attend a college fair.

NACAC's National College Fair program probably draws the greatest number of college representatives. NACAC sponsors thirty-six fairs in different parts of the country, which attract more than 300,000 students each year. Contact them at National Association for College Admission Counseling, 1631 Prince Street, Alexandria, Virginia 22314-2818; telephone: 703-836-2222; fax: 703-836-8015; or look at their Web site (www.nacac.com/) to receive an up-to-date list of college fairs.

What Do You Need to Know About Application Forms?

BASIC AID APPLICATION FORMS

FAFSA

Because the federal government provides about 75 percent of all aid awarded, the Free Application for Federal Student Aid (FAFSA) and the Federal Methodology (FM) are the most important application forms and need analysis process with which you will have to deal. The information on the FAFSA—parental and student income and assets, the number of family members, and the number attending college as well as other variables—is analyzed to derive the Expected Family Contribution. This one form is required by every college. It is also the basis for almost all student financial aid provided by state governments and colleges themselves.

The FAFSA is available from any college financial aid office as well as most high school guidance offices. Students and families can apply for federal student aid over the Internet using the interactive FAFSA on the Web. Most applicants will find the Web version of the FAFSA relatively easy and fast. FAFSA on the Web can be accessed at www.fafsa.ed.gov/ and does not require users to download programs or install software.

Submit the FAFSA after January 1 to meet the earliest deadline of your state, college, or private aid program. The aid decision process favors those who apply on time. Once you have passed the deadline, your application may not be considered. Because of early program deadlines, you may have to use an estimated tax return to complete the FAFSA. This is permitted, and even advisable. Far too many parents and students wait to submit the FAFSA and lose their chance at thousands of financial aid dollars. Many colleges provide the option to apply for early decision admission. If you apply for this before January 1, follow the college's aid application instructions.

You should be prepared when you start to complete the FAFSA. Here are the records that you will need (all income records are for the year immediately prior to college start):

- Federal tax returns (if available)
- If no tax return is available, a complete record of all taxable income
- Untaxed income (including Earned Income Credit; Social Security benefits; child support)
- Bank statements for checking, savings, money market, and CD accounts
- Investment statements concerning interest, dividends, and capital gains
- Second home or rental property value and debt records
- Business value and debt records
- Farm investment value and debt records

PROFILE®

Some colleges require an aid application in addition to the FAFSA. Among the approximately 2,000 four-year colleges, about 600 are private institutions with more than $2 billion of their own scholarships. Many of these colleges feel that the federal aid system (FAFSA and FM) does not collect or evaluate information thoroughly enough to be used to award their own funds. These colleges have made an arrangement with the College Scholarship Service, a branch of the College Board, to establish a separate application system called PROFILE®.

The need formula connected to PROFILE® is the Institutional Methodology (IM). If you apply for financial aid at one of the colleges that uses PROFILE®, the admission material will state that PROFILE® is required in addition to the FAFSA. You should read this information carefully and file PROFILE® to meet the earliest deadline among the colleges involved. Before you can receive the PROFILE® form, however, you must register, providing enough basic information so the PROFILE® package can be designed specifically for you. Also, while the FAFSA is free, there is a charge for PROFILE®.

In addition to the requirement by certain colleges that you submit both the FAFSA and PROFILE® (PROFILE® is always in addition to the FAFSA; it does not replace it), you should also realize that each system has its own method for analyzing family ability to pay for college. The main differences between PROFILE®'s Institutional Methodology and FAFSA's Federal Methodology are as follows:

- PROFILE® includes equity in the family home as an asset; the FAFSA doesn't.
- PROFILE® expects a minimum student contribution, usually in the form of summer earnings. The FAFSA has no such minimum.

- PROFILE® allows for more professional judgment than the FAFSA. Medical expenses, private secondary school costs, and a variety of special circumstances are considered under PROFILE® subject to the discretion of the aid counselor on campus.
- PROFILE® collects information on the noncustodial parent; the FAFSA doesn't.
- PROFILE® collects information on assets not reported on the FAFSA, including life insurance, annuities, retirement plans, etc.

PROFILE®'s Institutional Methodology tends to be both more complete in its data collection and more rigorous in its analysis than the FAFSA's Federal Methodology. When IM results are compared to FM results for thousands of applicants, IM will usually come up with a somewhat higher Expected Family Contribution than FM.

To prepare to complete the PROFILE® application form, you will need to gather all of the information that you would need to complete the FAFSA. In addition, you will need to show the market value of your home less the outstanding mortgage.

After the applications are submitted, you will receive the aid award letter. Your aid package will show you how much to subtract from the college's cost of attendance to arrive at your actual contribution. If you are an aid recipient, it is not until you have calculated your "bottom line" that you will learn the actual cost of an individual college.

PRIVATE AID SCHOLARSHIP APPLICATIONS

The types of applications that you will need to apply for scholarships from the noninstitutional sector can be as varied as the sponsors themselves. Be prepared to spend some time and effort gathering the material that each application requires. The amount of time you have to do this should be a factor in considering how many scholarships you wish to pursue. Weigh this against the fact that the chances for most students of receiving a privately sponsored scholarship will likely be less than their chances of getting help from the federal government or the college.

Need-based scholarships, especially many state scholarships, use the FAFSA as the primary application. Application for state aid is automatically done when you complete the FAFSA. However, check the aid information for your specific state, because the sources and programs vary considerably. It is advisable to keep a record of your FAFSA and PROFILE® data in the event that you may wish to reproduce them for a noninstitutional sponsor or if questions arise.

Merit-based scholarship sponsors frequently require a secondary school transcript and one or more letters of recommendation. The source of the letter of recommendation may be specified in the sponsor's materials. If not, you will want to find one or more individuals of appropriate professional authority or credence in the area directly related to that which forms the basis for the award. If, for example, the award is given for academic quality, typically a teacher or school administrator should be sought; if community service, a leader or organizer of relevant community service projects is the best choice. A document written and signed by this individual will attest to the quality of an applicant's qualifications, work, character, abilities, or accomplishments. Usually it is preferable that the letter be specifically addressed, but if a number of similar awards are being sought, you may have to settle for a generically addressed letter to any recipient who may be interested. Sponsors may request that the signer send the letter directly to them. If so, follow the sponsor's directions.

The best advice in applying for private scholarships is to request descriptive information from the sponsor about the scholarship program that you may be interested in and review it carefully in respect to the scholarship's eligibility criteria, application requirements, and deadlines. If you do not precisely match the scholarship's eligibility criteria, you almost certainly will not receive the award. Be careful to supply *all* of the application forms and supporting documentation that the sponsor requests. Pay attention to deadlines; begin the process of gathering information and preparing letters and forms well in advance of the deadline, and try to beat the deadline by as much as you can. Many sponsors' procedures give some advantage to earlier applicants.

In addition to the application, your case usually can be enhanced by a concise cover letter. Provide basic information about your grade in school or year of college, graduation date, major, and goals. If the basis for the award is academic, information about your GPA and class rank is relevant. Test scores appropriate to your level and field of study will be needed. High school students may wish to provide their PSAT, SAT, ACT, and/or Advanced Placement scores.

SUMMARY

There are reasons to be optimistic about your prospects of finding the help you need to pay for college. Although the "sticker price" of a college education may be high, there is an extensive network available to help students and families pay for a college education. If typical financial aid packages are taken into consideration, the actual cost of four years of college is likely to be less than what most families spend on a car and, unlike a car, the value of a college education will increase as time goes on. The majority of students should *expect* to receive aid to make their college costs manageable, whether this comes from the government, the college, or the many noninstitutional sponsors that offer scholarships. There are many ways to manage college costs and many channels through which you can receive help. This process requires preparation, organization, and resourcefulness.

We wish you success in your quest and hope that Peterson's *Scholarship Almanac* proves to be helpful.

How to Use This Guide

WHAT ARE THE CRITERIA FOR SELECTING THE TOP 500 SCHOLARSHIPS?

Between January and April of each year, Peterson's conducts a survey of more than 5,000 organizations and agencies in the U.S. and Canada that sponsor scholarships, prizes, fellowships, grants, and forgivable loans for undergraduate- and graduate-level students.

Scholarship sponsors provide Peterson's with data about the number and dollar amounts of the awards they give in a year. These are frequently described as ranges. To determine the 500 largest scholarships available in the U.S. out of a list of thousands, we multiplied the highest number in the range representing the number of awards given in a year (never less than 1) by the highest number in the range representing the dollar amounts given.

The information is constructed from Peterson's questionnaires that went to the sponsoring bodies in December 2002. The information was verified and correct as of April 2003. The number of awards, funding amounts, and procedures can change at any time. There is no way to guarantee that the number of awards or dollar amounts reported by a sponsor will be duplicated in a new year. You should request written descriptive materials for the program in which you are interested directly from the sponsor.

HOW TO UNDERSTAND THE PROFILES

The 500 scholarships described in this book are organized into categories that represent the major factors used to determine eligibility for scholarship awards and prizes. To find a basic list of scholarships available to you, look under the specific category or categories that fit your particular academic goals, skills, personal characteristics, or background.

The categories are divided into two broad classes: **Academic/ Career Areas** and **Nonacademic/Noncareer Criteria**.

Because your major academic field of study and/or career goal has central importance in college planning, the *Academic/Career Areas* section appears first. The *Academic/Career Areas* category is subdivided into individual subject areas that are organized alphabetically.

These are:

Accounting
Agribusiness
Agriculture
Animal/Veterinary Sciences
Applied Sciences
Architecture
Arts
Aviation/Aerospace
Biology
Business/Consumer Services
Chemical Engineering
Civil Engineering
Communications
Computer Science/Data Processing
Dental Health/Services
Drafting
Earth Science
Economics
Education
Electrical Engineering/Electronics
Engineering-Related Technologies
Engineering/Technology
Fashion Design
Filmmaking
Fire Sciences
Food Science/Nutrition
Food Service/Hospitality
Foreign Language
Funeral Services/Mortuary Science
Geography
Graphics/Graphic Arts/Printing
Health Administration
Health and Medical Sciences
Health Information Management/
    Technology
History
Home Economics

Horticulture/Floriculture
Hospitality Management
Humanities
Interior Design
International Migration
Journalism
Landscape Architecture
Law Enforcement/Police
    Administration
Law/Legal Services
Literature/English/Writing
Materials Science, Engineering, and
    Metallurgy
Mechanical Engineering
Meteorology/Atmospheric Science
Music
Natural Resources
Natural Sciences
Nuclear Science
Nursing
Peace and Conflict Studies
Performing Arts
Physical Sciences and Math
Political Science
Religion/Theology
Science, Technology, and Society
Social Sciences
Social Services
Special Education
Sports-related
Surveying, Surveying Technology,
    Cartography, or Geographic
    Information Science
Therapy/Rehabilitation
Trade/Technical Specialties
TV/Radio Broadcasting

The second class of awards, *Nonacademic/Noncareer Criteria*, are those that are primarily based on a personal characteristic of the award recipient. We have organized these criteria into ten categories:

Civic, Professional, Social, or Union Affiliation
Corporate Affiliation
Employment Experience

Impairment
Military Service
Nationality or Ethnic Heritage
Religious Affiliation
State of Residence
Talent
Miscellaneous Criteria

Full descriptive profiles of scholarship awards are sequentially numbered from 1 through 500. This number appears in the upper right-hand corner of the profile with a bullet in front of it (it is this profile number, not the page number the award appears on, that is referenced in all indexes). A full profile of an award appears in only one location in the book. Most awards have more than one criterion that needs to be met before a student can be eligible. Cross-references by name and sequential number are made to the full program description from the other relevant criteria categories under which the award might also have been listed if one of its multiple criteria had not come earlier in the alphabet. The full description appears in the first relevant location, the cross-references in the later ones.

Cross-references are not provided from the *Nonacademic/ Noncareer Criteria* section to programs in the *Academic/Career Areas* section. You will be able to locate relevant awards in this section by any personal qualifying criteria through the indexes in the back of the book, which repeat the organizing scheme of the profiles.

For example, the numbered full profile of a scholarship for any kind of engineering student who resides in Ohio, Pennsylvania, or West Virginia may appear under *Aviation/Aerospace*, the alphabetically first relevant engineering category heading in the *Academic/ Career Areas* section of the book. Cross-references to this first listing, by name and number, may occur from any other relevant engineering or technological academic field subject areas, such as *Chemical Engineering, Civil Engineering, Engineering-Related Technologies, Engineering/Technology, Mechanical Engineering,* or *Nuclear Science.* There would not be a cross-reference from the *State of Residence* category. However, the name of the scholarship will appear in the Index under the State section. You will always want to check the relevant indexes to get the most out of the guide's listings.

Within the appropriate categories, the descriptive profiles are organized alphabetically by the name of the sponsoring organization. If more than one scholarship from the same organization appears in a particular section, the awards are then listed alphabetically by the name of the award under the name of the sponsor.

WHAT IS IN THE DESCRIPTIVE PROFILES?

Here are the elements of a full descriptive profile:

1. Name of sponsoring organization (In most instances acronyms are given as full names. However, occasionally a sponsor will refer to itself throughout by acronym, and in deference to this seeming preference, we present their name as an acronym.)
2. Award name and sequence number
3. Brief description of the award
4. Academic/Career Areas (this is only in the *Academic/Career Areas* section)
5. Award descriptors (Is it a scholarship? A prize for winning a competition? A forgivable loan? An internship? For what years of college can it be used? Is it renewable or is it for only one year? How many awards are given? For what amounts?)
6. Eligibility Requirements
7. Application Requirements, which also lists the application deadline
8. Sponsoring organization's Web site address
9. Contact name, address, phone and fax numbers, and e-mail address

A STRATEGY FOR FINDING RELEVANT AWARDS

Private scholarships and awards are frequently characterized by unpredictable, sometimes seemingly bizarre, criteria. Before you begin your search for a relevant award, draw up a personal profile of yourself that will help establish as many as possible criteria that might form the basis for your award grant. Here is a basic checklist of what you should give consideration to:

What is your career goal? Be both narrow and broad in your designation. If, for example, you have a career goal to be a TV news reporter, you will find many awards specific to this field in the *TV/Radio Broadcasting* section. However, collegiate broadcasting courses can be offered in departments or schools of communication. So, be sure to consider *Communications* as a relevant section for your search. Also, consider *Journalism* for the same reasons. Then, look under some more broadly inclusive, but possibly relevant areas, such as *Trade/Technical Specialties*. Or, possibly, check a related, but different field, such as *Performing Arts*. Finally, look under marginally related, basic academic fields, such as *Humanities, Social Sciences,* or *Political Science*. We make every attempt to provide superior cross-reference aids, but the nuances of specific awards can be difficult to capture with even the most flexible cross-referencing systems. You will need to be broadly associative in your thinking in order to get the most out of this wealth of information.

If you have no clear career goal at this stage of your life, browsing through the huge variety of academic/career awards may well spark new interest in a career path. Be open to imagining yourself filling different career roles that you may not have previously considered.

In what academic subject fields are you interested in majoring? Your educational experiences to this point or your sense about your personal talents or interests may have given you a good idea of what academic discipline you wish to pursue. Again, use both broad and narrow focuses in designing your search and look to related subject fields. For example, if you want to major in history, there is a *History* section. But be sure to also check out *Social Sciences* and *Humanities* and, maybe *Area/Ethnic Studies*. In addition, *Education* could also have the perfect scholarship for a future historian.

In what jobs, industries, or occupations have your parents or other members of your immediate family been engaged? What employment experiences do you have? Individual companies, employee organizations, trade unions, government agencies, and industry associations frequently set up scholarships for workers or children or other relatives of workers from specific companies or industries. These awards may sometimes require that you study to stay in the same career field, but most are offered regardless of the field of study you wish to undertake. Also, if one of your parents worked as a public service employee, especially as a firefighter or police officer, and most especially if he or she was killed or disabled in the line of duty, there are many relevant awards available.

Do you have any hobbies or special interests? Have you ever been an officer of an organization? Do you have special skills or talents? Have you won any competitions? Are you a good writer? From bowling to clarinet playing, from caddying to ham radio, from winning a beauty contest to simply "being interested in leadership," there are a host of special interests that can win for you awards from groups that wish to promote and/or reward these pursuits.

Where do you live? Where have you lived? Where are you going to college? Residence criteria are among the most common qualifications for scholarship aid. Local clubs and companies provide millions of dollars in scholarship aid to students who live in a particular state, province, region, or section of a state. This means that your residential identity puts you at the head of the line for these grants. State of residence can—depending on the sponsor's criteria—include the place of your official residence, the place you attend college, the place you were born, or any place you lived for more than a year.

What is your family's ethnic heritage? Hundreds of scholarships have been endowed for students who can claim a particular nationality or racial or ethnic descent. Partial ethnic descent frequently qualifies, so don't be put off if you do not think of yourself as having a specific "ethnic" background. There are awards for Colonial American, English, Welsh, Scottish, descendants of signers of the Declaration of Independence, European, and other backgrounds that students may be inclined to consider as not especially "ethnic."

Do you have any physical impairment? There are many awards given to individuals with physical impairments. In addition to commonly recognized impairments of mobility, sight, communication, and hearing, learning disabilities and chronic diseases, such as asthma and epilepsy, are criteria for some awards.

Are you now in, or have you served in, a branch of the armed services? Did one of your parents serve? In a war? Was one of your parents lost or disabled in the armed services? There are hundreds of awards that use one or more of these qualifications.

Do you belong to a civic association, union, or religious organization? Do your parents belong? Hundreds of clubs and religious groups provide scholarship assistance to members or children of members.

Are you male or female?

What is your age?

Do you qualify for need-based aid?

Did you graduate in the upper half, upper third, or upper quarter of your class?

Do you plan to attend a two-year college, a four-year college, or a vocational/technical school?

What year (freshman, sophomore, etc.) of school are you entering?

Be expansive in considering your possible qualifications. Although some awards may be small, you may qualify for more than one award, and these can add up significantly in the end.

ACADEMIC/CAREER AREAS

ACCOUNTING

HISPANIC COLLEGE FUND, INC.

DENNY'S/HISPANIC COLLEGE FUND SCHOLARSHIP   ● 1

One-time scholarship award open to full-time undergraduates of Hispanic descent pursuing a degree in business or a business-related major with a GPA of 3.0 or better. Eligible students who have applied to the Hispanic College Fund need not re-apply.

Academic/Career Areas Accounting; Architecture; Business/Consumer Services; Chemical Engineering; Communications; Computer Science/Data Processing; Economics; Electrical Engineering/Electronics; Engineering/Technology; Engineering-Related Technologies; Graphics/Graphic Arts/Printing; Hospitality Management.

Award Scholarship for use in freshman, sophomore, junior, or senior years; not renewable. *Number:* 80–100. *Amount:* $1000.

Eligibility Requirements: Applicant must be Hispanic and enrolled or expecting to enroll full-time at a two-year or four-year institution or university. Applicant must have 3.0 GPA or higher. Available to U.S. citizens.

Application Requirements Application, essay, financial need analysis, resume, references, test scores, transcript, college acceptance letter, copy of taxes, copy of SAR. *Deadline:* April 15.

World Wide Web: http://www.hispanicfund.org

Contact: Stina Augustsson, Program Manager
        Hispanic College Fund, Inc.
        1717 Pennsylvania Avenue, NW, Suite 460
        Washington, DC 20006
        Phone: 202-296-5400
        Fax: 202-296-3774
        E-mail: hispaniccollegefund@earthlink.net

NATIONAL ASSOCIATION OF BLACK ACCOUNTANTS, INC.

NATIONAL ASSOCIATION OF BLACK ACCOUNTANTS NATIONAL SCHOLARSHIP   ● 2

One-time award for minority college students to study, full-time, any business-related discipline at an accredited institution. Candidate must be a member of the National Association of Black Accountants with a minimum GPA of 2.5. Must submit a copy of visa, if a non-U.S. citizen.

Academic/Career Areas Accounting; Business/Consumer Services; Economics.

Award Scholarship for use in freshman, sophomore, junior, or senior years; not renewable. *Number:* 40. *Amount:* $500–$6000.

Eligibility Requirements: Applicant must be American Indian/Alaska Native, Asian/Pacific Islander, Black (non-Hispanic), or Hispanic and enrolled or expecting to enroll full-time at a four-year institution or university. Applicant or parent of applicant must be member of National Association of Black Accountants. Applicant must have 2.5 GPA or higher. Available to U.S. and non-U.S. citizens.

Application Requirements Application, autobiography, essay, financial need analysis, resume, transcript, visa, if non-U.S. citizen. *Deadline:* December 31.

World Wide Web: http://www.nabainc.org

Contact: Challenge Okiwe, Director, Center for Advancement of Minority
       Accountants
       National Association of Black Accountants, Inc.
       7249-A Hanover Parkway
       Greenbelt, MD 20770
       Phone: 301-474-6222 Ext. 114
       Fax: 301-474-3114
       E-mail: cokiwe@nabainc.org

NEW JERSEY SOCIETY OF CERTIFIED PUBLIC ACCOUNTANTS

NEW JERSEY SOCIETY OF CERTIFIED PUBLIC ACCOUNTANTS COLLEGE SCHOLARSHIP PROGRAM   • 3

Award for college juniors or those entering an accounting-related graduate program. Based upon academic merit. Must be a New Jersey resident attending a four-year New Jersey institution. Must be nominated by Accounting Department Chair or submit application directly. Minimum 3.5 GPA required. Interview required. One-time award of up to $3000.

Academic/Career Areas Accounting.

Award Scholarship for use in junior, or graduate years; not renewable. *Number:* 4–37. *Amount:* $2500–$3000.

Eligibility Requirements: Applicant must be enrolled or expecting to enroll full or part-time at a four-year institution or university; resident of New Jersey and studying in New Jersey. Applicant must have 3.5 GPA or higher. Available to U.S. citizens.

Application Requirements Interview, transcript. *Deadline:* January 18.

World Wide Web: http://www.njscpa.org

Contact: Ms. Janice Amatucci, Student Programs Coordinator
       New Jersey Society of Certified Public Accountants
       425 Eagle Rock Avenue
       Roseland, NJ 07068
       Phone: 973-226-4494
       Fax: 973-226-7425
       E-mail: jamatucci@njscpa.org

NEW JERSEY SOCIETY OF CERTIFIED PUBLIC ACCOUNTANTS HIGH SCHOOL SCHOLARSHIP PROGRAM • 4

This program is open to all NJ high school seniors. Selection is based on a one-hour aptitude exam and the highest scorers on this exam are invited for an interview. The winners receive accounting scholarships to the college of their choice. Five-year awards range in value from $6500-$8500.

Academic/Career Areas Accounting.

Award Scholarship for use in freshman year; renewable. *Number:* 15-20. *Amount:* $6500-$8500.

Eligibility Requirements: Applicant must be high school student; planning to enroll or expecting to enroll full-time at a four-year institution or university and resident of New Jersey. Available to U.S. citizens.

Application Requirements Interview, test scores. *Deadline:* October 31.

World Wide Web: http://www.njscpa.org

Contact: Janice Amatucci, Student Programs Coordinator
New Jersey Society of Certified Public Accountants
425 Eagle Rock Avenue
Roseland, NJ 07068
Phone: 973-226-4494
Fax: 973-226-7425
E-mail: jamatucci@njscpa.org

NEW YORK STATE SOCIETY OF CERTIFIED PUBLIC ACCOUNTANTS FOUNDATION FOR ACCOUNTING EDUCATION

FOUNDATION FOR ACCOUNTING EDUCATION SCHOLARSHIP • 5

Up to 200 $1500 scholarships will be given to college students to encourage them to pursue a career in accounting. Must be a New York resident studying in New York and maintaining a 3.0 GPA.

Academic/Career Areas Accounting.

Award Scholarship for use in junior or senior years; renewable. *Number:* 1-200. *Amount:* $1500.

Eligibility Requirements: Applicant must be enrolled or expecting to enroll full or part-time at a four-year institution or university; resident of New York and studying in New York. Applicant must have 3.0 GPA or higher. Available to U.S. citizens.

Application Requirements Application, financial need analysis, transcript. *Deadline:* Continuous.

World Wide Web: http://www.nysscpa.org

Contact: Bill Pape, Associate Director Member Relations
New York State Society of Certified Public Accountants
Foundation for Accounting Education
530 Fifth Avenue, Fifth Floor
New York, NY 10036-5101
Phone: 212-719-8420
E-mail: wpape@nysscpa.org

ORDEAN FOUNDATION

ORDEAN LOAN PROGRAM • 6

Renewable award for low-income students who are from Hermantown, Proctor, or Duluth. Students must be fully admitted into social work, management, education, accounting or nursing. Students must work in their designated field in the Duluth area for up to 3 years after graduation. Open to full-time junior or senior undergraduates. Must be U.S. citizens. Minimum 2.5 GPA required.

Academic/Career Areas Accounting; Education; Health Administration; Health Information Management/Technology; Nursing; Social Services.
Award Forgivable loan for use in junior or senior years; renewable. *Number:* 40-50. *Amount:* $1250-$2500.
Eligibility Requirements: Applicant must be enrolled or expecting to enroll full-time at a four-year institution; resident of Minnesota and studying in Minnesota. Applicant must have 2.5 GPA or higher. Available to U.S. citizens.
Application Requirements Application, financial need analysis, transcript. *Deadline:* Continuous.
Contact: Trish Johnson, Financial Aid Counselor
Ordean Foundation
College of Saint Scholastica
1200 Kenwood Avenue
Duluth, MN 55811
Phone: 218-723-7027
Fax: 218-733-2229
E-mail: tjohnson@css.edu

OSCPA EDUCATIONAL FOUNDATION

OSCPA EDUCATIONAL FOUNDATION SCHOLARSHIP PROGRAM • 7

One-time award for students majoring in accounting. Must attend an accredited Oregon college/university or community college on full-time basis. High school seniors must have a minimum 3.5 GPA. College students must have a minimum 3.2 GPA. Must be a U.S. citizen and Oregon resident. Deadline is February 7.

Academic/Career Areas Accounting.
Award Scholarship for use in freshman, sophomore, junior, senior, graduate, or postgraduate years; not renewable. *Number:* 50-100. *Amount:* $500-$3000.

OSCPA Educational Foundation Scholarship Program (continued)

Eligibility Requirements: Applicant must be enrolled or expecting to enroll full-time at a two-year or four-year institution or university; resident of Oregon and studying in Oregon. Applicant must have 3.5 GPA or higher. Available to U.S. citizens.

Application Requirements Application, resume, references, test scores, transcript. *Deadline:* February 7.

World Wide Web: http://www.orcpa.org

Contact: Tonna Hollis, Member Services/Manager
OSCPA Educational Foundation
PO Box 4555
Beaverton, OR 97076-4555
Phone: 503-641-7200 Ext. 29
Fax: 503-626-2942
E-mail: tonna@orcpa.org

PENNSYLVANIA INSTITUTE OF CERTIFIED PUBLIC ACCOUNTANTS

PENNSYLVANIA INSTITUTE OF CERTIFIED PUBLIC ACCOUNTANTS SOPHOMORE SCHOLARSHIP • 8

To promote the accounting profession and CPA credential as an exciting and rewarding career path, the PICPA awards $34,000 annually in new scholarships to full-time sophomore undergraduate students enrolled at Pennsylvania colleges and universities. Minimum 3.0 GPA required.

Academic/Career Areas Accounting.

Award Scholarship for use in sophomore year; renewable. *Number:* 18. *Amount:* $1000–$9000.

Eligibility Requirements: Applicant must be enrolled or expecting to enroll full-time at a two-year or four-year institution or university and studying in Pennsylvania. Applicant must have 3.0 GPA or higher. Available to U.S. and non-U.S. citizens.

Application Requirements Application, essay, resume, references, test scores. *Deadline:* March 15.

World Wide Web: http://www.picpa.org

Contact: Meghan Reday, Careers in Accounting Administrator
Pennsylvania Institute of Certified Public Accountants
1650 Arch Street
17th Floor
Philadelphia, PA 19103-2099
Phone: 215-496-9272

AGRIBUSINESS

CENEX HARVEST STATES FOUNDATION

COOPERATIVE STUDIES SCHOLARSHIPS • 9

Renewable awards for college juniors and seniors attending agricultural colleges of participating universities. Must be enrolled in courses on cooperative principles and business practices. Each university selects a recipient in the spring. If the award is given in the junior year, the student is eligible for an additional $750 in their senior year without reapplying provided that eligibility requirements are met. A maximum of $1500 will be awarded to any one student in the cooperative studies program.

Academic/Career Areas Agribusiness; Agriculture.

Award Scholarship for use in junior or senior years; renewable. *Number:* 82. *Amount:* $750–$1500.

Eligibility Requirements: Applicant must be enrolled or expecting to enroll full-time at a four-year institution; resident of Colorado, Idaho, Iowa, Kansas, Minnesota, Montana, Nebraska, North Dakota, Oklahoma, Oregon, South Dakota, Utah, Washington, Wisconsin, or Wyoming and studying in Colorado, Idaho, Iowa, Kansas, Minnesota, Montana, Nebraska, North Dakota, Oregon, South Dakota, Utah, or Washington. Available to U.S. and non-U.S. citizens.

Application Requirements Application, transcript. *Deadline:* April 15.

Contact: Mary Kaste, Scholarship Director
Cenex Harvest States Foundation
5500 Cenex Drive
Inver Grove Heights, MN 55077
Phone: 651-451-5129
Fax: 651-451-5073
E-mail: mkast@chsco-ops.com

HISPANIC COLLEGE FUND, INC.

FIRST IN MY FAMILY SCHOLARSHIP PROGRAM • 10

One-time scholarship open to full-time undergraduates of Hispanic descent pursuing a degree in business- or technology-related major. Must be a U.S. citizen residing in the United States and have a minimum 3.0 GPA. Eligible students who have applied to the Hispanic College Fund need not re-apply. Must be first in the family to attend college.

Academic/Career Areas Agribusiness; Business/Consumer Services; Chemical Engineering; Communications; Computer Science/Data Processing; Drafting; Economics; Electrical Engineering/Electronics; Engineering/Technology; Engineering-Related Technologies; Graphics/Graphic Arts/Printing; Mechanical Engineering.

Award Scholarship for use in freshman, sophomore, junior, or senior years; not renewable. *Number:* 30–60. *Amount:* $1000–$5000.

First in My Family Scholarship Program (continued)

Eligibility Requirements: Applicant must be of Hispanic, Latin American/ Caribbean, Mexican, Nicaraguan, or Spanish heritage and enrolled or expecting to enroll full-time at a two-year or four-year institution or university. Applicant must have 3.0 GPA or higher. Available to U.S. citizens.

Application Requirements Application, essay, financial need analysis, resume, references, test scores, transcript, college acceptance letter, copy of taxes, copy of SAR. *Deadline:* April 15.

World Wide Web: http://www.hispanicfund.org

Contact: Stina Augustsson, Program Manager
Hispanic College Fund, Inc.
1717 Pennsylvania Avenue, NW, Suite 460
Washington, DC 20006
Phone: 202-296-5400
Fax: 202-296-3774
E-mail: hispaniccollegefund@earthlink.net

HISPANIC COLLEGE FUND SCHOLARSHIP PROGRAM • 11

This program awards scholarships to full-time students of Hispanic origin who have demonstrated academic excellence, leadership skills and financial need to pursue an undergraduate degree in a business or technology-related field.

Academic/Career Areas Agribusiness; Business/Consumer Services; Chemical Engineering; Communications; Computer Science/Data Processing; Drafting; Economics; Electrical Engineering/Electronics; Engineering/Technology; Engineering-Related Technologies; Graphics/Graphic Arts/Printing; Mechanical Engineering.

Award Scholarship for use in freshman, sophomore, junior, or senior years; not renewable. *Number:* 400–600. *Amount:* $1000–$5000.

Eligibility Requirements: Applicant must be of Hispanic, Latin American/ Caribbean, Mexican, Nicaraguan, or Spanish heritage and enrolled or expecting to enroll full-time at a two-year or four-year institution or university. Applicant must have 3.0 GPA or higher. Available to U.S. citizens.

Application Requirements Application, essay, financial need analysis, resume, references, test scores, transcript, college acceptance letter, copy of taxes, copy of SAR. *Deadline:* April 15.

World Wide Web: http://www.hispanicfund.org

Contact: Stina Augustsson, Program Manager
Hispanic College Fund, Inc.
1717 Pennsylvania Avenue, NW, Suite 460
Washington, DC 20006
Phone: 202-296-5400
Fax: 202-296-3774
E-mail: hispaniccollegefund@earthlink.net

AGRICULTURE

CENEX HARVEST STATES FOUNDATION

COOPERATIVE STUDIES SCHOLARSHIPS — see number 9

MORRIS K. UDALL FOUNDATION

MORRIS K. UDALL SCHOLARS • 12

One-time award to full-time college sophomores or juniors for study of the environment and related fields. Must be nominated by college. Minimum GPA of at least "B" or the equivalent. Must be U.S. citizen, a permanent resident alien or U.S. national.

Academic/Career Areas Agriculture; Biology; Earth Science; Geography; History; Natural Resources; Nuclear Science; Political Science.

Award Scholarship for use in sophomore or junior years; not renewable. *Number:* up to 110. *Amount:* $350–$5000.

Eligibility Requirements: Applicant must be enrolled or expecting to enroll full-time at a two-year or four-year institution. Available to U.S. citizens.

Application Requirements Application, essay, references, transcript, nomination. *Deadline:* March 3.

World Wide Web: http://www.udall.gov

Contact: Morris K. Udall Foundation
130 South Scott Avenue, Suite 3350
Tucson, AZ 85701-1922

ANIMAL/VETERINARY SCIENCES

ARKANSAS DEPARTMENT OF HIGHER EDUCATION

ARKANSAS HEALTH EDUCATION GRANT PROGRAM (ARHEG) • 13

Award provides assistance to Arkansas residents pursuing professional degrees in dentistry, optometry, veterinary medicine, podiatry, chiropractic medicine, or osteopathic medicine at out-of-state, accredited institutions (programs that are unavailable in Arkansas).

Academic/Career Areas Animal/Veterinary Sciences; Dental Health/Services; Health and Medical Sciences.

Award Grant for use in sophomore, junior, senior, or graduate years; renewable. *Number:* 258–288. *Amount:* $5000–$14,600.

Arkansas Health Education Grant Program (ARHEG) (continued)

Eligibility Requirements: Applicant must be enrolled or expecting to enroll full-time at a four-year institution or university and resident of Arkansas. Available to U.S. citizens.

Application Requirements Application, affidavit of Arkansas residency. *Deadline:* Continuous.

World Wide Web: http://www.arscholarships.com

Contact: Ms. Judy McAinsh, Coordinator, Arkansas Health Education Grant Program
Arkansas Department of Higher Education
114 East Capitol
Little Rock, AR 72201-3818
Phone: 501-371-2013
Fax: 501-371-2002
E-mail: judym@adhe.arknet.edu

APPLIED SCIENCES_____

ASTRONAUT SCHOLARSHIP FOUNDATION

ASTRONAUT SCHOLARSHIP FOUNDATION • 14

Provides scholarships for deserving college science and engineering students.

Academic/Career Areas Applied Sciences; Aviation/Aerospace; Biology; Chemical Engineering; Computer Science/Data Processing; Earth Science; Electrical Engineering/Electronics; Engineering/Technology; Engineering-Related Technologies; Materials Science, Engineering and Metallurgy; Mechanical Engineering; Meteorology/Atmospheric Science.

Award Scholarship for use in junior, senior, graduate, or postgraduate years; renewable. *Number:* 17. *Amount:* $8500.

Eligibility Requirements: Applicant must be enrolled or expecting to enroll full-time at an institution or university. Available to U.S. citizens.

Application Requirements Financial need analysis, references, transcript. *Deadline:* April 15.

World Wide Web: http://www.astronautscholarship.org

Contact: Mr. Howard Benedict, Executive Director
Astronaut Scholarship Foundation
6225 Vectorspace Boulevard
Titusville, FL 32780
Phone: 321-269-6119
Fax: 321-267-3970
E-mail: mercurysvn@aol.com

BARRY M. GOLDWATER SCHOLARSHIP AND EXCELLENCE IN EDUCATION FOUNDATION

BARRY M. GOLDWATER SCHOLARSHIP AND EXCELLENCE IN EDUCATION PROGRAM • 15

One-time award to college juniors and seniors who will pursue advanced degrees in mathematics, natural sciences, or engineering. Students planning to study medicine are eligible if they plan a career in research. Candidates must be nominated by their college or university. Must be U.S. citizen or resident alien demonstrating intent to obtain U.S. citizenship. Minimum 3.0 GPA required. Nomination deadline: February 1. Please visit web site for further updates. (http://www.act.org/goldwater)

Academic/Career Areas Applied Sciences; Biology; Chemical Engineering; Civil Engineering; Computer Science/Data Processing; Earth Science; Engineering/Technology; Materials Science, Engineering and Metallurgy; Mechanical Engineering; Natural Sciences; Nuclear Science; Physical Sciences and Math.

Award Scholarship for use in junior or senior years; renewable. *Number:* up to 300. *Amount:* up to $7500.

Eligibility Requirements: Applicant must be enrolled or expecting to enroll full-time at a two-year or four-year institution or university. Applicant must have 3.0 GPA or higher. Available to U.S. citizens.

Application Requirements Application, autobiography, essay, references, transcript, school nomination. *Deadline:* February 1.

World Wide Web: http://www.act.org/goldwater

Contact: On-Campus Faculty Representative
Barry M. Goldwater Scholarship and Excellence in Education Foundation
6225 Brandon Avenue, Suite 315
Springfield, VA 22150-2519

HISPANIC COLLEGE FUND, INC.

NATIONAL HISPANIC EXPLORERS SCHOLARSHIP PROGRAM • 16

One-time scholarship award open to full-time undergraduates of Hispanic descent pursuing a degree in science, math, engineering, or NASA-related major. Must be a U.S. resident or U.S. citizen and have a minimum of a 3.0 GPA.

Academic/Career Areas Applied Sciences; Aviation/Aerospace; Biology; Chemical Engineering; Civil Engineering; Communications; Computer Science/Data Processing; Earth Science; Electrical Engineering/Electronics; Engineering/Technology; Engineering-Related Technologies; Food Science/Nutrition.

Award Scholarship for use in freshman, sophomore, junior, or senior years; not renewable. *Number:* 125–150. *Amount:* $2000–$3000.

Eligibility Requirements: Applicant must be Hispanic and enrolled or expecting to enroll full-time at a two-year or four-year institution or university. Applicant must have 3.0 GPA or higher. Available to U.S. and non-Canadian citizens.

National Hispanic Explorers Scholarship Program (continued)

Application Requirements Application, essay, financial need analysis, resume, references, test scores, transcript, college acceptance letter, copy of taxes, proof of US citizenship or residency. *Deadline:* April 15.

World Wide Web: http://www.hispanicfund.org

Contact: Stina Augustsson, Program Manager
Hispanic College Fund, Inc.
1717 Pennsylvania Avenue, NW, Suite 460
Washington, DC 20006
Phone: 202-296-5400
Fax: 202-296-3774
E-mail: hispaniccollegefund@earthlink.net

INTERNATIONAL SOCIETY FOR OPTICAL ENGINEERING-SPIE

SPIE EDUCATIONAL SCHOLARSHIPS IN OPTICAL SCIENCE AND ENGINEERING • 17

Application forms must show demonstrated personal commitment to and involvement of the applicant in the fields of optics, optical science and engineering, and indicate how the granting of the award will contribute to these fields. Applications will be judged by the SPIE Scholarship Committee on the basis of the long range contribution which the granting of the award will make to these fields.

Academic/Career Areas Applied Sciences; Aviation/Aerospace; Chemical Engineering; Electrical Engineering/Electronics; Engineering/Technology; Engineering-Related Technologies; Materials Science, Engineering and Metallurgy; Mechanical Engineering.

Award Scholarship for use in freshman, sophomore, junior, or senior years; not renewable. *Number:* 30–80. *Amount:* $1000–$10,000.

Eligibility Requirements: Applicant must be enrolled or expecting to enroll full-time at a two-year or four-year or technical institution or university. Available to U.S. and non-U.S. citizens.

Application Requirements Application, references, self-addressed stamped envelope. *Deadline:* January 31.

World Wide Web: http://www.spie.org/info/scholarships

Contact: Scholarship Committee
International Society for Optical Engineering-SPIE
PO Box 10
Bellingham, WA 98227
Phone: 360-676-3290
Fax: 360-647-1445
E-mail: scholarships@spie.org

LUCENT TECHNOLOGIES FOUNDATION

LUCENT GLOBAL SCIENCE SCHOLARS PROGRAM   • 18

Award competition is open to graduating high school seniors. Must excel in math and science and have an interest in careers related to information technology. Females and minorities are encouraged to apply. Students will work on team projects. Minimum 3.5 GPA required. Must be U.S. citizen. Visit web site for more information.

Academic/Career Areas Applied Sciences; Aviation/Aerospace; Chemical Engineering; Computer Science/Data Processing; Electrical Engineering/Electronics; Engineering/Technology; Engineering-Related Technologies; Physical Sciences and Math.

Award Prize for use in freshman year; not renewable. *Number:* 23. *Amount:* $5000.

Eligibility Requirements: Applicant must be high school student; planning to enroll or expecting to enroll full-time at a four-year institution and must have an interest in designated field specified by sponsor. Applicant must have 3.5 GPA or higher. Available to U.S. citizens.

Application Requirements Application, essay, interview, references, test scores, transcript. *Deadline:* February 18.

World Wide Web: http://www.iie.org/programs/lucent

Contact: Kim Samson, Program Administrator
Lucent Technologies Foundation
Institute of International Education
809 United Nations Plaza
New York, NY 10017
Phone: 212-984-5419
E-mail: sciencescholars@iie.org

ARCHITECTURE

ADELANTE! U.S. EDUCATION LEADERSHIP FUND

ADELANTE U.S. EDUCATION LEADERSHIP FUND   • 19

Renewable award for college juniors or seniors of Hispanic descent. Award primarily created to enhance the leadership qualities of the recipients for transition into postgraduate education, business and/or corporate America. Financial need is a factor for this award. Minimum 3.0 GPA required.

Academic/Career Areas Architecture.

Award Scholarship for use in senior year; renewable. *Number:* 20–30. *Amount:* $3000.

Eligibility Requirements: Applicant must be Hispanic and enrolled or expecting to enroll full-time at a four-year institution or university. Applicant must have 3.0 GPA or higher. Available to U.S. citizens.

Adelante U.S. Education Leadership Fund (continued)

Application Requirements Application, essay, financial need analysis, references, transcript. *Deadline:* Continuous.

Contact: Jan Angelini, Executive Director
Adelante! U.S. Education Leadership Fund
8415 Datapoint Drive
Suite 400
San Antonio, TX 78229
Phone: 210-692-1971
Fax: 210-692-1951
E-mail: jangelini@dcci.com

AMERICAN ARCHITECTURAL FOUNDATION

AMERICAN INSTITUTE OF ARCHITECTS/AMERICAN ARCHITECTURAL FOUNDATION SCHOLARSHIP FOR PROFESSIONAL DEGREE CANDIDATES
• 20

One-time award available to students in the final two years of a professional degree, NAAB-accredited program leading to a bachelor of arts or master's. Applications available from head of department. Cosponsored by AIA and AAF.

Academic/Career Areas Architecture.

Award Scholarship for use in junior, senior, or graduate years; not renewable. *Number:* 250. *Amount:* $500–$2500.

Eligibility Requirements: Applicant must be enrolled or expecting to enroll full-time at a four-year institution or university. Available to U.S. and non-U.S. citizens.

Application Requirements Application, essay, financial need analysis, references, transcript. *Deadline:* February 1.

World Wide Web: http://www.archfoundation.org

Contact: Mary Felber, Director of Scholarship Programs
American Architectural Foundation
1735 New York Avenue, NW
Washington, DC 20006-5292
Phone: 202-626-7511
Fax: 202-626-7509
E-mail: mfelber@archfoundation.org

HISPANIC COLLEGE FUND, INC.

DENNY'S/HISPANIC COLLEGE FUND SCHOLARSHIP
see number 1

INTERNATIONAL FACILITY MANAGEMENT ASSOCIATION FOUNDATION

IFMA FOUNDATION SCHOLARSHIPS • 21

One-time scholarship of up to $6000 awarded to students enrolled in full-time facility management programs. Minimum 2.5 GPA required. Application deadline is June 13.

Academic/Career Areas Architecture; Engineering-Related Technologies.

Award Scholarship for use in freshman, sophomore, junior, senior, graduate, or postgraduate years; not renewable. *Number:* 10–15. *Amount:* $1000–$6000.

Eligibility Requirements: Applicant must be enrolled or expecting to enroll full-time at a four-year institution or university. Applicant must have 2.5 GPA or higher. Available to U.S. and non-U.S. citizens.

Application Requirements Application, references, transcript, letter of intent. *Deadline:* June 13.

World Wide Web: http://www.ifma.org

Contact: Bonnie Montgomery, Foundation Manager
International Facility Management Association Foundation
One East Greenway Plaza, Suite 1100
Houston, TX 77046-0194
Phone: 713-623-4362
Fax: 713-623-6124
E-mail: bonnie.montgomery@ifma.org

NATIONAL ASSOCIATION OF WOMEN IN CONSTRUCTION

NAWIC UNDERGRADUATE SCHOLARSHIPS • 22

One-time award for any student having at least one year of study remaining in a construction-related program leading to an associate or higher degree. Awards range from $500-$2000. Submit application and transcript of grades.

Academic/Career Areas Architecture; Civil Engineering; Drafting; Electrical Engineering/Electronics; Engineering/Technology; Engineering-Related Technologies; Interior Design; Landscape Architecture; Mechanical Engineering; Trade/Technical Specialties.

Award Scholarship for use in sophomore, junior, or senior years; not renewable. *Number:* 40–50. *Amount:* $500–$2000.

Eligibility Requirements: Applicant must be enrolled or expecting to enroll full-time at a two-year or four-year or technical institution or university. Applicant must have 3.0 GPA or higher. Available to U.S. and non-U.S. citizens.

Application Requirements Application, essay, financial need analysis, interview, transcript. *Deadline:* February 1.

World Wide Web: http://nawic.org

NAWIC Undergraduate Scholarships (continued)
Contact: Scholarship Administrator
National Association of Women in Construction
327 South Adams Street
Fort Worth, TX 76104

WORLDSTUDIO FOUNDATION

WORLDSTUDIO FOUNDATION SCHOLARSHIP PROGRAM • 23

Worldstudio Foundation provides scholarships to minority and economically disadvantaged students who are studying the design/architecture/arts disciplines in American colleges and universities. Among the foundation's primary aims are to increase diversity in the creative professions and to foster social and environmental responsibility in the artists, designers, and studios of tomorrow. To this end, scholarship recipients are selected not only for their ability and their need, but also for their demonstrated commitment to giving back to the larger community through their work.

Academic/Career Areas Architecture; Arts; Fashion Design; Filmmaking; Graphics/Graphic Arts/Printing; Interior Design.

Award Scholarship for use in freshman, sophomore, junior, senior, graduate, or postgraduate years; not renewable. *Number:* 30–50. *Amount:* $1000–$5000.

Eligibility Requirements: Applicant must be enrolled or expecting to enroll full-time at a two-year or four-year or technical institution or university. Applicant must have 2.5 GPA or higher. Available to U.S. and non-U.S. citizens.

Application Requirements Application, essay, financial need analysis, photo, portfolio, references, self-addressed stamped envelope, transcript. *Deadline:* February 14.

World Wide Web: http://www.worldstudio.org

Contact: Scholarship Coordinator
Worldstudio Foundation
200 Varick Street, Suite 507
New York, NY 10014
Phone: 212-366-1317 Ext. 18
Fax: 212-807-0024
E-mail: scholarships@worldstudio.org

ARTS

ALLIANCE FOR YOUNG ARTISTS AND WRITERS, INC.

SCHOLASTIC ART AND WRITING AWARDS-ART SECTION • 24

Award for students in grades 7-12. Winners of preliminary judging advance to national level. Contact regarding application fee and deadlines, which vary.

Academic/Career Areas Arts; Literature/English/Writing.
Award Scholarship for use in freshman, sophomore, junior, or senior years; not renewable. *Number:* 800. *Amount:* $100–$20,000.
Eligibility Requirements: Applicant must be high school student; planning to enroll or expecting to enroll at an institution or university and must have an interest in art. Available to U.S. and Canadian citizens.
Application Requirements Application, applicant must enter a contest, essay, portfolio, references.
World Wide Web: http://www.artandwriting.org
Contact: Alliance for Young Artists and Writers, Inc.
557 Broadway
New York, NY 10012-1396
Phone: 212-343-6493
E-mail: a&wgeneralinfo@scholastic.org

SCHOLASTIC ART AND WRITING AWARDS-WRITING SECTION SCHOLARSHIP
• 25
Award for students in grades 7-12. Winners of preliminary judging advance to national level. Contact regarding application fee and deadlines, which vary.
Academic/Career Areas Arts; Literature/English/Writing.
Award Scholarship for use in freshman, sophomore, junior, or senior years; not renewable. *Number:* 400. *Amount:* $100–$10,000.
Eligibility Requirements: Applicant must be high school student; planning to enroll or expecting to enroll at an institution or university and must have an interest in writing. Available to U.S. and Canadian citizens.
Application Requirements Application, applicant must enter a contest, essay, manuscript.
World Wide Web: http://www.artandwriting.org
Contact: Alliance for Young Artists and Writers, Inc.
557 Broadway
New York, NY 10012-1396
Phone: 212-343-6493
E-mail: a&wgeneralinfo@scholastic.org

ELIZABETH GREENSHIELDS FOUNDATION

ELIZABETH GREENSHIELDS AWARD/GRANT
• 26
Award of CAN$12,500 available to candidates working in painting, drawing, printmaking, or sculpture. Work must be representational or figurative. Must submit at least one color slide of each of six works. Must reapply to renew. Applications from self-taught individuals are also accepted.
Academic/Career Areas Arts.
Award Grant for use in freshman, sophomore, junior, senior, or graduate years; not renewable. *Number:* 40–60. *Amount:* $12,500.
Eligibility Requirements: Applicant must be enrolled or expecting to enroll full or part-time at a two-year or four-year or technical institution or university and must have an interest in art. Available to U.S. and non-U.S. citizens.

Elizabeth Greenshields Award/Grant (continued)

Application Requirements Application, slides. *Deadline:* Continuous.

Contact: Diane Pitcher, Applications Coordinator
Elizabeth Greenshields Foundation
1814 Sherbrooke Street West, Suite 1
Montreal, QC H3H IE4
Canada
Phone: 514-937-9225
Fax: 514-937-0141
E-mail: egreen@total.net

WORLDSTUDIO FOUNDATION

WORLDSTUDIO FOUNDATION SCHOLARSHIP PROGRAM

see number 23

AVIATION/AEROSPACE

ASTRONAUT SCHOLARSHIP FOUNDATION

ASTRONAUT SCHOLARSHIP FOUNDATION   see number 14

HISPANIC COLLEGE FUND, INC.

NATIONAL HISPANIC EXPLORERS SCHOLARSHIP PROGRAM

see number 16

HISPANIC ENGINEER NATIONAL ACHIEVEMENT AWARDS CORPORATION (HENAAC)

HISPANIC ENGINEER NATIONAL ACHIEVEMENT AWARDS CORPORATION SCHOLARSHIP PROGRAM   • 27

Scholarships available to Hispanic students maintaining a 3.0 GPA. Must be studying an engineering or science related field. For more details and an application go to web site: http://www.henaac.org

Academic/Career Areas Aviation/Aerospace; Biology; Chemical Engineering; Civil Engineering; Computer Science/Data Processing; Electrical Engineering/Electronics; Engineering/Technology; Materials Science, Engineering and Metallurgy; Mechanical Engineering; Nuclear Science.

Award Scholarship for use in freshman, sophomore, junior, senior, or graduate years; not renewable. *Number:* 12–20. *Amount:* $2000–$5000.

Eligibility Requirements: Applicant must be of Hispanic heritage and enrolled or expecting to enroll full-time at a four-year institution or university. Applicant must have 3.0 GPA or higher. Available to U.S. and Canadian citizens.
Application Requirements Application, essay, resume, references, transcript. *Deadline:* April 21.
World Wide Web: http://www.henaac.org
Contact: application available at web site

INTERNATIONAL SOCIETY FOR OPTICAL ENGINEERING-SPIE

SPIE EDUCATIONAL SCHOLARSHIPS IN OPTICAL SCIENCE AND ENGINEERING
see number 17

LUCENT TECHNOLOGIES FOUNDATION

LUCENT GLOBAL SCIENCE SCHOLARS PROGRAM
see number 18

NAMEPA NATIONAL SCHOLARSHIP FOUNDATION

NATIONAL ASSOCIATION OF MINORITY ENGINEERING PROGRAM ADMINISTRATORS NATIONAL SCHOLARSHIP FUND • 28

NAMEPA offers one-time scholarships for African-American, Hispanic, and American-Indian students who have demonstrated potential and interest in pursuing an undergraduate degree in engineering. Must have a minimum 3.0 GPA. Must have a score above 25 on ACT, or above 1000 on SAT. Visit web site at http://www.namepa.org for application materials and further details.

Academic/Career Areas Aviation/Aerospace; Chemical Engineering; Civil Engineering; Computer Science/Data Processing; Electrical Engineering/ Electronics; Engineering/Technology; Engineering-Related Technologies; Materials Science, Engineering and Metallurgy; Mechanical Engineering.

Award Scholarship for use in freshman or junior years; not renewable. *Number:* 10–50. *Amount:* $1000–$5000.

Eligibility Requirements: Applicant must be American Indian/Alaska Native, Black (non-Hispanic), or Hispanic and enrolled or expecting to enroll full-time at a two-year or four-year institution or university. Applicant must have 3.0 GPA or higher. Available to U.S. and non-U.S. citizens.

Application Requirements Application, essay, resume, references, test scores, transcript. *Deadline:* March 30.
World Wide Web: http://www.namepa.org

National Association of Minority Engineering Program Administrators National Scholarship Fund (continued)

Contact: Latisha Moore, Administrative Assistant
NAMEPA National Scholarship Foundation
1133 West Morse Boulevard, Suite 201
Winter Park, FL 32789
Phone: 407-647-8839
Fax: 407-629-2502
E-mail: namepa@namepa.org

NASA NEVADA SPACE GRANT CONSORTIUM

UNIVERSITY AND COMMUNITY COLLEGE SYSTEM OF NEVADA NASA SPACE GRANT AND FELLOWSHIP PROGRAM ● 29

Nevada Space Grant provides graduate fellowships and undergraduate scholarship to qualified student majoring in aerospace science, technology and related fields. Must be Nevada resident studying at a Nevada college/university. Minimum 2.5 GPA required.

Academic/Career Areas Aviation/Aerospace; Chemical Engineering; Computer Science/Data Processing; Electrical Engineering/Electronics; Engineering/Technology; Meteorology/Atmospheric Science; Physical Sciences and Math.
Award Scholarship for use in freshman, sophomore, junior, senior, or graduate years; renewable. *Number:* 1–20. *Amount:* $2500–$25,000.
Eligibility Requirements: Applicant must be enrolled or expecting to enroll full-time at a two-year or four-year institution or university; resident of Nevada and studying in Nevada. Applicant must have 2.5 GPA or higher. Available to U.S. citizens.
Application Requirements Application, autobiography, essay, resume, references, transcript. *Deadline:* April 1.
World Wide Web: http://www.unr.edu/spacegrant
Contact: Lori Rountree, Program Coordinator
NASA Nevada Space Grant Consortium
University of Nevada, Reno
MS 172
Reno, NV 89557-0138
Phone: 775-784-6261
Fax: 775-327-2235
E-mail: lori@mines.unr.edu

BIOLOGY

ALBERTA HERITAGE SCHOLARSHIP FUND

ALBERTA HERITAGE SCHOLARSHIP FUND ABORIGINAL HEALTH CAREERS BURSARY ● 30

Award for aboriginal students in Alberta entering their second or subsequent year of postsecondary education in a health field. Must be Indian, Inuit, or

Métis and a resident of Alberta for a minimum of three years prior to applying. Awards are valued up to CAN$13,000. Deadline: May 15. Must be ranked in upper half of class or have a minimum 2.5 GPA.

Academic/Career Areas Biology; Dental Health/Services; Health Administration; Health and Medical Sciences; Nursing; Therapy/Rehabilitation.

Award Scholarship for use in sophomore, junior, senior, or graduate years; not renewable. *Number:* 20–40. *Amount:* $1000–$13,000.

Eligibility Requirements: Applicant must be Canadian citizenship; American Indian/Alaska Native; enrolled or expecting to enroll full-time at a two-year or four-year or technical institution or university and resident of Alberta. Applicant must have 2.5 GPA or higher.

Application Requirements Application, essay, financial need analysis, references, transcript. *Deadline:* May 15.

World Wide Web: http://www.alis.gov.ab.ca/scholarships

Contact: Alberta Heritage Scholarship Fund
9940 106th Street, 9th Floor, Box 28000 Station Main
Edmonton, AB T5J 4R4
Canada
Phone: 780-427-8640
Fax: 780-422-4516
E-mail: heritage@gov.ab.ca

ARKANSAS DEPARTMENT OF HIGHER EDUCATION

EMERGENCY SECONDARY EDUCATION LOAN PROGRAM ● 31

Must be Arkansas resident enrolled full-time in approved Arkansas institution. Renewable award for students majoring in secondary math, chemistry, physics, biology, physical science, general science, special education, or foreign language. Must teach in Arkansas at least five years. Must rank in upper half of class or have a minimum 2.5 GPA.

Academic/Career Areas Biology; Education; Foreign Language; Physical Sciences and Math; Special Education.

Award Forgivable loan for use in sophomore, junior, senior, or graduate years; renewable. *Number:* up to 50. *Amount:* up to $2500.

Eligibility Requirements: Applicant must be enrolled or expecting to enroll full-time at a two-year or four-year institution or university; resident of Arkansas and studying in Arkansas. Applicant must have 2.5 GPA or higher. Available to U.S. citizens.

Application Requirements Application, transcript. *Deadline:* April 1.

World Wide Web: http://www.arscholarships.com

Contact: Lillian K. Williams, Assistant Coordinator
Arkansas Department of Higher Education
114 East Capitol
Little Rock, AR 72201
Phone: 501-371-2050
Fax: 501-371-2001

ASTRONAUT SCHOLARSHIP FOUNDATION

ASTRONAUT SCHOLARSHIP FOUNDATION   see number 14

BARRY M. GOLDWATER SCHOLARSHIP AND EXCELLENCE IN EDUCATION FOUNDATION

BARRY M. GOLDWATER SCHOLARSHIP AND EXCELLENCE IN EDUCATION PROGRAM   see number 15

BUSINESS AND PROFESSIONAL WOMEN'S FOUNDATION

BPW CAREER ADVANCEMENT SCHOLARSHIP PROGRAM FOR WOMEN   • 32

Scholarships ranging from $1000-$5000 each are awarded for full-or part-time study. Applicant must be studying in one of the following fields: biological sciences, teacher education certification, engineering, social science, paralegal studies, humanities, business studies, mathematics, computer science, physical sciences, or for a professional degree (JD, MD, DDS). The Career Advancement Scholarship Program was established to assist women seeking the education necessary for entry or re-entry into the work force, or advancement within a career field. Must be 25 or over. Send self-addressed double-stamped envelope between January 1 and April 1 for application.

Academic/Career Areas Biology; Computer Science/Data Processing; Dental Health/Services; Education; Engineering/Technology; Engineering-Related Technologies; Health and Medical Sciences; Humanities; Law/Legal Services; Physical Sciences and Math; Social Sciences.

Award Scholarship for use in junior, senior, or graduate years; not renewable. *Number:* up to 100. *Amount:* $1000–$5000.

Eligibility Requirements: Applicant must be age 25; enrolled or expecting to enroll full or part-time at a two-year or four-year or technical institution or university and female. Applicant must have 2.5 GPA or higher. Available to U.S. citizens.

Application Requirements Application, essay, financial need analysis, references, self-addressed stamped envelope, transcript. *Deadline:* April 15.

World Wide Web: http://www.bpwusa.org

Contact: Diane Thurston Frye, Development and Scholarship Manager
Business and Professional Women's Foundation
1900 M Street, NW, Suite 310
Washington, DC 20036
Phone: 202-293-1100 Ext. 182
Fax: 202-861-0298

HISPANIC COLLEGE FUND, INC.

NATIONAL HISPANIC EXPLORERS SCHOLARSHIP PROGRAM
see number 16

HISPANIC ENGINEER NATIONAL ACHIEVEMENT AWARDS CORPORATION (HENAAC)

HISPANIC ENGINEER NATIONAL ACHIEVEMENT AWARDS CORPORATION SCHOLARSHIP PROGRAM
see number 27

MORRIS K. UDALL FOUNDATION

MORRIS K. UDALL SCHOLARS
see number 12

NATIONAL FISH AND WILDLIFE FOUNDATION

BUDWEISER CONSERVATION SCHOLARSHIP PROGRAM   • 33

One-time award supports and promotes innovative research or study that seeks to respond to today's most pressing conservation issues. This competitive scholarship program is designed to respond to many of the most significant challenges in fish, wildlife, and plant conservation in the United States by providing scholarships to eligible graduate and undergraduate students who are poised to make a significant contribution to the field of conservation.

Academic/Career Areas Biology; Geography; Natural Resources; Natural Sciences; Political Science; Surveying; Surveying Technology, Cartography, or Geographic Information Science.

Award Scholarship for use in sophomore, junior, senior, or graduate years; not renewable. *Number:* 10–20. *Amount:* $10,000.

Eligibility Requirements: Applicant must be enrolled or expecting to enroll full-time at a four-year institution or university. Available to U.S. citizens.

Application Requirements Application, essay, references, transcript, title of proposed research and a short abstract. *Deadline:* January 18.

World Wide Web: http://www.nfwf.org

Contact: Tom Kelsch, Director, Conservation Education
National Fish and Wildlife Foundation
1120 Connecticut Avenue, NW
Suite 900
Washington, DC 20036
Phone: 202-857-0166
Fax: 202-857-0162
E-mail: tom.kelsch@nfwf.org

UNITED NEGRO COLLEGE FUND

MERCK SCIENCE INITIATIVE   • 34

Scholarship for undergraduate juniors, graduate students, or postdoctoral fellows majoring in the life or physical sciences. 3.3 GPA required. Visit web site at http://www.uncf.org/merck for details. Prospective applicants should complete the Student Profile found at web site: http://www.uncf.org.

Academic/Career Areas Biology; Health and Medical Sciences; Physical Sciences and Math.

Award Scholarship for use in junior, graduate, or postgraduate years; not renewable. *Number:* 37. *Amount:* up to $7000.

Eligibility Requirements: Applicant must be Black (non-Hispanic) and enrolled or expecting to enroll at a four-year institution or university. Available to U.S. citizens.

Application Requirements Application, financial need analysis. *Deadline:* December 16.

World Wide Web: http://www.uncf.org

Contact: Program Services Department
United Negro College Fund
8260 Willow Oaks Corporate Drive
Fairfax, VA 22031

UNITED STATES DEPARTMENT OF HEALTH AND HUMAN SERVICES

NIH UNDERGRADUATE SCHOLARSHIP FOR INDIVIDUALS FROM DISADVANTAGED BACKGROUNDS   • 35

Renewable awards of up to $20,000 per year for individuals from disadvantaged backgrounds to pursue degrees in physical and life sciences (including chemistry). Must complete one year of National Institutes of Health employment for each year of scholarship plus ten weeks during each year of scholarship. Minimum 3.5 GPA required.

Academic/Career Areas Biology; Health and Medical Sciences; Physical Sciences and Math.

Award Scholarship for use in freshman, sophomore, junior, or senior years; renewable. *Number:* 15–20. *Amount:* up to $20,000.

Eligibility Requirements: Applicant must be enrolled or expecting to enroll full-time at a four-year institution or university. Applicant must have 3.5 GPA or higher.

Application Requirements Application, essay, financial need analysis, references, transcript. *Deadline:* March 31.

World Wide Web: http://helix.nih.gov:8001/oe/student/ugsp.html

Contact: Dr. Alfred C. Johnson, Director of Undergraduate Scholarship
Program
United States Department of Health and Human Services
2 Center Drive, Room 2E30
Bethesda, MD 20892-0230
Phone: 800-528-7689
Fax: 301-402-8098
E-mail: ugsp@nih.gov

BUSINESS/CONSUMER SERVICES_____

AMERICAN FLORAL ENDOWMENT

VICTOR AND MARGARET BALL PROGRAM • 36

Award for undergraduate students majoring in business, floriculture, and
ornamental horticulture. A paid training experience for students who are
interested in a "production related" career (growing), and up to a $6000 grant
upon satisfactory completion of six months of training. Deadlines: March 1 for
fall/winter training; November 1 for spring/summer training.

Academic/Career Areas Business/Consumer Services; Horticulture/
Floriculture.

Award Scholarship for use in freshman, sophomore, junior, or senior years;
not renewable. *Number:* 20. *Amount:* $3000–$6000.

Eligibility Requirements: Applicant must be enrolled or expecting to enroll
full-time at a two-year or four-year institution or university. Applicant must
have 2.5 GPA or higher. Available to U.S. and non-U.S. citizens.

Application Requirements Application, photo, references, transcript.

World Wide Web: http://www.endowment.org

Contact: Steve F. Martinez, Executive Vice President
American Floral Endowment
11 Glen-Ed Professional Park
Glen Carbon, IL 62034
Phone: 618-692-0045
Fax: 618-692-4045
E-mail: afe@endowment.org

APICS- EDUCATIONAL AND RESEARCH FOUNDATION, INC.

DONALD W. FOGARTY INTERNATIONAL STUDENT PAPER COMPETITION • 37

Annual competition on topics pertaining to resource management only. Must
be original work of one or more authors. May submit one paper only. Must be

Donald W. Fogarty International Student Paper Competition (continued)
in English. Open to full- and part-time undergraduate and graduate students. High school students ineligible. All queries are directed to web site. Other queries must submit e-mail address and SASE.

Academic/Career Areas Business/Consumer Services; Natural Resources.

Award Prize for use in freshman, sophomore, junior, senior, or graduate years; not renewable. *Number:* up to 90. *Amount:* $100–$1750.

Eligibility Requirements: Applicant must be enrolled or expecting to enroll full or part-time at a four-year institution or university. Available to U.S. and non-U.S. citizens.

Application Requirements Application, applicant must enter a contest, essay, self-addressed stamped envelope. *Deadline:* May 15.

World Wide Web: http://www.apics.org/E&R

Contact: Dr. Steven A. Melnyk, Professor Supply Chain Management, Dept. of Marketing
E-mail: foundation@apicshq.org

CASUALTY ACTUARIAL SOCIETY/SOCIETY OF ACTUARIES JOINT COMMITTEE ON MINORITY RECRUITING

ACTUARIAL SCHOLARSHIPS FOR MINORITY STUDENTS   • 38

Award for underrepresented minority students planning careers in actuarial science or mathematics. Applicants should have taken the ACT Assessment or the SAT. Number and amount of awards vary with merit and financial need. Must be a U.S. citizen or permanent resident. All scholarship information including application is available online. Do not send award inquiries to address.

Academic/Career Areas Business/Consumer Services.

Award Scholarship for use in freshman, sophomore, junior, senior, or graduate years; not renewable. *Number:* 20–40. *Amount:* $500–$3000.

Eligibility Requirements: Applicant must be American Indian/Alaska Native, Black (non-Hispanic), or Hispanic and enrolled or expecting to enroll full or part-time at a two-year or four-year institution or university. Available to U.S. citizens.

Application Requirements Application, financial need analysis, references, test scores, transcript. *Deadline:* May 1.

World Wide Web: http://www.BeAnActuary.org

Contact: Frank Lupo, Minority Scholarship Coordinator
Casualty Actuarial Society/Society of Actuaries Joint Committee on Minority Recruiting
475 North Martingale Road, Suite 800
Schaumburg, IL 60173-2226
Phone: 703-276-3100
E-mail: flupo@casact.org

CATCHING THE DREAM

MATH, ENGINEERING, SCIENCE, BUSINESS, EDUCATION, COMPUTERS SCHOLARSHIPS • 39

Renewable scholarships for Native-Americans students planning to study math, engineering, science, business, education, and computers, or presently studying in these fields. Study of social science, humanities and liberal arts also funded. Scholarships are awarded on merit and on the basis of likelihood of recipient improving the lives of Indian people. Deadlines are March 15, April 15, and September 15. Scholarships are available nationwide.

Academic/Career Areas Business/Consumer Services; Computer Science/ Data Processing; Education; Engineering/Technology; Humanities; Physical Sciences and Math; Science, Technology and Society; Social Sciences.

Award Scholarship for use in freshman, sophomore, junior, senior, graduate, or postgraduate years; renewable. *Number:* 180. *Amount:* $500–$5000.

Eligibility Requirements: Applicant must be American Indian/Alaska Native and enrolled or expecting to enroll full-time at a two-year or four-year institution or university. Applicant must have 3.0 GPA or higher. Available to U.S. citizens.

Application Requirements Application, essay, financial need analysis, photo, references, test scores, transcript, certificate of Indian blood.

Contact: Recruiter
Catching the Dream
8200 Mountain Road, NE
Suite 203
Albuquerque, NM 87110
Phone: 505-262-2351
Fax: 505-262-0534
E-mail: nscholarsh@aol.com

NATIVE AMERICAN LEADERSHIP IN EDUCATION (NALE) • 40

Renewable scholarships available for Native-Americans and Alaskan Native students. Must be at least one-quarter Native-Americans from a federally recognized, state recognized or terminated tribe. Must be U.S. citizen. Must demonstrate high academic achievement, depth of character, leadership, seriousness of purpose, and service orientation. Application deadlines are March 15, April 15, and September 15.

Academic/Career Areas Business/Consumer Services; Education; Humanities; Physical Sciences and Math; Science, Technology and Society.

Award Scholarship for use in freshman, sophomore, junior, or senior years; renewable. *Number:* up to 30. *Amount:* $500–$5000.

Eligibility Requirements: Applicant must be American Indian/Alaska Native and enrolled or expecting to enroll full-time at a four-year institution or university. Available to U.S. citizens.

Application Requirements Application, essay, references, transcript.

Native American Leadership in Education (NALE) (continued)
Contact: Recruitment Office
Catching the Dream
8200 Mountain Road, NE
Suite 203
Albuquerque, NM 87110
Phone: 505-262-2351
Fax: 505-262-0534
E-mail: nscholarsh@aol.com

CUBAN AMERICAN NATIONAL FOUNDATION
MAS FAMILY SCHOLARSHIPS   • 41
Graduate and undergraduate scholarships in the fields of engineering, business, international relations, economics, communications, and journalism. Applicants must be Cuban-American and have graduated in the top 10% of high school class or have minimum 3.5 college GPA. Selection based on need, academic performance, leadership. Those who have already received awards and maintained high level of performance are given preference over new applicants.

Academic/Career Areas Business/Consumer Services; Chemical Engineering; Communications; Economics; Electrical Engineering/Electronics; Engineering/Technology; Engineering-Related Technologies; Journalism; Mechanical Engineering; Political Science.

Award Scholarship for use in freshman, sophomore, junior, or senior years; renewable. *Number:* 10–15. *Amount:* $1000–$10,000.

Eligibility Requirements: Applicant must be of Latin American/Caribbean heritage; enrolled or expecting to enroll full-time at a two-year or four-year institution or university and must have an interest in leadership. Applicant must have 3.5 GPA or higher. Available to U.S. citizens.

Application Requirements Application, autobiography, essay, financial need analysis, references, test scores, transcript. *Deadline:* March 31.

Contact: Director
Cuban American National Foundation
Mas Family Scholarships
1312 SW 27th Avenue, 3rd Floor
Miami, FL 33145
Phone: 305-592-7768
Fax: 305-592-7889

DECA (DISTRIBUTIVE EDUCATION CLUBS OF AMERICA)
HARRY A. APPLEGATE SCHOLARSHIP   • 42
Available to current DECA members for undergraduate or graduate study. Must major in marketing education, merchandising, and/or management.

Nonrenewable award for high school students based on DECA activities, grades, and need. Submit application to state office by state application deadline. National office must receive applications by the second Monday in March.

Academic/Career Areas Business/Consumer Services; Education; Food Service/Hospitality.

Award Scholarship for use in freshman, sophomore, junior, senior, or graduate years; not renewable. *Number:* 30–100. *Amount:* $1000–$1500.

Eligibility Requirements: Applicant must be high school student; planning to enroll or expecting to enroll full or part-time at a two-year or four-year institution or university and must have an interest in leadership. Applicant or parent of applicant must be member of Distribution Ed Club or Future Business Leaders of America. Applicant must have 2.5 GPA or higher. Available to U.S. and Canadian citizens.

Application Requirements Application, references, test scores, transcript.

World Wide Web: http://www.deca.org

Contact: Kathy Onion, Marketing Specialist
DECA (Distributive Education Clubs of America)
1908 Association Drive
Reston, VA 20191-4013
Phone: 703-860-5000 Ext. 248
Fax: 703-860-4013
E-mail: kathy_onion@deca.org

HISPANIC COLLEGE FUND, INC.

DENNY'S/HISPANIC COLLEGE FUND SCHOLARSHIP   see number 1

FIRST IN MY FAMILY SCHOLARSHIP PROGRAM   see number 10

HISPANIC COLLEGE FUND SCHOLARSHIP PROGRAM   see number 11

HISPANIC COLLEGE FUND/INROADS/SPRINT SCHOLARSHIP PROGRAM   • 43

One-time award open to undergraduates of Hispanic descent pursuing a degree in a business- or technology-related major. Must be a U.S. citizen and have a minimum 3.0 GPA. Recipients will participate in INROADS Leadership Development Training while interning at Sprint during the summer.

Academic/Career Areas Business/Consumer Services; Communications; Computer Science/Data Processing; Economics; Electrical Engineering/Electronics; Engineering/Technology; Engineering-Related Technologies; Mechanical Engineering.

Award Scholarship for use in freshman, sophomore, junior, or senior years; not renewable. *Number:* 10–20. *Amount:* $1000–$5000.

Eligibility Requirements: Applicant must be of Hispanic, Latin American/Caribbean, Mexican, Nicaraguan, or Spanish heritage and enrolled or expecting to enroll full-time at a two-year or four-year institution or university. Applicant must have 3.0 GPA or higher. Available to U.S. citizens.

Hispanic College Fund/INROADS/Sprint Scholarship Program (continued)
Application Requirements Application, essay, financial need analysis, resume, references, test scores, transcript, college acceptance letter, copy of taxes, copy of SAR. *Deadline:* April 15.
World Wide Web: http://www.hispanicfund.org
Contact: Stina Augustsson, Program Manager
Hispanic College Fund, Inc.
1717 Pennsylvania Avenue, NW, Suite 460
Washington, DC 20006
Phone: 202-296-5400
Fax: 202-296-3774
E-mail: hispaniccollegefund@earthlink.net

HISPANIC SCHOLARSHIP FUND

HSF/GENERAL MOTORS SCHOLARSHIP   • 44
Scholarships are available to Hispanic students pursuing a degree in business or engineering at an accredited U.S. four-year college. For more details, deadlines and an application see web site: http://www.hsf.net.
Academic/Career Areas Business/Consumer Services; Chemical Engineering; Civil Engineering; Electrical Engineering/Electronics; Engineering/Technology; Engineering-Related Technologies; Mechanical Engineering.
Award Scholarship for use in freshman, sophomore, junior, or senior years; not renewable. *Number:* 83. *Amount:* $2500.
Eligibility Requirements: Applicant must be Hispanic and enrolled or expecting to enroll full-time at a four-year institution or university. Applicant must have 3.0 GPA or higher. Available to U.S. citizens.
Application Requirements Application.
World Wide Web: http://www.hsf.net
Contact: application available at web site

MARYLAND ASSOCIATION OF PRIVATE CAREER SCHOOLS

MARYLAND ASSOCIATION OF PRIVATE CAREER SCHOOLS SCHOLARSHIP   • 45
Awards for study at trade schools only. Must enter school same year high school is completed. For use only in Maryland and by Maryland residents. Write for further information. One-time award of $1000 to $18,000.
Academic/Career Areas Business/Consumer Services; Computer Science/Data Processing; Dental Health/Services; Engineering/Technology; Food Science/Nutrition; Home Economics; Trade/Technical Specialties; TV/Radio Broadcasting.
Award Scholarship for use in freshman year; not renewable. *Number:* 38. *Amount:* $1000–$18,000.
Eligibility Requirements: Applicant must be high school student; planning to enroll or expecting to enroll full-time at a technical institution; resident of Maryland and studying in Maryland. Available to U.S. citizens.

Application Requirements Application, references, transcript. *Deadline:* April 18.

Contact: Administrative Assistant
Maryland Association of Private Career Schools
1205 Stonewood Court
Annapolis, MD 21401
Phone: 410-282-4012
Fax: 410-282-4012

NATIONAL ASSOCIATION OF BLACK ACCOUNTANTS, INC.

NATIONAL ASSOCIATION OF BLACK ACCOUNTANTS NATIONAL SCHOLARSHIP
see number 2

NORTH CAROLINA CPA FOUNDATION, INC.

NORTH CAROLINA CPA FOUNDATION ACCOUNTING SCHOLARSHIP PROGRAM
• 46

Awards are made to juniors, seniors and fifth-year students pursuing undergraduate and graduate degrees in accounting. The essay requests the students describe the "CPA of the Future" and why they want to become one. The amount of the award will be determined by the best essay. Applicants must be a North Carolina resident attending a North Carolina four-year college or university.

Academic/Career Areas Business/Consumer Services.
Award Scholarship for use in junior, senior, or graduate years; not renewable. *Number:* 20–30. *Amount:* $1000–$3000.
Eligibility Requirements: Applicant must be enrolled or expecting to enroll full-time at a four-year institution or university; resident of North Carolina and studying in North Carolina. Applicant must have 2.5 GPA or higher. Available to U.S. citizens.
Application Requirements Application, applicant must enter a contest, essay, transcript. *Deadline:* January 31.
World Wide Web: http://www.ncacpa.org
Contact: Jim Ahler, CAE, Executive Director
North Carolina CPA Foundation, Inc.
PO Box 80188
Raleigh, NC 27623-0188
Phone: 919-469-1040
Fax: 919-469-3959
E-mail: jtahler@ncacpa.org

SOCIETY OF PLASTICS ENGINEERS (SPE) FOUNDATION

SOCIETY OF PLASTICS ENGINEERS SCHOLARSHIP PROGRAM • 47

The SPE Foundation offers scholarships to full-time students who have demonstrated or expressed an interest in the plastics industry. They must be majoring in or taking courses that would be beneficial to a career in the plastics industry.

Academic/Career Areas Business/Consumer Services; Chemical Engineering; Civil Engineering; Engineering/Technology; Materials Science, Engineering and Metallurgy; Mechanical Engineering; Trade/Technical Specialties.

Award Scholarship for use in freshman, sophomore, junior, senior, or graduate years; not renewable. *Number:* 19. *Amount:* $1000–$5000.

Eligibility Requirements: Applicant must be enrolled or expecting to enroll full-time at a two-year or four-year or technical institution or university. Available to U.S. and non-U.S. citizens.

Application Requirements Application, essay, financial need analysis, references, transcript. *Deadline:* January 15.

World Wide Web: http://www.4spe.org

Contact: Gail Bristol, Managing Director
Society of Plastics Engineers (SPE) Foundation
14 Fairfield Drive
Brookfield, CT 06804
Phone: 203-740-5447
Fax: 203-775-1157
E-mail: grbristol@4spe.org

UNITED NEGRO COLLEGE FUND

COLLEGE FUND/COCA COLA CORPORATE INTERN PROGRAM • 48

Provides educational opportunities for minority students. Must be rising college juniors with a minimum GPA of 3.0. Scholarship based on successful internship performance. Open to majors in engineering, business, finance, information technology, chemistry, communications, and human resources. Prospective applicants should complete the Student Profile found at web site: http://www.uncf.org.

Academic/Career Areas Business/Consumer Services; Communications; Computer Science/Data Processing; Engineering/Technology.

Award Scholarship for use in junior year; not renewable. *Number:* up to 50. *Amount:* $10,000.

Eligibility Requirements: Applicant must be American Indian/Alaska Native, Asian/Pacific Islander, Black (non-Hispanic), or Hispanic and enrolled or expecting to enroll full-time at a four-year institution or university. Applicant must have 3.0 GPA or higher.

Application Requirements Application, references, transcript. *Deadline:* December 16.

World Wide Web: http://www.uncf.org
Contact: Program Services Department
United Negro College Fund
8260 Willow Oaks Corporate Drive
Fairfax, VA 22031

HOUSEHOLD INTERNATIONAL CORPORATE SCHOLARS   • 49
Scholarship provides opportunities for minority sophomores and juniors majoring in business, finance, accounting, marketing, computer science or human resources. Must attend a UNCF member college or university or a selected historically black college or university. Minimum 3.0 GPA required. Prospective applicants should complete the Student Profile found at web site: http://www.uncf.org.

Academic/Career Areas Business/Consumer Services; Computer Science/Data Processing.

Award Scholarship for use in sophomore or junior years; not renewable. *Number:* up to 30. *Amount:* up to $10,000.

Eligibility Requirements: Applicant must be American Indian/Alaska Native, Asian/Pacific Islander, Black (non-Hispanic), or Hispanic and enrolled or expecting to enroll at a four-year institution or university. Applicant must have 3.0 GPA or higher.

Application Requirements Application, financial need analysis. *Deadline:* March 1.

World Wide Web: http://www.uncf.org
Contact: Program Services Department
United Negro College Fund
8260 Willow Oaks Corporate Drive
Fairfax, VA 22031

CHEMICAL ENGINEERING_____

AEA-OREGON COUNCIL

AEA TECHNOLOGY SCHOLARSHIP PROGRAM   • 50
Over 30 scholarships given annually to Oregon high school seniors who plan to major in engineering, computer science or a closely related field and attend one of seven Oregon University system campuses. Must be U.S. citizen. Deadline is March 1.

Academic/Career Areas Chemical Engineering; Civil Engineering; Computer Science/Data Processing; Electrical Engineering/Electronics; Engineering/Technology; Engineering-Related Technologies; Materials Science, Engineering and Metallurgy; Mechanical Engineering.

Award Scholarship for use in freshman, sophomore, junior, or senior years; renewable. *Number:* 30–35. *Amount:* $2500.

AeA Technology Scholarship Program (continued)

Eligibility Requirements: Applicant must be high school student; planning to enroll or expecting to enroll full-time at an institution or university; resident of Oregon and studying in Oregon. Available to U.S. citizens.

Application Requirements Application, essay, references, test scores, transcript. *Deadline:* March 1.

World Wide Web: http://www.ous.edu/ecs/scholarships

Contact: Gary Lietke, AeA Scholarship Program Manager
AeA-Oregon Council
18640 NW Walker Road #1027
Beaverton, OR 97006
Phone: 503-725-2920
Fax: 503-725-2921
E-mail: geaschol@capital.ous.edu

AMERICAN CHEMICAL SOCIETY

AMERICAN CHEMICAL SOCIETY SCHOLARS PROGRAM • 51

Renewable award for minority students pursuing studies in chemistry, biochemistry, chemical technology, chemical engineering or any chemical sciences. Must be U.S. citizen or permanent resident and have minimum 3.0 GPA. Must be Native-Americans, African-American, or Hispanic. Scholarship amount for freshmen is up to $2500, and up to $3000 for sophomores, juniors and seniors.

Academic/Career Areas Chemical Engineering; Materials Science, Engineering and Metallurgy; Natural Sciences.

Award Scholarship for use in freshman, sophomore, or junior years; renewable. *Number:* 100–200. *Amount:* up to $3000.

Eligibility Requirements: Applicant must be American Indian/Alaska Native, Black (non-Hispanic), or Hispanic and enrolled or expecting to enroll full-time at a two-year or four-year or technical institution or university. Applicant must have 3.0 GPA or higher. Available to U.S. citizens.

Application Requirements Application, financial need analysis, references, test scores, transcript. *Deadline:* February 15.

World Wide Web: http://www.chemistry.org

Contact: Robert Hughes, Manager
American Chemical Society
1155 16th Street, NW
Washington, DC 20036
Phone: 202-872-6048
Fax: 202-776-8003
E-mail: scholars@acs.org

ASTRONAUT SCHOLARSHIP FOUNDATION

ASTRONAUT SCHOLARSHIP FOUNDATION   see number 14

BARRY M. GOLDWATER SCHOLARSHIP AND EXCELLENCE IN EDUCATION FOUNDATION

BARRY M. GOLDWATER SCHOLARSHIP AND EXCELLENCE IN EDUCATION PROGRAM see number 15

CUBAN AMERICAN NATIONAL FOUNDATION

MAS FAMILY SCHOLARSHIPS see number 41

HISPANIC COLLEGE FUND, INC.

DENNY'S/HISPANIC COLLEGE FUND SCHOLARSHIP see number 1

FIRST IN MY FAMILY SCHOLARSHIP PROGRAM see number 10

HISPANIC COLLEGE FUND SCHOLARSHIP PROGRAM see number 11

NATIONAL HISPANIC EXPLORERS SCHOLARSHIP PROGRAM see number 16

HISPANIC ENGINEER NATIONAL ACHIEVEMENT AWARDS CORPORATION (HENAAC)

HISPANIC ENGINEER NATIONAL ACHIEVEMENT AWARDS CORPORATION SCHOLARSHIP PROGRAM see number 27

HISPANIC SCHOLARSHIP FUND

HSF/GENERAL MOTORS SCHOLARSHIP see number 44

INTERNATIONAL SOCIETY FOR OPTICAL ENGINEERING-SPIE

SPIE EDUCATIONAL SCHOLARSHIPS IN OPTICAL SCIENCE AND ENGINEERING see number 17

LUCENT TECHNOLOGIES FOUNDATION

LUCENT GLOBAL SCIENCE SCHOLARS PROGRAM see number 18

MICRON TECHNOLOGY FOUNDATION

MICRON SCIENCE AND TECHNOLOGY SCHOLARS • 52

Merit-based scholarship competition for high school seniors recognizing excellence in academics and leadership. One, top prize of a $55,000 college scholarship and twelve $16,500 scholarships available each year. Two scholars are selected from each of the five select states, with up to three floating scholarships awarded within those states. See web site for details.

Academic/Career Areas Chemical Engineering; Computer Science/Data Processing; Electrical Engineering/Electronics; Engineering/Technology; Engineering-Related Technologies; Materials Science, Engineering and Metallurgy; Mechanical Engineering.

Award Scholarship for use in freshman, sophomore, junior, or senior years; renewable. *Number:* up to 13. *Amount:* $16,500–$55,000.

Eligibility Requirements: Applicant must be high school student; planning to enroll or expecting to enroll full-time at a four-year institution or university; resident of Colorado, Idaho, Texas, Utah, or Virginia and must have an interest in leadership. Applicant must have 3.5 GPA or higher. Available to U.S. citizens.

Application Requirements Application, essay, interview, references, test scores, transcript. *Deadline:* January 20.

World Wide Web: http://www.micron.com/scholars

Contact: Micron Technology Foundation
8000 South Federal Way
Boise, ID 83716

NAMEPA NATIONAL SCHOLARSHIP FOUNDATION

NATIONAL ASSOCIATION OF MINORITY ENGINEERING PROGRAM ADMINISTRATORS NATIONAL SCHOLARSHIP FUND see number 28

NASA NEVADA SPACE GRANT CONSORTIUM

UNIVERSITY AND COMMUNITY COLLEGE SYSTEM OF NEVADA NASA SPACE GRANT AND FELLOWSHIP PROGRAM see number 29

SOCIETY OF PLASTICS ENGINEERS (SPE) FOUNDATION

SOCIETY OF PLASTICS ENGINEERS SCHOLARSHIP PROGRAM
see number 47

CIVIL ENGINEERING_____

AEA-OREGON COUNCIL

AEA TECHNOLOGY SCHOLARSHIP PROGRAM   see number 50

ASSOCIATED GENERAL CONTRACTORS EDUCATION AND RESEARCH FOUNDATION

AGC EDUCATION AND RESEARCH FOUNDATION UNDERGRADUATE SCHOLARSHIPS   • 53

Fifty-five or more named scholarships are available to college freshmen, first- or second-year students at a two-year school who plan to transfer to a four-year program for the fall term, or college freshman, sophomores, juniors, or beginning seniors in a five-year program. Junior- and senior-level applicants must have one full academic year of coursework remaining at the beginning of the fall term. Applicant must pursue a BS degree in construction or construction/civil engineering. Must be a U.S. citizen or permanent resident. Maximum award of $2,000 per year is renewable for up to four years. Application and complete guidelines are available on the web.

Academic/Career Areas Civil Engineering; Engineering/Technology; Trade/Technical Specialties.

Award Scholarship for use in freshman, sophomore, junior, or senior years; renewable. *Number:* 55. *Amount:* up to $2000.

Eligibility Requirements: Applicant must be enrolled or expecting to enroll full-time at a four-year institution. Available to U.S. citizens.

Application Requirements Application, essay, references, transcript. *Deadline:* November 1.

World Wide Web: http://www.agcfoundation.org

Contact: Floretta Slade, Director of Programs
Associated General Contractors Education and Research
Foundation
1957 E Street, NW
Washington, DC 20006
Phone: 703-837-5342
Fax: 703-837-5402
E-mail: sladef@agc.org

BARRY M. GOLDWATER SCHOLARSHIP AND EXCELLENCE IN EDUCATION FOUNDATION

BARRY M. GOLDWATER SCHOLARSHIP AND EXCELLENCE IN EDUCATION PROGRAM   see number 15

HISPANIC COLLEGE FUND, INC.
NATIONAL HISPANIC EXPLORERS SCHOLARSHIP PROGRAM
see number 16

HISPANIC ENGINEER NATIONAL ACHIEVEMENT AWARDS CORPORATION (HENAAC)
HISPANIC ENGINEER NATIONAL ACHIEVEMENT AWARDS CORPORATION SCHOLARSHIP PROGRAM
see number 27

HISPANIC SCHOLARSHIP FUND
HSF/GENERAL MOTORS SCHOLARSHIP
see number 44

KENTUCKY TRANSPORTATION CABINET
KENTUCKY TRANSPORTATION CABINET CIVIL ENGINEERING SCHOLARSHIP PROGRAM • 54
Scholarships are available to eligible applicants at 4 ABET-accredited universities in Kentucky. Our mission is to continually pursue statewide recruitment and retention of bright, motivated civil engineers in the Kentucky Transportation Cabinet.

Academic/Career Areas Civil Engineering.

Award Scholarship for use in freshman, sophomore, junior, senior, or graduate years; renewable. *Number:* 15–20. *Amount:* $7200–$8000.

Eligibility Requirements: Applicant must be enrolled or expecting to enroll full-time at an institution or university; resident of Kentucky and studying in Kentucky. Available to U.S. citizens.

Application Requirements Application, essay, interview, references, test scores, transcript. *Deadline:* March 1.

World Wide Web: http://www.kytc.state.ky.us/person/ScholarshipProgram.htm

Contact: Jo Anne Tingle, Scholarship Program Manager
Kentucky Transportation Cabinet
Attn: Scholarship Coordinator, State Office Building
501 High Street, Room 913
Frankfort, KY 40622
Phone: 877-273-5222
Fax: 502-564-6683
E-mail: jo.tingle@mail.state.ky.us

NAMEPA NATIONAL SCHOLARSHIP FOUNDATION

NATIONAL ASSOCIATION OF MINORITY ENGINEERING PROGRAM ADMINISTRATORS NATIONAL SCHOLARSHIP FUND   see number 28

NATIONAL ASSOCIATION OF WOMEN IN CONSTRUCTION

NAWIC UNDERGRADUATE SCHOLARSHIPS   see number 22

SOCIETY OF PLASTICS ENGINEERS (SPE) FOUNDATION

SOCIETY OF PLASTICS ENGINEERS SCHOLARSHIP PROGRAM
see number 47

TEXAS DEPARTMENT OF TRANSPORTATION

CONDITIONAL GRANT PROGRAM   • 55

A grant that provides female minorities financial education assistance up to $6,000 per year for approved degree plans. At present, it is for civil engineering or computer science degrees. Must be a Texas resident and study in Texas.

Academic/Career Areas Civil Engineering; Computer Science/Data Processing.
Award Grant for use in freshman, sophomore, junior, or senior years; renewable. *Number:* 25. *Amount:* up to $6000.
Eligibility Requirements: Applicant must be American Indian/Alaska Native, Asian/Pacific Islander, Black (non-Hispanic), or Hispanic; enrolled or expecting to enroll full-time at a four-year institution; female; resident of Texas and studying in Texas. Applicant must have 2.5 GPA or higher. Available to U.S. citizens.
Application Requirements Application, essay, interview, references, test scores, transcript. *Deadline:* March 1.
World Wide Web: http://www.dot.state.tx.us
Contact: Minnie Brown, Program Coordinator
Texas Department of Transportation
125 East 11th Street
Austin, TX 78701-2483
Phone: 512-416-4979
Fax: 512-416-4980
E-mail: mbrown2@dot.state.tx.us

TRIMMER EDUCATION FOUNDATION

TRIMMER SCHOLARSHIPS • 56

Scholarships are available to students in a major related to the construction industry.

Academic/Career Areas Civil Engineering; Electrical Engineering/Electronics; Engineering/Technology; Engineering-Related Technologies; Mechanical Engineering.

Award Scholarship for use in sophomore, junior, senior, graduate, or postgraduate years; not renewable. *Number:* 50–75. *Amount:* up to $2500.

Eligibility Requirements: Applicant must be enrolled or expecting to enroll full-time at a two-year or four-year institution or university. Applicant must have 2.5 GPA or higher. Available to U.S. citizens.

Application Requirements Application, financial need analysis, references, transcript. *Deadline:* June 30.

World Wide Web: http://www.abc.org

Contact: Cristine Hess
Trimmer Education Foundation
1300 North 17th Street, 8th Floor
Rosslyn, VA 22209
Phone: 703-812-2008
Fax: 703-812-8234

COMMUNICATIONS

CUBAN AMERICAN NATIONAL FOUNDATION

MAS FAMILY SCHOLARSHIPS see number 41

HISPANIC COLLEGE FUND, INC.

DENNY'S/HISPANIC COLLEGE FUND SCHOLARSHIP see number 1

FIRST IN MY FAMILY SCHOLARSHIP PROGRAM see number 10

HISPANIC COLLEGE FUND SCHOLARSHIP PROGRAM see number 11

HISPANIC COLLEGE FUND/INROADS/SPRINT SCHOLARSHIP PROGRAM see number 43

NATIONAL HISPANIC EXPLORERS SCHOLARSHIP PROGRAM see number 16

JOHN BAYLISS BROADCAST FOUNDATION

JOHN BAYLISS BROADCAST RADIO SCHOLARSHIP • 57

One-time award for college juniors, seniors, or graduate students majoring in broadcast communications with a concentration in radio broadcasting. Must have history of radio-related activities and a GPA of at least 3.0. Essay outlining future broadcasting goals required. Request information by mail, including stamped, self-addressed envelope, or by e-mail rather than by telephone. Must be attending school in U.S. Application is available at web site: http://www. baylissfoundation.org.

Academic/Career Areas Communications; Journalism; TV/Radio Broadcasting.
Award Scholarship for use in junior, senior, or graduate years; not renewable. *Number:* 15–20. *Amount:* up to $5000.
Eligibility Requirements: Applicant must be enrolled or expecting to enroll full-time at a four-year institution or university. Applicant must have 3.0 GPA or higher. Available to U.S. and Canadian citizens.
Application Requirements Application, essay, references, self-addressed stamped envelope, transcript. *Deadline:* April 30.
World Wide Web: http://www.baylissfoundation.org
Contact: Kit Hunter Franke, Executive Director
John Bayliss Broadcast Foundation
PO Box 51126
Pacific Grove, CA 93950
E-mail: info@baylissfoundation.org

UNITED NEGRO COLLEGE FUND

COLLEGE FUND/COCA COLA CORPORATE INTERN PROGRAM
see number 48

COMPUTER SCIENCE/DATA PROCESSING_____

AEA-OREGON COUNCIL
AEA TECHNOLOGY SCHOLARSHIP PROGRAM
see number 50

ASTRONAUT SCHOLARSHIP FOUNDATION
ASTRONAUT SCHOLARSHIP FOUNDATION
see number 14

BARRY M. GOLDWATER SCHOLARSHIP AND EXCELLENCE IN EDUCATION FOUNDATION
BARRY M. GOLDWATER SCHOLARSHIP AND EXCELLENCE IN EDUCATION PROGRAM
see number 15

BUSINESS AND PROFESSIONAL WOMEN'S FOUNDATION

BPW CAREER ADVANCEMENT SCHOLARSHIP PROGRAM FOR WOMEN
see number 32

CATCHING THE DREAM

MATH, ENGINEERING, SCIENCE, BUSINESS, EDUCATION, COMPUTERS SCHOLARSHIPS
see number 39

EATON CORPORATION

EATON CORPORATION MULTICULTURAL SCHOLARS PROGRAM
• 58

Renewable award of up to $3000. Award for minorities who are full-time students in freshman or sophomore year at a four-year college or university. Applicant must be studying computer science, electrical/mechanical engineering or related engineering field. Minimum 3.0 GPA required.

Academic/Career Areas Computer Science/Data Processing; Electrical Engineering/Electronics; Engineering/Technology; Engineering-Related Technologies; Mechanical Engineering.

Award Scholarship for use in freshman or sophomore years; renewable. *Number:* up to 50. *Amount:* $500–$3000.

Eligibility Requirements: Applicant must be American Indian/Alaska Native, Asian/Pacific Islander, Black (non-Hispanic), or Hispanic and enrolled or expecting to enroll at an institution or university. Applicant must have 3.0 GPA or higher.

Application Requirements Application, essay, financial need analysis, interview, test scores. *Deadline:* December 31.

World Wide Web: http://www.eaton.com

Contact: Mildred Neumann, Scholarship Coordinator
Eaton Corporation
Eaton Center
1111 Superior Avenue
Cleveland, OH 44114
Phone: 216-523-4354
Fax: 216-479-7354
E-mail: mildredneumann@eaton.com

HISPANIC COLLEGE FUND, INC.

DENNY'S/HISPANIC COLLEGE FUND SCHOLARSHIP
see number 1

FIRST IN MY FAMILY SCHOLARSHIP PROGRAM
see number 10

HISPANIC COLLEGE FUND SCHOLARSHIP PROGRAM   see number 11

HISPANIC COLLEGE FUND/INROADS/SPRINT SCHOLARSHIP
PROGRAM   see number 43

NATIONAL HISPANIC EXPLORERS SCHOLARSHIP PROGRAM
see number 16

HISPANIC ENGINEER NATIONAL ACHIEVEMENT AWARDS CORPORATION (HENAAC)

HISPANIC ENGINEER NATIONAL ACHIEVEMENT AWARDS
CORPORATION SCHOLARSHIP PROGRAM   see number 27

LUCENT TECHNOLOGIES FOUNDATION

LUCENT GLOBAL SCIENCE SCHOLARS PROGRAM   see number 18

MARYLAND ASSOCIATION OF PRIVATE CAREER SCHOOLS

MARYLAND ASSOCIATION OF PRIVATE CAREER SCHOOLS
SCHOLARSHIP   see number 45

MICRON TECHNOLOGY FOUNDATION

MICRON SCIENCE AND TECHNOLOGY SCHOLARS   see number 52

NAMEPA NATIONAL SCHOLARSHIP FOUNDATION

NATIONAL ASSOCIATION OF MINORITY ENGINEERING PROGRAM
ADMINISTRATORS NATIONAL SCHOLARSHIP FUND   see number 28

NASA NEVADA SPACE GRANT CONSORTIUM

UNIVERSITY AND COMMUNITY COLLEGE SYSTEM OF NEVADA
NASA SPACE GRANT AND FELLOWSHIP PROGRAM   see number 29

TEXAS DEPARTMENT OF TRANSPORTATION

CONDITIONAL GRANT PROGRAM
see number 55

UNITED NEGRO COLLEGE FUND

COLLEGE FUND/COCA COLA CORPORATE INTERN PROGRAM
see number 48

HOUSEHOLD INTERNATIONAL CORPORATE SCHOLARS
see number 49

UTAH STATE BOARD OF REGENTS

UTAH ENGINEERING AND COMPUTER SCIENCE PROGRAM (UECLP)
● **59**

A loan forgiveness program to recruit and train engineering, computer science and related technology students to assist in providing for and advancing the intellectual and economic welfare of the state.

Academic/Career Areas Computer Science/Data Processing; Engineering/Technology; Engineering-Related Technologies.

Award Forgivable loan for use in junior or senior years; renewable. *Number:* 90–110. *Amount:* $1500–$5000.

Eligibility Requirements: Applicant must be enrolled or expecting to enroll full-time at a four-year institution or university; resident of Utah and studying in Utah. Applicant must have 3.0 GPA or higher. Available to U.S. citizens.

Application Requirements Application, test scores, transcript. *Deadline:* Continuous.

World Wide Web: http://www.uheaa.org

Contact: Chalmers Gail Norris, Executive Director of UHEAA of the Utah
State Board of Regents
Utah State Board of Regents
60 South 400 West
Salt Lake City, UT 84101
Fax: 801-321-7299

DENTAL HEALTH/SERVICES_____

ALBERTA HERITAGE SCHOLARSHIP FUND

ALBERTA HERITAGE SCHOLARSHIP FUND ABORIGINAL HEALTH CAREERS BURSARY
see number 30

ARKANSAS DEPARTMENT OF HIGHER EDUCATION

ARKANSAS HEALTH EDUCATION GRANT PROGRAM (ARHEG)
see number 13

BUSINESS AND PROFESSIONAL WOMEN'S FOUNDATION

BPW CAREER ADVANCEMENT SCHOLARSHIP PROGRAM FOR WOMEN
see number 32

HEALTH PROFESSIONS EDUCATION FOUNDATION

HEALTH PROFESSIONS EDUCATION SCHOLARSHIP PROGRAM
• 60

The scholarship is awarded to students pursuing a career as a dentist, dental hygienist, nurse practitioner, certified nurse midwives or physician assistant. Eligible scholarship applicants may receive $10,000 per year in financial assistance. Applicants must agree to practice in a medically under-served area of California for a minimum of two years. Deadline: March 27. Must be a resident of CA and U.S. citizen. Minimum 2.0 GPA.

Academic/Career Areas Dental Health/Services; Health and Medical Sciences; Nursing.

Award Scholarship for use in senior, graduate, or postgraduate years; not renewable. *Number:* 10–15. *Amount:* $5000–$10,000.

Eligibility Requirements: Applicant must be enrolled or expecting to enroll full or part-time at an institution or university; resident of California and studying in California. Available to U.S. citizens.

Application Requirements Application, driver's license, financial need analysis, references, transcript, 2 copies of application. *Deadline:* March 27.

World Wide Web: http://www.healthprofessions.ca.gov

Contact: Charles Gray, Program Director
Health Professions Education Foundation
818 K Street, Suite 210
Sacramento, CA 95814
Phone: 916-324-6500

MARYLAND ASSOCIATION OF PRIVATE CAREER SCHOOLS

MARYLAND ASSOCIATION OF PRIVATE CAREER SCHOOLS SCHOLARSHIP
see number 45

MARYLAND HIGHER EDUCATION COMMISSION

GRADUATE AND PROFESSIONAL SCHOLARSHIP PROGRAM-MARYLAND • 61

Graduate and professional scholarships provide need-based financial assistance to students attending a Maryland school of medicine, dentistry, law, pharmacy, social work, or nursing. Funds are provided to specific Maryland colleges and universities. Students must demonstrate financial need and be Maryland residents. Contact institution financial aid office for more information.

Academic/Career Areas Dental Health/Services; Health and Medical Sciences; Law/Legal Services; Nursing; Social Services.

Award Scholarship for use in freshman, sophomore, junior, senior, graduate, or postgraduate years; renewable. *Number:* 40–200. *Amount:* $1000–$5000.

Eligibility Requirements: Applicant must be enrolled or expecting to enroll full or part-time at a four-year institution or university; resident of Maryland and studying in Maryland. Available to U.S. citizens.

Application Requirements Application, financial need analysis. *Deadline:* March 1.

World Wide Web: http://www.mhec.state.md.us

Contact: Maryland Higher Education Commission
839 Bestgate Road
Suite 400
Annapolis, MD 21401-3013

NEW MEXICO COMMISSION ON HIGHER EDUCATION

ALLIED HEALTH STUDENT LOAN PROGRAM-NEW MEXICO • 62

Renewable loans for New Mexico residents enrolled in an undergraduate allied health program. Loans can be forgiven through service in a medically underserved area or can be repaid. Penalties apply for failure to provide service. May borrow up to $12,000 per year for four years.

Academic/Career Areas Dental Health/Services; Health and Medical Sciences; Nursing; Social Sciences; Therapy/Rehabilitation.

Award Forgivable loan for use in freshman, sophomore, junior, or senior years; renewable. *Number:* 1–40. *Amount:* up to $12,000.

Eligibility Requirements: Applicant must be enrolled or expecting to enroll full or part-time at a two-year or four-year institution or university; resident of New Mexico and studying in New Mexico. Available to U.S. citizens.

Application Requirements Application, financial need analysis, transcript, FAFSA. *Deadline:* July 1.

World Wide Web: http://www.nmche.org

Contact: Maria Barele, Financial Specialist
New Mexico Commission on Higher Education
PO Box 15910
Santa Fe, NM 87506-5910
Phone: 505-827-4026
Fax: 505-827-7392

STATE OF GEORGIA

SERVICE-CANCELABLE STAFFORD LOAN-GEORGIA • 63

To assist Georgia students enrolled in critical fields of study in allied health (e.g., nursing, physical therapy). For use at GSFA-approved schools. $3500 forgivable loan for dentistry students only. Contact school financial aid officer for more details.

Academic/Career Areas Dental Health/Services; Health and Medical Sciences; Nursing.

Award Forgivable loan for use in freshman, sophomore, junior, senior, or graduate years; not renewable. *Number:* 500–1200. *Amount:* $2000–$4500.

Eligibility Requirements: Applicant must be enrolled or expecting to enroll full or part-time at a two-year or four-year or technical institution or university; resident of Georgia and studying in Georgia. Available to U.S. citizens.

Application Requirements Application, financial need analysis. *Deadline:* Continuous.

World Wide Web: http://www.gsfc.org

Contact: Peggy Matthews, Manager/GSFA Originations
State of Georgia
2082 East Exchange Place, Suite 230
Tucker, GA 30084-5305
Phone: 770-724-9230
Fax: 770-724-9263
E-mail: peggy@mail.gsfc.state.ga.us

DRAFTING_____

HISPANIC COLLEGE FUND, INC.

FIRST IN MY FAMILY SCHOLARSHIP PROGRAM   see number 10

HISPANIC COLLEGE FUND SCHOLARSHIP PROGRAM   see number 11

NATIONAL ASSOCIATION OF WOMEN IN CONSTRUCTION

NAWIC UNDERGRADUATE SCHOLARSHIPS   see number 22

EARTH SCIENCE_____

ASTRONAUT SCHOLARSHIP FOUNDATION

ASTRONAUT SCHOLARSHIP FOUNDATION   see number 14

BARRY M. GOLDWATER SCHOLARSHIP AND EXCELLENCE IN EDUCATION FOUNDATION

BARRY M. GOLDWATER SCHOLARSHIP AND EXCELLENCE IN EDUCATION PROGRAM   see number 15

HISPANIC COLLEGE FUND, INC.

NATIONAL HISPANIC EXPLORERS SCHOLARSHIP PROGRAM
                    see number 16

MORRIS K. UDALL FOUNDATION

MORRIS K. UDALL SCHOLARS   see number 12

ECONOMICS_____

CUBAN AMERICAN NATIONAL FOUNDATION

MAS FAMILY SCHOLARSHIPS   see number 41

HISPANIC COLLEGE FUND, INC.

DENNY'S/HISPANIC COLLEGE FUND SCHOLARSHIP   see number 1

FIRST IN MY FAMILY SCHOLARSHIP PROGRAM   see number 10

HISPANIC COLLEGE FUND SCHOLARSHIP PROGRAM   see number 11

HISPANIC COLLEGE FUND/INROADS/SPRINT SCHOLARSHIP PROGRAM   see number 43

NATIONAL ASSOCIATION OF BLACK ACCOUNTANTS, INC.

NATIONAL ASSOCIATION OF BLACK ACCOUNTANTS NATIONAL SCHOLARSHIP   see number 2

EDUCATION_____

ALASKA COMMISSION ON POSTSECONDARY EDUCATION

ALASKA COMMISSION ON POSTSECONDARY EDUCATION
TEACHER EDUCATION LOAN • 64

Renewable loans for graduates of an Alaskan high school pursuing teaching careers in rural elementary and secondary schools in Alaska. Must be nominated by rural school district. Eligible for 100% forgiveness if loan recipient teaches in rural Alaska upon graduation. Several awards of up to $7500 each. Must maintain good standing at institution.

Academic/Career Areas Education.

Award Forgivable loan for use in freshman, sophomore, junior, or senior years; renewable. *Number:* 100. *Amount:* up to $7500.

Eligibility Requirements: Applicant must be enrolled or expecting to enroll full-time at a four-year institution or university. Available to U.S. citizens.

Application Requirements Application, transcript. *Deadline:* July 1.

World Wide Web: http://www.state.ak.us/acpe/

Contact: Lori Stedman, Administrative Assistant, Special Programs
Alaska Commission on Postsecondary Education
3030 Vintage Boulevard
Juneau, AK 99801-7100
Phone: 907-465-6741
Fax: 907-465-5316

ARKANSAS DEPARTMENT OF HIGHER EDUCATION

ARKANSAS MINORITY TEACHER SCHOLARS PROGRAM • 65

Renewable award for Native-Americans, African-American, Hispanic and Asian-American students who have completed at least 60 semester hours and are enrolled full-time in a teacher education program in Arkansas. Award may be renewed for one year. Must be Arkansas resident with minimum 2.5 GPA. Must teach for three to five years in Arkansas to repay scholarship funds received. Must pass PPST exam.

Academic/Career Areas Education.

Award Forgivable loan for use in junior or senior years; renewable. *Number:* up to 100. *Amount:* up to $5000.

Eligibility Requirements: Applicant must be American Indian/Alaska Native, Asian/Pacific Islander, Black (non-Hispanic), or Hispanic; enrolled or expecting to enroll full-time at a four-year institution or university; resident of Arkansas and studying in Arkansas. Applicant must have 2.5 GPA or higher. Available to U.S. citizens.

Application Requirements Application, transcript. *Deadline:* June 1.

Arkansas Minority Teacher Scholars Program (continued)
World Wide Web: http://www.arscholarships.com
Contact: Lillian Williams, Assistant Coordinator
Arkansas Department of Higher Education
114 East Capitol
Little Rock, AR 72201
Phone: 501-371-2050
Fax: 501-371-2001

EMERGENCY SECONDARY EDUCATION LOAN PROGRAM
see number 31

BUSINESS AND PROFESSIONAL WOMEN'S FOUNDATION

BPW CAREER ADVANCEMENT SCHOLARSHIP PROGRAM FOR WOMEN
see number 32

CATCHING THE DREAM

MATH, ENGINEERING, SCIENCE, BUSINESS, EDUCATION, COMPUTERS SCHOLARSHIPS
see number 39

NATIVE AMERICAN LEADERSHIP IN EDUCATION (NALE)
see number 40

DECA (DISTRIBUTIVE EDUCATION CLUBS OF AMERICA)

HARRY A. APPLEGATE SCHOLARSHIP
see number 42

DELAWARE HIGHER EDUCATION COMMISSION

CHRISTA MCAULIFFE TEACHER SCHOLARSHIP LOAN-DELAWARE
• 66

Award for Delaware residents who are pursuing teaching careers. Must agree to teach in Delaware public schools as repayment of loan. Minimum award is $1000 and is renewable for up to four years. Available only at Delaware colleges. Based on academic merit. Must be ranked in upper half of class, and have a score of 1050 on SAT or 25 on the ACT.

Academic/Career Areas Education.

Award Forgivable loan for use in freshman, sophomore, junior, or senior years; renewable. *Number:* 1–60. *Amount:* $1000–$5000.

Eligibility Requirements: Applicant must be enrolled or expecting to enroll full-time at a four-year institution or university; resident of Delaware and studying in Delaware. Applicant must have 2.5 GPA or higher. Available to U.S. citizens.

Application Requirements Application, essay, test scores, transcript. *Deadline:* March 31.

World Wide Web: http://www.doe.state.de.us/high-ed

Contact: Donna Myers, Higher Education Analyst
Delaware Higher Education Commission
820 North French Street
5th Floor
Wilmington, DE 19711-3509
Phone: 302-577-3240
Fax: 302-577-6765
E-mail: dhec@doe.k12.de.us

FLORIDA DEPARTMENT OF EDUCATION

CRITICAL TEACHER SHORTAGE TUITION REIMBURSEMENT-FLORIDA • 67

One-time awards for full-time Florida public school employees who are certified to teach in Florida and are teaching or preparing to teach in critical teacher shortage subject areas. Must earn minimum grade of 3.0 in approved courses. May receive tuition reimbursement up to 9 semester hours or equivalent per academic year, not to exceed $78 per semester hour, for maximum 36 hours. Must be resident of Florida.

Academic/Career Areas Education.

Award Scholarship for use in freshman, sophomore, junior, senior, or graduate years; not renewable. *Number:* 1000–1200. *Amount:* up to $234.

Eligibility Requirements: Applicant must be enrolled or expecting to enroll part-time at a two-year or four-year institution or university; resident of Florida and studying in Florida. Applicant or parent of applicant must have employment or volunteer experience in teaching. Applicant must have 3.0 GPA or higher. Available to U.S. citizens.

Application Requirements Application, financial need analysis. *Deadline:* September 15.

World Wide Web: http://www.floridastudentfinancialaid.org

Contact: Scholarship Information
Florida Department of Education
Office of Student Financial Assistance
1940 North Monroe, Suite 70
Tallahassee, FL 32303-4759
Phone: 888-827-2004
E-mail: osfa@fldoe.org

GEORGIA STUDENT FINANCE COMMISSION

GEORGIA PROMISE TEACHER SCHOLARSHIP PROGRAM • 68

Renewable, forgivable loans for junior undergraduates at Georgia colleges who have been accepted for enrollment into a teacher education program leading to initial certification. Minimum cumulative 3.0 GPA required. Recipient must teach at a Georgia public school for one year for each $1500 awarded. Available to seniors for renewal only. Write for deadlines.

Academic/Career Areas Education.

Award Forgivable loan for use in junior or senior years; renewable. *Number:* 700–1400. *Amount:* $3000–$6000.

Eligibility Requirements: Applicant must be enrolled or expecting to enroll full or part-time at a four-year institution or university and studying in Georgia. Applicant must have 3.0 GPA or higher. Available to U.S. citizens.

Application Requirements Application, transcript. *Deadline:* Continuous.

World Wide Web: http://www.gsfc.org

Contact: Stan DeWitt, Manager of Teacher Scholarships
Georgia Student Finance Commission
2082 East Exchange Place, Suite 100
Tucker, GA 30084
Phone: 770-724-9060
Fax: 770-724-9031

GOLDEN APPLE FOUNDATION

GOLDEN APPLE SCHOLARS OF ILLINOIS • 69

Between 75 and 100 forgivable loans are given to undergraduate students. Loans are $7,000 a year for 4 years. Applicants must be between 17 and 21 and carry a minimum GPA of 2.5. Eligible applicants will be residents of Illinois who are studying in Illinois. The deadline is December 1. Recipients must agree to teach in high-need Illinois schools.

Academic/Career Areas Education.

Award Forgivable loan for use in freshman, sophomore, junior, or senior years; renewable. *Number:* 75–100. *Amount:* $7000.

Eligibility Requirements: Applicant must be age 17-21; enrolled or expecting to enroll full-time at a four-year institution or university; resident of Illinois and studying in Illinois. Applicant must have 2.5 GPA or higher. Available to U.S. citizens.

Application Requirements Application, autobiography, essay, interview, photo, references, test scores, transcript. *Deadline:* December 1.

World Wide Web: http://www.goldenapple.org

Contact: Pat Kilduff, Director of Recruitment and Placement
Golden Apple Foundation
8 South Michigan Avenue, Suite 700
Chicago, IL 60603-3318
Phone: 312-407-0006 Ext. 105
Fax: 312-407-0344
E-mail: patnk@goldenapple.org

ILLINOIS STUDENT ASSISTANCE COMMISSION (ISAC)

ITEACH TEACHER SHORTAGE SCHOLARSHIP PROGRAM • 70

Award to assist Illinois students planning to teach at an Illinois pre-school, elementary school, or high school in a teacher shortage discipline. Must agree to teach one year in teacher shortage area for each year of award assistance received. Deadline: May 1.

Academic/Career Areas Education; Special Education.

Award Forgivable loan for use in freshman, sophomore, junior, senior, or graduate years; not renewable. *Number:* 500–600. *Amount:* $4000–$5000.

Eligibility Requirements: Applicant must be enrolled or expecting to enroll full or part-time at a two-year or four-year institution or university; resident of Illinois and studying in Illinois. Applicant must have 2.5 GPA or higher. Available to U.S. and non-U.S. citizens.

Application Requirements Application, transcript. *Deadline:* May 1.

World Wide Web: http://www.isac-online.org

Contact: Dave Barinholtz, Client Information
Illinois Student Assistance Commission (ISAC)
1755 Lake Cook Road
Deerfield, IL 60015-5209
Phone: 847-948-8500 Ext. 2385
E-mail: cssupport@isac.org

MINORITY TEACHERS OF ILLINOIS SCHOLARSHIP PROGRAM • 71

Award for minority students planning to teach at an approved Illinois preschool, elementary, or secondary school. Deadline: May 1. Must be Illinois resident.

Academic/Career Areas Education; Special Education.

Award Forgivable loan for use in freshman, sophomore, junior, senior, graduate, or postgraduate years; renewable. *Number:* 450–550. *Amount:* $4000–$5000.

Eligibility Requirements: Applicant must be American Indian/Alaska Native, Asian/Pacific Islander, Black (non-Hispanic), or Hispanic; enrolled or expecting to enroll full-time at a two-year or four-year institution or university; resident of Illinois and studying in Illinois. Applicant must have 2.5 GPA or higher. Available to U.S. and non-U.S. citizens.

Application Requirements Application. *Deadline:* May 1.

World Wide Web: http://www.isac-online.org

Contact: David Barinholtz, Client Information
Illinois Student Assistance Commission (ISAC)
1755 Lake Cook Road
Deerfield, IL 60015-5209
Phone: 847-948-8500 Ext. 2385
E-mail: cssupport@isac.org

KANSAS BOARD OF REGENTS

KANSAS TEACHER SERVICE SCHOLARSHIP • 72

Several scholarships for Kansas residents pursuing teaching careers. Must teach in a hard-to-fill discipline or underserved area of the state of Kansas for one year for each award received. Renewable award of $5000. Application fee is $10. Deadline: May 1. Must be U.S. citizen.

Academic/Career Areas Education.

Award Forgivable loan for use in freshman, sophomore, junior, or senior years; renewable. *Number:* 60–80. *Amount:* $5000.

Eligibility Requirements: Applicant must be enrolled or expecting to enroll full-time at a two-year or four-year institution or university; resident of Kansas and studying in Kansas. Applicant must have 3.0 GPA or higher. Available to U.S. citizens.

Application Requirements Application, references, test scores, transcript. *Fee:* $10. *Deadline:* May 1.

World Wide Web: http://www.kansasregents.org

Contact: Diane Lindeman, Director of Student Financial Assistance
Kansas Board of Regents
1000 Southwest Jackson, Suite 520
Topeka, KS 66612-1368
Phone: 785-296-3517
Fax: 785-296-0983
E-mail: dlindeman@ksbor.org

KENTUCKY HIGHER EDUCATION ASSISTANCE AUTHORITY (KHEAA)

KENTUCKY TEACHER SCHOLARSHIP PROGRAM • 73

Award for Kentucky resident attending Kentucky institutions and pursuing initial teacher certification. Must teach one semester for each semester of award received. In critical shortage areas, must teach one semester for every two semesters of award received. Repayment obligation if teaching requirement not met. Submit Free Application for Federal Student Aid and Teacher Scholarship Application by May 1.

Academic/Career Areas Education; Special Education.

Award Forgivable loan for use in freshman, sophomore, junior, senior, or graduate years; not renewable. *Number:* 600–700. *Amount:* $100–$5000.

Eligibility Requirements: Applicant must be enrolled or expecting to enroll full-time at a two-year or four-year institution or university; resident of Kentucky and studying in Kentucky. Available to U.S. citizens.

Application Requirements Application, financial need analysis. *Deadline:* May 1.

World Wide Web: http://www.kheaa.com

Contact: Pam Polly, Program Coordinator
Kentucky Higher Education Assistance Authority (KHEAA)
PO Box 798
Frankfort, KY 40602-0798
Phone: 502-696-7392
Fax: 502-696-7373
E-mail: ppolly@kheaa.com

MARION D. AND EVA S. PEEPLES FOUNDATION TRUST SCHOLARSHIP PROGRAM

MARION D. AND EVA S. PEEPLES SCHOLARSHIPS • 74

Award for study in nursing, dietetics, and teaching in industrial arts renewable annually up to four years. Applicant must reapply each year for renewal. Recipient must maintain 2.5 GPA and take at least 12 credit hours per semester. Minimum 1100 on SAT if high school student. Must be Indiana resident and attending an Indiana school.

Academic/Career Areas Education; Engineering/Technology; Food Science/Nutrition; Nursing; Trade/Technical Specialties.

Award Scholarship for use in freshman, sophomore, junior, or senior years; renewable. *Number:* 15–30. *Amount:* $500–$4000.

Eligibility Requirements: Applicant must be enrolled or expecting to enroll full-time at a two-year or four-year or technical institution or university; resident of Indiana and studying in Indiana. Applicant must have 2.5 GPA or higher. Available to U.S. citizens.

Application Requirements Application, autobiography, financial need analysis, interview, references, self-addressed stamped envelope, test scores, transcript. *Deadline:* March 1.

World Wide Web: http://www.jccf.org

Contact: Cheryl Morphew, Director of Grants and Scholarships
Marion D. and Eva S. Peeples Foundation Trust Scholarship
Program
398 South Main Street
Franklin, IN 46131
Phone: 317-738-2213
Fax: 317-738-9113
E-mail: cheryls@iquest.net

MARYLAND HIGHER EDUCATION COMMISSION

CHILD CARE PROVIDER PROGRAM-MARYLAND • 75

Forgivable loan provides assistance for Maryland undergraduates attending a Maryland institution and pursuing studies in a child development program or

Child Care Provider Program-Maryland (continued)

an early childhood education program. Must serve as a professional day care provider in Maryland for one year for each year award received. Must maintain minimum 2.0 GPA. Contact for further information.

Academic/Career Areas Education.

Award Forgivable loan for use in freshman, sophomore, junior, or senior years; renewable. *Number:* 100–150. *Amount:* $500–$2000.

Eligibility Requirements: Applicant must be enrolled or expecting to enroll full or part-time at a two-year or four-year institution or university; resident of Maryland and studying in Maryland. Available to U.S. citizens.

Application Requirements Application, transcript. *Deadline:* June 15.

World Wide Web: http://www.mhec.state.md.us

Contact: Margaret Crutchley, Office of Student Financial Assistance
Maryland Higher Education Commission
839 Bestgate Road, Suite 400
Annapolis, MD 21401-3013
Phone: 410-260-4545
Fax: 410-260-3203
E-mail: ofsamail@mhec.state.md.us

DISTINGUISHED SCHOLAR-TEACHER EDUCATION AWARDS • 76

Up to $3,000 award for Maryland high school seniors who have received the Distinguished Scholar Award. Recipient must enroll as a full-time undergraduate in a Maryland institution and pursue a program of study leading to a Maryland teaching certificate. Must maintain annual 3.0 GPA for renewal. Must teach in a Maryland public school one year for each year award is received.

Academic/Career Areas Education.

Award Forgivable loan for use in freshman, sophomore, junior, or senior years; renewable. *Number:* 20–80. *Amount:* up to $3000.

Eligibility Requirements: Applicant must be high school student; planning to enroll or expecting to enroll full-time at a two-year or four-year institution or university; resident of Maryland and studying in Maryland. Applicant must have 3.0 GPA or higher. Available to U.S. citizens.

Application Requirements Application, test scores, transcript, must be recipient of the Distinguished Scholar Award. *Deadline:* Continuous.

World Wide Web: http://www.mhec.state.md.us

Contact: Monica Tipton, Office of Student Financial Assistance
Maryland Higher Education Commission
839 Bestgate Road, Suite 400
Annapolis, MD 21401-3013
Phone: 410-260-4568
Fax: 410-260-3200
E-mail: ofsamail@mhec.state.md.us

JANET L. HOFFMANN LOAN ASSISTANCE REPAYMENT PROGRAM • 77

Provides assistance for repayment of loan debt to Maryland residents working full-time in non-profit organizations and state or local governments. Must submit Employment Verification Form and Lender verification form.

Academic/Career Areas Education; Law/Legal Services; Nursing; Social Services; Therapy/Rehabilitation.

Award Grant for use in freshman, sophomore, junior, senior, or graduate years; not renewable. *Number:* up to 400. *Amount:* up to $7500.

Eligibility Requirements: Applicant must be enrolled or expecting to enroll at an institution or university; resident of Maryland and studying in Maryland. Available to U.S. citizens.

Application Requirements Application, transcript, IRS 1040 form. *Deadline:* September 30.

World Wide Web: http://www.mhec.state.md.us

Contact: Marie Janiszewski, Office of Student Financial Assistance
Maryland Higher Education Commission
839 Bestgate Road, Suite 400
Annapolis, MD 21401
Phone: 410-260-4569
Fax: 410-260-3203
E-mail: osfamail@mhec.state.md.us

SHARON CHRISTA MCAULIFFE TEACHER EDUCATION-CRITICAL SHORTAGE GRANT PROGRAM • 78

Renewable awards for Maryland residents who are college juniors, seniors, or graduate students enrolled in a Maryland teacher education program. Must agree to enter profession in a subject designated as a critical shortage area. Must teach in Maryland for one year for each award year. Renewable for one year.

Academic/Career Areas Education.

Award Forgivable loan for use in junior, senior, or graduate years; renewable. *Number:* up to 137. *Amount:* $200–$12,981.

Eligibility Requirements: Applicant must be enrolled or expecting to enroll full or part-time at a four-year institution or university; resident of Maryland and studying in Maryland. Applicant must have 3.0 GPA or higher. Available to U.S. citizens.

Application Requirements Application, essay, resume, transcript. *Deadline:* December 31.

World Wide Web: http://www.mhec.state.md.us

Sharon Christa McAuliffe Teacher Education-Critical Shortage Grant Program (continued)

Contact: Margaret Crutchley, Office of Student Financial Assistance
Maryland Higher Education Commission
839 Bestgate Road, Suite 400
Annapolis, MD 21401-3013
Phone: 410-260-4545
Fax: 410-260-3203
E-mail: ofsamail@mhec.state.md.us

MISSOURI DEPARTMENT OF ELEMENTARY AND SECONDARY EDUCATION

MISSOURI MINORITY TEACHING SCHOLARSHIP   • 79

Award may be used any year up to four years at an approved, participating Missouri institution. Scholarship is for minority Missouri residents in teaching programs. Recipients must commit to teach for five years in a Missouri public elementary or secondary school. Graduate students must teach math or science. Otherwise, award must be repaid.

Academic/Career Areas Education.

Award Scholarship for use in freshman, sophomore, junior, senior, or graduate years; renewable. *Number:* 100. *Amount:* $3000.

Eligibility Requirements: Applicant must be of African, Chinese, Hispanic, Indian, or Japanese heritage; American Indian/Alaska Native, Asian/Pacific Islander, or Black (non-Hispanic); enrolled or expecting to enroll full-time at a two-year or four-year institution or university; resident of Missouri and studying in Missouri. Applicant must have 3.5 GPA or higher. Available to U.S. citizens.

Application Requirements Application, essay, financial need analysis, references, test scores, transcript. *Deadline:* February 15.

World Wide Web: http://www.dese.state.mo.us

Contact: Laura Harrison, Administrative Assistant II
Missouri Department of Elementary and Secondary Education
PO Box 480
Jefferson City, MO 65102-0480
Phone: 573-751-1668
Fax: 573-526-3580
E-mail: lharriso@mail.dese.state.mo.us

MISSOURI TEACHER EDUCATION SCHOLARSHIP (GENERAL)   • 80

Nonrenewable award for Missouri high school seniors or Missouri resident college students. Must attend approved teacher training program at Missouri institution. Nonrenewable. Must rank in top 15 % of high school class on ACT/SAT. Merit-based award.

Academic/Career Areas Education.

Award Scholarship for use in freshman, sophomore, junior, or senior years; not renewable. *Number:* 200–240. *Amount:* $2000.

Eligibility Requirements: Applicant must be enrolled or expecting to enroll full-time at a two-year or four-year institution or university; resident of Missouri and studying in Missouri. Applicant must have 3.5 GPA or higher. Available to U.S. citizens.

Application Requirements Application, essay, references, test scores, transcript. *Deadline:* February 15.

World Wide Web: http://www.dese.state.mo.us

Contact: Laura Harrison, Administrative Assistant II
Missouri Department of Elementary and Secondary Education
PO Box 480
Jefferson City, MO 65102-0480
Phone: 573-751-1668
Fax: 573-526-3580
E-mail: lharriso@mail.dese.state.mo.us

NORTH CAROLINA TEACHING FELLOWS COMMISSION

NORTH CAROLINA TEACHING FELLOWS SCHOLARSHIP PROGRAM • 81

Renewable award for North Carolina high school seniors pursuing teaching careers. Must agree to teach in a North Carolina public or government school for four years or repay award. Must attend one of the 14 approved schools in North Carolina. Merit-based. Must interview at the local level and at the regional level as a finalist.

Academic/Career Areas Education.

Award Forgivable loan for use in freshman, sophomore, junior, or senior years; renewable. *Number:* up to 400. *Amount:* $6500.

Eligibility Requirements: Applicant must be high school student; planning to enroll or expecting to enroll full-time at a four-year institution; resident of North Carolina and studying in North Carolina. Applicant must have 3.5 GPA or higher. Available to U.S. citizens.

Application Requirements Application, essay, interview, references, test scores, transcript. *Deadline:* October 31.

World Wide Web: http://www.teachingfellows.org

Contact: Ms. Sherry Woodruff, Program Officer
North Carolina Teaching Fellows Commission
3739 National Drive, Suite 210
Raleigh, NC 27612
Phone: 919-781-6833 Ext. 103
Fax: 919-781-6527
E-mail: tfellows@ncforum.org

ORDEAN FOUNDATION

ORDEAN LOAN PROGRAM
see number 6

PHI DELTA KAPPA INTERNATIONAL

SCHOLARSHIP GRANTS FOR PROSPECTIVE EDUCATORS • 82

One-time award available to high school seniors in the top 50% of their graduating class. Applicants must plan to major in education and pursue a teaching career. Contact local Phi Delta Kappa chapter for more information. Do not send application to headquarters. Must have minimum 2.5 GPA.

Academic/Career Areas Education.

Award Grant for use in freshman year; not renewable. *Number:* 30. *Amount:* $1000–$5000.

Eligibility Requirements: Applicant must be high school student and planning to enroll or expecting to enroll full-time at a two-year or four-year institution or university. Applicant must have 2.5 GPA or higher. Available to U.S. and non-U.S. citizens.

Application Requirements Application, essay, references, self-addressed stamped envelope, transcript. *Deadline:* January 15.

World Wide Web: http://www.pdkintl.org

Contact: contact local chapter for information

SOUTH CAROLINA STUDENT LOAN CORPORATION

SOUTH CAROLINA TEACHER LOAN PROGRAM • 83

One-time awards for South Carolina residents attending four-year postsecondary institutions in South Carolina. Recipients must teach in the South Carolina public school system in a critical-need area after graduation. 20% of loan forgiven for each year of service. Write for additional requirements.

Academic/Career Areas Education; Special Education.

Award Forgivable loan for use in freshman, sophomore, junior, senior, or graduate years; not renewable. *Number:* up to 1121. *Amount:* $2500–$5000.

Eligibility Requirements: Applicant must be enrolled or expecting to enroll full or part-time at a four-year institution or university; resident of South Carolina and studying in South Carolina. Applicant must have 3.0 GPA or higher.

Application Requirements Application, test scores. *Deadline:* June 1.

World Wide Web: http://www.slc.sc.edu

Contact: Jennifer Jones-Gaddy, Vice President
South Carolina Student Loan Corporation
PO Box 21487
Columbia, SC 29221
Phone: 803-798-0916
Fax: 803-772-9410
E-mail: jgaddy@slc.sc.edu

STATE OF UTAH

TERREL H. BELL TEACHING INCENTIVE LOAN • 84

Designed to provide financial assistance to outstanding Utah students pursuing a degree in education. The incentive loan funds full-time tuition and general fees for eight semesters. After graduation/certification the loan may be forgiven if the recipient teaches in a Utah public school or accredited private school (K-12). Loan forgiveness is done on a year-for-year basis. For more details see web site: http://www.utahsbr.edu.

Academic/Career Areas Education.

Award Forgivable loan for use in freshman, sophomore, junior, or senior years; renewable. *Number:* 365. *Amount:* $600–$1500.

Eligibility Requirements: Applicant must be enrolled or expecting to enroll full-time at a two-year or four-year institution or university; resident of Utah and studying in Utah. Available to U.S. citizens.

Application Requirements Application, essay, test scores, transcript. *Deadline:* March 31.

World Wide Web: http://www.utahsbr.edu

Contact: Angie Loving, Manager for Programs and Administration
State of Utah
3 Triad Center, Suite 550
Salt Lake City, UT 84180
Phone: 801-321-7124
Fax: 801-321-7199
E-mail: aloving@utahsbr.edu

STATE STUDENT ASSISTANCE COMMISSION OF INDIANA (SSACI)

INDIANA MINORITY TEACHER AND SPECIAL EDUCATION SERVICES SCHOLARSHIP PROGRAM • 85

For Black or Hispanic students seeking teaching certification or for students seeking special education teaching certification or occupational or physical therapy certification. Must be a U.S. citizen and Indiana resident enrolled full-time at an eligible Indiana institution. Must teach in an Indiana-accredited elementary or secondary school after graduation. Contact institution for application and deadline. Minimum 2.0 GPA required.

Academic/Career Areas Education; Special Education; Therapy/Rehabilitation.

Award Scholarship for use in freshman, sophomore, junior, or senior years; not renewable. *Number:* 330–370. *Amount:* $1000–$4000.

Eligibility Requirements: Applicant must be Black (non-Hispanic) or Hispanic; enrolled or expecting to enroll full-time at a four-year institution or university; resident of Indiana and studying in Indiana. Available to U.S. citizens.

Application Requirements Application, financial need analysis. *Deadline:* Continuous.

World Wide Web: http://www.ssaci.in.gov

Indiana Minority Teacher and Special Education Services Scholarship Program (continued)

Contact: Ms. Yvonne Heflin, Director, Special Programs
State Student Assistance Commission of Indiana (SSACI)
150 West Market Street, Suite 500
Indianapolis, IN 46204-2805
Phone: 317-232-2350
Fax: 317-232-3260
E-mail: grants@ssaci.state.un.is

TENNESSEE STUDENT ASSISTANCE CORPORATION

MINORITY TEACHING FELLOWS PROGRAM/TENNESSEE ● 86

Forgivable loan for minority Tennessee residents pursuing teaching careers. High school applicant minimum 2.75 GPA. Must be in the top quarter of the class or score an 18 on ACT. College applicant minimum 2.50 GPA. Submit statement of intent, test scores, and transcripts with application and two letters of recommendation. Must teach one year per year of award or repay as a loan.

Academic/Career Areas Education; Special Education.
Award Forgivable loan for use in freshman, sophomore, junior, or senior years; renewable. *Number:* 19–29. *Amount:* $5000.
Eligibility Requirements: Applicant must be American Indian/Alaska Native, Asian/Pacific Islander, Black (non-Hispanic), or Hispanic; enrolled or expecting to enroll full-time at a two-year or four-year institution or university; resident of Tennessee and studying in Tennessee. Available to U.S. citizens.
Application Requirements Application, essay, references, test scores, transcript. *Deadline:* April 15.
World Wide Web: http://www.state.tn.us/tsac
Contact: Kathy Stripling, Scholarship Coordinator
Tennessee Student Assistance Corporation
404 James Robertson Parkway, Suite 1950, Parkway Towers
Nashville, TN 37243-0820
Phone: 615-741-1346
Fax: 615-741-6101
E-mail: kathy.stripling@state.tn.us

TENNESSEE TEACHING SCHOLARS PROGRAM ● 87

Forgivable loan for college juniors, seniors, and college graduates admitted to an education program in Tennessee with a minimum GPA of 2.5. Students must commit to teach in a Tennessee public school one year for each year of the award.

Academic/Career Areas Education.
Award Forgivable loan for use in junior, senior, or graduate years; not renewable. *Number:* 30–250. *Amount:* $1000–$4200.

Eligibility Requirements: Applicant must be enrolled or expecting to enroll full or part-time at a four-year institution or university; resident of Tennessee and studying in Tennessee. Applicant must have 2.5 GPA or higher. Available to U.S. citizens.

Application Requirements Application, references, test scores, transcript, letter of intent. *Deadline:* April 15.

World Wide Web: http://www.state.tn.us/tsac

Contact: Mike McCormack, Scholarship Administrator
Tennessee Student Assistance Corporation
Suite 1950, Parkway Towers
Nashville, TN 37243-0820
Phone: 615-741-1346
Fax: 615-741-6101
E-mail: mike.mccormack@state.tn.us

WEST VIRGINIA HIGHER EDUCATION POLICY COMMISSION-OFFICE OF FINANCIAL AID AND OUTREACH SERVICES

UNDERWOOD-SMITH TEACHER SCHOLARSHIP PROGRAM • 88

For West Virginia residents at West Virginia institutions pursuing teaching careers. Must have a 3.25 GPA after completion of two years of course work. Must teach two years in West Virginia public schools for each year the award is received. Recipients will be required to sign an agreement acknowledging an understanding of the program's requirements and their willingness to repay the award if appropriate teaching service is not rendered.

Academic/Career Areas Education.

Award Scholarship for use in junior, senior, or graduate years; renewable. *Number:* 53. *Amount:* up to $5000.

Eligibility Requirements: Applicant must be enrolled or expecting to enroll full-time at a four-year institution or university; resident of West Virginia and studying in West Virginia. Available to U.S. citizens.

Application Requirements Application, essay, references. *Deadline:* March 1.

World Wide Web: http://www.hepc.wvnet.edu

Contact: Michelle Wicks, Scholarship Coordinator
West Virginia Higher Education Policy Commission-Office of
Financial Aid and Outreach Services
1018 Kanawha Boulevard East, Suite 700
Charleston, WV 25301
Phone: 304-558-4618
Fax: 304-558-4622
E-mail: wicks@hepc.wvnet.edu

ELECTRICAL ENGINEERING/ ELECTRONICS

AEA-OREGON COUNCIL
AEA TECHNOLOGY SCHOLARSHIP PROGRAM   see number 50

ASTRONAUT SCHOLARSHIP FOUNDATION
ASTRONAUT SCHOLARSHIP FOUNDATION   see number 14

CUBAN AMERICAN NATIONAL FOUNDATION
MAS FAMILY SCHOLARSHIPS   see number 41

EATON CORPORATION
EATON CORPORATION MULTICULTURAL SCHOLARS PROGRAM
    see number 58

HISPANIC COLLEGE FUND, INC.
DENNY'S/HISPANIC COLLEGE FUND SCHOLARSHIP   see number 1

FIRST IN MY FAMILY SCHOLARSHIP PROGRAM   see number 10

HISPANIC COLLEGE FUND SCHOLARSHIP PROGRAM   see number 11

HISPANIC COLLEGE FUND/INROADS/SPRINT SCHOLARSHIP
PROGRAM   see number 43

NATIONAL HISPANIC EXPLORERS SCHOLARSHIP PROGRAM
    see number 16

HISPANIC ENGINEER NATIONAL ACHIEVEMENT AWARDS CORPORATION (HENAAC)
HISPANIC ENGINEER NATIONAL ACHIEVEMENT AWARDS
CORPORATION SCHOLARSHIP PROGRAM   see number 27

HISPANIC SCHOLARSHIP FUND
HSF/GENERAL MOTORS SCHOLARSHIP   see number 44

INTERNATIONAL SOCIETY FOR OPTICAL ENGINEERING-SPIE

SPIE EDUCATIONAL SCHOLARSHIPS IN OPTICAL SCIENCE AND ENGINEERING
see number 17

LUCENT TECHNOLOGIES FOUNDATION

LUCENT GLOBAL SCIENCE SCHOLARS PROGRAM   see number 18

MICRON TECHNOLOGY FOUNDATION

MICRON SCIENCE AND TECHNOLOGY SCHOLARS   see number 52

NAMEPA NATIONAL SCHOLARSHIP FOUNDATION

NATIONAL ASSOCIATION OF MINORITY ENGINEERING PROGRAM ADMINISTRATORS NATIONAL SCHOLARSHIP FUND   see number 28

NASA NEVADA SPACE GRANT CONSORTIUM

UNIVERSITY AND COMMUNITY COLLEGE SYSTEM OF NEVADA NASA SPACE GRANT AND FELLOWSHIP PROGRAM   see number 29

NATIONAL ASSOCIATION OF WOMEN IN CONSTRUCTION

NAWIC UNDERGRADUATE SCHOLARSHIPS   see number 22

TRIMMER EDUCATION FOUNDATION

TRIMMER SCHOLARSHIPS   see number 56

WEST VIRGINIA HIGHER EDUCATION POLICY COMMISSION-OFFICE OF FINANCIAL AID AND OUTREACH SERVICES

WEST VIRGINIA ENGINEERING, SCIENCE & TECHNOLOGY SCHOLARSHIP PROGRAM
• 89

For students attending West Virginia institutions full time pursuing a career in engineering, science or technology. Must have a 3.0 GPA on a 4.0 scale. Must

West Virginia Engineering, Science & Technology Scholarship Program (continued)
work in the fields of engineering, science or technology in West Virginia one year for each year the award is received.

Academic/Career Areas Electrical Engineering/Electronics; Engineering/Technology; Engineering-Related Technologies; Science, Technology and Society.

Award Scholarship for use in freshman, sophomore, junior, or senior years; renewable. *Number:* 300. *Amount:* up to $3000.

Eligibility Requirements: Applicant must be enrolled or expecting to enroll full-time at a two-year or four-year or technical institution or university and studying in West Virginia. Applicant must have 3.0 GPA or higher. Available to U.S. citizens.

Application Requirements Application, essay, test scores, transcript. *Deadline:* March 1.

World Wide Web: http://www.hepc.wvnet.edu

Contact: Michelle Wicks, Scholarship Coordinator
West Virginia Higher Education Policy Commission-Office of
Financial Aid and Outreach Services
1018 Kanawha Boulevard East, Suite 700
Charleston, WV 25301
Phone: 304-558-4618
Fax: 304-558-4622
E-mail: wicks@hepc.wvnet.edu

ENGINEERING-RELATED TECHNOLOGIES

AEA-OREGON COUNCIL

AEA TECHNOLOGY SCHOLARSHIP PROGRAM   see number 50

AMERICAN WELDING SOCIETY

AMERICAN WELDING SOCIETY DISTRICT SCHOLARSHIP PROGRAM   • 90

Award for students in vocational training, community college, or a degree program in welding or a related field of study. Applicants must be high school graduates or equivalent. Must reside in the U.S. and attend a U.S. institution. Recipients may reapply. Must include personal statement of career goals. Also must rank in upper half of class or have a minimum GPA of 2.5.

Academic/Career Areas Engineering-Related Technologies; Trade/Technical Specialties.

Award Scholarship for use in freshman, sophomore, junior, or senior years; not renewable. *Number:* 66–150. *Amount:* $500–$1000.

Eligibility Requirements: Applicant must be age 18 and enrolled or expecting to enroll full or part-time at a two-year or four-year or technical institution or university. Applicant must have 2.5 GPA or higher. Available to U.S. and non-U.S. citizens.

Application Requirements Application, autobiography, financial need analysis, photo, transcript. *Deadline:* March 1.

World Wide Web: http://www.aws.org

Contact: Ms. Jo Ann Castrillo, Development Coordinator
American Welding Society
550 NW Le Jeune Road
Miami, FL 33126
Phone: 800-443-9353 Ext. 461
Fax: 305-443-7559
E-mail: joann@aws.org

ASTRONAUT SCHOLARSHIP FOUNDATION

ASTRONAUT SCHOLARSHIP FOUNDATION   see number 14

BUSINESS AND PROFESSIONAL WOMEN'S FOUNDATION

BPW CAREER ADVANCEMENT SCHOLARSHIP PROGRAM FOR WOMEN   see number 32

CUBAN AMERICAN NATIONAL FOUNDATION

MAS FAMILY SCHOLARSHIPS   see number 41

EATON CORPORATION

EATON CORPORATION MULTICULTURAL SCHOLARS PROGRAM   see number 58

HISPANIC COLLEGE FUND, INC.

DENNY'S/HISPANIC COLLEGE FUND SCHOLARSHIP   see number 1

FIRST IN MY FAMILY SCHOLARSHIP PROGRAM   see number 10

HISPANIC COLLEGE FUND SCHOLARSHIP PROGRAM   see number 11

HISPANIC COLLEGE FUND/INROADS/SPRINT SCHOLARSHIP PROGRAM   see number 43

NATIONAL HISPANIC EXPLORERS SCHOLARSHIP PROGRAM
see number 16

HISPANIC SCHOLARSHIP FUND
HSF/GENERAL MOTORS SCHOLARSHIP
see number 44

INTERNATIONAL FACILITY MANAGEMENT ASSOCIATION FOUNDATION
IFMA FOUNDATION SCHOLARSHIPS
see number 21

INTERNATIONAL SOCIETY FOR OPTICAL ENGINEERING-SPIE
SPIE EDUCATIONAL SCHOLARSHIPS IN OPTICAL SCIENCE AND ENGINEERING
see number 17

LUCENT TECHNOLOGIES FOUNDATION
LUCENT GLOBAL SCIENCE SCHOLARS PROGRAM
see number 18

MICRON TECHNOLOGY FOUNDATION
MICRON SCIENCE AND TECHNOLOGY SCHOLARS
see number 52

NAMEPA NATIONAL SCHOLARSHIP FOUNDATION
NATIONAL ASSOCIATION OF MINORITY ENGINEERING PROGRAM ADMINISTRATORS NATIONAL SCHOLARSHIP FUND
see number 28

NATIONAL ASSOCIATION OF WOMEN IN CONSTRUCTION
NAWIC UNDERGRADUATE SCHOLARSHIPS
see number 22

TRIMMER EDUCATION FOUNDATION
TRIMMER SCHOLARSHIPS
see number 56

UTAH STATE BOARD OF REGENTS

UTAH ENGINEERING AND COMPUTER SCIENCE PROGRAM
(UECLP)
see number 59

WEST VIRGINIA HIGHER EDUCATION POLICY COMMISSION-OFFICE OF FINANCIAL AID AND OUTREACH SERVICES

WEST VIRGINIA ENGINEERING, SCIENCE & TECHNOLOGY
SCHOLARSHIP PROGRAM
see number 89

ENGINEERING/TECHNOLOGY_____

AEA-OREGON COUNCIL

AEA TECHNOLOGY SCHOLARSHIP PROGRAM
see number 50

ASSOCIATED GENERAL CONTRACTORS EDUCATION AND RESEARCH FOUNDATION

AGC EDUCATION AND RESEARCH FOUNDATION
UNDERGRADUATE SCHOLARSHIPS
see number 53

ASTRONAUT SCHOLARSHIP FOUNDATION

ASTRONAUT SCHOLARSHIP FOUNDATION
see number 14

BARRY M. GOLDWATER SCHOLARSHIP AND EXCELLENCE IN EDUCATION FOUNDATION

BARRY M. GOLDWATER SCHOLARSHIP AND EXCELLENCE IN
EDUCATION PROGRAM
see number 15

BUSINESS AND PROFESSIONAL WOMEN'S FOUNDATION

BPW CAREER ADVANCEMENT SCHOLARSHIP PROGRAM FOR
WOMEN
see number 32

CATCHING THE DREAM

MATH, ENGINEERING, SCIENCE, BUSINESS, EDUCATION, COMPUTERS SCHOLARSHIPS   see number 39

CUBAN AMERICAN NATIONAL FOUNDATION

MAS FAMILY SCHOLARSHIPS   see number 41

EATON CORPORATION

EATON CORPORATION MULTICULTURAL SCHOLARS PROGRAM
see number 58

HISPANIC COLLEGE FUND, INC.

DENNY'S/HISPANIC COLLEGE FUND SCHOLARSHIP   see number 1

FIRST IN MY FAMILY SCHOLARSHIP PROGRAM   see number 10

HISPANIC COLLEGE FUND SCHOLARSHIP PROGRAM   see number 11

HISPANIC COLLEGE FUND/INROADS/SPRINT SCHOLARSHIP
PROGRAM   see number 43

NATIONAL HISPANIC EXPLORERS SCHOLARSHIP PROGRAM
see number 16

HISPANIC ENGINEER NATIONAL ACHIEVEMENT AWARDS CORPORATION (HENAAC)

HISPANIC ENGINEER NATIONAL ACHIEVEMENT AWARDS
CORPORATION SCHOLARSHIP PROGRAM   see number 27

HISPANIC SCHOLARSHIP FUND

HSF/GENERAL MOTORS SCHOLARSHIP   see number 44

INTERNATIONAL SOCIETY FOR OPTICAL ENGINEERING-SPIE

SPIE EDUCATIONAL SCHOLARSHIPS IN OPTICAL SCIENCE AND
ENGINEERING   see number 17

LUCENT TECHNOLOGIES FOUNDATION

LUCENT GLOBAL SCIENCE SCHOLARS PROGRAM   see number 18

MARION D. AND EVA S. PEEPLES FOUNDATION TRUST SCHOLARSHIP PROGRAM

MARION D. AND EVA S. PEEPLES SCHOLARSHIPS   see number 74

MARYLAND ASSOCIATION OF PRIVATE CAREER SCHOOLS

MARYLAND ASSOCIATION OF PRIVATE CAREER SCHOOLS SCHOLARSHIP   see number 45

MICRON TECHNOLOGY FOUNDATION

MICRON SCIENCE AND TECHNOLOGY SCHOLARS   see number 52

NAMEPA NATIONAL SCHOLARSHIP FOUNDATION

NATIONAL ASSOCIATION OF MINORITY ENGINEERING PROGRAM ADMINISTRATORS NATIONAL SCHOLARSHIP FUND   see number 28

NASA NEVADA SPACE GRANT CONSORTIUM

UNIVERSITY AND COMMUNITY COLLEGE SYSTEM OF NEVADA NASA SPACE GRANT AND FELLOWSHIP PROGRAM   see number 29

NATIONAL ASSOCIATION OF WOMEN IN CONSTRUCTION

NAWIC UNDERGRADUATE SCHOLARSHIPS   see number 22

SOCIETY OF PLASTICS ENGINEERS (SPE) FOUNDATION

SOCIETY OF PLASTICS ENGINEERS SCHOLARSHIP PROGRAM   see number 47

TAU BETA PI ASSOCIATION

TAU BETA PI SCHOLARSHIP PROGRAM • 91

One-time award for initiated members of Tau Beta Pi in their senior year of full-time undergraduate engineering study. Submit typewritten application and two letters of recommendation. Contact for complete details.

Academic/Career Areas Engineering/Technology.
Award Scholarship for use in senior year; not renewable. *Number:* 30–50. *Amount:* $2000.
Eligibility Requirements: Applicant must be enrolled or expecting to enroll full-time at a four-year institution or university. Applicant must have 3.5 GPA or higher. Available to U.S. and non-U.S. citizens.
Application Requirements Application, references. *Deadline:* March 1.
World Wide Web: http://www.tbp.org/
Contact: D. Stephen Pierre, Jr., Director of Fellowships
Tau Beta Pi Association
PO Box 2697
Knoxville, TN 37901-2697
Fax: 334-694-2310
E-mail: dspierre@southernco.com

TRIMMER EDUCATION FOUNDATION

TRIMMER SCHOLARSHIPS see number 56

UNITED NEGRO COLLEGE FUND

COLLEGE FUND/COCA COLA CORPORATE INTERN PROGRAM
see number 48

UTAH STATE BOARD OF REGENTS

UTAH ENGINEERING AND COMPUTER SCIENCE PROGRAM (UECLP) see number 59

WEST VIRGINIA HIGHER EDUCATION POLICY COMMISSION-OFFICE OF FINANCIAL AID AND OUTREACH SERVICES

WEST VIRGINIA ENGINEERING, SCIENCE & TECHNOLOGY SCHOLARSHIP PROGRAM see number 89

FASHION DESIGN_____

WORLDSTUDIO FOUNDATION
WORLDSTUDIO FOUNDATION SCHOLARSHIP PROGRAM
see number 23

FILMMAKING_____

PRINCESS GRACE FOUNDATION-USA
PRINCESS GRACE SCHOLARSHIPS IN DANCE, THEATER, AND FILM
• 92

Scholarships are offered as follows: Dance for any year of training after the first year; Theater for last year of study in acting, directing, designing; Film for senior/master's thesis projects. Must be a U.S. citizen or permanent resident. Must include a video and nominator's statements. Deadlines: Theater: March 31, Dance: April 30, and Film: June 2.

Academic/Career Areas Filmmaking; Performing Arts.
Award Scholarship for use in senior, or graduate years; not renewable. *Number:* 15–20. *Amount:* $5000–$25,000.
Eligibility Requirements: Applicant must be enrolled or expecting to enroll full-time at a four-year institution or university. Available to U.S. citizens.
Application Requirements Application, essay, photo, portfolio, resume, references, self-addressed stamped envelope, nomination.
World Wide Web: http://www.pgfusa.com
Contact: Ms. Toby Boshak, Executive Director
Princess Grace Foundation-USA
150 East 58th Street, 21st Floor
New York, NY 10155
Phone: 212-317-1470
Fax: 212-317-1473
E-mail: tboshak@pgfusa.com

WORLDSTUDIO FOUNDATION
WORLDSTUDIO FOUNDATION SCHOLARSHIP PROGRAM
see number 23

FIRE SCIENCES

MARYLAND HIGHER EDUCATION COMMISSION

FIREFIGHTER, AMBULANCE, AND RESCUE SQUAD MEMBER TUITION REIMBURSEMENT PROGRAM-MARYLAND • 93

Award intended to reimburse members of rescue organizations serving Maryland communities for tuition costs of course work towards a degree or certificate in fire service or medical technology. Must attend a two- or four-year school in Maryland. Minimum 2.0 GPA.

Academic/Career Areas Fire Sciences; Health and Medical Sciences; Trade/Technical Specialties.

Award Scholarship for use in freshman, sophomore, junior, or senior years; not renewable. *Number:* 100–300. *Amount:* $200–$4000.

Eligibility Requirements: Applicant must be enrolled or expecting to enroll full or part-time at a two-year or four-year institution or university; resident of Maryland and studying in Maryland. Applicant or parent of applicant must have employment or volunteer experience in police/firefighting. Available to U.S. citizens.

Application Requirements Application, transcript. *Deadline:* July 1.

World Wide Web: http://www.mhec.state.md.us

Contact: Gerrie Rogers, Office of Student Financial Assistance
Maryland Higher Education Commission
839 Bestgate Road, Suite 400
Annapolis, MD 21401-3013
Phone: 410-260-4574
Fax: 410-260-3203
E-mail: ofsamail@mhec.state.md.us

FOOD SCIENCE/NUTRITION

HISPANIC COLLEGE FUND, INC.

NATIONAL HISPANIC EXPLORERS SCHOLARSHIP PROGRAM
see number 16

INSTITUTE OF FOOD TECHNOLOGISTS

INSTITUTE OF FOOD TECHNOLOGISTS FOOD ENGINEERING DIVISION JUNIOR/SENIOR SCHOLARSHIP • 94

One-time award for junior or senior-level students in an Institute of Food Technologists-approved program, with demonstrated intent to pursue professional activities in food science or food technology. Submit recommendation. Applications must be sent to department head of educational institution, not IFT.

Academic/Career Areas Food Science/Nutrition.
Award Scholarship for use in sophomore, junior, or senior years; not renewable. *Number:* 59. *Amount:* $1000–$2250.
Eligibility Requirements: Applicant must be enrolled or expecting to enroll at a four-year institution or university. Available to U.S. citizens.
Application Requirements Application, references, transcript. *Deadline:* February 1.
World Wide Web: http://www.ift.org
Contact: Administrator
Institute of Food Technologists
525 West Van Buren Street, Suite 1000
Chicago, IL 60607
Phone: 312-782-8424
Fax: 312-782-8348

INTERNATIONAL ASSOCIATION OF CULINARY PROFESSIONALS FOUNDATION (IACPF)

IACP FOUNDATION CULINARY SCHOLARSHIPS • 95

Scholarships for beginning students, continuing education, culinary professionals and independent research. Applicants must have at least two years of foodservice experience (paid, volunteer or combination of both), a minimum 3.0 GPA and write an essay. There is a $25 application fee.

Academic/Career Areas Food Science/Nutrition; Food Service/Hospitality.
Award Scholarship for use in freshman, sophomore, junior, senior, graduate, or postgraduate years; not renewable. *Number:* 18. *Amount:* $500–$10,000.
Eligibility Requirements: Applicant must be enrolled or expecting to enroll full or part-time at a two-year or four-year or technical institution or university. Applicant or parent of applicant must have employment or volunteer experience in food service. Applicant must have 3.0 GPA or higher. Available to U.S. and non-U.S. citizens.
Application Requirements Application, essay, references, transcript. *Fee:* $25. *Deadline:* December 15.
World Wide Web: http://www.iacpfoundation.org
Contact: Trina Gribbins, Program Coordinator
International Association of Culinary Professionals Foundation
(IACPF)
304 West Liberty Street, Suite 201
Louisville, KY 40202-3068
Phone: 502-581-9786 Ext. 264
Fax: 502-589-3602
E-mail: tgribbins@hqtrs.com

JAMES BEARD FOUNDATION, INC.

JAMES BEARD FOUNDATION GENERAL SCHOLARSHIPS   • 96

One-time award towards tuition at an accredited culinary school of student's choice. The amount of each scholarship will be at the discretion of the James Beard Foundation scholarship committee. Candidates must demonstrate a strong commitment to the culinary arts, an exceptional academic or work record, and financial need. See web site at http://www.jamesbeard.org for further details.

Academic/Career Areas Food Science/Nutrition.

Award Scholarship for use in freshman, sophomore, junior, senior, or graduate years; not renewable. *Number:* up to 50. *Amount:* $1000–$2000.

Eligibility Requirements: Applicant must be enrolled or expecting to enroll at an institution or university. Available to U.S. and non-U.S. citizens.

Application Requirements Application, essay, financial need analysis, references, transcript. *Deadline:* May 1.

World Wide Web: http://www.jamesbeard.org

Contact: Caroline Stuart, Scholarship Director
James Beard Foundation, Inc.
167 West 12th Street
New York, NY 10011
Phone: 212-675-4984 Ext. 311
Fax: 212-645-1438
E-mail: jamesbeardfound@hotmail.com

MARION D. AND EVA S. PEEPLES FOUNDATION TRUST SCHOLARSHIP PROGRAM

MARION D. AND EVA S. PEEPLES SCHOLARSHIPS   see number 74

MARYLAND ASSOCIATION OF PRIVATE CAREER SCHOOLS

MARYLAND ASSOCIATION OF PRIVATE CAREER SCHOOLS SCHOLARSHIP   see number 45

NATIONAL RESTAURANT ASSOCIATION EDUCATIONAL FOUNDATION

NATIONAL RESTAURANT ASSOCIATION EDUCATIONAL FOUNDATION UNDERGRADUATE SCHOLARSHIPS FOR HIGH SCHOOL SENIORS • 97

This scholarship is awarded to high school students who have demonstrated a commitment to both postsecondary hospitality education and to a career in the industry. Must have 250 hours of industry experience, age 17-19 with a 2.75 GPA.

Academic/Career Areas Food Science/Nutrition.

Award Scholarship for use in freshman year; not renewable. *Number:* 50–100. *Amount:* $2000.

Eligibility Requirements: Applicant must be high school student; age 17-19 and planning to enroll or expecting to enroll full-time at an institution or university. Applicant or parent of applicant must have employment or volunteer experience in food service.

Application Requirements Application, essay, references, transcript. *Deadline:* March 1.

World Wide Web: http://www.nraef.org

Contact: Emilee N. Rogan, Director, Scholarship Program
National Restaurant Association Educational Foundation
175 West Jackson Boulevard, Suite 1500
Chicago, IL 60604-2702
Phone: 800-765-2122
Fax: 312-715-1362
E-mail: scholars@foodtrain.org

FOOD SERVICE/HOSPITALITY_____

DECA (DISTRIBUTIVE EDUCATION CLUBS OF AMERICA)

HARRY A. APPLEGATE SCHOLARSHIP   see number 42

ILLINOIS RESTAURANT ASSOCIATION EDUCATIONAL FOUNDATION

ILLINOIS RESTAURANT ASSOCIATION EDUCATIONAL FOUNDATION SCHOLARSHIPS • 98

Scholarship available to Illinois residents enrolled in a food service management, culinary arts, or hospitality management concentration in an accredited program of a two- or four-year college or university. Must be a U.S. citizen. Deadline is May 15.

Illinois Restaurant Association Educational Foundation Scholarships (continued)
Academic/Career Areas Food Service/Hospitality; Hospitality Management.
Award Scholarship for use in freshman, sophomore, junior, or senior years; not renewable. *Number:* 40–60. *Amount:* $500–$10,000.
Eligibility Requirements: Applicant must be enrolled or expecting to enroll full or part-time at a two-year or four-year institution or university and resident of Illinois. Available to U.S. citizens.
Application Requirements Application, references, transcript. *Deadline:* May 15.
World Wide Web: http://www.illinoisrestaurants.org
Contact: Susanne Gilbert, Program and Operations Manager
Illinois Restaurant Association Educational Foundation
200 North LaSalle, Suite 880
Chicago, IL 60601-1014
Phone: 312-787-4000
Fax: 312-787-4792
E-mail: edfound@illinoisrestaurants.org

INTERNATIONAL ASSOCIATION OF CULINARY PROFESSIONALS FOUNDATION (IACPF)

IACP FOUNDATION CULINARY SCHOLARSHIPS   see number 95

NATIONAL RESTAURANT ASSOCIATION EDUCATIONAL FOUNDATION

NATIONAL RESTAURANT ASSOCIATION EDUCATIONAL FOUNDATION UNDERGRADUATE SCHOLARSHIPS FOR COLLEGE STUDENTS   • 99

This scholarship is awarded to college students who have demonstrated a commitment to both postsecondary hospitality education and to a career in the industry with 750 hours of industry work experience. Must have a 2.75 GPA, and be enrolled for a full academic term for the school year beginning in fall.

Academic/Career Areas Food Service/Hospitality.
Award Scholarship for use in sophomore, junior, or senior years; not renewable. *Number:* 159–200. *Amount:* $2000.
Eligibility Requirements: Applicant must be enrolled or expecting to enroll full-time at an institution or university. Applicant or parent of applicant must have employment or volunteer experience in food service. Available to U.S. citizens.
Application Requirements Application, essay, transcript. *Deadline:* March 1.
World Wide Web: http://www.nraef.org

Contact: Emilee N. Rogan, Director, Scholarship Program
National Restaurant Association Educational Foundation
175 West Jackson Boulevard, Suite 1500
Chicago, IL 60604-2702
Phone: 800-765-2122
Fax: 312-715-1362
E-mail: scholars@foodtrain.org

FOREIGN LANGUAGE

ARKANSAS DEPARTMENT OF HIGHER EDUCATION

EMERGENCY SECONDARY EDUCATION LOAN PROGRAM

see number 31

ROTARY FOUNDATION OF ROTARY INTERNATIONAL

ROTARY FOUNDATION CULTURAL AMBASSADORIAL SCHOLARSHIP

• 100

One-time award funds three or six months (depending on availability through sponsoring Rotary district) of intensive language study and cultural immersion abroad. Applicant must have completed at least two years of university course work or one year in proposed language of study. Application through local Rotary club; appearances before clubs required during award period. Applications accepted March through July. See web site at http://www.rotary.org for updated information.

Academic/Career Areas Foreign Language.
Award Scholarship for use in junior, senior, or graduate years; not renewable. *Number:* 150–200. *Amount:* $12,000–$19,000.
Eligibility Requirements: Applicant must be enrolled or expecting to enroll at an institution or university and must have an interest in leadership.
Application Requirements Application, autobiography, essay, interview, references, transcript.
World Wide Web: http://www.rotary.org
Contact: Scholarship Program
Rotary Foundation of Rotary International
1560 Sherman Avenue
Evanston, IL 60201
Phone: 847-866-4459

SOCIEDAD HONORARIA HISPÁNICA

JOSEPH S. ADAMS SCHOLARSHIP • 101

Applicants must be members of the Sociedad Honoraria Hispánica and a high school senior. Must have major/career interest in Spanish/Portuguese. Applicants must demonstrate high academic achievement, depth of character, leadership, patriotism, seriousness of purpose. Award available to citizens of other countries as long as they are members of the Sacred Honoraria Hispánica. For information contact local sponsor of Sociedad Honoraria Hispánica. For high school students only.

Academic/Career Areas Foreign Language.

Award Scholarship for use in freshman year; not renewable. *Number:* 44. *Amount:* $1000–$2000.

Eligibility Requirements: Applicant must be high school student; planning to enroll or expecting to enroll full-time at a four-year institution or university and must have an interest in Portuguese language or Spanish language. Available to U.S. and non-U.S. citizens.

World Wide Web: http://www.sociedadhonorariahispanica.org

Contact: local sponsor of SHH at high school

FUNERAL SERVICES/MORTUARY SCIENCE

CHAFFER SCHOLARSHIP TRUST

CHAFFER SCHOLARSHIP TRUST • 102

The Chaffer Trust is designated for university music majors in their junior, senior, or graduate school years attending Idaho institutions, or are Idahoans attending school out-of-state. They must major in piano, organ, or harpsichord, or Music Education with their main instrument one of the three mentioned. Trust awards are for a maximum of 2 years.

Academic/Career Areas Funeral Services/Mortuary Science.

Award Scholarship for use in junior, senior, graduate, or postgraduate years; renewable. *Number:* 22–25. *Amount:* $700–$4800.

Eligibility Requirements: Applicant must be enrolled or expecting to enroll full-time at a four-year institution or university and must have an interest in music. Available to U.S. and non-U.S. citizens.

Application Requirements Application, tape or CD of applicant playing 3 piano/organ/harpsichord pieces from 3 different music periods. *Deadline:* April 1.

Contact: Gay Pool, Chairman of Chaffer Trust
Chaffer Scholarship Trust
c/o Wells Fargo Bank
119 North Ninth Street, PO Box 2618
Boise, ID 83701
Phone: 208-383-9216
E-mail: gpiano83712@earthlink.net

GEOGRAPHY

MORRIS K. UDALL FOUNDATION
MORRIS K. UDALL SCHOLARS
see number 12

NATIONAL FISH AND WILDLIFE FOUNDATION
BUDWEISER CONSERVATION SCHOLARSHIP PROGRAM
see number 33

GRAPHICS/GRAPHIC ARTS/PRINTING

HISPANIC COLLEGE FUND, INC.
DENNY'S/HISPANIC COLLEGE FUND SCHOLARSHIP
see number 1
FIRST IN MY FAMILY SCHOLARSHIP PROGRAM
see number 10
HISPANIC COLLEGE FUND SCHOLARSHIP PROGRAM
see number 11

PRINT AND GRAPHIC SCHOLARSHIP FOUNDATION
PRINT AND GRAPHICS SCHOLARSHIPS
• 103

Applicant must be interested in a career in graphic communications, printing technology, printing management or publishing. Must have and maintain a 3.0 cumulative GPA. Selection based on academic record, class rank, recommendations, biographical information and extracurricular activities. Deadline for high school students is March 1 and April 1 for enrolled college students.

Print and Graphics Scholarships (continued)

Award available to citizens outside U.S. as long as they are attending a U.S. institution. Application may be obtained from web site and may be submitted between November 1 and April 1.

Academic/Career Areas Graphics/Graphic Arts/Printing.

Award Scholarship for use in freshman, sophomore, junior, senior, or graduate years; renewable. *Number:* 20–320. *Amount:* $500–$3000.

Eligibility Requirements: Applicant must be enrolled or expecting to enroll full-time at a two-year or four-year or technical institution or university and must have an interest in designated field specified by sponsor. Applicant must have 3.0 GPA or higher. Available to U.S. and non-U.S. citizens.

Application Requirements Application, essay, references, self-addressed stamped envelope, test scores, transcript.

World Wide Web: http://www.pgsf.org

Contact: Bernadine Eckert, Scholarship Administrator
Print and Graphic Scholarship Foundation
200 Deer Run Road
Sewickley, PA 15143-2600
Phone: 412-741-6860
Fax: 412-741-2311
E-mail: pgsf@gatf.org

WORLDSTUDIO FOUNDATION

WORLDSTUDIO FOUNDATION SCHOLARSHIP PROGRAM
see number 23

HEALTH ADMINISTRATION_____

ALBERTA HERITAGE SCHOLARSHIP FUND

ALBERTA HERITAGE SCHOLARSHIP FUND ABORIGINAL HEALTH CAREERS BURSARY
see number 30

CONGRESSIONAL BLACK CAUCUS SPOUSES PROGRAM

CONGRESSIONAL BLACK CAUCUS SPOUSES HEALTH INITIATIVE
• 104

Award made to students who reside or attend school in a congressional district represented by an African-American member of Congress. Must be full-time undergraduate enrolled in health-related program. Minimum 2.5 GPA required. Contact the congressional office in the appropriate district for information and applications. Visit http://www.cbcfinc.org for a list of district offices.

Academic/Career Areas Health Administration; Health and Medical Sciences; Health Information Management/Technology.

Award Scholarship for use in freshman, sophomore, junior, or senior years; renewable. *Number:* 200. *Amount:* $500–$4000.

Eligibility Requirements: Applicant must be enrolled or expecting to enroll full-time at a two-year or four-year or technical institution or university. Applicant must have 2.5 GPA or higher. Available to U.S. citizens.

Application Requirements Application, essay, financial need analysis, interview, photo, references, transcript. *Deadline:* Continuous.

World Wide Web: http://cbcfinc.org

Contact: Appropriate Congressional District Office

ORDEAN FOUNDATION

ORDEAN LOAN PROGRAM
see number 6

HEALTH AND MEDICAL SCIENCES___

ALBERTA HERITAGE SCHOLARSHIP FUND

ALBERTA HERITAGE SCHOLARSHIP FUND ABORIGINAL HEALTH CAREERS BURSARY
see number 30

ALICE M. YARNOLD AND SAMUEL YARNOLD SCHOLARSHIP TRUST

ALICE M. AND SAMUEL YARNOLD SCHOLARSHIP • 105

Must be a New Hampshire resident, attending school in any state; applicant must already have begun postsecondary education (graduating high school seniors not eligible); must major in medicine, nursing or health-related field but not in management within those fields.

Academic/Career Areas Health and Medical Sciences; Nursing; Therapy/Rehabilitation.

Award Scholarship for use in sophomore, junior, senior, graduate, or postgraduate years; not renewable. *Number:* 20–30. *Amount:* $1000–$3000.

Eligibility Requirements: Applicant must be enrolled or expecting to enroll full or part-time at a two-year or four-year or technical institution or university and resident of New Hampshire. Available to U.S. citizens.

Application Requirements Application, essay, financial need analysis, references, transcript. *Deadline:* May 10.

Alice M. and Samuel Yarnold Scholarship (continued)
Contact: Ms. Jacqueline Lambert, Assistant to Trustees of Yarnold Trust
Alice M. Yarnold and Samuel Yarnold Scholarship Trust
180 Locust Street
Dover, NH 03820
Phone: 603-749-5535
Fax: 603-749-1187

ARKANSAS DEPARTMENT OF HIGHER EDUCATION

ARKANSAS HEALTH EDUCATION GRANT PROGRAM (ARHEG)

see number 13

BUREAU OF HEALTH PROFESSIONS

NATIONAL HEALTH SERVICE CORPS SCHOLARSHIP PROGRAM

• 106

Federal scholarships for U.S. citizens pursuing allopathic (MD) or osteopathic (DO) medicine, dentistry, family nurse practitioner, nurse midwifery, or physician assistant education. Two-year to four-year service commitment required. Scholarship includes tuition, fees, monthly stipends, and payment for educational expenses. Monthly stipend is taxable. Federal income tax only withheld from monthly stipend. Application deadline: March 28.

Academic/Career Areas Health and Medical Sciences; Nursing.
Award Scholarship for use in freshman, sophomore, junior, senior, or graduate years; renewable. *Number:* 300–320. *Amount:* $67,500–$135,000.
Eligibility Requirements: Applicant must be enrolled or expecting to enroll full-time at a four-year institution or university. Available to U.S. citizens.
Application Requirements Application, interview. *Deadline:* March 28.
World Wide Web: http://nhsc.bhpr.hrsa.gov/Get_Invoved/scholarships.html
Contact: c/o IQ Solutions
Bureau of Health Professions
11300 Rockville Pike, Suite 801
Rockville, MD 20852
Phone: 800-638-0824

BUSINESS AND PROFESSIONAL WOMEN'S FOUNDATION

BPW CAREER ADVANCEMENT SCHOLARSHIP PROGRAM FOR WOMEN

see number 32

CONGRESSIONAL BLACK CAUCUS SPOUSES PROGRAM

CONGRESSIONAL BLACK CAUCUS SPOUSES HEALTH INITIATIVE
see number 104

HEALTH PROFESSIONS EDUCATION FOUNDATION

HEALTH PROFESSIONS EDUCATION SCHOLARSHIP PROGRAM
see number 60

KAISER PERMANENTE ALLIED HEALTHCARE SCHOLARSHIP • 107

One-time award to all students enrolled in or accepted to California accredited allied health education programs for school related expenses. Priority is given to students enrolled in the following fields: medical imaging, occupational therapy, physical therapy, respiratory care, social work, pharmacy, pharmacy technician, medical laboratory technologist, surgical technician, ultrasound technician and diagnostic medical sonography. Eligible applicants may receive up to $2,500 per year in financial assistance. Deadlines: March 27 and September 11. Must be resident of CA and U.S. citizen.

Academic/Career Areas Health and Medical Sciences; Social Services; Therapy/Rehabilitation.

Award Scholarship for use in freshman, sophomore, junior, or senior years; not renewable. *Number:* 20–40. *Amount:* $2000–$2500.

Eligibility Requirements: Applicant must be enrolled or expecting to enroll full or part-time at a two-year or four-year or technical institution or university; resident of California and studying in California. Applicant must have 2.5 GPA or higher. Available to U.S. citizens.

Application Requirements Application, driver's license, financial need analysis, references, transcript.

World Wide Web: http://www.healthprofessions.ca.gov

Contact: Charles Gray, Program Director
Health Professions Education Foundation
818 K Street, Suite 210
Sacramento, CA 95814
Phone: 916-324-6500

YOUTH FOR ADOLESCENT PREGNANCY PREVENTION LEADERSHIP RECOGNITION PROGRAM • 108

The Youth for Adolescent Pregnancy Prevention (YAPP) Leadership Recognition Program (LRP) will recognize youths throughout California who have made an outstanding contribution to their communities by promoting healthy adolescent sexuality and teen pregnancy prevention. Youths selected to receive this scholarship award will receive up to $5,000 per year for up to five years

Youth for Adolescent Pregnancy Prevention Leadership Recognition Program (continued) to assist them in pursing careers in the health field (e.g., medicine, ancillary services, dentistry, mental health). Must be resident of CA and U.S. citizen between the ages of 16-24.

Academic/Career Areas Health and Medical Sciences; Nursing.

Award Scholarship for use in freshman, sophomore, junior, or senior years; not renewable. *Number:* 8. *Amount:* $25,000.

Eligibility Requirements: Applicant must be age 16-24; enrolled or expecting to enroll full or part-time at a two-year or four-year or technical institution or university; resident of California and studying in California. Available to U.S. citizens.

Application Requirements Application, financial need analysis, interview, photo, references, transcript, 2 copies of application. *Deadline:* January 23.

World Wide Web: http://www.healthprofessions.ca.gov

Contact: Charles Gray, Project Officer
Health Professions Education Foundation
818 K Street, Suite 210
Sacramento, CA 95814
Phone: 916-324-6500
Fax: 916-324-6585
E-mail: cgray@oshpd.state.ca.us

J.D. ARCHBOLD MEMORIAL HOSPITAL

ARCHBOLD SCHOLARSHIP PROGRAM • 109

Service cancelable loan awarded for a clinical degree. Awarded to residents of Southwest Georgia and North Florida. Specific clinical degree may vary, depending on need in area. Must agree to full-time employment for 1-3 years upon graduation.

Academic/Career Areas Health and Medical Sciences; Nursing.

Award Forgivable loan for use in junior year; not renewable. *Number:* 50. *Amount:* $600–$6000.

Eligibility Requirements: Applicant must be enrolled or expecting to enroll full or part-time at a two-year or four-year or technical institution or university and resident of Florida or Georgia. Available to U.S. citizens.

Application Requirements Application, interview, transcript. *Deadline:* Continuous.

World Wide Web: http://www.archbold.org

Contact: Donna McMillan, Education Coordinator
J.D. Archbold Memorial Hospital
PO Box 1018
Thomasville, GA 31799
Phone: 229-228-2795
Fax: 229-228-8584

MARYLAND HIGHER EDUCATION COMMISSION

DEVELOPMENTAL DISABILITIES AND MENTAL HEALTH WORKFORCE TUITION ASSISTANCE PROGRAM • 110

Provides tuition assistance to students who are service employees that provide direct support or care to individuals with developmental disabilities or mental disorders. Must be a Maryland resident attending a Maryland college. Minimum 2.0 GPA.

Academic/Career Areas Health and Medical Sciences; Nursing; Social Services; Special Education; Therapy/Rehabilitation.

Award Forgivable loan for use in freshman, sophomore, junior, senior, or graduate years; renewable. *Number:* 300–400. *Amount:* $500–$3000.

Eligibility Requirements: Applicant must be enrolled or expecting to enroll full or part-time at a two-year or four-year institution or university; resident of Maryland and studying in Maryland. Applicant or parent of applicant must have employment or volunteer experience in designated career field. Available to U.S. citizens.

Application Requirements Application, transcript. *Deadline:* July 1.

World Wide Web: http://www.mhec.state.md.us

Contact: Gerrie Rogers, Office of Student Financial Assistance
Maryland Higher Education Commission
839 Bestgate Road, Suite 400
Annapolis, MD 21401
Phone: 410-260-4574
Fax: 410-260-3203
E-mail: osfamail@mhec.state.md.us

FIREFIGHTER, AMBULANCE, AND RESCUE SQUAD MEMBER TUITION REIMBURSEMENT PROGRAM-MARYLAND see number 93

GRADUATE AND PROFESSIONAL SCHOLARSHIP PROGRAM-MARYLAND see number 61

NATIONAL AMBUCS, INC.

AMBUCS SCHOLARS-SCHOLARSHIPS FOR THERAPISTS • 111

Scholarships are open to students who are U.S. citizens at a junior level or above in college. Must be enrolled in an accredited program by the appropriate health therapy profession authority in physical therapy, occupational therapy, speech-language pathology, or audiology and must demonstrate a financial need. Application available on web site at http://www.ambucs.com. Paper applications are not accepted.

Academic/Career Areas Health and Medical Sciences; Therapy/Rehabilitation.

Award Scholarship for use in junior, senior, graduate, or postgraduate years; not renewable. *Number:* 300. *Amount:* $500–$6000.

AMBUCS Scholars-Scholarships for Therapists (continued)

Eligibility Requirements: Applicant must be enrolled or expecting to enroll full-time at a four-year institution or university. Available to U.S. citizens.

Application Requirements Application, essay, financial need analysis, enrollment certification form. *Deadline:* April 15.

World Wide Web: http://www.ambucs.com

Contact: Janice Blankenship, Scholarship Coordinator
National AMBUCS, Inc.
PO Box 5127
High Point, NC 27262
Phone: 336-869-2166
Fax: 336-887-8451
E-mail: janiceb@ambucs.com

NEW MEXICO COMMISSION ON HIGHER EDUCATION

ALLIED HEALTH STUDENT LOAN PROGRAM-NEW MEXICO
see number 62

PHYSICIAN ASSISTANT FOUNDATION

PHYSICIAN ASSISTANT FOUNDATION ANNUAL SCHOLARSHIP
• 112

One-time award for student members of the American Academy of Physician Assistants enrolled in an ARC PA accredited physician assistant programs. Award based on financial need, academic achievement, and goals. Must submit two passport-type photographs for promotional reasons.

Academic/Career Areas Health and Medical Sciences.

Award Scholarship for use in junior or senior years; not renewable. *Number:* 50–75. *Amount:* $2000–$3000.

Eligibility Requirements: Applicant must be enrolled or expecting to enroll full or part-time at a two-year or four-year institution or university. Applicant or parent of applicant must be member of American Academy of Physicians Assistants. Available to U.S. and non-U.S. citizens.

Application Requirements Application, essay, financial need analysis, photo, transcript. *Deadline:* February 1.

World Wide Web: http://www.aapa.org

Contact: Physician Assistant Foundation
950 North Washington Street
Alexandria, VA 22304-1552
Phone: 703-836-2272
Fax: 703-684-1924

STATE OF GEORGIA

SERVICE-CANCELABLE STAFFORD LOAN-GEORGIA   see number 63

UNITED NEGRO COLLEGE FUND

MERCK SCIENCE INITIATIVE
see number 34

UNITED STATES DEPARTMENT OF HEALTH AND HUMAN SERVICES

NIH UNDERGRADUATE SCHOLARSHIP FOR INDIVIDUALS FROM DISADVANTAGED BACKGROUNDS
see number 35

HEALTH INFORMATION MANAGEMENT/ TECHNOLOGY

AMERICAN HEALTH INFORMATION MANAGEMENT ASSOCIATION/FOUNDATION OF RESEARCH AND EDUCATION

FOUNDATION OF RESEARCH AND EDUCATION UNDERGRADUATE MERIT SCHOLARSHIPS
• 113

Multiple scholarships for undergraduate Health Information Management students. One standard application for all available scholarships. Must have a 3.0 GPA. Applications can be downloaded at http://www.ahima.org. Must be a member of AHIMA.

Academic/Career Areas Health Information Management/Technology.

Award Scholarship for use in freshman, sophomore, junior, senior, graduate, or postgraduate years; not renewable. *Number:* 40–60. *Amount:* $1000– $5000.

Eligibility Requirements: Applicant must be enrolled or expecting to enroll full or part-time at a two-year or four-year or technical institution or university. Applicant or parent of applicant must be member of American Health Information Management Association. Applicant must have 3.0 GPA or higher. Available to U.S. and non-U.S. citizens.

Application Requirements Application, essay, references, transcript. *Deadline:* May 30.

World Wide Web: http://www.ahima.org

Contact: Ms. Alison Bergum, Donor Relations and Grants Associate
American Health Information Management Association/Foundation of Research and Education
233 North Michigan Avenue, Suite 2150
Chicago, IL 60601-5800
Phone: 312-233-1100
E-mail: fore@ahima.org

CONGRESSIONAL BLACK CAUCUS SPOUSES PROGRAM

CONGRESSIONAL BLACK CAUCUS SPOUSES HEALTH INITIATIVE
see number 104

ORDEAN FOUNDATION

ORDEAN LOAN PROGRAM
see number 6

HISTORY_____

HUGH FULTON BYAS MEMORIAL FUNDS, INC.

HUGH FULTON BYAS MEMORIAL GRANT • 114

Grants for United Kingdom citizens who are full-time students intending to pursue a course of study in the United States devoted to world peace, journalism, Anglo-American relations, or the creative arts.

Academic/Career Areas History; International Migration; Journalism; Peace and Conflict Studies.

Award Grant for use in sophomore, junior, senior, graduate, or postgraduate years; renewable. *Number:* 3–10. *Amount:* $1000–$25,000.

Eligibility Requirements: Applicant must be English citizenship and enrolled or expecting to enroll full-time at a four-year institution or university. Available to citizens of countries other than the U.S. or Canada.

Application Requirements Application, essay, financial need analysis, photo, self-addressed stamped envelope, transcript, United Kingdom passport. *Deadline:* Continuous.

Contact: Linda Maffei, Administrator
Hugh Fulton Byas Memorial Funds, Inc.
261 Bradley Street
New Haven, CT 06511
Phone: 203-777-8356
Fax: 203-562-6288

MORRIS K. UDALL FOUNDATION

MORRIS K. UDALL SCHOLARS
see number 12

HOME ECONOMICS_____

FAMILY, CAREER AND COMMUNITY LEADERS OF AMERICA-TEXAS ASSOCIATION

FCCLA HOUSTON LIVESTOCK SHOW AND RODEO SCHOLARSHIP
• 115

Ten, four-year $10,000 scholarships to be awarded to outstanding members of the Texas FCCLA. Applicants should visit the web site (http://www.texasfccla. org) or write to Texas FCCLA for complete information, submission guidelines, and restrictions. Minimum 3.5 GPA required. Must be Texas resident and attend a Texas institution.

Academic/Career Areas Home Economics.
Award Scholarship for use in freshman, sophomore, junior, or senior years; not renewable. *Number:* 10. *Amount:* $10,000.
Eligibility Requirements: Applicant must be high school student; planning to enroll or expecting to enroll full-time at a four-year institution or university; resident of Texas and studying in Texas. Applicant or parent of applicant must be member of Family, Career and Community Leaders of America. Applicant must have 3.5 GPA or higher. Available to U.S. citizens.
Application Requirements Application, essay, photo, references, test scores, transcript. *Deadline:* March 1.
World Wide Web: http://www.texasfccla.org
Contact: FCCLA Staff
Family, Career and Community Leaders of America-Texas
Association
3530 Bee Caves Road, #101
Austin, TX 78766
Phone: 512-306-0099
Fax: 512-306-0041
E-mail: fccla@texasfccla.org

MARYLAND ASSOCIATION OF PRIVATE CAREER SCHOOLS

MARYLAND ASSOCIATION OF PRIVATE CAREER SCHOOLS SCHOLARSHIP
see number 45

HORTICULTURE/FLORICULTURE_____

AMERICAN FLORAL ENDOWMENT

VICTOR AND MARGARET BALL PROGRAM
see number 36

HOSPITALITY MANAGEMENT_____

HISPANIC COLLEGE FUND, INC.

DENNY'S/HISPANIC COLLEGE FUND SCHOLARSHIP   see number 1

ILLINOIS RESTAURANT ASSOCIATION EDUCATIONAL FOUNDATION

ILLINOIS RESTAURANT ASSOCIATION EDUCATIONAL FOUNDATION SCHOLARSHIPS   see number 98

HUMANITIES_____

BUSINESS AND PROFESSIONAL WOMEN'S FOUNDATION

BPW CAREER ADVANCEMENT SCHOLARSHIP PROGRAM FOR WOMEN   see number 32

CATCHING THE DREAM

MATH, ENGINEERING, SCIENCE, BUSINESS, EDUCATION, COMPUTERS SCHOLARSHIPS   see number 39

NATIVE AMERICAN LEADERSHIP IN EDUCATION (NALE)   see number 40

INTERIOR DESIGN_____

NATIONAL ASSOCIATION OF WOMEN IN CONSTRUCTION

NAWIC UNDERGRADUATE SCHOLARSHIPS   see number 22

WORLDSTUDIO FOUNDATION

WORLDSTUDIO FOUNDATION SCHOLARSHIP PROGRAM
see number 23

INTERNATIONAL MIGRATION_____

HUGH FULTON BYAS MEMORIAL FUNDS, INC.

HUGH FULTON BYAS MEMORIAL GRANT
see number 114

JOURNALISM_____

CUBAN AMERICAN NATIONAL FOUNDATION

MAS FAMILY SCHOLARSHIPS
see number 41

FREEDOM FORUM

AL NEUHARTH FREE SPIRIT SCHOLARSHIP   • 116

One-time award for high school seniors interested in pursuing a career in journalism. Must be actively involved in high school journalism and demonstrate qualities such as being a visionary, an innovative leader, an entrepreneur, or a courageous achiever. Deadline is October 31. See web site at http://www.freedomforum.org for further information.

Academic/Career Areas Journalism.

Award Scholarship for use in freshman year; not renewable. *Number:* 102. *Amount:* $1000.

Eligibility Requirements: Applicant must be high school student and planning to enroll or expecting to enroll at an institution or university.

Application Requirements Application, essay, photo, references, transcript, sample of journalistic work. *Deadline:* October 31.

Contact: Freedom Forum
       1101 Wilson Boulevard
       Arlington, VA 22209

HUGH FULTON BYAS MEMORIAL FUNDS, INC.

HUGH FULTON BYAS MEMORIAL GRANT
see number 114

JOHN BAYLISS BROADCAST FOUNDATION

JOHN BAYLISS BROADCAST RADIO SCHOLARSHIP   see number 57

LANDSCAPE ARCHITECTURE_____

NATIONAL ASSOCIATION OF WOMEN IN CONSTRUCTION

NAWIC UNDERGRADUATE SCHOLARSHIPS   see number 22

LAW ENFORCEMENT/POLICE ADMINISTRATION_____

SOUTH CAROLINA POLICE CORPS

SOUTH CAROLINA POLICE CORPS SCHOLARSHIP   • 117

Tuition reimbursement scholarship available to a full time student of an U.S. accredited college. Must agree to serve for four years on community patrol with a participating South Carolina police or sheriff's department. Up to $7500 per academic year with a limit of $30,000 per student.

Academic/Career Areas Law Enforcement/Police Administration.

Award Scholarship for use in junior, senior, or graduate years; renewable. *Number:* 20. *Amount:* $7500–$30,000.

Eligibility Requirements: Applicant must be enrolled or expecting to enroll full-time at a four-year institution or university. Available to U.S. citizens.

Application Requirements Application, autobiography, driver's license, essay, financial need analysis, interview, portfolio, resume, references, test scores, transcript. *Deadline:* Continuous.

World Wide Web: http://www.citadel.edu/scpolicecorps/info.html

Contact: Thomas Adams, Program Coordinator
South Carolina Police Corps
The Citadel, MSC 67
171 Moultrie Street
Charleston, SC 29409
Phone: 843-953-6908
Fax: 843-953-6993
E-mail: adamst@citadel.edu

UTAH POLICE CORPS

UTAH POLICE CORPS SCHOLARSHIP PROGRAM • 118

Once accepted into this program we will pay up to $7500 per academic year for a degree with any major. Years completed before acceptance into our program are reimbursed for a total of up to $30,000. Students must attend and pass our police training academy and complete four years with one of Utah's sponsoring law enforcement agencies.

Academic/Career Areas Law Enforcement/Police Administration.

Award Scholarship for use in senior, graduate, or postgraduate years; renewable. *Number:* 30. *Amount:* $7500–$30,000.

Eligibility Requirements: Applicant must be enrolled or expecting to enroll full-time at a four-year institution or university. Available to U.S. citizens.

Application Requirements Application, autobiography, driver's license, interview, photo, resume, references, test scores, transcript. *Deadline:* Continuous.

World Wide Web: http://www.policecorps.utah.gov

Contact: Arlene Bobowski, Office Specialist
Utah Police Corps
4525 South 2700 West
Salt Lake City, UT 84119-1775
Phone: 801-965-4650
Fax: 801-965-4292
E-mail: abobowski@utah.gov

LAW/LEGAL SERVICES_____

BUSINESS AND PROFESSIONAL WOMEN'S FOUNDATION

BPW CAREER ADVANCEMENT SCHOLARSHIP PROGRAM FOR WOMEN
see number 32

MARYLAND HIGHER EDUCATION COMMISSION

GRADUATE AND PROFESSIONAL SCHOLARSHIP PROGRAM-MARYLAND
see number 61

JANET L. HOFFMANN LOAN ASSISTANCE REPAYMENT PROGRAM
see number 77

LITERATURE/ENGLISH/WRITING_____

ALLIANCE FOR YOUNG ARTISTS AND WRITERS, INC.

SCHOLASTIC ART AND WRITING AWARDS-ART SECTION
see number 24

SCHOLASTIC ART AND WRITING AWARDS-WRITING SECTION SCHOLARSHIP
see number 25

MATERIALS SCIENCE, ENGINEERING, AND METALLURGY_____

AEA-OREGON COUNCIL

AEA TECHNOLOGY SCHOLARSHIP PROGRAM
see number 50

AMERICAN CHEMICAL SOCIETY

AMERICAN CHEMICAL SOCIETY SCHOLARS PROGRAM
see number 51

ASTRONAUT SCHOLARSHIP FOUNDATION

ASTRONAUT SCHOLARSHIP FOUNDATION
see number 14

BARRY M. GOLDWATER SCHOLARSHIP AND EXCELLENCE IN EDUCATION FOUNDATION

BARRY M. GOLDWATER SCHOLARSHIP AND EXCELLENCE IN EDUCATION PROGRAM
see number 15

HISPANIC ENGINEER NATIONAL ACHIEVEMENT AWARDS CORPORATION (HENAAC)

HISPANIC ENGINEER NATIONAL ACHIEVEMENT AWARDS CORPORATION SCHOLARSHIP PROGRAM
see number 27

INTERNATIONAL SOCIETY FOR OPTICAL ENGINEERING-SPIE

SPIE EDUCATIONAL SCHOLARSHIPS IN OPTICAL SCIENCE AND ENGINEERING
see number 17

MICRON TECHNOLOGY FOUNDATION

MICRON SCIENCE AND TECHNOLOGY SCHOLARS
see number 52

NAMEPA NATIONAL SCHOLARSHIP FOUNDATION

NATIONAL ASSOCIATION OF MINORITY ENGINEERING PROGRAM ADMINISTRATORS NATIONAL SCHOLARSHIP FUND
see number 28

SOCIETY OF PLASTICS ENGINEERS (SPE) FOUNDATION

SOCIETY OF PLASTICS ENGINEERS SCHOLARSHIP PROGRAM
see number 47

MECHANICAL ENGINEERING_____

AEA-OREGON COUNCIL

AEA TECHNOLOGY SCHOLARSHIP PROGRAM
see number 50

ASTRONAUT SCHOLARSHIP FOUNDATION

ASTRONAUT SCHOLARSHIP FOUNDATION
see number 14

BARRY M. GOLDWATER SCHOLARSHIP AND EXCELLENCE IN EDUCATION FOUNDATION

BARRY M. GOLDWATER SCHOLARSHIP AND EXCELLENCE IN EDUCATION PROGRAM
see number 15

CUBAN AMERICAN NATIONAL FOUNDATION

MAS FAMILY SCHOLARSHIPS — see number 41

EATON CORPORATION

EATON CORPORATION MULTICULTURAL SCHOLARS PROGRAM — see number 58

HISPANIC COLLEGE FUND, INC.

FIRST IN MY FAMILY SCHOLARSHIP PROGRAM — see number 10

HISPANIC COLLEGE FUND SCHOLARSHIP PROGRAM — see number 11

HISPANIC COLLEGE FUND/INROADS/SPRINT SCHOLARSHIP PROGRAM — see number 43

HISPANIC ENGINEER NATIONAL ACHIEVEMENT AWARDS CORPORATION (HENAAC)

HISPANIC ENGINEER NATIONAL ACHIEVEMENT AWARDS CORPORATION SCHOLARSHIP PROGRAM — see number 27

HISPANIC SCHOLARSHIP FUND

HSF/GENERAL MOTORS SCHOLARSHIP — see number 44

INTERNATIONAL SOCIETY FOR OPTICAL ENGINEERING-SPIE

SPIE EDUCATIONAL SCHOLARSHIPS IN OPTICAL SCIENCE AND ENGINEERING — see number 17

MICRON TECHNOLOGY FOUNDATION

MICRON SCIENCE AND TECHNOLOGY SCHOLARS — see number 52

NAMEPA NATIONAL SCHOLARSHIP FOUNDATION

NATIONAL ASSOCIATION OF MINORITY ENGINEERING PROGRAM ADMINISTRATORS NATIONAL SCHOLARSHIP FUND — see number 28

NATIONAL ASSOCIATION OF WOMEN IN CONSTRUCTION

NAWIC UNDERGRADUATE SCHOLARSHIPS see number 22

SOCIETY OF PLASTICS ENGINEERS (SPE) FOUNDATION

SOCIETY OF PLASTICS ENGINEERS SCHOLARSHIP PROGRAM
see number 47

TRIMMER EDUCATION FOUNDATION

TRIMMER SCHOLARSHIPS see number 56

METEOROLOGY/ATMOSPHERIC SCIENCE

ASTRONAUT SCHOLARSHIP FOUNDATION

ASTRONAUT SCHOLARSHIP FOUNDATION see number 14

NASA NEVADA SPACE GRANT CONSORTIUM

UNIVERSITY AND COMMUNITY COLLEGE SYSTEM OF NEVADA
NASA SPACE GRANT AND FELLOWSHIP PROGRAM see number 29

MUSIC

INTERNATIONALER MUSIKWETTBEWERB

INTERNATIONAL MUSIC COMPETITION OF THE ARD
MUNICH • 119

Twelve prizes will be awarded at the International Music Competition of the ARD Munich. The competition is held annually in September. Prizes are awarded in various categories.

Academic/Career Areas Music.

International Music Competition of the ARD Munich (continued)

Award Prize for use in senior, or graduate years; not renewable. *Number:* 12. *Amount:* $5000–$10,000.

Eligibility Requirements: Applicant must be age 20-29 and enrolled or expecting to enroll full or part-time at an institution or university. Available to U.S. and non-U.S. citizens.

Application Requirements Application, applicant must enter a contest, references. *Fee:* $80. *Deadline:* April 20.

World Wide Web: http://www.ard-musikwettbewerb.de

Contact: Ingeborg Krause, Head of Organization
Internationaler Musikwettbewerb
Bayerischer Rundfink
Munich 80300
Germany
Phone: 49-89-59002471
Fax: 49-89-59003573
E-mail: ard.musikwettbewerb@brnet.de

NATURAL RESOURCES

APICS- EDUCATIONAL AND RESEARCH FOUNDATION, INC.

DONALD W. FOGARTY INTERNATIONAL STUDENT PAPER COMPETITION
see number 37

GREATER KANAWHA VALLEY FOUNDATION

LEOPOLD AND ELIZABETH MARMET FUND • 120

Renewable award open to students pursuing a degree in science, production or conservation of energy or natural resources. Preference given to graduate students. Go to our web site at http://www.tgkvf.org for more information. May apply for two Foundation scholarships, but will only be chosen for one. Must be a resident of West Virginia.

Academic/Career Areas Natural Resources.

Award Scholarship for use in freshman, sophomore, junior, senior, or graduate years; renewable. *Number:* 40. *Amount:* $2500.

Eligibility Requirements: Applicant must be enrolled or expecting to enroll full-time at a four-year institution or university and resident of West Virginia. Applicant must have 2.5 GPA or higher. Available to U.S. citizens.

Application Requirements Application, essay, financial need analysis, references, self-addressed stamped envelope, test scores, transcript. *Deadline:* February 13.

World Wide Web: http://www.tgkvf.org
Contact: Susan Hoover, Scholarship Coordinator
Greater Kanawha Valley Foundation
PO Box 3041
Charleston, WV 25331
Phone: 304-346-3620
Fax: 304-346-3640

MORRIS K. UDALL FOUNDATION

MORRIS K. UDALL SCHOLARS
see number 12

NATIONAL FISH AND WILDLIFE FOUNDATION

BUDWEISER CONSERVATION SCHOLARSHIP PROGRAM
see number 33

UNITED STATES ENVIRONMENTAL PROTECTION AGENCY

NATIONAL NETWORK FOR ENVIRONMENTAL MANAGEMENT STUDIES FELLOWSHIP
• 121

The NNEMS Fellowship Program is designed to provide undergraduate and graduate students with research opportunities at one of EPA's facilities nationwide. EPA awards approximately 80-90 NNEMS fellowships per year. Selected students receive a stipend for performing their research project. EPA develops an annual catalog of research projects available for student application. Submit a complete application package as described in the annual catalog. Minimum 3.0 GPA required.

Academic/Career Areas Natural Resources.
Award Grant for use in freshman, sophomore, junior, senior, or graduate years; not renewable. *Number:* 80–90. *Amount:* $5564–$9600.
Eligibility Requirements: Applicant must be enrolled or expecting to enroll full or part-time at a two-year or four-year institution or university. Applicant must have 3.0 GPA or higher. Available to U.S. citizens.
Application Requirements Application, applicant must enter a contest, resume, references, transcript, application package. *Deadline:* February 24.
World Wide Web: http://www.epa.gov/enviroed/students.html
Contact: Sheri Jojokian, Environmental Education Specialist
United States Environmental Protection Agency
Office of Environmental Education, 1200 Pennsylvania Avenue,
NW (1704A)
Washington, DC 20460
Phone: 202-564-0452
Fax: 202-564-2754
E-mail: jojokian.sheri@epa.gov

NATURAL SCIENCES_____

AMERICAN CHEMICAL SOCIETY

AMERICAN CHEMICAL SOCIETY SCHOLARS PROGRAM

see number 51

BARRY M. GOLDWATER SCHOLARSHIP AND EXCELLENCE IN EDUCATION FOUNDATION

BARRY M. GOLDWATER SCHOLARSHIP AND EXCELLENCE IN EDUCATION PROGRAM

see number 15

NATIONAL FISH AND WILDLIFE FOUNDATION

BUDWEISER CONSERVATION SCHOLARSHIP PROGRAM

see number 33

NUCLEAR SCIENCE_____

BARRY M. GOLDWATER SCHOLARSHIP AND EXCELLENCE IN EDUCATION FOUNDATION

BARRY M. GOLDWATER SCHOLARSHIP AND EXCELLENCE IN EDUCATION PROGRAM

see number 15

HISPANIC ENGINEER NATIONAL ACHIEVEMENT AWARDS CORPORATION (HENAAC)

HISPANIC ENGINEER NATIONAL ACHIEVEMENT AWARDS CORPORATION SCHOLARSHIP PROGRAM

see number 27

MORRIS K. UDALL FOUNDATION

MORRIS K. UDALL SCHOLARS

see number 12

NURSING

ALBERTA HERITAGE SCHOLARSHIP FUND

ALBERTA HERITAGE SCHOLARSHIP FUND ABORIGINAL HEALTH CAREERS BURSARY
see number 30

ALICE M. YARNOLD AND SAMUEL YARNOLD SCHOLARSHIP TRUST

ALICE M. AND SAMUEL YARNOLD SCHOLARSHIP
see number 105

AMERICAN ASSOCIATION OF CRITICAL-CARE NURSES (AACN)

AACN EDUCATIONAL ADVANCEMENT SCHOLARSHIPS-BSN COMPLETION • 122

One-time award for juniors and seniors currently enrolled in a nursing program accredited by State Board of Nursing. Must be AACN member with active RN license who is currently or has recently worked in critical care. Must have 3.0 GPA. Supports RN members completing a baccalaureate degree in nursing.

Academic/Career Areas Nursing.

Award Scholarship for use in junior or senior years; not renewable. *Number:* 50–100. *Amount:* $1500.

Eligibility Requirements: Applicant must be enrolled or expecting to enroll full or part-time at a four-year institution or university. Applicant or parent of applicant must be member of American Association of Critical Care Nurses. Applicant or parent of applicant must have employment or volunteer experience in designated career field. Applicant must have 3.0 GPA or higher. Available to U.S. and Canadian citizens.

Application Requirements Application, essay, transcript, verification of critical care experience. *Deadline:* April 1.

World Wide Web: http://www.aacn.org

Contact: Lisa Mynes, Member Relations and Services Specialist
American Association of Critical-Care Nurses (AACN)
101 Columbia
Aliso Viejo, CA 92656
Phone: 800-899-2226
Fax: 949-448-5502
E-mail: lisa.mynes@aacn.org

BUREAU OF HEALTH PROFESSIONS

NATIONAL HEALTH SERVICE CORPS SCHOLARSHIP PROGRAM
see number 106

DELAWARE HIGHER EDUCATION COMMISSION

DELAWARE NURSING INCENTIVE SCHOLARSHIP LOAN • 123

Award for Delaware residents pursuing a nursing career. Must be repaid with nursing practice at a Delaware state-owned hospital. Based on academic merit. Must have minimum 2.5 GPA. Renewable for up to four years.

Academic/Career Areas Nursing.

Award Forgivable loan for use in freshman, sophomore, junior, or senior years; renewable. *Number:* 1–40. *Amount:* $1000–$5000.

Eligibility Requirements: Applicant must be enrolled or expecting to enroll full-time at a two-year or four-year institution or university and resident of Delaware. Applicant must have 2.5 GPA or higher. Available to U.S. citizens.

Application Requirements Application, essay, test scores, transcript. *Deadline:* March 31.

World Wide Web: http://www.doe.state.de.us/high-ed

Contact: Donna Myers, Higher Education Analyst
Delaware Higher Education Commission
820 North French Street
5th Floor
Wilmington, DE 19711-3509
Phone: 302-577-3240
Fax: 302-577-6765
E-mail: dhec@doe.k12.de.us

FLORIDA DEPARTMENT OF HEALTH

NURSING SCHOLARSHIP PROGRAM • 124

Provides financial assistance for Florida residents who are full- or part-time nursing students enrolled in an approved nursing program in Florida. Awards are for a maximum of two years and must be repaid through full-time service.

Academic/Career Areas Nursing.

Award Scholarship for use in junior, senior, or graduate years; renewable. *Number:* 15–30. *Amount:* $8000–$12,000.

Eligibility Requirements: Applicant must be enrolled or expecting to enroll full or part-time at a two-year or four-year institution or university; resident of Florida and studying in Florida. Available to U.S. and non-U.S. citizens.

Application Requirements Application. *Deadline:* Continuous.

Contact: Florida Department of Health
Division of EMS and Community Health Resources
4052 Bald Cypress Way, Mail Bin C-15
Tallahassee, FL 32399-1735

FOUNDATION OF THE NATIONAL STUDENT NURSES' ASSOCIATION

FOUNDATION OF THE NATIONAL STUDENT NURSES' ASSOCIATION GENERAL SCHOLARSHIPS • 125

One-time award for National Student Nurses' Association members and nonmembers enrolled in nursing programs leading to RN license. Based on need, academic ability, and health-related nursing school or community involvement. Send self-addressed stamped envelope with two stamps for application. Graduating high school seniors are not eligible.

Academic/Career Areas Nursing.

Award Scholarship for use in freshman, sophomore, junior, or senior years; not renewable. *Number:* 50–100. *Amount:* $1000–$5000.

Eligibility Requirements: Applicant must be enrolled or expecting to enroll full-time at a two-year or four-year institution or university. Applicant must have 2.5 GPA or higher. Available to U.S. citizens.

Application Requirements Application, financial need analysis, self-addressed stamped envelope, transcript. *Deadline:* January 31.

World Wide Web: http://www.nsna.org
Contact: application available at web site
     E-mail: receptionist@nsna.org

HEALTH PROFESSIONS EDUCATION FOUNDATION

ASSOCIATE DEGREE NURSING SCHOLARSHIP PROGRAM • 126

One-time award to nursing students accepted to or enrolled in associate degree nursing programs and who agree to obtain a BSN at a nursing program in California within five years of obtaining an ADN Eligible applicants may receive up to $4,000 per year in financial assistance. Deadlines: March 27 and September 11. Must be a resident of California. Minimum 2.0 GPA.

Academic/Career Areas Nursing.

Award Scholarship for use in freshman or sophomore years; not renewable. *Number:* 30. *Amount:* up to $4000.

Eligibility Requirements: Applicant must be enrolled or expecting to enroll full or part-time at a two-year or technical institution or university; resident of California and studying in California. Available to U.S. citizens.

Application Requirements Application, driver's license, financial need analysis, references, transcript.

World Wide Web: http://www.healthprofessions.ca.gov
Contact: Monique Voss, Project Officer
     Health Professions Education Foundation
     818 K Street, Suite 210
     Sacramento, CA 95814
     Phone: 916-324-6500

CENTRAL VALLEY NURSING SCHOLARSHIP   • 127

One-time award for California residents studying nursing at a California institution. Scholarship is part of the Central Valley Nursing Work Force Diversity Initiative. Minimum 2.0 GPA. Application deadlines are March 26 and October 9.

Academic/Career Areas Nursing.

Award Scholarship for use in freshman, sophomore, junior, senior, graduate, or postgraduate years; not renewable. *Number:* 90–140. *Amount:* $8000–$12,000.

Eligibility Requirements: Applicant must be enrolled or expecting to enroll full or part-time at a two-year or four-year or technical institution or university; resident of California and studying in California. Available to U.S. citizens.

Application Requirements Application, driver's license, financial need analysis, transcript.

World Wide Web: http://www.healthprofessions.ca.gov

Contact: Charles Gray, Program Director
Health Professions Education Foundation
818 K Street, Suite 210
Sacramento, CA 95814
Phone: 916-324-6500

HEALTH PROFESSIONS EDUCATION SCHOLARSHIP PROGRAM
see number 60

REGISTERED NURSE EDUCATION LOAN REPAYMENT PROGRAM   • 128

Repays governmental and commercial loans that were obtained for tuition expenses, books, equipment and reasonable living expenses associated with attending college. In return for the repayment of educational debt, loan repayment recipients are required to practice full-time in direct patient care in a medically underserved area or county health facility. Eligible applicants may receive up to $19,000 for repayment of educational debt. Deadlines: March 27 and September 11. Must be resident of CA and U.S. citizen.

Academic/Career Areas Nursing.

Award Grant for use in senior, or postgraduate years; not renewable. *Number:* 50–70. *Amount:* $4000–$8000.

Eligibility Requirements: Applicant must be enrolled or expecting to enroll full or part-time at a four-year institution or university; resident of California and studying in California. Available to U.S. citizens.

Application Requirements Application, driver's license, financial need analysis, references, transcript.

World Wide Web: http://www.healthprofessions.ca.gov

Contact: Monique Voss, Project Officer
Health Professions Education Foundation
818 K Street, Suite 210
Sacramento, CA 95814
Phone: 916-324-6500
E-mail: mjoss@oshpd.state.ca.gov

RN EDUCATION SCHOLARSHIP PROGRAM ● 129

One-time award to nursing students accepted to or enrolled in baccalaureate degree nursing programs in California. Eligible applicants may receive up to $8,000 per year in financial assistance. Deadlines: March 27 and September 11. Must be resident of California and a U.S. citizen. Minimum 2.0 GPA.

Academic/Career Areas Nursing.

Award Scholarship for use in freshman, sophomore, junior, or senior years; not renewable. *Number:* 50–70. *Amount:* $6000–$8000.

Eligibility Requirements: Applicant must be enrolled or expecting to enroll full or part-time at a four-year or technical institution or university; resident of California and studying in California. Available to U.S. citizens.

Application Requirements Application, driver's license, financial need analysis, references, transcript.

World Wide Web: http://www.healthprofessions.ca.gov

Contact: Monique Voss, Project Officer
Health Professions Education Foundation
818 K Street, Suite 210
Sacramento, CA 95814
Phone: 916-324-6500

YOUTH FOR ADOLESCENT PREGNANCY PREVENTION LEADERSHIP RECOGNITION PROGRAM
see number 108

J.D. ARCHBOLD MEMORIAL HOSPITAL

ARCHBOLD SCHOLARSHIP PROGRAM
see number 109

KANSAS BOARD OF REGENTS

KANSAS NURSING SERVICE SCHOLARSHIP PROGRAM ● 130

This program is designed to encourage Kansans to enroll in nursing programs and commit to practicing in Kansas. Recipients sign agreements to practice nursing at specific facilities one year for each year of support. Application fee is $10. Deadline: May 1.

Academic/Career Areas Nursing.

Award Forgivable loan for use in freshman, sophomore, junior, or senior years; renewable. *Number:* 100–200. *Amount:* $2500–$3500.

Eligibility Requirements: Applicant must be enrolled or expecting to enroll full-time at a two-year or four-year institution or university; resident of Kansas and studying in Kansas. Available to U.S. citizens.

Kansas Nursing Service Scholarship Program (continued)
Application Requirements Application, financial need analysis, sponsor agreement form. *Fee:* $10. *Deadline:* May 1.
World Wide Web: http://www.kansasregents.org
Contact: Diane Lindeman, Director of Student Financial Assistance
　　　　　　Kansas Board of Regents
　　　　　　1000 Southwest Jackson, Suite 520
　　　　　　Topeka, KS 66612-1368
　　　　　　Phone: 785-296-3517
　　　　　　Fax: 785-296-0983
　　　　　　E-mail: dlindeman@ksbor.org

MARION D. AND EVA S. PEEPLES FOUNDATION TRUST SCHOLARSHIP PROGRAM

MARION D. AND EVA S. PEEPLES SCHOLARSHIPS see number 74

MARYLAND HIGHER EDUCATION COMMISSION

DEVELOPMENTAL DISABILITIES AND MENTAL HEALTH WORKFORCE TUITION ASSISTANCE PROGRAM see number 110

GRADUATE AND PROFESSIONAL SCHOLARSHIP PROGRAM-MARYLAND see number 61

JANET L. HOFFMANN LOAN ASSISTANCE REPAYMENT PROGRAM see number 77

MARYLAND STATE NURSING SCHOLARSHIP AND LIVING EXPENSES GRANT • 131

Renewable grant for Maryland residents enrolled in a two-or four-year Maryland institution nursing degree program. Recipients must agree to serve as a full-time nurse in a Maryland shortage area and must maintain a 3.0 GPA in college. Application deadline is June 30. Submit Free Application for Federal Student Aid.

Academic/Career Areas Nursing.
Award Forgivable loan for use in freshman, sophomore, junior, senior, or graduate years; renewable. *Number:* up to 600. *Amount:* $200–$3000.
Eligibility Requirements: Applicant must be enrolled or expecting to enroll full or part-time at a two-year or four-year institution or university; resident of Maryland and studying in Maryland. Applicant must have 3.0 GPA or higher. Available to U.S. citizens.
Application Requirements Application, financial need analysis, transcript. *Deadline:* June 30.

World Wide Web: http://www.mhec.state.md.us

Contact: Marie Janiszewski, Office of Student Financial Assistance
Maryland Higher Education Commission
839 Bestgate Road, Suite 400
Annapolis, MD 21401-3013
Phone: 410-260-4569
Fax: 410-260-3203
E-mail: ofsamail@mhec.state.md.us

NEW MEXICO COMMISSION ON HIGHER EDUCATION

ALLIED HEALTH STUDENT LOAN PROGRAM-NEW MEXICO

see number 62

NORTH CAROLINA STATE EDUCATION ASSISTANCE AUTHORITY

NURSE SCHOLARS PROGRAM—UNDERGRADUATE (NORTH CAROLINA)
• 132

Forgivable loans to residents of North Carolina who have gained full acceptance to a North Carolina institution of higher education that offers a nursing program. Must apply to the North Carolina State Education and Welfare division. Must serve as a registered nurse in North Carolina for one year for each year of funding. Minimum 3.0 GPA required.

Academic/Career Areas Nursing.

Award Forgivable loan for use in freshman, sophomore, junior, or senior years; renewable. *Number:* up to 450. *Amount:* $3000–$5000.

Eligibility Requirements: Applicant must be enrolled or expecting to enroll full-time at a two-year or four-year institution or university; resident of North Carolina and studying in North Carolina. Applicant must have 3.0 GPA or higher. Available to U.S. citizens.

Application Requirements Application, essay, references, test scores, transcript.

World Wide Web: http://www.cfnc.org

Contact: Christy Campbell, Manager-Health, Education and Welfare
North Carolina State Education Assistance Authority
PO Box 14223
Research Triangle, NC 27709-3663
Phone: 919-549-8614
Fax: 919-248-4687

NORTH DAKOTA BOARD OF NURSING

NORTH DAKOTA BOARD OF NURSING EDUCATION LOAN PROGRAM
• 133

One-time loan for North Dakota residents pursuing a nursing degree. Must sign repayment note agreeing to repay loan by nursing employment in North

North Dakota Board of Nursing Education Loan Program (continued)
Dakota after graduation. Repayment rate is $1 per hour of employment. For juniors, seniors, and graduate students.

Academic/Career Areas Nursing.

Award Forgivable loan for use in junior, senior, or graduate years; not renewable. *Number:* 30–35. *Amount:* $2000–$5000.

Eligibility Requirements: Applicant must be enrolled or expecting to enroll full or part-time at a two-year or four-year institution or university and resident of North Dakota. Applicant must have 2.5 GPA or higher. Available to U.S. citizens.

Application Requirements Application, financial need analysis, references, transcript. *Fee:* $15. *Deadline:* July 1.

World Wide Web: http://www.ndbon.org

Contact: Ms. Constance Kalanek, Executive Director
North Dakota Board of Nursing
919 South 7th Street, Suite 504
Bismarck, ND 58504-5881
Phone: 701-328-9777
Fax: 701-328-9785
E-mail: executivedir@nbdon.org

ORDEAN FOUNDATION

ORDEAN LOAN PROGRAM
see number 6

STATE OF GEORGIA

NORTHEAST GEORGIA PILOT NURSE SERVICE CANCELABLE LOAN
• 134

Up to 100 forgivable loans between $2,500 and $4,500 will be awarded to undergraduate students who are residents of Georgia studying nursing at a four-year school in Georgia. Loans can be repaid by working as a nurse in northeast Georgia.

Academic/Career Areas Nursing.

Award Forgivable loan for use in freshman, sophomore, junior, or senior years; not renewable. *Number:* up to 100. *Amount:* $2500–$4500.

Eligibility Requirements: Applicant must be enrolled or expecting to enroll full or part-time at a four-year institution; resident of Georgia and studying in Georgia. Available to U.S. citizens.

Application Requirements Application, financial need analysis. *Deadline:* Continuous.

World Wide Web: http://www.gsfc.org

Contact: Peggy Matthews, Manager/GSFA Originations
State of Georgia
2082 East Exchange Place, Suite 230
Tucker, GA 30084-5305
Phone: 770-724-9230
Fax: 770-724-9263
E-mail: peggy@mail.gsfc.state.ga.us

SERVICE-CANCELABLE STAFFORD LOAN-GEORGIA   see number 63

STATE STUDENT ASSISTANCE COMMISSION OF INDIANA (SSACI)

INDIANA NURSING SCHOLARSHIP FUND   • 135

Need-based tuition funding for nursing students enrolled full- or part-time at an eligible Indiana institution. Must be an Indiana resident and have a minimum 2.0 GPA or meet the minimum requirements for the nursing program. Upon graduation, recipients must practice as a nurse in an Indiana health care setting for two years.

Academic/Career Areas Nursing.
Award Scholarship for use in freshman, sophomore, junior, or senior years; not renewable. *Number:* 510–690. *Amount:* $200–$5000.
Eligibility Requirements: Applicant must be enrolled or expecting to enroll full or part-time at a two-year or four-year institution or university; resident of Indiana and studying in Indiana. Available to U.S. citizens.
Application Requirements Application, financial need analysis. *Deadline:* Continuous.
World Wide Web: http://www.ssaci.in.gov
Contact: Ms. Yvonne Heflin, Director, Special Programs
State Student Assistance Commission of Indiana (SSACI)
150 West Market Street, Suite 500
Indianapolis, IN 46204-2805
Phone: 317-232-2350
Fax: 317-232-3260

VIRGINIA DEPARTMENT OF HEALTH, OFFICE OF HEALTH POLICY AND PLANNING

MARY MARSHALL REGISTERED NURSING PROGRAM SCHOLARSHIPS   • 136

Award for registered nursing students who are Virginia residents. Must attend a nursing program in Virginia. Recipient must agree to work in Virginia after graduation. Minimum 3.0 GPA required. Recipient may reapply up to three years for an award.

Academic/Career Areas Nursing.

Mary Marshall Registered Nursing Program Scholarships (continued)

Award Scholarship for use in freshman, sophomore, junior, or senior years; not renewable. *Number:* 60–100. *Amount:* $1200–$2000.

Eligibility Requirements: Applicant must be enrolled or expecting to enroll full or part-time at a two-year or four-year institution or university; resident of Virginia and studying in Virginia. Applicant must have 3.0 GPA or higher. Available to U.S. citizens.

Application Requirements Application, financial need analysis, references, transcript. *Deadline:* June 30.

World Wide Web: http://www.vdh.state.va.us/primcare/index.html

Contact: Norma Marrin, Business Manager/Policy Analyst
Virginia Department of Health, Office of Health Policy and
Planning
PO Box 2448
Richmond, VA 23218-2448
Phone: 804-371-4090
Fax: 804-371-0116
E-mail: nmarrin@udh.state.va.us

PEACE AND CONFLICT STUDIES⸺

HUGH FULTON BYAS MEMORIAL FUNDS, INC.

HUGH FULTON BYAS MEMORIAL GRANT   see number 114

PERFORMING ARTS⸺

AMERICAN SOCIETY OF COMPOSERS, AUTHORS, AND PUBLISHERS FOUNDATION

ASCAP FOUNDATION MORTON GOULD YOUNG COMPOSER AWARDS   • 137

Cash grants for U.S. citizens or permanent residents or those with U.S. student visas, up to age 30 as of December 31. Applicants must be composers and must submit score, with or without tape or CD recording, for competition. Original music of any style will be considered. Works that have earned national prizes are ineligible, as are arrangements.

Academic/Career Areas Performing Arts.

Award Prize for use in freshman, sophomore, junior, senior, graduate, or postgraduate years; not renewable. *Number:* 20–25. *Amount:* $250–$3500.

Eligibility Requirements: Applicant must be age 30 or under; enrolled or expecting to enroll at a two-year or four-year institution or university and must have an interest in music/singing. Available to U.S. and Canadian citizens.

Application Requirements Application, applicant must enter a contest, autobiography, self-addressed stamped envelope, music score. *Deadline:* December 31.

World Wide Web: http://www.ascap.com

Contact: Frances Richard, Vice President and Director of Concert Music
American Society of Composers, Authors, and Publishers
    Foundation
One Lincoln Plaza
New York, NY 10023
Phone: 212-621-6327
Fax: 212-621-6504
E-mail: frichard@ascap.com

CLARICE SMITH PERFORMING ARTS CENTER AT MARYLAND

WILLIAM KAPELL INTERNATIONAL PIANO COMPETITION AND FESTIVAL • 138

Quadrennial international piano competition for ages 18-33. $80 application fee. Competition takes place at the Clarice Smith Performing Arts Center at the University of Maryland July 16-25, 2003. Next competition will be in 2007.

Academic/Career Areas Performing Arts.

Award Prize for use in freshman, sophomore, junior, senior, graduate, or postgraduate years; not renewable. *Number:* up to 12. *Amount:* $1000–$20,000.

Eligibility Requirements: Applicant must be age 18-33; enrolled or expecting to enroll at an institution or university and must have an interest in music. Available to U.S. and non-U.S. citizens.

Application Requirements Application, applicant must enter a contest, autobiography, photo, portfolio, references, CD or audiocassette of performance. *Fee:* $80. *Deadline:* February 1.

World Wide Web: http://www.claricesmithcenter.umd.edu

Contact: Dr. Christopher Patton, Coordinator
Clarice Smith Performing Arts Center at Maryland
Suite 3800, University of Maryland
College Park, MD 20742-1625
Phone: 301-405-8174
Fax: 301-405-5977
E-mail: kapell@deans.umd.edu

GINA BACHAUER INTERNATIONAL PIANO FOUNDATION

GINA BACHAUER INTERNATIONAL ARTISTS PIANO COMPETITION AWARD ● 139

Piano competition sponsored every four years. Includes solo, and orchestral performances. Prizes include cash awards, concerts, CD recording, and residency in various countries. Submit birth certificate copy, passport copy, tapes of last two year's programs, and audition tape. May also audition live.

Academic/Career Areas Performing Arts.

Award Prize for use in freshman, sophomore, junior, senior, graduate, or postgraduate years; not renewable. *Number:* 6. *Amount:* $4000–$30,000.

Eligibility Requirements: Applicant must be enrolled or expecting to enroll at an institution or university and must have an interest in music/singing. Available to U.S. and non-U.S. citizens.

Application Requirements Application, applicant must enter a contest, photo, tapes, passport and birth certificate copies. *Fee:* $50. *Deadline:* December 1.

World Wide Web: http://www.bachauer.com

Contact: Paul Pollei, Artistic Director
Gina Bachauer International Piano Foundation
PO Box 11664
Salt Lake City, UT 84147-1664
Phone: 801-297-4250
Fax: 801-521-9202
E-mail: gina@bachauer.com

PRINCESS GRACE FOUNDATION-USA

PRINCESS GRACE SCHOLARSHIPS IN DANCE, THEATER, AND FILM
see number 92

YOUNG MUSICIANS FOUNDATION

YMF SCHOLARSHIP PROGRAM ● 140

Applicants must demonstrate exceptional talent and financial need, and must be residents of Southern California. Instrumentalists must be under 18 years of age and not beyond junior year in high school at audition time. Vocalists must be under 26 at audition time. Application fee: $15.

Academic/Career Areas Performing Arts.

Award Scholarship for use in freshman, sophomore, or junior years; not renewable. *Number:* 40–60. *Amount:* $500–$2500.

Eligibility Requirements: Applicant must be age 8-25; enrolled or expecting to enroll full or part-time at a two-year or four-year or technical institution or university; resident of California; studying in California and must have an interest in music/singing. Available to U.S. citizens.

Application Requirements Application, applicant must enter a contest, financial need analysis, references, audition. *Fee:* $15. *Deadline:* May 1.
World Wide Web: http://www.ymf.org
Contact: Programs Director
Young Musicians Foundation
195 South Beverly Drive, Suite 414
Beverly Hills, CA 90212
Phone: 310-859-7668
E-mail: info@ymf.org

PHYSICAL SCIENCES AND MATH_____

ARKANSAS DEPARTMENT OF HIGHER EDUCATION
EMERGENCY SECONDARY EDUCATION LOAN PROGRAM
see number 31

BARRY M. GOLDWATER SCHOLARSHIP AND EXCELLENCE IN EDUCATION FOUNDATION
BARRY M. GOLDWATER SCHOLARSHIP AND EXCELLENCE IN EDUCATION PROGRAM
see number 15

BUSINESS AND PROFESSIONAL WOMEN'S FOUNDATION
BPW CAREER ADVANCEMENT SCHOLARSHIP PROGRAM FOR WOMEN
see number 32

CATCHING THE DREAM
MATH, ENGINEERING, SCIENCE, BUSINESS, EDUCATION, COMPUTERS SCHOLARSHIPS
see number 39
NATIVE AMERICAN LEADERSHIP IN EDUCATION (NALE)
see number 40

LUCENT TECHNOLOGIES FOUNDATION
LUCENT GLOBAL SCIENCE SCHOLARS PROGRAM
see number 18

NASA NEVADA SPACE GRANT CONSORTIUM

UNIVERSITY AND COMMUNITY COLLEGE SYSTEM OF NEVADA NASA SPACE GRANT AND FELLOWSHIP PROGRAM   see number 29

SOCIETY OF PHYSICS STUDENTS

SOCIETY OF PHYSICS STUDENTS SCHOLARSHIPS   • 141

Scholarships available to Society of Physics Students (SPS) members. Award based on scholarship and/or need, and SPS participation. For more details visit: http://www.spsnational.org.

Academic/Career Areas Physical Sciences and Math.
Award Scholarship for use in sophomore, junior, or senior years; not renewable. *Number:* 17–22. *Amount:* $1000–$4000.
Eligibility Requirements: Applicant must be enrolled or expecting to enroll full-time at a four-year institution. Available to U.S. and non-U.S. citizens.
Application Requirements Application, references, transcript. *Deadline:* February 15.
World Wide Web: http://www.spsnational.org
Contact: SPS Scholarship Committee
Society of Physics Students
One Physics Ellipse
College Park, MD 20740
Phone: 301-209-3077
Fax: 301-209-0839
E-mail: sps@aip.org

UNITED NEGRO COLLEGE FUND

MERCK SCIENCE INITIATIVE   see number 34

UNITED STATES DEPARTMENT OF HEALTH AND HUMAN SERVICES

NIH UNDERGRADUATE SCHOLARSHIP FOR INDIVIDUALS FROM DISADVANTAGED BACKGROUNDS   see number 35

POLITICAL SCIENCE_____

CUBAN AMERICAN NATIONAL FOUNDATION

MAS FAMILY SCHOLARSHIPS   see number 41

MORRIS K. UDALL FOUNDATION

MORRIS K. UDALL SCHOLARS
see number 12

NATIONAL FISH AND WILDLIFE FOUNDATION

BUDWEISER CONSERVATION SCHOLARSHIP PROGRAM
see number 33

RELIGION/THEOLOGY

ED E. AND GLADYS HURLEY FOUNDATION

ED E. AND GLADYS HURLEY FOUNDATION SCHOLARSHIP • 142

The Hurley Foundation provides scholarships (maximum of $1,000/year per student) to worthy and deserving young men and women, residing in any state, who wish to study at a school within the State of Texas to become ministers, missionaries or religious workers of the Protestant faith. Contact institution's financial aid office for more information.

Academic/Career Areas Religion/Theology.

Award Scholarship for use in freshman, sophomore, junior, senior, graduate, or postgraduate years; not renewable. *Number:* 100–150. *Amount:* up to $1000.

Eligibility Requirements: Applicant must be Protestant; enrolled or expecting to enroll full or part-time at a two-year or four-year institution or university and studying in Texas. Available to U.S. citizens.

Application Requirements Application, financial need analysis, references. *Deadline:* April 30.

Contact: financial aid office at school for application

MARY E. BIVINS FOUNDATION

MARY E. BIVINS RELIGIOUS SCHOLARSHIP • 143

Scholarships provided to young men who are permanent residents of the Texas Panhandle pursuing an undergraduate degree in a field preparing them to preach the Christian religion. Write for details.

Academic/Career Areas Religion/Theology.

Award Scholarship for use in freshman, sophomore, junior, or senior years; renewable. *Number:* up to 65. *Amount:* $1000–$3000.

Eligibility Requirements: Applicant must be Christian; enrolled or expecting to enroll full-time at a two-year or four-year institution or university; male and resident of Texas. Applicant must have 2.5 GPA or higher. Available to U.S. citizens.

Mary E. Bivins Religious Scholarship (continued)

Application Requirements Application, essay, references, test scores, transcript, proof of residence. *Deadline:* June 15.

World Wide Web: http://www.bivinsfoundation.org

Contact: Linda Pitner, Grant and Scholarship Program Coordinator
Mary E. Bivins Foundation
Attn: Linda Pitner, Grant and Scholarships Program Coordinator
Post Office Box 1727
Amarillo, TX 79105
Phone: 806-379-9400
Fax: 806-379-9404
E-mail: linda@bivinsfoundation.org

UNITED METHODIST CHURCH

ERNEST AND EURICE MILLER BASS SCHOLARSHIP FUND • 144

One-time award for undergraduate student enrolled at an accredited institution and entering United Methodist Church ministry as a deacon or elder. Must be an active member of United Methodist Church for at least one year. Merit-based award. Minimum 3.0 GPA required.

Academic/Career Areas Religion/Theology.

Award Scholarship for use in freshman, sophomore, junior, or senior years; not renewable. *Number:* 75–80. *Amount:* $800–$1200.

Eligibility Requirements: Applicant must be Methodist and enrolled or expecting to enroll full-time at a two-year or four-year institution or university. Applicant must have 3.0 GPA or higher. Available to U.S. citizens.

Application Requirements Application, essay, references, transcript. *Deadline:* June 1.

World Wide Web: http://www.umc.org/

Contact: Patti J. Zimmerman, Scholarships Administrator
United Methodist Church
PO Box 34007
Nashville, TN 37203-0007
Phone: 615-340-7344
E-mail: pzimmer@gbhem.org

SCIENCE, TECHNOLOGY, AND SOCIETY

CATCHING THE DREAM

MATH, ENGINEERING, SCIENCE, BUSINESS, EDUCATION, COMPUTERS SCHOLARSHIPS
see number 39

NATIVE AMERICAN LEADERSHIP IN EDUCATION (NALE)
see number 40

WEST VIRGINIA HIGHER EDUCATION POLICY COMMISSION-OFFICE OF FINANCIAL AID AND OUTREACH SERVICES

WEST VIRGINIA ENGINEERING, SCIENCE & TECHNOLOGY SCHOLARSHIP PROGRAM
see number 89

SOCIAL SCIENCES_____

BUSINESS AND PROFESSIONAL WOMEN'S FOUNDATION

BPW CAREER ADVANCEMENT SCHOLARSHIP PROGRAM FOR WOMEN
see number 32

CATCHING THE DREAM

MATH, ENGINEERING, SCIENCE, BUSINESS, EDUCATION, COMPUTERS SCHOLARSHIPS
see number 39

NEW MEXICO COMMISSION ON HIGHER EDUCATION

ALLIED HEALTH STUDENT LOAN PROGRAM-NEW MEXICO
see number 62

SOCIAL SERVICES_____

HEALTH PROFESSIONS EDUCATION FOUNDATION

KAISER PERMANENTE ALLIED HEALTHCARE SCHOLARSHIP
see number 107

MARYLAND HIGHER EDUCATION COMMISSION

DEVELOPMENTAL DISABILITIES AND MENTAL HEALTH WORKFORCE TUITION ASSISTANCE PROGRAM
see number 110

GRADUATE AND PROFESSIONAL SCHOLARSHIP PROGRAM-MARYLAND
see number 61

JANET L. HOFFMANN LOAN ASSISTANCE REPAYMENT PROGRAM
see number 77

ORDEAN FOUNDATION

ORDEAN LOAN PROGRAM
see number 6

SPECIAL EDUCATION

ARKANSAS DEPARTMENT OF HIGHER EDUCATION

EMERGENCY SECONDARY EDUCATION LOAN PROGRAM
see number 31

ILLINOIS STUDENT ASSISTANCE COMMISSION (ISAC)

ITEACH TEACHER SHORTAGE SCHOLARSHIP PROGRAM
see number 70

MINORITY TEACHERS OF ILLINOIS SCHOLARSHIP PROGRAM
see number 71

KENTUCKY HIGHER EDUCATION ASSISTANCE AUTHORITY (KHEAA)

KENTUCKY TEACHER SCHOLARSHIP PROGRAM
see number 73

MARYLAND HIGHER EDUCATION COMMISSION

DEVELOPMENTAL DISABILITIES AND MENTAL HEALTH WORKFORCE TUITION ASSISTANCE PROGRAM
see number 110

SOUTH CAROLINA STUDENT LOAN CORPORATION

SOUTH CAROLINA TEACHER LOAN PROGRAM
see number 83

STATE STUDENT ASSISTANCE COMMISSION OF INDIANA (SSACI)

INDIANA MINORITY TEACHER AND SPECIAL EDUCATION SERVICES SCHOLARSHIP PROGRAM
see number 85

TENNESSEE STUDENT ASSISTANCE CORPORATION

MINORITY TEACHING FELLOWS PROGRAM/TENNESSEE
see number 86

SPORTS-RELATED

NATIONAL ATHLETIC TRAINERS' ASSOCIATION

NATIONAL ATHLETIC TRAINER'S ASSOCIATION RESEARCH AND EDUCATION FOUNDATION SCHOLARSHIP PROGRAM • 145

One-time award available to full-time students who are members of NATA. Minimum 3.2 GPA required. Open to undergraduate upperclassmen and graduate/post-graduate students.

Academic/Career Areas Sports-related.

Award Scholarship for use in junior, senior, graduate, or postgraduate years; not renewable. *Number:* 55–60. *Amount:* $2000.

Eligibility Requirements: Applicant must be enrolled or expecting to enroll full-time at a four-year institution or university. Available to U.S. and non-U.S. citizens.

Application Requirements Application, essay, references, transcript. *Deadline:* February 10.

World Wide Web: http://www.natafoundation.org

Contact: Barbara Niland, Scholarship Coordinator
National Athletic Trainers' Association
2952 Stemmons Freeway, Suite 200
Dallas, TX 75247-6103
Phone: 214-637-6282 Ext. 121
Fax: 214-637-2206
E-mail: barbara@nata.org

SURVEYING; SURVEYING TECHNOLOGY, CARTOGRAPHY, OR GEOGRAPHIC INFORMATION SCIENCE_____

NATIONAL FISH AND WILDLIFE FOUNDATION

BUDWEISER CONSERVATION SCHOLARSHIP PROGRAM
see number 33

THERAPY/REHABILITATION_____

ALBERTA HERITAGE SCHOLARSHIP FUND

ALBERTA HERITAGE SCHOLARSHIP FUND ABORIGINAL HEALTH CAREERS BURSARY
see number 30

ALICE M. YARNOLD AND SAMUEL YARNOLD SCHOLARSHIP TRUST

ALICE M. AND SAMUEL YARNOLD SCHOLARSHIP
see number 105

HEALTH PROFESSIONS EDUCATION FOUNDATION

KAISER PERMANENTE ALLIED HEALTHCARE SCHOLARSHIP
see number 107

MARYLAND HIGHER EDUCATION COMMISSION

DEVELOPMENTAL DISABILITIES AND MENTAL HEALTH WORKFORCE TUITION ASSISTANCE PROGRAM
see number 110

JANET L. HOFFMANN LOAN ASSISTANCE REPAYMENT PROGRAM
see number 77

NATIONAL AMBUCS, INC.

AMBUCS SCHOLARS-SCHOLARSHIPS FOR THERAPISTS
see number 111

NEW MEXICO COMMISSION ON HIGHER EDUCATION

ALLIED HEALTH STUDENT LOAN PROGRAM-NEW MEXICO
see number 62

STATE STUDENT ASSISTANCE COMMISSION OF INDIANA (SSACI)

INDIANA MINORITY TEACHER AND SPECIAL EDUCATION SERVICES SCHOLARSHIP PROGRAM
see number 85

TRADE/TECHNICAL SPECIALTIES_____

AMERICAN WELDING SOCIETY

AMERICAN WELDING SOCIETY DISTRICT SCHOLARSHIP PROGRAM
see number 90

ASSOCIATED GENERAL CONTRACTORS EDUCATION AND RESEARCH FOUNDATION

AGC EDUCATION AND RESEARCH FOUNDATION UNDERGRADUATE SCHOLARSHIPS
see number 53

KANSAS BOARD OF REGENTS

VOCATIONAL EDUCATION SCHOLARSHIP PROGRAM-KANSAS
• 146

Several scholarships for Kansas residents who graduated from a Kansas accredited high school. Must be enrolled in a vocational education program at an eligible Kansas institution. Based on ability and aptitude. Deadline is July 1. Renewable award of $500. Must be U.S. citizen.

Academic/Career Areas Trade/Technical Specialties.
Award Scholarship for use in freshman or sophomore years; renewable. *Number:* 100–200. *Amount:* $500.

Vocational Education Scholarship Program-Kansas (continued)

Eligibility Requirements: Applicant must be enrolled or expecting to enroll full-time at a two-year or technical institution; resident of Kansas and studying in Kansas. Available to U.S. citizens.

Application Requirements Application, test scores. *Deadline:* July 1.

World Wide Web: http://www.kansasregents.org

Contact: Diane Lindeman, Director of Student Financial Assistance
Kansas Board of Regents
1000 Southwest Jackson, Suite 520
Topeka, KS 66612-1368
Phone: 785-296-3517
Fax: 785-296-0983
E-mail: dlindeman@ksbor.org

MARION D. AND EVA S. PEEPLES FOUNDATION TRUST SCHOLARSHIP PROGRAM

MARION D. AND EVA S. PEEPLES SCHOLARSHIPS see number 74

MARYLAND ASSOCIATION OF PRIVATE CAREER SCHOOLS

MARYLAND ASSOCIATION OF PRIVATE CAREER SCHOOLS SCHOLARSHIP see number 45

MARYLAND HIGHER EDUCATION COMMISSION

FIREFIGHTER, AMBULANCE, AND RESCUE SQUAD MEMBER TUITION REIMBURSEMENT PROGRAM-MARYLAND see number 93

NATIONAL ASSOCIATION OF WOMEN IN CONSTRUCTION

NAWIC UNDERGRADUATE SCHOLARSHIPS see number 22

SOCIETY OF PLASTICS ENGINEERS (SPE) FOUNDATION

SOCIETY OF PLASTICS ENGINEERS SCHOLARSHIP PROGRAM see number 47

STATE OF GEORGIA

INTELLECTUAL CAPITAL PARTNERSHIP PROGRAM, ICAPP • 147

Forgivable loans will be awarded to undergraduate students who are residents of Georgia studying high-tech related fields at a Georgia institution. Repayment for every $2500 that is awarded is one-year service in a high-tech field in Georgia. Can be enrolled in a certificate or degree program.

Academic/Career Areas Trade/Technical Specialties.

Award Forgivable loan for use in freshman, sophomore, junior, or senior years; not renewable. *Number:* up to 328. *Amount:* $7000–$10,000.

Eligibility Requirements: Applicant must be enrolled or expecting to enroll full or part-time at a two-year or four-year institution or university; resident of Georgia and studying in Georgia. Available to U.S. citizens.

Application Requirements Application, financial need analysis. *Deadline:* Continuous.

World Wide Web: http://www.gsfc.org

Contact: Peggy Matthews, Manager/GSFA Originations
State of Georgia
2082 East Exchange Place, Suite 230
Tucker, GA 30084-5305
Phone: 770-724-9230
Fax: 770-724-9263
E-mail: peggy@mail.gsfc.state.ga.us

TV/RADIO BROADCASTING_____

JOHN BAYLISS BROADCAST FOUNDATION

JOHN BAYLISS BROADCAST RADIO SCHOLARSHIP   see number 57

MARYLAND ASSOCIATION OF PRIVATE CAREER SCHOOLS

MARYLAND ASSOCIATION OF PRIVATE CAREER SCHOOLS SCHOLARSHIP
see number 45

NONACADEMIC/NONCAREER CRITERIA

CIVIC, PROFESSIONAL, SOCIAL, OR UNION AFFILIATION_____

AMERICAN FOREIGN SERVICE ASSOCIATION

AMERICAN FOREIGN SERVICE ASSOCIATION (AFSA) FINANCIAL AID AWARD PROGRAM • 148

Need-based financial aid scholarship program open to children whose parents are in the U.S. Government Foreign Service. Must attend a U.S. school full-time and maintain a "C" average. Children whose parents are in the military and international students are not eligible.

Award Scholarship for use in freshman, sophomore, junior, or senior years; not renewable. *Number:* 50–60. *Amount:* $500–$3000.

Eligibility Requirements: Applicant must be enrolled or expecting to enroll full-time at a two-year or four-year or technical institution or university and single. Applicant or parent of applicant must be member of American Foreign Service Association. Applicant or parent of applicant must have employment or volunteer experience in U.S. government foreign service. Applicant must have 2.5 GPA or higher. Available to U.S. citizens.

Application Requirements Application, financial need analysis, transcript, CSS Profile. *Deadline:* February 6.

World Wide Web: http://www.afsa.org

Contact: Ms. Lori Dec, Scholarship Administrator
American Foreign Service Association
2101 E Street, NW
Washington, DC 20037
Phone: 202-944-5504
Fax: 202-338-6820
E-mail: dec@afsa.org

AMERICAN QUARTER HORSE FOUNDATION (AQHF)

AMERICAN QUARTER HORSE FOUNDATION YOUTH SCHOLARSHIPS • 149

$8,000 scholarships to AQHYA members who have belonged for three or more years. The recipient will receive $2,000 per year for four years. Minimum 2.5 GPA required.

Award Scholarship for use in freshman year; renewable. *Number:* 1–25. *Amount:* $8000.

Eligibility Requirements: Applicant must be enrolled or expecting to enroll full-time at a two-year or four-year or technical institution or university. Applicant or parent of applicant must be member of American Quarter Horse Association. Applicant must have 2.5 GPA or higher. Available to U.S. and Canadian citizens.

Application Requirements Application, financial need analysis, photo, references, transcript. *Deadline:* February 1.

World Wide Web: http://www.aqha.org/aqhya

Contact: Laura Owens, Scholarship Coordinator
American Quarter Horse Foundation (AQHF)
2601 I-40 East
Amarillo, TX 79104
Phone: 806-376-5181
Fax: 806-376-1005
E-mail: lowens@aqha.org

DELTA DELTA DELTA FOUNDATION

DELTA DELTA DELTA UNDERGRADUATE SCHOLARSHIP   • 150

One-time award based on academic achievement, campus, chapter, and community involvement. Any initiated sophomore or junior member-in-good-standing of Delta Delta Delta may apply. Application and information available at web site http://www.tridelta.org.

Award Scholarship for use in junior or senior years; not renewable. *Number:* 48–50. *Amount:* $500–$2000.

Eligibility Requirements: Applicant must be enrolled or expecting to enroll full-time at a four-year institution or university and single female. Applicant or parent of applicant must have employment or volunteer experience in community service.

Application Requirements Application, references, transcript. *Deadline:* February 1.

World Wide Web: http://www.tridelta.org

Contact: Joyce Allen, Foundation Coordinator of Scholarships and Financial Services
Delta Delta Delta Foundation
PO Box 5987
Arlington, TX 76005
Phone: 817-633-8001
Fax: 817-652-0212
E-mail: jallen@trideltaeo.org

ELKS NATIONAL FOUNDATION

ELKS NATIONAL FOUNDATION LEGACY AWARDS   • 151

Up to five hundred $1000 one-year scholarships for children and grandchildren of Elks in good standing. Parent or grandparent must have been an Elk for two

Elks National Foundation Legacy Awards (continued)

years. Contact local Elks Lodge for an application or send a SASE to Foundation or see home page (http://www.elks.org, keyword: scholarship). Deadline is January 10.

Award Scholarship for use in freshman year; not renewable. *Number:* up to 500. *Amount:* $1000.

Eligibility Requirements: Applicant must be high school student and planning to enroll or expecting to enroll full-time at a two-year or four-year institution or university. Applicant or parent of applicant must be member of Elks Club. Available to U.S. citizens.

Application Requirements Application, essay, references, self-addressed stamped envelope, test scores, transcript. *Deadline:* January 10.

World Wide Web: http://www.elks.org/enf

Contact: Ms. Jeannine Kunz, Scholarship Coordinator
Elks National Foundation
2750 North Lakeview Avenue
Chicago, IL 60614-1889
Phone: 773-755-4732
Fax: 773-755-4733
E-mail: scholarship@elks.org

FRATERNAL ORDER OF EAGLES

FRATERNAL ORDER OF EAGLES MEMORIAL FOUNDATION • 152

Award for children of members of the Fraternal Order of Eagles and Ladies Auxiliary who died from injuries or diseases incurred or aggravated in line of duty. Grant may be renewed until a total of $30,000 is reached. May be used for cost of college, vocational school, fees, books, or course-related supplies. Eligible until 25 years of age unless married and self-supporting before then. Must maintain a "C" average. Contact for deadlines.

Award Grant for use in freshman, sophomore, junior, or senior years; renewable. *Number:* 35. *Amount:* $6000.

Eligibility Requirements: Applicant must be age 25 or under and enrolled or expecting to enroll full or part-time at a two-year or four-year or technical institution or university. Applicant or parent of applicant must be member of Fraternal Order of Eagles. Available to U.S. citizens.

Application Requirements Application.

Contact: Fraternal Order of Eagles
4710 14th Street West
Bradenton, FL 34207

GOLDEN KEY INTERNATIONAL HONOUR SOCIETY

UNDERGRADUATE SCHOLARSHIP • 153

Two $500 scholarships are awarded at each chapter every year to members of Golden Key International Honour Society. Minimum 3.5 GPA required. Must be a member of Golden Key International Honour Society to be eligible for awards. Please visit web site (http://goldenkey.gsu.edu) for more information. Offered in conjunction with the Ford Motor Company.

Award Scholarship for use in junior or senior years; not renewable. *Number:* 690. *Amount:* $500–$700.

Eligibility Requirements: Applicant must be enrolled or expecting to enroll full-time at an institution or university. Applicant or parent of applicant must be member of Golden Key National Honor Society. Applicant must have 3.5 GPA or higher. Available to U.S. and non-U.S. citizens.

Application Requirements Application, interview, transcript. *Deadline:* January 15.

World Wide Web: http://goldenkey.gsu.edu

Contact: Luke Anderson, Coordinator of Scholarships and Awards
Golden Key International Honour Society
1189 Ponce de Leon Avenue
Atlanta, GA 30306-4624
Phone: 404-377-2400
Fax: 404-373-7033
E-mail: scholarships@goldenkey.gsu.edu

HEBREW IMMIGRANT AID SOCIETY

HEBREW IMMIGRANT AID SOCIETY SCHOLARSHIP AWARDS COMPETITION
• 154

Must be Hebrew Immigrant Aid Society-assisted refugee or child thereof who immigrated to the U.S. Must have completed two semesters at a U.S. high school, college, or graduate school. Send self-addressed stamped envelope for application after December 15. Application and information are available at web site http://www.hias.org. Postmark deadline for competition is March 15.

Award Scholarship for use in freshman, sophomore, junior, senior, or graduate years; not renewable. *Number:* 100. *Amount:* $1500.

Eligibility Requirements: Applicant must be enrolled or expecting to enroll full or part-time at a two-year or four-year or technical institution or university. Applicant or parent of applicant must be member of Hebrew Immigrant Aid Society. Available to U.S. citizens.

Application Requirements Application, essay, financial need analysis, self-addressed stamped envelope, test scores, transcript. *Deadline:* March 15.

World Wide Web: http://www.hias.org

Contact: Ms. Irina Reyn, Associate Director of Scholarship
Hebrew Immigrant Aid Society
333 Seventh Avenue
New York, NY 10001-5004
Phone: 212-613-1358
Fax: 212-629-0921
E-mail: irina_reyn@hias.org

KAPPA ALPHA THETA FOUNDATION

KAPPA ALPHA THETA FOUNDATION MERIT BASED SCHOLARSHIP PROGRAM • 155

Foundation scholarships are awarded to either graduate or undergraduate members of Kappa Alpha Theta. All scholarships are merit-based. Application postmark date is February 1. Applications may be downloaded from the web site or may be obtained by calling 1-888-526-1870 ext. 336.

Award Scholarship for use in sophomore, junior, senior, graduate, or postgraduate years; not renewable. *Number:* 120–140. *Amount:* $1000–$8000.

Eligibility Requirements: Applicant must be enrolled or expecting to enroll full or part-time at a four-year institution or university and female. Available to U.S. and non-U.S. citizens.

Application Requirements Application, resume, references, transcript. *Deadline:* February 1.

World Wide Web: http://www.kappaalphatheta.org

Contact: Mrs. Jeni Hilgedag, Director of Programs
Kappa Alpha Theta Foundation
8740 Founders Road
Indianapolis, IN 46268
Phone: 317-876-1870 Ext. 110
Fax: 317-876-1925
E-mail: info@kappaalphatheta.org

KAPPA ALPHA THETA FOUNDATION NAMED TRUST GRANT PROGRAM • 156

The Kappa Alpha Theta Foundation named Trust Grant program was established to provide monies for undergraduate and alumna members of the Fraternity for leadership training and non-degree educational opportunities. Applications may be downloaded from the web site. Application is due 90 days prior to event, workshop or program.

Award Grant for use in freshman, sophomore, junior, or senior years; not renewable. *Number:* up to 50. *Amount:* $100–$5000.

Eligibility Requirements: Applicant must be enrolled or expecting to enroll at an institution or university and female. Available to U.S. and non-U.S. citizens.

Application Requirements Application, resume, references, budget, proposal, narrative. *Deadline:* Continuous.

World Wide Web: http://www.kappaalphatheta.org

Contact: Mrs. Jeni Hilgedag, Director of Programs
Kappa Alpha Theta Foundation
8740 Founders Road
Indianapolis, IN 46268
Phone: 317-876-1870 Ext. 110
Fax: 317-876-1925
E-mail: info@kappaalphatheta.org

KAPPA SIGMA ENDOWMENT FUND

SCHOLARSHIP-LEADERSHIP AWARDS PROGRAM • 157

Scholarships are given to outstanding undergraduate Kappa Sigma members who excel in the classroom, on campus and within the fraternity. Must have a 2.5 GPA. Applications can be downloaded at http://www.ksefnet.org.

Award Scholarship for use in freshman, sophomore, junior, or senior years; not renewable. *Number:* 275–280. *Amount:* $500–$2500.

Eligibility Requirements: Applicant must be enrolled or expecting to enroll full-time at a four-year institution or university and male. Applicant must have 2.5 GPA or higher. Available to U.S. and non-U.S. citizens.

Application Requirements Application, transcript. *Deadline:* October 3.

World Wide Web: http://www.ksefnet.org

Contact: James Eldridge, Director of Annual Giving
Kappa Sigma Endowment Fund
PO Box 5643
Charlottesville, VA 22905-5643
Phone: 434-979-5733 Ext. 125
Fax: 434-296-5733
E-mail: jamese@imh.kappasigma.org

KNIGHTS OF COLUMBUS

FOURTH DEGREE PRO DEO AND PRO PATRIA SCHOLARSHIPS • 158

Renewable award available to students entering freshman year at a Catholic university or college. Applicant must be a member or child of a member of Knights of Columbus or Columbian Squires. Scholarships are awarded on the basis of academic excellence. Minimum 3.0 GPA required.

Award Scholarship for use in freshman year; renewable. *Number:* 62. *Amount:* $1500.

Eligibility Requirements: Applicant must be Roman Catholic and enrolled or expecting to enroll full-time at a four-year institution. Applicant or parent of applicant must be member of Columbian Squires or Knights of Columbus. Applicant must have 3.0 GPA or higher. Available to U.S. citizens.

Application Requirements Application, autobiography, essay, references, test scores, transcript. *Deadline:* March 1.

Contact: Rev. Donald Barry, Director of Scholarship Aid
Knights of Columbus
PO Box 1670
New Haven, CT 06507-0901
Phone: 203-752-4332
Fax: 203-752-4103

MODERN WOODMEN OF AMERICA

MODERN WOODMEN OF AMERICA FRATERNAL COLLEGE SCHOLARSHIP PROGRAM • 159

Available to high school seniors who have been beneficial members of Modern Woodmen of America for two years by September 30 of senior year. Selection based on scholarship, extracurricular activities, and character. Include photo. Renewable for four years. Must submit biographical questionnaire and a form from official of applicant's high school.

Award Scholarship for use in freshman, sophomore, junior, or senior years; renewable. *Number:* up to 75. *Amount:* up to $4000.

Eligibility Requirements: Applicant must be high school student and planning to enroll or expecting to enroll full-time at a four-year institution or university. Applicant or parent of applicant must be member of Modern Woodmen. Applicant must have 2.5 GPA or higher.

Application Requirements Application, essay, photo, references, test scores, transcript. *Deadline:* January 1.

World Wide Web: http://www.modern-woodmen.org

Contact: Byron Carlson, Fraternal Scholarship Administrator
Modern Woodmen of America
1701 1st Avenue
PO Box 2005
Rock Island, IL 61204

NATIONAL ASSOCIATION OF SECONDARY SCHOOL PRINCIPALS, AND PRUDENTIAL FINANCIALS, INC.

NATIONAL HONOR SOCIETY SCHOLARSHIPS • 160

One-time award available only to high school seniors who are National Honor Society members, for use at an accredited two- or four-year college or university in the U.S. Based on outstanding scholarship, leadership, service, and character. Application fee $6. Contact school counselor or NHS chapter adviser. Minimum 3.0 GPA.

Award Scholarship for use in freshman year; not renewable. *Number:* 200. *Amount:* $1000.

Eligibility Requirements: Applicant must be high school student and planning to enroll or expecting to enroll full-time at a two-year or four-year institution or university. Applicant or parent of applicant must be member of National Honor Society. Applicant must have 3.0 GPA or higher. Available to U.S. and non-U.S. citizens.

Application Requirements Application, essay, references, test scores, transcript. *Fee:* $6. *Deadline:* January 23.

World Wide Web: http://www.principals.org

Contact: local school's NHS chapter adviser

UNION PLUS SCHOLARSHIP PROGRAM

UNION PLUS SCHOLARSHIP PROGRAM   • 161

One-time cash award for AFL-CIO union members, their spouses, or dependent children. Based upon academic achievement, character, leadership, career goals, social awareness, and financial need. Must be from Canada or U.S. including Puerto Rico. Members must download application from web site. Applications are available from September 1 to January 15.

Award Scholarship for use in freshman, sophomore, junior, or senior years; not renewable. *Number:* 110–130. *Amount:* $500–$4000.

Eligibility Requirements: Applicant must be enrolled or expecting to enroll full or part-time at a two-year or four-year or technical institution or university. Applicant or parent of applicant must be member of AFL-CIO. Available to U.S. and Canadian citizens.

Application Requirements Application, essay, financial need analysis, references, test scores, transcript. *Deadline:* January 31.

World Wide Web: http://www.unionplus.org

Contact: visit web site for application and information

YOUNG AMERICAN BOWLING ALLIANCE (YABA)

PEPSI-COLA YOUTH BOWLING CHAMPIONSHIPS   • 162

Awarded to members of the Young American Bowling Alliance. Must win state or provincial tournaments to be eligible for international championships. U.S. citizens abroad may participate through military affiliate. Application fee varies by state. Contact Youth Director at local bowling center.

Award Scholarship for use in freshman, sophomore, junior, or senior years; not renewable. *Number:* 292. *Amount:* $500–$3000.

Eligibility Requirements: Applicant must be enrolled or expecting to enroll full or part-time at an institution or university and must have an interest in bowling. Applicant or parent of applicant must be member of Young American Bowling Alliance. Available to U.S. and non-U.S. citizens.

Application Requirements Applicant must enter a contest. *Deadline:* February 28.

World Wide Web: http://www.bowl.com

Contact: Young American Bowling Alliance (YABA)
5301 South 76th Street
Greendale, WI 53129-1192

CORPORATE AFFILIATION_____

ALCOA FOUNDATION

ALCOA FOUNDATION SONS AND DAUGHTERS SCHOLARSHIP PROGRAM • 163

Open to children of Alcoa, Inc., employees. Apply in senior year of high school through parent's employment location. Merit is considered.

Award Scholarship for use in freshman year; renewable. *Number:* 100–150. *Amount:* $1500.

Eligibility Requirements: Applicant must be high school student and planning to enroll or expecting to enroll full-time at a two-year or four-year or technical institution or university. Applicant or parent of applicant must be affiliated with Aluminum Company of America. Available to U.S. and non-U.S. citizens.

Application Requirements Application, applicant must enter a contest, essay, references, test scores, transcript. *Deadline:* January 22.

Contact: Ms. Carol Greco, Data Analyst
Alcoa Foundation
201 Isabella Street
Pittsburgh, PA 15212-5858
Phone: 412-553-4786
Fax: 412-553-4532
E-mail: carol.greco@alcoa.com

BRIDGESTONE/FIRESTONE TRUST FUND

BRIDGESTONE/FIRESTONE TRUST FUND SCHOLARSHIPS • 164

Award for sons and daughters of Bridgestone/Firestone, Inc., employees and retirees. Must be high school student in junior year. Must be a U.S. citizen. Must also meet all requirements for participation that are published in the PSAT/NMSQT Student Bulletin.

Award Scholarship for use in freshman year; not renewable. *Number:* up to 50. *Amount:* $4000.

Eligibility Requirements: Applicant must be high school student and planning to enroll or expecting to enroll full-time at a four-year institution or university. Applicant or parent of applicant must be affiliated with Bridgestone/Firestone. Applicant or parent of applicant must have employment or volunteer experience in designated career field. Available to U.S. citizens.

Application Requirements Application. *Deadline:* February 1.

Contact: Bernice Csaszar, Administrator
Bridgestone/Firestone Trust Fund
535 Marriott Drive
Nashville, TN 37214-0990
Phone: 615-937-1415
Fax: 615-937-1414
E-mail: bfstrustfund@bfusa.com

CLARA ABBOTT FOUNDATION

SCHOLARSHIP PROGRAM • 165

Scholarships are available to the children of Abbott Laboratories' employees and retirees. Must be under 29 years of age and planning to attend an accredited undergraduate program. Must reapply each year. Requirements: Completed application, copies of W2 and IRS 1040 form, and student's most recent grade report. Based on financial need. The deadline is the second Monday of December.

Award Grant for use in freshman, sophomore, junior, or senior years; not renewable. *Number:* 4000. *Amount:* $250–$13,000.

Eligibility Requirements: Applicant must be age 17-29 and enrolled or expecting to enroll full or part-time at a two-year or four-year or technical institution or university. Applicant or parent of applicant must be affiliated with Abbott Laboratories. Applicant or parent of applicant must have employment or volunteer experience in designated career field. Available to U.S. and non-U.S. citizens.

Application Requirements Application, financial need analysis, transcript, copies of W2's, 1040's.

World Wide Web: http://clara.abbott.com/
Contact: Kate O'Brian, Scholarship Coordinator
Clara Abbott Foundation
200 Abbott Park Road, D579, J37
Abbott Park, IL 60064
Phone: 847-935-8196
Fax: 847-938-6511
E-mail: jo.jakubowicz@abbott.com

DUKE ENERGY CORPORATION

DUKE ENERGY SCHOLARS PROGRAM • 166

Scholarship is open to graduating high school seniors who are children of eligible employees and retirees of Duke Energy and its subsidiaries. Fifteen four-year scholarships of up to $20,000 and five $1,000 awards given annually. Recipients selected by 5-member outside committee.

Award Scholarship for use in freshman, sophomore, junior, or senior years; renewable. *Number:* 5-15. *Amount:* $1000–$20,000.

Eligibility Requirements: Applicant must be high school student and planning to enroll or expecting to enroll full-time at a two-year or four-year or technical institution or university. Applicant or parent of applicant must be affiliated with Duke Energy Corporation. Applicant or parent of applicant must have employment or volunteer experience in designated career field. Available to U.S. and Canadian citizens.

Application Requirements Application, autobiography, essay, financial need analysis, references, test scores, transcript. *Deadline:* December 1.

World Wide Web: http://www.duke-energy.com

Duke Energy Scholars Program (continued)
Contact: Dianne S. Wilson, Scholarship Administrator
Duke Energy Corporation
PO Box 1642
Houston, TX 77251-1642
Phone: 713-627-4608
Fax: 713-627-4061
E-mail: dswilson@duke-energy.com

HUMANA FOUNDATION

HUMANA FOUNDATION SCHOLARSHIP PROGRAM • 167

Up to 75 scholarships are given to full-time undergraduate students. Eligible applicants must be under 25 and a United States citizen. The deadline is February 1. Must be a dependent of a Humana employee.

Award Scholarship for use in freshman, sophomore, or junior years; renewable. *Number:* up to 75. *Amount:* $1250–$2500.
Eligibility Requirements: Applicant must be age 25 or under and enrolled or expecting to enroll full-time at a two-year or four-year institution. Applicant or parent of applicant must be affiliated with Humana Foundation. Available to U.S. citizens.
Application Requirements Application, transcript. *Deadline:* February 1.
World Wide Web: http://www.humanafoundation.org/scholarship.html
Contact: Charles Jackson, Program Manager
Humana Foundation
Attention: Scholarship Program, 500 West Main Street
Room 208
Louisville, KY 40202
Phone: 502-580-1245
Fax: 502-580-1256
E-mail: cjackson@humana.com

JOHNSON CONTROLS, INC.

JOHNSON CONTROLS FOUNDATION SCHOLARSHIP PROGRAM • 168

Available to high school seniors who are children of Johnson Controls, Inc., employees. Award is distributed over four years of undergraduate study. Renewable scholarships of up to $8000 each based on merit.

Award Scholarship for use in freshman, sophomore, junior, or senior years; renewable. *Number:* up to 50. *Amount:* $2000–$8000.
Eligibility Requirements: Applicant must be high school student and planning to enroll or expecting to enroll full-time at a four-year institution. Applicant or parent of applicant must be affiliated with Johnson Controls, Inc. Applicant must have 3.0 GPA or higher. Available to U.S. citizens.
Application Requirements Application, transcript. *Deadline:* February 15.

World Wide Web: http://www.johnsoncontrols.com
Contact: Valerie Adisek, Scholarship Coordinator
Johnson Controls, Inc.
5757 North Green Bay Avenue, X-46
Milwaukee, WI 53209
Phone: 414-524-2296

PROCTER & GAMBLE FUND

PROCTER & GAMBLE FUND SCHOLARSHIP COMPETITION FOR EMPLOYEES' CHILDREN • 169

Award for high school seniors who are dependents of eligible employees, including deceased employees, and retirees of Procter and Gamble Company. All winners receive a one-time-only award of $2500. Deadline: January 15 of applicant's senior year of high school.

Award Scholarship for use in freshman year; not renewable. *Number:* 250. *Amount:* $2500.

Eligibility Requirements: Applicant must be high school student and planning to enroll or expecting to enroll full-time at a two-year or four-year or technical institution or university. Applicant or parent of applicant must be affiliated with Procter & Gamble Company. Applicant or parent of applicant must have employment or volunteer experience in designated career field. Available to U.S. citizens.

Application Requirements Application, applicant must enter a contest, essay, references, test scores, transcript. *Deadline:* January 15.
World Wide Web: http://www.pg.com
Contact: Tawnia True, Coordinator, P&G Employee Scholarship Fund
Procter & Gamble Fund
PO Box 599
Cincinnati, OH 45201-0599
Phone: 513-983-2139
Fax: 513-983-2173
E-mail: pgfund.im@pg.com

WAL-MART FOUNDATION

WAL-MART ASSOCIATE SCHOLARSHIPS • 170

Awards for college-bound high school seniors who work for Wal-Mart or whose parents are part-time Wal-Mart associates or have not been with the company for one year. Based on ACT or SAT scores, counselor recommendations, transcripts, class rank, activities, and financial need. One-time award of $1000. For use at an accredited two- or four-year U.S. institution.

Award Scholarship for use in freshman year; not renewable. *Number:* 150–300. *Amount:* $1000.

Eligibility Requirements: Applicant must be high school student and planning to enroll or expecting to enroll full-time at a two-year or four-year

Wal-Mart Associate Scholarships (continued)

institution or university. Applicant or parent of applicant must be affiliated with Wal-Mart Foundation. Applicant or parent of applicant must have employment or volunteer experience in designated career field. Available to U.S. citizens.

Application Requirements Application, test scores, transcript, federal income tax return. *Deadline:* February 1.

World Wide Web: http://www.walmartfoundation.org

Contact: Jenny Harral
Wal-Mart Foundation
702 Southwest 8th Street
Bentonville, AR 72716-0150
Phone: 800-530-9925
Fax: 501-273-6850

WALTON FAMILY FOUNDATION SCHOLARSHIP • 171

Award for high-school seniors who are children of a Wal-Mart associate who has been employed as a full-time associate for at least one year. $8000 undergraduate scholarship payable over four years. Must submit latest federal income tax return. Contact a member of Wal-Mart management for an application starting in November each year.

Award Scholarship for use in freshman, sophomore, junior, or senior years; renewable. *Number:* 100–120. *Amount:* $8000.

Eligibility Requirements: Applicant must be high school student and planning to enroll or expecting to enroll full-time at a two-year or four-year institution or university. Applicant or parent of applicant must be affiliated with Wal-Mart Foundation. Available to U.S. citizens.

Application Requirements Application, financial need analysis, test scores, transcript, federal income tax return. *Deadline:* February 1.

World Wide Web: http://www.walmartfoundation.org

Contact: Jenny Harral
Wal-Mart Foundation
702 Southwest 8th Street
Bentonville, AR 72716-0150
Phone: 800-530-9925
Fax: 501-273-6850

WEYERHAEUSER COMPANY FOUNDATION

WEYERHAEUSER COMPANY FOUNDATION SCHOLARSHIPS • 172

Renewable awards for children of Weyerhaeuser Company employees. Twenty scholarships for use at two-year schools are offered at $1000 per year. Forty-five scholarships for use at four-year schools are offered at $1000 to $4000 per year. Must apply by January 15 of senior year in high school.

Award Scholarship for use in freshman year; renewable. *Number:* 65. *Amount:* $1000–$4000.

Eligibility Requirements: Applicant must be high school student and planning to enroll or expecting to enroll at a two-year or four-year or technical institution. Applicant or parent of applicant must be affiliated with Weyerhauser Company.

Application Requirements Application. *Deadline:* January 15.

Contact: Penny Paul, Program Manager
Weyerhaeuser Company Foundation
EC-22A8
PO Box 9777
Federal Way, WA 98063-9777
Phone: 253-924-2629
Fax: 253-924-3658

EMPLOYMENT EXPERIENCE_____

ALABAMA COMMISSION ON HIGHER EDUCATION

POLICE OFFICERS AND FIREFIGHTERS SURVIVORS EDUCATION ASSISTANCE PROGRAM-ALABAMA   • 173

Provides tuition, fees, books, and supplies to dependents of full-time police officers and firefighters killed in the line of duty. Must attend any Alabama public college as an undergraduate. Must be Alabama resident. Renewable.

Award Grant for use in freshman, sophomore, junior, or senior years; renewable. *Number:* 15–30. *Amount:* $2000–$5000.

Eligibility Requirements: Applicant must be enrolled or expecting to enroll full or part-time at a two-year or four-year or technical institution or university; single; resident of Alabama and studying in Alabama. Applicant or parent of applicant must have employment or volunteer experience in police/firefighting. Available to U.S. citizens.

Application Requirements Application, transcript. *Deadline:* Continuous.

World Wide Web: http://www.ache.state.al.us

Contact: Dr. William Wall, Associate Executive Director for Student
Assistance, ACHE
Alabama Commission on Higher Education
PO Box 302000
Montgomery, AL 36130-2000

AMERICAN FOREIGN SERVICE ASSOCIATION

AMERICAN FOREIGN SERVICE ASSOCIATION (AFSA) FINANCIAL AID AWARD PROGRAM   see number 148

BRIDGESTONE/FIRESTONE TRUST FUND

BRIDGESTONE/FIRESTONE TRUST FUND SCHOLARSHIPS
see number 164

CALIFORNIA CORRECTIONAL PEACE OFFICERS ASSOCIATION

CALIFORNIA CORRECTIONAL PEACE OFFICERS ASSOCIATION JOE HARPER SCHOLARSHIP • 174

A scholarship program for immediate relatives and/or correctional officers in California.

Award Scholarship for use in freshman, sophomore, junior, senior, or graduate years; not renewable. *Number:* 100. *Amount:* $1000.

Eligibility Requirements: Applicant must be enrolled or expecting to enroll full or part-time at a two-year or four-year or technical institution or university and resident of California. Applicant or parent of applicant must have employment or volunteer experience in designated career field. Applicant must have 3.5 GPA or higher. Available to U.S. citizens.

Application Requirements Application, autobiography, essay, financial need analysis, photo, references, test scores, transcript. *Deadline:* April 30.

Contact: Marcia Bartlett, Bookkeeper
California Correctional Peace Officers Association
755 Riverpoint Drive, Suite 200
West Sacremento, CA 95605
Phone: 916-372-6060
Fax: 916-372-6623

CHAIRSCHOLARS FOUNDATION, INC.

CHAIRSCHOLARS FOUNDATION, INC. SCHOLARSHIPS • 175

Award for students who are severely physically challenged. Applicants may be high school seniors or college freshmen. Must be outstanding citizen with history of public service. Minimum 3.5 GPA required. Ten to twelve renewable awards of $5000. Must be under 21 years old.

Award Scholarship for use in freshman or sophomore years; renewable. *Number:* 10–12. *Amount:* $5000–$20,000.

Eligibility Requirements: Applicant must be age 21 or under and enrolled or expecting to enroll full-time at a two-year or four-year or technical institution or university. Applicant or parent of applicant must have employment or volunteer experience in community service. Applicant must be hearing impaired, physically disabled, or visually impaired. Applicant must have 3.5 GPA or higher. Available to U.S. citizens.

Application Requirements Application, autobiography, essay, financial need analysis, photo, portfolio, references, self-addressed stamped envelope, test scores, transcript, parents' tax return from previous year. *Deadline:* February 28.

World Wide Web: http://www.chairscholars.org
Contact: Hugo Keim
Chairscholars Foundation, Inc.
16101 Carencia Lane
Odessa, FL 33556
Phone: 813-920-2737
E-mail: hugokeim@earthlink.net

CLARA ABBOTT FOUNDATION

SCHOLARSHIP PROGRAM
see number 165

COLLEGE ASSISTANCE MIGRANT PROGRAM

COLLEGE ASSISTANCE MIGRANT PROGRAM AT ST. EDWARD'S UNIVERSITY
• 176

The purpose of CAMP is to provide migrant/seasonal farm workers who have completed high school requirements an opportunity to work toward a four-year baccalaureate degree. This program offers the eligible student financial, academic and other supportive assistance necessary for successful completion of the first two semesters of college. Must be U.S. citizen. Application deadline is February 1.

Award Grant for use in freshman year; not renewable. *Number:* 40. *Amount:* $20,500.

Eligibility Requirements: Applicant must be enrolled or expecting to enroll full-time at an institution or university. Applicant or parent of applicant must have employment or volunteer experience in agriculture. Available to U.S. citizens.

Application Requirements Application, essay, financial need analysis, references, test scores, transcript, certification of migrant eligibility. *Deadline:* February 1.

World Wide Web: http://www.stedwards.edu/camp
Contact: Esther Quinones Yacono, Director
College Assistance Migrant Program
3001 South Congress Avenue
Austin, TX 78704
Phone: 512-448-8625
Fax: 512-464-8830
E-mail: esthery@admin.stedwards.edu

DELTA DELTA DELTA FOUNDATION

DELTA DELTA DELTA UNDERGRADUATE SCHOLARSHIP
see number 150

DUKE ENERGY CORPORATION

DUKE ENERGY SCHOLARS PROGRAM
see number 166

EXPLOSIVE ORDNANCE DISPOSAL MEMORIAL COMMITTEE

EXPLOSIVE ORDNANCE DISPOSAL SCHOLARSHIP • 177

One-time award based on academic merit, community involvement, and financial need for the children and spouses of Explosive Ordnance Disposal technicians. Applications are only available on the web site at http://www.eodmemorial. org.

Award Scholarship for use in freshman, sophomore, junior, or senior years; not renewable. *Number:* 20–60. *Amount:* $1500–$2000.

Eligibility Requirements: Applicant must be enrolled or expecting to enroll full-time at a two-year or four-year or technical institution or university. Applicant or parent of applicant must have employment or volunteer experience in explosive ordinance disposal. Available to U.S. citizens. Applicant or parent must meet one or more of the following requirements: general military experience; retired from active duty; disabled or killed as a result of military service; prisoner of war; or missing in action.

Application Requirements Application, financial need analysis, transcript. *Deadline:* March 1.

World Wide Web: http://www.eodmemorial.org

Contact: Mary McKinley, Administrator
Explosive Ordnance Disposal Memorial Committee
PO Box 594
Niceville, FL 32588
Phone: 850-729-2401
Fax: 850-729-2401
E-mail: admin@eodmorial.org

ILLINOIS STUDENT ASSISTANCE COMMISSION (ISAC)

GRANT PROGRAM FOR DEPENDENTS OF POLICE, FIRE, OR CORRECTIONAL OFFICERS • 178

Award for dependents of police, fire, and corrections officers killed or disabled in line of duty. Provides for tuition and fees at approved Illinois institutions. Must be resident of Illinois. Continuous deadline. Provide proof of status.

Award Grant for use in freshman, sophomore, junior, senior, graduate, or postgraduate years; renewable. *Number:* 50–55. *Amount:* $3000–$4000.

Eligibility Requirements: Applicant must be enrolled or expecting to enroll at a two-year or four-year or technical institution or university; resident of Illinois and studying in Illinois. Applicant or parent of applicant must have employment or volunteer experience in police/firefighting. Available to U.S. and non-U.S. citizens.

Application Requirements Application, proof of status. *Deadline:* Continuous.

World Wide Web: http://www.isac-online.org

Contact: David Barinholtz, Client Information
Illinois Student Assistance Commission (ISAC)
1755 Lake Cook Road
Deerfield, IL 60015-5209
Phone: 847-948-8500 Ext. 2385
E-mail: cssupport@isac.org

J. WOOD PLATT CADDIE SCHOLARSHIP TRUST

J. WOOD PLATT CADDIE SCHOLARSHIP TRUST • 179

Renewable award for high school seniors or college undergraduates who have caddied at least one year at a member club of the Golf Association of Philadelphia. Submit transcript and financial need analysis with application. Interview required.

Award Scholarship for use in freshman, sophomore, junior, senior, or graduate years; renewable. *Number:* 200–300. *Amount:* $200–$7000.

Eligibility Requirements: Applicant must be enrolled or expecting to enroll full-time at a two-year or four-year institution or university and must have an interest in golf. Applicant or parent of applicant must have employment or volunteer experience in private club/caddying. Available to U.S. and non-U.S. citizens.

Application Requirements Application, financial need analysis, interview, references, test scores, transcript. *Deadline:* April 25.

World Wide Web: http://www.gapgolf.org

Contact: Robert Caucci, Program Administrator
J. Wood Platt Caddie Scholarship Trust
Drawer 808
Southeastern, PA 19399-0808
Phone: 610-687-2340 Ext. 21
Fax: 610-687-2082

NATIONAL BURGLAR AND FIRE ALARM ASSOCIATION

NBFAA/SECURITY DEALER YOUTH SCHOLARSHIP PROGRAM• 180

Scholarship program provides cash college scholarship awards to deserving sons or daughters of police and fire officials. Applicants should contact state NBFAA chapters.

Award Scholarship for use in freshman year; not renewable. *Number:* 32. *Amount:* $500–$6500.

Eligibility Requirements: Applicant must be high school student; age 15-20; planning to enroll or expecting to enroll full-time at a four-year institution or university and resident of California, Connecticut, Georgia, Indiana, Kentucky, Louisiana, Maryland, Minnesota, New Jersey, North Carolina, Pennsylvania,

NBFAA/Security Dealer Youth Scholarship Program (continued)
Puerto Rico, Tennessee, Virginia, or Washington. Applicant or parent of applicant must have employment or volunteer experience in fire service or police/firefighting. Available to U.S. and non-Canadian citizens.

Application Requirements Application, essay, test scores, transcript. *Deadline:* March 1.

World Wide Web: http://www.alarm.org

Contact: Melynda Cutler, Marketing Coordinator
National Burglar and Fire Alarm Association
8380 Colesville Road
Suite 750
Silver Spring, MD 20910
Phone: 301-585-1855 Ext. 117
Fax: 301-585-1866
E-mail: melyndac@alarm.org

NATIONAL FEDERATION OF THE BLIND

NATIONAL FEDERATION OF THE BLIND SCHOLARSHIPS • 181

Award for legally blind students pursuing postsecondary education in the U.S. Must submit recommendation from state officer of the National Federation of the Blind. Award based on academic excellence, service to the community, and financial need. One award given to a person working full-time and attending or planning to attend a part-time course of study to broaden opportunities in work.

Award Scholarship for use in freshman, sophomore, junior, or senior years; not renewable. *Number:* 18. *Amount:* $3000–$7000.

Eligibility Requirements: Applicant must be enrolled or expecting to enroll full or part-time at a four-year institution or university. Applicant or parent of applicant must have employment or volunteer experience in community service. Applicant must be visually impaired. Available to U.S. and non-U.S. citizens.

Application Requirements Application, essay, financial need analysis, references, transcript. *Deadline:* March 31.

World Wide Web: http://www.nfb.org

Contact: Peggy Elliot, Chairman, Scholarship Committee
National Federation of the Blind
805 Fifth Avenue
Grinnell, IA 50112
Phone: 641-236-3366

NEW JERSEY STATE GOLF ASSOCIATION

NEW JERSEY STATE GOLF ASSOCIATION CADDIE SCHOLARSHIP • 182

Must caddie for at least one year at a member club of the New Jersey State Golf Association. Based on grades, test scores, references, and financial need. Renewable award for undergraduate use.

Award Scholarship for use in freshman, sophomore, junior, or senior years; renewable. *Number:* 200. *Amount:* $1500–$3000.

Eligibility Requirements: Applicant must be enrolled or expecting to enroll full-time at a two-year or four-year institution or university. Applicant or parent of applicant must have employment or volunteer experience in private club/caddying.

Application Requirements Application, financial need analysis, references, test scores, transcript. *Deadline:* May 1.

World Wide Web: http://www.njsga.org

Contact: Education Director
New Jersey State Golf Association
PO Box 6947
Freehold, NJ 07728

PROCTER & GAMBLE FUND

PROCTER & GAMBLE FUND SCHOLARSHIP COMPETITION FOR EMPLOYEES' CHILDREN
see number 169

SID RICHARDSON MEMORIAL FUND

SID RICHARDSON MEMORIAL FUND
• 183

Eligible applicants are children or grandchildren of persons presently employed (or retired) at a Sid Bass/Richardson company or its subsidiaries. Employee must have a minimum of three years of full-time employment. High school seniors may apply for incoming freshman year. Minimum GPA 2.0.

Award Scholarship for use in freshman year; not renewable. *Number:* 50–60. *Amount:* $500–$7000.

Eligibility Requirements: Applicant must be enrolled or expecting to enroll full or part-time at a two-year or four-year or technical institution or university. Applicant or parent of applicant must have employment or volunteer experience in designated career field. Available to U.S. and non-U.S. citizens.

Application Requirements Application, essay, financial need analysis, test scores, transcript. *Deadline:* May 31.

Contact: Jo Helen Rosasker, Administrator
Sid Richardson Memorial Fund
309 Main Street
Fort Worth, TX 76102
Phone: 817-336-0494
Fax: 817-332-2176
E-mail: jhrosacker@sidrichardson.org

SUBMARINE OFFICERS' WIVES CLUB

BOWFIN MEMORIAL SCHOLARSHIP
• 184

Bowfin Memorial Scholarships are available to Hawaii submariners and their families. Academic scholarships are for children of submariners under 23 years old and Continuing Education Scholarships are for submariners and their dependents.

Bowfin Memorial Scholarship (continued)

Award Scholarship for use in freshman, sophomore, junior, or senior years; not renewable. *Number:* 8–40. *Amount:* $500–$2500.

Eligibility Requirements: Applicant must be enrolled or expecting to enroll full or part-time at a two-year or four-year or technical institution or university and resident of Hawaii. Applicant or parent of applicant must have employment or volunteer experience in designated career field. Available to U.S. citizens. Applicant must have served in the Navy.

Application Requirements Application, essay, financial need analysis, interview, references, transcript. *Deadline:* March 1.

Contact: Scholarship Coordinator
Submarine Officers' Wives Club
121 McGrew Loop
Aiea, HI 96701
Phone: 808-423-1341

TEXAS HIGHER EDUCATION COORDINATING BOARD

TRAIN OUR TEACHERS AWARD • 185

Awarded to employed child care workers seeking credentials or an associate degree in child development. Must agree to work 18 consecutive months in a licensed child care facility. Must attend a Texas institution. For more details and deadlines see web site: http://www.collegefortexans.com.

Award Scholarship for use in freshman or sophomore years; not renewable. *Number:* up to 2000. *Amount:* up to $1000.

Eligibility Requirements: Applicant must be enrolled or expecting to enroll at an institution or university and studying in Texas. Applicant or parent of applicant must have employment or volunteer experience in designated career field.

Application Requirements Application.

World Wide Web: http://www.collegefortexans.com

Contact: Financial Aid Office at college
Texas Higher Education Coordinating Board
PO Box 12788
Austin, TX 78711-2788
Phone: 512-427-6101
Fax: 512-427-6127
E-mail: grantinfo@thecb.state.tx.us

TUITION EXCHANGE, INC.

TUITION EXCHANGE SCHOLARSHIPS • 186

The Tuition Exchange is an association of 530 colleges and universities awarding over 3,400 full or substantial scholarships each year for children and other family members of faculty and staff employed at participating institutions. See web site for complete list of participating institutions. Application procedures and deadlines vary per school. Contact Tuition Exchange Liaison Officer at home institution for details.

Award Scholarship for use in freshman, sophomore, junior, senior, graduate, or postgraduate years; renewable. *Number:* 3400–4000. *Amount:* up to $19,650.

Eligibility Requirements: Applicant must be enrolled or expecting to enroll full or part-time at a two-year or four-year institution or university. Applicant or parent of applicant must have employment or volunteer experience in designated career field. Available to U.S. and non-U.S. citizens.

Application Requirements Application.

World Wide Web: http://www.tuitionexchange.org

Contact: Tuition Exchange Liaison Officer at the college or university where your parent is employed

TWO/TEN INTERNATIONAL FOOTWEAR FOUNDATION

TWO/TEN INTERNATIONAL FOOTWEAR FOUNDATION SCHOLARSHIP
• 187

Renewable, merit- and need-based award available to students who have 500 hours work experience in footwear, leather, or allied industries during year of application, or have a parent employed in one of these fields for at least one year. Must have proof of employment and maintain 2.0 GPA.

Award Scholarship for use in freshman, sophomore, junior, or senior years; renewable. *Number:* 200–250. *Amount:* $200–$3000.

Eligibility Requirements: Applicant must be enrolled or expecting to enroll full-time at a two-year or four-year or technical institution or university. Applicant or parent of applicant must have employment or volunteer experience in leather/footwear. Available to U.S. citizens.

Application Requirements Application, essay, financial need analysis, references, transcript. *Deadline:* January 1.

World Wide Web: http://www.twoten.org

Contact: Catherine Nelson, Scholarship Director
Two/Ten International Footwear Foundation
1466 Main Street
Waltham, MA 02451-1623
Phone: 800-346-3210
Fax: 781-736-1555
E-mail: scholarship@twoten.org

WAL-MART FOUNDATION

WAL-MART ASSOCIATE SCHOLARSHIPS
see number 170

IMPAIRMENT

AMERICAN COUNCIL OF THE BLIND

AMERICAN COUNCIL OF THE BLIND SCHOLARSHIPS • 188

Merit-based award available to undergraduate, graduate, vocational or technical students who are legally blind in both eyes. Submit certificate of legal blindness and proof of acceptance at an accredited postsecondary institution.

Award Scholarship for use in freshman, sophomore, junior, senior, or graduate years; not renewable. *Number:* 30. *Amount:* $500–$5000.

Eligibility Requirements: Applicant must be enrolled or expecting to enroll full-time at a two-year or four-year or technical institution or university. Applicant must be visually impaired. Applicant must have 3.5 GPA or higher.

Application Requirements Application, autobiography, essay, references, transcript. *Deadline:* March 1.

World Wide Web: http://www.acb.org

Contact: Terry Pacheco, Affiliate and Membership Services
American Council of the Blind
1155 15th Street, NW, Suite 1004
Washington, DC 20005
Phone: 202-467-5081
Fax: 202-467-5085
E-mail: info@acb.org

CHAIRSCHOLARS FOUNDATION, INC.

CHAIRSCHOLARS FOUNDATION, INC. SCHOLARSHIPS

see number 175

CYSTIC FIBROSIS SCHOLARSHIP FOUNDATION

CYSTIC FIBROSIS FOUNDATION SCHOLARSHIP • 189

Awards for young adults with cystic fibrosis to be used to further their education after high school. Awards may be used for tuition, books and fees. Awards are for one year. Students may reapply in subsequent years.

Award Scholarship for use in freshman, sophomore, junior, or senior years; not renewable. *Number:* 40–50. *Amount:* $1000–$2000.

Eligibility Requirements: Applicant must be enrolled or expecting to enroll full or part-time at a two-year or four-year or technical institution or university. Applicant must be physically disabled. Available to U.S. citizens.

Application Requirements Application, essay, financial need analysis, references, test scores, transcript. *Deadline:* March 15.

Contact: Mary K. Bottorff, President
Cystic Fibrosis Scholarship Foundation
2814 Grant Street
Evanston, IL 60201
Phone: 847-328-0127
Fax: 847-328-0127
E-mail: mkbcfsf@aol.com

IOWA DIVISION OF VOCATIONAL REHABILITATION SERVICES

IOWA VOCATIONAL REHABILITATION • 190

Provides vocational rehabilitation services to individuals with disabilities who need these services in order to maintain, retain, or obtain employment compatible with their disabilities. Must be Iowa resident.

Award Grant for use in freshman, sophomore, junior, senior, graduate, or postgraduate years; renewable. *Number:* up to 5000. *Amount:* $500–$4000.
Eligibility Requirements: Applicant must be enrolled or expecting to enroll full or part-time at a two-year or four-year or technical institution or university and resident of Iowa. Applicant must be hearing impaired, learning disabled, physically disabled, or visually impaired. Available to U.S. and non-U.S. citizens.
Application Requirements Application, interview. *Deadline:* Continuous.
World Wide Web: http://www.dvrs.state.ia.us
Contact: Ralph Childers, Policy and Workforce Initiatives Coordinator
Iowa Division of Vocational Rehabilitation Services
Division of Vocational Rehabilitation Services
510 East 12th Street
Des Moines, IA 50319
Phone: 515-281-4151
Fax: 515-281-4703
E-mail: rchilders@dvrs.state.ia.us

NATIONAL FEDERATION OF THE BLIND

NATIONAL FEDERATION OF THE BLIND SCHOLARSHIPS
see number 181

MILITARY SERVICE: AIR FORCE_____

AIR FORCE AID SOCIETY

GENERAL HENRY H. ARNOLD EDUCATION GRANT PROGRAM • 191

$1500 grant provided to selected sons and daughters of active duty, Title 10 AGR/Reserve, Title 32 AGR performing full-time active duty, retired reserve

General Henry H. Arnold Education Grant Program (continued)
and deceased Air Force members; spouses (stateside) of active members and Title 10 AGR/Reservist; and surviving spouses of deceased personnel for their undergraduate studies. Dependent children must be unmarried and under the age of 23. High school seniors may apply. Minimum 2.0 GPA is required. Applicant must reapply for subsequent years.

Award Grant for use in freshman, sophomore, junior, or senior years; not renewable. *Number:* 4000–5000. *Amount:* $1500.

Eligibility Requirements: Applicant must be age 23 or under; enrolled or expecting to enroll full-time at a two-year or four-year or technical institution or university and single. Available to U.S. citizens. Applicant or parent must meet one or more of the following requirements: Air Force or Air Force National Guard experience; retired from active duty; disabled or killed as a result of military service; prisoner of war; or missing in action.

Application Requirements Application, financial need analysis, self-addressed stamped envelope, transcript, program's own financial forms, USAF military orders (member/parent). *Deadline:* March 14.

World Wide Web: http://www.afas.org
Contact: Education Assistance Department
Air Force Aid Society
1745 Jefferson Davis Highway, Suite 202
Arlington, VA 22202-3410
Phone: 800-429-9475
Fax: 703-607-3022
E-mail: ed@afas-hq.org

MILITARY SERVICE: AIR FORCE NATIONAL GUARD

GENERAL HENRY H. ARNOLD EDUCATION GRANT PROGRAM
see number 191

DEPARTMENT OF MILITARY AFFAIRS

WISCONSIN NATIONAL GUARD TUITION GRANT • 192

Renewable award for active members of the Wisconsin National Guard in good standing, who successfully complete a course of study at a qualifying school. Award covers full tuition, excluding fees, not to exceed undergraduate tuition charged by University of Wisconsin-Madison. Must have a minimum 2.0 GPA.

Award Grant for use in freshman, sophomore, junior, or senior years; renewable. *Number:* up to 4000. *Amount:* up to $1927.

Eligibility Requirements: Applicant must be enrolled or expecting to enroll full or part-time at a two-year or four-year or technical institution or university and resident of Wisconsin. Applicant must have 2.5 GPA or higher. Available to U.S. citizens. Applicant must have served in the Air Force National Guard or Army National Guard.

Application Requirements Application. *Deadline:* Continuous.

World Wide Web: http://wisconsinguard.com

Contact: Karen Behling, Tuition Grant Administrator
Department of Military Affairs
PO Box 14587
Madison, WI 53714-0587
Phone: 608-242-3159
Fax: 608-242-3154
E-mail: karen.behling@dma.state.wi.us

ILLINOIS STUDENT ASSISTANCE COMMISSION (ISAC)

ILLINOIS NATIONAL GUARD GRANT PROGRAM • 193

Award for qualified National Guard personnel which pays tuition and fees at Illinois public universities and community colleges. Must provide documentation of service. Deadline: September 15.

Award Grant for use in freshman, sophomore, junior, or senior years; renewable. *Number:* 2000–3000. *Amount:* $1300–$1700.

Eligibility Requirements: Applicant must be enrolled or expecting to enroll full or part-time at a two-year or four-year institution or university; resident of Illinois and studying in Illinois. Available to U.S. and non-U.S. citizens. Applicant must have served in the Air Force National Guard or Army National Guard.

Application Requirements Application, documentation of service. *Deadline:* September 15.

World Wide Web: http://www.isac-online.org

Contact: David Barinholtz, Client Information
Illinois Student Assistance Commission (ISAC)
1755 Lake Cook Road
Deerfield, IL 60015-5209
Phone: 847-948-8500 Ext. 2385
E-mail: cssupport@isac.org

KANSAS NATIONAL GUARD EDUCATIONAL ASSISTANCE PROGRAM

KANSAS NATIONAL GUARD EDUCATIONAL ASSISTANCE AWARD PROGRAM • 194

Service scholarship for enlisted soldiers in the Kansas National Guard. Pays up to 100% of tuition and fees based on funding. Must attend a state-supported institution. Recipients will be required to serve in the KNG for four years after the last payment of state tuition assistance. Must not have over 15 years of

Kansas National Guard Educational Assistance Award Program (continued)
service at time of application. Deadlines are January 15 and August 20. Contact KNG Education Services Specialist for further information. Must be Kansas resident.

Award Scholarship for use in freshman, sophomore, junior, or senior years; not renewable. *Number:* up to 400. *Amount:* $250–$3500.

Eligibility Requirements: Applicant must be enrolled or expecting to enroll full or part-time at a two-year or four-year or technical institution or university; resident of Kansas and studying in Kansas. Available to U.S. citizens. Applicant must have served in the Air Force National Guard or Army National Guard.

Application Requirements Application.

Contact: Steve Finch, Education Services Specialist
Kansas National Guard Educational Assistance Program
Attn: AGKS-DOP-ESO, The Adjutant General of Kansas
2800 South West Topeka Boulevard
Topeka, KS 66611-1287
Phone: 785-274-1060
Fax: 785-274-1617
E-mail: steve.finch@ks.ngb.army.mil

OHIO NATIONAL GUARD

OHIO NATIONAL GUARD SCHOLARSHIP PROGRAM • 195

Scholarships are for undergraduate studies at an approved Ohio postsecondary institution. Applicants must enlist for six years of Selective Service Reserve Duty in the Ohio National Guard. Scholarship pays 100% instructional and general fees for public institutions and an average of cost of public schools is available for private schools. Must be 18 years of age or older. Award is renewable. Deadlines: July 1, November 1, February 1, April 1.

Award Scholarship for use in freshman, sophomore, junior, or senior years; renewable. *Number:* 3500–10,000. *Amount:* up to $3000.

Eligibility Requirements: Applicant must be age 18; enrolled or expecting to enroll full or part-time at a two-year or four-year or technical institution or university and studying in Ohio. Available to U.S. citizens. Applicant must have served in the Air Force National Guard or Army National Guard.

Application Requirements Application.

Contact: Mrs. Toni Davis, Grants Administrator
Ohio National Guard
2825 West Dublin Granville Road
Columbus, OH 43235-2789
Phone: 614-336-7032
Fax: 614-336-7318
E-mail: toni.davis@tagoh.org

STATE OF GEORGIA

GEORGIA NATIONAL GUARD SERVICE CANCELABLE LOAN PROGRAM • 196

Forgivable loans will be awarded to residents of Georgia maintaining good military standing as an eligible member of the Georgia National Guard who are enrolled at least half-time in an undergraduate degree program at an eligible college, university or technical school within the state of Georgia.

Award Forgivable loan for use in freshman, sophomore, junior, or senior years; not renewable. *Number:* 200–250. *Amount:* $150–$1395.

Eligibility Requirements: Applicant must be enrolled or expecting to enroll full or part-time at a two-year or four-year or technical institution or university; resident of Georgia and studying in Georgia. Available to U.S. citizens. Applicant must have served in the Air Force National Guard or Army National Guard.

Application Requirements Application, financial need analysis. *Deadline:* Continuous.

World Wide Web: http://www.gsfc.org

Contact: Peggy Matthews, Manager/GSFA Originations
State of Georgia
2082 East Exchange Place, Suite 230
Tucker, GA 30084-5305
Phone: 770-724-9230
Fax: 770-724-9263
E-mail: peggy@mail.gsfc.state.ga.us

STATE STUDENT ASSISTANCE COMMISSION OF INDIANA (SSACI)

INDIANA NATIONAL GUARD SUPPLEMENTAL GRANT • 197

One-time award, which is a supplement to the Indiana Higher Education Grant program. Applicants must be members of the Indiana National Guard. All Guard paperwork must be completed prior to the start of each semester. The FAFSA must be received by March 10. Award covers tuition and fees at select public colleges.

Award Grant for use in freshman, sophomore, junior, or senior years; not renewable. *Number:* 350–870. *Amount:* $200–$5314.

Eligibility Requirements: Applicant must be enrolled or expecting to enroll full or part-time at a two-year or four-year institution or university; resident of Indiana and studying in Indiana. Available to U.S. citizens. Applicant must have served in the Air Force National Guard or Army National Guard.

Application Requirements Application, financial need analysis. *Deadline:* March 10.

World Wide Web: http://www.ssaci.in.gov

Indiana National Guard Supplemental Grant (continued)
Contact: Grants Counselor
State Student Assistance Commission of Indiana (SSACI)
150 West Market Street, Suite 500
Indianapolis, IN 46204-2805
Phone: 317-232-2350
Fax: 317-232-2360
E-mail: grants@ssaci.state.in.us

WASHINGTON NATIONAL GUARD

WASHINGTON NATIONAL GUARD SCHOLARSHIP PROGRAM • 198

A state funded retention incentive/loan program for both Washington Army and Air Guard members meeting all eligibility requirements. The loans are forgiven if the soldier/airman completes their service requirements. Failure to meet/complete service obligations incurs the requirement to repay the loan plus 8% interest. Minimum 2.5 GPA required. Deadline is April 30.

Award Forgivable loan for use in freshman, sophomore, junior, or senior years; not renewable. *Number:* up to 60. *Amount:* $200–$4000.

Eligibility Requirements: Applicant must be enrolled or expecting to enroll full or part-time at a two-year or four-year or technical institution or university and resident of Washington. Applicant must have 2.5 GPA or higher. Available to U.S. and non-U.S. citizens. Applicant must have served in the Air Force National Guard or Army National Guard.

Application Requirements Application, transcript, enlistment/extension documents. *Deadline:* April 30.

World Wide Web: http://www.washingtonguard.com/education/education. htm

Contact: Mark Rhoden, Educational Services Officer
Washington National Guard
Building 15, Camp Murray
Tacoma, WA 98430-5073
Phone: 253-512-8899
Fax: 253-512-8936
E-mail: mark.rhoden@wa.ngb.army.mil

MILITARY SERVICE: ARMY_____

DEPARTMENT OF THE ARMY

ARMY ROTC HISTORICALLY BLACK COLLEGES AND UNIVERSITIES PROGRAM
• 199

One-time award for students attending college for the first time or freshmen in a documented five-year degree program. Must attend a historically black college or university and must join school's ROTC program. Must pass physical. Must have a qualifying SAT or ACT score and submit a teacher evaluation. Applicant must be 18 by October 1 and under 27 years of age on June 30 in the year of graduation.

Award Scholarship for use in freshman or sophomore years; not renewable. *Number:* 180–250. *Amount:* $5000–$16,000.

Eligibility Requirements: Applicant must be age 18-26 and enrolled or expecting to enroll full-time at a four-year institution or university. Applicant must have 2.5 GPA or higher. Available to U.S. citizens. Applicant must have served in the Army or Army National Guard.

Application Requirements Application, essay, interview, references, test scores, transcript. *Deadline:* November 16.

World Wide Web: http://www.rotc.monroe.army.mil

Contact: Goldquest Center, Army ROTC Scholarships
Department of the Army
U.S. Army Cadet Command
Fort Monroe, VA 23651-5000
Phone: 800-USA-ROTC
E-mail: rotcinfo@monroe.army.mil

ARMY ROTC TWO-YEAR, THREE-YEAR AND FOUR-YEAR SCHOLARSHIPS FOR ACTIVE DUTY ARMY ENLISTED PERSONNEL
• 200

Award for freshman, sophomore, and junior year for use at a four-year institution for Army enlisted personnel. Merit considered. Must also be member of the school's ROTC program. Must pass physical and have completed two years of active duty. Applicant must be 18 years of age by October 1 and under 27 years of age on June 30 in the year of graduation. Submit recommendations from Commanding Officer and Field Grade Commander. Include DODMERB Physical Forms and DA Form 2A.

Award Scholarship for use in freshman, sophomore, or junior years; not renewable. *Number:* 150–350. *Amount:* $5000–$16,000.

Eligibility Requirements: Applicant must be age 18-26 and enrolled or expecting to enroll full-time at a four-year institution or university. Applicant must have 2.5 GPA or higher. Available to U.S. citizens. Applicant must have served in the Army or Army National Guard.

Application Requirements Application, essay, photo, references, test scores, transcript, DA Form 2A, DODMERB physical, APFT, GT. *Deadline:* April 1.

World Wide Web: http://www.rotc.monroe.army.mil

Contact: Goldquest Center, Army ROTC Scholarships
Department of the Army
U.S. Army Cadet Command
Fort Monroe, VA 23651-5000
Phone: 800-USA-ROTC
E-mail: rotcinfo@monroe.army.mil

FOUR-YEAR AND THREE-YEAR ADVANCE DESIGNEES SCHOLARSHIP • 201

One-time award for students entering college for the first time or freshmen in a documented five-year degree program. Must join school's ROTC program. Must pass physical and submit teacher evaluations. Must be a U.S. citizen and have a qualifying SAT or ACT score. Applicant must be 18 years of age by October 1 and under 27 years of age on June 30 in the year of graduation. On-line application available.

Award Scholarship for use in freshman or sophomore years; not renewable. *Number:* 700–3000. *Amount:* $5000–$20,000.

Eligibility Requirements: Applicant must be age 18-26 and enrolled or expecting to enroll full-time at a four-year institution. Applicant must have 2.5 GPA or higher. Available to U.S. citizens. Applicant must have served in the Army or Army National Guard.

Application Requirements Application, essay, interview, references, test scores, transcript. *Deadline:* November 15.

World Wide Web: http://www.rotc.monroe.army.mil

Contact: Goldquest Center, Army ROTC Scholarships
Department of the Army
U.S. Army Cadet Command
Fort Monroe, VA 23651-5000
Phone: 800-USA-ROTC
E-mail: rotcinfo@monroe.army.mil

TWO- AND THREE-YEAR CAMPUS-BASED SCHOLARSHIPS • 202

One-time award for college sophomores or juniors or students with BA who need two years to obtain graduate degree. Must be a member of school's ROTC program. Must pass physical. Minimum 2.5 GPA required. Professor of military science must submit application. Applicant must be 18 years of age by October 1 and under 27 years of age on June 30 in the year of graduation. Deadline for college sophomores is April 15 and for college juniors and graduate students is June 1.

Award Scholarship for use in sophomore, junior, or graduate years; not renewable. *Number:* 250–1500. *Amount:* $5000–$16,000.

Eligibility Requirements: Applicant must be age 18-26 and enrolled or expecting to enroll full-time at a four-year institution. Applicant must have 2.5 GPA or higher. Available to U.S. citizens. Applicant must have served in the Army or Army National Guard.

Application Requirements Application, test scores, transcript.

World Wide Web: http://www.rotc.monroe.army.mil

Contact: Goldquest Center, Army ROTC Scholarships
Department of the Army
U.S. Army Cadet Command
Fort Monroe, VA 23651-5000
Phone: 800-USA-ROTC
E-mail: rotcinfo@monroe.army.mil

MILITARY SERVICE: ARMY NATIONAL GUARD

DEPARTMENT OF MILITARY AFFAIRS

WISCONSIN NATIONAL GUARD TUITION GRANT
see number 192

DEPARTMENT OF THE ARMY

ARMY ROTC HISTORICALLY BLACK COLLEGES AND UNIVERSITIES PROGRAM
see number 199

ARMY ROTC TWO-YEAR, THREE-YEAR AND FOUR-YEAR SCHOLARSHIPS FOR ACTIVE DUTY ARMY ENLISTED PERSONNEL
see number 200

DEDICATED MILITARY JUNIOR COLLEGE PROGRAM • 203

One-time award for high school graduates who wish to attend a two-year military junior college. Must serve simultaneously in the Army National Guard or Reserve and qualify for the ROTC Advanced Course. Must have a minimum GPA of 2.5. Must also be 18 years of age by October 1 and under 27 years of age on June 30 in the year of graduation. On-line application available. Deadline: August 25. Must be used at one of five military junior colleges.

Award Scholarship for use in freshman year; not renewable. *Number:* 60. *Amount:* up to $20,000.

Eligibility Requirements: Applicant must be age 18-26 and enrolled or expecting to enroll full-time at a two-year institution. Applicant must have 2.5 GPA or higher. Available to U.S. citizens. Applicant must have served in the Army National Guard.

Application Requirements Application, essay, interview, test scores, transcript. *Deadline:* August 25.

World Wide Web: http://www.rotc.monroe.army.mil

Contact: Goldquest Center, Army ROTC Scholarships
Department of the Army
U.S. Army Cadet Command
Fort Monroe, VA 23651-5000
Phone: 800-USA-ROTC
E-mail: rotcinfo@monroe.army.mil

FOUR-YEAR AND THREE-YEAR ADVANCE DESIGNEES SCHOLARSHIP
see number 201

TWO- AND THREE-YEAR CAMPUS-BASED SCHOLARSHIPS
see number 202

TWO-YEAR RESERVE FORCES DUTY SCHOLARSHIPS • 204

One-time award for college juniors or two-year graduate degree students. Must be a member of school's ROTC program. Must pass physical. Minimum 2.5 GPA required. Applicant must be 18 years of age by October 1 and under 27 years of age on June 30 in the year of graduation.

Award Scholarship for use in junior, or graduate years; not renewable. *Number:* 140–300. *Amount:* $5000–$16,000.

Eligibility Requirements: Applicant must be age 18-26 and enrolled or expecting to enroll full-time at a four-year institution or university. Applicant must have 2.5 GPA or higher. Available to U.S. citizens. Applicant must have served in the Army National Guard.

Application Requirements Application, transcript. *Deadline:* April 16.

World Wide Web: http://www.rotc.monroe.army.mil

Contact: Goldquest Center, Army ROTC Scholarships
Department of the Army
U.S. Army Cadet Command
Fort Monroe, VA 23651-5000
Phone: 800-USA-ROTC
E-mail: rotcinfo@monroe.army.mil

ILLINOIS STUDENT ASSISTANCE COMMISSION (ISAC)

ILLINOIS NATIONAL GUARD GRANT PROGRAM   see number 193

KANSAS NATIONAL GUARD EDUCATIONAL ASSISTANCE PROGRAM

KANSAS NATIONAL GUARD EDUCATIONAL ASSISTANCE AWARD PROGRAM   see number 194

OHIO NATIONAL GUARD

OHIO NATIONAL GUARD SCHOLARSHIP PROGRAM   see number 195

STATE OF GEORGIA

GEORGIA NATIONAL GUARD SERVICE CANCELABLE LOAN PROGRAM   see number 196

STATE STUDENT ASSISTANCE COMMISSION OF INDIANA (SSACI)

INDIANA NATIONAL GUARD SUPPLEMENTAL GRANT   see number 197

WASHINGTON NATIONAL GUARD

WASHINGTON NATIONAL GUARD SCHOLARSHIP PROGRAM
see number 198

MILITARY SERVICE: GENERAL___

AMERICAN LEGION, DEPARTMENT OF ALABAMA

AMERICAN LEGION DEPARTMENT OF ALABAMA SCHOLARSHIP PROGRAM
• 205

Renewable award for Alabama residents directly related to any war veteran. Parents must be legal residents of Alabama. Send self-addressed stamped envelope to receive scholarship application, list of available schools, and instructions.

Award Scholarship for use in freshman, sophomore, junior, or senior years; renewable. *Number:* 150. *Amount:* $850.

Eligibility Requirements: Applicant must be enrolled or expecting to enroll full or part-time at a four-year institution or university; resident of Alabama and studying in Alabama. Available to U.S. citizens. Applicant or parent must meet one or more of the following requirements: general military experience; retired from active duty; disabled or killed as a result of military service; prisoner of war; or missing in action.

Application Requirements Application, photo, references, self-addressed stamped envelope, test scores, transcript. *Deadline:* May 1.

World Wide Web: http://www.alabamalegion.org

Contact: Braxton Bridgers, Department Adjutant
American Legion, Department of Alabama
PO Box 1069
Montgomery, AL 36101-1069
Phone: 334-285-2225
E-mail: allegion@bellsouth.net

EXPLOSIVE ORDNANCE DISPOSAL MEMORIAL COMMITTEE

EXPLOSIVE ORDNANCE DISPOSAL SCHOLARSHIP
see number 177

ILLINOIS STUDENT ASSISTANCE COMMISSION (ISAC)

ILLINOIS VETERAN GRANT PROGRAM—IVG   • 206

Award for qualified veterans for tuition and fees at Illinois public universities and community colleges. Must provide documentation of service (DD214). Deadline is continuous.

Award Grant for use in freshman, sophomore, junior, or senior years; renewable. *Number:* 11,000–13,000. *Amount:* $1400–$1600.

Eligibility Requirements: Applicant must be enrolled or expecting to enroll full or part-time at a two-year or four-year institution or university; resident of Illinois and studying in Illinois. Available to U.S. and non-U.S. citizens. Applicant must have general military experience.

Application Requirements Application, documentation of service. *Deadline:* Continuous.

World Wide Web: http://www.isac-online.org

Contact: David Barinholtz, Client Information
           Illinois Student Assistance Commission (ISAC)
           1755 Lake Cook Road
           Deerfield, IL 60015-5209
           Phone: 847-948-8500 Ext. 2385
           E-mail: cssupport@isac.org

MILITARY OFFICERS ASSOCIATION OF AMERICA (MOAA)

MOAA BASE/POST SCHOLARSHIP   • 207

Recipients are randomly selected from dependent sons and daughters of active duty officers and enlisted military personnel. Eligible applicants will be under the age of 24. For more details and an application go to web site: http://www.moaa.org.

Award Scholarship for use in freshman, sophomore, junior, or senior years; not renewable. *Number:* 100. *Amount:* $1000.

Eligibility Requirements: Applicant must be age 23 or under; enrolled or expecting to enroll full-time at a two-year or four-year institution or university and single. Available to U.S. citizens. Applicant or parent must meet one or more of the following requirements: general military experience; retired from active duty; disabled or killed as a result of military service; prisoner of war; or missing in action.

Application Requirements Application, test scores, transcript, service parent's Leave and Earning Statement (LES). *Deadline:* March 1.

World Wide Web: http://www.moaa.org

Contact: application available at web site

NORTH CAROLINA DIVISION OF VETERANS' AFFAIRS

NORTH CAROLINA VETERANS' SCHOLARSHIPS CLASS II • 208

Renewable awards for children of veterans rated by U.S.DVA as much as 20% but less than 100% disabled due to wartime service as defined in the law, or was awarded Purple Heart Medal for wounds received. Parent must have been a North Carolina resident at time of entry into service. Duration of the scholarship is four academic years (8 semesters) if used within 8 years. Free tuition and exemption from certain mandatory fees as set forth in the law in Public, Community & Technical Colleges/Institutions. See web site for details and where to procure an application. $4500 per nine month academic year in Private Colleges & Junior Colleges. 100 awarded each year. Deadline is March 31.

Award Scholarship for use in freshman, sophomore, junior, or senior years; renewable. *Number:* 100. *Amount:* up to $4500.

Eligibility Requirements: Applicant must be enrolled or expecting to enroll full or part-time at a two-year or four-year or technical institution or university and studying in North Carolina. Available to U.S. citizens. Applicant or parent must meet one or more of the following requirements: general military experience; retired from active duty; disabled or killed as a result of military service; prisoner of war; or missing in action.

Application Requirements Application, financial need analysis, interview, transcript. *Deadline:* March 31.

Contact: Charles Smith, Director
North Carolina Division of Veterans' Affairs
325 North Salisbury Street
Raleigh, NC 27603
Phone: 919-733-3851
Fax: 919-733-2834

NORTH CAROLINA VETERANS' SCHOLARSHIPS CLASS III • 209

Renewable awards for children of a veteran who died or was, at time of death, drawing a pension for total and permanent disability as rated by U.S.DVA, was honorably discharged and does not a qualify for Class I, II, or IV, scholarships, or served in a combat zone or waters adjacent to a combat zone and received a campaign badge or medal and does not qualify under Class I, II, IV, or V. Parent must have been a North Carolina resident at time of entry into service. Duration of the scholarship is four academic years (8 semesters) if used within eight years. Free tuition and exemption from certain mandatory fees as set forth in the law in Public, Community & Technical Colleges/Institutions. $4500 per nine month academic year in Private Colleges & Junior Colleges. See web site for details and where to procure an application. 100 awarded each year. Deadline is March 31.

Award Scholarship for use in freshman, sophomore, junior, or senior years; renewable. *Number:* 100. *Amount:* up to $4500.

North Carolina Veterans' Scholarships Class III (continued)

Eligibility Requirements: Applicant must be enrolled or expecting to enroll full or part-time at a two-year or four-year or technical institution or university and studying in North Carolina. Available to U.S. citizens. Applicant or parent must meet one or more of the following requirements: general military experience; retired from active duty; disabled or killed as a result of military service; prisoner of war; or missing in action.

Application Requirements Application, financial need analysis, interview, transcript. *Deadline:* March 31.

Contact: Charles Smith, Director
North Carolina Division of Veterans' Affairs
325 North Salisbury Street
Raleigh, NC 27603
Phone: 919-733-3851
Fax: 919-733-2834

RED RIVER VALLEY ASSOCIATION, INC.

RED RIVER VALLEY ASSOCIATION SCHOLARSHIP GRANT PROGRAM
• 210

Annual college tuition grants for legal dependents of U.S. military members listed as Killed in Action or Missing in Action; or of military aircrew members killed while performing aircrew duties on non-combat missions. Must submit DD Form 1300. Amount of award varies.

Award Grant for use in freshman, sophomore, junior, senior, or graduate years; not renewable. *Number:* 10–40. *Amount:* $500–$4000.

Eligibility Requirements: Applicant must be enrolled or expecting to enroll full or part-time at a two-year or four-year or technical institution or university. Available to U.S. citizens. Applicant or parent must meet one or more of the following requirements: general military experience; retired from active duty; disabled or killed as a result of military service; prisoner of war; or missing in action.

Application Requirements Application, financial need analysis, photo, references, test scores, transcript. *Deadline:* May 15.

World Wide Web: http://www.river-rats.org

Contact: Col. Al Bache, Executive Director
Red River Valley Association, Inc.
PO Box 882
Boothbay Harbor, ME 04538-0882
Phone: 207-633-0333
Fax: 207-633-0330
E-mail: afbridger@aol.com

MILITARY SERVICE: MARINES_____

UNITED STATES MARINE CORPS SCHOLARSHIP FOUNDATION, INC.

MARINE CORPS SCHOLARSHIP FOUNDATION • 211

Available to undergraduate dependent children of current or former Marine Corps members whose family income does not exceed $54,000. Must submit proof of parent's service and should send for applications in the winter.

Award Scholarship for use in freshman, sophomore, junior, or senior years; not renewable. *Number:* 1000. *Amount:* $500–$2500.

Eligibility Requirements: Applicant must be enrolled or expecting to enroll at a two-year or four-year or technical institution or university. Available to U.S. citizens. Applicant or parent must meet one or more of the following requirements: Marine Corp experience; retired from active duty; disabled or killed as a result of military service; prisoner of war; or missing in action.

Application Requirements Application, essay, financial need analysis, photo, transcript. *Deadline:* April 1.

World Wide Web: http://www.marine-scholars.org

Contact: United States Marine Corps Scholarship Foundation, Inc.
PO Box 3008
Princeton, NJ 08543-3008

MILITARY SERVICE: NAVY_____

DOLPHIN SCHOLARSHIP FOUNDATION

DOLPHIN SCHOLARSHIPS • 212

Renewable award for undergraduate students under 24 years of age. Must be dependent children or stepchildren of members or former members of Submarine Force-qualified submariners who served for a minimum of eight years, or of Navy members who served minimum ten years in submarine support. Based on academic merit, need, and leadership.

Award Scholarship for use in freshman, sophomore, junior, or senior years; renewable. *Number:* 25–30. *Amount:* up to $3000.

Eligibility Requirements: Applicant must be age 23 or under; enrolled or expecting to enroll full-time at a four-year institution or university and single. Available to U.S. citizens. Applicant or parent must meet one or more of the following requirements: Navy experience; retired from active duty; disabled or killed as a result of military service; prisoner of war; or missing in action.

Application Requirements Application, essay, financial need analysis, references, self-addressed stamped envelope, test scores, transcript. *Deadline:* March 15.

Dolphin Scholarships (continued)
World Wide Web: http://www.dolphinscholarship.org
Contact: Tomi Roeske, Scholarship Administrator
Dolphin Scholarship Foundation
5040 Virginia Beach Boulevard, Suite 104A
Virginia Beach, VA 23462
Phone: 757-671-3200
Fax: 757-671-3330

SEABEE MEMORIAL SCHOLARSHIP ASSOCIATION, INC.

SEABEE MEMORIAL ASSOCIATION SCHOLARSHIP • 213

Award available to children or grandchildren of current or former members of the Naval Construction Force (Seabees) or Naval Civil Engineer Corps. High school students may apply. Not available for graduate study or to great-grandchildren of Seabees.

Award Scholarship for use in freshman, sophomore, junior, or senior years; renewable. *Number:* 86. *Amount:* $2200.

Eligibility Requirements: Applicant must be enrolled or expecting to enroll full-time at a four-year institution. Available to U.S. citizens. Applicant or parent must meet one or more of the following requirements: Navy experience; retired from active duty; disabled or killed as a result of military service; prisoner of war; or missing in action.

Application Requirements Application, essay, financial need analysis, test scores, transcript. *Deadline:* May 1.

World Wide Web: http://www.seabee.org
Contact: Sheryl Chiogioji, Administrative Assistant
Seabee Memorial Scholarship Association, Inc.
PO Box 6574
Silver Spring, MD 20916
Phone: 301-570-2850
Fax: 301-570-2873
E-mail: smsa@erols.com

SUBMARINE OFFICERS' WIVES CLUB

BOWFIN MEMORIAL SCHOLARSHIP   see number 184

NATIONALITY OR ETHNIC HERITAGE___

ALBERTA HERITAGE SCHOLARSHIP FUND

ADULT HIGH SCHOOL EQUIVALENCY SCHOLARSHIPS • 214

Designed to recognize outstanding achievement in the attainment of high school equivalency. Students are eligible if they have been out of high school for three years, have achieved a minimum average of 80 per cent as a full-time student in courses required for entry into a postsecondary program, and are nominated by their institution. Two hundred awards of CAN$500. Must study in and be a resident of Alberta, Canada. Nomination deadline: September 1.

Award Scholarship for use in freshman year; not renewable. *Number:* 200. *Amount:* $500.

Eligibility Requirements: Applicant must be Canadian citizenship; enrolled or expecting to enroll full-time at a two-year or four-year or technical institution or university; resident of Alberta and studying in Alberta. Applicant must have 3.0 GPA or higher.

Application Requirements Application. *Deadline:* September 1.

World Wide Web: http://www.alis.gov.ab.ca/scholarships

Contact: Alberta Heritage Scholarship Fund
9940 106th Street, 9th Floor, Box 28000 Station Main
Edmonton, AB T5J 4R4
Canada
Phone: 780-427-8640
Fax: 780-422-4516
E-mail: heritage@gov.ab.ca

ALEXANDER RUTHERFORD SCHOLARSHIPS FOR HIGH SCHOOL ACHIEVEMENT
● 215

The scholarships are awarded to students earning a minimum of 80% in five designated subjects in grades 10, 11, and 12. The scholarships are valued at CAN$400 for grade 10; CAN$800 for grade 11; and CAN$1300 for grade 12. Applicants must be Alberta residents who plan to enroll in a full-time postsecondary program. May 1 deadline for September entry; December 1 deadline for January entry.

Award Scholarship for use in freshman year; not renewable. *Number:* 7500. *Amount:* $400–$2500.

Eligibility Requirements: Applicant must be Canadian citizenship; high school student; planning to enroll or expecting to enroll full-time at a two-year or four-year or technical institution or university and resident of Alberta. Applicant must have 3.0 GPA or higher.

Application Requirements Application, transcript.

World Wide Web: http://www.alis.gov.ab.ca/scholarships

Contact: Alberta Heritage Scholarship Fund
9940 106th Street, 9th Floor, Box 28000 Station Main
Edmonton, AB T5J 4R4
Canada
Phone: 780-427-8640
Fax: 780-422-4516
E-mail: heritage@gov.ab.ca

FELLOWSHIPS FOR FULL-TIME STUDIES IN FRENCH-UNIVERSITY   • 216

One-time awards for Canadian citizens who are Alberta residents pursuing full-time postsecondary studies in French in any discipline at a Canadian university. Travel grant is available for studies outside of Alberta. Awards valued at CAN$1000 per semester.

Award Scholarship for use in freshman, sophomore, junior, or senior years; not renewable. *Number:* 300. *Amount:* up to $2000.

Eligibility Requirements: Applicant must be Canadian citizenship; enrolled or expecting to enroll full-time at a four-year institution or university and resident of Alberta.

Application Requirements Application, transcript. *Deadline:* November 15.

World Wide Web: http://www.alis.gov.ab.ca/scholarships

Contact: Director
Alberta Heritage Scholarship Fund
9940 106th Street, 9th Floor, Box 28000 Station Main
Edmonton, AB T5J 4R4
Canada
Phone: 780-427-8640
Fax: 780-422-4516
E-mail: heritage@gov.ab.ca

JIMMIE CONDON ATHLETIC SCHOLARSHIPS   • 217

One-time award for Canadian citizens who are residents of Alberta and are full-time students in Alberta and members of sports teams. Must be nominated and maintaining at least a 65% average.

Award Scholarship for use in freshman, sophomore, junior, senior, or graduate years; not renewable. *Number:* 1800. *Amount:* $1800.

Eligibility Requirements: Applicant must be Canadian citizenship; enrolled or expecting to enroll full-time at a two-year or four-year or technical institution or university; resident of Alberta; studying in Alberta and must have an interest in athletics/sports. Applicant must have 2.5 GPA or higher.

Application Requirements Application. *Deadline:* November 1.

World Wide Web: http://www.alis.gov.ab.ca/scholarships

Contact: Alberta Heritage Scholarship Fund
9940 106th Street, 9th Floor, Box 28000 Station Main
Edmonton, AB T5J 4R4
Canada
Phone: 780-427-8640
Fax: 780-422-4516
E-mail: heritage@gov.ab.ca

LOUISE MCKINNEY POSTSECONDARY SCHOLARSHIPS   • 218

Students enrolled in programs within Alberta are nominated by the awards office of their institution. Albertans enrolled in programs outside the province because their program of study is not offered in Alberta should contact the

Alberta Heritage Scholarship Fund office. Must be a resident of Alberta. Must be ranked in upper quarter of class or have a minimum 3.5 GPA.

Award Scholarship for use in sophomore, junior, senior, or graduate years; renewable. *Number:* 950. *Amount:* $2500.

Eligibility Requirements: Applicant must be Canadian citizenship; enrolled or expecting to enroll full-time at a two-year or four-year institution or university and resident of Alberta. Applicant must have 3.5 GPA or higher.

Application Requirements Application, transcript. *Deadline:* June 1.

World Wide Web: http://www.alis.gov.ab.ca/scholarships

Contact: Alberta Heritage Scholarship Fund
9940 106th Street, 9th Floor, Box 28000 Station Main
Edmonton, AB T5J 4R4
Canada
Phone: 780-427-8640
Fax: 780-422-4516
E-mail: heritage@gov.ab.ca

NORTHERN ALBERTA DEVELOPMENT COUNCIL BURSARIES • 219

Applicants must have been residents of Alberta for a minimum of three years prior to applying. Students should also be in their latter years of academic study. Recipients are required to live and work for one year within the Northern Alberta Development Council boundary upon graduation.

Award Scholarship for use in junior, senior, or graduate years; not renewable. *Number:* 200–250. *Amount:* up to $3000.

Eligibility Requirements: Applicant must be Canadian citizenship; enrolled or expecting to enroll full-time at a two-year or four-year or technical institution or university and resident of Alberta. Applicant must have 2.5 GPA or higher.

Application Requirements Application, essay, financial need analysis, transcript. *Deadline:* May 15.

World Wide Web: http://www.alis.gov.ab.ca/scholarships

Contact: Alberta Heritage Scholarship Fund
9940 106th Street, 9th Floor, Box 28000 Station Main
Edmonton, AB T5J 4R4
Canada
Phone: 780-427-8640
Fax: 780-422-4516
E-mail: heritage@gov.ab.ca

PERSONS CASE SCHOLARSHIPS • 220

Awards recognize students whose studies will contribute to the advancement of women, or who are studying in fields where members of their sex are traditionally few in number. Selection is based on program of studies, academic achievement and financial need. Awards range from CAN$1000 to CAN$5000. A maximum of CAN$20,000 is available each year. Must study in and be a resident of Alberta, Canada. Must be ranked in upper third of class or have a minimum 3.0 GPA.

Persons Case Scholarships (continued)

Award Scholarship for use in freshman, sophomore, junior, or senior years; not renewable. *Number:* 5–20. *Amount:* $1000–$5000.

Eligibility Requirements: Applicant must be Canadian citizenship; enrolled or expecting to enroll full-time at a two-year or four-year or technical institution or university; resident of Alberta and studying in Alberta. Applicant must have 3.0 GPA or higher.

Application Requirements Application, essay, transcript. *Deadline:* September 30.

World Wide Web: http://www.alis.gov.ab.ca/scholarships

Contact: Alberta Heritage Scholarship Fund
9940 106th Street, 9th Floor, Box 28000 Station Main
Edmonton, AB T5J 4R4
Canada
Phone: 780-427-8640
Fax: 780-422-4516
E-mail: heritage@gov.ab.ca

AMERICAN INSTITUTE FOR FOREIGN STUDY

AMERICAN INSTITUTE FOR FOREIGN STUDY MINORITY SCHOLARSHIPS

● **221**

Applications will be accepted from African-Americans, Asian-Americans, Native-Americans, Hispanic-Americans and Pacific Islanders who are currently enrolled as undergraduates at a U.S. institution applying to an AIFS study abroad program. Applicants must demonstrate financial need, leadership ability, and academic accomplishment and meet program requirements. One full scholarship and three runners-up scholarships are awarded each semester. Submit application by April 15 for fall or October 15 for spring. Application fees are $75.

Award Scholarship for use in sophomore, junior, or senior years; not renewable. *Number:* 8. *Amount:* $2000–$11,500.

Eligibility Requirements: Applicant must be American Indian/Alaska Native, Asian/Pacific Islander, Black (non-Hispanic), or Hispanic; age 17; enrolled or expecting to enroll full-time at a two-year or four-year institution or university and must have an interest in leadership. Applicant must have 3.0 GPA or higher. Available to U.S. and non-U.S. citizens.

Application Requirements Application, essay, financial need analysis, photo, references, transcript. *Fee:* $75.

World Wide Web: http://www.aifsabroad.com

Contact: David Mauro, Admissions Counselor
American Institute for Foreign Study
River Plaza, 9 West Broad Street
Stamford, CT 06902-3788
Phone: 800-727-2437 Ext. 5163
Fax: 203-399-5598
E-mail: college.info@aifs.com

ARMENIAN STUDENTS ASSOCIATION OF AMERICA, INC.

ARMENIAN STUDENTS ASSOCIATION OF AMERICA, INC. SCHOLARSHIPS
• 222

One-time award for students of Armenian descent. Must be undergraduate in sophomore, junior, or senior years, or graduate student, attending accredited U.S. institution full-time. Award based on need, merit, and character. Show proof of tuition costs and enrollment. Application fee: $15.

Award Scholarship for use in sophomore, junior, senior, or graduate years; not renewable. *Number:* 30. *Amount:* $1000–$3500.

Eligibility Requirements: Applicant must be of Armenian heritage and enrolled or expecting to enroll full-time at a four-year institution or university.

Application Requirements Application, essay, financial need analysis, references, transcript. *Fee:* $15. *Deadline:* March 15.

Contact: Nathalie Yaghoobian, Scholarship Administrator
Armenian Students Association of America, Inc.
333 Atlantic Avenue
Warwick, RI 02888
Phone: 401-461-6114
Fax: 401-461-6112
E-mail: headasa.com@aol.com

ASSOCIATION OF UNIVERSITIES AND COLLEGES OF CANADA

FAIRFAX FINANCIAL HOLDINGS LIMITED SCHOLARSHIP PROGRAM
• 223

At least sixty scholarships (36 at university level and 24 at college level). Students enrolled in undergraduate university program receive CAN$5000. Students pursuing college diploma receiveCAN$3500. Must be Canadian citizen or permanent resident. Applications are by nomination only; each eligible institution may nominate only one candidate.

Award Scholarship for use in freshman, sophomore, junior, or senior years; renewable. *Number:* 60. *Amount:* $3500–$5000.

Eligibility Requirements: Applicant must be Canadian citizenship and enrolled or expecting to enroll full-time at a two-year or four-year institution or university.

Application Requirements Application, financial need analysis, references, transcript. *Deadline:* July 2.

World Wide Web: http://www.aucc.ca/

Contact: Higher Education Scholarships
Association of Universities and Colleges of Canada
350 Albert Street, Suite 600
Ottawa, ON K1R 1B1
Canada
E-mail: awards@aucc.ca

BLACKFEET NATION HIGHER EDUCATION PROGRAM

BLACKFEET NATION HIGHER EDUCATION GRANT   • 224

Up to 140 grants of up to $3500 will be awarded to students who are enrolled members of the Blackfeet Tribe and actively pursuing an undergraduate degree. Must submit a certification of Blackfeet blood. The deadline is March 1.

Award Grant for use in freshman, sophomore, junior, or senior years; renewable. *Number:* 140. *Amount:* $3500.

Eligibility Requirements: Applicant must be American Indian/Alaska Native and enrolled or expecting to enroll full-time at a two-year or four-year institution or university. Available to U.S. citizens.

Application Requirements Application, essay, financial need analysis, transcript, certification of Blackfeet blood. *Deadline:* March 1.

World Wide Web: http://www.blackfeetnation.com

Contact: Conrad Lafromboise, Director, Blackfeet Higher Education
Blackfeet Nation Higher Education Program
PO Box 850
Browning, MT 59417
Phone: 406-338-7539
Fax: 406-338-7530
E-mail: bhep@blackfeetnation.com

CAP FOUNDATION

RON BROWN SCHOLAR PROGRAM   • 225

Program seeks to identify African-American students who will make significant contributions to society. Applicants must excel academically, show exceptional leadership potential, participate in community service activities and demonstrate financial need. Must be a U.S. citizen or hold permanent resident visa.

Award Scholarship for use in freshman, sophomore, junior, or senior years; renewable. *Number:* 10–20. *Amount:* $10,000–$40,000.

Eligibility Requirements: Applicant must be Black (non-Hispanic); high school student; planning to enroll or expecting to enroll full-time at a four-year institution or university and must have an interest in leadership. Applicant must have 3.5 GPA or higher. Available to U.S. citizens.

Application Requirements Application, essay, financial need analysis, interview, photo, references, test scores, transcript. *Deadline:* January 9.

World Wide Web: http://www.ronbrown.org

Contact: Fran Hardey, Executive Assistant, Ron Brown Scholar Program
CAP Foundation
1160 Pepsi Place, Suite 206
Charlottesville, VA 22901
Phone: 434-964-1588
Fax: 434-964-1589
E-mail: franh@ronbrown.org

CHEROKEE NATION OF OKLAHOMA

CHEROKEE NATION HIGHER EDUCATION • 226

A supplementary program that provides financial assistance to Cherokee Nation Members only. It is a need-based program which provides assistance in seeking a bachelor's degree.

Award Grant for use in freshman, sophomore, junior, or senior years; renewable. *Number:* 1200–1500. *Amount:* $500–$1000.

Eligibility Requirements: Applicant must be American Indian/Alaska Native and enrolled or expecting to enroll full-time at a two-year or four-year institution or university. Available to U.S. citizens.

Application Requirements Application, financial need analysis, test scores, transcript, written request for the application. *Deadline:* June 28.

World Wide Web: http://www.cherokee.org

Contact: Bill Miller, Higher Education Specialist
Cherokee Nation of Oklahoma
PO Box 948
Tahlequah, OK 74465
Phone: 918-456-0671
Fax: 918-458-6195

ESPERANZA, INC.

ESPERANZA SCHOLARSHIPS • 227

The Esperanza Scholarship is a one-year award valid only for full-time tuition and/or books at an accredited college or university. Recipients are eligible to apply yearly until they have completed their curriculum.

Award Scholarship for use in freshman, sophomore, junior, senior, graduate, or postgraduate years; not renewable. *Number:* 45–60. *Amount:* $500–$1500.

Eligibility Requirements: Applicant must be of Hispanic heritage; enrolled or expecting to enroll full-time at a two-year or four-year institution or university and resident of Ohio. Applicant must have 2.5 GPA or higher. Available to U.S. and non-U.S. citizens.

Application Requirements Application, essay, interview, references, test scores, transcript. *Deadline:* March 1.

World Wide Web: http://www.esperanzainc.com

Contact: Olga Ferrer, Office Assistant
Esperanza, Inc.
4115 Bridge Avenue
Room 108
Cleveland, OH 44113
Phone: 216-651-7178
Fax: 216-651-7183
E-mail: hope4ed@aol.com

FIRST CATHOLIC SLOVAK LADIES ASSOCIATION

FIRST CATHOLIC SLOVAK LADIES ASSOCIATION FRATERNAL SCHOLARSHIP AWARD FOR COLLEGE AND GRADUATE STUDY • 228

Must be FCSLA member in good standing for at least three years. Must attend accredited college in the U.S. or Canada in undergraduate or graduate degree program. Must submit certified copy of college acceptance. One-time tuition award; win once as undergraduate, up to $1250; once as graduate, up to $1750.

Award Scholarship for use in freshman, sophomore, junior, senior, or graduate years; not renewable. *Number:* 100. *Amount:* up to $1750.

Eligibility Requirements: Applicant must be Roman Catholic; of Slavic/Czech heritage and enrolled or expecting to enroll full-time at a two-year or four-year institution or university. Available to U.S. and non-U.S. citizens.

Application Requirements Application, autobiography, photo, references, test scores, transcript. *Deadline:* March 1.

World Wide Web: http://www.fcsla.com

Contact: Ms. Irene Drotleff, Director of Fraternal Scholarships
First Catholic Slovak Ladies Association
24950 Chagrin Boulevard
Beachwood, OH 44122
Phone: 216-464-8015
Fax: 216-464-8717

FLORIDA DEPARTMENT OF EDUCATION

JOSE MARTI SCHOLARSHIP CHALLENGE GRANT FUND • 229

Award available to Hispanic-American students who were born in or whose parent was born in an Hispanic country. Must have lived in Florida for one year, be enrolled full-time in Florida at an eligible school, and have a GPA of 3.0 or above. Must be U.S. citizen or eligible non-citizen. Renewable award of $2000. Application must be postmarked by April 1. Free Application for Federal Student Aid must be processed by May 15.

Award Scholarship for use in freshman, or graduate years; renewable. *Number:* 75. *Amount:* $2000.

Eligibility Requirements: Applicant must be Hispanic; enrolled or expecting to enroll full-time at a two-year or four-year institution or university; resident of Florida and studying in Florida. Applicant must have 3.0 GPA or higher. Available to U.S. citizens.

Application Requirements Application, financial need analysis, FAFSA. *Deadline:* April 1.

World Wide Web: http://www.floridastudentfinancialaid.org

Contact: Scholarship Information
Florida Department of Education
Office of Student Financial Assistance
1940 North Monroe, Suite 70
Tallahassee, FL 32303-4759
Phone: 888-827-2004
E-mail: osfa@fldoe.org

ROSEWOOD FAMILY SCHOLARSHIP FUND ● 230

Renewable award for eligible minority students to attend a Florida public postsecondary institution on a full-time basis. Preference given to direct descendants of African-American Rosewood families affected by the incidents of January 1923. Must be Black, Hispanic, Asian, Pacific Islander, American-Indian, or Alaska Native. Free Application for Federal Student Aid (and Student Aid Report for nonresidents of Florida) must be processed by May 15.

Award Scholarship for use in freshman, sophomore, junior, or senior years; renewable. *Number:* up to 25. *Amount:* up to $4000.

Eligibility Requirements: Applicant must be American Indian/Alaska Native, Asian/Pacific Islander, Black (non-Hispanic), or Hispanic; enrolled or expecting to enroll full-time at a two-year or four-year or technical institution or university and studying in Florida. Available to U.S. citizens.

Application Requirements Application, financial need analysis. *Deadline:* April 1.

World Wide Web: http://www.floridastudentfinancialaid.org

Contact: Scholarship Information
Florida Department of Education
Office of Student Financial Assistance
1940 North Monroe, Suite 70
Tallahassee, FL 32303-4759
Phone: 888-827-2004
E-mail: osfa@fldoe.org

FOND DU LAC RESERVATION

FOND DU LAC SCHOLARSHIP PROGRAM ● 231

Must be enrolled tribal member and have high school diploma or GED. Must be accepted for admission at accredited college, university or technical school. Must complete FAFSA and all other required applications. All recipients must submit grades at the end of each term, must maintain 2.0 GPA for continued funding.

Award Scholarship for use in freshman, sophomore, junior, senior, graduate, or postgraduate years; renewable. *Number:* 75–125. *Amount:* $500–$12,000.

Eligibility Requirements: Applicant must be American Indian/Alaska Native and enrolled or expecting to enroll full or part-time at a two-year or four-year or technical institution or university. Available to U.S. citizens.

Application Requirements Application, financial need analysis, transcript. *Deadline:* May 15.

Fond du Lac Scholarship Program (continued)
World Wide Web: http://www.fdlrez.com
Contact: Bonnie Wallace, Scholarship Director
Fond Du Lac Reservation
1720 Big Lake Road, Federal Tribal Center
Cloquet, MN 55720
Phone: 218-879-4593 Ext. 2681
Fax: 218-878-7529
E-mail: scholarships@fdlrez.com

GENERAL BOARD OF GLOBAL MINISTRIES

NATIONAL LEADERSHIP DEVELOPMENT GRANTS • 232

Award for racial and ethnic minority members of the United Methodist Church who are pursuing undergraduate study. Must be U.S. citizen or resident alien or reside in U.S. as a refugee. Renewable award of $500 to $5000. Deadline: May 31.

Award Grant for use in freshman, sophomore, junior, or senior years; renewable. *Number:* 75. *Amount:* $500–$5000.
Eligibility Requirements: Applicant must be Methodist; American Indian/Alaska Native, Asian/Pacific Islander, Black (non-Hispanic), or Hispanic and enrolled or expecting to enroll full-time at a two-year or four-year or technical institution or university. Available to U.S. and non-U.S. citizens.
Application Requirements Application, essay, financial need analysis, photo, references, transcript. *Deadline:* May 31.
World Wide Web: http://www.gbgm-umc.org
Contact: Scholarship Office
General Board of Global Ministries
475 Riverside Drive
Room 1351
New York, NY 10115
Phone: 212-870-3787
Fax: 212-870-3932
E-mail: scholars@gbgm-umc.org

HELLENIC TIMES SCHOLARSHIP FUND

HELLENIC TIMES SCHOLARSHIP FUND • 233

One-time award to students of Greek/Hellenic descent. Must be between the ages of 17-30. For use in any year of undergraduate education. Deadline is February 15.

Award Scholarship for use in freshman, sophomore, junior, or senior years; not renewable. *Number:* 30–40. *Amount:* $500–$10,000.
Eligibility Requirements: Applicant must be of Greek heritage; age 17-30 and enrolled or expecting to enroll full or part-time at a two-year or four-year or technical institution or university. Available to U.S. and non-U.S. citizens.

Application Requirements Application, financial need analysis, resume, references, transcript. *Deadline:* February 15.
World Wide Web: http://www.htsfund.org
Contact: Nick Katsoris
Hellenic Times Scholarship Fund
823 Eleventh Avenue, 5th Floor
New York, NY 10019-3535
Phone: 212-986-6881
Fax: 212-977-3662
E-mail: htsfund@aol.com

HENRY SACHS FOUNDATION

HENRY SACHS FOUNDATION GRANTS • 234

Grants up to $7000 are awarded to graduating high school seniors who are African-American and residents of Colorado. Must demonstrate financial need and maintain a 3.5 GPA.

Award Grant for use in senior year; renewable. *Number:* 30–40. *Amount:* $2000–$7000.

Eligibility Requirements: Applicant must be Black (non-Hispanic); high school student; planning to enroll or expecting to enroll full-time at a two-year or four-year institution or university and resident of Colorado. Applicant must have 3.5 GPA or higher. Available to U.S. citizens.

Application Requirements Application, financial need analysis, interview, photo, references, self-addressed stamped envelope, test scores, transcript. *Deadline:* March 1.

World Wide Web: http://www.frii.com/~sachs
Contact: Lisa M. Harris, Scholarship Coordinator
Henry Sachs Foundation
90 South Cascade Avenue, Suite 1410
Colorado Springs, CO 80903
E-mail: sachs@frii.com

HISPANIC HERITAGE FOUNDATION AWARDS

HHAF CHASE AND MASTERCARD ACADEMIC EXCELLENCE YOUTH AWARD • 235

Educational grants are awarded to two Hispanic students in each of twelve regions for demonstrated academic excellence. One student will receive $2000 and the other will receive $1000. One national winner will receive a $5000 educational grant from the pool of regional winners. For more details or an application see web site: http://www.hispanicheritageawards.org.

Award Grant for use in freshman year; not renewable. *Number:* 25. *Amount:* $1000–$5000.

HHAF Chase and Mastercard Academic Excellence Youth Award (continued)

Eligibility Requirements: Applicant must be of Hispanic heritage; high school student and planning to enroll or expecting to enroll at an institution or university. Available to U.S. citizens.

Application Requirements Application. *Deadline:* March 6.

World Wide Web: http://www.hispanicheritageawards.org

Contact: application available at web site

HHAF DR. PEPPER LEADERSHIP AND COMMUNITY SERVICE YOUTH AWARD • 236

Educational grants are awarded to two Hispanic students in each of twelve regions for demonstrated interest in leadership, community service and academic excellence in general. One student will receive $2000 and the other will receive $1000. One national winner will receive a $5000 educational grant from the pool of regional winners. For more details or an application see web site: http://www.hispanicheritageawards.org.

Award Grant for use in freshman year; not renewable. *Number:* 25. *Amount:* $1000–$5000.

Eligibility Requirements: Applicant must be of Hispanic heritage; high school student and planning to enroll or expecting to enroll at an institution or university. Available to U.S. citizens.

Application Requirements Application. *Deadline:* March 6.

World Wide Web: http://www.hispanicheritageawards.org

Contact: application available at web site

HHAF EXXON MOBIL MATHEMATICS YOUTH AWARD • 237

Educational grants are awarded to two Hispanic students in each of twelve regions for demonstrated interest in mathematics and academics excellence in general. One student will receive $2000 and the other will receive $1000. One national winner will receive a $5000 educational grant from the pool of regional winners. For more details or an application see web site: http://www. hispanicheritageawards.org.

Award Grant for use in freshman year; not renewable. *Number:* 25. *Amount:* $1000–$5000.

Eligibility Requirements: Applicant must be of Hispanic heritage; high school student and planning to enroll or expecting to enroll at an institution or university. Available to U.S. citizens.

Application Requirements Application. *Deadline:* March 6.

World Wide Web: http://www.hispanicheritageawards.org

Contact: application available at web site

HHAF GLAXO SMITH KLINE HEALTH AND SCIENCE YOUTH AWARD • 238

Educational grants are awarded to two Hispanic students in each of twelve regions for demonstrated interest in Health and Science and academic excellence in general. One student will receive $2000 and the other will receive

$1000. One national winner will receive a $5000 educational grant from the pool of regional winners. For more details or an application see web site: http://www.hispanicheritageawards.org.

Award Grant for use in freshman year; not renewable. *Number:* 25. *Amount:* $1000–$5000.

Eligibility Requirements: Applicant must be of Hispanic heritage; high school student and planning to enroll or expecting to enroll at an institution or university. Available to U.S. citizens.

Application Requirements Application. *Deadline:* March 6.

World Wide Web: http://www.hispanicheritageawards.org

Contact: application available at web site

HHAF NBC JOURNALISM YOUTH AWARD • 239

Educational grants are awarded to two Hispanic students in each of twelve regions for demonstrated interest in journalism and academic excellence in general. One student will receive $2000 and the other will receive $1000. One national winner will receive a $5000 educational grant from the pool of regional winners. For more details or an application see web site: http://www. hispanicheritageawards.org.

Award Grant for use in freshman year; not renewable. *Number:* 25. *Amount:* $1000–$5000.

Eligibility Requirements: Applicant must be of Hispanic heritage; high school student and planning to enroll or expecting to enroll at an institution or university. Available to U.S. citizens.

Application Requirements Application. *Deadline:* March 6.

World Wide Web: http://www.hispanicheritageawards.org

Contact: application available at web site

HHAF SPORTS YOUTH AWARD • 240

Educational grants are awarded to two Hispanic students in each of twelve regions for demonstrated interest in sports and academic excellence in general. One student will receive $2000 and the other will receive $1000. One national winner will receive a $5000 educational grant from the pool of regional winners. For more details or an application see web site: http://www. hispanicheritageawards.org.

Award Grant for use in freshman year; not renewable. *Number:* 25. *Amount:* $1000–$5000.

Eligibility Requirements: Applicant must be of Hispanic heritage; high school student and planning to enroll or expecting to enroll at an institution or university. Available to U.S. citizens.

Application Requirements Application. *Deadline:* March 6.

World Wide Web: http://www.hispanicheritageawards.org

Contact: application available at web site

HISPANIC SCHOLARSHIP FUND

COLLEGE SCHOLARSHIP PROGRAM • 241

Awards available to full-time undergraduate or graduate students of Hispanic origin. Applicants must have 12 college units with a minimum 2.7 GPA before applying. Merit-based award for U.S. citizens or permanent residents. Must include financial aid award letter and SAR.

Award Scholarship for use in sophomore, junior, senior, or graduate years; not renewable. *Number:* 2900–3500. *Amount:* $1000–$3000.

Eligibility Requirements: Applicant must be of Latin American/Caribbean, Mexican, or Spanish heritage; Hispanic and enrolled or expecting to enroll full-time at a two-year or four-year institution or university. Available to U.S. citizens.

Application Requirements Application, essay, financial need analysis, references, self-addressed stamped envelope, transcript. *Deadline:* October 15.

World Wide Web: http://www.hsf.net

Contact: Art Taylor, Program Officer-College Scholarship
Hispanic Scholarship Fund
55 Second Street, Suite 1500
San Francisco, CA 94105
Phone: 415-808-2300
Fax: 415-808-2301
E-mail: info@hsf.net

HOPI TRIBE

BIA HIGHER EDUCATION GRANT • 242

Grant provides financial support for eligible Hopi individuals pursuing postsecondary education. Minimum 2.5 GPA required. Deadlines are July 31 for fall, and November 30 for spring.

Award Grant for use in freshman, sophomore, junior, or senior years; not renewable. *Number:* 1–130. *Amount:* $50–$2500.

Eligibility Requirements: Applicant must be American Indian/Alaska Native and enrolled or expecting to enroll full or part-time at a two-year or four-year institution or university. Applicant must have 2.5 GPA or higher. Available to U.S. citizens.

Application Requirements Application, financial need analysis, test scores, transcript, certificate of Indian blood.

Contact: Hopi Tribe
PO Box 123
Kykotsmovi, AZ 86039-0123

HOPI SUPPLEMENTAL GRANT • 243

Grant provides financial support for eligible Hopi individuals pursuing postsecondary education. Minimum 2.5 GPA required. Deadlines are April 30 for summer, July 31 for fall, and November 30 for spring.

Award Grant for use in freshman, sophomore, junior, or senior years; not renewable. *Number:* 1–400. *Amount:* $50–$1500.

Eligibility Requirements: Applicant must be American Indian/Alaska Native and enrolled or expecting to enroll full or part-time at a two-year or four-year institution or university. Applicant must have 2.5 GPA or higher. Available to U.S. citizens.

Application Requirements Application, financial need analysis, test scores, transcript, certificate of Indian blood.

Contact: Hopi Tribe
PO Box 123
Kykotsmovi, AZ 86039-0123

PEABODY SCHOLARSHIP • 244

Scholarship provides financial support for eligible Hopi individuals pursuing postsecondary education. Minimum 3.0 GPA required. Deadline is July 31.

Award Scholarship for use in freshman, sophomore, junior, senior, graduate, or postgraduate years; not renewable. *Number:* 1–90. *Amount:* $50–$1000.

Eligibility Requirements: Applicant must be American Indian/Alaska Native and enrolled or expecting to enroll full-time at a two-year or four-year institution or university. Applicant must have 3.0 GPA or higher. Available to U.S. citizens.

Application Requirements Application, financial need analysis, test scores, transcript, certificate of Indian blood. *Deadline:* July 31.

Contact: Hopi Tribe
PO Box 123
Kykotsmovi, AZ 86039-0123

INDIAN HEALTH SERVICES, UNITED STATES DEPARTMENT OF HEALTH AND HUMAN SERVICES

HEALTH PROFESSIONS SCHOLARSHIP PROGRAM • 245

Renewable scholarship available for undergraduate, graduate, or doctoral study in health professions and allied health professions programs. Minimum 2.0 GPA required. Award averages $18,500. New applicants must first submit to Area Scholarship Coordinator. There are service obligations and payback requirements that the recipient incurs upon acceptance of the scholarship funding. Contact office for more information.

Award Scholarship for use in freshman, sophomore, junior, senior, or graduate years; renewable. *Number:* up to 393. *Amount:* $18,500.

Eligibility Requirements: Applicant must be American Indian/Alaska Native and enrolled or expecting to enroll full or part-time at a two-year or four-year or technical institution or university. Available to U.S. citizens.

Application Requirements Application, applicant must enter a contest, essay, references, transcript. *Deadline:* April 1.

World Wide Web: http://www.ihs.gov

Health Professions Scholarship Program (continued)
Contact: Ms. Patricia Yee-Spencer, Acting Chief, Scholarship Branch
Indian Health Services, United States Department of Health and
 Human Services
801 Thompson Avenue, Suite 120
Rockville, MD 20852
Phone: 301-443-6197
Fax: 301-443-6048

JACKIE ROBINSON FOUNDATION

JACKIE ROBINSON SCHOLARSHIP · 246

Scholarship for graduating minority high school seniors who have been accepted
to accredited four-year colleges or universities. Must be U.S. citizen and show
financial need, leadership potential and a high level of academic achievement.
Application deadline: April 1.

Award Scholarship for use in freshman year; renewable. *Number:* 50–60.
Amount: up to $6000.
Eligibility Requirements: Applicant must be American Indian/Alaska Native,
Asian/Pacific Islander, Black (non-Hispanic), or Hispanic; high school student
and planning to enroll or expecting to enroll full-time at a four-year institution.
Available to U.S. citizens.
Application Requirements Application, essay, financial need analysis, refer-
ences, test scores, transcript, school certification. *Deadline:* April 1.
World Wide Web: http://www.jackierobinson.org
Contact: Scholarship Program
Jackie Robinson Foundation
3 West 35th Street, 11th Floor
New York, NY 10001-2204
Phone: 212-290-8600
Fax: 212-290-8081

JOSE MARTI SCHOLARSHIP CHALLENGE GRANT FUND

JOSE MARTI SCHOLARSHIP CHALLENGE GRANT · 247

Must apply as a senior in high school or as graduate student. Must be resident
of Florida and study in Florida. Need-based, merit scholarship. Must be U.S.
citizen or eligible non-citizen. Applicant must certify minimum 3.0 GPA and
Hispanic origin.

Award Scholarship for use in freshman, sophomore, junior, senior, or graduate years; renewable. *Number:* 50. *Amount:* $2000.
Eligibility Requirements: Applicant must be of Hispanic heritage; enrolled
or expecting to enroll full-time at a two-year or four-year institution or university;
resident of Florida and studying in Florida. Applicant must have 3.0 GPA or
higher. Available to U.S. citizens.

Application Requirements Application, financial need analysis. *Deadline:* April 1.

World Wide Web: http://www.floridastudentfinancialaid.org

Contact: Jose Marti Scholarship Challenge Grant Fund
1940 North Monroe Street, Suite 70
Tallahassee, FL 32303-4759
Phone: 888-827-2004

KANSAS BOARD OF REGENTS

ETHNIC MINORITY SCHOLARSHIP PROGRAM   • 248

This program is designed to assist financially needy, academically competitive students who are identified as members of the following ethnic/racial groups: African-American; American-Indian or Alaskan Native; Asian or Pacific Islander; or Hispanic. Must be resident of Kansas and attend college in Kansas. Application fee is $10. Deadline: May 1. Minimum 3.0 GPA required. Must be U.S. citizen.

Award Scholarship for use in freshman, sophomore, junior, or senior years; renewable. *Number:* 200–250. *Amount:* $1850.

Eligibility Requirements: Applicant must be American Indian/Alaska Native, Asian/Pacific Islander, Black (non-Hispanic), or Hispanic; enrolled or expecting to enroll full-time at a two-year or four-year institution or university; resident of Kansas and studying in Kansas. Applicant must have 3.0 GPA or higher. Available to U.S. citizens.

Application Requirements Application, financial need analysis, test scores, transcript. *Fee:* $10. *Deadline:* May 1.

World Wide Web: http://www.kansasregents.org

Contact: Diane Lindeman, Director of Student Financial Assistance
Kansas Board of Regents
1000 Southwest Jackson, Suite 520
Topeka, KS 66612-1368
Phone: 785-296-3517
Fax: 785-296-0983
E-mail: dlindeman@ksbor.org

LEAGUE OF UNITED LATIN AMERICAN CITIZENS NATIONAL EDUCATIONAL SERVICE CENTERS, INC.

LULAC NATIONAL SCHOLARSHIP FUND   • 249

LULAC Councils will award scholarships to qualified Hispanic students who are enrolled or are planning to enroll in accredited colleges or universities in the United States. Applicants must be U.S. citizens or legal residents. Scholarships may be used for the payment of tuition, academic fees, room, board and the purchase of required educational materials. For additional information

LULAC National Scholarship Fund (continued)
applicants should check LULAC web site at http://www.lnesc.org to see a list of participating councils or send a self-addressed stamped envelope.

Award Scholarship for use in freshman, sophomore, junior, senior, or graduate years; not renewable. *Number:* 1500–2000. *Amount:* $250–$1000.

Eligibility Requirements: Applicant must be Hispanic and enrolled or expecting to enroll full-time at a two-year or four-year institution or university. Available to U.S. citizens.

Application Requirements Application, autobiography, essay, financial need analysis, interview, references, self-addressed stamped envelope, test scores, transcript. *Deadline:* March 31.

World Wide Web: http://www.lnesc.org

Contact: Scholarship Administrator
League of United Latin American Citizens National Educational
    Service Centers, Inc.
2000 L Street, NW
Suite 610
Washington, DC 20036

MENOMINEE INDIAN TRIBE OF WISCONSIN

MENOMINEE INDIAN TRIBE OF WISCONSIN HIGHER EDUCATION GRANTS • 250

Renewable award for enrolled Menominee tribal member to use at a two- or four-year college or university. Must be at least 1/4 Menominee and show proof of Indian blood. Must complete financial aid form. Contact for deadline information.

Award Grant for use in freshman, sophomore, junior, or senior years; renewable. *Number:* 136. *Amount:* $100–$1100.

Eligibility Requirements: Applicant must be American Indian/Alaska Native and enrolled or expecting to enroll full or part-time at a two-year or four-year institution or university. Available to U.S. citizens.

Application Requirements Application, financial need analysis. *Deadline:* Continuous.

World Wide Web: http://www.menominee.nsn.us/educationindex/educationhomepage.htm

Contact: Virginia Nuske, Education Director
Menominee Indian Tribe of Wisconsin
PO Box 910
Keshena, WI 54135
Phone: 715-799-5110
Fax: 715-799-1364
E-mail: vnuske@mitw.org

MONTANA GUARANTEED STUDENT LOAN PROGRAM, OFFICE OF COMMISSIONER OF HIGHER EDUCATION

INDIAN STUDENT FEE WAIVER • 251

Fee waiver awarded by the Montana University System to undergraduate and graduate students meeting the criteria. Amount varies depending upon the tuition and registration fee at each participating college. Students must provide documentation of one-fourth Indian blood or more; must be a resident of Montana for at least one year prior to enrolling in school and must demonstrate financial need. Full-or part-time study qualifies. Complete and submit the FAFSA by March 1 and a Montana Indian Fee Waiver application form. Contact the financial aid office at the college of attendance to determine eligibility.

Award Scholarship for use in freshman, sophomore, junior, senior, or graduate years; renewable. *Number:* 600. *Amount:* $2000.

Eligibility Requirements: Applicant must be American Indian/Alaska Native; enrolled or expecting to enroll full or part-time at a two-year or four-year institution or university; resident of Montana and studying in Montana. Available to U.S. citizens.

Application Requirements Application, financial need analysis, FAFSA. *Deadline:* March 1.

World Wide Web: http://www.mgslp.state.mt.us

Contact: Sally Speer, Grants and Scholarship Coordinator
Montana Guaranteed Student Loan Program, Office of
   Commissioner of Higher Education
2500 Broadway
PO Box 203101
Helena, MT 59620-3101
Phone: 406-444-0638
Fax: 406-444-1869
E-mail: sspeer@mgslp.state.mt.us

NATIONAL MERIT SCHOLARSHIP CORPORATION

NATIONAL ACHIEVEMENT SCHOLARSHIP PROGRAM • 252

Competition of African-American students for recognition and undergraduate scholarships. Students enter by taking the Preliminary SAT/National Merit Scholar Qualifying Test and by meeting other participation requirements. Half of the awards are one-time scholarships of $2,500; others are renewable for four years, and valued between $500 and $2,000 or more. Contact high school counselor by fall of junior year. Those qualifying for recognition are notified through their high school. Participation requirements are available in the PSAT/NMSQT Student Bulletin and on the NMSC web site.

Award Scholarship for use in freshman year; renewable. *Number:* 700. *Amount:* $500–$2500.

National Achievement Scholarship Program (continued)
Eligibility Requirements: Applicant must be Black (non-Hispanic); high school student and planning to enroll or expecting to enroll full-time at a four-year institution or university. Available to U.S. citizens.
Application Requirements Application, autobiography, essay, references, test scores, transcript.
World Wide Web: http://www.nationalmerit.org
Contact: student's high school counselor

NATIVE AMERICAN EDUCATION GRANTS

NATIVE AMERICAN EDUCATION GRANTS • 253
Must prove tribal membership, show financial need, make satisfactory academic progress.
Award Grant for use in freshman, sophomore, junior, senior, graduate, or postgraduate years; renewable. *Number:* 50. *Amount:* $2500.
Eligibility Requirements: Applicant must be American Indian/Alaska Native and enrolled or expecting to enroll full-time at a two-year or four-year or technical institution or university. Applicant must have 2.5 GPA or higher. Available to U.S. citizens.
Application Requirements Application, essay, financial need analysis, test scores, transcript, tribal membership. *Deadline:* June 3.
World Wide Web: http://www.pcusa.org/financialaid
Contact: Frances Cook, Associate, Financial Aid
　　　　　Native American Education Grants
　　　　　Financial Aid for Studies
　　　　　100 Witherspoon Street, MO65
　　　　　Louisville, KY 40202-1396
　　　　　Phone: 888-728-7228 Ext. 5776
　　　　　Fax: 502-569-8766
　　　　　E-mail: fcook@pcusa.org

NORTH CAROLINA COMMISSION OF INDIAN AFFAIRS

INCENTIVE SCHOLARSHIP FOR NATIVE AMERICANS • 254
Merit-based award with a required public service component. Maximum award $3000 per academic year. Must be graduate of a North Carolina high school enrolled at North Carolina institution. Must submit tribal enrollment card. Minimum 2.5 GPA required.

Award Scholarship for use in freshman, sophomore, junior, or senior years; renewable. *Number:* up to 200. *Amount:* up to $3000.
Eligibility Requirements: Applicant must be American Indian/Alaska Native; enrolled or expecting to enroll full-time at a four-year institution; resident of North Carolina and studying in North Carolina. Applicant must have 2.5 GPA or higher. Available to U.S. citizens.

Application Requirements Application, financial need analysis, tribal enrollment card. *Deadline:* Continuous.

Contact: Ms. Mickey Locklear, Director, Education Talent Search
North Carolina Commission of Indian Affairs
217 West Jones Street
Raleigh, NC 27603
Phone: 919-733-5998
Fax: 919-733-1207
E-mail: mickey.locklear@ncmail.net

NORTH DAKOTA UNIVERSITY SYSTEM

NORTH DAKOTA INDIAN COLLEGE SCHOLARSHIP PROGRAM
• 255

Renewable award to Native-Americans residents of North Dakota. Priority given to full-time undergraduate students. Minimum 2.0 GPA required.

Award Scholarship for use in freshman, sophomore, junior, senior, or graduate years; renewable. *Number:* up to 150. *Amount:* $700–$2000.

Eligibility Requirements: Applicant must be American Indian/Alaska Native; enrolled or expecting to enroll full-time at a two-year or four-year or technical institution or university and resident of North Dakota. Available to U.S. citizens.

Application Requirements Application, financial need analysis, transcript, proof of tribal enrollment. *Deadline:* July 15.

World Wide Web: http://www.ndus.nodak.edu

Contact: Rhonda Schauer, SAA Director
North Dakota University System
600 East Boulevard Avenue
Department 215
Bismarck, ND 58505-0230
Phone: 701-328-9661

NORTHERN CHEYENNE TRIBAL EDUCATION DEPARTMENT

HIGHER EDUCATION SCHOLARSHIP PROGRAM
• 256

Scholarships are only provided for enrolled Northern Cheyenne Tribal Members who meet the requirements listed in the higher education guidelines. Must be U.S. citizen enrolled in a postsecondary institution. Minimum 2.5 GPA required. Deadline is March 1.

Award Grant for use in freshman, sophomore, junior, or senior years; renewable. *Number:* 72. *Amount:* $50–$6000.

Eligibility Requirements: Applicant must be American Indian/Alaska Native and enrolled or expecting to enroll full or part-time at a two-year or four-year institution or university. Applicant must have 2.5 GPA or higher. Available to U.S. citizens.

Higher Education Scholarship Program (continued)

Application Requirements Application, essay, financial need analysis, references, test scores, transcript. *Deadline:* March 1.

Contact: Norma Bixby, Director
Northern Cheyenne Tribal Education Department
Box 307
Lame deer, MT 59043
Phone: 406-477-6602
Fax: 406-477-8150
E-mail: norma@rangeweb.net

PAGE EDUCATION FOUNDATION

PAGE EDUCATION FOUNDATION GRANT • 257

Grants are available to Minnesota students of color who attend Minnesota postsecondary institutions. Students must be willing to provide a minimum of 50 hours of service each year they accept a grant. This service is focused on K-8th grade children of color and encourages the youngsters to value learning and education. Page scholars are tutors, mentors and role models. Mentors are also provided for the page scholars.

Award Grant for use in freshman, sophomore, junior, or senior years; renewable. *Number:* 500–600. *Amount:* $900–$2500.

Eligibility Requirements: Applicant must be American Indian/Alaska Native, Asian/Pacific Islander, Black (non-Hispanic), or Hispanic; enrolled or expecting to enroll full-time at a two-year or four-year or technical institution or university; resident of Minnesota and studying in Minnesota. Available to U.S. citizens.

Application Requirements Application, essay, financial need analysis, references, transcript. *Deadline:* May 1.

World Wide Web: http://www.page-ed.org

Contact: Ramona Harristhal, Administrative Director
Page Education Foundation
PO Box 581254
Minneapolis, MN 55458-1254
Phone: 612-332-0406
Fax: 612-332-0403
E-mail: pagemail@mtn.org

POLISH NATIONAL ALLIANCE

POLISH NATIONAL ALLIANCE SCHOLARSHIP AWARD • 258

This program is awarded to Polish National Alliance members only. Must have a 3.0 GPA. Must currently be enrolled full-time in an accredited college as an undergraduate sophomore, junior or senior.

Award Scholarship for use in sophomore, junior, or senior years; renewable. *Number:* 200. *Amount:* $500.

Eligibility Requirements: Applicant must be of Polish heritage and enrolled or expecting to enroll full-time at a four-year institution. Applicant must have 3.0 GPA or higher. Available to U.S. citizens.

Application Requirements Application, photo, test scores, transcript. *Deadline:* April 15.

Contact: Polish National Alliance
Education Department
6100 North Cicero Avenue
Chicago, IL 60646

PRESBYTERIAN CHURCH (USA)

STUDENT OPPORTUNITY SCHOLARSHIP-PRESBYTERIAN CHURCH (U.S.A.)
• 259

Available to graduating high school seniors. Applicants must be members of racial minority and be communicant members of the Presbyterian Church (U.S.A.). Renewable award based on academics and financial need. Must be a U.S. citizen. Minimum 2.5 GPA.

Award Scholarship for use in freshman, sophomore, junior, or senior years; renewable. *Number:* up to 200. *Amount:* $100–$1000.

Eligibility Requirements: Applicant must be Presbyterian; American Indian/Alaska Native, Asian/Pacific Islander, Black (non-Hispanic), or Hispanic; high school student and planning to enroll or expecting to enroll full-time at a two-year or four-year or technical institution or university. Applicant must have 2.5 GPA or higher. Available to U.S. citizens.

Application Requirements Application, autobiography, essay, financial need analysis, references, test scores, transcript. *Deadline:* May 1.

World Wide Web: http://www.pcusa.org/financialaid

Contact: Kathy Smith, Program Assistant, Undergraduate Grants
Presbyterian Church (USA)
100 Witherspoon Street
Louisville, KY 40202-1396
Phone: 888-728-7228 Ext. 5745
Fax: 502-569-8766
E-mail: ksmith@ctr.pcusa.org

PUEBLO OF ISLETA, DEPARTMENT OF EDUCATION

HIGHER EDUCATION SUPPLEMENTAL SCHOLARSHIP
• 260

Enrolled tribal members of the Isleta Pueblo may apply for this scholarship if they also apply for additional scholarships from different sources. Deadlines: Summer, April 1; Spring, October 1; Fall, July 1.

Award Scholarship for use in freshman, sophomore, junior, senior, graduate, or postgraduate years; not renewable. *Number:* up to 150. *Amount:* $500–$6000.

Higher Education Supplemental Scholarship (continued)

Eligibility Requirements: Applicant must be American Indian/Alaska Native and enrolled or expecting to enroll full or part-time at a two-year or four-year institution or university. Applicant must have 2.5 GPA or higher. Available to U.S. citizens.

Application Requirements Application, financial need analysis, transcript, certificate of Indian blood, class schedule.

World Wide Web: http://www.isletaeducation.org

Contact: Joanna Garcia, Higher Education Director
Pueblo of Isleta, Department of Education
PO Box 1270
Isleta, NM 87022
Fax: 505-869-7690
E-mail: isletahighered@yahoo.com

SACHS FOUNDATION

SACHS FOUNDATION SCHOLARSHIPS • 261

Award for black high school seniors who have been residents of Colorado for at least five years. Based on financial need and GPA of 3.60 or higher. Deadline: February 15.

Award Scholarship for use in freshman year; renewable. *Number:* 30. *Amount:* $4000.

Eligibility Requirements: Applicant must be Black (non-Hispanic); high school student; planning to enroll or expecting to enroll full-time at a two-year or four-year institution or university and resident of Colorado. Available to U.S. citizens.

Application Requirements Application, financial need analysis, interview, photo, references, transcript. *Deadline:* February 15.

World Wide Web: http://www.frii.com/~sachs

Contact: Lisa Harris, Secretary and Treasurer
SACHS Foundation
90 South Cascade Avenue, Suite 1410
Colorado Springs, CO 80903
Phone: 719-633-2353
E-mail: sachs@frii.com

SALVADORAN AMERICAN LEADERSHIP AND EDUCATIONAL FUND

FULFILLING OUR DREAMS SCHOLARSHIP FUND • 262

Up to sixty scholarships ranging from $500-$2500 will be awarded to students who come from a Hispanic heritage. Must have a 2.5 GPA. See web site for more details: http://www.salef.org

Award Scholarship for use in freshman, sophomore, junior, senior, graduate, or postgraduate years; not renewable. *Number:* 40–60. *Amount:* $500–$2500.

Eligibility Requirements: Applicant must be of Hispanic or Latin American/Caribbean heritage and enrolled or expecting to enroll full-time at a four-year institution or university. Applicant must have 2.5 GPA or higher. Available to U.S. and non-Canadian citizens.

Application Requirements Application, essay, financial need analysis, interview, photo, resume, references, self-addressed stamped envelope, test scores, transcript. *Deadline:* June 28.

World Wide Web: http://www.salef.org

Contact: Mayra Soriano, Educational and Youth Programs Manager
Salvadoran American Leadership and Educational Fund
1625 West Olympic Boulevard, Suite 706
Los Angeles, CA 90015
Phone: 213-480-1052
Fax: 213-487-2530
E-mail: msoriano@salef.org

SOCIETY FOR ADVANCEMENT OF CHICANOS AND NATIVE AMERICANS IN SCIENCE (SACNAS)

SACNAS FINANCIAL AID: LODGING AND TRAVEL AWARD • 263

Undergraduate and graduate students are encouraged to apply for lodging and travel to attend the SACNAS National Conference. The conference offers students the opportunity to be mentored, to present their research, attend scientific symposiums in all science disciplines, and professional development sessions to enhance their educational careers.

Award Scholarship for use in freshman, sophomore, junior, or senior years; not renewable. *Number:* 400–550. *Amount:* $800–$1000.

Eligibility Requirements: Applicant must be American Indian/Alaska Native, Asian/Pacific Islander, Black (non-Hispanic), or Hispanic and enrolled or expecting to enroll full or part-time at a two-year or four-year or technical institution or university. Applicant must have 2.5 GPA or higher. Available to U.S. citizens.

Application Requirements Application, essay, references, current enrollment verification. *Deadline:* June 3.

World Wide Web: http://www.sacnas.org

Contact: Rosalina Aranda, Student Program Manager
Society for Advancement of Chicanos and Native Americans in Science (SACNAS)
333 Front Street
Suite 104
Santa Cruz, CA 95060
Phone: 831-459-0170 Ext. 224
Fax: 831-459-0194
E-mail: rosalina@sacnas.org

SONS OF ITALY FOUNDATION

SONS OF ITALY FOUNDATION NATIONAL LEADERSHIP GRANTS   • 264

Scholarships for full-time-student of Italian-American descent. Must demonstrate commitment to academic excellence and potential for leadership. Must submit resume. Application fee: $25 (money orders only).

Award Scholarship for use in freshman, sophomore, junior, senior, graduate, or postgraduate years; not renewable. *Number:* 10–13. *Amount:* $4000–$25,000.

Eligibility Requirements: Applicant must be of Italian heritage and enrolled or expecting to enroll full-time at a four-year institution or university. Available to U.S. citizens.

Application Requirements Application, applicant must enter a contest, essay, resume, references, test scores, transcript. *Fee:* $25. *Deadline:* February 28.

World Wide Web: http://www.osia.org

Contact: Gina M. Guiducci, Scholarship Coordinator
Sons of Italy Foundation
219 E Street, NE
Washington, DC 20002
Phone: 202-547-5106
Fax: 202-546-8168
E-mail: scholarships@osia.org

STATE OF NORTH DAKOTA

NORTH DAKOTA INDIAN SCHOLARSHIP PROGRAM   • 265

Assists Native-Americans North Dakota residents in obtaining a college education. Priority given to full-time undergraduate students and those having a 3.5 GPA or higher. Certification of tribal enrollment required. For use at North Dakota institution.

Award Scholarship for use in freshman, sophomore, junior, senior, or graduate years; renewable. *Number:* 120–150. *Amount:* $700–$2000.

Eligibility Requirements: Applicant must be American Indian/Alaska Native; enrolled or expecting to enroll at a two-year or four-year institution or university; resident of North Dakota and studying in North Dakota. Applicant must have 3.5 GPA or higher.

Application Requirements Application, financial need analysis, transcript. *Deadline:* July 15.

World Wide Web: http://www.ndus.nodak.edu

Contact: Rhonda Schauer, Coordinator of American Indian Higher Education
State of North Dakota
600 East Boulevard, Department 215
Bismarck, ND 58505-0230
Phone: 701-328-2166

SWISS BENEVOLENT SOCIETY OF NEW YORK

PELLEGRINI SCHOLARSHIP GRANTS • 266

Award to students who have a minimum 3.0 GPA, and show financial need. Must submit proof of Swiss nationality or descent. Must be a resident of Connecticut, Delaware, New Jersey, New York, or Pennsylvania. Fifty grants of up to $2500.

Award Grant for use in freshman, sophomore, junior, senior, or graduate years; not renewable. *Number:* 50. *Amount:* $500–$2500.

Eligibility Requirements: Applicant must be of Swiss heritage; enrolled or expecting to enroll full or part-time at a two-year or four-year or technical institution or university and resident of Connecticut, Delaware, New Jersey, New York, or Pennsylvania. Applicant must have 3.0 GPA or higher.

Application Requirements Application, financial need analysis, references, test scores, transcript. *Deadline:* March 31.

World Wide Web: http://www.swissbenevolentny.com

Contact: Anne Marie Gilman, Scholarship Director
Swiss Benevolent Society of New York
608 Fifth Avenue, #309
New York, NY 10020

TERRY FOX HUMANITARIAN AWARD PROGRAM

TERRY FOX HUMANITARIAN AWARD • 267

Award granted to Canadian students entering postsecondary education. Criteria includes commitment to voluntary humanitarian work, courage in overcoming obstacles and excellence in academics, fitness and amateur sports. Must also show involvement in extracurricular activities. Value of award is $6000 awarded annually for maximum of four years. For those who attend institution that does not charge tuition fees, award is $3500 a year. Must be no older than 25.

Award Scholarship for use in freshman, sophomore, or junior years; renewable. *Number:* 20. *Amount:* $3500–$6000.

Eligibility Requirements: Applicant must be Canadian citizenship; age 25 or under and enrolled or expecting to enroll full-time at a two-year or four-year or technical institution or university.

Application Requirements Application, references, self-addressed stamped envelope, transcript. *Deadline:* February 1.

World Wide Web: http://www.terryfox.org

Contact: Melissa Ratcliff, Administrative Assistant
Terry Fox Humanitarian Award Program
AQ 5003, 8888 University Drive
Burnaby, BC V5A 1S6
Phone: 604-291-3057
Fax: 604-291-3311
E-mail: terryfox@sfu.ca

UNITED METHODIST CHURCH

UNITED METHODIST CHURCH ETHNIC SCHOLARSHIP • 268

Awards for minority students pursuing undergraduate degree. Must have been certified members of the United Methodist Church for one year. Proof of membership and pastor's statement required. One-time award but is renewable by application each year. Minimum 2.5 GPA required.

Award Scholarship for use in freshman, sophomore, junior, or senior years; not renewable. *Number:* 430–500. *Amount:* $800–$1000.

Eligibility Requirements: Applicant must be Methodist; American Indian/Alaska Native, Asian/Pacific Islander, Black (non-Hispanic), or Hispanic and enrolled or expecting to enroll full-time at a two-year or four-year institution or university. Applicant must have 2.5 GPA or higher. Available to U.S. and non-Canadian citizens.

Application Requirements Application, essay, references, transcript, membership proof, pastor's statement. *Deadline:* May 1.

World Wide Web: http://www.umc.org/

Contact: Patti J. Zimmerman, Scholarships Administrator
United Methodist Church
PO Box 340007
Nashville, TN 37203-0007
Phone: 615-340-7344
E-mail: pzimmer@gbhem.org

UNITED METHODIST CHURCH HISPANIC, ASIAN, AND NATIVE AMERICAN SCHOLARSHIP • 269

Award for members of United Methodist Church who are Hispanic, Asian, Native-Americans, or Pacific Islander college juniors, seniors, or graduate students. Need membership proof and pastor's letter. Minimum 2.8 GPA required.

Award Scholarship for use in junior, senior, or graduate years; not renewable. *Number:* 200–250. *Amount:* $1000–$3000.

Eligibility Requirements: Applicant must be Methodist; American Indian/Alaska Native, Asian/Pacific Islander, or Hispanic and enrolled or expecting to enroll full-time at a four-year institution or university. Available to U.S. citizens.

Application Requirements Application, essay, references, transcript, membership proof, pastor's letter. *Deadline:* April 1.

World Wide Web: http://www.umc.org/

Contact: Patti J. Zimmerman, Scholarships Administrator
United Methodist Church
PO Box 340007
Nashville, TN 37203-0007
Phone: 615-340-7344
E-mail: pzimmer@gbhem.org

WHITE EARTH TRIBAL COUNCIL

WHITE EARTH SCHOLARSHIP PROGRAM • 270

Renewable scholarship of at least $3000 awarded to Native-Americans Indian students. Financial need is considered. To be used for any undergraduate or graduate year of a trade/technical institution, two- or four-year college or university. Minimum 2.5 GPA required. Deadline is May 31.

Award Scholarship for use in freshman, sophomore, junior, senior, graduate, or postgraduate years; renewable. *Number:* 200. *Amount:* $3000.

Eligibility Requirements: Applicant must be American Indian/Alaska Native and enrolled or expecting to enroll full or part-time at a two-year or four-year or technical institution or university. Applicant must have 2.5 GPA or higher. Available to U.S. citizens.

Application Requirements Application, financial need analysis, transcript. *Deadline:* May 31.

Contact: Leslie Nessman, Scholarship Manager
White Earth Tribal Council
PO Box 418
White Earth, MN 56591-0418
Phone: 218-983-3285 Ext. 1227
Fax: 218-983-4299

YAKAMA NATION

YAKAMA NATION SCHOLARSHIP PROGRAM • 271

Scholarship is for enrolled Yakama tribal members studying for a college degree (non-vocational) at an accredited two-year or four-year college institution. Applicant must be member of Yakama Nation.

Award Scholarship for use in freshman, sophomore, junior, senior, or graduate years; renewable. *Number:* 150–180. *Amount:* $2000.

Eligibility Requirements: Applicant must be American Indian/Alaska Native and enrolled or expecting to enroll full or part-time at a two-year or four-year institution or university. Available to U.S. citizens.

Application Requirements Application, financial need analysis, transcript. *Deadline:* July 1.

Contact: Program Manager
Yakama Nation
PO Box 151
Toppenish, WA 98948

RELIGIOUS AFFILIATION_____

CATHOLIC AID ASSOCIATION

CATHOLIC AID ASSOCIATION COLLEGE TUITION SCHOLARSHIP
• 272

Applicants must have been a Catholic Aid Association member for at least two years. $300 scholarships for state and non-Catholic institutions, $500 for Catholic Colleges and Universities. Must be a member of the Catholic Aid Association.

Award Scholarship for use in freshman or sophomore years; not renewable. *Number:* 100–250. *Amount:* $300–$500.

Eligibility Requirements: Applicant must be Roman Catholic and enrolled or expecting to enroll full-time at a two-year or four-year institution or university. Available to U.S. citizens.

Application Requirements Application, essay, references, transcript. *Deadline:* January 15.

World Wide Web: http://www.catholicaid.com

Contact: Ann Goserud, Fraternal Department Assistant
Catholic Aid Association
3499 North Lexington Avenue
St. Paul, MN 55126-8098
Phone: 651-490-0170
E-mail: agoserud@catholicaid.com

FIRST CATHOLIC SLOVAK LADIES ASSOCIATION

FIRST CATHOLIC SLOVAK LADIES ASSOCIATION FRATERNAL SCHOLARSHIP AWARD FOR COLLEGE AND GRADUATE STUDY
see number 228

GENERAL BOARD OF GLOBAL MINISTRIES

NATIONAL LEADERSHIP DEVELOPMENT GRANTS
see number 232

ITALIAN CATHOLIC FEDERATION, INC.

ICF COLLEGE SCHOLARSHIPS TO HIGH SCHOOL SENIORS
• 273

Renewable awards for high school students who are residents of California, Illinois, Arizona and Nevada and plan to pursue postsecondary education. Must have minimum 3.2 GPA. Must be a U.S. citizen, Catholic, and of Italian descent or if non-Italian the student's parents or grandparents must be members of the Federation for the student to qualify. Applicants must submit the last two pages of parents' income tax return, along with other required materials as listed on the application.

Award Scholarship for use in freshman, sophomore, junior, or senior years; renewable. *Number:* 170–200. *Amount:* $400–$1000.

Eligibility Requirements: Applicant must be Roman Catholic; high school student; planning to enroll or expecting to enroll full-time at a two-year or four-year or technical institution or university and resident of Arizona, California, Illinois, or Nevada. Available to U.S. citizens.

Application Requirements Application, essay, references, transcript. *Deadline:* March 15.

World Wide Web: http://www.icf.org

Contact: Scholarship Director
Italian Catholic Federation, Inc.
675 Hegenberger Road, Suite 230
Oakland, CA 94621
Phone: 510-633-9058
Fax: 510-633-9758

KNIGHTS OF COLUMBUS

FOURTH DEGREE PRO DEO AND PRO PATRIA SCHOLARSHIPS
see number 158

PRESBYTERIAN CHURCH (USA)

APPALACHIAN SCHOLARSHIPS • 274

Renewable scholarship to assist students who are full-time residents of Appalachia. Must be high school graduate or GED recipient and U.S. citizen. Must be member of Presbyterian Church (U.S.A). Must rank in upper third of class or have a minimum 3.0 GPA. Deadline is July 1. Must be a full-time student. High school seniors may apply.

Award Scholarship for use in freshman, sophomore, junior, or senior years; renewable. *Number:* 100–150. *Amount:* $100–$1500.

Eligibility Requirements: Applicant must be Presbyterian; enrolled or expecting to enroll full-time at a two-year or four-year or technical institution or university and resident of Alabama, Georgia, Kentucky, Maryland, Mississippi, New York, North Carolina, Ohio, Pennsylvania, South Carolina, Tennessee, Virginia, or West Virginia. Applicant must have 3.0 GPA or higher. Available to U.S. citizens.

Application Requirements Application, autobiography, essay, financial need analysis, references, test scores, transcript. *Deadline:* July 1.

World Wide Web: http://www.pcusa.org/financialaid

Appalachian Scholarships (continued)

Contact: Kathy Smith, Program Assistant, Undergraduate Grants
Presbyterian Church (USA)
100 Witherspoon Street
Louisville, KY 40202-1396
Phone: 888-728-7228 Ext. 5745
Fax: 502-569-8766
E-mail: ksmith@ctr.pcusa.org

NATIONAL PRESBYTERIAN COLLEGE SCHOLARSHIP • 275

Available to high school seniors who are members of the Presbyterian Church (U.S.A.) and plan to attend a participating college related to the Presbyterian Church (U.S.A.). Must be a U.S. citizen. Merit-based. Must have 3.0 GPA minimum. Deadline is December 1.

Award Scholarship for use in freshman, sophomore, junior, or senior years; renewable. *Number:* 200. *Amount:* $500–$1400.

Eligibility Requirements: Applicant must be Presbyterian; high school student and planning to enroll or expecting to enroll full-time at a four-year institution. Applicant must have 3.0 GPA or higher. Available to U.S. citizens.

Application Requirements Application, autobiography, essay, financial need analysis, references, test scores, transcript. *Deadline:* December 1.

World Wide Web: http://www.pcusa.org/financialaid

Contact: Megan Willman, Program Assistant
Presbyterian Church (USA)
100 Witherspoon Street
Louisville, KY 40202-1396
Phone: 888-728-7228 Ext. 8235
Fax: 502-569-8766
E-mail: megan_willman@yahoo.com

STUDENT OPPORTUNITY SCHOLARSHIP-PRESBYTERIAN CHURCH (U.S.A.)
see number 259

UNITED METHODIST CHURCH

UNITED METHODIST CHURCH ETHNIC SCHOLARSHIP see number 268

UNITED METHODIST CHURCH HISPANIC, ASIAN, AND NATIVE AMERICAN SCHOLARSHIP
see number 269

STATE OF RESIDENCE_____

ALABAMA COMMISSION ON HIGHER EDUCATION

POLICE OFFICERS AND FIREFIGHTERS SURVIVORS EDUCATION ASSISTANCE PROGRAM-ALABAMA
see number 173

ROBERT C. BYRD HONORS SCHOLARSHIP-ALABAMA • 276

Approximately 105 awards. Must be Alabama resident and a high school senior. Minimum 3.5 GPA. Contact school guidance counselor for an application and deadlines.

Award Scholarship for use in freshman, sophomore, junior, or senior years; renewable. *Number:* 105. *Amount:* $1500.

Eligibility Requirements: Applicant must be high school student; planning to enroll or expecting to enroll full-time at a two-year or four-year institution or university and resident of Alabama. Applicant must have 3.5 GPA or higher. Available to U.S. citizens.

Application Requirements Application, test scores, transcript.

World Wide Web: http://www.ache.state.al.us

Contact: Dr. William Wall, Assoc. Executive Director for Student Assistance
Alabama Commission on Higher Education
PO Box 302000
Montgomery, AL 36130

ALBERTA HERITAGE SCHOLARSHIP FUND

ADULT HIGH SCHOOL EQUIVALENCY SCHOLARSHIPS
see number 214

ALBERTA APPRENTICESHIP AND INDUSTRY TRAINING SCHOLARSHIP • 277

A $1000 scholarship is available for apprentices in a trade and trainees in a designated occupation to encourage recipients to complete their apprenticeship or occupational training programs. Must be a Canadian citizen and Alberta resident. For more details see web site: http://www.alis.gov.ab.ca.

Award Scholarship for use in freshman year; not renewable. *Number:* 160. *Amount:* $1000.

Eligibility Requirements: Applicant must be enrolled or expecting to enroll full-time at a technical institution and resident of Alberta. Available to Canadian citizens.

Application Requirements Application. *Deadline:* July 31.

World Wide Web: http://www.alis.gov.ab.ca/scholarships

Alberta Apprenticeship and Industry Training Scholarship (continued)

Contact: Director
Alberta Heritage Scholarship Fund
9940 106th Street, 9th Floor
Box 28000, Station Main
Edmonton, AB T5J 4R4
Canada
Phone: 780-427-8640
Fax: 780-422-4516
E-mail: heritage@gov.ab.ca

ALEXANDER RUTHERFORD SCHOLARSHIPS FOR HIGH SCHOOL ACHIEVEMENT
see number 215

FELLOWSHIPS FOR FULL-TIME STUDIES IN FRENCH-UNIVERSITY
see number 216

JASON LANG SCHOLARSHIP • 278

A $1000 scholarship will be awarded for the outstanding academic achievement of Alberta postsecondary students who are continuing full-time into their second, third or fourth year of an undergraduate program. Must be a Canadian citizen and Alberta resident. For more details and deadlines see web site: http://www.alis.gov.ab.ca.

Award Scholarship for use in sophomore, junior, or senior years; not renewable. *Number:* 7500. *Amount:* $1000.

Eligibility Requirements: Applicant must be enrolled or expecting to enroll full-time at an institution or university; resident of Alberta and studying in Alberta. Available to Canadian citizens.

Application Requirements Application, transcript. *Deadline:* Continuous.

World Wide Web: http://www.alis.gov.ab.ca/scholarships

Contact: Director
Alberta Heritage Scholarship Fund
9940 106th Street, 9th Floor
Box 28000, Station Main
Edmonton, AB T5J 4R4
Canada
Phone: 780-427-8640
Fax: 780-422-4516
E-mail: heritage@gov.ab.ca

JIMMIE CONDON ATHLETIC SCHOLARSHIPS
see number 217

LOUISE MCKINNEY POSTSECONDARY SCHOLARSHIPS
see number 218

NORTHERN ALBERTA DEVELOPMENT COUNCIL BURSARIES
see number 219

PERSONS CASE SCHOLARSHIPS   see number 220

ALBUQUERQUE COMMUNITY FOUNDATION

SUSSMAN-MILLER EDUCATIONAL ASSISTANCE FUND · 279

Program to provide financial aid to enable students to continue with an undergraduate program. This is a "gap" program based on financial need. Must be resident of New Mexico. Do not write or call for information. Please visit web site: http://www.albuquerquefoundation.org for complete information. Minimum 3.0 GPA required. Deadlines vary.

Award Grant for use in freshman, sophomore, junior, or senior years; not renewable. *Number:* 40–60. *Amount:* $500–$4000.

Eligibility Requirements: Applicant must be enrolled or expecting to enroll full-time at a four-year institution or university and resident of New Mexico. Applicant must have 3.0 GPA or higher. Available to U.S. citizens.

Application Requirements Application, autobiography, essay, financial need analysis, resume, references, test scores, transcript.

World Wide Web: http://www.albuquerquefoundation.org

Contact: Program Director
Albuquerque Community Foundation
PO Box 36960
Albuquerque, NM 87176-6960

AMERICAN CANCER SOCIETY, FLORIDA DIVISION, INC.

AMERICAN CANCER SOCIETY, FLORIDA DIVISION COLLEGE SCHOLARSHIP PROGRAM · 280

To be eligible for an American Cancer Society Florida Division Scholarship applicants must have had a personal diagnosis of cancer, be under 21, be a Florida resident, and plan to attend college in Florida. Awards will be based on financial need, scholarship, leadership and community service.

Award Grant for use in freshman, sophomore, junior, or senior years; renewable. *Number:* 120–150. *Amount:* $1850–$2300.

Eligibility Requirements: Applicant must be age 20 or under; enrolled or expecting to enroll full or part-time at a two-year or four-year or technical institution or university; resident of Florida and studying in Florida. Available to U.S. citizens.

Application Requirements Application, essay, financial need analysis, interview, resume, references, test scores, transcript. *Deadline:* April 10.

World Wide Web: http://www.cancer.org

American Cancer Society, Florida Division College Scholarship Program (continued)
Contact: Marilyn Westley, Director of Childhood Cancer Programs
American Cancer Society, Florida Division, Inc.
3709 West Jetton Avenue
Tampa, FL 33629
Phone: 813-253-0541
Fax: 813-254-5857
E-mail: mwestley@cancer.org

AMERICAN LEGION, DEPARTMENT OF ALABAMA

AMERICAN LEGION DEPARTMENT OF ALABAMA SCHOLARSHIP PROGRAM
see number 205

AMERICAN LEGION, DEPARTMENT OF NEW YORK

AMERICAN LEGION DEPARTMENT OF NEW YORK STATE HIGH SCHOOL ORATORICAL CONTEST
● 281

Oratorical contest open to students under the age of twenty in 9th-12th grades of any accredited New York high school. Speech contests begin in November at post levels and continue on to national competition. Contact local American Legion post for deadlines. Must be U.S. citizen or lawful permanent resident. Payments are made directly to college and are awarded over a four-year period.

Award Scholarship for use in freshman year; not renewable. *Number:* 65. *Amount:* $75–$6000.

Eligibility Requirements: Applicant must be high school student; age 20 or under; planning to enroll or expecting to enroll at an institution or university; resident of New York and must have an interest in public speaking. Available to U.S. citizens.

Application Requirements Application, applicant must enter a contest.

World Wide Web: http://www.ny.legion.org

Contact: Richard Pedro, Department Adjutant
American Legion, Department of New York
112 State Street, Suite 400
Albany, NY 12207
Phone: 518-463-2215
Fax: 518-427-8443
E-mail: newyork@legion.org

ARKANSAS DEPARTMENT OF HIGHER EDUCATION

ARKANSAS STUDENT ASSISTANCE GRANT PROGRAM • 282

Award for Arkansas residents attending a college within the state. Must be enrolled full-time, have financial need, and maintain satisfactory progress. One-time award for undergraduate use only. Application is the FAFSA.

Award Grant for use in freshman, sophomore, junior, or senior years; not renewable. *Number:* 600–5500. *Amount:* $600.

Eligibility Requirements: Applicant must be enrolled or expecting to enroll full-time at a two-year or four-year or technical institution or university; resident of Arkansas and studying in Arkansas. Available to U.S. citizens.

Application Requirements Application, financial need analysis, FAFSA. *Deadline:* April 1.

World Wide Web: http://www.arscholarships.com

Contact: Assistant Coordinator
Arkansas Department of Higher Education
114 East Capitol
Little Rock, AR 72201
Phone: 501-371-2050
Fax: 501-371-2001

GOVERNOR'S SCHOLARS-ARKANSAS • 283

Awards for outstanding Arkansas high school seniors. Must be an Arkansas resident and have a high school GPA of at least 3.5 or have scored at least 27 on the ACT. Award is $4000 per year for four years of full-time undergraduate study. Applicants who attain 32 or above on ACT, 1410 or above on SAT and have an academic 3.50 GPA, or are selected as National Merit or National Achievement finalists may receive an award equal to tuition, mandatory fees, room, and board up to $10,000 per year at any Arkansas institution.

Award Scholarship for use in freshman, sophomore, junior, or senior years; renewable. *Number:* 75–250. *Amount:* $4000–$10,000.

Eligibility Requirements: Applicant must be high school student; planning to enroll or expecting to enroll full-time at a two-year or four-year institution or university; resident of Arkansas and studying in Arkansas. Applicant must have 3.5 GPA or higher. Available to U.S. citizens.

Application Requirements Application, test scores, transcript. *Deadline:* February 1.

World Wide Web: http://www.arscholarships.com

Contact: Philip Axelroth, Assistant Coordinator of Financial Aid
Arkansas Department of Higher Education
114 East Capitol
Little Rock, AR 72201
Phone: 501-371-2050
Fax: 501-371-2001
E-mail: phila@adhe.arknet.edu

BARBARA ALICE MOWER MEMORIAL SCHOLARSHIP COMMITTEE

BARBARA ALICE MOWER MEMORIAL SCHOLARSHIP • 284

Award for women residents of Hawaii who are committed to using their education to help other women, especially women of Hawaii. Must be junior or senior level undergraduate. Graduate level also eligible.

Award Scholarship for use in junior, senior, graduate, or postgraduate years; not renewable. *Number:* 1–25. *Amount:* $1000–$3500.

Eligibility Requirements: Applicant must be enrolled or expecting to enroll full-time at a four-year institution or university; female and resident of Hawaii. Available to U.S. citizens.

Application Requirements Application, essay, references, transcript. *Deadline:* May 1.

Contact: Nancy Mower
Barbara Alice Mower Memorial Scholarship Committee
1536 Kamole Street
Honolulu, HI 96821
Phone: 808-373-2901
E-mail: nmower@hawaii.edu

BIG 33 SCHOLARSHIP FOUNDATION, INC.

BIG 33 SCHOLARSHIP FOUNDATION, INC. SCHOLARSHIPS • 285

Open to all high school seniors in Pennsylvania and Ohio. Quantity of scholarships awarded, dollar amount of each and type of scholarships varies each year. One-time award only. Minimum 2.0 GPA required. Applications are available at web site: http://www.big33.org

Award Scholarship for use in freshman year; not renewable. *Number:* 150–200. *Amount:* $500–$4500.

Eligibility Requirements: Applicant must be high school student; planning to enroll or expecting to enroll full-time at a two-year or four-year or technical institution or university and resident of Ohio or Pennsylvania. Available to U.S. citizens.

Application Requirements Application, essay, transcript. *Deadline:* February 1.

World Wide Web: http://www.big33.org

Contact: Mickey Minnich, Executive Director
Big 33 Scholarship Foundation, Inc.
511 Bridge Street
PO Box 213
New Cumberland, PA 17070
Phone: 717-774-3303
Fax: 717-774-1749
E-mail: info@big33.org

BIG Y FOODS, INC.

BIG Y SCHOLARSHIPS • 286

Awards are for customers or dependents of customers of Big Y Foods. Big Y Trade area covers western and central Massachusetts and Connecticut. Also awards for Big Y employees and dependents of employees. Awards are based on academic excellence. Grades, board scores and three letters of recommendation required.

Award Scholarship for use in freshman, sophomore, junior, senior, or graduate years; not renewable. *Number:* 250. *Amount:* $500–$2000.

Eligibility Requirements: Applicant must be enrolled or expecting to enroll full or part-time at a two-year or four-year institution or university and resident of Connecticut or Massachusetts. Available to U.S. citizens.

Application Requirements Application, references, test scores, transcript. *Deadline:* February 1.

World Wide Web: http://www.bigy.com

Contact: Gail Borkosky, Scholarship Administrator
Big Y Foods, Inc.
2145 Roosevelt Avenue
Springfield, MA 01102-7840
Phone: 413-504-4062

BOETTCHER FOUNDATION

BOETTCHER FOUNDATION SCHOLARSHIPS • 287

The Boettcher Scholarship is the most prestigious merit-based scholarship available to graduating seniors in the state of Colorado. Selection based on class rank (top 5%), test scores, leadership, and service. Renewable for four years and can be used at any Colorado university or college. Includes full tuition and fees, living stipend of $2,800 per year and a stipend for books.

Award Scholarship for use in freshman, sophomore, junior, or senior years; renewable. *Number:* 40. *Amount:* $40,000–$120,000.

Eligibility Requirements: Applicant must be high school student; planning to enroll or expecting to enroll full-time at a four-year institution or university; resident of Colorado and studying in Colorado. Applicant must have 3.5 GPA or higher. Available to U.S. citizens.

Application Requirements Application, essay, interview, references, test scores, transcript. *Deadline:* November 1.

World Wide Web: http://www.boettcherfoundation.org

Contact: Jennie Kenney, Scholarship Administrative Assistant
Boettcher Foundation
600 17th Street, Suite 2210 S
Denver, CO 80202-5422
Phone: 303-285-6207
E-mail: scholarships@boettcherfoundation.org

BUFFETT FOUNDATION

BUFFETT FOUNDATION SCHOLARSHIP • 288

Scholarship provides assistance for tuition and fees (only) up to $2500 per semester. Must be used at a Nebraska state school or a two-year college or trade school within Nebraska. High school applicant must have maintained a 2.5 GPA, college students a 2.0. Must have already applied for federal financial aid and have printed results. Strict deadlines apply. March 1st for requesting mail applications which must be returned by April 10. Must be Nebraska resident.

Award Scholarship for use in freshman, sophomore, junior, or senior years; renewable. *Number:* 30–50. *Amount:* up to $2500.

Eligibility Requirements: Applicant must be enrolled or expecting to enroll full-time at a two-year or four-year or technical institution or university; resident of Nebraska and studying in Nebraska. Applicant must have 2.5 GPA or higher. Available to U.S. citizens.

Application Requirements Application, autobiography, essay, financial need analysis, references, transcript, federal tax return. *Deadline:* April 10.

World Wide Web: http://www.buffettscholarships.org

Contact: Devon Buffett, Director of Scholarships
Buffett Foundation
PO Box 4508
Decatur, IL 62525
Phone: 402-451-6011
E-mail: buffettfound@aol.com

CALIFORNIA ASSOCIATION OF PRIVATE POSTSECONDARY SCHOOLS

CAPPS SCHOLARSHIP PROGRAM • 289

Schools participating in the CAPPS Scholarship Program offer both full- and partial-tuition scholarships to graduating high school students and adults wishing to pursue their education at a private career school. Scholarships are for tuition only. Applications are sent to the school of the applicant's choice; that school selects scholarship recipients using their own criterion. Among other qualifications listed on the application, recipients must meet that school's admissions requirements and be a California resident and a U.S. legal citizen to qualify. Written inquiries must include a self-addressed stamped envelope for reply.

Award Scholarship for use in freshman year; not renewable. *Number:* 250–500. *Amount:* $1000–$10,000.

Eligibility Requirements: Applicant must be enrolled or expecting to enroll full or part-time at a two-year or technical institution or university and resident of California. Available to U.S. citizens.

Application Requirements Application, self-addressed stamped envelope. *Deadline:* May 30.

World Wide Web: http://www.cappsonline.org

Contact: Lola Noren, Scholarship Coordinator
California Association of Private Postsecondary Schools
921 11th Street #619
Sacramento, CA 95814-2821
E-mail: info@cappsoline.org

CALIFORNIA CORRECTIONAL PEACE OFFICERS ASSOCIATION

CALIFORNIA CORRECTIONAL PEACE OFFICERS ASSOCIATION JOE HARPER SCHOLARSHIP
see number 174

CALIFORNIA JUNIOR MISS SCHOLARSHIP PROGRAM

CALIFORNIA JUNIOR MISS SCHOLARSHIP PROGRAM • 290

Scholarship program to recognize and reward outstanding high school junior girls in the areas of academics, leadership, athletics, public speaking and the arts. Must be single, female, a U.S. citizen, and resident of California. Minimum 3.0 GPA required.

Award Scholarship for use in freshman year; not renewable. *Number:* 10–20. *Amount:* $300–$10,000.

Eligibility Requirements: Applicant must be high school student; planning to enroll or expecting to enroll full-time at a two-year or four-year institution or university; single female; resident of California and must have an interest in leadership. Applicant must have 3.0 GPA or higher. Available to U.S. citizens.

Application Requirements Application, applicant must enter a contest, interview, test scores, transcript. *Deadline:* January 1.

World Wide Web: http://www.ajm.org/california

Contact: Becky Jo Peterson, California State Chairman
California Junior Miss Scholarship Program
3523 Glenbrook Lane
Napa, CA 94558
Phone: 707-224-5112
E-mail: caljrmiss@aol.com

CALIFORNIA STUDENT AID COMMISSION

ASSUMPTION PROGRAMS OF LOANS FOR EDUCATION • 291

The APLE is a competitive teacher loan assumption program designed to encourage outstanding students and out-of-state teachers to become California teachers with in subject areas where a teacher shortage has been identified or in schools meeting specific criteria identified annually. Participants may receive up to $19,000 towards outstanding student loans.

Assumption Programs of Loans for Education (continued)
Award Forgivable loan for use in junior, senior, or graduate years; renewable.
Number: up to 6500. *Amount:* up to $19,000.
Eligibility Requirements: Applicant must be enrolled or expecting to enroll full or part-time at a four-year institution or university; resident of California and studying in California. Available to U.S. citizens.
Application Requirements Application, references. *Deadline:* June 30.
World Wide Web: http://www.csac.ca.gov
Contact: California Student Aid Commission
P O Box 419027
Rancho Cordova, CA 95741-9027
Phone: 916-526-7590
Fax: 916-526-8002
E-mail: custsvcs@csac.ca.gov

CAL GRANT C • 292

Award for California residents who are enrolled in a short-term vocational training program. Program must lead to a recognized degree or certificate. Course length must be a minimum of 4 months and no longer than 24 months. Students must be attending an approved California institution and show financial need.

Award Grant for use in freshman, sophomore, junior, or senior years; renewable. *Number:* up to 7761. *Amount:* $576–$3168.
Eligibility Requirements: Applicant must be enrolled or expecting to enroll full or part-time at a two-year or technical institution; resident of California and studying in California. Available to U.S. citizens.
Application Requirements Application, financial need analysis. *Deadline:* March 2.
World Wide Web: http://www.csac.ca.gov
Contact: California Student Aid Commission
P O Box 419027
Rancho Cordova, CA 95741-9027
Phone: 916-526-7590
Fax: 916-526-8002
E-mail: custsvs@csac.ca.gov

CHILD DEVELOPMENT TEACHER AND SUPERVISOR GRANT PROGRAM • 293

Award is for those students pursuing an approved course of study leading to a Child Development Permit issued by the California Commission on Teacher Credentialing. In exchange for each year funding is received, recipients agree to provide one year of service in a licensed childcare center.

Award Grant for use in freshman, sophomore, junior, or senior years; renewable. *Number:* 100–200. *Amount:* $1000–$2000.
Eligibility Requirements: Applicant must be enrolled or expecting to enroll full or part-time at a two-year or four-year or technical institution or university; resident of California and studying in California. Available to U.S. citizens.

Application Requirements Application, financial need analysis, references, FAFSA. *Deadline:* June 1.

World Wide Web: http://www.csac.ca.gov

Contact: California Student Aid Commission
PO Box 419027
Rancho Cordova, CA 95741-9027
Phone: 916-526-7590
Fax: 916-526-8002
E-mail: custsvcs@csac.ca.gov

COMPETITIVE CAL GRANT A • 294

Award for California residents who are not recent high school graduates attending an approved college or university within the state. Must show financial need and meet minimum 3.0 GPA requirements.

Award Grant for use in freshman, sophomore, junior, or senior years; renewable. *Number:* up to 22,500. *Amount:* $1572–$9708.

Eligibility Requirements: Applicant must be enrolled or expecting to enroll full or part-time at a two-year or four-year or technical institution or university; resident of California and studying in California. Applicant must have 3.0 GPA or higher. Available to U.S. citizens.

Application Requirements Application, financial need analysis. *Deadline:* March 2.

World Wide Web: http://www.csac.ca.gov

Contact: California Student Aid Commission
P O Box 41907
Rancho Cordova, CA 95741-9027
Phone: 916-526-7590
Fax: 916-526-8002
E-mail: custsvcs@csac.ca.gov

COMPETITIVE CAL GRANT B • 295

Award is for California residents who are not recent high school graduates attending an approved college or university within the state. Must show financial need and meet the minimum 2.0 GPA requirements.

Award Grant for use in freshman, sophomore, or junior years; renewable. *Number:* up to 22,500. *Amount:* $700–$11,259.

Eligibility Requirements: Applicant must be enrolled or expecting to enroll full or part-time at a two-year or four-year or technical institution or university; resident of California and studying in California. Available to U.S. citizens.

Application Requirements Application, financial need analysis, GPA Verification. *Deadline:* March 2.

World Wide Web: http://www.csac.ca.gov

Competitive Cal Grant B (continued)
Contact: California Student Aid Commission
PO Box 419027
Rancho Cordova, CA 95741-9027
Phone: 916-526-7590
Fax: 916-526-8002
E-mail: custsvcs@gsac.ca.gov

ROBERT C. BYRD SCHOLARSHIP • 296

Federally funded award is available to California high school seniors. Students are awarded based on outstanding academic merit. Students must be nominated by their high school.

Award Scholarship for use in freshman, sophomore, junior, or senior years; renewable. *Number:* 700–800. *Amount:* $1500.
Eligibility Requirements: Applicant must be high school student; planning to enroll or expecting to enroll full-time at a four-year institution or university and resident of California. Applicant must have 3.5 GPA or higher. Available to U.S. citizens.
Application Requirements Application, financial need analysis, test scores. *Deadline:* April 30.
World Wide Web: http://www.csac.ca.gov
Contact: California Student Aid Commission
P O Box 419027
Rancho Cordova, CA 95741-9027
Phone: 916-526-7590
Fax: 916-526-8002
E-mail: custsvcs@csa.ca.gov

CAREER COLLEGES AND SCHOOLS OF TEXAS

CAREER COLLEGES AND SCHOOLS OF TEXAS SCHOLARSHIP PROGRAM • 297

One-time award available to graduating high school seniors who plan to attend a Texas trade or technical institution. Must be a Texas resident. Criteria selection, which is determined independently by each school's guidance counselors, may be based on academic excellence, financial need or student leadership. Must be U.S. citizen.

Award Scholarship for use in freshman year; not renewable. *Number:* up to 6000. *Amount:* up to $1000.
Eligibility Requirements: Applicant must be high school student; planning to enroll or expecting to enroll full or part-time at a technical institution; resident of Texas and studying in Texas. Available to U.S. citizens.
Application Requirements Determined by high school. *Deadline:* Continuous.
World Wide Web: http://www.colleges-schools.org

Contact: High School counselors
Career Colleges and Schools of Texas
6460 Hiller, Suite D
El Paso, TX 79925

CENTRAL SCHOLARSHIP BUREAU

MARY RUBIN AND BENJAMIN M. RUBIN SCHOLARSHIP FUND • 298

Renewable scholarship for tuition only to women who are attending a college, university or other institution of higher learning. Must be a resident of Maryland. Have a GPA of 3.0 or better and meet the financial requirements. Contact for application or download from web site.

Award Scholarship for use in freshman, sophomore, junior, senior, graduate, or postgraduate years; renewable. *Number:* 30–35. *Amount:* $500–$2500.

Eligibility Requirements: Applicant must be enrolled or expecting to enroll full or part-time at a two-year or four-year or technical institution or university; female and resident of Maryland. Applicant must have 3.0 GPA or higher. Available to U.S. citizens.

Application Requirements Application, essay, financial need analysis, references, transcript. *Deadline:* March 1.

World Wide Web: http://www.centralsb.org

Contact: Roberta Goldman, Program Director
Central Scholarship Bureau
1700 Reisterstown Road
Suite 220
Baltimore, MD 21208-2903
Phone: 410-415-5558
Fax: 410-415-5501
E-mail: roberta@centralsb.org

COLORADO COMMISSION ON HIGHER EDUCATION

COLORADO LEVERAGING EDUCATIONAL ASSISTANCE PARTNERSHIP (CLEAP) AND SLEAP • 299

Renewable awards for Colorado residents who are attending Colorado state-supported postsecondary institutions at the undergraduate level. Must document financial need. Contact colleges for complete information and deadlines.

Award Grant for use in freshman, sophomore, junior, or senior years; not renewable. *Number:* 5000. *Amount:* $50–$900.

Eligibility Requirements: Applicant must be enrolled or expecting to enroll full or part-time at a two-year or four-year or technical institution or university; resident of Colorado and studying in Colorado. Available to U.S. citizens.

Application Requirements Application, financial need analysis.

World Wide Web: http://www.state.co.us/cche

Colorado Leveraging Educational Assistance Partnership (CLEAP) and SLEAP (continued)
Contact: Financial Aid Office at college/institution
Colorado Commission on Higher Education
1380 Lawrence Street, Suite 1200
Denver, CO 80204-2059

COLORADO UNDERGRADUATE MERIT SCHOLARSHIPS • 300

Renewable awards for students attending Colorado state-supported institutions at the undergraduate level. Must demonstrate superior scholarship or talent. Contact college financial aid office for complete information and deadlines.

Award Scholarship for use in freshman, sophomore, junior, or senior years; renewable. *Number:* 10,823. *Amount:* $1230.

Eligibility Requirements: Applicant must be enrolled or expecting to enroll full or part-time at a two-year or four-year or technical institution or university; resident of Colorado and studying in Colorado. Applicant must have 3.0 GPA or higher.

Application Requirements Application, test scores, transcript.

World Wide Web: http://www.state.co.us/cche

Contact: Financial Aid Office at college/institution
Colorado Commission on Higher Education
1380 Lawrence Street, Suite 1200
Denver, CO 80204-2059

GOVERNOR'S OPPORTUNITY SCHOLARSHIP • 301

Scholarship available for the most needy first-time freshmen whose parents' adjusted gross income is less than $26,000. Must be U.S. citizen for permanent legal resident. Work-study is part of the program.

Award Scholarship for use in freshman, sophomore, junior, or senior years; renewable. *Number:* up to 1052. *Amount:* $5665.

Eligibility Requirements: Applicant must be high school student; planning to enroll or expecting to enroll full-time at a two-year or four-year or technical institution or university; resident of Colorado and studying in Colorado. Available to U.S. citizens.

Application Requirements Application, financial need analysis, test scores, transcript. *Deadline:* Continuous.

World Wide Web: http://www.state.co.us/cche

Contact: Financial Aid Office at college/institution
Colorado Commission on Higher Education
1380 Lawrence Street, Suite 1200
Denver, CO 80204-2059

COMMUNITY FOUNDATION FOR GREATER ATLANTA, INC.

NANCY PENN LYONS SCHOLARSHIP • 302

Scholarship supports students graduating from a high school in Georgia who have been accepted for enrollment at highly selective or out-of-state colleges and universities. Awards are made to students for their freshman year and can be renewed with continued academic progress.

Award Scholarship for use in freshman, sophomore, junior, or senior years; renewable. *Number:* 5–20. *Amount:* up to $5000.

Eligibility Requirements: Applicant must be high school student; planning to enroll or expecting to enroll full-time at a four-year institution or university and resident of Georgia. Applicant must have 3.0 GPA or higher. Available to U.S. citizens.

Application Requirements Application, essay, financial need analysis, resume, references, test scores, transcript. *Deadline:* April 15.

World Wide Web: http://www.atlcf.org/

Contact: Claudette Clark
Community Foundation for Greater Atlanta, Inc.
50 Hurt Plaza, Suite 449
Atlanta, GA 30303
Phone: 404-688-5525
Fax: 404-688-3060
E-mail: cclarke@atlcf.org

COMMUNITY FOUNDATION FOR GREATER BUFFALO

COMMUNITY FOUNDATION FOR GREATER BUFFALO SCHOLARSHIPS • 303

Scholarships restricted to current residents of western New York (several only to Erie County), who have been accepted for admission to any nonprofit school in the United States for full-time study at the undergraduate level. Must maintain a "C" average. Must submit estimated family contribution as indicated on Student Aid Report from FAFSA form.

Award Scholarship for use in freshman, sophomore, junior, or senior years; not renewable. *Number:* 125. *Amount:* $200–$4500.

Eligibility Requirements: Applicant must be enrolled or expecting to enroll full-time at a two-year or four-year institution or university and resident of New York. Available to U.S. and non-U.S. citizens.

Application Requirements Application, essay, financial need analysis, references, self-addressed stamped envelope, transcript. *Deadline:* June 1.

World Wide Web: http://www.cfgb.org

Community Foundation for Greater Buffalo Scholarships (continued)

Contact: Program Officer
Community Foundation for Greater Buffalo
712 Main Street
Buffalo, NY 14202

COMMUNITY FOUNDATION OF WESTERN MASSACHUSETTS

JAMES Z. NAURISON SCHOLARSHIP • 304

For undergraduate and graduate students who are residents of Hampden, Kampshire, Franklin, and Berkshire Counties in Massachusetts and Enfield and Suffield, Connecticut. May be awarded up to four years based upon discretion of the scholarship committee. Deadline: April 16. Visit http://www.communityfoundation.org.

Award Scholarship for use in freshman, sophomore, junior, senior, or graduate years; renewable. *Number:* 655. *Amount:* $1000.

Eligibility Requirements: Applicant must be enrolled or expecting to enroll at an institution or university and resident of Connecticut or Massachusetts. Available to U.S. citizens.

Application Requirements Application, financial need analysis, references, transcript, personal statement. *Deadline:* April 16.

World Wide Web: http://www.communityfoundation.org

Contact: Community Foundation of Western Massachusetts
1500 Main Street, PO Box 15769
Springfield, MA 01115

DC GOVERNMENT, EXECUTIVE OFFICE OF THE MAYOR, STATE OFFICE OF EDUCATION

DC LEVERAGING EDUCATIONAL ASSISTANCE PARTNERSHIP • 305

Need-based program awarding grants to high-need applicants, DC residents enrolled in undergraduate degree programs. Applicants must submit SAR. Awards made to applicants with unmet need equal to or greater than $1,500.

Award Grant for use in freshman, sophomore, junior, or senior years; not renewable. *Number:* 2500–3000. *Amount:* $1500.

Eligibility Requirements: Applicant must be enrolled or expecting to enroll full or part-time at a two-year or four-year or technical institution or university and resident of District of Columbia. Available to U.S. citizens.

Application Requirements Application, financial need analysis, Student Aid Report (SAR). *Deadline:* June 28.

World Wide Web: http://www.seo.dc.gov

Contact: Angela M. March, Program Manager, D.C. LEAP
DC Government, Executive Office of the Mayor, State Office of
Education
DC State Education Office, 441 4th Street NW, Suite 350 North
Washington, DC 20001
Phone: 202-724-7803
Fax: 202-727-2019
E-mail: angela.march@dc.gov

DC TUITION ASSISTANCE GRANT PROGRAM   • 306

Federally funded and legislated grant pays the difference between in-state and
out-of-state tuition at any public college in the U.S., up to $10,000 per year.
Students attending private colleges in DC Metropolitan area or private HBCU's,
nationwide, are eligible for a grant of up to $2,500 per year. Must be a DC
resident to be eligible. The program is not need-based.

Award Grant for use in freshman, sophomore, junior, or senior years; not
renewable. *Number:* up to 4000. *Amount:* $2500–$10,000.

Eligibility Requirements: Applicant must be enrolled or expecting to enroll
full or part-time at a two-year or four-year institution or university and resident
of District of Columbia. Available to U.S. citizens.

Application Requirements Application, proof of domicile. *Deadline:* June
30.

World Wide Web: http://www.seo.dc.gov

Contact: DC Government, Executive Office of the Mayor, State Office of
Education
441 4th Street, NW, Room 350N
Washington, DC 20001
Phone: 202-727-2824
Fax: 202-727-2834

DE VRY, INC.

DEVRY COMMUNITY COLLEGE SCHOLARSHIPS   • 307

Each of DeVry's 25 campuses awards four half-tuition Community College
Scholarships each year. A student who has received an associate's degree in
the past year and is applying to a DeVry University's bachelor's degree program
is eligible to apply. The winners are chosen by committees at each campus on
the basis of applicants' academics, records, two letters of recommendation,
and an essay on a topic chosen by the committee.

Award Scholarship for use in freshman, sophomore, junior, or senior years;
renewable. *Number:* 75. *Amount:* $5000–$8000.

Eligibility Requirements: Applicant must be enrolled or expecting to enroll
full-time at an institution or university and studying in Arizona, California,
Colorado, Florida, Georgia, Illinois, Missouri, New Jersey, New York, Ohio,
Texas, or Virginia. Applicant must have 3.0 GPA or higher. Available to U.S.
and Canadian citizens.

DeVry Community College Scholarships (continued)
Application Requirements Application, essay, interview, references, transcript.
Deadline: Continuous.
World Wide Web: http://www.devry.edu
Contact: Scholarship Coordinator
De Vry, Inc.
One Tower Lane
Oak Brook Terrace, IL 60181
Phone: 630-571-7700
Fax: 630-571-0317

DEVRY COMMUNITY SCHOLARS PROGRAM • 308

DeVry University's Community Scholars Program will provide scholarships to approximately 1600 graduates from public high schools in the 18 metropolitan areas served by DeVry's campuses. One graduating senior from each eligible high school will receive $1000 per semester or $3000 per calendar year for the duration of the DeVry degree program. Recipients of this award must demonstrate proficiency in mathematics and rank in the upper one-third of their class.

Award Scholarship for use in freshman, sophomore, junior, or senior years; renewable. *Number:* 1600. *Amount:* up to $3000.
Eligibility Requirements: Applicant must be high school student; planning to enroll or expecting to enroll full-time at an institution or university and studying in Arizona, California, Colorado, Florida, Georgia, Illinois, Missouri, New Jersey, New York, Ohio, Texas, or Virginia. Applicant must have 3.0 GPA or higher. Available to U.S. and Canadian citizens.
Application Requirements Application, interview, references, test scores, transcript. *Deadline:* Continuous.
World Wide Web: http://www.devry.edu
Contact: Scholarship Coordinator
De Vry, Inc.
One Tower Lane
Oak Brook Terrace, IL 60181
Phone: 630-571-7700
Fax: 630-571-0317

DEVRY PRESIDENTIAL SCHOLARSHIPS • 309

Two full-tuition Presidential Scholarships are awarded by each of the 25 DeVry University campuses each year. Contenders are chosen from those who receive a Dean's Scholarship. Winners are determined by committees at each campus on the basis of their academic records, SAT or ACT scores, and an essay on a topic chosen by the committee.

Award Scholarship for use in freshman, sophomore, junior, or senior years; renewable. *Number:* 50. *Amount:* $10,000–$15,000.
Eligibility Requirements: Applicant must be high school student; planning to enroll or expecting to enroll full-time at an institution or university and studying in Arizona, California, Colorado, Florida, Georgia, Illinois, Missouri,

New Jersey, New York, Ohio, Texas, or Virginia. Applicant must have 3.0 GPA or higher. Available to U.S. and Canadian citizens.

Application Requirements Application, essay, interview, test scores, transcript. *Deadline:* Continuous.

World Wide Web: http://www.devry.edu

Contact: Scholarship Coordinator
De Vry, Inc.
One Tower Lane
Oak Brook Terrace, IL 60181
Phone: 630-571-7700
Fax: 630-571-0317

DELAWARE HIGHER EDUCATION COMMISSION

DIAMOND STATE SCHOLARSHIP   • 310

Renewable award for Delaware high school seniors enrolling full-time at an accredited college or university. Must be ranked in upper quarter of class and score 1200 on SAT or 27 on the ACT.

Award Scholarship for use in freshman year; renewable. *Number:* 50–200. *Amount:* $1250.

Eligibility Requirements: Applicant must be high school student; planning to enroll or expecting to enroll full-time at a four-year institution or university and resident of Delaware. Applicant must have 3.5 GPA or higher. Available to U.S. citizens.

Application Requirements Application, essay, test scores, transcript. *Deadline:* March 31.

World Wide Web: http://www.doe.state.de.us/high-ed

Contact: Donna Myers, Higher Education Analyst
Delaware Higher Education Commission
820 North French Street
5th Floor
Wilmington, DE 19711-3509
Phone: 302-577-3240
Fax: 302-577-6765
E-mail: dhec@doe.k12.de.us

LEGISLATIVE ESSAY SCHOLARSHIP   • 311

Must be a senior in high school and Delaware resident. Submit an essay of 500 to 2000 words on a designated historical topic (changes annually). Deadline: November 16. For more information visit: http://www.doe.state.de.us/high-ed.

Award Scholarship for use in freshman year; not renewable. *Number:* 62. *Amount:* $500–$5500.

Legislative Essay Scholarship (continued)
Eligibility Requirements: Applicant must be high school student; planning to enroll or expecting to enroll full or part-time at a two-year or four-year or technical institution or university and resident of Delaware. Available to U.S. citizens.
Application Requirements Application, applicant must enter a contest, essay. *Deadline:* November 16.
World Wide Web: http://www.doe.state.de.us/high-ed
Contact: Donna Myers, Higher Education Analyst
Delaware Higher Education Commission
820 North French Street
5th Floor
Wilmington, DE 19711-3509
Phone: 302-577-3240
Fax: 302-577-6765
E-mail: dhec@doe.k12.de.us

ROBERT C. BYRD HONORS SCHOLARSHIP-DELAWARE • 312

Available to Delaware residents who are graduating high school seniors. Based on outstanding academic merit. Awards are renewable up to four years. Must be ranked in upper quarter of class and have a score of 1200 on SAT or 27 on ACT.
Award Scholarship for use in freshman year; renewable. *Number:* 16–80. *Amount:* $1500.
Eligibility Requirements: Applicant must be high school student; planning to enroll or expecting to enroll full-time at a two-year or four-year institution or university and resident of Delaware. Applicant must have 3.5 GPA or higher. Available to U.S. citizens.
Application Requirements Application, essay, test scores, transcript. *Deadline:* March 31.
World Wide Web: http://www.doe.state.de.us/high-ed
Contact: Donna Myers, Higher Education Analyst
Delaware Higher Education Commission
820 North French Street
5th Floor
Wilmington, DE 19711-3509
Phone: 302-577-3240
Fax: 302-577-6765
E-mail: dhec@doe.k12.de.us

SCHOLARSHIP INCENTIVE PROGRAM-DELAWARE • 313

One-time award for Delaware residents with financial need. May be used at an institution in Delaware or Pennsylvania, or at another out-of-state institution if a program is not available at a publicly-supported school in Delaware. Must have minimum 2.5 GPA.
Award Grant for use in freshman, sophomore, junior, or senior years; not renewable. *Number:* 1000–1300. *Amount:* $700–$2200.

Eligibility Requirements: Applicant must be enrolled or expecting to enroll full-time at a two-year or four-year institution or university; resident of Delaware and studying in Delaware or Pennsylvania. Applicant must have 2.5 GPA or higher. Available to U.S. citizens.

Application Requirements Application, financial need analysis, transcript. *Deadline:* April 15.

World Wide Web: http://www.doe.state.de.us/high-ed

Contact: Donna Myers, Higher Education Analyst
Delaware Higher Education Commission
820 North French Street
5th Floor
Wilmington, DE 19711-3509
Phone: 302-577-3240
Fax: 302-577-6765
E-mail: dhec@doe.k12.de.us

DEPARTMENT OF MILITARY AFFAIRS

WISCONSIN NATIONAL GUARD TUITION GRANT   see number 192

DISTRICT OF COLUMBIA STATE EDUCATION OFFICE

DC LEVERAGING EDUCATIONAL ASSISTANCE PARTNERSHIP PROGRAM (LEAP)   • 314

Available to Washington, D.C. residents who have financial need. Must also apply for the Federal Pell Grant. Must attend an eligible college at least half-time. Contact financial aid office or local library for more information. Proof of residency may be required. Deadline is last Friday in June.

Award Scholarship for use in freshman, sophomore, junior, or senior years; not renewable. *Number:* 1200–1500. *Amount:* $500–$1500.

Eligibility Requirements: Applicant must be enrolled or expecting to enroll full or part-time at a two-year or four-year or technical institution or university and resident of District of Columbia. Available to U.S. citizens.

Application Requirements Application, financial need analysis, Student Aid Report (SAR). *Deadline:* June 28.

World Wide Web: http://www.seo.dc.gov

Contact: Angela March, Program Manager
District of Columbia State Education Office
441 4th Street NW, Suite 350 North
Washington, DC 20001
Phone: 202-727-6436
Fax: 202-727-2019
E-mail: angela.march@dc.gov

EAST LOS ANGELES COMMUNITY UNION (TELACU) EDUCATION FOUNDATION

TELACU SCHOLARSHIP PROGRAM • 315

Scholarships available to low-income applicants from the Greater East Side of Los Angeles. Must be U.S. citizen or permanent resident. Must be a resident of one of the following communities: East Los Angeles, Bell Gardens, Commerce, Huntington Park, Montebello, Monterey Park, Pico Rivera, Santa Ana, South Gate, and the City of Los Angeles. Must be the first generation in their family to achieve a college degree. Must have a record of community service.

Award Scholarship for use in freshman, sophomore, junior, or senior years; not renewable. *Number:* up to 100. *Amount:* $500–$1000.

Eligibility Requirements: Applicant must be enrolled or expecting to enroll full-time at a two-year or four-year institution or university; resident of California and studying in California. Applicant must have 2.5 GPA or higher. Available to U.S. citizens.

Application Requirements Application, essay, financial need analysis, interview, references, transcript. *Deadline:* April 6.

Contact: Michael A. Alvarado, Director
      Phone: 323-721-1655

EDMUND F. MAXWELL FOUNDATION

EDMUND F. MAXWELL FOUNDATION SCHOLARSHIP • 316

Scholarships awarded to residents of western Washington to attend accredited independent colleges or universities. Awards of up to $3500 per year based on need, merit, citizenship, and activities. Renewable for up to four years if academic progress is suitable and financial need is unchanged.

Award Scholarship for use in freshman year; renewable. *Number:* 110. *Amount:* $1000–$3500.

Eligibility Requirements: Applicant must be enrolled or expecting to enroll full-time at a four-year institution or university and resident of Washington. Available to U.S. citizens.

Application Requirements Application, essay, financial need analysis, test scores, transcript, employment history. *Deadline:* April 30.

World Wide Web: http://www.maxwell.org

Contact: Administrator
      Edmund F. Maxwell Foundation
      PO Box 22537
      Seattle, WA 98122
      E-mail: admin@maxwell.com

ESPERANZA, INC.

ESPERANZA SCHOLARSHIPS

see number 227

FINANCE AUTHORITY OF MAINE

MAINE STATE GRANT • 317

Scholarships for residents of Maine attending an eligible school, full time, in Connecticut, Maine, Massachusetts, New Hampshire, Pennsylvania, Rhode Island, Washington, D.C., or Vermont. Award based on need. Must apply annually. Complete Free Application for Federal Student Aid to apply. One-time award of $500-$1250 for undergraduate study.

Award Grant for use in freshman, sophomore, junior, or senior years; not renewable. *Number:* 8900–12,500. *Amount:* $500–$1250.

Eligibility Requirements: Applicant must be enrolled or expecting to enroll full-time at a two-year or four-year or technical institution or university; resident of Maine and studying in Connecticut, District of Columbia, Maine, Massachusetts, New Hampshire, Pennsylvania, Rhode Island, or Vermont.

Application Requirements Application, financial need analysis, FAFSA. *Deadline:* May 1.

World Wide Web: http://www.famemaine.com

Contact: Claude Roy, Program Officer
Finance Authority of Maine
5 Community Drive
Augusta, ME 04332-0949
Phone: 800-228-3734
Fax: 207-623-0095
E-mail: claude@famemaine.com

FLORIDA ASSOCIATION OF POSTSECONDARY SCHOOLS AND COLLEGES

FLORIDA ASSOCIATION OF POSTSECONDARY SCHOOLS AND COLLEGES SCHOLARSHIP PROGRAM • 318

Full and partial scholarship to private career schools in Florida are awarded to students either graduating from high school or receiving GED in the current school year. Must be a resident of Florida. Minimum 2.5 GPA required.

Award Scholarship for use in freshman year; not renewable. *Number:* 100–200. *Amount:* $3500.

Eligibility Requirements: Applicant must be high school student; planning to enroll or expecting to enroll at a technical institution; resident of Florida and studying in Florida. Applicant must have 2.5 GPA or higher. Available to U.S. citizens.

Application Requirements Application, essay, references, transcript. *Deadline:* March 1.

World Wide Web: http://www.fapsc.org

Florida Association of Postsecondary Schools and Colleges Scholarship Program (continued)

Contact: Heather Fuselier, Membership Director
Florida Association of Postsecondary Schools and Colleges
200 West College Avenue
Tallahassee, FL 32301
Phone: 850-577-3139
Fax: 850-577-3133
E-mail: scholarship@fapsc.org

FLORIDA DEPARTMENT OF EDUCATION

JOSE MARTI SCHOLARSHIP CHALLENGE GRANT FUND

see number 229

MARY MCLEOD BETHUNE SCHOLARSHIP • 319

Available to Florida students with a GPA of 3.0 or above who will attend Florida Agricultural and Mechanical University, Edward Waters College, Bethune-Cookman College, or Florida Memorial College. Based on need and merit. Further information, deadlines and applications available at the financial aid office at the school.

Award Scholarship for use in freshman, sophomore, junior, or senior years; not renewable. *Number:* 160. *Amount:* $3000.

Eligibility Requirements: Applicant must be enrolled or expecting to enroll full-time at a four-year institution; resident of Florida and studying in Florida. Applicant must have 3.0 GPA or higher. Available to U.S. citizens.

Application Requirements Application, financial need analysis.

World Wide Web: http://www.floridastudentfinancialaid.org

Contact: Scholarship Information
Florida Department of Education
Office of Student Financial Assistance
1940 North Monroe, Suite 70
Tallahassee, FL 32303-4759
Phone: 888-827-2004
E-mail: osfa@fldoe.org

ROBERT C. BYRD HONORS SCHOLARSHIP PROGRAM-FLORIDA • 320

One applicant per high school may be nominated. Must be Florida resident. Must be U.S. citizen or eligible non-citizen. Application must be submitted in the same year as graduation. Must meet Selective Service System registration requirements. May attend any postsecondary accredited institution.

Award Scholarship for use in freshman, sophomore, junior, or senior years; renewable. *Number:* 1200. *Amount:* up to $1500.

Eligibility Requirements: Applicant must be high school student; planning to enroll or expecting to enroll full-time at a two-year or four-year or technical institution or university and resident of Florida. Available to U.S. citizens.

Application Requirements Application, financial need analysis, references, test scores, transcript. *Deadline:* April 15.
World Wide Web: http://www.floridastudentfinancialaid.org
Contact: Scholarship Information
Florida Department of Education
Office of Student Financial Assistance
1940 North Monroe, Suite 70
Tallahassee, FL 32303-4759
Phone: 888-827-2004
E-mail: osfa@fldoe.org

ROSEWOOD FAMILY SCHOLARSHIP FUND   see number 230

FLORIDA LEADER MAGAZINE/COLLEGE STUDENT OF THE YEAR, INC.

FLORIDA COLLEGE STUDENT OF THE YEAR AWARD   • 321

This award recognizes Florida's finest campus leaders for their service to their campuses and communities. Available to students enrolled at least part-time in a Florida postsecondary school. Must have completed at least eighteen credit hours with minimum GPA of 3.25. Based primarily on leadership activities but academic merit and work history are considered. Applicant may be in high school if concurrently enrolled in postsecondary institution. Submit statement of financial self-reliance.

Award Scholarship for use in sophomore, junior, senior, graduate, or postgraduate years; not renewable. *Number:* 20. *Amount:* $1500–$4500.

Eligibility Requirements: Applicant must be enrolled or expecting to enroll full or part-time at a two-year or four-year or technical institution or university; studying in Florida and must have an interest in leadership. Available to U.S. and non-U.S. citizens.

Application Requirements Application, autobiography, essay, photo, resume, references, self-addressed stamped envelope, transcript. *Deadline:* February 1.
World Wide Web: http://www.floridaleader.com/soty
Contact: W. H. Oxendine, Jr., Publisher/Editor-in-Chief
Florida Leader Magazine/College Student of the Year, Inc.
PO Box 14081
Gainesville, FL 32604-2081
Phone: 352-373-6907
Fax: 352-373-8120
E-mail: info@studentleader.com

GEORGIA STUDENT FINANCE COMMISSION

GEORGIA LEVERAGING EDUCATIONAL ASSISTANCE PARTNERSHIP GRANT PROGRAM   • 322

Based on financial need. Recipients must be eligible for the Federal Pell Grant. Renewable award for Georgia residents enrolled in a state postsecondary institution. Must be U.S. citizen.

Georgia Leveraging Educational Assistance Partnership Grant Program (continued)

Award Grant for use in freshman, sophomore, junior, or senior years; renewable. *Number:* 3000–3500. *Amount:* $370.

Eligibility Requirements: Applicant must be enrolled or expecting to enroll full or part-time at a two-year or four-year or technical institution or university; resident of Georgia and studying in Georgia. Available to U.S. citizens.

Application Requirements Application, financial need analysis. *Deadline:* Continuous.

World Wide Web: http://www.gsfc.org

Contact: William Flook, Director of Scholarships and Grants
Georgia Student Finance Commission
2082 East Exchange Place, Suite 100
Tucker, GA 30084
Phone: 770-724-9050
Fax: 770-724-9031

GEORGIA TUITION EQUALIZATION GRANT (GTEG) • 323

Award for Georgia residents pursuing undergraduate study at an accredited two- or four-year Georgia private institution. Complete the Georgia Student Grant Application. Award is $1045 per academic year. Deadlines vary.

Award Grant for use in freshman, sophomore, junior, or senior years; renewable. *Number:* 25,000–32,000. *Amount:* $1045.

Eligibility Requirements: Applicant must be enrolled or expecting to enroll full-time at a two-year or four-year institution or university; resident of Georgia and studying in Georgia. Available to U.S. citizens.

Application Requirements Application. *Deadline:* Continuous.

World Wide Web: http://www.gsfc.org

Contact: William Flook, Director of Scholarships and Grants Division
Georgia Student Finance Commission
2082 East Exchange Place, Suite 100
Tucker, GA 30084
Phone: 770-724-9050
Fax: 770-724-9031

GOVERNOR'S SCHOLARSHIP-GEORGIA • 324

Award to assist students selected as Georgia scholars, STAR students, valedictorians, and salutatorians. For use at two- and four-year colleges and universities in Georgia. Recipients are selected as entering freshmen. Renewable award of up to $1575. Minimum 3.5 GPA required.

Award Scholarship for use in freshman, sophomore, junior, or senior years; renewable. *Number:* 2000–3000. *Amount:* up to $1575.

Eligibility Requirements: Applicant must be high school student; planning to enroll or expecting to enroll full-time at a two-year or four-year institution or university; resident of Georgia and studying in Georgia. Applicant must have 3.5 GPA or higher. Available to U.S. citizens.

Application Requirements Application, transcript. *Deadline:* Continuous.

World Wide Web: http://www.gsfc.org

Contact: William Flook, Director of Scholarships and Grants Division
Georgia Student Finance Commission
2082 East Exchange Place, Suite 100
Tucker, GA 30084
Phone: 770-724-9050
Fax: 770-724-9031

HOPE—HELPING OUTSTANDING PUPILS EDUCATIONALLY • 325

Grant program for Georgia residents who are college undergraduates to attend an accredited two- or four-year Georgia institution. Tuition and fees may be covered by the grant. Minimum 3.0 GPA required. Renewable if student maintains grades and reapplies. Write for deadlines.

Award Scholarship for use in freshman, sophomore, junior, or senior years; renewable. *Number:* 140,000–170,000. *Amount:* $300–$3000.

Eligibility Requirements: Applicant must be enrolled or expecting to enroll full or part-time at a two-year or four-year institution or university; resident of Georgia and studying in Georgia. Applicant must have 3.0 GPA or higher. Available to U.S. citizens.

Application Requirements Application. *Deadline:* Continuous.

World Wide Web: http://www.gsfc.org

Contact: William Flook, Director of Scholarships and Grants Division
Georgia Student Finance Commission
2082 East Exchange Place, Suite 100
Tucker, GA 30084
Phone: 770-724-9050
Fax: 770-724-9031

ROBERT C. BYRD HONORS SCHOLARSHIP-GEORGIA • 326

Complete the application provided by the Georgia Department of Education. Renewable awards for outstanding graduating Georgia high school seniors to be used for full-time undergraduate study at eligible U.S. institution.

Award Scholarship for use in freshman, sophomore, junior, or senior years; renewable. *Number:* 600–700. *Amount:* $1500.

Eligibility Requirements: Applicant must be high school student; planning to enroll or expecting to enroll full-time at a two-year or four-year institution or university and resident of Georgia. Available to U.S. citizens.

Application Requirements Application, transcript. *Deadline:* April 1.

World Wide Web: http://www.gsfc.org

Contact: William Flook, Director of Scholarships and Grants Division
Georgia Student Finance Commission
2082 East Exchange Place, Suite 100
Tucker, GA 30084
Phone: 770-724-9050
Fax: 770-724-9031

GRAND LODGE OF IOWA, AF AND AM

GRAND LODGE OF IOWA MASONIC SCHOLARSHIP • 327

One-time awards for graduating seniors of Iowa public high schools. The scholarship is for the freshman year of college. The application must be submitted by February 1 on an original application provided by the Grand Lodge of Iowa.

Award Scholarship for use in freshman year; not renewable. *Number:* 60–70. *Amount:* $2000.

Eligibility Requirements: Applicant must be high school student; planning to enroll or expecting to enroll full-time at a four-year institution or university and resident of Iowa. Available to U.S. and non-U.S. citizens.

Application Requirements Application, autobiography, essay, interview, references, transcript. *Deadline:* February 1.

World Wide Web: http://gl-iowa.org

Contact: William Crawford, Grand Secretary
Grand Lodge of Iowa, AF and AM
PO Box 279
Cedar Rapids, IA 52406-0279
Phone: 319-365-1438
Fax: 319-365-1439
E-mail: gs@gl-iowa.org

GREATER BRIDGEPORT AREA FOUNDATION

SCHOLARSHIP AWARD PROGRAM • 328

The Greater Bridgeport Area Foundation Scholarship Award program primarily supports high school seniors entering their freshman year in college. Scholarships average $1100 for one year. Some graduate school scholarships are available. Awards given to students from towns in GBAF service area: Bridgeport, Easton, Fairfield, Milford, Monroe, Shelton, Stratford, Trumbull, and Westport.

Award Scholarship for use in freshman year; not renewable. *Number:* 100–150. *Amount:* up to $1100.

Eligibility Requirements: Applicant must be high school student; planning to enroll or expecting to enroll full-time at a four-year institution or university and resident of Connecticut. Available to U.S. citizens.

Application Requirements Application, essay, references, transcript. *Deadline:* March 28.

World Wide Web: http://www.gbafoundation.org

Contact: Education Associate
Greater Bridgeport Area Foundation
211 State Street, 3rd Floor
Bridgeport, CT 06604
Phone: 203-334-7511
Fax: 203-333-4652
E-mail: info@gbafoundation.org

GREATER KANAWHA VALLEY FOUNDATION

W. P. BLACK SCHOLARSHIP FUND • 329

Renewable award for West Virginia residents who demonstrate academic excellence and financial need and who are enrolled in an undergraduate program in any accredited college or university. May apply for two Foundation scholarships but will only be chosen for one.

Award Scholarship for use in freshman, sophomore, junior, or senior years; renewable. *Number:* 98. *Amount:* $1000.

Eligibility Requirements: Applicant must be enrolled or expecting to enroll at a two-year or four-year institution or university and resident of West Virginia. Applicant must have 2.5 GPA or higher. Available to U.S. citizens.

Application Requirements Application, essay, financial need analysis, references, self-addressed stamped envelope, test scores, transcript. *Deadline:* February 13.

World Wide Web: http://www.tgkvf.org

Contact: Susan Hoover, Scholarship Coordinator
Greater Kanawha Valley Foundation
PO Box 3041
Charleston, WV 25331
Phone: 304-346-3620
Fax: 304-346-3640

HENRY SACHS FOUNDATION

HENRY SACHS FOUNDATION GRANTS see number 234

HERBERT HOOVER PRESIDENTIAL LIBRARY ASSOCIATION

HERBERT HOOVER UNCOMMON STUDENT AWARD • 330

Only juniors in an Iowa high school or home school program may apply. Grades and test scores are not evaluated. Applicants are chosen on the basis of project proposals they submit. Those chosen complete their project and make a presentation. All receive $750. Three are chosen for $5000 award.

Award Scholarship for use in freshman year; not renewable. *Number:* 18. *Amount:* $750–$5000.

Eligibility Requirements: Applicant must be high school student; planning to enroll or expecting to enroll full-time at a two-year or four-year institution and resident of Iowa. Available to U.S. and non-U.S. citizens.

Application Requirements Application, references, project proposal. *Deadline:* March 31.

World Wide Web: http://www.hooverassociation.org

Herbert Hoover Uncommon Student Award (continued)

Contact: Patricia Hand, Academic Programs Manager
Herbert Hoover Presidential Library Association
PO Box 696
West Branch, IA 52358-0696
Phone: 319-643-5327
Fax: 319-643-2391
E-mail: info@hooverassociation.org

IDAHO STATE BOARD OF EDUCATION

IDAHO MINORITY AND "AT RISK" STUDENT SCHOLARSHIP • 331

Renewable award for Idaho residents who are disabled or members of a minority group and have financial need. Must attend one of eight postsecondary institutions in the state for undergraduate study. Deadlines vary by institution. Must be a U.S. citizen and be a graduate of an Idaho high school. Contact college financial aid office.

Award Scholarship for use in freshman, sophomore, junior, or senior years; renewable. *Number:* 38–40. *Amount:* $3000.

Eligibility Requirements: Applicant must be enrolled or expecting to enroll full-time at a two-year or four-year institution or university; resident of Idaho and studying in Idaho. Available to U.S. citizens.

Application Requirements Application, financial need analysis.

World Wide Web: http://www.idahoboardofed.org

Contact: Financial Aid Office

IDAHO PROMISE CATEGORY A SCHOLARSHIP PROGRAM • 332

Renewable award available to Idaho residents who are graduating high school seniors. Must attend an approved Idaho college full-time. Based on class rank (must be verified by school official), GPA, and ACT scores. Professional-technical student applicants must take COMPASS.

Award Scholarship for use in freshman, sophomore, junior, or senior years; renewable. *Number:* 25–30. *Amount:* $3000.

Eligibility Requirements: Applicant must be high school student; planning to enroll or expecting to enroll full-time at a two-year or four-year or technical institution or university; resident of Idaho and studying in Idaho. Applicant must have 3.5 GPA or higher. Available to U.S. citizens.

Application Requirements Application, test scores. *Deadline:* December 15.

World Wide Web: http://www.idahoboardofed.org

Contact: Lynn Humphrey, Scholarship Assistant
Idaho State Board of Education
PO Box 83720
Boise, ID 83720-0037
Phone: 208-332-1574
Fax: 208-334-2632
E-mail: lhumphre@osbe.state.id.us

ROBERT C. BYRD HONORS SCHOLARSHIP PROGRAM-IDAHO
• **333**

Renewable scholarships available to Idaho residents based on outstanding academic achievement. Students must apply as high school seniors.

Award Scholarship for use in freshman, sophomore, junior, or senior years; renewable. *Number:* 90. *Amount:* $1500.

Eligibility Requirements: Applicant must be high school student; planning to enroll or expecting to enroll full-time at a two-year or four-year or technical institution and resident of Idaho. Applicant must have 3.5 GPA or higher. Available to U.S. citizens.

Application Requirements Application, references, test scores, transcript. *Deadline:* March 20.

World Wide Web: http://www.idahoboardofed.org

Contact: Sally Tiel, Department of Education, Counseling and Assessment
Idaho State Board of Education
PO Box 83720
Boise, ID 83720-0027
Phone: 208-332-6800
Fax: 208-334-2228

ILLINOIS STUDENT ASSISTANCE COMMISSION (ISAC)

GRANT PROGRAM FOR DEPENDENTS OF POLICE, FIRE, OR CORRECTIONAL OFFICERS
see number 178

HIGHER EDUCATION LICENSE PLATE PROGRAM—HELP
• **334**

Need-based grants for students at institutions participating in program whose funds are raised by sale of special license plates commemorating the institutions. Deadline: June 30. Must be Illinois resident.

Award Grant for use in freshman, sophomore, junior, or senior years; not renewable. *Number:* 175–200. *Amount:* up to $2000.

Eligibility Requirements: Applicant must be enrolled or expecting to enroll full or part-time at a two-year or four-year institution or university; resident of Illinois and studying in Illinois. Available to U.S. and non-U.S. citizens.

Application Requirements Financial need analysis. *Deadline:* June 30.

World Wide Web: http://www.isac-online.org

Contact: David Barinholtz, Client Information
Illinois Student Assistance Commission (ISAC)
1755 Lake Cook Road
Deerfield, IL 60015-5209
Phone: 847-948-8500 Ext. 2385
E-mail: cssupport@isac.org

ILLINOIS COLLEGE SAVINGS BOND BONUS INCENTIVE GRANT PROGRAM • 335

Program offers holders of Illinois College Savings Bonds a $20 grant for each year of bond maturity payable upon bond redemption if at least 70% of proceeds are used to attend college in Illinois. May not be used by students attending religious or divinity schools.

Award Grant for use in freshman, sophomore, junior, senior, graduate, or postgraduate years; not renewable. *Number:* 1200–1400. *Amount:* $40–$220.

Eligibility Requirements: Applicant must be enrolled or expecting to enroll full or part-time at a two-year or four-year or technical institution or university and studying in Illinois. Available to U.S. and non-U.S. citizens.

Application Requirements Application. *Deadline:* Continuous.

World Wide Web: http://www.isac-online.org

Contact: David Barinholtz, Client Information
Illinois Student Assistance Commission (ISAC)
1755 Lake Cook Road
Deerfield, IL 60015-5209
Phone: 847-948-8500 Ext. 2385
E-mail: cssupport@isac.org

ILLINOIS INCENTIVE FOR ACCESS PROGRAM • 336

Award for eligible first-time freshmen enrolling in approved Illinois institutions. One-time grant of up to $500 may be used for any educational expense. Deadline: October 1.

Award Grant for use in freshman year; not renewable. *Number:* 19,000–22,000. *Amount:* $300–$500.

Eligibility Requirements: Applicant must be enrolled or expecting to enroll full or part-time at a two-year or four-year or technical institution or university; resident of Illinois and studying in Illinois. Available to U.S. and non-U.S. citizens.

Application Requirements Financial need analysis. *Deadline:* October 1.

World Wide Web: http://www.isac-online.org

Contact: David Barinholtz, Client Information
Illinois Student Assistance Commission (ISAC)
1755 Lake Cook Road
Deerfield, IL 60015-5209
Phone: 847-948-8500 Ext. 2385
E-mail: cssupport@isac.org

ILLINOIS MONETARY AWARD PROGRAM • 337

Award for eligible students attending Illinois public universities, private colleges and universities, community colleges, and some proprietary institutions. Applicable only to tuition and fees. Based on financial need. Deadline: October 1.

Award Grant for use in freshman, sophomore, junior, or senior years; not renewable. *Number:* 135,000–145,000. *Amount:* $300–$4320.

Eligibility Requirements: Applicant must be enrolled or expecting to enroll full or part-time at a two-year or four-year or technical institution or university; resident of Illinois and studying in Illinois. Available to U.S. and non-U.S. citizens.

Application Requirements Financial need analysis. *Deadline:* October 1.

World Wide Web: http://www.isac-online.org

Contact: David Barinholtz, Client Information
Illinois Student Assistance Commission (ISAC)
1755 Lake Cook Road
Deerfield, IL 60015-5209
Phone: 847-948-8500 Ext. 2385
E-mail: cssupport@isac.org

ILLINOIS NATIONAL GUARD GRANT PROGRAM   see number 193

ILLINOIS STUDENT-TO-STUDENT PROGRAM OF MATCHING GRANTS
• 338

Award provides matching funds for need-based grants at participating Illinois public universities and community colleges. Deadline: October 1.

Award Grant for use in freshman, sophomore, junior, or senior years; not renewable. *Number:* 2000–4000. *Amount:* $300–$500.

Eligibility Requirements: Applicant must be enrolled or expecting to enroll full or part-time at a two-year or four-year institution or university; resident of Illinois and studying in Illinois. Available to U.S. and non-U.S. citizens.

Application Requirements Financial need analysis. *Deadline:* October 1.

World Wide Web: http://www.isac-online.org

Contact: David Barinholtz, Client Information
Illinois Student Assistance Commission (ISAC)
1755 Lake Cook Road
Deerfield, IL 60015-5209
Phone: 847-948-8500 Ext. 2385
E-mail: cssupport@isac.org

ILLINOIS VETERAN GRANT PROGRAM—IVG   see number 206

MERIT RECOGNITION SCHOLARSHIP (MRS) PROGRAM   • 339

Award for Illinois high school seniors graduating in the top 5% of their class and attending Illinois postsecondary institution. Deadline: June 15. Contact for application procedures.

Award Scholarship for use in freshman year; not renewable. *Number:* 5000–6000. *Amount:* $900–$1000.

Eligibility Requirements: Applicant must be high school student; planning to enroll or expecting to enroll full or part-time at a two-year or four-year institution or university; resident of Illinois and studying in Illinois. Applicant must have 3.5 GPA or higher. Available to U.S. and non-U.S. citizens.

Application Requirements Application. *Deadline:* June 15.

World Wide Web: http://www.isac-online.org

Merit Recognition Scholarship (MRS) Program (continued)

Contact: David Barinholtz, Client Information
Illinois Student Assistance Commission (ISAC)
1755 Lake Cook Road
Deerfield, IL 60015-5209
Phone: 847-948-8500 Ext. 2385
E-mail: cssupport@isac.org

ROBERT C. BYRD HONORS SCHOLARSHIP-ILLINOIS • 340

Available to Illinois residents who are graduating high school seniors. Based on outstanding academic merit. Awards are renewable up to four years. Must be accepted on a full-time basis as an undergraduate student.

Award Scholarship for use in freshman, sophomore, junior, or senior years; renewable. *Number:* 1100–1200. *Amount:* $1400–$1500.

Eligibility Requirements: Applicant must be high school student; planning to enroll or expecting to enroll full-time at a two-year or four-year institution or university and resident of Illinois. Applicant must have 3.5 GPA or higher. Available to U.S. and non-U.S. citizens.

Application Requirements Application, test scores, transcript. *Deadline:* January 15.

World Wide Web: http://www.isac-online.org

Contact: David Barinholtz, Client Information
Illinois Student Assistance Commission (ISAC)
1755 Lake Cook Road
Deerfield, IL 60015-5209
Phone: 847-948-8500 Ext. 2385
E-mail: cssupport@isac.org

INDEPENDENT COLLEGES OF WASHINGTON

CORPORATE SPONSORED SCHOLARSHIP PROGRAM • 341

All scholarships restricted to students attending one of ten independent colleges located in Washington State. Colleges include Gonzaga University, Heritage College, Pacific Lutheran University, Saint Martin's College, Seattle Pacific University, Seattle University, University of Puget Sound, Walla Walla College, Whitman College, Whitworth College. For more details see web site: http://www.icwashington.org.

Award Scholarship for use in freshman, sophomore, junior, or senior years; not renewable. *Number:* 20–70. *Amount:* $400–$3500.

Eligibility Requirements: Applicant must be enrolled or expecting to enroll full-time at a four-year institution and studying in Washington. Available to U.S. and non-U.S. citizens.

Application Requirements Application, essay, resume, references, transcript.

World Wide Web: http://www.ICWashington.org

Contact: Independent Colleges of Washington
600 Tower Building
1809 Seventh Avenue
Seattle, WA 98101

IOWA COLLEGE STUDENT AID COMMISSION

ROBERT C. BYRD HONORS SCHOLARSHIP   • 342

Scholarships up to $1500 are awarded to exceptionally able Iowa high school seniors who show promise of continued academic excellence. Must have a minimum of a 28 ACT or 1240 SAT, a 3.5 GPA and rank in the top 10% of the student's high school graduating class. For more details see web site: http://www.iowacollegeaid.org.

Award Scholarship for use in freshman year; renewable. *Number:* up to 70. *Amount:* up to $1500.

Eligibility Requirements: Applicant must be high school student; planning to enroll or expecting to enroll at an institution or university and resident of Iowa. Applicant must have 3.5 GPA or higher. Available to U.S. citizens.

Application Requirements Application, test scores, transcript. *Deadline:* February 1.

World Wide Web: http://www.iowacollegeaid.org

Contact: Julie Leeper, Director, State Student Aid Programs
Iowa College Student Aid Commission
200 10th Street, 4th Floor
Des Moines, IA 50309-3609
Phone: 515-242-3370
Fax: 515-242-3388
E-mail: icsac@max.state.ia.us

STATE OF IOWA SCHOLARSHIP PROGRAM   • 343

Program provides recognition and financial honorarium to Iowa's academically talented high school seniors. Honorary scholarships are presented to all qualified candidates. Approximately 1700 top-ranking candidates are designated State of Iowa Scholars every March, from an applicant pool of nearly 5000 high school seniors. Must be used at an Iowa postsecondary institution. Minimum 3.5 GPA required.

Award Scholarship for use in freshman year; not renewable. *Number:* up to 1700. *Amount:* up to $400.

Eligibility Requirements: Applicant must be high school student; planning to enroll or expecting to enroll full-time at a two-year or four-year or technical institution or university; resident of Iowa and studying in Iowa. Applicant must have 3.5 GPA or higher. Available to U.S. citizens.

Application Requirements Application, test scores. *Deadline:* November 1.

World Wide Web: http://www.iowacollegeaid.org

State of Iowa Scholarship Program (continued)

Contact: Julie Leeper, Director, State Student Aid Programs
Iowa College Student Aid Commission
200 10th Street, 4th Floor
Des Moines, IA 50309-3609
Phone: 515-242-3370
Fax: 515-242-3388
E-mail: icsac@max.state.ia.us

IOWA DIVISION OF VOCATIONAL REHABILITATION SERVICES

IOWA VOCATIONAL REHABILITATION

see number 190

ITALIAN CATHOLIC FEDERATION, INC.

ICF COLLEGE SCHOLARSHIPS TO HIGH SCHOOL SENIORS

see number 273

JAMES F. BYRNES FOUNDATION

JAMES F. BYRNES SCHOLARSHIP • 344

Renewable award for residents of South Carolina ages 17-22 with one or both parents deceased. Must show financial need; a satisfactory scholastic record; and qualities of character, ability, and enterprise. Award is for undergraduate study. Results of SAT must be provided.

Award Scholarship for use in freshman, sophomore, junior, or senior years; renewable. *Number:* 50–60. *Amount:* $2000–$2750.

Eligibility Requirements: Applicant must be age 17-22; enrolled or expecting to enroll full-time at a four-year institution and resident of South Carolina. Available to U.S. citizens.

Application Requirements Application, autobiography, financial need analysis, interview, photo, references, test scores, transcript. *Deadline:* February 15.

World Wide Web: http://www.byrnesscholars.org

Contact: Mrs. Genny White, Executive Secretary
James F. Byrnes Foundation
PO Box 6781
Columbia, SC 29260-6781
Phone: 803-254-9325
Fax: 803-254-9354
E-mail: info@byrnesscholars.org

JEWISH FEDERATION OF METROPOLITAN CHICAGO (JFMC)

JEWISH FEDERATION OF METROPOLITAN CHICAGO ACADEMIC SCHOLARSHIP PROGRAM • 345

Available for Jewish students only in the Chicago metropolitan area. Award available for undergraduates who have entered their junior year in career-specific programs which require no postgraduate education for professional level employment, or students enrolled in graduate or professional school. Students in a vocational program with a specific educational goal in the helping professions also are eligible.

Award Scholarship for use in junior, senior, or graduate years; renewable. *Number:* 75. *Amount:* $5000.

Eligibility Requirements: Applicant must be enrolled or expecting to enroll full-time at an institution or university and resident of Illinois. Available to U.S. and non-U.S. citizens.

Application Requirements Application, essay, financial need analysis, interview, references, transcript. *Deadline:* March 1.

World Wide Web: http://www.jvschicago.org

Contact: Lea Gruhn, Scholarship Secretary
Jewish Federation of Metropolitan Chicago (JFMC)
1 South Franklin Street
Chicago, IL 60606
Phone: 312-357-4521
Fax: 312-553-5544
E-mail: jvsscholarship@jvschicago.org

JOSE MARTI SCHOLARSHIP CHALLENGE GRANT FUND

JOSE MARTI SCHOLARSHIP CHALLENGE GRANT   see number 247

KANSAS BOARD OF REGENTS

ETHNIC MINORITY SCHOLARSHIP PROGRAM   see number 248

KANSAS COMPREHENSIVE GRANT PROGRAM • 346

Grants available for Kansas residents attending public or private baccalaureate colleges or universities in Kansas. Based on financial need. Must file Free Application for Federal Student Aid to apply. Renewable award based on continuing eligibility. Up to $3000 for undergraduate use. Deadline: April 1.

Award Grant for use in freshman, sophomore, junior, or senior years; renewable. *Number:* 7000–8200. *Amount:* $1100–$3000.

Eligibility Requirements: Applicant must be enrolled or expecting to enroll full-time at a four-year institution or university; resident of Kansas and studying in Kansas. Available to U.S. citizens.

Kansas Comprehensive Grant Program (continued)
Application Requirements Financial need analysis. *Deadline:* April 1.
World Wide Web: http://www.kansasregents.org
Contact: Diane Lindeman, Director of Student Financial Assistance
Kansas Board of Regents
1000 Southwest Jackson, Suite 520
Topeka, KS 66612-1368
Phone: 785-296-3517
Fax: 785-296-0983
E-mail: dlindeman@ksbor.org

KANSAS STATE SCHOLARSHIP PROGRAM • 347

The Kansas State Scholarship Program provides assistance to financially needy, academically outstanding students who attend Kansas postsecondary institutions. Must be Kansas resident. Minimum 3.0 GPA required for renewal. Application fee is $10. Deadline: May 1.

Award Scholarship for use in freshman, sophomore, junior, or senior years; renewable. *Number:* 1000–1500. *Amount:* $1000.
Eligibility Requirements: Applicant must be enrolled or expecting to enroll full-time at a two-year or four-year institution or university; resident of Kansas and studying in Kansas. Applicant must have 3.0 GPA or higher. Available to U.S. citizens.
Application Requirements Application, financial need analysis, test scores, transcript. *Fee:* $10. *Deadline:* May 1.
World Wide Web: http://www.kansasregents.org
Contact: Diane Lindeman, Director of Student Financial Assistance
Kansas Board of Regents
1000 Southwest Jackson, Suite 520
Topeka, KS 66612-1368
Phone: 785-296-3517
Fax: 785-296-0983
E-mail: dlindeman@ksbor.org

KANSAS NATIONAL GUARD EDUCATIONAL ASSISTANCE PROGRAM

KANSAS NATIONAL GUARD EDUCATIONAL ASSISTANCE AWARD PROGRAM
see number 194

KENTUCKY HIGHER EDUCATION ASSISTANCE AUTHORITY (KHEAA)

COLLEGE ACCESS PROGRAM (CAP) GRANT • 348

Award for U.S. citizen and Kentucky resident with no previous college degree. Provides $53 per semester hour for a minimum of six hours per semester.

Applicants seeking degrees in religion are not eligible. Must demonstrate financial need and submit Free Application for Federal Student Aid. Priority deadline is March 15.

Award Grant for use in freshman, sophomore, junior, or senior years; not renewable. *Number:* 30,000–35,000. *Amount:* up to $1260.

Eligibility Requirements: Applicant must be enrolled or expecting to enroll full or part-time at a two-year or four-year or technical institution or university; resident of Kentucky and studying in Kentucky. Available to U.S. citizens.

Application Requirements Financial need analysis. *Deadline:* Continuous.

World Wide Web: http://www.kheaa.com

Contact: Allan Osborne, Program Coordinator
Kentucky Higher Education Assistance Authority (KHEAA)
PO Box 798
Frankfort, KY 40602-0798
Phone: 502-696-7394
Fax: 502-696-7373
E-mail: aosborne@kheaa.com

KENTUCKY EDUCATIONAL EXCELLENCE SCHOLARSHIP (KEES)
• 349

Annual award based on GPA and highest ACT or SAT score received by high school graduation. Awards are renewable if required cumulative GPA maintained at a Kentucky postsecondary school. Must be a Kentucky resident.

Award Scholarship for use in freshman, sophomore, junior, or senior years; renewable. *Number:* 40,000–50,000. *Amount:* $125–$2000.

Eligibility Requirements: Applicant must be high school student; planning to enroll or expecting to enroll full or part-time at a two-year or four-year or technical institution or university; resident of Kentucky and studying in Kentucky. Applicant must have 2.5 GPA or higher. Available to U.S. citizens.

Application Requirements Test scores, transcript.

World Wide Web: http://www.kheaa.com

Contact: Tim Phelps, KEES Program Coordinator
Kentucky Higher Education Assistance Authority (KHEAA)
PO Box 798
Frankfort, KY 40602-0798
Phone: 502-696-7397
Fax: 502-696-7373
E-mail: tphelps@kheaa.com

KENTUCKY TUITION GRANT (KTG)
• 350

Available to Kentucky residents who are full-time undergraduates at an independent college within the state. Must not be enrolled in a religion program. Based on financial need. Submit Free Application for Federal Student Aid. Priority deadline is March 15.

Award Grant for use in freshman, sophomore, junior, or senior years; not renewable. *Number:* 9000–10,000. *Amount:* $50–$1800.

Kentucky Tuition Grant (KTG) (continued)
Eligibility Requirements: Applicant must be enrolled or expecting to enroll full-time at a two-year or four-year institution or university; resident of Kentucky and studying in Kentucky. Available to U.S. citizens.
Application Requirements Financial need analysis. *Deadline:* Continuous.
World Wide Web: http://www.kheaa.com
Contact: Allan Osborne, Program Coordinator
Kentucky Higher Education Assistance Authority (KHEAA)
PO Box 798
Frankfort, KY 40602-0798
Phone: 502-696-7394
Fax: 502-696-7373
E-mail: aosborne@kheaa.com

KNIGHTS OF AK-SAR-BEN

AK-SAR-BEN LEADERSHIP SCHOLARSHIP • 351
Scholarships are awarded to outstanding and talented graduates of "Heartland" (Nebraska and Western Iowa) high schools. Must be a graduating high school senior and a resident of Nebraska or Western Iowa. For more details and an application see web site: http://www.aksarben.org.

Award Scholarship for use in freshman, sophomore, junior, or senior years; renewable. *Number:* 20. *Amount:* $10,000.
Eligibility Requirements: Applicant must be high school student; planning to enroll or expecting to enroll full-time at a four-year institution or university and resident of Iowa or Nebraska. Available to U.S. citizens.
Application Requirements Application, essay, financial need analysis, references, test scores, transcript. *Deadline:* February 1.
World Wide Web: http://www.aksarben.org/programs/scholarship.htm
Contact: application available at web site

LINCOLN COMMUNITY FOUNDATION

DUNCAN E. AND LILLIAN M. MCGREGOR SCHOLARSHIP • 352
Scholarship for graduating seniors or former graduates of the high schools in Ansley, Arcadia, Gibbon, Ord, Shelton or Sayen high schools in Nebraska. Must have resided in a community served by and maintained an exchange served by the Nebraska Central Telephone Company during his/her high school education.

Award Scholarship for use in freshman, sophomore, junior, or senior years; not renewable. *Number:* 80–100. *Amount:* $500–$1000.
Eligibility Requirements: Applicant must be enrolled or expecting to enroll full-time at a two-year or four-year or technical institution or university and resident of Nebraska. Applicant must have 2.5 GPA or higher. Available to U.S. citizens.
Application Requirements Application, financial need analysis, test scores, transcript. *Deadline:* April 15.

World Wide Web: http://www.lcf.org
Contact: application available at web site

LONG & FOSTER REAL ESTATE, INC.

LONG & FOSTER SCHOLARSHIP PROGRAM • 353

One-time award for residents of MD, PA, DC , VA and DE. Students may pursue any academic major they desire. The Scholarship Committee will be seeking academically strong high school seniors who are well rounded and demonstrate leadership and involvement in a variety of school activities. Must be U.S. citizen. Minimum 3.0 GPA required.

Award Scholarship for use in freshman year; not renewable. *Number:* up to 125. *Amount:* $1000.

Eligibility Requirements: Applicant must be high school student; planning to enroll or expecting to enroll full-time at a four-year institution or university and resident of Delaware, District of Columbia, Maryland, Pennsylvania, or Virginia. Applicant must have 3.0 GPA or higher. Available to U.S. citizens.

Application Requirements Application, essay, financial need analysis, references, test scores, transcript. *Deadline:* March 3.

World Wide Web: http://www.longandfoster.com
Contact: Colleen Park, Public Relations Coordinator
Long & Foster Real Estate, Inc.
11351 Random Hills Road
Fairfax, VA 22030-6082
Phone: 703-359-1750
Fax: 703-591-5493
E-mail: colleen.park@longandfoster.com

LOUISIANA OFFICE OF STUDENT FINANCIAL ASSISTANCE

LEVERAGING EDUCATIONAL ASSISTANCE PROGRAM (LEAP) • 354

LEAP program provides federal and state funds to provide need-based grants to academically qualified students. Individual award determined by Financial Aid Office and governed by number of applicants and availability of funds. File Free Application for Federal Student aid by school deadline to apply each year. For Louisiana students attending Louisiana postsecondary institutions.

Award Grant for use in freshman, sophomore, junior, or senior years; not renewable. *Number:* 3000. *Amount:* $200–$2000.

Eligibility Requirements: Applicant must be enrolled or expecting to enroll full or part-time at a two-year or four-year or technical institution or university; resident of Louisiana and studying in Louisiana. Available to U.S. citizens.

Application Requirements Application, financial need analysis.
World Wide Web: http://www.osfa.state.la.us

Leveraging Educational Assistance Program (LEAP) (continued)

Contact: Public Information
Louisiana Office of Student Financial Assistance
PO Box 91202
Baton Rouge, LA 70821-9202
Phone: 800-259-5626 Ext. 1012
E-mail: custserv@osfa.state.la.us

MAINE COMMUNITY FOUNDATION, INC.

MAINE COMMUNITY FOUNDATION SCHOLARSHIP PROGRAMS   • 355

Several scholarships are available for Maine residents attending secondary, postsecondary and graduate programs. Application deadlines vary. Complete list of scholarships available at http://www.mainecf.org/scholar.html.

Award Scholarship for use in freshman, sophomore, junior, senior, or graduate years; not renewable. *Number:* 150–700. *Amount:* $500–$5000.

Eligibility Requirements: Applicant must be enrolled or expecting to enroll full or part-time at a two-year or four-year or technical institution or university and resident of Maine. Available to U.S. citizens.

Application Requirements Application.

World Wide Web: http://www.mainecf.org

Contact: Education Coordinator
Maine Community Foundation, Inc.
245 Main Street
Ellsworth, ME 04605
Phone: 207-667-9735
Fax: 207-667-0447

MARYLAND HIGHER EDUCATION COMMISSION

DELEGATE SCHOLARSHIP PROGRAM-MARYLAND   • 356

Delegate scholarships help Maryland residents attending Maryland degree-granting institutions, certain career schools, or nursing diploma schools. May attend out-of-state institution if Maryland Higher Education Commission deems major to be unique and not offered at a Maryland institution. Free Application for Federal Student Aid may be required. Students interested in this program should apply by contacting their legislative district delegate.

Award Scholarship for use in freshman, sophomore, junior, senior, or graduate years; not renewable. *Number:* up to 3500. *Amount:* $200–$12,981.

Eligibility Requirements: Applicant must be enrolled or expecting to enroll full or part-time at a two-year or four-year or technical institution or university; resident of Maryland and studying in Maryland. Available to U.S. citizens.

Application Requirements Application, financial need analysis. *Deadline:* Continuous.

World Wide Web: http://www.mhec.state.md.us

Contact: Barbara Fantom, Office of Student Financial Assistance
Maryland Higher Education Commission
839 Bestgage Road, Suite 400
Annapolis, MD 21401-3013
Phone: 410-260-4547
Fax: 410-260-3200
E-mail: osfamail@mhec.state.md.us

DISTINGUISHED SCHOLAR AWARD-MARYLAND • 357

Renewable award for Maryland students enrolled full-time at Maryland
institutions. National Merit Scholar Finalists automatically offered award. Others may qualify for the award in satisfying criteria of a minimum 3.7 GPA or in
combination with high test scores, or for Talent in Arts competition in categories
of music, drama, dance, or visual arts. Must maintain annual 3.0 GPA in college
for award to be renewed. Contact for further details.

Award Scholarship for use in freshman, sophomore, junior, or senior years;
renewable. *Number:* up to 2000. *Amount:* up to $3000.

Eligibility Requirements: Applicant must be high school student; planning
to enroll or expecting to enroll full-time at a two-year or four-year institution
or university; resident of Maryland and studying in Maryland. Available to U.S.
citizens.

Application Requirements Application, test scores, transcript. *Deadline:*
March 1.

World Wide Web: http://www.mhec.state.md.us

Contact: Monica Tipton, Office of Student Financial Assistance
Maryland Higher Education Commission
839 Bestgate Road, Suite 400
Annapolis, MD 21401-3013
Phone: 410-260-4568
Fax: 410-260-3200
E-mail: ofsamail@mhec.state.md.us

EDUCATIONAL ASSISTANCE GRANTS-MARYLAND • 358

Award for Maryland residents accepted or enrolled in a full-time undergraduate degree or certificate program at a Maryland institution or hospital nursing
school. Must submit financial aid form by March 1. Must earn 2.0 GPA in
college to maintain award.

Award Grant for use in freshman, sophomore, junior, or senior years;
renewable. *Number:* 11,000–20,000. *Amount:* $400–$2700.

Eligibility Requirements: Applicant must be enrolled or expecting to enroll
full-time at a two-year or four-year institution or university; resident of Maryland
and studying in Maryland. Available to U.S. citizens.

Application Requirements Application, financial need analysis. *Deadline:*
March 1.

World Wide Web: http://www.mhec.state.md.us

Educational Assistance Grants-Maryland (continued)

Contact: Barbara Fantom, Office of Student Financial Assistance
Maryland Higher Education Commission
839 Bestgate Road, Suite 400
Annapolis, MD 21401-3013
Phone: 410-260-4547
Fax: 410-260-3200
E-mail: osfamail@mhec.state.md.us

EDWARD T. CONROY MEMORIAL SCHOLARSHIP PROGRAM • 359

Scholarship for dependents of deceased or 100% disabled U.S. Armed Forces personnel, the son, daughter, or surviving spouse of a victim of the September 11, 2001, terrorist attacks who died as a result of the attacks on the World Trade Center in New York City, the attack on the Pentagon in Virginia, or the crash of United Airlines Flight 93 in Pennsylvania; a POW/MIA of the Vietnam Conflict or his/her son or daughter; the son, daughter or surviving spouse (who has not remarried),of a state or local public safety employee or volunteer who died in the line of duty; or a state or local public safety employee or volunteer who was 100% disabled in the line of duty. Must be Maryland resident at time of disability. Submit applicable VA certification. Must be at least 16 years of age and attend Maryland institution.

Award Scholarship for use in freshman, sophomore, junior, senior, or graduate years; renewable. *Number:* up to 70. *Amount:* up to $12,981.

Eligibility Requirements: Applicant must be age 16-24; enrolled or expecting to enroll full or part-time at a two-year or four-year institution or university; resident of Maryland and studying in Maryland. Available to U.S. citizens.

Application Requirements Application, birth and death certificate, and disability papers. *Deadline:* July 30.

World Wide Web: http://www.mhec.state.md.us

Contact: Margaret Crutchley, Office of Student Financial Assistance
Maryland Higher Education Commission
839 Bestgate Road, Suite 400
Annapolis, MD 21401-3013
Phone: 410-260-4545
Fax: 410-260-3203
E-mail: osfamail@mhec.state.md.us

GUARANTEED ACCESS GRANT-MARYLAND • 360

Award for Maryland resident enrolling full-time in an undergraduate program at a Maryland institution. Must be under 22 at time of first award and begin college within one year of completing high school in Maryland with a minimum 2.5 GPA. Must have an annual family income less than 130% of the federal poverty level guideline.

Award Grant for use in freshman, sophomore, junior, or senior years; renewable. *Number:* up to 1000. *Amount:* $400–$10,200.

Eligibility Requirements: Applicant must be enrolled or expecting to enroll full-time at a two-year or four-year institution or university; resident of Maryland and studying in Maryland. Applicant must have 2.5 GPA or higher. Available to U.S. citizens.

Application Requirements Application, financial need analysis, transcript. *Deadline:* Continuous.

World Wide Web: http://www.mhec.state.md.us

Contact: Theresa Lowe, Office of Student Financial Assistance
Maryland Higher Education Commission
839 Bestgate Road, Suite 400
Annapolis, MD 21401-3013
Phone: 410-260-4555
Fax: 410-260-3200
E-mail: osfamail@mhec.state.md.us

J.F. TOLBERT MEMORIAL STUDENT GRANT PROGRAM   • 361

Available to Maryland residents attending a private career school in Maryland with at least 18 clock hours per week.

Award Grant for use in freshman or sophomore years; not renewable. *Number:* 1000. *Amount:* up to $300.

Eligibility Requirements: Applicant must be enrolled or expecting to enroll at a technical institution; resident of Maryland and studying in Maryland. Available to U.S. citizens.

Application Requirements Application, financial need analysis. *Deadline:* Continuous.

World Wide Web: http://www.mhec.state.md.us

Contact: Carla Rich, Office of Student Financial Assistance
Maryland Higher Education Commission
839 Bestgate Road, Suite 400
Annapolis, MD 21401-3013
Phone: 410-260-4513
Fax: 410-260-3200
E-mail: osfamail@mhec.state.md.us

PART-TIME GRANT PROGRAM-MARYLAND   • 362

Funds provided to Maryland colleges and universities. Eligible students must be enrolled on a part-time basis (6-11 credits) in an undergraduate degree program. Must demonstrate financial need and also be Maryland resident. Contact financial aid office at institution for more information.

Award Grant for use in freshman, sophomore, junior, or senior years; renewable. *Number:* 1800–9000. *Amount:* $200–$1000.

Eligibility Requirements: Applicant must be enrolled or expecting to enroll part-time at a two-year or four-year institution or university; resident of Maryland and studying in Maryland. Available to U.S. citizens.

Application Requirements Application, financial need analysis. *Deadline:* March 1.

Part-time Grant Program-Maryland (continued)
World Wide Web: http://www.mhec.state.md.us
Contact: Maryland Higher Education Commission
839 Bestgate Road
Suite 400
Annapolis, MD 21401-3013

SENATORIAL SCHOLARSHIPS-MARYLAND • 363

Renewable award for Maryland residents attending a Maryland degree-granting institution, nursing diploma school, or certain private career schools. May be used out-of-state only if Maryland Higher Education Commission deems major to be unique and not offered at Maryland institution.

Award Scholarship for use in freshman, sophomore, junior, senior, or graduate years; renewable. *Number:* up to 7000. *Amount:* $200–$2000.

Eligibility Requirements: Applicant must be enrolled or expecting to enroll full or part-time at a two-year or four-year or technical institution or university; resident of Maryland and studying in Maryland. Available to U.S. citizens.

Application Requirements Financial need analysis, test scores, application to Legislative District Senator. *Deadline:* March 1.

World Wide Web: http://www.mhec.state.md.us
Contact: Barbara Fantom, Office of Student Financial Assistance
Maryland Higher Education Commission
839 Bestgate Road, Suite 400
Annapolis, MD 21401-3013
Phone: 410-260-4547
Fax: 410-260-3202
E-mail: osfamail@mhec.state.md.us

MASONIC GRAND LODGE CHARITIES OF RHODE ISLAND

RHODE ISLAND MASONIC GRAND LODGE SCHOLARSHIP • 364

One-time scholarships for Rhode Island residents who have lived in Rhode Island for more than five years and who are enrolled in undergraduate studies. Awards may also be given to students who do not live in Rhode Island but have an association with the Rhode Island Masonic organization. High school students may apply.

Award Scholarship for use in freshman, sophomore, junior, or senior years; not renewable. *Number:* 200–250. *Amount:* $750–$2500.

Eligibility Requirements: Applicant must be enrolled or expecting to enroll full-time at a two-year or four-year institution or university and resident of Rhode Island. Available to U.S. and non-U.S. citizens.

Application Requirements Application, financial need analysis, transcript. *Deadline:* March 14.

Contact: Scholarship Committee
Masonic Grand Lodge Charities of Rhode Island
222 Taunton Avenue
East Providence, RI 02914-4556

MASSACHUSETTS OFFICE OF STUDENT FINANCIAL ASSISTANCE

MASSACHUSETTS ASSISTANCE FOR STUDENT SUCCESS PROGRAM • 365

Provides need-based financial assistance to Massachusetts residents to attend undergraduate postsecondary institutions in Connecticut, Maine, Massachusetts, New Hampshire, Pennsylvania, Rhode Island, Vermont, and District of Columbia. High school seniors may apply. Timely filing of FAFSA required.

Award Grant for use in freshman, sophomore, junior, or senior years; not renewable. *Number:* 32,000–35,000. *Amount:* $300–$2900.

Eligibility Requirements: Applicant must be enrolled or expecting to enroll full-time at a two-year or four-year or technical institution or university; resident of Massachusetts and studying in Connecticut, District of Columbia, Maine, Massachusetts, New Hampshire, Pennsylvania, Rhode Island, or Vermont. Available to U.S. citizens.

Application Requirements Financial need analysis, FAFSA. *Deadline:* May 1.

World Wide Web: http://www.osfa.mass.edu

Contact: Scholarship Information
Massachusetts Office of Student Financial Assistance
454 Broadway
Suite 200
Revere, MA 02151

MELLINGER EDUCATIONAL FOUNDATION

MELLINGER SCHOLARSHIPS • 366

Scholarships for undergraduates residing in western Illinois and eastern Iowa.

Award Scholarship for use in freshman, sophomore, junior, or senior years; renewable. *Number:* 300–350. *Amount:* $300–$1200.

Eligibility Requirements: Applicant must be enrolled or expecting to enroll full or part-time at a two-year or four-year or technical institution or university and resident of Illinois or Iowa. Available to U.S. citizens.

Application Requirements Application, financial need analysis, test scores, transcript. *Deadline:* May 1.

World Wide Web: http://www.mellinger.org

Contact: David Fleming, President
Mellinger Educational Foundation
1025 East Broadway, Box 770
Monmouth, IL 61462
Phone: 309-734-2419
Fax: 309-734-4435

MINNESOTA HIGHER EDUCATION SERVICES OFFICE

ADVANCED PLACEMENT/INTERNATIONAL BACCALAUREATE DEGREE PROGRAM • 367

A non-need-based grant available for incoming Freshman who had an average score of 3 or higher on five AP courses or an average score of 4 or higher on 5 IB courses. Must be a Minnesota resident and attend a college in Minnesota.

Award Grant for use in freshman or sophomore years; not renewable. *Number:* 300. *Amount:* $300–$700.

Eligibility Requirements: Applicant must be high school student; planning to enroll or expecting to enroll full or part-time at a two-year or four-year institution or university; resident of Minnesota and studying in Minnesota. Available to U.S. citizens.

Application Requirements Application, test scores. *Deadline:* Continuous.

World Wide Web: http://www.mheso.state.mn.us

Contact: Brenda Larter
Minnesota Higher Education Services Office
1450 Energy Park Drive, Suite 350
St. Paul, MN 55108-5227
Phone: 651-642-0567 Ext. 3417
Fax: 651-642-0675
E-mail: larter@heso.state.mn.us

MINNESOTA STATE GRANT PROGRAM • 368

Need-based grant program available for Minnesota residents attending Minnesota colleges. Student covers 46% of cost with remainder covered by Pell Grant, parent contribution and state grant. Students apply with FAFSA and college administers the program on campus.

Award Grant for use in freshman, sophomore, junior, or senior years; not renewable. *Number:* 71,000. *Amount:* $100–$7770.

Eligibility Requirements: Applicant must be age 17; enrolled or expecting to enroll full or part-time at a two-year or four-year or technical institution or university; resident of Minnesota and studying in Minnesota. Available to U.S. citizens.

Application Requirements Application, financial need analysis. *Deadline:* June 30.

World Wide Web: http://www.mheso.state.mn.us

Contact: Minnesota Higher Education Services Office
1450 Energy Park Drive, Suite 350
St. Paul, MN 55108
Phone: 651-642-0567 Ext. 1

MISSOURI DEPARTMENT OF ELEMENTARY AND SECONDARY EDUCATION

ROBERT C. BYRD HONORS SCHOLARSHIP • 369

Award for Missouri high school seniors who are residents of Missouri. The amount of the award per student each year depends on the amount the state is allotted by the U.S. Department of Education. The highest amount of award per student is $1500. Students must rank in top 10% of high school class and score in top 10% of ACT test.

Award Scholarship for use in freshman year; renewable. *Number:* 150–190. *Amount:* up to $1500.

Eligibility Requirements: Applicant must be high school student; planning to enroll or expecting to enroll full-time at a two-year or four-year or technical institution or university and resident of Missouri. Applicant must have 3.5 GPA or higher. Available to U.S. and non-Canadian citizens.

Application Requirements Application, test scores, transcript, 7th semester transcripts. *Deadline:* April 15.

World Wide Web: http://www.dese.state.mo.us

Contact: Laura Harrison, Administrative Assistant
Missouri Department of Elementary and Secondary Education
PO Box 480
Jefferson City, MO 65102-0480
Phone: 573-751-1668
Fax: 573-526-3580
E-mail: lharriso@mail.dese.state.mo.us

MITCHELL INSTITUTE

SENATOR GEORGE J. MITCHELL SCHOLARSHIP RESEARCH INSTITUTE SCHOLARSHIPS • 370

The Mitchell Institute awards 160 $4,000 scholarships each year to Maine students entering colleges. One Mitchell Scholar is chosen from every public high school in the state, 15 awarded to private/parochial school students, home-school students, and non-traditional students. Fifteen scholarships are available to Maine seniors going out of state.

Award Scholarship for use in freshman, sophomore, junior, or senior years; renewable. *Number:* 160. *Amount:* $4000.

Eligibility Requirements: Applicant must be high school student; planning to enroll or expecting to enroll full or part-time at a two-year or four-year or technical institution or university and resident of Maine. Available to U.S. citizens.

Application Requirements Application, essay, financial need analysis, photo, references, transcript. *Deadline:* April 1.

World Wide Web: http://www.mitchellinstitute.org

Senator George J. Mitchell Scholarship Research Institute Scholarships (continued)
Contact: Ms. Patricia Higgins, Director of Scholarship Programs
Mitchell Institute
22 Monument Square, Suite 200
Portland, ME 04106
Phone: 207-773-7700
Fax: 207-773-1133

MONTANA GUARANTEED STUDENT LOAN PROGRAM, OFFICE OF COMMISSIONER OF HIGHER EDUCATION

HIGH SCHOOL HONOR SCHOLARSHIP • 371

Scholarship provides a one-year non-renewable fee waiver of tuition and registration and is awarded to graduating high school seniors from accredited high schools in Montana. 500 scholarships are awarded each year averaging $2,000 per recipient. The value of the award varies, depending on the tuition and registration fee at each participating college. Must have a minimum 3.0 GPA, meet all college preparatory requirements and be enrolled in an accredited high school for at least three years prior to graduation. Awarded to highest-ranking student in class attending a participating school. Contact high school counselor to apply. Deadline: April 15.

Award Scholarship for use in freshman year; not renewable. *Number:* 500. *Amount:* $2000.

Eligibility Requirements: Applicant must be high school student; planning to enroll or expecting to enroll full or part-time at a two-year or four-year institution or university; resident of Montana and studying in Montana. Applicant must have 3.0 GPA or higher. Available to U.S. citizens.

Application Requirements Application, transcript. *Deadline:* April 15.

World Wide Web: http://www.mgslp.state.mt.us

Contact: high school counselor

INDIAN STUDENT FEE WAIVER see number 251

MONTANA HIGHER EDUCATION OPPORTUNITY GRANT • 372

This grant is awarded based on need to undergraduate students attending either part-time or full-time who are residents of Montana and attending participating Montana schools. Awards are limited to the most needy students. A specific major or program of study is not required. This grant does not need to be repaid, and students may apply each year. Apply by filing a Free Application for Federal Student Aid by March 1 and contacting the financial aid office at the admitting college.

Award Grant for use in freshman, sophomore, junior, or senior years; not renewable. *Number:* 500. *Amount:* $400–$600.

Eligibility Requirements: Applicant must be enrolled or expecting to enroll full or part-time at a two-year or four-year institution or university; resident of Montana and studying in Montana. Available to U.S. citizens.

Application Requirements Financial need analysis, FAFSA. *Deadline:* March 1.
World Wide Web: http://www.mgslp.state.mt.us
Contact: Sally Speer, Grants and Scholarship Coordinator
Montana Guaranteed Student Loan Program, Office of
Commissioner of Higher Education
2500 Broadway
PO Box 203101
Helena, MT 59620-3101
Phone: 406-444-0638
Fax: 406-444-1869
E-mail: sspeer@mgslp.state.mt.us

NASA FLORIDA SPACE GRANT CONSORTIUM

FLORIDA SPACE RESEARCH AND EDUCATION GRANT PROGRAM • 373

One-time award for aerospace and technology research. Must be U.S. citizen. Grant is for research in Florida only. Submit research proposal with budget. Application deadline is March 1.

Award Grant for use in freshman, sophomore, junior, senior, graduate, or postgraduate years; not renewable. *Number:* 9–12. *Amount:* $10,000–$30,000.
Eligibility Requirements: Applicant must be enrolled or expecting to enroll full or part-time at a four-year institution or university and studying in Florida. Available to U.S. citizens.
Application Requirements Proposal with budget. *Deadline:* March 1.
World Wide Web: http://fsgc.engr.ucf.edu
Contact: Dr. Jaydeep Mukherjee, Administrator
NASA Florida Space Grant Consortium
Mail Stop: FSGC
Kennedy Space Center, FL 32899
Phone: 321-452-4301
Fax: 321-449-0739
E-mail: jmukherj@mail.ucf.edu

NATIONAL BURGLAR AND FIRE ALARM ASSOCIATION

NBFAA/SECURITY DEALER YOUTH SCHOLARSHIP PROGRAM
see number 180

NEVADA DEPARTMENT OF EDUCATION

NEVADA DEPARTMENT OF EDUCATION ROBERT C. BYRD HONORS SCHOLARSHIP PROGRAM • 374

Award for senior graduating from public or private Nevada high school. Must be Nevada resident and Nevada High School Scholars Program recipient.

Nevada Department of Education Robert C. Byrd Honors Scholarship Program (continued)

Renewable award of $1500. No application necessary. Nevada scholars are chosen from a database supplied by ACT and SAT. Please request SAT score be mailed to 2707 on your registration form. SAT scores of 1100 and above qualify as initial application. ACT score is automatically submitted for a score of 25 or greater. GPA (unweighted) must be 3.5 or higher.

Award Scholarship for use in freshman, sophomore, junior, or senior years; renewable. *Number:* 40–60. *Amount:* $1500.

Eligibility Requirements: Applicant must be high school student; planning to enroll or expecting to enroll full-time at a two-year or four-year or technical institution or university and resident of Nevada. Applicant must have 3.5 GPA or higher.

Application Requirements Test scores, transcript. *Deadline:* Continuous.

Contact: Financial Aid Office at local college
Nevada Department of Education
700 East 5th Street
Carson City, NV 89701

NEVADA STUDENT INCENTIVE GRANT • 375

Award available to Nevada residents for use at an accredited Nevada college or university. Must show financial need. Any field of study eligible. High school students may not apply. One-time award of up to $5000. Contact financial aid office at local college.

Award Grant for use in freshman, sophomore, junior, or senior years; not renewable. *Number:* 400–800. *Amount:* $100–$5000.

Eligibility Requirements: Applicant must be enrolled or expecting to enroll full or part-time at a two-year or four-year or technical institution or university; resident of Nevada and studying in Nevada. Available to U.S. citizens.

Application Requirements Application, financial need analysis. *Deadline:* Continuous.

Contact: Financial Aid Office at local college
Nevada Department of Education
700 East 5th Street
Carson City, NV 89701

NEVADA WOMEN'S FUND

NEVADA WOMEN'S FUND SCHOLARSHIPS • 376

Awards for women for a variety of academic and vocational training scholarships. Must be a resident of Nevada. Preference given to applicants from northern Nevada. Renewable award of $500 to $5000. Application deadline is the last Friday in February. Application can be downloaded from web site (http://www.nevadawomensfund.org).

Award Scholarship for use in freshman, sophomore, junior, or senior years; renewable. *Number:* 50–80. *Amount:* $500–$5000.

Eligibility Requirements: Applicant must be enrolled or expecting to enroll full or part-time at a two-year or four-year or technical institution or university; female and resident of Nevada.
Application Requirements Application, financial need analysis, references, transcript.
World Wide Web: http://www.nevadawomensfund.org
Contact: Fritsi Ericson, President and CEO
Nevada Women's Fund
770 Smithridge Drive, Suite 300
Reno, NV 89502
Phone: 775-786-2335
Fax: 775-786-8152
E-mail: fritsi@nevadawomensfund.org

NEW HAMPSHIRE CHARITABLE FOUNDATION

ADULT STUDENT AID PROGRAM • 377
Award for New Hampshire residents who are at least 24 years old, or who have served in the military, are wards of the court, have not been claimed by their parents for two consecutive years, are married, or who have dependent children. Application deadlines are August 15, December 15, and May 15. Application fee is $15. Further information and application available at web site http://www.nhcf.org.

Award Grant for use in freshman, sophomore, junior, or senior years; not renewable. *Number:* 100–200. *Amount:* $100–$1500.
Eligibility Requirements: Applicant must be enrolled or expecting to enroll full or part-time at a two-year or four-year or technical institution or university and resident of New Hampshire. Available to U.S. citizens.
Application Requirements Application, financial need analysis, resume, references. *Fee:* $15.
World Wide Web: http://www.nhcf.org
Contact: Norma Daviault, Program Assistant
New Hampshire Charitable Foundation
37 Pleasant Street
Concord, NH 03301-4005
Phone: 603-225-6641 Ext. 226
E-mail: nd@nhcf.org

CAREER AID TO TECHNOLOGY STUDENTS PROGRAM • 378
Awards for New Hampshire residents enrolled in any accredited vocational or technical program that does not lead to a four-year baccalaureate degree. Must be financially needy and planning to enroll at least half time. Application deadline is June 27. See web site at http://www.nhcf.org for further information and application.

Award Grant for use in freshman, sophomore, or junior years; not renewable. *Number:* 300. *Amount:* $100–$2500.

Career Aid to Technology Students Program (continued)
Eligibility Requirements: Applicant must be enrolled or expecting to enroll at a two-year or technical institution and resident of New Hampshire. Available to U.S. citizens.
Application Requirements Application, financial need analysis, transcript. *Deadline:* June 27.
World Wide Web: http://www.nhcf.org
Contact: CATS Program
New Hampshire Charitable Foundation
37 Pleasant Street
Concord, NH 03301-4005
Phone: 800-464-6641

NHCF STATEWIDE STUDENT AID PROGRAM   • 379

Awards available to New Hampshire residents enrolled at accredited institutions. Some awards are renewable. Application fee is $20. Students must be enrolled at least half time, carrying 6 or more hours. Further information and application available at web site http://www.nhcf.org.

Award Grant for use in freshman, sophomore, junior, senior, or graduate years; not renewable. *Number:* 300–400. *Amount:* $100–$2500.
Eligibility Requirements: Applicant must be enrolled or expecting to enroll at a four-year institution or university and resident of New Hampshire. Available to U.S. citizens.
Application Requirements Application, essay, financial need analysis, resume, references, test scores, transcript. *Fee:* $20. *Deadline:* April 5.
World Wide Web: http://www.nhcf.org
Contact: Norma Davaiult, Program Assistant
New Hampshire Charitable Foundation
37 Pleasant Street
Concord, NH 03301-4005
Phone: 603-225-6641 Ext. 226
E-mail: nd@nhcf.org

NEW HAMPSHIRE POSTSECONDARY EDUCATION COMMISSION

NEW HAMPSHIRE INCENTIVE PROGRAM (NHIP)   • 380

One-time grants for New Hampshire residents attending school in New Hampshire, Connecticut, Maine, Massachusetts, Rhode Island, or Vermont. Must have financial need. Deadline is May 1. Complete Free Application for Federal Student Aid. Grant is not automatically renewable. Applicant must reapply.

Award Grant for use in freshman, sophomore, junior, or senior years; not renewable. *Number:* 3000–3500. *Amount:* $125–$1000.
Eligibility Requirements: Applicant must be enrolled or expecting to enroll full or part-time at a two-year or four-year or technical institution or university;

resident of New Hampshire and studying in Connecticut, Maine, Massachusetts, New Hampshire, Rhode Island, or Vermont. Available to U.S. citizens.
Application Requirements Application, financial need analysis. *Deadline:* May 1.
World Wide Web: http://www.state.nh.us/postsecondary
Contact: Sherrie Tucker, Program Assistant
New Hampshire Postsecondary Education Commission
3 Barrell Court, Suite 300
Concord, NH 03301-8512
Phone: 603-271-2555 Ext. 355
Fax: 603-271-2696
E-mail: stucker@pec.state.nh.us

NEW YORK COUNCIL FOR THE HUMANITIES
YOUNG SCHOLARS CONTEST • 381
The Young Scholars Contest is a research essay competition on a predetermined theme in the humanities. New York State high school students who are legal residents of the state are eligible. Further information, guidelines and deadlines are available at web site http://www.nyhumanities.org.

Award Scholarship for use in freshman year; not renewable. *Number:* 6–18. *Amount:* $250–$5000.
Eligibility Requirements: Applicant must be high school student; planning to enroll or expecting to enroll full-time at a two-year or four-year institution or university and resident of New York. Available to U.S. and non-U.S. citizens.
Application Requirements Applicant must enter a contest, essay.
World Wide Web: http://www.nyhumanities.org
Contact: New York Council for the Humanities
150 Broadway, Suite 1700
New York, NY 10038

NEW YORK STATE EDUCATION DEPARTMENT
ROBERT C. BYRD HONORS SCHOLARSHIP-NEW YORK • 382
Award for outstanding high school seniors accepted to U.S. college or university. Based on SAT score and high school average. Minimum 3.5 GPA required; minimum 1250 combined SAT score from one sitting. Must be legal resident of New York and a U.S. citizen. Renewable for up to four years. General Education Degree holders eligible.

Award Scholarship for use in freshman, sophomore, junior, or senior years; renewable. *Number:* 410. *Amount:* $1500.
Eligibility Requirements: Applicant must be high school student; planning to enroll or expecting to enroll full-time at a two-year or four-year institution or university and resident of New York. Applicant must have 3.5 GPA or higher. Available to U.S. citizens.

Robert C. Byrd Honors Scholarship-New York (continued)
Application Requirements Application, test scores, transcript. *Deadline:* March 1.
Contact: Lewis J. Hall, Coordinator
New York State Education Department
Room 1078 EBA
Albany, NY 12234
Phone: 518-486-1319
Fax: 518-486-5346

NEW YORK STATE HIGHER EDUCATION SERVICES CORPORATION

NEW YORK STATE TUITION ASSISTANCE PROGRAM • 383
Award for New York state residents attending New York postsecondary institution. Must be full-time student in approved program with tuition over $200 per year. Must show financial need and not be in default in any other state program. Renewable award of $500-$5000.

Award Grant for use in freshman, sophomore, junior, or senior years; renewable. *Number:* 300,000–320,000. *Amount:* $500–$5000.
Eligibility Requirements: Applicant must be enrolled or expecting to enroll full-time at a two-year or four-year institution or university; resident of New York and studying in New York.
Application Requirements Application, financial need analysis. *Deadline:* May 1.
World Wide Web: http://www.hesc.com
Contact: Student Information
New York State Higher Education Services Corporation
99 Washington Avenue, Room 1320
Albany, NY 12255

SCHOLARSHIPS FOR ACADEMIC EXCELLENCE • 384
Renewable awards of up to $1500 for academically outstanding New York State high school graduates planning to attend an approved postsecondary institution in New York State. For full-time study only. Contact high school guidance counselor to apply.

Award Scholarship for use in freshman, sophomore, junior, or senior years; renewable. *Number:* 8000. *Amount:* $500–$1500.
Eligibility Requirements: Applicant must be high school student; planning to enroll or expecting to enroll full-time at a four-year institution or university; resident of New York and studying in New York. Available to U.S. citizens.
Application Requirements Application.
World Wide Web: http://www.hesc.com
Contact: Student Information
New York State Higher Education Services Corporation
99 Washington Avenue, Room 1320
Albany, NY 12255

NORTH CAROLINA COMMISSION OF INDIAN AFFAIRS

INCENTIVE SCHOLARSHIP FOR NATIVE AMERICANS see number 254

NORTH CAROLINA DIVISION OF VETERANS' AFFAIRS

NORTH CAROLINA VETERANS' SCHOLARSHIPS CLASS II
see number 208

NORTH CAROLINA VETERANS' SCHOLARSHIPS CLASS III
see number 209

NORTH CAROLINA STATE EDUCATION ASSISTANCE AUTHORITY

AUBREY LEE BROOKS SCHOLARSHIPS • 385

Renewable award for high school seniors who are residents of designated North Carolina counties and are planning to attend North Carolina State University, the University of North Carolina at Chapel Hill or the University of North Carolina at Greensboro. Award provides approximately half of the cost of an undergraduate education. Write for further details and deadlines, or visit web site: http://www.cfnc.org.

Award Scholarship for use in freshman, sophomore, junior, or senior years; renewable. *Number:* 17–54. *Amount:* $7700.

Eligibility Requirements: Applicant must be high school student; planning to enroll or expecting to enroll full-time at an institution or university; resident of North Carolina and studying in North Carolina. Applicant must have 3.0 GPA or higher. Available to U.S. citizens.

Application Requirements Application, essay, financial need analysis, interview, photo, references, test scores, transcript. *Deadline:* February 1.

World Wide Web: http://www.cfnc.org

Contact: Bill Carswell, Manager of Scholarship and Grant Division
North Carolina State Education Assistance Authority
PO Box 13663
Research Triangle, NC 27709-3663
Phone: 919-549-8614
Fax: 919-549-4687
E-mail: carswellb@ncseaa.edu

NORTH DAKOTA UNIVERSITY SYSTEM

NORTH DAKOTA INDIAN COLLEGE SCHOLARSHIP PROGRAM
see number 255

OHIO ASSOCIATION OF CAREER COLLEGES AND SCHOOLS

LEGISLATIVE SCHOLARSHIP • 386

Renewable award to full-time students attending a trade/technical institution in Ohio. Must be U.S. citizen. Minimum 2.5 GPA required. Must be graduating high school senior.

Award Scholarship for use in freshman or sophomore years; renewable. *Number:* 80. *Amount:* $2600–$13,448.

Eligibility Requirements: Applicant must be high school student; planning to enroll or expecting to enroll full-time at a technical institution; resident of Ohio and studying in Ohio. Applicant must have 2.5 GPA or higher. Available to U.S. citizens.

Application Requirements Application, essay, references, transcript. *Deadline:* February 21.

Contact: Max Lerner, Executive Director
Ohio Association of Career Colleges and Schools
1857 Northwest Boulevard
The Annex
Columbus, OH 43212
Phone: 614-487-8180
Fax: 614-487-8190

OHIO BOARD OF REGENTS

OHIO ACADEMIC SCHOLARSHIP PROGRAM • 387

Award for academically outstanding Ohio residents planning to attend an approved Ohio college. Must be a high school senior intending to enroll full-time. Award is renewable for up to four years. Must rank in upper quarter of class or have a minimum GPA of 3.5.

Award Scholarship for use in freshman, sophomore, junior, or senior years; renewable. *Number:* 1000. *Amount:* $2000.

Eligibility Requirements: Applicant must be high school student; planning to enroll or expecting to enroll full-time at a two-year or four-year institution; resident of Ohio and studying in Ohio. Applicant must have 3.5 GPA or higher. Available to U.S. citizens.

Application Requirements Application, test scores, transcript. *Deadline:* February 23.

World Wide Web: http://www.regents.state.oh.us

Contact: Sarina Wilks, Program Administrator
Ohio Board of Regents
PO Box 182452
Columbus, OH 43218-2452
Phone: 614-752-9528
Fax: 614-752-5903
E-mail: swilks@regents.state.oh.us

OHIO NATIONAL GUARD

OHIO NATIONAL GUARD SCHOLARSHIP PROGRAM   see number 195

OKLAHOMA STATE REGENTS FOR HIGHER EDUCATION

OKLAHOMA TUITION AID GRANT • 388

Award for Oklahoma residents enrolled at an Oklahoma institution at least part-time per semester in a degree program. May be enrolled in two- or four-year or approved vocational-technical institution. Award of up to $1000 per year. Application is made through FAFSA.

Award Grant for use in freshman, sophomore, junior, senior, or graduate years; renewable. *Number:* 23,000. *Amount:* $200–$1000.

Eligibility Requirements: Applicant must be enrolled or expecting to enroll full or part-time at a two-year or four-year or technical institution or university; resident of Oklahoma and studying in Oklahoma. Available to U.S. citizens.

Application Requirements Application, financial need analysis, FAFSA. *Deadline:* April 30.

World Wide Web: http://www.okhighered.org

Contact: Oklahoma State Regents for Higher Education
PO Box 3020
Oklahoma City, OK 73101-3020
Phone: 405-225-9456
Fax: 405-225-9392
E-mail: otaginfo@otag.org

WILLIAM P. WILLIS SCHOLARSHIP • 389

Renewable award for Oklahoma residents attending an Oklahoma institution. Contact institution financial aid office for application deadline.

Award Scholarship for use in freshman, sophomore, junior, or senior years; renewable. *Number:* 32. *Amount:* $2000–$3000.

Eligibility Requirements: Applicant must be enrolled or expecting to enroll full-time at a two-year or four-year institution or university; resident of Oklahoma and studying in Oklahoma.

World Wide Web: http://www.okhighered.org

Contact: Oklahoma State Regents for Higher Education
PO Box 108850
Oklahoma City, OK 73101-8850
Phone: 800-858-1840
Fax: 405-225-9230
E-mail: studentinfo@osrhe.edu

PAGE EDUCATION FOUNDATION

PAGE EDUCATION FOUNDATION GRANT   see number 257

PENNSYLVANIA HIGHER EDUCATION ASSISTANCE AGENCY

PENNSYLVANIA STATE GRANT
• 390

Award for Pennsylvania residents attending an approved postsecondary institution as undergraduates in a program of at least two years duration. Renewable for up to eight semesters if applicants show continued need and academic progress. Submit Free Application for Federal Student Aid.

Award Grant for use in freshman, sophomore, junior, or senior years; renewable. *Number:* up to 151,000. *Amount:* $300–$3300.

Eligibility Requirements: Applicant must be enrolled or expecting to enroll full or part-time at a two-year or four-year or technical institution or university and resident of Pennsylvania. Available to U.S. and Canadian citizens.

Application Requirements Application, financial need analysis. *Deadline:* May 1.

World Wide Web: http://www.pheaa.org

Contact: Keith New, Director of Communications and Press Office
Pennsylvania Higher Education Assistance Agency
1200 North Seventh Street
Harrisburg, PA 17102-1444
Phone: 717-720-2509
Fax: 717-720-3903
E-mail: knew@pheaa.org

POTLATCH FOUNDATION FOR HIGHER EDUCATION SCHOLARSHIP

POTLATCH FOUNDATION FOR HIGHER EDUCATION SCHOLARSHIP
• 391

Granted to students living within 30 miles of a major Potlatch facility and based on financial need.

Award Scholarship for use in freshman, sophomore, junior, or senior years; renewable. *Number:* 50–80. *Amount:* $1400.

Eligibility Requirements: Applicant must be enrolled or expecting to enroll full-time at a two-year or four-year or technical institution or university and resident of Arkansas, Idaho, Minnesota, or Washington. Available to U.S. citizens.

Application Requirements Application, financial need analysis, transcript. *Deadline:* July 1.

World Wide Web: http://www.potlatchcorp.com

Contact: Sharon Pegau, Corporate Programs and Board Administrator
Potlatch Foundation For Higher Education Scholarship
601 West Riverside Avenue
Suite 1100
Spokane, WA 99201
Phone: 509-835-1515
Fax: 509-835-1566
E-mail: foundation@potlatchcorp.com

PRESBYTERIAN CHURCH (USA)

APPALACHIAN SCHOLARSHIPS
see number 274

R.O.S.E. FUND

R.O.S.E. FUND SCHOLARSHIP PROGRAM
• 392

The R.O.S.E. scholarship program acknowledges women who are survivors of violence or abuse. Primarily awarded to women who have successfully completed one year of undergraduate studies. Scholarships are for tuition and expenses at any accredited college or university in New England. Must be U.S. residents. Deadlines are June 17 for the fall semester, December 3 for the spring semester.

Award Scholarship for use in sophomore, junior, or senior years; renewable. *Number:* 10–15. *Amount:* $500–$10,000.

Eligibility Requirements: Applicant must be age 18; enrolled or expecting to enroll full or part-time at a two-year or four-year institution or university; female and studying in Connecticut, Maine, Massachusetts, New Hampshire, Rhode Island, or Vermont. Applicant must have 2.5 GPA or higher. Available to U.S. and non-U.S. citizens.

Application Requirements Application, autobiography, essay, financial need analysis, interview, references, test scores, transcript.

World Wide Web: http://www.rosefund.org

Contact: Alison Justus, Director of Programs
R.O.S.E. Fund
175 Federal Street, Suite 455
Boston, MA 02110
Phone: 617-482-5400 Ext. 11
Fax: 617-482-3443
E-mail: ajustus@rosefund.org

RHODE ISLAND HIGHER EDUCATION ASSISTANCE AUTHORITY

COLLEGE BOUND FUND ACADEMIC PROMISE SCHOLARSHIP
• 393

One-time award to graduating high school seniors. Eligibility based on financial need and SAT/ACT scores. Must maintain specified grade point averages each

College Bound Fund Academic Promise Scholarship (continued)
year for renewal. Must be Rhode Island resident and attend college full time. Application and FAFSA deadline is March 1.

Award Scholarship for use in freshman, sophomore, junior, or senior years; not renewable. *Number:* 100. *Amount:* $2500.

Eligibility Requirements: Applicant must be high school student; planning to enroll or expecting to enroll full-time at a two-year or four-year or technical institution or university and resident of Rhode Island. Available to U.S. citizens.

Application Requirements Application, financial need analysis, test scores. *Deadline:* March 1.

World Wide Web: http://www.riheaa.org

Contact: Mary Ann Welch, Director of Program Administration
Rhode Island Higher Education Assistance Authority
560 Jefferson Boulevard
Warwick, RI 02886
Phone: 401-736-1170
Fax: 401-732-3541
E-mail: mawelch@riheaa.org

RHODE ISLAND HIGHER EDUCATION GRANT PROGRAM • 394

Grants for residents of Rhode Island attending an approved school in the U.S., Canada, or Mexico. Based on need. Renewable for up to four years if in good academic standing. Applications accepted January 1 through March 1. Several awards of variable amounts. Must be U.S. citizen or registered alien.

Award Grant for use in freshman, sophomore, junior, or senior years; not renewable. *Number:* 10,000–12,000. *Amount:* $250–$750.

Eligibility Requirements: Applicant must be enrolled or expecting to enroll full or part-time at a two-year or four-year or technical institution or university and resident of Rhode Island. Available to U.S. citizens.

Application Requirements Application, financial need analysis. *Deadline:* March 1.

World Wide Web: http://www.riheaa.org

Contact: Mary Ann Welch, Director of Program Administration
Rhode Island Higher Education Assistance Authority
560 Jefferson Boulevard
Warwick, RI 02886
Phone: 401-736-1170
Fax: 401-732-3541
E-mail: mawelch@riheaa.org

SACHS FOUNDATION

SACHS FOUNDATION SCHOLARSHIPS   see number 261

SHOPKO STORES, INC.

SHOPKO SCHOLARS PROGRAM • 395

Must live within 100 miles of a ShopKo store. Scholars selected on the basis of academic record, potential to succeed, leadership, and participation in school and community activates, honors, work, experience, a statement of educational and career goals, and an outside appraisal. Financial need is not considered.

Award Scholarship for use in freshman, sophomore, junior, or senior years; not renewable. *Number:* 100–110. *Amount:* $1000.

Eligibility Requirements: Applicant must be enrolled or expecting to enroll at a two-year or four-year or technical institution or university and resident of California, Colorado, Idaho, Illinois, Iowa, Michigan, Minnesota, Montana, Nebraska, Nevada, Oregon, South Dakota, Utah, Washington, or Wisconsin. Available to U.S. citizens.

Application Requirements Application, essay, photo, references, self-addressed stamped envelope, transcript. *Deadline:* December 1.

World Wide Web: http://www.shopko.com/

Contact: Amy Anderson, Communications Specialist
ShopKo Stores, Inc.
700 Pilgrim Way
PO Box 19060
Green Bay, WI 54307-9060
Phone: 920-429-4328
Fax: 920-429-4363
E-mail: aanderso@shopko.com

SOUTH CAROLINA DEPARTMENT OF EDUCATION

ROBERT C. BYRD HONORS SCHOLARSHIP-SOUTH CAROLINA • 396

Renewable award of $1500 for graduating high school seniors from South Carolina who will be attending a two-year or four-year institution. Applicants should be superior students who demonstrate academic achievement and show promise of continued success at a postsecondary institution.

Award Scholarship for use in freshman, sophomore, junior, or senior years; renewable. *Number:* 96. *Amount:* $1500.

Eligibility Requirements: Applicant must be high school student; planning to enroll or expecting to enroll full-time at a two-year or four-year institution and resident of South Carolina. Applicant must have 3.5 GPA or higher. Available to U.S. citizens.

Application Requirements Application, references, test scores, transcript, extracurricular activities. *Deadline:* February 4.

Robert C. Byrd Honors Scholarship-South Carolina (continued)

Contact: Mrs. Beth Cope, Program Coordinator
South Carolina Department of Education
1424 Senate Street
Columbia, SC 29201
Phone: 803-734-8116
Fax: 803-734-0702
E-mail: bcope@sde.state.sc.us

SOUTH CAROLINA TUITION GRANTS COMMISSION

SOUTH CAROLINA TUITION GRANTS PROGRAM • 397

Assists South Carolina residents attending one of twenty approved South Carolina Independent colleges. Freshmen must be in upper 3/4 of high school class or have SAT score of at least 900. Upper-class students must complete 24 semester hours per year to be eligible.

Award Grant for use in freshman, sophomore, junior, or senior years; renewable. *Number:* up to 11,000. *Amount:* $100–$3240.

Eligibility Requirements: Applicant must be enrolled or expecting to enroll full-time at a two-year or four-year institution; resident of South Carolina and studying in South Carolina. Available to U.S. citizens.

Application Requirements Application, financial need analysis, test scores, transcript, FAFSA. *Deadline:* June 30.

World Wide Web: http://www.sctuitiongrants.com

Contact: Toni Cave, Financial Aid Counselor
South Carolina Tuition Grants Commission
101 Business Park Boulevard, Suite 2100
Columbia, SC 29203-9498
Phone: 803-896-1120
Fax: 803-896-1126
E-mail: toni@sctuitiongrants.org

SOUTH DAKOTA DEPARTMENT OF EDUCATION AND CULTURAL AFFAIRS

ROBERT C. BYRD HONORS SCHOLARSHIP-SOUTH DAKOTA • 398

For South Dakota residents in their senior year of high school. Must have a minimum 3.5 GPA and a minimum ACT score of 24. Awards are renewable up to four years. Contact high school guidance office for more details.

Award Scholarship for use in freshman, sophomore, junior, or senior years; renewable. *Number:* up to 80. *Amount:* $1500.

Eligibility Requirements: Applicant must be high school student; planning to enroll or expecting to enroll full-time at a two-year or four-year or technical institution or university and resident of South Dakota. Applicant must have 3.5 GPA or higher. Available to U.S. citizens.

Application Requirements Application, test scores, transcript. *Deadline:* May 1.
World Wide Web: http://www.state.sd.us/deca
Contact: Roxie Thielen, Financial Aid Administrator
South Dakota Department of Education and Cultural Affairs
700 Governors Drive
Pierre, SD 57501-2291
Phone: 605-773-5669
Fax: 605-773-6139
E-mail: roxie.thielen@state.sd.us

SOUTHERN SCHOLARSHIP FOUNDATION, INC.

SOUTHERN SCHOLARSHIP FOUNDATION • 399

The scholarship is for rent-free cooperative living in our houses located at Florida State University, University of Florida, Florida A & M, and (for men only) at Bethune-Cookman College. Students share all household duties while maintaining high academic standards.

Award Scholarship for use in freshman, sophomore, junior, or senior years; renewable. *Number:* 431. *Amount:* $550–$650.
Eligibility Requirements: Applicant must be enrolled or expecting to enroll full-time at a four-year institution or university; single and studying in Florida. Applicant must have 3.0 GPA or higher. Available to U.S. and non-U.S. citizens.
Application Requirements Application, autobiography, essay, financial need analysis, photo, references, test scores, transcript, college acceptance letter. *Deadline:* March 1.
World Wide Web: http://www.scholarships.org/ssf
Contact: Southern Scholarship Foundation, Inc.
322 Stadium Drive
Tallahassee, FL 32304
Phone: 850-222-3833
Fax: 850-222-6750
E-mail: tpitcock@scholarships.org

STATE COUNCIL OF HIGHER EDUCATION FOR VIRGINIA

VIRGINIA TUITION ASSISTANCE GRANT PROGRAM (PRIVATE INSTITUTIONS) • 400

Renewable awards of approximately $3,000 each for undergraduate, graduate, and first professional degree students attending an approved private, nonprofit college within Virginia. Must be a Virginia resident and be enrolled full-time. Not to be used for religious study. Preferred deadline July 31. Others are wait-listed. Contact college financial aid office. The application process is handled by the participating colleges' financial aid office.

Virginia Tuition Assistance Grant Program (Private Institutions) (continued)
Award Grant for use in freshman, sophomore, junior, senior, or graduate years; renewable. *Number:* 15,000. *Amount:* $3000.
Eligibility Requirements: Applicant must be enrolled or expecting to enroll full-time at a four-year institution; resident of Virginia and studying in Virginia.
Application Requirements Application. *Deadline:* July 31.
World Wide Web: http://www.schev.edu
Contact: Financial Aid Office at participating institution
State Council of Higher Education for Virginia
James Monroe Building, 10th Floor
101 North 14th Street
Richmond, VA 23219

STATE OF GEORGIA

GEORGIA NATIONAL GUARD SERVICE CANCELABLE LOAN PROGRAM
see number 196

STATE OF NORTH DAKOTA

NORTH DAKOTA INDIAN SCHOLARSHIP PROGRAM   see number 265

NORTH DAKOTA STUDENT FINANCIAL ASSISTANCE GRANTS
• 401

Aids North Dakota residents attending an approved college or university in North Dakota. Must be enrolled in a program of at least nine months in length.

Award Grant for use in freshman, sophomore, junior, or senior years; not renewable. *Number:* 2500–2600. *Amount:* up to $600.
Eligibility Requirements: Applicant must be enrolled or expecting to enroll full-time at a two-year or four-year institution or university; resident of North Dakota and studying in North Dakota. Available to U.S. citizens.
Application Requirements Application, financial need analysis. *Deadline:* April 15.
World Wide Web: http://www.ndus.nodak.edu
Contact: Peggy Wipf, Director of Financial Aid
State of North Dakota
600 East Boulevard, Department 215
Bismarck, ND 58505-0230
Phone: 701-328-4114

STATE STUDENT ASSISTANCE COMMISSION OF INDIANA (SSACI)

HOOSIER SCHOLAR AWARD
• 402

The Hoosier Scholar Award is a $500 nonrenewable award. Based on the size of the senior class, one to three scholars are selected by the guidance counselor(s). The award is based on academic merit and may be used for any educational expense at an eligible Indiana institution of higher education.

Award Scholarship for use in freshman year; not renewable. *Number:* 790–840. *Amount:* $500.

Eligibility Requirements: Applicant must be high school student; planning to enroll or expecting to enroll full-time at a two-year or four-year institution or university; resident of Indiana and studying in Indiana. Applicant must have 3.5 GPA or higher. Available to U.S. citizens.

Application Requirements *Deadline:* March 1.

World Wide Web: http://www.ssaci.in.gov

Contact: Ms. Ada Sparkman, Program Coordinator
State Student Assistance Commission of Indiana (SSACI)
150 West Market Street, Suite 500
Indianapolis, IN 46204-2805
Phone: 317-232-2350
Fax: 317-232-3260

INDIANA FREEDOM OF CHOICE GRANT • 403

The Freedom of Choice Grant is a need-based, tuition-restricted program for students attending Indiana private institutions seeking a first undergraduate degree. It is awarded in addition to the Higher Education Award. Students (and parents of dependent students) who are U.S. citizens and Indiana residents must file the FAFSA yearly by the March 10 deadline.

Award Grant for use in freshman, sophomore, junior, or senior years; not renewable. *Number:* 10,000–11,830. *Amount:* $200–$3906.

Eligibility Requirements: Applicant must be enrolled or expecting to enroll full-time at a four-year institution or university; resident of Indiana and studying in Indiana. Available to U.S. citizens.

Application Requirements Application, financial need analysis, FAFSA. *Deadline:* March 10.

World Wide Web: http://www.ssaci.in.gov

Contact: Grant Counselor
State Student Assistance Commission of Indiana (SSACI)
150 West Market Street, Suite 500
Indianapolis, IN 46204-2805
Phone: 317-232-2350
Fax: 317-232-3260
E-mail: grants@ssaci.state.in.us

INDIANA HIGHER EDUCATION AWARD • 404

The Higher Education Award is a need-based, tuition-restricted program for students attending Indiana public, private or proprietary institutions seeking a first undergraduate degree. Students (and parents of dependent students) who are U.S. citizens and Indiana residents must file the FAFSA yearly by the March 10 deadline.

Award Grant for use in freshman, sophomore, junior, or senior years; not renewable. *Number:* 38,000–43,660. *Amount:* $200–$4734.

Indiana Higher Education Award (continued)

Eligibility Requirements: Applicant must be enrolled or expecting to enroll full-time at a two-year or four-year or technical institution or university; resident of Indiana and studying in Indiana. Available to U.S. citizens.

Application Requirements Application, financial need analysis, FAFSA. *Deadline:* March 10.

World Wide Web: http://www.ssaci.in.gov

Contact:　Grant Counselors
State Student Assistance Commission of Indiana (SSACI)
150 West Market Street, Suite 500
Indianapolis, IN 46204-2805
Phone: 317-232-2350
Fax: 317-232-3260
E-mail: grants@ssaci.state.in.us

INDIANA NATIONAL GUARD SUPPLEMENTAL GRANT　see number 197

PART-TIME GRANT PROGRAM　● 405

Program is designed to encourage part-time undergraduates to start and complete their associate or baccalaureate degrees or certificates by subsidizing part-time tuition costs. It is a term-based award that is based on need. State residency requirements must be met and a FAFSA must be filed. Eligibility is determined at the institutional level subject to approval by SSACI.

Award Grant for use in freshman, sophomore, junior, or senior years; not renewable. *Number:* 4000–6366. *Amount:* $50–$4000.

Eligibility Requirements: Applicant must be enrolled or expecting to enroll part-time at a two-year or four-year or technical institution or university; resident of Indiana and studying in Indiana. Available to U.S. citizens.

Application Requirements Application, financial need analysis. *Deadline:* Continuous.

World Wide Web: http://www.ssaci.in.gov

Contact:　Grant Division
State Student Assistance Commission of Indiana (SSACI)
150 West Market Street, Suite 500
Indianapolis, IN 46204-2805
Phone: 317-232-2350
Fax: 317-232-3260
E-mail: grants@ssaci.state.in.us

ROBERT C. BYRD HONORS SCHOLARSHIP-INDIANA　● 406

Scholarship is designed to recognize academic achievement and requires a minimum SAT score of 1300 or ACT score of 31, or recent GED score of 65. The scholarship is awarded equally among Indiana's congressional districts. The amount of the scholarship varies depending upon federal funding and is automatically renewed if the institution's satisfactory academic progress requirements are met.

Award Scholarship for use in freshman, sophomore, junior, or senior years; renewable. *Number:* 550–570. *Amount:* $1500.

Eligibility Requirements: Applicant must be enrolled or expecting to enroll full-time at a two-year or four-year institution or university and resident of Indiana. Applicant must have 3.5 GPA or higher. Available to U.S. citizens.

Application Requirements Application, test scores, transcript. *Deadline:* April 24.

World Wide Web: http://www.ssaci.in.gov

Contact: Ms. Yvonne Heflin, Director, Special Programs
State Student Assistance Commission of Indiana (SSACI)
150 West Market Street, Suite 500
Indianapolis, IN 46204-2805
Phone: 317-232-2350
Fax: 317-232-3260

TWENTY-FIRST CENTURY SCHOLARS AWARD • 407

Income-eligible 7th graders who enroll in the program fulfill a pledge of good citizenship and complete the Affirmation Form are guaranteed tuition for four years at any participating public institution. If the student attends a private institution, the state will award an amount comparable to that of a public institution. If the student attends a participating proprietary school, the state will award a tuition scholarship equal to that of Ivy Tech State College. FAFSA and affirmation form must be filed yearly by March 10. Applicant must be resident of Indiana.

Award Scholarship for use in freshman, sophomore, junior, or senior years; not renewable. *Number:* 2800–8100. *Amount:* $1000–$5314.

Eligibility Requirements: Applicant must be enrolled or expecting to enroll full-time at a two-year or four-year or technical institution or university; resident of Indiana and studying in Indiana. Applicant must have 2.5 GPA or higher. Available to U.S. citizens.

Application Requirements Application, financial need analysis, affirmation form. *Deadline:* March 10.

World Wide Web: http://www.ssaci.in.gov

Contact: Twenty-first Century Scholars Program Counselors
State Student Assistance Commission of Indiana (SSACI)
150 West Market Street, Suite 500
Indianapolis, IN 46204-2805
Phone: 317-233-2100
Fax: 317-232-3260

SUBMARINE OFFICERS' WIVES CLUB

BOWFIN MEMORIAL SCHOLARSHIP see number 184

SWISS BENEVOLENT SOCIETY OF NEW YORK

PELLEGRINI SCHOLARSHIP GRANTS see number 266

TENNESSEE STUDENT ASSISTANCE CORPORATION

NED MCWHERTER SCHOLARS PROGRAM • 408

Assists Tennessee residents with high academic ability. Must have high school GPA of at least 3.5 and have scored in top 5% of SAT or ACT. Must attend college in Tennessee. Only high school seniors may apply.

Award Scholarship for use in freshman, sophomore, junior, or senior years; renewable. *Number:* 55. *Amount:* $6000.

Eligibility Requirements: Applicant must be high school student; planning to enroll or expecting to enroll full-time at a two-year or four-year institution or university; resident of Tennessee and studying in Tennessee. Applicant must have 3.5 GPA or higher. Available to U.S. citizens.

Application Requirements Application, test scores, transcript. *Deadline:* February 15.

World Wide Web: http://www.state.tn.us/tsac

Contact: Kathy Stripling, Scholarship Coordinator
Tennessee Student Assistance Corporation
Suite 1950, Parkway Towers
Nashville, TN 37243-0820
Phone: 615-741-1346
Fax: 615-741-6101
E-mail: kathy.stripling@state.tn.us

ROBERT C. BYRD HONORS SCHOLARSHIP-TENNESSEE • 409

Available to Tennessee residents graduating from high school. Must have at least a 3.5 GPA. May also qualify with a 24 ACT or 1090 SAT. Renewable up to four years. Those with GED Test score of 57 or above may also apply.

Award Scholarship for use in freshman, sophomore, junior, or senior years; renewable. *Number:* 125. *Amount:* $1100–$1500.

Eligibility Requirements: Applicant must be high school student; planning to enroll or expecting to enroll full-time at a two-year or four-year institution or university and resident of Tennessee. Applicant must have 3.5 GPA or higher. Available to U.S. citizens.

Application Requirements Application, test scores, transcript. *Deadline:* March 1.

World Wide Web: http://www.state.tn.us/tsac

Contact: Kathy Stripling, Scholarship Coordinator
Tennessee Student Assistance Corporation
404 James Robertson Parkway, Suite 1950, Parkway Towers
Nashville, TN 37243-0820
Phone: 615-741-1346
Fax: 615-741-6101
E-mail: kathy.stripling@state.tn.us

TENNESSEE STUDENT ASSISTANCE AWARD PROGRAM   • 410

Assists Tennessee residents attending an approved college or university within the state. Complete a Free Application for Federal Student Aid form. Apply January 1. FAFSA must be processed by May 1 for priority consideration.

Award Grant for use in freshman, sophomore, junior, or senior years; renewable. *Number:* 26,000. *Amount:* $100–$2130.

Eligibility Requirements: Applicant must be enrolled or expecting to enroll full or part-time at a two-year or four-year or technical institution or university; resident of Tennessee and studying in Tennessee. Available to U.S. citizens.

Application Requirements Application, financial need analysis. *Deadline:* May 1.

World Wide Web: http://www.state.tn.us/tsac

Contact: Naomi Derryberry, Grant and Scholarship Administrator
Tennessee Student Assistance Corporation
Suite 1950, Parkway Towers
Nashville, TN 37243-0820
Phone: 615-741-1346
Fax: 615-741-6101
E-mail: naomi.derryberry@state.tn.us

TEXAS 4-H YOUTH DEVELOPMENT FOUNDATION

TEXAS 4-H OPPORTUNITY SCHOLARSHIP   • 411

Renewable award for Texas 4-H members to attend a Texas college or university. Minimum GPA of 2.5 required. Must attend full-time. Deadline is February 1.

Award Scholarship for use in freshman, sophomore, junior, or senior years; renewable. *Number:* 100. *Amount:* $1500–$15,000.

Eligibility Requirements: Applicant must be enrolled or expecting to enroll full-time at a two-year or four-year or technical institution or university; resident of Texas and studying in Texas. Applicant must have 2.5 GPA or higher. Available to U.S. citizens.

Application Requirements Application, essay, financial need analysis, interview, references, test scores, transcript. *Deadline:* February 1.

World Wide Web: http://texas4-h.tamu.edu

Contact: Philip Pearce, Executive Director
Texas 4-H Youth Development Foundation
Texas A&M University
7606 Eastmark Drive, Suite 101, Box 4-H
College Station, TX 77843-2473
Phone: 979-845-1213
Fax: 979-845-6495
E-mail: p-pearce@tamu.edu

TEXAS HIGHER EDUCATION COORDINATING BOARD

TRAIN OUR TEACHERS AWARD   see number 185

TRIANGLE COMMUNITY FOUNDATION

GLAXO SMITH KLINE OPPORTUNITIES SCHOLARSHIP   • 412

Renewable award for any type of education or training program. Must be a legal resident of the United States with a permanent residence in Durham, Orange, Wake, or Chatham counties. No income limitations. Application deadline is March 15. For further information see web site at http://www.tranglecf.org.

Award Scholarship for use in freshman, sophomore, junior, senior, or graduate years; renewable. *Number:* 1–5. *Amount:* $1000–$20,000.

Eligibility Requirements: Applicant must be enrolled or expecting to enroll full-time at a two-year or four-year institution or university; resident of North Carolina and studying in North Carolina. Available to U.S. citizens.

Application Requirements Application, autobiography, essay, financial need analysis, references, test scores, transcript, proof of U.S. citizenship. *Deadline:* March 15.

World Wide Web: http://www.trianglecf.org

Contact: application available at web site

UNITED FEDERATION OF TEACHERS

ALBERT SHANKER COLLEGE SCHOLARSHIP FUND OF THE UNITED FEDERATION OF TEACHERS   • 413

Renewable award for eligible students graduating from New York City public high schools to pursue undergraduate studies. Scholarship is $1250 a year for four years. Submit transcript, autobiography, essay, references, and financial need analysis with application. Deadline is third week of December. There are nine graduate awards including a renewable medical and a renewable law award. Applicants must be current undergraduate award winners.

Award Scholarship for use in freshman, sophomore, junior, senior, or graduate years; renewable. *Number:* 250. *Amount:* $1250.

Eligibility Requirements: Applicant must be enrolled or expecting to enroll full-time at a two-year or four-year institution or university and resident of New York. Available to U.S. citizens.

Application Requirements Application, autobiography, essay, financial need analysis, references, transcript.

Contact: Jeffrey A. Huart, Director
United Federation of Teachers
52 Broadway, 11th Floor
New York, NY 10004-1603

UTAH STATE BOARD OF REGENTS

LEVERAGING EDUCATIONAL ASSISTANCE PARTNERSHIP (LEAP)
• 414

Available to students with substantial financial need for use at participating Utah schools. Contact Financial Aid Office of specific school for application requirements and deadlines. Must be Utah resident.

Award Grant for use in freshman, sophomore, junior, or senior years; renewable. *Number:* up to 3000. *Amount:* up to $2500.

Eligibility Requirements: Applicant must be enrolled or expecting to enroll full or part-time at a two-year or four-year or technical institution or university; resident of Utah and studying in Utah. Available to U.S. citizens.

Application Requirements Application, financial need analysis. *Deadline:* Continuous.

World Wide Web: http://www.uheaa.org

Contact: Financial Aid Office

VIRGINIA DEPARTMENT OF EDUCATION

LEE-JACKSON FOUNDATION SCHOLARSHIP
• 415

Essay contest for junior and senior Virginia high school students. Must demonstrate appreciation for the exemplary character and soldierly virtues of Generals Robert E. Lee and Thomas J. "Stonewall" Jackson. Three one-time awards of $1000 in each of Virginia's eight regions. A bonus scholarship of $1000 will be awarded to the author of the best essay in each of the eight regions. An additional award of $8000 will go to the essay judged the best in the state.

Award Scholarship for use in freshman year; not renewable. *Number:* 27. *Amount:* $1000–$8000.

Eligibility Requirements: Applicant must be high school student; planning to enroll or expecting to enroll at a four-year institution; resident of Virginia and must have an interest in writing. Available to U.S. citizens.

Application Requirements Application, applicant must enter a contest, essay, transcript. *Deadline:* December 21.

World Wide Web: http://www.pen.k12.va.us

Contact: Robert Almond, Director, Office of Grants and Special Projects
Virginia Department of Education
PO Box 2120
Richmond, VA 23218-2120
Phone: 804-225-3349
Fax: 804-371-2456
E-mail: ralmond@pen.k12.va.us

WASHINGTON NATIONAL GUARD

WASHINGTON NATIONAL GUARD SCHOLARSHIP PROGRAM
see number 198

WASHINGTON STATE WORKFORCE TRAINING AND EDUCATION COORDINATING BOARD

WASHINGTON AWARD FOR VOCATIONAL EXCELLENCE • 416

Tuition-only award for those completing a vocational education program as graduating seniors or community/technical college students who have completed first year of a two-year program. The scholarship is for 6 quarters or 4 semesters. Three are awarded in each of 49 legislative districts in the state. Must be a Washington State resident attending a postsecondary institution in Washington State.

Award Grant for use in freshman or sophomore years; renewable. *Number:* 147. *Amount:* $3486–$7796.

Eligibility Requirements: Applicant must be enrolled or expecting to enroll full or part-time at a two-year or four-year or technical institution or university; resident of Washington and studying in Washington. Available to U.S. and non-U.S. citizens.

Application Requirements Application, essay, references. *Deadline:* March 1.

World Wide Web: http://www.wtb.wa.gov/wave-abt.html

Contact: Lee Williams, Program Administrator
Washington State Workforce Training and Education Coordinating Board
128 Tenth Avenue SW
PO Box 43105
Olympia, WA 98504-3105
Phone: 360-586-3321
Fax: 360-586-5862
E-mail: lwilliams@wtb.wa.gov

WATERBURY FOUNDATION

REGIONAL AND RESTRICTED SCHOLARSHIP AWARD PROGRAM • 417

Supports accredited college or university study for residents of the Waterbury Foundation's twenty-one town service area. Regional awards are restricted to Connecticut colleges/universities only. Twenty-five restricted award programs are based on specific fund criteria (residency, ethnicity or course of study).

Award Scholarship for use in freshman, sophomore, junior, or senior years; renewable. *Number:* 175–220. *Amount:* $250–$10,000.

Eligibility Requirements: Applicant must be enrolled or expecting to enroll full or part-time at a two-year or four-year institution or university and resident of Connecticut. Applicant must have 2.5 GPA or higher. Available to U.S. citizens.

Application Requirements Application, essay, financial need analysis, references, transcript. *Deadline:* April 1.

World Wide Web: http://www.waterburyfoundation.org

Contact: Jill Stone, Program Officer
Waterbury Foundation
81 West Main Street
Waterbury, CT 06702
Phone: 203-753-1315
Fax: 203-756-3054
E-mail: jstone@waterburyfoundation.org

WEST VIRGINIA HIGHER EDUCATION POLICY COMMISSION-OFFICE OF FINANCIAL AID AND OUTREACH SERVICES

PROMISE SCHOLARSHIP • 418

Renewable award for West Virginia residents. Minimum 3.0 GPA and combined ACT score of 21 or 1000 on the SAT. Provides full-tuition scholarship to a state college or university in West Virginia or an equivalent scholarship to an in-state private college. Financial resources are not a factor.

Award Scholarship for use in freshman, sophomore, junior, or senior years; renewable. *Number:* 3500. *Amount:* $3000.

Eligibility Requirements: Applicant must be high school student; planning to enroll or expecting to enroll full-time at a two-year or four-year institution or university; resident of West Virginia and studying in West Virginia. Applicant must have 3.0 GPA or higher. Available to U.S. citizens.

Application Requirements Application, financial need analysis, test scores, transcript. *Deadline:* January 31.

World Wide Web: http://www.hepc.wvnet.edu

Contact: Robert Morgenstern, Executive Director
West Virginia Higher Education Policy Commission-Office of
Financial Aid and Outreach Services
Promise Scholarship, 1018 Kanawha Boulevard, Suite 700
Charleston, WV 25301
Phone: 304-558-4417
Fax: 304-558-3264
E-mail: morgenstern@hepc.wvnet.edu

WEST VIRGINIA HIGHER EDUCATION GRANT PROGRAM • 419

For West Virginia residents attending an approved nonprofit degree-granting college or university in West Virginia or Pennsylvania. Must be enrolled full-time. Based on financial need and academic merit. Award covers tuition and fees.

Award Grant for use in freshman, sophomore, junior, or senior years; renewable. *Number:* 10,500–10,800. *Amount:* $350–$2718.

Eligibility Requirements: Applicant must be enrolled or expecting to enroll full-time at a two-year or four-year institution or university; resident of West Virginia and studying in Pennsylvania or West Virginia. Available to U.S. citizens.

West Virginia Higher Education Grant Program (continued)

Application Requirements Application, financial need analysis, test scores, transcript. *Deadline:* March 1.

World Wide Web: http://www.hepc.wvnet.edu

Contact: Robert Long, Grant Program Coordinator
West Virginia Higher Education Policy Commission-Office of
Financial Aid and Outreach Services
1018 Kanawha Boulevard East, Suite 700
Charleston, WV 25301-2827
Phone: 888-825-5707
Fax: 304-558-4622
E-mail: long@hepc.wvnet.edu

WILLIAM G. AND MARIE SELBY FOUNDATION

SELBY SCHOLAR PROGRAM • 420

Scholarships awarded up to $5000 annually, not to exceed 1/3 of individual's financial need. Renewable for four years if student is full-time undergraduate at accredited college or university. Must demonstrate values of leadership and service to the community. Must reside in Sarasota, Manatee, Charlotte or DeSoto counties in Florida.

Award Scholarship for use in freshman, sophomore, junior, or senior years; renewable. *Number:* 30. *Amount:* up to $5000.

Eligibility Requirements: Applicant must be high school student; planning to enroll or expecting to enroll full-time at a four-year institution or university and resident of Florida. Applicant must have 3.0 GPA or higher. Available to U.S. citizens.

Application Requirements Application, essay, financial need analysis, interview, references, test scores, transcript. *Deadline:* April 1.

World Wide Web: http://www.selbyfdn.org

Contact: Jan Noah, Grants Manager
William G. and Marie Selby Foundation
1800 Second Street, Suite 750
Sarasota, FL 34236
Phone: 941-957-0442
Fax: 941-957-3135
E-mail: jnoah@selbyfdn.org

WISCONSIN FOUNDATION FOR INDEPENDENT COLLEGES, INC.

UPS SCHOLARSHIP • 421

Applicants must attend one of Wisconsin's private colleges and maintain a 3.0 GPA. Each school can award one to three UPS scholarships. Application deadline is May 1.

Award Scholarship for use in freshman, sophomore, junior, or senior years; not renewable. *Number:* 21–63. *Amount:* $1050–$3150.

Eligibility Requirements: Applicant must be enrolled or expecting to enroll full-time at a four-year institution or university and studying in Wisconsin. Applicant must have 3.0 GPA or higher. Available to U.S. citizens.

Application Requirements Application, autobiography, references. *Deadline:* May 1.

World Wide Web: http://www.wficweb.org

Contact: Christy Miller, Marketing Program Manager
Wisconsin Foundation for Independent Colleges, Inc.
735 North Water Street, Suite 600
Milwaukee, WI 53202
Phone: 414-273-5980
Fax: 414-273-5995
E-mail: wfic@execpc.com

TALENT

ALBERTA HERITAGE SCHOLARSHIP FUND

JIMMIE CONDON ATHLETIC SCHOLARSHIPS see number 217

AMERICAN INSTITUTE FOR FOREIGN STUDY

AMERICAN INSTITUTE FOR FOREIGN STUDY INTERNATIONAL SCHOLARSHIPS • 422

Awards are available to undergraduates on an AIFS study abroad program. Applicants must demonstrate leadership potential, have a minimum 3.0 cumulative GPA and meet program requirements. Up to 100 $1,000 scholarships are awarded per semester and up to 50 $750 scholarships are awarded each summer. Submit application by March 15 for summer, April 15 for fall or October 15 for spring. The application fee is $75.

Award Scholarship for use in freshman, sophomore, junior, or senior years; not renewable. *Number:* up to 150. *Amount:* $750–$1000.

Eligibility Requirements: Applicant must be age 17; enrolled or expecting to enroll full-time at a two-year or four-year institution or university and must have an interest in leadership. Applicant must have 3.0 GPA or higher. Available to U.S. and non-U.S. citizens.

Application Requirements Application, essay, photo, references, transcript. *Fee:* $75.

World Wide Web: http://www.aifsabroad.com

American Institute for Foreign Study International Scholarships (continued)
Contact: David Mauro, Admissions Counselor
American Institute for Foreign Study
River Plaza, 9 West Broad Street
Stamford, CT 06902-3788
Phone: 800-727-2437 Ext. 5163
Fax: 203-399-5598
E-mail: college.info@aifs.com

AMERICAN INSTITUTE FOR FOREIGN STUDY MINORITY SCHOLARSHIPS
see number 221

AMERICAN LEGION, DEPARTMENT OF NEW YORK

AMERICAN LEGION DEPARTMENT OF NEW YORK STATE HIGH SCHOOL ORATORICAL CONTEST
see number 281

AMERICAN LEGION, NATIONAL HEADQUARTERS

AMERICAN LEGION NATIONAL HEADQUARTERS NATIONAL HIGH SCHOOL ORATORICAL CONTEST
• 423

Several prizes awarded to high school students (freshmen through seniors) who give a speech lasting eight to ten minutes on the U.S. Constitution and an assigned topic speech of three to five minutes. Winners advance to higher level. Contact local chapter for entry information. One-time award of $1500-$18,000.

Award Scholarship for use in freshman, sophomore, junior, senior, or graduate years; not renewable. *Number:* 54. *Amount:* $1500–$18,000.
Eligibility Requirements: Applicant must be high school student; planning to enroll or expecting to enroll full-time at a two-year or four-year institution or university and must have an interest in public speaking. Available to U.S. citizens.
Application Requirements Application. *Deadline:* December 1.
World Wide Web: http://www.legion.org
Contact: Michael Buss, Assistant Director
American Legion, National Headquarters
PO Box 1055
Indianapolis, IN 46206-1055
Phone: 317-630-1249
Fax: 317-630-1369
E-mail: acy@legion.org

AMERICAN STRING TEACHERS ASSOCIATION

NATIONAL SOLO COMPETITION • 424

Twenty-six individual awards totaling $30,000 will be awarded. Instrument categories are violin, viola, cello, double bass, classical guitar and harp. Applicants competing in Junior Division must be under age 19. Senior Division competitors must be ages 19-25. Application fee is $60. Visit web site for application forms. Applicant must be a member of ASTA.

Award Prize for use in freshman, sophomore, junior, senior, or graduate years; not renewable. *Number:* 26. *Amount:* $600–$4500.

Eligibility Requirements: Applicant must be enrolled or expecting to enroll full-time at an institution or university and must have an interest in music. Available to U.S. and Canadian citizens.

Application Requirements Application, applicant must enter a contest, proof of age. *Fee:* $60.

World Wide Web: http://www.astaweb.com

Contact: American String Teachers Association
4153 Chain Bridge Road
Fairfax, VA 22030
Phone: 703-279-2113
Fax: 703-279-2114
E-mail: asta@astaweb.com

AYN RAND INSTITUTE

ATLAS SHRUGGED ESSAY COMPETITION • 425

Forty-nine awards totaling $10,000 for essays demonstrating an outstanding grasp of the philosophical meaning of "Atlas Shrugged." Students must be enrolled in either an undergraduate or graduate program. Essay should be between 1000 to 1200 words in length. Winners announced October 21. For more information, contact your scholarship office. All information necessary to enter the contest is available at web site http://www.aynrand.org/contests.

Award Prize for use in freshman, sophomore, junior, senior, or graduate years; not renewable. *Number:* 49. *Amount:* $50–$5000.

Eligibility Requirements: Applicant must be enrolled or expecting to enroll full-time at a two-year or four-year or technical institution or university and must have an interest in writing. Available to U.S. and non-U.S. citizens.

Application Requirements Applicant must enter a contest, essay. *Deadline:* September 16.

World Wide Web: http://www.aynrand.org/contests

Contact: Ayn Rand Institute
PO Box 57044
Irvine, CA 92619-7044

AYN RAND INSTITUTE COLLEGE SCHOLARSHIP ESSAY CONTEST BASED ON AYN RAND'S NOVELETTE, "ANTHEM" • 426

Entrant must be in the 9th or 10th grade. Essays will be judged on both style and content. Winning essays must demonstrate an outstanding grasp of the

Ayn Rand Institute College Scholarship Essay Contest Based on Ayn Rand's Novelette, "Anthem" (continued)

philosophical meaning of Ayn Rand's novelette, "Anthem." Contest deadline is March 18. Winners announced June 4. All information necessary to enter the contest is at http://www.aynrand.org/contests.

Award Prize for use in freshman year; not renewable. *Number:* 251. *Amount:* $30–$2000.

Eligibility Requirements: Applicant must be high school student; planning to enroll or expecting to enroll at an institution or university and must have an interest in writing. Available to U.S. and non-U.S. citizens.

Application Requirements Applicant must enter a contest, essay. *Deadline:* March 18.

World Wide Web: http://www.aynrand.org/contests

Contact: Ayn Rand Institute
PO Box 57044
Irvine, CA 92169-7044
E-mail: essay@aynrand.org

FOUNTAINHEAD COLLEGE SCHOLARSHIP ESSAY CONTEST • 427

251 prizes totaling $37,500 awarded to 11th and 12th grades for essays on Ayn Rand's "Fountainhead". Essay should be between 800 and 1600 words. Winners announced June 4. Semifinalist and finalist prizes also awarded. All information necessary to enter the contest is available at http://www.aynrand.org/contests.

Award Prize for use in freshman year; not renewable. *Number:* 251. *Amount:* $50–$10,000.

Eligibility Requirements: Applicant must be high school student; planning to enroll or expecting to enroll at an institution or university and must have an interest in writing. Available to U.S. and non-U.S. citizens.

Application Requirements Applicant must enter a contest, essay. *Deadline:* April 15.

World Wide Web: http://www.aynrand.org/contests

Contact: Ayn Rand Institute
PO Box 57044
Irvine, CA 92619-7044
E-mail: essay@aynrand.org

CALIFORNIA JUNIOR MISS SCHOLARSHIP PROGRAM

CALIFORNIA JUNIOR MISS SCHOLARSHIP PROGRAM

see number 290

CAP FOUNDATION

RON BROWN SCHOLAR PROGRAM

see number 225

COCA-COLA SCHOLARS FOUNDATION, INC.

COCA-COLA SCHOLARS PROGRAM • 428

Awards based on leadership, academic performance, extracurricular activities, employment, and community involvement. Finalists represent every state in the U.S. 40% of the recipients are minorities. Must apply in senior year of high school. Deadline is October 31. Recipient has six years in which to use award. Two hundred $4000 awards and fifty $20000 awards granted annually. Must apply through web site: http://www.coca-colascholars.org. Paper applications not offered.

Award Scholarship for use in freshman, sophomore, junior, or senior years; renewable. *Number:* 250. *Amount:* $4000–$20,000.

Eligibility Requirements: Applicant must be high school student; planning to enroll or expecting to enroll full or part-time at a two-year or four-year or technical institution or university and must have an interest in leadership. Applicant must have 3.0 GPA or higher. Available to U.S. citizens.

Application Requirements Application, essay, interview, references, transcript. *Deadline:* October 31.

World Wide Web: http://www.coca-colascholars.org

Contact: Mark Davis, President
Coca-Cola Scholars Foundation, Inc.
PO Box 442
Atlanta, GA 30301-0442
Phone: 800-306-2653
Fax: 404-733-5439
E-mail: scholars@na.ko.com

COCA-COLA TWO-YEAR COLLEGES SCHOLARSHIP • 429

Awards based on community involvement, leadership, and academic performance. Finalists represent every state in the U.S. Must pursue a two-year degree. Deadline is March 31. Each institution may nominate up to two applicants. Minimum 2.5 GPA is required. See web site: http://www.coca-colascholars.org for additional information.

Award Scholarship for use in freshman or sophomore years; not renewable. *Number:* 400. *Amount:* $1000.

Eligibility Requirements: Applicant must be enrolled or expecting to enroll full or part-time at a two-year or technical institution and must have an interest in leadership. Applicant must have 2.5 GPA or higher. Available to U.S. citizens.

Application Requirements Application, essay, nomination from institution. *Deadline:* March 31.

World Wide Web: http://www.coca-colascholars.org

Coca-Cola Two-Year Colleges Scholarship (continued)
Contact: Ryan Rodriguez, Program Facilitator
Coca-Cola Scholars Foundation, Inc.
PO Box 442
Atlanta, GA 30301-0442
Phone: 800-306-2653
Fax: 404-733-5439
E-mail: scholars@na.ko.com

CULTURAL SERVICES OF THE FRENCH EMBASSY

TEACHING ASSISTANTSHIP IN FRANCE   • 430

Grants support American students as they teach English in the French school system. For more details, deadlines and applications go to web site: http://www.frenchculture.org.

Award Grant for use in freshman, sophomore, junior, senior, graduate, or postgraduate years; renewable. *Number:* 1000–1500. *Amount:* up to $6750.
Eligibility Requirements: Applicant must be age 20-30; enrolled or expecting to enroll full or part-time at a two-year or four-year or technical institution or university; single and must have an interest in French language. Available to U.S. and Canadian citizens.
Application Requirements Application, photo, references, self-addressed stamped envelope, transcript.
World Wide Web: http://www.frenchculture.org
Contact: Benedicty Alessandra, Assistantship Coordinator
Cultural Services of the French Embassy
4101 Reservoir Road
Washington, DC 20007
Phone: 202-944-6294
Fax: 202-944-6268
E-mail: alessandra.benedicty@diplomatie.fr

EXECUTIVE WOMEN INTERNATIONAL

EXECUTIVE WOMEN INTERNATIONAL SCHOLARSHIP PROGRAM   • 431

Competitive award to high school juniors planning careers in any business or professional field of study which requires a four-year college degree. Award is renewable based on continuing eligibility. All awards are given through local chapters of the EWI. Applicant must apply through nearest chapter and live within 100 miles of it. Student must have a sponsoring teacher and school to be considered. For more details visit web site: http://www.executivewomen.org.

Award Scholarship for use in freshman, sophomore, junior, or senior years; renewable. *Number:* 130. *Amount:* $50–$10,000.

Eligibility Requirements: Applicant must be high school student; planning to enroll or expecting to enroll full-time at a four-year institution or university and must have an interest in designated field specified by sponsor.
Application Requirements Application, autobiography, interview, references, transcript. *Deadline:* March 1.
World Wide Web: http://www.executivewomen.org
Contact: application information available at web site

FLORIDA LEADER MAGAZINE/COLLEGE STUDENT OF THE YEAR, INC.

FLORIDA COLLEGE STUDENT OF THE YEAR AWARD   see number 321

J. WOOD PLATT CADDIE SCHOLARSHIP TRUST

J. WOOD PLATT CADDIE SCHOLARSHIP TRUST   see number 179

LIEDERKRANZ FOUNDATION

LIEDERKRANZ FOUNDATION SCHOLARSHIP AWARD FOR VOICE
● 432

Non-renewable awards for voice for both full- and part-time study. Those studying general voice must be between ages 20 to 35 years old while those studying Wagnerian voice must be between ages 25 to 45 years old. Application fee: $40. Applications not available before August/September. Deadline: November 15.

Award Scholarship for use in freshman, sophomore, junior, senior, or graduate years; not renewable. *Number:* 14–18. *Amount:* $1000–$5000.
Eligibility Requirements: Applicant must be enrolled or expecting to enroll full or part-time at an institution or university and must have an interest in music/singing. Available to U.S. and non-U.S. citizens.
Application Requirements Application, applicant must enter a contest, driver's license, self-addressed stamped envelope, proof of age. *Fee:* $40. *Deadline:* November 15.
Contact: C. Kessel, Administrative Assistant
Liederkranz Foundation
6 East 87th Street
New York, NY 10128
Phone: 212-534-0880
Fax: 212-828-5372

NATIONAL ASSOCIATION OF SECONDARY SCHOOL PRINCIPALS, AND PRUDENTIAL FINANCIALS, INC.

PRINCIPAL'S LEADERSHIP AWARD • 433

One-time award available to high school seniors only, for use at an accredited two- or four-year college or university. Based on leadership and school or community involvement. Application fee: $6. Deadline is December 1. Contact school counselor or principal. Citizens of countries other than the U.S. may only apply if they are attending a United States overseas institution. Minimum GPA 3.0.

Award Scholarship for use in freshman year; not renewable. *Number:* 150. *Amount:* $1000.

Eligibility Requirements: Applicant must be high school student; planning to enroll or expecting to enroll full-time at a two-year or four-year institution or university and must have an interest in leadership. Applicant must have 3.0 GPA or higher. Available to U.S. and non-Canadian citizens.

Application Requirements Application, essay, references, test scores, transcript. *Fee:* $6. *Deadline:* December 1.

World Wide Web: http://www.principals.org

Contact: local school principal or guidance counselor

ROTARY FOUNDATION OF ROTARY INTERNATIONAL

ROTARY FOUNDATION ACADEMIC-YEAR AMBASSADORIAL SCHOLARSHIPS • 434

One-time award funds travel, tuition, room and board for one academic year of study in foreign country. Applicant must have completed at least two years of university course work and be proficient in language of host country. Application through local Rotary club; appearances before clubs required during award period. Deadlines vary (March-July). See web site at http://www. rotary.org for updated information.

Award Scholarship for use in junior, senior, graduate, or postgraduate years; not renewable. *Number:* 900–1000. *Amount:* up to $25,000.

Eligibility Requirements: Applicant must be enrolled or expecting to enroll at a four-year institution or university and must have an interest in foreign language.

Application Requirements Application, autobiography, essay, interview, references, transcript.

World Wide Web: http://www.rotary.org

Contact: Scholarship Program
Rotary Foundation of Rotary International
1560 Sherman Avenue
Evanston, IL 60201
Phone: 847-866-4459

ROTARY MULTI-YEAR AMBASSADORIAL SCHOLARSHIPS • 435

Awarded for two or three years (depending on availability through sponsoring Rotary district) of degree-oriented study in another country. Applicant must have completed at least two years of university course work and be proficient in language of host country. Application through local Rotary club; appearances before clubs required during award period. Applications are accepted March through July. See web site at http://www.rotary.org for updated information.

Award Scholarship for use in junior, senior, or graduate years; not renewable. *Number:* 100–150. *Amount:* $12,000.

Eligibility Requirements: Applicant must be enrolled or expecting to enroll full-time at a four-year institution or university and must have an interest in foreign language.

Application Requirements Application, autobiography, essay, interview, references, transcript.

World Wide Web: http://www.rotary.org

Contact: Scholarship Program
Rotary Foundation of Rotary International
1560 Sherman Avenue
Evanston, IL 60201
Phone: 847-866-4459

SAN ANTONIO INTERNATIONAL PIANO COMPETITION

SAN ANTONIO INTERNATIONAL PIANO COMPETITION • 436

International piano competition for 10 semi-finalists, ages 20-32. Cash awards, ranging from $1000 for 5th prize to $15,000 for 1st prize, are determined through a series of daily concerts, with an additional award for the best performance of a commissioned work. Application fee: $65. Deadline: March 31. Additional awards: $500. Competition held every three years.

Award Prize for use in freshman, sophomore, junior, senior, graduate, or postgraduate years; not renewable. *Number:* 7–12. *Amount:* $500–$15,000.

Eligibility Requirements: Applicant must be age 20-32; enrolled or expecting to enroll at an institution or university and must have an interest in music/singing. Available to U.S. and non-U.S. citizens.

Application Requirements Application, applicant must enter a contest, autobiography, driver's license, photo, portfolio, references, self-addressed stamped envelope, tape recording, certified proof of date of birth, clippings and programs from previous performances. *Fee:* $65. *Deadline:* March 31.

World Wide Web: http://www.saipc.org

San Antonio International Piano Competition (continued)
Contact: Ms. Virginia Lawrence, Registrar
San Antonio International Piano Competition
PO Box 39636
San Antonio, TX 78218
Phone: 210-655-0766
Fax: 210-824-5094
E-mail: info@saipc.org

SCIENCE SERVICE, INC.

DISCOVERY CHANNEL YOUNG SCIENTIST CHALLENGE   • 437

Scholarship for students in the fifth through eighth grade to be used for future college enrollment. Must be a U.S. citizen. Must participate in a science fair. For additional information, visit web site: http://www.discovery.com/dysc

Award Scholarship for use in freshman year; renewable. *Number:* up to 40. *Amount:* $500–$15,000.

Eligibility Requirements: Applicant must be enrolled or expecting to enroll full-time at an institution or university and must have an interest in designated field specified by sponsor. Available to U.S. citizens.

Application Requirements Application, applicant must enter a contest, essay, interview, references. *Deadline:* June 4.

World Wide Web: http://www.sciserv.org

Contact: Michele Glidden, DYSC Program
Science Service, Inc.
1719 N Street, NW
Washington, DC 20036
Phone: 202-785-2255
Fax: 202-785-1243
E-mail: mglidden@sciserv.org

INTEL SCIENCE TALENT SEARCH   • 438

Forty scholarships ranging from $5000 to $100,000 will be awarded to the top high school science competition winners. Deadline: December 1. Write for more details. Applicants who are not U.S. citizens must be living in the U.S. and attending a U.S. high school. Visit web site for additional information: http://www.discovery.com/dysc

Award Scholarship for use in freshman, sophomore, junior, or senior years; renewable. *Number:* 40. *Amount:* $5000–$100,000.

Eligibility Requirements: Applicant must be high school student; planning to enroll or expecting to enroll full-time at a four-year institution or university and must have an interest in designated field specified by sponsor. Available to U.S. citizens.

Application Requirements Application, applicant must enter a contest, autobiography, essay, references, test scores, transcript. *Deadline:* December 1.

World Wide Web: http://www.sciserv.org

Contact: Intel STS Program Manager
Science Service, Inc.
1719 N Street, NW
Washington, DC 20036
Phone: 202-872-5149
Fax: 202-785-1243
E-mail: kstafford@scicerv.org

VIRGINIA DEPARTMENT OF EDUCATION

LEE-JACKSON FOUNDATION SCHOLARSHIP   see number 415

WASHINGTON CROSSING FOUNDATION

WASHINGTON CROSSING FOUNDATION SCHOLARSHIP   • 439

Renewable, merit-based awards available to high school seniors who are planning a career in government service. Must write an essay stating reason for deciding on a career in public service. Minimum 3.0 GPA required. Write for details.

Award Scholarship for use in freshman, sophomore, junior, or senior years; renewable. *Number:* 5–10. *Amount:* $1000–$20,000.

Eligibility Requirements: Applicant must be high school student; planning to enroll or expecting to enroll full-time at a four-year institution and must have an interest in designated field specified by sponsor. Applicant must have 3.0 GPA or higher. Available to U.S. citizens.

Application Requirements Application, essay, references, test scores, transcript. *Deadline:* January 15.

World Wide Web: http://www.gwcf.org

Contact: Eugene Fish, Vice Chairman
Washington Crossing Foundation
PO Box 503
Levittown, PA 19058-0503
Phone: 215-949-8841

WILLIAM RANDOLPH HEARST FOUNDATION

UNITED STATES SENATE YOUTH PROGRAM   • 440

For high school juniors and seniors holding elected student offices. Must attend high school in state of parents' or guardians' legal residence. Two students selected from each state and the selection process will vary by state. Contact school principal or state department of education for information. Application deadline is in the early fall of each year for most states but the actual date will vary by state. Program is open to citizens and permanent residents of the United States Department of Defense schools overseas and the District of Columbia (not the territories). More information at web site, http://www.ussenateyouth.org.

United States Senate Youth Program (continued)

Award Scholarship for use in freshman, sophomore, junior, or senior years; not renewable. *Number:* 104. *Amount:* $5000.

Eligibility Requirements: Applicant must be high school student; planning to enroll or expecting to enroll full or part-time at a two-year or four-year or technical institution or university and must have an interest in designated field specified by sponsor. Available to U.S. citizens.

Application Requirements Application procedures will vary by state.

World Wide Web: http://www.ussenateyouth.org

Contact: Ms. Rita Almon, Program Director
William Randolph Hearst Foundation
90 New Montgomery Street, Suite 1212
San Francisco, CA 94105-4504
Phone: 800-841-7048
Fax: 415-243-0760
E-mail: ussyp@hearstfdn.org

WOMEN'S SPORTS FOUNDATION

TRAVEL AND TRAINING FUND • 441

Award to provide financial assistance to aspiring female athletes with successful competitive regional or national records who have the potential to achieve even higher performance levels and rankings. Must be a U.S. citizen or legal resident.

Award Grant for use in freshman, sophomore, junior, or senior years; not renewable. *Number:* 90–100. *Amount:* $500–$2000.

Eligibility Requirements: Applicant must be enrolled or expecting to enroll full or part-time at an institution or university; female and must have an interest in athletics/sports. Available to U.S. citizens.

Application Requirements Application, references. *Deadline:* December 31.

World Wide Web: http://www.womenssportsfoundation.org

Contact: Women's Sports Foundation
Eisenhower Park
East Meadow, NY 11554
Phone: 800-227-3988
E-mail: wosport@aol.com

WOMEN'S WESTERN GOLF FOUNDATION

WOMEN'S WESTERN GOLF FOUNDATION SCHOLARSHIP • 442

Scholarships for female high school seniors for use at a four-year college or university. Based on academic record, financial need, character, and involvement in golf. (Golf skill not a criterion.) Twenty awards annually for incoming freshmen; approximately 60 scholarships renewed. Must maintain 2.5 GPA as freshman; 3.0 upperclassman GPA. Must continue to have financial need. Award is $2000 per student per year. Applicant must be 17-18 years of age.

Award Scholarship for use in freshman, sophomore, junior, or senior years; renewable. *Number:* up to 80. *Amount:* $2000.

Eligibility Requirements: Applicant must be high school student; age 17-18; planning to enroll or expecting to enroll full-time at a four-year institution or university; female and must have an interest in golf. Applicant must have 3.0 GPA or higher. Available to U.S. citizens.

Application Requirements Application, essay, financial need analysis, self-addressed stamped envelope, test scores, transcript. *Deadline:* April 5.

Contact: Mrs. Richard Willis, Scholarship Chairman
Women's Western Golf Foundation
393 Ramsay Road
Deerfield, IL 60015

WRITER'S DIGEST

WRITER'S DIGEST ANNUAL WRITING COMPETITION • 443

Annual writing competition. Only original, unpublished entries in any of the ten categories. Send self-addressed stamped envelope for guidelines and entry form. Deadline is May 15. Application fee: $10.

Award Prize for use in freshman, sophomore, junior, senior, or graduate years; not renewable. *Number:* 1001. *Amount:* $25–$1500.

Eligibility Requirements: Applicant must be enrolled or expecting to enroll full or part-time at a two-year or four-year or technical institution or university and must have an interest in writing. Available to U.S. and non-U.S. citizens.

Application Requirements Application, applicant must enter a contest, self-addressed stamped envelope. *Fee:* $10. *Deadline:* May 15.

World Wide Web: http://www.writersdigest.com

Contact: Terri Boes, Promotion Assistant
Writer's Digest
4700 East Galbraith Road
Cincinnati, OH 45236
Phone: 513-531-2690
Fax: 513-531-0798
E-mail: competitions@fwpubs.com

YOUNG AMERICAN BOWLING ALLIANCE (YABA)

PEPSI-COLA YOUTH BOWLING CHAMPIONSHIPS   see number 162

MISCELLANEOUS CRITERIA

AMERICAN ASSOCIATION OF SCHOOL ADMINISTRATORS/DISCOVER CARD TRIBUTE AWARD PROGRAM

DISCOVER CARD TRIBUTE AWARD SCHOLARSHIP PROGRAM • 444

Applicants should be current high school juniors with minimum 2.75 GPA. Nine scholarships available in each state and Washington, D.C. Nine $25,000 awards at the national level in three categories. Must plan to further education beyond high school in any accredited certification, licensing or training program or institution of higher education. Must demonstrate outstanding accomplishments in three of four areas: special talents, leadership, obstacles overcome, and community service. Visit web site for application and more information: http://www.aasa.org/discover.htm

Award Scholarship for use in freshman year; not renewable. *Number:* up to 478. *Amount:* $2500–$25,000.

Eligibility Requirements: Applicant must be high school student and planning to enroll or expecting to enroll full or part-time at a two-year or four-year or technical institution or university. Available to U.S. and non-U.S. citizens.

Application Requirements Application, essay, references, transcript. *Deadline:* January 9.

World Wide Web: http://www.aasa.org/discover.htm

Contact: Program Director
American Association of School Administrators/Discover Card
    Tribute Award Program
PO Box 9338
Arlington, VA 22219
Phone: 703-875-0708
E-mail: tributeaward@aasa.org

AMERICAN AUTOMOBILE ASSOCIATION

NATIONAL SENIOR HIGH COMMUNICATION CONTEST • 445

Contest for graduating high school seniors. Competition areas include graphic arts, writing, and audiovisual. Contact local AAA or CAA for details.

Award Scholarship for use in freshman, sophomore, junior, or senior years; not renewable. *Number:* 30–40. *Amount:* $100–$5000.

Eligibility Requirements: Applicant must be high school student and planning to enroll or expecting to enroll full or part-time at a two-year or four-year or technical institution or university. Available to U.S. and Canadian citizens.

Application Requirements Applicant must enter a contest. *Deadline:* January 27.

World Wide Web: http://aaapublicaffairs.com
Contact: Steve Meyer, Educational Technologist
American Automobile Association
1000 AAA Drive
Heathrow, FL 32746-5063
Phone: 407-444-7916
Fax: 407-444-7150
E-mail: smeyer@national.aaa.com

AMERICAN DIETETIC ASSOCIATION

AMERICAN DIETETIC ASSOCIATION FOUNDATION SCHOLARSHIP PROGRAM
• **446**

ADAF scholarships are available for undergraduate and graduate students enrolled in programs, including dietetic internships, preparing for entry to dietetics practice as well as dietetics professionals engaged in continuing education at the graduate level. Scholarship funds are provided by many state dietetic associations, dietetic practice groups, past ADA leaders, and corporate donors. All scholarships require ADA membership.

Award Scholarship for use in sophomore, junior, senior, graduate, or postgraduate years; not renewable. *Number:* 200. *Amount:* $500–$5000.

Eligibility Requirements: Applicant must be enrolled or expecting to enroll full or part-time at a two-year or four-year institution or university. Available to U.S. citizens.

Application Requirements Application, essay, financial need analysis, references, transcript. *Deadline:* February 15.

World Wide Web: http://www.adaf.org
Contact: Eva Donovan, Education Coordinator
American Dietetic Association
216 West Jackson Boulevard
Chicago, IL 60606-6695
Phone: 312-899-0040 Ext. 4876
Fax: 312-899-4817
E-mail: education@eatright.org

AMERICAN GI FORUM OF THE UNITED STATES

AMERICAN GI FORUM OF THE UNITED STATES HISPANIC EDUCATION FOUNDATION MATCHING SCHOLARSHIPS
• **447**

Renewable scholarship of up to $1000. Not restricted to, but priority given to Hispanics. Priority may be given to veterans and their families. Please contact local chapters for qualifications and deadline dates.

Award Scholarship for use in freshman, sophomore, junior, senior, graduate, or postgraduate years; renewable. *Number:* 50–200. *Amount:* $250–$1000.

American GI Forum of the United States Hispanic Education Foundation Matching Scholarships (continued)

Eligibility Requirements: Applicant must be enrolled or expecting to enroll full or part-time at a two-year or four-year or technical institution or university. Available to U.S. and non-U.S. citizens.

World Wide Web: http://www.agifnat.org

Contact: Local American GI Forum
American GI Forum of the United States
Attn: Hispanic Education Foundation
PO Box 952
Ulysses, KS 67880

ASSOCIATION OF INTERNATIONAL EDUCATION, JAPAN (AIEJ)

SHORT-TERM STUDENT EXCHANGE PROMOTION PROGRAM SCHOLARSHIP • 448

Scholarship available for qualified students accepted by Japanese universities under the student exchange agreement on a short-term basis from three months to one year. Scholarship includes a $645 monthly stipend, a $200 settling-in allowance, and round-trip, economy-class airfare. Application should be filed by Japanese host institution. Inquiries should be addressed to the international office of the home institution. Deadline decided by host institution.

Award Scholarship for use in freshman, sophomore, junior, senior, or graduate years; not renewable. *Number:* 1950. *Amount:* up to $7900.

Eligibility Requirements: Applicant must be enrolled or expecting to enroll full-time at a four-year institution or university. Available to U.S. and non-U.S. citizens.

World Wide Web: http://www.aiej.or.jp

Contact: Chika Hotta, Program Coordinator, Office for Cooperation with
Extrabudgetary Funding Sources, AIEJ
Association of International Education, Japan (AIEJ)
4-5-29 Komaba, Meguro-ku
Tokyo 153-8503
Japan
Phone: 81-3-54545290
Fax: 81-3-54545299
E-mail: efs@aiej.or.jp

ASSOCIATION OF TEACHERS OF JAPANESE BRIDGING CLEARINGHOUSE FOR STUDY ABROAD IN JAPAN

BRIDGING SCHOLARSHIPS • 449

Scholarships for U.S. students studying in Japan on semester or year-long programs. Deadlines are April 3 and October 3.

Award Scholarship for use in sophomore, junior, or senior years; not renewable. *Number:* 40–80. *Amount:* $2500–$4000.

Eligibility Requirements: Applicant must be enrolled or expecting to enroll full-time at a two-year or four-year institution or university. Available to U.S. citizens.

Application Requirements Application, essay, references, transcript.

World Wide Web: http://www.colorado.edu/ealld/atj/Bridging/scholarships.html

Contact: Susan Schmidt, Executive Director
Association of Teachers of Japanese Bridging Clearinghouse for
Study Abroad in Japan
279 UCB
Boulder, CO 80309-0279
Phone: 303-492-5487
Fax: 303-492-5856
E-mail: atj@colorado.edu

ASSOCIATION OF UNIVERSITIES AND COLLEGES OF CANADA

FAIRFAX FINANCIAL HOLDINGS LIMITED SCHOLARSHIP PROGRAM
see number 223

BOY SCOUTS OF AMERICA, EAGLE SCOUT SERVICE

NATIONAL EAGLE SCOUT HALL / MCELWAIN MERIT SCHOLARSHIP
• 450

Must be an Eagle Scout. Only graduating high school seniors through college juniors may apply. Application is available at the web site. (http://www.scouting.org/nesa/scholar)

Award Scholarship for use in freshman, sophomore, junior, or senior years; not renewable. *Number:* 80. *Amount:* $1500.

Eligibility Requirements: Applicant must be enrolled or expecting to enroll full-time at a four-year institution or university and male. Available to U.S. citizens.

Application Requirements Application, references. *Deadline:* February 28.

World Wide Web: http://www.scouting.org/nesa/scholar

Contact: Ann Dimond, Manager
Boy Scouts of America, Eagle Scout Service
1325 West Walnut Hill Lane
Box 152079
Irving, TX 75015-2079

CAREER TRAINING FOUNDATION

IMAGINE AMERICA SCHOLARSHIP • 451

One-time award available to graduating high school seniors. Must attend an accredited private postsecondary institution. Must be nominated by school counselor or principal. Must enroll by October 31. See web site, http://www. petersons.com/cca. Contact the guidance counselor at high school.

Award Scholarship for use in freshman year; not renewable. *Number:* up to 10,000. *Amount:* $1000.

Eligibility Requirements: Applicant must be high school student; age 17-18 and planning to enroll or expecting to enroll full-time at a two-year or four-year or technical institution. Applicant must have 2.5 GPA or higher. Available to U.S. citizens.

Application Requirements Applicant must enter a contest, financial need analysis, nomination. *Deadline:* October 31.

World Wide Web: http://www.petersons.com/cca/

Contact: Robert Martin, Executive Director/Vice President
Career Training Foundation
10 G Street, NE, Suite 750
Washington, DC 20002-4213
Phone: 202-336-6800
Fax: 202-408-8102
E-mail: scholarships@career.org

COMMISSION FRANCO-AMERICAINE D'ECHANGES UNIVERSITAIRES ET CULTURELS

FULBRIGHT PROGRAM • 452

Fulbright program offered to senior scholars, advanced students, professionals and exchange teachers to carry out research, and/or lecture, study or teach in the United States or France. Program provides grants to approximately 100 nationals from both countries. Applicants must submit proof of their affiliation with their host institution. Grant is only available to American and French citizens. For French citizens, photo must accompany application. Application deadlines: August 1 (for U.S. applicants) and December 15 (for French applicants). For more information, see web site: http://www.fulbright-france. org.

Award Grant for use in senior, graduate, or postgraduate years; not renewable. *Number:* 80–100. *Amount:* $1000–$20,000.

Eligibility Requirements: Applicant must be enrolled or expecting to enroll full or part-time at a four-year institution or university. Available to U.S. and non-Canadian citizens.

Application Requirements Application, essay, interview, photo, references, test scores, transcript.

World Wide Web: http://www.fulbright-france.org

Contact: Dr. Amy Tondu, Program Officer
Commission Franco-Americaine d'Echanges Universitaires et
    Culturels
Fulbright Commission
9 Rue Chardin
Paris 75016
France
Phone: 33-1-44145364
Fax: 33-1-42880479
E-mail: atondu@fulbright-france.org

CONGRESSIONAL BLACK CAUCUS SPOUSES PROGRAM

CONGRESSIONAL BLACK CAUCUS SPOUSES EDUCATION SCHOLARSHIP FUND
• **453**

Award made to students who reside or attend school in a Congressional district represented by an African-American member of Congress. Contact the Congressional office in the appropriate district for information and applications. Any correspondence sent to the CBC Foundation Office on Pennsylvania Avenue will be discarded and may disqualify applicant for the award. See web site for more details: http://www.cbcfinc.org.

Award Scholarship for use in freshman, sophomore, junior, or senior years; renewable. *Number:* 200. *Amount:* $500–$4000.

Eligibility Requirements: Applicant must be enrolled or expecting to enroll full-time at a two-year or four-year or technical institution or university. Applicant must have 2.5 GPA or higher. Available to U.S. citizens.

Application Requirements Application, essay, financial need analysis, interview, photo, references, transcript. *Deadline:* Continuous.

World Wide Web: http://cbcfinc.org

Contact: Appropriate Congressional District Office

CONNECTICUT POLICE CORPS

CONNECTICUT POLICE CORPS PROGRAM
• **454**

Full-time college students accepted into the Police Corps can receive up to $7,500 a year to cover the expenses of study toward a baccalaureate or graduate degree. Students may receive up to $30,000 under this program. Students may choose to study criminal justice, or may pursue degrees in other fields.

Award Scholarship for use in freshman, sophomore, junior, senior, or graduate years; renewable. *Number:* 10–15. *Amount:* up to $7500.

Eligibility Requirements: Applicant must be enrolled or expecting to enroll full-time at a four-year institution or university. Available to U.S. and non-U.S. citizens.

Application Requirements Application. *Deadline:* May 1.

Connecticut Police Corps Program (continued)
World Wide Web: http://www.post.state.ct.us/police%20corps.htm
Contact: application available at web site

DAVIS-PUTTER SCHOLARSHIP FUND

DAVIS-PUTTER SCHOLARSHIP FUND • 455
Provides need-based grants to student activists who are able to do academic work at the college level and are actively involved in building the movement for social and economic justice. For details regarding eligibility and instructions for receiving an application, contact: davisputter@hotmail.com.

Award Scholarship for use in freshman, sophomore, junior, senior, graduate, or postgraduate years; not renewable. *Number:* 25–30. *Amount:* up to $6000.
Eligibility Requirements: Applicant must be enrolled or expecting to enroll full or part-time at a two-year or four-year institution or university. Available to U.S. and non-U.S. citizens.
Application Requirements Application, essay, financial need analysis, photo, references, self-addressed stamped envelope, transcript. *Deadline:* April 1.
Contact: Jan Phillips, Secretary
Davis-Putter Scholarship Fund
PO Box 7307
New York, NY 10116
E-mail: davisputter@hotmail.com

EDUCATIONAL COMMUNICATIONS SCHOLARSHIP FOUNDATION

EDUCATIONAL COMMUNICATIONS SCHOLARSHIP • 456
Award based on scholarship, financial need, leadership, and extracurricular activity. Must be high school student and legal resident of U.S. to apply. Must have a minimum 3.0 GPA and have taken ACT or SAT exam. Semifinalists submit financial need analysis and essay; finalists submit transcript. Application fee is $3.50. Applications are available only at high school guidance offices. For application go to http://www.ecsf.org.

Award Scholarship for use in freshman year; not renewable. *Number:* 200. *Amount:* $1000.
Eligibility Requirements: Applicant must be high school student and planning to enroll or expecting to enroll full or part-time at a two-year or four-year or technical institution or university. Applicant must have 3.0 GPA or higher. Available to U.S. citizens.
Application Requirements Application, essay, financial need analysis, test scores, transcript. *Fee:* $3.5. *Deadline:* May 15.
World Wide Web: http://www.honoring.com/highschool/frame.html

Contact: Shelly M. White, Scholarship Coordinator
Educational Communications Scholarship Foundation
1701 Directors Boulevard, Suite 920
Austin, TX 78744
Phone: 512-440-2705
Fax: 512-447-1687
E-mail: scholar@ecsf.org

ELKS NATIONAL FOUNDATION

ELKS MOST VALUABLE STUDENT CONTEST • 457

Five hundred four-year awards are allocated for graduating high school seniors nationally by state quota. Based on scholarship, leadership, and financial need. Renewable awards with first place awards at $60,000, second place awards at $40,000 and third place awards at $20,000. This will be distributed over four years. The remainder of the 494 awards will continue to be worth $4000 over four years. Applications available at local Elks Lodge, at the web site (http://www.elks.org) (keyword: scholarship) or by sending a SASE to the Foundation.

Award Scholarship for use in freshman, sophomore, junior, or senior years; renewable. *Number:* 500. *Amount:* $4000–$60,000.

Eligibility Requirements: Applicant must be high school student and planning to enroll or expecting to enroll full-time at a two-year or four-year institution or university. Available to U.S. citizens.

Application Requirements Application, applicant must enter a contest, essay, financial need analysis, references, self-addressed stamped envelope, test scores, transcript. *Deadline:* January 10.

World Wide Web: http://www.elks.org/enf

Contact: Robin Edison, Scholarship Coordinator
Elks National Foundation
2750 North Lakeview Avenue
Chicago, IL 60614-1889
Phone: 773-755-4732
Fax: 773-755-4733
E-mail: scholarship@elks.org

EPSILON SIGMA ALPHA FOUNDATION

EPSILON SIGMA ALPHA SCHOLARSHIPS • 458

Awards for various fields of study. Some scholarships are restricted by gender, residency, grade point average, or location of school. Applications must be sent to the Epsilon Sigma Alpha designated state counselor. See web site at http://www.esaintl.com/esaf for further information, application forms, and a list of state counselors. Application deadline is February 1.

Award Scholarship for use in freshman, sophomore, junior, senior, or graduate years; not renewable. *Number:* up to 100. *Amount:* $500–$1500.

Eligibility Requirements: Applicant must be enrolled or expecting to enroll full or part-time at an institution or university.

Epsilon Sigma Alpha Scholarships (continued)
Application Requirements Application. *Deadline:* February 1.
World Wide Web: http://www.esaintl.com/esaf
Contact: application available at web site

FINANCIAL SERVICE CENTERS OF AMERICA, INC.

FINANCIAL SERVICE CENTERS OF AMERICA SCHOLARSHIP FUND   • 459

The FISCA Scholarship Program awards cash grants of at least $2,500 to two students from each of the 5 geographic regions across the country. Criteria is based on academic achievement, financial need, leadership skills in schools and the community, and an essay written expressly for the competition. Applicant must be single.

Award Grant for use in freshman year; not renewable. *Number:* 10–20. *Amount:* $2500–$5000.

Eligibility Requirements: Applicant must be high school student; planning to enroll or expecting to enroll full-time at a two-year or four-year institution or university and single. Available to U.S. citizens.

Application Requirements Application, essay, financial need analysis, photo, references, transcript. *Deadline:* June 15.

World Wide Web: http://www.fisca.org

Contact: Henry Shyne, Executive Director
        Financial Service Centers of America, Inc.
        25 Main Street
        PO Box 647
        Hackensack, NJ 07602
        Phone: 201-487-0412
        Fax: 201-487-3954
        E-mail: fiscahfs@aol.com

FLORIDA POLICE CORPS

FLORIDA POLICE CORPS SCHOLARSHIPS   • 460

One-time award that covers undergraduate or graduate expenses. Requires a four-year commitment to a Florida law enforcement agency. Candidate must meet the employment standards of the agency where he or she will serve. Twenty-four week training period at Jacksonville Policy Academy.

Award Scholarship for use in junior year; not renewable. *Number:* 60. *Amount:* up to $30,000.

Eligibility Requirements: Applicant must be enrolled or expecting to enroll full-time at a four-year institution or university. Available to U.S. citizens.

Application Requirements Application, driver's license, interview, photo, references, transcript. *Deadline:* Continuous.

World Wide Web: http://www.floridapolicecorps.com

Contact: Steven Richardson, Recruiting Coordinator/Lead Instructor
Florida Police Corps
4715 Capper Road
Jacksonville, FL 32218
Phone: 877-863-6731
Fax: 904-713-4820
E-mail: 3202sar@jaxsheriff.com

GUARDIAN LIFE INSURANCE COMPANY OF AMERICA

GIRLS GOING PLACES SCHOLARSHIP PROGRAM • 461

Rewards the enterprising spirits of girls ages 12 to 16 who demonstrate budding entrepreneurship, are taking the first steps toward financial independence, and make a difference in their school and community.

Award Prize for use in freshman year; not renewable. *Number:* 15. *Amount:* $1000–$10,000.

Eligibility Requirements: Applicant must be high school student; age 12-16; planning to enroll or expecting to enroll full-time at a two-year or four-year or technical institution or university and single female. Available to U.S. citizens.

Application Requirements Application, essay. *Deadline:* February 28.

World Wide Web: http://www.girlsgoingplaces.com

Contact: Diana Acevedo, Project Manager
Guardian Life Insurance Company of America
7 Hanover Square 26-C
New York, NY 10004
Phone: 212-598-7881
Fax: 212-919-2586
E-mail: diana_acevedo@glic.com

GUIDEPOSTS MAGAZINE

GUIDEPOSTS YOUNG WRITER'S CONTEST • 462

Entrants must be either a high school junior or senior. Submit a first-person story about a memorable or moving experience; story must be the true personal experience of the writer. Authors of top ten manuscripts receive a scholarship. First Prize: $10,000; Second Prize: $8,000; Third Prize: $6,000; Fourth Prize: $4,000; Fifth Prize: $3,000; Sixth through Tenth Prizes: $1,000; Eleventh through Twentieth Prizes receive $250 gift certificate for college supplies. The deadline is the Monday before Thanksgiving.

Award Prize for use in freshman year; not renewable. *Number:* 20. *Amount:* $250–$10,000.

Eligibility Requirements: Applicant must be high school student and planning to enroll or expecting to enroll full-time at a two-year or four-year or technical institution or university. Available to U.S. and non-U.S. citizens.

Application Requirements Applicant must enter a contest, manuscript (maximum 1200 words).

GUIDEPOSTS Young Writer's Contest (continued)
World Wide Web: http://www.guideposts.com
Contact: Christine Pisani, Secretary
GUIDEPOSTS Magazine
16 East 34th Street, 21st Floor
New York, NY 10016
Phone: 212-251-8100
Fax: 212-684-0679
E-mail: cpisani@guideposts.org

HERSCHEL C. PRICE EDUCATIONAL FOUNDATION

HERSCHEL C. PRICE EDUCATIONAL FOUNDATION SCHOLARSHIPS • 463

Open to undergraduates, graduates, and high school seniors. Must be a U.S. citizen, resident of West Virginia or attending a West Virginia college. Based on academic achievement and financial need. Deadlines are April 1 for fall and October 1 for spring. Undergraduates are shown preference.

Award Scholarship for use in freshman, sophomore, junior, senior, or graduate years; renewable. *Number:* 200–300. *Amount:* $500–$10,000.
Eligibility Requirements: Applicant must be enrolled or expecting to enroll full or part-time at a two-year or four-year institution or university. Available to U.S. citizens.
Application Requirements Application, financial need analysis, interview, test scores, transcript.
Contact: Jonna Hughes, Trustee/Director
Herschel C. Price Educational Foundation
PO Box 412
Huntington, WV 25708-0412
Phone: 304-529-3852

HORATIO ALGER ASSOCIATION OF DISTINGUISHED AMERICANS

HORATIO ALGER ASSOCIATION SCHOLARSHIP PROGRAM • 464

The Horatio Alger Association provides financial assistance to students in the United States who have exhibited integrity and perseverance in overcoming personal adversity and who aspire to pursue higher education. Renewable award for full-time students seeking undergraduate degree. Minimum 2.0 GPA required.

Award Scholarship for use in freshman, sophomore, junior, or senior years; renewable. *Number:* up to 1200. *Amount:* $1000–$10,000.
Eligibility Requirements: Applicant must be high school student and planning to enroll or expecting to enroll full-time at a two-year or four-year institution or university. Available to U.S. citizens.

Application Requirements Application, essay, references, transcript. *Deadline:* October 15.

World Wide Web: http://www.horatioalger.org

Contact: Scholarship Coordinator
Horatio Alger Association of Distinguished Americans
99 Canal Center Plaza, Suite 320
Alexandria, VA 22314
E-mail: programs@horatioalger.com

INSTITUTE OF INTERNATIONAL EDUCATION

NATIONAL SECURITY EDUCATION PROGRAM DAVID L. BOREN UNDERGRADUATE SCHOLARSHIPS ● 465

The National Security Education Program (NSEP) awards scholarships to American undergraduate students for study abroad in regions critical to U.S. national interest. Emphasized world areas include Africa, Asia, Central and Eastern Europe, the NIS, Latin America and the Caribbean, and the Middle East. NSEP scholarship recipients incur a service agreement. Must be a U.S. citizen.

Award Scholarship for use in freshman, sophomore, junior, or senior years; not renewable. *Number:* 150–200. *Amount:* $2500–$20,000.

Eligibility Requirements: Applicant must be enrolled or expecting to enroll full or part-time at a two-year or four-year institution or university. Available to U.S. citizens.

Application Requirements Application, essay, financial need analysis, references, transcript, campus review. *Deadline:* February 14.

World Wide Web: http://www.iie.org

Contact: Amy VanDyke, NSEP Program Officer
Institute of International Education
1400 K Street NW, Suite 650
Washington, DC 20005-2403
Phone: 800-618-6737
Fax: 202-326-7698
E-mail: nsep@iie.org

INTERNATIONAL ASSOCIATION OF FIRE CHIEFS FOUNDATION

INTERNATIONAL ASSOCIATION OF FIRE CHIEFS FOUNDATION SCHOLARSHIP AWARD ● 466

One-time award open to any person who is an active member (volunteer or paid) of an emergency or fire department. Must be studying at a recognized institution of higher education. Application deadline is August 1.

Award Scholarship for use in freshman, sophomore, junior, senior, graduate, or postgraduate years; not renewable. *Number:* 10–30. *Amount:* $350–$4000.

International Association of Fire Chiefs Foundation Scholarship Award (continued)

Eligibility Requirements: Applicant must be enrolled or expecting to enroll full or part-time at a two-year or four-year or technical institution or university. Available to U.S. and non-U.S. citizens.

Application Requirements Application, essay. *Deadline:* August 1.

Contact: International Association of Fire Chiefs Foundation
PO Box 1818
Windermere, FL 34786

JACK KENT COOKE FOUNDATION

JACK KENT COOKE UNDERGRADUATE SCHOLARSHIP PROGRAM
• 467

Students must be nominated by the faculty representative at his/her institution. Eligible students enrolled at an accredited four-year college or university must: be a junior in the Fall term, and have a cumulative GPA of 3.0 or higher. Eligible students enrolled at an accredited two-year or community college in the U.S. must: have completed freshman year credits by December, be transferring to an accredited four-year institution for the Fall following term, and have a cumulative GPA of 3.3 or higher. Financial need is critical.

Award Scholarship for use in junior or senior years; renewable. *Number:* 60. *Amount:* up to $30,000.

Eligibility Requirements: Applicant must be enrolled or expecting to enroll full-time at a two-year or four-year institution or university. Available to U.S. and non-U.S. citizens.

Application Requirements Application, essay, financial need analysis, references, transcript. *Deadline:* February 1.

World Wide Web: http://www.jackkentcookefoundation.org/bridge/index.html

Contact: Jack Kent Cooke Foundation
2255 North Dubuque Road
PO Box 4030
Iowa City, IA 52243-4030
Phone: 800-498-6478
Fax: 319-337-1204
E-mail: jkc@act.org

MASSACHUSETTS POLICE CORPS

MASSACHUSETTS POLICE CORPS FEDERAL SCHOLARSHIP • 468

The program offers Federal educational assistance to college students who agree to serve 4 years as police officers in MA. In return for this commitment, the Massachusetts Police Corps will award participants scholarships to cover college expenses including tuition, fees, books, supplies, transportation, housing, meals, and other expenses. Participants can receive up to $7,500 per academic year with a limit of $30,000 per student.

Award Scholarship for use in freshman, sophomore, junior, or senior years; renewable. *Number:* up to 50. *Amount:* up to $7500.

Eligibility Requirements: Applicant must be enrolled or expecting to enroll full-time at a four-year institution or university. Available to U.S. citizens.

Application Requirements Application, essay, interview, references, test scores, transcript. *Deadline:* Continuous.

World Wide Web: http://www.masspolicecorps.com

Contact: Lt. Doris Thompson, Training Manager
Massachusetts Police Corps
484 Shea Memorial Drive
South Weymouth, MA 02190
Phone: 781-337-6311
Fax: 781-337-6245
E-mail: dthompson@masspolicecorps.com

MISSISSIPPI POLICE CORPS

MISSISSIPPI POLICE CORPS SCHOLARSHIP   • 469

Program designed to motivate highly qualified young people to serve as police officers and sheriffs' deputies in the municipalities and counties that need them the most. Federal scholarships offered on a competitive basis to college students who agree to serve where needed on community patrol for at least four years. Participants who seek baccalaureate degrees begin their work as officers shortly after graduation from college. Those who pursue graduate study complete their service in advance. Minimum 2.75 GPA required.

Award Scholarship for use in sophomore, junior, senior, graduate, or postgraduate years; not renewable. *Number:* 65. *Amount:* $30,000.

Eligibility Requirements: Applicant must be enrolled or expecting to enroll full-time at a four-year institution or university. Available to U.S. citizens.

Application Requirements Application, driver's license, essay, interview, resume, references, test scores, transcript. *Deadline:* Continuous.

World Wide Web: http://www.mississippipolicecorps.org

Contact: Rick Weaver, Training Specialist
Mississippi Police Corps
c/o University of Southern Mississippi
Box 5084
Hattiesburg, MS 39406-5084
Phone: 601-266-6770
Fax: 601-266-6786
E-mail: rick.weaver@usm.edu

NATIONAL ACADEMY OF AMERICAN SCHOLARS

NAAS-USA AWARDS   • 470

A series of pure, merit-based scholarships available for tuition, room, board, books, and academically-related supplies. Applicants must be high school

NAAS-USA Awards (continued)

seniors or equivalent home-school seniors and be U.S. citizen or permanent resident. Application periods are September 15 to May 1. For further information and applications, download applications from web site at http://www. naas.org/senior1.htm or visit http://www.naas.org/. Application fee varies, up to $22. Applicants that request an application by mail must enclose a $3 handling fee and a self addressed stamped envelope.

Award Scholarship for use in freshman year; renewable. *Number:* 10–14. *Amount:* $200–$10,000.

Eligibility Requirements: Applicant must be high school student and planning to enroll or expecting to enroll full-time at a four-year institution or university. Available to U.S. citizens.

Application Requirements Application, self-addressed stamped envelope, download forms from web site. *Deadline:* May 1.

World Wide Web: http://www.naas.org

Contact: Merit Committee, NAAS-I
National Academy of American Scholars
5196 Benito Street, Suite #15, Room A
Montclair, CA 91763-2891
E-mail: staff@naas.org

NATIONAL ALLIANCE FOR EXCELLENCE

NATIONAL ALLIANCE FOR EXCELLENCE HONORED SCHOLARS AND ARTISTS PROGRAM • 471

National competition in four categories: academics, visual arts, performing arts, and technological innovations. Students in arts competitions must send slides or videos of their work. Minimum 1300 SAT and 3.7 GPA for non-arts categories. $5 application fee. All awards are given out in ceremonies with government officials, prominent artists, or business leaders as presenters. Highly competitive. Must send SASE or download application at http://www. excellence.org.

Award Scholarship for use in freshman, sophomore, junior, or senior years; not renewable. *Number:* 20–40. *Amount:* $1000–$5000.

Eligibility Requirements: Applicant must be enrolled or expecting to enroll full-time at a four-year institution or university. Available to U.S. citizens.

Application Requirements Application, applicant must enter a contest, essay, portfolio, resume, references, self-addressed stamped envelope, test scores, transcript. *Fee:* $5. *Deadline:* Continuous.

World Wide Web: http://www.excellence.org

Contact: Linda Paras, President
National Alliance for Excellence
1070-H Highway 34, #205
Matawan, NJ 07747
Phone: 732-765-1730
Fax: 732-765-1732
E-mail: info@excellence.org

NATIONAL BETA CLUB

NATIONAL BETA CLUB SCHOLARSHIP • 472

Applicant must be in 12th grade and a member of the National Beta Club. Must be nominated by school chapter of the National Beta Club, therefore, applications will not be sent to the individual students. Renewable and nonrenewable awards available. Contact school Beta Club sponsor for more information. Application fee: $10.

Award Scholarship for use in freshman year; renewable. *Number:* 208. *Amount:* $1000–$3750.

Eligibility Requirements: Applicant must be high school student and planning to enroll or expecting to enroll full-time at a two-year or four-year institution or university.

Application Requirements Application, essay, references, test scores, transcript. *Fee:* $10. *Deadline:* December 10.

World Wide Web: http://www.betaclub.org

Contact: Beta Club Sponsor (School Faculty Adviser)
National Beta Club
151 Beta Club Way
Spartanburg, SC 29306-3012

NATIONAL FFA ORGANIZATION

NATIONAL FFA COLLEGE AND VOCATIONAL/TECHNICAL SCHOOL SCHOLARSHIP PROGRAM • 473

The National FFA College and Vocational/Technical Scholarship Program currently offers nearly $2 million in money for students who are high school seniors planning to enroll in a full-time course of study at an accredited vocational-technical school, college or university. A smaller number of scholarships are also available to currently enrolled sophomores, juniors and seniors. Most of the awards require that you are an FFA member. However, there are awards offered to non-FFA and former FFA members who are going into the career fields mentioned above. In order to be considered, you will be judged on your academic record, extracurricular activities, volunteer community activities, work experience, a statement of career and educational goals, a counselor or advisor's evaluation and your degree of financial need. Majors may vary from the following career areas: Agriculture, Natural Resources, Communication, Education Specialists, Management, Financial Specialists, Marketing, Engineering, Science, Social Service Professionals and Related Industries.

Award Scholarship for use in freshman, sophomore, junior, or senior years; not renewable. *Number:* up to 1700. *Amount:* $1000–$15,000.

Eligibility Requirements: Applicant must be enrolled or expecting to enroll full-time at a two-year or four-year or technical institution or university. Available to U.S. citizens.

Application Requirements Application. *Deadline:* February 15.

World Wide Web: http://www.ffa.org

National FFA College and Vocational/Technical School Scholarship Program (continued)

Contact: Scholarship Coordinator
National FFA Organization
PO Box 68960
Indianapolis, IN 46268-0960
Phone: 317-802-6060
Fax: 317-802-6061

NATIONAL INSTITUTES OF HEALTH

NIH UNDERGRADUATE SCHOLARSHIP PROGRAM FOR STUDENTS FROM DISADVANTAGED BACKGROUNDS • 474

The NIH Undergraduate Scholarship Program offers competitive scholarships to exceptional students from disadvantaged backgrounds who are committed to biomedical, behavioral and social science research careers at the NIH. Applicants must be U.S. citizens, nationals, or qualified permanent residents.

Award Scholarship for use in freshman, sophomore, junior, or senior years; renewable. *Number:* 10–20. *Amount:* up to $20,000.

Eligibility Requirements: Applicant must be enrolled or expecting to enroll full-time at a four-year institution or university. Available to U.S. citizens.

Application Requirements Application, essay, financial need analysis, references, transcript. *Deadline:* February 28.

World Wide Web: http://ugsp.info.nih.gov

Contact: NIH Undergraduate Scholarship Program Director
National Institutes of Health
2 Center Drive, Room 2E30, MSC 0230
Bethesda, MD 20892-0230
Phone: 800-528-7689
Fax: 301-480-5481
E-mail: ugsp@nih.gov

NATIONAL INVENTORS HALL OF FAME

COLLEGIATE INVENTORS COMPETITION • 475

The Collegiate Inventors Competition is a national competition designed to encourage college students to be active in science, engineering, mathematics, technology and creative invention, while stimulating their problem-solving abilities. This prestigious challenge recognizes the working relationship between a student and his or her advisor who are involved in projects leading to inventions that can be patented. The grand prize-winning student—or student team—receives a $50,000 cash prize. Advisors each receive a $10,000 cash prize.

Award Prize for use in freshman, sophomore, junior, or senior years; not renewable. *Number:* up to 5. *Amount:* up to $50,000.

Eligibility Requirements: Applicant must be enrolled or expecting to enroll full or part-time at a two-year or four-year institution or university. Available to U.S. and non-U.S. citizens.

Application Requirements Application, applicant must enter a contest, essay. *Deadline:* June 1.
World Wide Web: http://www.invent.org/collegiate
Contact: Ray DePuy, Program Coordinator
National Inventors Hall of Fame
221 South Broadway Street
Akron, OH 44308-1505
Phone: 330-849-6887
Fax: 330-762-6313
E-mail: rdepuy@invent.org

NATIONAL MERIT SCHOLARSHIP CORPORATION

NATIONAL MERIT SCHOLARSHIP PROGRAM • 476

High school students enter by taking the Preliminary SAT/National Merit Scholar Qualifying Test, and by meeting other participation requirements. Those eligible are contacted through high school. Selection based on test scores, academic abilities, essay, activities, and recommendations. Some awards are renewable. Contact counselor by fall of junior year for deadline. Participation requirements are available in the PAST/NMSQT Student Bulletin and on NMSE's web site.

Award Scholarship for use in freshman year; renewable. *Number:* 9600. *Amount:* $500–$2000.
Eligibility Requirements: Applicant must be high school student and planning to enroll or expecting to enroll full-time at a four-year institution or university. Available to U.S. citizens.
Application Requirements Application, autobiography, essay, references, test scores, transcript.
World Wide Web: http://www.nationalmerit.org
Contact: student's high school counselor

NATIONAL SCIENCE TEACHERS ASSOCIATION

TOSHIBA/NSTA EXPLORAVISION AWARDS PROGRAM • 477

Teams of students in grades K-12 consider the impact that science and technology have on society and how innovative thinking can change the future, then use their imaginations and the tools of science to envision new technologies. Students develop written proposals and web pages.

Award Prize for use in freshman year; not renewable. *Number:* 16–32. *Amount:* $5000–$10,000.
Eligibility Requirements: Applicant must be age 21 or under and enrolled or expecting to enroll full-time at an institution or university. Available to U.S. and Canadian citizens.

Toshiba/NSTA ExploraVision Awards Program (continued)
Application Requirements Application, applicant must enter a contest, essay. *Deadline:* February 4.
World Wide Web: http://www.nsta.org
Contact: Explora Vision
National Science Teachers Association
1840 Wilson Boulevard
Arlington, VA 22201
Phone: 800-EXP-LOR9
Fax: 703-243-7177
E-mail: exploravision@nsta.org

NATIONAL TEEN-AGER SCHOLARSHIP FOUNDATION

NATIONAL TEEN-AGER SCHOLARSHIP FOUNDATION   • 478

One-time award for young women of leadership and intellect. Award based on school and community leadership, communication skills, academics and personal presentation. 3-5 awards per state. Awards come in the form of savings bonds from $500-1000 and in cash from $5000-10,000. Must be between the ages of 12-18 and be a U.S. citizen. Minimum 3.0 GPA required. $20 application fee. Deadline varies by state. For more details see web site: http://www.nationalteen.com.

Award Scholarship for use in freshman year; not renewable. *Number:* 250–1510. *Amount:* $1000–$10,000.

Eligibility Requirements: Applicant must be age 12-18; enrolled or expecting to enroll full-time at a two-year or four-year institution or university and single female. Applicant must have 3.0 GPA or higher. Available to U.S. citizens.

Application Requirements Application, applicant must enter a contest, interview, photo, self-addressed stamped envelope, transcript. *Fee:* $20.

World Wide Web: http://www.nationalteen.com

Contact: Cheryl Snow, National Director
National Teen-Ager Scholarship Foundation
4708 Mill Crossing West
Colleyville, TX 76034
Phone: 817-577-2220
Fax: 817-428-7232
E-mail: csnow@dallas.net

NEVADA POLICE CORPS

NEVADA POLICE CORPS PROGRAM   • 479

Renewable award available to upper level, full-time undergraduates or graduate students. Must complete four year degree, complete required training and agree to serve a Nevada law enforcement agency for four years. Must be a U.S. citizen. Minimum 2.5 GPA required.

Award Scholarship for use in junior, senior, or graduate years; renewable. *Number:* 10–20. *Amount:* up to $30,000.

Eligibility Requirements: Applicant must be enrolled or expecting to enroll full-time at an institution or university. Applicant must have 2.5 GPA or higher. Available to U.S. citizens.

Application Requirements Application, driver's license, essay, interview, references, transcript, peace officer selection process. *Deadline:* Continuous.

World Wide Web: http://www.nevadapolicecorps.state.nv.us

Contact: Greg Befort, Director
Nevada Police Corps
WNCC, Cedar Building Room 309-312
2201 West College Parkway
Carson City, NV 89703
Phone: 775-684-8720
Fax: 775-684-8775
E-mail: gbefort@post.state.nv.us

NINETY-NINES, INC.

AMELIA EARHART MEMORIAL CAREER SCHOLARSHIP FUND
• 480

Scholarships are awarded to members of The Ninety-Nines, Inc., who hold a current medical certificate appropriate for the use of the certificate sought. Applicants must meet the requirements for pilot currency (Flight Review or non-U.S. equivalent) and have financial need. Applicants must agree to complete the course, training and meet the requirements for ratings/certificates specific to the country where training will occur.

Award Scholarship for use in freshman, sophomore, junior, or senior years; not renewable. *Number:* 15–18. *Amount:* $2000–$10,000.

Eligibility Requirements: Applicant must be enrolled or expecting to enroll full-time at an institution or university and female. Available to U.S. and non-U.S. citizens.

Application Requirements Application, financial need analysis, photo, resume, references. *Deadline:* December 31.

World Wide Web: http://ninety-nines.org

Contact: Charlene H. Falkenberg, Chairman, Permanent Trustee
Ninety-Nines, Inc.
618 South Washington Street
Hobart, IN 46342-5026
Phone: 219-942-8887
Fax: 219-942-8887
E-mail: charf@prodigy.net

NORTH CAROLINA POLICE CORPS

NORTH CAROLINA POLICE CORPS SCHOLARSHIP
• 481

Selected participants must attend a four-year institution full-time. May receive up to $10,000 per year with a maximum of $30,000. Complete 24-week

North Carolina Police Corps Scholarship (continued)
training course receiving $400 per week while in residence and serve four years in selected law enforcement agency. Must have physical, background investigation, drug test, and psychological evaluation.

Award Scholarship for use in freshman, sophomore, junior, senior, or graduate years; renewable. *Number:* 15–30. *Amount:* $7500–$10,000.

Eligibility Requirements: Applicant must be enrolled or expecting to enroll full-time at a four-year institution or university. Available to U.S. citizens.

Application Requirements Application, autobiography, essay, interview, photo, references, test scores, transcript. *Deadline:* November 15.

World Wide Web: http://www.ncpolicecorps.org

Contact: Neil Woodcock, Director, NC Police Corps
North Carolina Police Corps
NC Department of Crime Control and Public Safety, 4710 Mail
Service Center
Raleigh, NC 27699-4710
Phone: 919-773-2823
Fax: 919-773-2845
E-mail: nwoodcock@nccrimecontrol.org

OPTIMIST INTERNATIONAL FOUNDATION

ESSAY CONTEST   • 482

$650 college scholarship is offered at the district level; $2,000-$5,000 scholarships are offered at the international level. Eligible students are under 19 as of December 31 of the current school year. Open to residents of the U.S., Canada and the Caribbean. Must be conducted through a local Optimist Club. Visit web site at http://www.optimist.org for additional information.

Award Scholarship for use in freshman, sophomore, junior, or senior years; not renewable. *Number:* 53. *Amount:* up to $10,000.

Eligibility Requirements: Applicant must be high school student; age 19 or under and planning to enroll or expecting to enroll full-time at a two-year or four-year or technical institution or university. Available to U.S. and non-U.S. citizens.

Application Requirements Application, applicant must enter a contest. *Deadline:* January 15.

World Wide Web: http://www.optimist.org/

Contact: Amy Haker, International Programs Coordinator
Optimist International Foundation
4494 Lindell Boulevard
St. Louis, MO 63108
Phone: 314-371-6000 Ext. 224
Fax: 314-371-6006
E-mail: hakera@optimist.org

ORATORICAL CONTEST • 483

$1,500 scholarship offered at the district level. Student shall not have attained the age of 16 years prior to or on January 1 of current school year. No minimum age. Must be conducted through a local Optimist Club. Open to citizens of the U.S., Canada or a Caribbean nation. Visit web site at http://www.optimist.org for additional information.

Award Scholarship for use in freshman or sophomore years; not renewable. *Number:* 106. *Amount:* $1500.

Eligibility Requirements: Applicant must be age 16 or under and enrolled or expecting to enroll full-time at a two-year or four-year or technical institution or university. Available to U.S. and non-U.S. citizens.

Application Requirements Application, applicant must enter a contest. *Deadline:* April 1.

World Wide Web: http://www.optimist.org/

Contact: Amy Haker, International Programs Coordinator
Optimist International Foundation
4494 Lindell Boulevard
St. Louis, MO 63108
Phone: 314-371-6000 Ext. 224
Fax: 314-371-6006
E-mail: hakera@optimist.org

ORPHAN FOUNDATION OF AMERICA

OFA 2002 NATIONAL SCHOLARSHIP/CASEY FAMILY SCHOLARS • 484

Scholarships are given to young people who were in foster care for at least one year at the time of their 18th birthday. Must be under 25 years old. Must have been accepted into an accredited postsecondary school or program. Must not currently be a Casey Family Program CEJT participant.

Award Scholarship for use in freshman, sophomore, junior, or senior years; not renewable. *Number:* 350. *Amount:* $2000–$6000.

Eligibility Requirements: Applicant must be age 24 or under and enrolled or expecting to enroll full or part-time at a two-year or four-year or technical institution or university. Available to U.S. and non-U.S. citizens.

Application Requirements Application, essay, financial need analysis, photo, references, transcript. *Deadline:* April 15.

World Wide Web: http://www.orphan.org

Contact: Tina Raheem, Office Manager
Orphan Foundation of America
12020—D North Shore Drive
Reston, VA 20190-4507
Phone: 571-203-0270
Fax: 571-203-0273
E-mail: tinar@orphan.org

PHILLIPS FOUNDATION

PHILLIPS FOUNDATION RONALD REAGAN FUTURE LEADERS PROGRAM • 485

The program offers renewable cash grants to college juniors and seniors who demonstrate leadership on behalf of the cause of freedom, American values, and constitutional principles. Winners will receive a grant for their junior year and may apply for renewal before their senior year.

Award Grant for use in junior or senior years; not renewable. *Number:* 10–20. *Amount:* $2500–$10,000.

Eligibility Requirements: Applicant must be enrolled or expecting to enroll full-time at a four-year institution or university. Available to U.S. citizens.

Application Requirements Application, essay, references. *Deadline:* January 15.

World Wide Web: http://www.thephillipsfoundation.org

Contact: Jeff Hollingsworth, Assistant Secretary
Phillips Foundation
7811 Montrose Road, Suite 100
Potomac, MD 20854
Phone: 301-340-7788 Ext. 6028
E-mail: jhollingsworth@phillips.com

POLONIA GLOBAL FUND 9-11 SCHOLARSHIP FUND

POLONIA GLOBAL FUND 9-11 SCHOLARSHIP • 486

Funding granted to victims and families of victims of the 9-11 tragedy. Ten one-time awards for both full- or part-time study in any year of undergraduate study.

Award Scholarship for use in freshman, sophomore, junior, or senior years; not renewable. *Number:* up to 10. *Amount:* up to $10,000.

Eligibility Requirements: Applicant must be enrolled or expecting to enroll full or part-time at a two-year or four-year or technical institution or university. Available to U.S. and non-U.S. citizens.

Application Requirements Application, autobiography, financial need analysis, interview, references. *Deadline:* Continuous.

World Wide Web: http://www.pgf.cc

Contact: James Konicki, Co-Chair
Polonia Global Fund 9-11 Scholarship Fund
PO Box 13833
Albany, NY 12212-3833
Phone: 518-765-2657
Fax: 518-765-2657
E-mail: administrator@pgf.cc

PRESIDENTIAL FREEDOM SCHOLARSHIP

PRESIDENTIAL FREEDOM SCHOLARSHIP • 487

The Presidential Freedom Scholarship program is designed to highlight and promote service and citizenship by students and to recognize students for their leadership in those areas. Each high school in the county may select up to 2 students to receive a $1,000 scholarship. With funds appropriated by Congress, the Corporation for National and Community Service provides $500, which must be matched with $500 secured by the school from the community.

Award Scholarship for use in freshman year; not renewable. *Number:* 10,000. *Amount:* $1000.

Eligibility Requirements: Applicant must be high school student and planning to enroll or expecting to enroll full or part-time at a two-year or four-year or technical institution or university. Available to U.S. citizens.

Application Requirements Application. *Deadline:* June 30.

World Wide Web: http://www.nationalservice.org/scholarships

Contact: Presidential Freedom Scholarship
Presidential Freedom Scholarship
1150 Connecticut Avenue, NW, Suite 1100
Washington, DC 20036
Phone: 866-291-7700
E-mail: info@studentservicescholarship.org

PUERTO RICO DEPARTMENT OF EDUCATION

ROBERT C. BYRD HONOR SCHOLARSHIPS • 488

This grant is sponsored by the Puerto Rico Department of Education and is granted to gifted students. These are students chosen from public and private schools who graduate from high school and are admitted to an accredited university in Puerto Rico or in the United States and who show promise to complete a college career. It is granted for a period of four years if the student maintains a satisfactory academic progress. Must be a U.S. citizen and rank in the upper quarter of class or have a minimum 3.5 GPA.

Award Scholarship for use in freshman, sophomore, junior, or senior years; renewable. *Number:* 74–85. *Amount:* $1500.

Eligibility Requirements: Applicant must be high school student and planning to enroll or expecting to enroll full-time at a four-year institution or university. Applicant must have 3.5 GPA or higher. Available to U.S. citizens.

Application Requirements Application, financial need analysis, interview, portfolio, references, test scores, transcript. *Deadline:* May 30.

World Wide Web: http://www.de.gobierno.pr/eduportal/default.htm

Robert C. Byrd Honor Scholarships (continued)
Contact: Eligio Hernandez, Director
Puerto Rico Department of Education
PO Box 190759
San Juan, PR 00919-0759
Phone: 787-754-1015
Fax: 787-758-2281
E-mail: hernandez_eli@de.gobierno.pr

ROOTHBERT FUND, INC.

ROOTHBERT FUND, INC. SCHOLARSHIP • 489

Award for those pursuing undergraduate degree or higher in U.S. institution and satisfying academic standards. Non-U.S. citizens must be living in U.S. Must travel at own expense to interview in Philadelphia, New Haven, or Washington, D.C. Deadline: February 1. Provide SASE when requesting an application.

Award Scholarship for use in freshman, sophomore, junior, senior, or graduate years; renewable. *Number:* 50. *Amount:* $2000–$5000.

Eligibility Requirements: Applicant must be enrolled or expecting to enroll full-time at a two-year or four-year or technical institution or university. Available to U.S. and non-U.S. citizens.

Application Requirements Application, autobiography, essay, financial need analysis, interview, photo, references, self-addressed stamped envelope, test scores, transcript. *Deadline:* February 1.

World Wide Web: http://www.roothbertfund.org

Contact: Roothbert Fund, Inc.
475 Riverside Drive, Room 252
New York, NY 10115
Phone: 212-870-3116

STEPHEN PHILLIPS MEMORIAL SCHOLARSHIP FUND

STEPHEN PHILLIPS MEMORIAL SCHOLARSHIP FUND • 490

Award open to full-time undergraduate students with financial need who display academic excellence, strong citizenship and character, and a desire to make a meaningful contribution to society. While preference is given to students from a small number of cities and towns north of Boston, all qualified applicants are considered for an award. For more details see web site: http://www.phillips-scholarship.org.

Award Scholarship for use in freshman, sophomore, junior, or senior years; renewable. *Number:* 150–200. *Amount:* $3000–$5000.

Eligibility Requirements: Applicant must be enrolled or expecting to enroll full-time at a four-year institution or university. Applicant must have 3.0 GPA or higher. Available to U.S. citizens.

Application Requirements Application, essay, financial need analysis, references, test scores, transcript. *Deadline:* May 1.
World Wide Web: http://www.phillips-scholarship.org
Contact: Karen Emery, Scholarship Coordinator
Stephen Phillips Memorial Scholarship Fund
PO Box 870
Salem, MA 01970
E-mail: info@spscholars.org

SUNSHINE LADY FOUNDATION, INC.

WOMEN'S INDEPENDENCE SCHOLARSHIP PROGRAM   • 491

Scholarship for female survivors of domestic violence (partner abuse) who are U.S. citizens or permanent legal residents with critical financial need to return to school to gain skills to become independent and self-sufficient. Requires sponsorship by non-profit domestic violence service agency. First priority candidates are single mothers with young children.

Award Scholarship for use in freshman, sophomore, junior, or senior years; renewable. *Number:* 500. *Amount:* $250–$5000.
Eligibility Requirements: Applicant must be enrolled or expecting to enroll full or part-time at a two-year or four-year or technical institution or university and female. Available to U.S. citizens.
Application Requirements Application, essay, financial need analysis, references, sponsor. *Deadline:* Continuous.
World Wide Web: http://www.sunshineladyfdn.org
Contact: Nancy Soward, Program Coordinator
Sunshine Lady Foundation, Inc.
4900 Randall Parkway
Suite H
Wilmington, NC 28403
Phone: 910-397-7742
Fax: 910-397-0023
E-mail: sunlady1@bellsouth.net

TALBOTS CHARITABLE FOUNDATION

TALBOTS WOMEN'S SCHOLARSHIP FUND   • 492

One-time scholarship for women who earned their high school diploma or GED at least 10 years ago, and who are now seeking an undergraduate college degree. Deadline is March 3.

Award Scholarship for use in freshman, sophomore, junior, or senior years; not renewable. *Number:* 5–50. *Amount:* $1000–$10,000.
Eligibility Requirements: Applicant must be enrolled or expecting to enroll full or part-time at a two-year or four-year or technical institution or university and female. Available to U.S. citizens.
Application Requirements Application, essay, financial need analysis, references, transcript. *Deadline:* March 3.

Talbots Women's Scholarship Fund (continued)
World Wide Web: http://www.talbots.com
Contact: Deb Johnson, Citizens Scholarship Foundation
Talbots Charitable Foundation
1505 Riverview Road, PO Box 297
Saint Peter, MN 56082
Phone: 507-931-0452
Fax: 507-931-9278
E-mail: debj@csfa.org

TERRY FOX HUMANITARIAN AWARD PROGRAM

TERRY FOX HUMANITARIAN AWARD see number 267

THIRD WAVE FOUNDATION

SCHOLARSHIP FOR YOUNG WOMEN • 493

Our scholarship program is available to all full-time or part-time female students aged 17-30 who are enrolled in, or have been accepted to, an accredited university, college, or community college in the U.S. The primary criterion for funding is financial need. Students should also be involved as activists, artists, or cultural workers working on issues such as racism, homophobia, sexism, or other forms of inequality. Application available at web site http://www. thirdwavefoundation.org. Application deadlines are April 1 and October 1.

Award Scholarship for use in freshman, sophomore, junior, or senior years; not renewable. *Number:* 20-30. *Amount:* $500-$5000.

Eligibility Requirements: Applicant must be age 17-30; enrolled or expecting to enroll full or part-time at a two-year or four-year or technical institution or university and female. Applicant must have 2.5 GPA or higher. Available to U.S. and non-U.S. citizens.

Application Requirements Application, essay, financial need analysis, resume, references, transcript.

World Wide Web: http://www.thirdwavefoundation.org
Contact: Mia Herndon, Network Coordinator
Third Wave Foundation
511 West 25th Street, Suite 301
New York, NY 10001
Phone: 212-675-0700
Fax: 212-255-6653
E-mail: info@thirdwavefoundation.org

THURGOOD MARSHALL SCHOLARSHIP FUND

THURGOOD MARSHALL SCHOLARSHIP • 494

Merit scholarships for students attending 1 of 45 member HBPCU's (historically black public colleges, universities) including 5 member law schools.

Must maintain an average of 3.0 and have a financial need. Must be a U.S. citizen. 3.0 GPA required to renew. No applications accepted at TMSF. Must apply through the HBPCUs, through a campus scholarship coordinator.

Award Scholarship for use in freshman, sophomore, junior, senior, or graduate years; not renewable. *Number:* 50–100. *Amount:* $4000.

Eligibility Requirements: Applicant must be enrolled or expecting to enroll full-time at a four-year institution or university. Applicant must have 3.0 GPA or higher. Available to U.S. citizens.

Application Requirements Application, essay, interview, photo, references, test scores, transcript. *Deadline:* Continuous.

World Wide Web: http://www.thurgoodmarshallfund.org

Contact: Damian Travier, Programs Officer
Thurgood Marshall Scholarship Fund
100 Park Avenue, 10th Floor
New York, NY 10017
Phone: 917-663-2276
Fax: 917-633-2988
E-mail: dtravier@tmsf.org

UNITED STATES JUNIOR CHAMBER OF COMMERCE

JAYCEE WAR MEMORIAL FUND SCHOLARSHIP • 495

Students who are U.S. citizens, possess academic potential and leadership qualities, and show financial need are eligible to apply. To receive an application, send $5 application fee and stamped, self-addressed envelope between July 1 and February 1. Application deadline is March 1.

Award Scholarship for use in freshman, sophomore, junior, or senior years; not renewable. *Number:* 25–30. *Amount:* $1000–$5000.

Eligibility Requirements: Applicant must be enrolled or expecting to enroll full-time at a two-year or four-year or technical institution or university. Available to U.S. citizens.

Application Requirements Application, financial need analysis, self-addressed stamped envelope, transcript. *Fee:* $5. *Deadline:* March 1.

World Wide Web: http://www.usjaycees.org

Contact: Bob Guest, Director of Operations
United States Junior Chamber of Commerce
PO Box 7
Tulsa, OK 74194
Phone: 918-584-2484
Fax: 918-584-4422

WAL-MART FOUNDATION

SAM WALTON COMMUNITY SCHOLARSHIP • 496

Award for high school seniors not affiliated with Wal-Mart stores. Based on academic merit, financial need, and school or work activities. Each store

Sam Walton Community Scholarship (continued)
awards one nonrenewable scholarship. For use at an accredited two- or four-year U.S. institution. Must have 2.5 GPA. Applications available only through local Wal-Mart or Sam's Club stores starting in December. Applications are not available from the corporate office.

Award Scholarship for use in freshman year; not renewable. *Number:* 2900–3400. *Amount:* $1000.

Eligibility Requirements: Applicant must be high school student and planning to enroll or expecting to enroll full-time at a two-year or four-year institution or university. Applicant must have 2.5 GPA or higher. Available to U.S. citizens.

Application Requirements Application, essay, financial need analysis, test scores, transcript. *Deadline:* February 1.

World Wide Web: http://www.walmartfoundation.org

Contact: Jenny Harral
Wal-Mart Foundation
702 Southwest 8th Street
Bentonville, AR 72716-0150
Phone: 800-530-9925
Fax: 501-273-6850

WASHINGTON STATE PARENT TEACHER ASSOCIATION SCHOLARSHIPS FOUNDATION

WASHINGTON STATE PARENT TEACHER ASSOCIATION SCHOLARSHIPS FOUNDATION
• 497

One-time scholarships for students who have graduated from a public high school in state of Washington, and who greatly need financial help to begin full-time postsecondary education. For entering freshmen only.

Award Scholarship for use in freshman year; not renewable. *Number:* 60–80. *Amount:* $1000–$2000.

Eligibility Requirements: Applicant must be enrolled or expecting to enroll full-time at a two-year or four-year or technical institution or university. Available to U.S. and non-U.S. citizens.

Application Requirements Application, essay, financial need analysis, references, transcript. *Deadline:* March 1.

World Wide Web: http://www.wastatepta.org

Contact: Jean Carpenter, Executive Director
Washington State Parent Teacher Association Scholarships
Foundation
2003 65th Avenue, West
Tacoma, WA 98466-6215

WELLS FARGO EDUCATION FINANCIAL SERVICES

COLLEGESTEPS SCHOLARSHIP PROGRAM • 498

The Wells Fargo CollegeSTEPS Scholarship Program offers high school seniors the chance to win one of a hundred $1000 scholarships to be given away during the 2003-2004 school year. Winners are chosen through random drawings, so all students have an equal chance to win. Register at http://www. wellsfargo.com/collegesteps

Award Scholarship for use in freshman year; not renewable. *Number:* 100. *Amount:* $1000.

Eligibility Requirements: Applicant must be high school student and planning to enroll or expecting to enroll full or part-time at a two-year or four-year or technical institution or university. Available to U.S. citizens.

Application Requirements Application. *Deadline:* Continuous.

World Wide Web: http://www.wellsfargo.com/collegesteps

Contact: Wells Fargo Education Financial Services
301 East 58th Street North
Sioux Falls, SD 57104-0422
Phone: 800-658-3567
Fax: 605-575-4550
E-mail: collegesteps@wellsfargoefs.com

WOODMEN OF THE WORLD

WOODMEN OF THE WORLD SCHOLARSHIP PROGRAM • 499

One-time award for full-time study at a trade/technical school, two-year college, four-year college or university. Applicant must be a member, child of a member or grandchild of a member of Woodman of the World of Denver, Colorado. Applicant must have minimum 2.5 GPA.

Award Scholarship for use in freshman, sophomore, junior, senior, or graduate years; not renewable. *Number:* 65. *Amount:* $500–$2500.

Eligibility Requirements: Applicant must be enrolled or expecting to enroll full-time at a two-year or four-year or technical institution or university. Applicant must have 2.5 GPA or higher. Available to U.S. citizens.

Application Requirements Application, essay, photo, transcript. *Deadline:* March 15.

World Wide Web: http://www.denverwoodmen.com

Contact: Scholarship Committee
Woodmen of the World
PO Box 266000
Highlands Ranch, CO 80163-6000
Phone: 303-792-9777
Fax: 303-792-9793

WORLDFEST INTERNATIONAL FILM AND VIDEO FESTIVAL

WORLDFEST STUDENT FILM AWARD   • **500**

This is a cash award program for student films, both shorts and features. Film must be entered by December 15 to be considered for an award. Application fee is $45.

Award Prize for use in freshman, sophomore, junior, senior, or graduate years; not renewable. *Number:* 10. *Amount:* $1000–$10,000.

Eligibility Requirements: Applicant must be enrolled or expecting to enroll full or part-time at a two-year or four-year or technical institution or university. Available to U.S. and non-U.S. citizens.

Application Requirements Application, applicant must enter a contest, film/tape entry. *Fee:* $45. *Deadline:* December 15.

World Wide Web: http://www.worldfest.org

Contact: Hunter Todd, Executive Director
Worldfest International Film and Video Festival
PO Box 56566
Houston, TX 77256-6566
Phone: 713-965-9955
Fax: 713-965-9960
E-mail: hunter@worldfest.org

Profiles of State-Sponsored Programs

Each state government has established one or more financial aid programs for qualified students. In many instances, these state programs are restricted to legal residents of the state. However, some are available to out-of-state students attending colleges within the state. In addition to residential status, other qualifications frequently exist.

Each of the fifty states' and District of Columbia's gift aid and forgivable loan programs that are open to undergraduate students are described in this section. They are arranged in alphabetical order, first by state name, then by program name. The annotation for each program provides information about the program, eligibility, and the contact addresses for applications or further information.

Students or parents should write to the address given for each program to request that award details for 2003–04 be sent to them as soon as these are available. Descriptive information brochures and application forms for state scholarship programs are usually available in your high school guidance office or from a college financial aid office in your state. Increasingly, state government agencies are putting state scholarship information on their Web sites. Also, the financial aid page of state-administered college or university sites frequently has a list of state-sponsored scholarships and financial aid programs. College and university Web sites can be accessed easily through Peterson's Education Center (www.petersons.com).

Names of scholarship program frequently are used inconsistently or become abbreviated in use. Many programs have variant names by which they are known. The program's sponsor has approved the title of the program that Peterson's uses. However, this name sometimes differs from the program's official name or from the most commonly used name.

States may also offer internship or work-study programs, graduate fellowships and grants, or low-interest loans in addition to the grant aid and forgivable loans programs listed here. If you are interested in learning more about these other kinds of programs, the state higher education office should be able to provide information.

ALABAMA

Alabama G.I. Dependents Scholarship Program. Full scholarship for dependents of Alabama disabled, prisoner of war, or missing-in-action veterans. Child or stepchild must initiate training before 26th birthday; age 30 deadline may apply in certain situations. No age deadline for spouses or widows. Contact for application procedures and deadline. *Award:* Scholarship for use in freshman, sophomore, junior, senior, or graduate year; renewable. *Award amount:* up to $7000. *Eligibility Requirements:* Applicant must be enrolled or expecting to enroll full or part-time at a two-year, four-year, or technical institution or university; resident of Alabama and studying in Alabama. Available to U.S. and non-U.S. citizens. Applicant or parent must meet one or more of the following requirements: general military experience; retired from active duty; disabled or killed as a result of military service; prisoner of war; or missing in action. *Application Requirements:* Application.

Contact Willie E. Moore, Scholarship Administrator, Alabama Department of Veterans Affairs, PO Box 1509, Montgomery, AL 36102-1509. *E-mail:* wmoore@ va.state.al.us. *Phone:* 334-242-5077. *Fax:* 334-242-5102. *Web site:* www.va.state.al.us/scholarship.htm.

Alabama National Guard Educational Assistance Program. Renewable award aids Alabama residents who are members of the Alabama National Guard and are enrolled in an accredited college in Alabama. Forms must be signed by a representative of the Alabama Military Department and financial aid officer. Recipient must be in a degree-seeking program. *Award:* Grant for use in freshman, sophomore, junior, senior, or graduate year; renewable. *Award amount:* up to $1000. *Eligibility Requirements:* Applicant must be enrolled or expecting to enroll full or part-time at a two-year, four-year, or technical institution or university; resident of Alabama and studying in Alabama. Available to U.S. citizens. Applicant must have served in the Air Force National Guard or Army National Guard. *Application Requirements:* Application. **Deadline:** continuous.

Contact Dr. William Wall, Associate Executive Director for Student Assistance, Alabama Commission on Higher Education, PO Box 302000, Montgomery, AL 36130-2000. *Web site:* www.ache.state.al.us.

Alabama Scholarship for Dependents of Blind Parents. Scholarship given to defray the cost of books and fees for children of blind parents. Must be accepted or enrolled in a Alabama state supported school. Must be Alabama resident. Financial need is considered. Family income must be less than 1.5 times the federal poverty guideline for size of family unit. *Award:* Scholarship for use in freshman, sophomore, junior, or senior year; renewable. *Number of awards:* 10–15. *Eligibility Requirements:* Applicant must be age 28 or under; enrolled or expecting to enroll full-time at a two-year, four-year, or technical institution or university; resident of Alabama and studying in Alabama. Available to U.S. citizens. *Application Requirements:* Application, financial need analysis. **Deadline:** continuous.

Contact Don Sims, Rehabilitation Specialist for the Blind, Alabama Department of Rehabilitation Services, Alabama Scholarship for Dependents of Blind Parents, 2129 East South Boulevard, Montgomery, AL 36111. *Phone:* 800-441-7607.

Alabama Student Grant Program. Renewable awards available to Alabama residents for undergraduate study at certain independent colleges within the state. Both full-time and half-time students are eligible. Deadlines: September 15, January 15, and February 15. *Award:* Grant for use in freshman, sophomore, junior, or senior year; renewable. *Award amount:* up to $1200. *Eligibility Requirements:* Applicant must be enrolled or expecting to enroll full or part-time at a four-year institution; resident of Alabama and studying in Alabama. Available to U.S. citizens. *Application Requirements:* Application.

Contact Dr. William Wall, Associate Executive Director for Student Assistance, ACHE, Alabama Commission on Higher Education, PO Box 302000, Montgomery, AL 36130-2000. *Web site:* www.ache.state.al.us.

American Legion Department of Alabama Scholarship Program. Renewable award for Alabama residents directly related to any war veteran. Parents must be legal residents of Alabama. Send self-addressed stamped envelope to receive scholarship application, list of available schools, and instructions. *Award:* Scholarship for use in freshman, sophomore, junior, or senior year; renewable. *Award amount:* $850. *Number of awards:* 150. *Eligibility Requirements:* Applicant must be enrolled or expecting to enroll full or part-time at a four-year institution or university; resident of Alabama and studying in Alabama. Available to U.S. citizens. Applicant or parent must meet one or more of the following requirements: general military experience; retired from active duty; disabled or killed as a result of military service; prisoner of war; or missing in action. *Application Requirements:* Application, photo, references, self-addressed stamped envelope, test scores, transcript. **Deadline:** May 1.

Contact Braxton Bridgers, Department Adjutant, American Legion, Department of Alabama, PO Box 1069, Montgomery, AL 36101-1069. *E-mail:* allegion@bellsouth.net. *Phone:* 334-285-2225. *Web site:* www.alabamalegion.org.

Math and Science Scholarship Program for Alabama Teachers. For full-time students pursuing teaching certificates in mathematics, general science, biology, or physics. Applicants must agree to teach for five years (if a position is offered) in a targeted system with critical needs. Renewable if recipient continues to meet the requirements. Minimum 3.0 GPA required. Must be resident of Alabama and attend school in Alabama. *Academic/Career Areas:* Biology; Earth Science; Meteorology/Atmospheric Science; Natural Sciences; Physical Sciences and Math. *Award:* Forgivable loan for use in junior or senior year; renewable. *Award amount:* $2000–$12,000. *Eligibility Requirements:* Applicant must be enrolled or expecting to enroll full-time at an institution or university; resident of Alabama and studying in Alabama. Applicant must have 3.0 GPA or higher. Available to U.S. citizens. *Application Requirements:* Application.

Contact Dr. Jayne Meyer, Assistant Superintendent, Alabama State Department of Education, Special Education Services, PO Box 302101, Montgomery, AL 36130-2101. *Phone:* 334-242-9560.

Police Officers and Firefighters Survivors Education Assistance Program—Alabama. Provides tuition, fees, books, and supplies to dependents of full-time police officers and firefighters killed in the line of duty. Must attend any Alabama public college as an undergraduate. Must be Alabama resident. Renewable. *Award:* Grant for use in freshman, sophomore, junior, or senior year; renewable. *Award amount:* $2000–$5000. *Number of awards:* 15–30. *Eligibility Requirements:* Applicant must be enrolled or expecting to enroll full or part-time at a two-year, four-year, or technical institution or university; single; resident of Alabama and studying in Alabama. Applicant or parent of applicant must have employment or volunteer experience in police/firefighting. Available to U.S. citizens. *Application Requirements:* Application, transcript. **Deadline:** continuous.

Contact Dr. William Wall, Associate Executive Director for Student Assistance, ACHE, Alabama Commission on Higher Education, PO Box 302000, Montgomery, AL 36130-2000. *Web site:* www.ache.state.al.us.

ALASKA

A.W. "Winn" Brindle Memorial Scholarship Loans. Renewable loan for study of approved curriculum in fisheries, seafood processing, food technology or related fields for Alaska residents. Must maintain good standing at institution. Eligible for up to 50% forgiveness if recipient returns to Alaska for employment in fisheries-related field. *Academic/Career Areas:* Agribusiness; Animal/Veterinary Sciences; Biology; Food Science/Nutrition; Natural Resources. *Award:* Forgivable loan for use in freshman, sophomore, junior, senior, or graduate year; renewable. *Eligibility Requirements:* Applicant must be enrolled or expecting to enroll full-time at a two-year, four-year, or technical institution or university and resident of Alaska. Available to U.S. citizens. *Application Requirements:* Application, essay. **Deadline:** May 15.

Contact Lori Stedman, Administrative Assistant, Special Programs, Alaska Commission on Postsecondary Education, 3030 Vintage Boulevard, Juneau, AK 99801-7100. *Phone:* 907-465-6741. *Fax:* 907-465-5316. *Web site:* www.state.ak.us/acpe/.

Alaska Commission on Postsecondary Education Teacher Education Loan. Renewable loans for graduates of an Alaskan high school pursuing teaching careers in rural elementary and secondary schools in Alaska. Must be nominated by rural school district. Eligible for 100% forgiveness if loan recipient teaches in rural Alaska upon graduation. Several awards of up to $7500 each. Must maintain good standing at institution. *Academic/Career Areas:* Education. *Award:* Forgivable loan for use in freshman, sophomore, junior, or senior year; renewable. *Award amount:* up to $7500. *Number of awards:* 100. *Eligibility Requirements:* Applicant must be enrolled or expecting to enroll full-time at a four-year institution or university. Available to U.S. citizens. *Application Requirements:* Application, transcript. **Deadline:** July 1.

Contact Lori Stedman, Administrative Assistant, Special Programs, Alaska Commission on Postsecondary Education, 3030 Vintage Boulevard, Juneau, AK 99801-7100. *Phone:* 907-465-6741. *Fax:* 907-465-5316. *Web site:* www.state.ak.us/acpe/.

Western Undergraduate Exchange (WUE) Program. Program allowing Alaska residents to enroll at two-or four-year institutions in participating states at a reduced tuition level, which is the in-state tuition plus a percentage of that amount. To be used for full-time undergraduate studies. See web site at http://www.state.ak.us/acpe for further information, a list of eligible institutions, and deadlines. **Award:** Grant for use in freshman, sophomore, junior, or senior year; renewable. *Eligibility Requirements:* Applicant must be enrolled or expecting to enroll full-time at a two-year or four-year institution or university; resident of Alaska and studying in Arizona, Colorado, Hawaii, Idaho, Montana, Nevada, New Mexico, North Dakota, Oregon, South Dakota, Utah, or Washington. Available to U.S. citizens.

Contact college admissions office, for further information, Alaska Commission on Postsecondary Education. *Web site:* www.state.ak.us/acpe/.

ARIZONA

Arizona Private Postsecondary Education Student Financial Assistance Program. Provides grants to financially needy Arizona Community College graduates to attend a private postsecondary baccalaureate degree-granting institution. *Award:* Forgivable loan for use in junior or senior year; renewable. *Award amount:* $750–$1500. *Eligibility Requirements:* Applicant must be enrolled or expecting to enroll full-time at a four-year institution or university; resident of Arizona and studying in Arizona. Available to U.S. and non-Canadian citizens. *Application Requirements:* Application, promissory note. **Deadline:** continuous.

Contact Danny Lee, PFAP Program Manager, Arizona Commission for Postsecondary Education, 2020 North Central Avenue, Suite 550, Phoenix, AZ 85004-4503. *E-mail:* danny_lee@azhighered.org. *Phone:* 602-258-2435 Ext. 103. *Fax:* 602-258-2483. *Web site:* www.acpe.asu.edu.

Leveraging Educational Assistance Partnership. LEAP provides grants to financially needy students who enroll in and attend postsecondary education or training in Arizona schools. LEAP Program was formerly known as the State Student Incentive Grant or SSIG Program. *Award:* Grant for use in freshman, sophomore, junior, senior, or graduate year; not renewable. *Award amount:* $100–$2500. *Eligibility Requirements:* Applicant must be enrolled or expecting to enroll full or part-time at a two-year, four-year, or technical institution or university; resident of Arizona and studying in Arizona. Available to U.S. and non-Canadian citizens. *Application Requirements:* Application. **Deadline:** continuous.

Contact Mila A. Zaporteza, Business Manager/LEAP Financial Aid Management, Arizona Commission for Postsecondary Education, 2020 North Central Avenue, Suite 550, Phoenix, AZ 85004-4503. *E-mail:* mila@azhighered.org. *Phone:* 602-258-2435 Ext. 102. *Fax:* 602-258-2483. *Web site:* www.acpe.asu.edu.

ARKANSAS

Arkansas Academic Challenge Scholarship Program. Awards for Arkansas residents who are graduating high school seniors to study at an Arkansas institution. Must have at least a 2.75 GPA, meet minimum ACT composite score standards, and have financial need. Renewable up to three additional years. *Award:* Scholarship for use in freshman, sophomore, junior, or senior year; renewable. *Award amount:* up to $2500. *Eligibility Requirements:* Applicant must be high school student; planning to enroll or expecting to enroll full-time at a two-year or four-year institution or university; resident of Arkansas and studying in Arkansas. Available to U.S. citizens. *Application Requirements:* Application, financial need analysis, test scores, transcript. **Deadline:** June 1.

Contact Assistant Coordinator, Arkansas Department of Higher Education, 114 East Capitol, Little Rock, AR 72201. *Phone:* 501-371-2050. *Fax:* 501-371-2001. *Web site:* www.arscholarships.com.

Arkansas Health Education Grant Program (ARHEG). Award provides assistance to Arkansas residents pursuing professional degrees in dentistry, optometry, veterinary medicine, podiatry, chiropractic medicine, or osteopathic medicine at out-of-state, accredited institutions (programs that are unavailable in Arkansas). *Academic/Career Areas:* Animal/Veterinary Sciences; Dental Health/Services; Health and Medical Sciences. *Award:* Grant for use in sophomore, junior, senior, or graduate year; renewable. *Award amount:* $5000–$14,600. *Number of awards:* 258–288. *Eligibility Requirements:* Applicant must be enrolled or expecting to enroll full-time at a four-year institution or university and resident of Arkansas. Available to U.S. citizens. *Application Requirements:* Application, affidavit of Arkansas residency. **Deadline:** continuous.

Contact Ms. Judy McAinsh, Coordinator, Arkansas Health Education Grant Program, Arkansas Department of Higher Education, 114 East Capitol, Little Rock, AR 72201-3818. *E-mail:* judym@adhe.arknet.edu. *Phone:* 501-371-2013. *Fax:* 501-371-2002. *Web site:* www.arscholarships.com.

Arkansas Minority Teacher Scholars Program. Renewable award for Native-Americans, African-American, Hispanic and Asian-American students who have completed at least 60 semester hours and are enrolled full-time in a teacher education program in Arkansas. Award may be renewed for one year. Must be Arkansas resident with minimum 2.5 GPA. Must teach for three to five years in Arkansas to repay scholarship funds received. Must pass PPST exam. *Academic/Career Areas:* Education. *Award:* Forgivable loan for use in junior or senior year; renewable. *Award amount:* up to $5000. *Number of awards:* up to 100. *Eligibility Requirements:* Applicant must be American Indian/Alaska Native, Asian/Pacific Islander, Black (non-Hispanic), or Hispanic; enrolled or expecting to enroll full-time at a four-year institution or university; resident of Arkansas and studying in Arkansas. Applicant must have 2.5 GPA or higher. Available to U.S. citizens. *Application Requirements:* Application, transcript. **Deadline:** June 1.

Contact Lillian Williams, Assistant Coordinator, Arkansas Department of Higher Education, 114 East Capitol, Little Rock, AR 72201. *Phone:* 501-371-2050. *Fax:* 501-371-2001. *Web site:* www.arscholarships.com.

Arkansas Student Assistance Grant Program. Award for Arkansas residents attending a college within the state. Must be enrolled full-time, have financial need, and maintain satisfactory progress. One-time award for undergraduate use only. Application is the FAFSA. *Award:* Grant for use in freshman, sophomore, junior, or senior year; not renewable. *Award amount:* $600. *Number of awards:* 600–5500. *Eligibility Requirements:* Applicant must be enrolled or expecting to enroll full-time at a two-year, four-year, or technical institution or university; resident of Arkansas and studying in Arkansas. Available to U.S. citizens. *Application Requirements:* Application, financial need analysis, FAFSA. **Deadline:** April 1.

Contact Assistant Coordinator, Arkansas Department of Higher Education, 114 East Capitol, Little Rock, AR 72201. *Phone:* 501-371-2050. *Fax:* 501-371-2001. *Web site:* www.arscholarships.com.

Emergency Secondary Education Loan Program. Must be Arkansas resident enrolled full-time in approved Arkansas institution. Renewable award for students majoring in secondary math, chemistry, physics, biology, physical science, general science, special education, or foreign language. Must teach in Arkansas at least five years. Must rank in upper half of class or have a minimum 2.5 GPA. *Academic/Career Areas:* Biology; Education; Foreign Language; Physical Sciences and Math; Special Education. *Award:* Forgivable loan for use in sophomore, junior, senior, or graduate year; renewable. *Award amount:* up to $2500. *Number of awards:* up to 50. *Eligibility Requirements:* Applicant must be enrolled or expecting to enroll full-time at a two-year or four-year institution or university; resident of Arkansas and studying in Arkansas. Applicant must have 2.5 GPA or higher. Available to U.S. citizens. *Application Requirements:* Application, transcript. **Deadline:** April 1.

Contact Lillian K. Williams, Assistant Coordinator, Arkansas Department of Higher Education, 114 East Capitol, Little Rock, AR 72201. *Phone:* 501-371-2050. *Fax:* 501-371-2001. *Web site:* www.arscholarships.com.

Governor's Scholars—Arkansas. Awards for outstanding Arkansas high school seniors. Must be an Arkansas resident and have a high school GPA of at least 3.5 or have scored at least 27 on the ACT. Award is $4000 per year for four years of full-time undergraduate study. Applicants who attain 32 or above on ACT, 1410 or above on SAT and have an academic 3.50 GPA, or are selected as National Merit or National Achievement finalists may receive an award equal to tuition, mandatory fees, room, and board up to $10,000 per year at any Arkansas institution. *Award:* Scholarship for use in freshman, sophomore, junior, or senior year; renewable. *Award amount:* $4000–$10,000. *Number of awards:* 75–250. *Eligibility Requirements:* Applicant must be high school student; planning to enroll or expecting to enroll full-time at a two-year or four-year institution or university; resident of Arkansas and studying in Arkansas. Applicant must have 3.5 GPA or higher. Available to U.S. citizens. *Application Requirements:* Application, test scores, transcript. **Deadline:** February 1.

Contact Philip Axelroth, Assistant Coordinator of Financial Aid, Arkansas Department of Higher Education, 114 East Capitol, Little Rock, AR 72201. *E-mail:* phila@adhe.arknet.edu. *Phone:* 501-371-2050. *Fax:* 501-371-2001. *Web site:* www.arscholarships.com.

Law Enforcement Officers' Dependents Scholarship-Arkansas. For dependents, under 23 years old, of Arkansas law-enforcement officers killed or permanently disabled in the line of duty. Renewable award is a waiver of tuition, fees, and room at two- or four-year Arkansas institution. Submit birth certificate, death certificate, and claims commission report of findings of fact. Proof of disability from State Claims Commission may also be submitted. *Award:* Scholarship for use in freshman, sophomore, junior, or senior year; renewable. *Award amount:* $2000–$2500. *Number of awards:* 27–32. *Eligibility Requirements:* Applicant must be age 23 or under; enrolled or expecting to enroll full or part-time at a two-year or four-year institution or university; resident of Arkansas and studying in Arkansas. Applicant or parent of applicant must have employment or volunteer experience in police/firefighting. Available to U.S. citizens. *Application Requirements:* Application. **Deadline:** continuous.

Contact Lillian Williams, Assistant Coordinator, Arkansas Department of Higher Education, 114 East Capitol, Little Rock, AR 72201. *E-mail:* lillianw@adhe.arknet. edu. *Phone:* 501-371-2050. *Fax:* 501-371-2001. *Web site:* www.arscholarships.com.

Missing in Action/Killed in Action Dependent's Scholarship—Arkansas. Available to Arkansas residents whose parent or spouse was classified either as missing in action, killed in action or a prisoner-of-war. Must attend state-supported institution in Arkansas. Renewable waiver of tuition, fees, room and board. Submit proof of casualty. *Award:* Scholarship for use in freshman, sophomore, junior, or senior year; renewable. *Award amount:* up to $2500. *Eligibility Requirements:* Applicant must be enrolled or expecting to enroll full-time at a two-year, four-year, or technical institution or university; resident of Arkansas and studying in Arkansas. Available to U.S. citizens. Applicant or parent must meet one or more of the following requirements: general military experience; retired from active duty; disabled or killed as a result of military service; prisoner of war; or missing in action. *Application Requirements:* Application, report of casualty. **Deadline:** continuous.

Contact Lillian K. Williams, Assistant Coordinator, Arkansas Department of Higher Education, 114 East Capitol, Little Rock, AR 72201. *Phone:* 501-371-2050. *Fax:* 501-371-2001. *Web site:* www.arscholarships.com.

Second Effort Scholarship. Awarded to those scholars who achieved one of the 10 highest scores on the Arkansas High School Diploma Test (GED). Must be at least age 18 and not have graduated from high school. Students do not apply for this award, they are contacted by the Arkansas Department of Higher Education. *Award:* Scholarship for use in freshman, sophomore, junior, or senior year; renewable. *Award amount:* up to $1000. *Number of awards:* 10. *Eligibility Requirements:* Applicant must be age 18; enrolled or expecting to enroll full or part-time at a two-year or four-year institution or university; resident of Arkansas and studying in Arkansas. Applicant must have 2.5 GPA or higher. *Application Requirements:* Application.

Contact Arkansas Department of Higher Education. *Phone:* 501-371-2050. *Fax:* 501-371-2001. *Web site:* www.arscholarships.com.

CALIFORNIA

Assumption Programs of Loans for Education. The APLE is a competitive teacher loan assumption program designed to encourage outstanding students and out-of-state teachers to become California teachers with in subject areas where a teacher shortage has been identified or in schools meeting specific criteria identified annually. Participants may receive up to $19,000 towards outstanding student loans. *Award:* Forgivable loan for use in junior, senior, or graduate year; renewable. *Award amount:* up to $19,000. *Number of awards:* up to 6500. *Eligibility Requirements:* Applicant must be enrolled or expecting to enroll full or part-time at a four-year institution or university; resident of California and studying in California. Available to U.S. citizens. *Application Requirements:* Application, references. **Deadline:** June 30.

Contact California Student Aid Commission, P O Box 419027, Rancho Cordova, CA 95741-9027. *E-mail:* custsvcs@csac.ca.gov. *Phone:* 916-526-7590. *Fax:* 916-526-8002. *Web site:* www.csac.ca.gov.

Cal Grant C. Award for California residents who are enrolled in a short-term vocational training program. Program must lead to a recognized degree or certificate. Course length must be a minimum of 4 months and no longer than 24 months. Students must be attending an approved California institution and show financial need. *Award:* Grant for use in freshman, sophomore, junior, or senior year; renewable. *Award amount:* $576-$3168. *Number of awards:* up to 7761. *Eligibility Requirements:* Applicant must be enrolled or expecting to enroll full or part-time at a two-year or technical institution; resident of California and studying in California. Available to U.S. citizens. *Application Requirements:* Application, financial need analysis. **Deadline:** March 2.

Contact California Student Aid Commission, P O Box 419027, Rancho Cordova, CA 95741-9027. *E-mail:* custsvs@csac.ca.gov. *Phone:* 916-526-7590. *Fax:* 916-526-8002. *Web site:* www.csac.ca.gov.

Child Development Teacher and Supervisor Grant Program. Award is for those students pursuing an approved course of study leading to a Child Development Permit issued by the California Commission on Teacher Credentialing. In exchange for each year funding is received, recipients agree to provide one year of service in a licensed childcare center. *Award:* Grant for use in freshman, sophomore, junior, or senior year; renewable. *Award amount:* $1000-$2000. *Number of awards:* 100-200. *Eligibility Requirements:* Applicant must be enrolled or expecting to enroll full or part-time at a two-year, four-year, or technical institution or university; resident of California and studying in California. Available to U.S. citizens. *Application Requirements:* Application, financial need analysis, references, FAFSA. **Deadline:** June 1.

Contact California Student Aid Commission, PO Box 419027, Rancho Cordova, CA 95741-9027. *E-mail:* custsvcs@csac.ca.gov. *Phone:* 916-526-7590. *Fax:* 916-526-8002. *Web site:* www.csac.ca.gov.

Competitive Cal Grant A. Award for California residents who are not recent high school graduates attending an approved college or university within the state. Must show financial need and meet minimum 3.0 GPA requirements. *Award:* Grant for use in freshman, sophomore, junior, or senior year; renewable. *Award amount:* $1572–$9708. *Number of awards:* up to 22,500. *Eligibility Requirements:* Applicant must be enrolled or expecting to enroll full or part-time at a two-year, four-year, or technical institution or university; resident of California and studying in California. Applicant must have 3.0 GPA or higher. Available to U.S. citizens. *Application Requirements:* Application, financial need analysis. **Deadline:** March 2.

Contact California Student Aid Commission, P O Box 41907, Rancho Cordova, CA 95741-9027. *E-mail:* custsvcs@csac.ca.gov. *Phone:* 916-526-7590. *Fax:* 916-526-8002. *Web site:* www.csac.ca.gov.

Competitive Cal Grant B. Award is for California residents who are not recent high school graduates attending an approved college or university within the state. Must show financial need and meet the minimum 2.0 GPA requirements. *Award:* Grant for use in freshman, sophomore, or junior year; renewable. *Award amount:* $700–$11,259. *Number of awards:* up to 22,500. *Eligibility Requirements:* Applicant must be enrolled or expecting to enroll full or part-time at a two-year, or technical institution or university; resident of California and studying in California. Available to U.S. citizens. *Application Requirements:* Application, financial need analysis, GPA Verification. **Deadline:** March 2.

Contact California Student Aid Commission, PO Box 419027, Rancho Cordova, CA 95741-9027. *E-mail:* custsvcs@gsac.ca.gov. *Phone:* 916-526-7590. *Fax:* 916-526-8002. *Web site:* www.csac.ca.gov.

Cooperative Agencies Resources for Education Program. Renewable award available to California resident attending a two-year California community college. Must have no more than 70 degree-applicable units, currently receive CALWORKS/TANF, and have at least one child under 14 years of age. Must be in EOPS, single head of household, and 18 or older. Contact local college EOPS-CARE office. *Award:* Grant for use in freshman or sophomore year; renewable. *Number of awards:* 11,000. *Eligibility Requirements:* Applicant must be age 18; enrolled or expecting to enroll full-time at a two-year institution; single; resident of California and studying in California. Applicant or parent of applicant must be member of Extended Opportunity Program Service. Available to U.S. citizens. *Application Requirements:* Application, financial need analysis, test scores, transcript. **Deadline:** continuous.

Contact Local Community College EOPS/CARE Program, California Community Colleges, 1102 Q Street, Sacramento, CA 95814-6511. *Web site:* www.cccco.edu.

Entitlement Cal Grant A. Award is for California residents who are recent high school graduates attending an approved college or university within the state. Must show financial need and meet the minimum 3.0 GPA requirements. *Award:* Grant for use in freshman, sophomore, junior, or senior year; renewable. *Award amount:* $1572–$9708. *Eligibility Requirements:* Applicant must be enrolled or expecting to enroll full or part-time at a two-year, four-year, or technical institution or university; resident of California and studying in California. Applicant must have 3.0 GPA or higher. Available to U.S. citizens. *Application Requirements:* Application, financial need analysis, GPA Verification. **Deadline:** March 2.

Contact California Student Aid Commission, PO Box 419027, Rancho Cordova, CA 95741-9027. *E-mail:* custsvcs@csac.ca.gov. *Phone:* 916-526-7590. *Fax:* 916-526-8002. *Web site:* www.csac.ca.gov.

Entitlement Cal Grant B. Award for California residents who are high school graduates attending an approved college or university within the state. Must show financial need and meet the minimum 2.0 GPA requirements. *Award:* Grant for use in freshman, sophomore, junior, or senior year; renewable. *Award amount:* $700–$11,259. *Eligibility Requirements:* Applicant must be enrolled or expecting to enroll full or part-time at a two-year, four-year, or technical institution or university; resident of California and studying in California. Available to U.S. citizens. *Application Requirements:* Application, financial need analysis. **Deadline:** March 2.

Contact California Student Aid Commission, P O Box 419027, Rancho Cordova, CA 95741-9027. *E-mail:* custsvcs@csac.ca.gov. *Phone:* 916-526-7590. *Fax:* 916-526-8002. *Web site:* www.csac.ca.gov.

Governor's Distinguished Mathematics and Science Scholars Award. One-time scholarship for California public high school students who, in addition to receiving the Governor's Scholars Award, attain required scores on certain Advanced Placement exams, International Baccalaureate exams, or Golden State exams. See web site at http://www.scholarshare.com for further details. **Award:** Scholarship for use in freshman, sophomore, junior, senior, or graduate year; not renewable. *Award amount:* $2500. *Eligibility Requirements:* Applicant must be high school student; planning to enroll or expecting to enroll at a two-year, four-year, or technical institution or university and resident of California. *Application Requirements:* Test scores.

Contact application available at web site, ScholarShare Investment Board. *Web site:* www.scholarshare.com/gsp/index.html.

Governor's Scholars Award. Award to California students who demonstrate high academic achievement on certain exams in the Standardized Testing and Reporting program in the 9th, 10th, or 11th grades. For use at any postsecondary institution eligible to participate in federal Title IV financial aid programs, including schools outside the country. See web site at http://www.scholarshare.com for further details. **Award:** Scholarship for use in freshman, sophomore, junior, senior, or graduate year; not renewable. *Award amount:* $1000. *Eligibility Requirements:* Applicant must be high school student; planning to enroll or expecting to enroll at a two-year, four-year, or technical institution or university and resident of California. *Application Requirements:* Test scores.

Contact application available at web site, ScholarShare Investment Board. *Web site:* www.scholarshare.com/gsp/index.html.

Law Enforcement Personnel Development Scholarship. The Law Enforcement Personnel Dependents Scholarship Program provides college grants to needy dependents of California law enforcement officers, officers and employees of the Department of Corrections and Department of Youth Authority, and firefighters killed or disabled in the line of duty. *Award:* Grant for use in freshman, sophomore, junior, or senior year; renewable. *Award amount:* $100–$11,259. *Eligibility Requirements:* Applicant must be enrolled or expecting to enroll full or part-time at a two-year, four-year, or technical institution or university; resident of California and studying in California. Applicant or parent of applicant must have employment or volunteer experience in police/firefighting. Available to U.S. citizens. *Application Requirements:* Application, financial need analysis. **Deadline:** continuous.

Contact California Student Aid Commission, PO Box 419027, Rancho Cordova, CA 95741-9027. *E-mail:* custsvcs@csac.ca.gov. *Phone:* 916-526-7590. *Fax:* 916-526-8002. *Web site:* www.csac.ca.gov.

COLORADO

Colorado Leveraging Educational Assistance Partnership (CLEAP) and SLEAP. Renewable awards for Colorado residents who are attending Colorado state-supported postsecondary institutions at the undergraduate level. Must document financial need. Contact colleges for complete information and deadlines. *Award:* Grant for use in freshman, sophomore, junior, or senior year; not renewable. *Award amount:* $50–$900. *Number of awards:* 5000. *Eligibility Requirements:* Applicant must be enrolled or expecting to enroll full or part-time at a two-year, four-year, or technical institution or university; resident of Colorado and studying in Colorado. Available to U.S. citizens. *Application Requirements:* Application, financial need analysis.

Contact Financial Aid Office at college/institution, Colorado Commission on Higher Education, 1380 Lawrence Street, Suite 1200, Denver, CO 80204-2059. *Web site:* www.state.co.us/cche.

Colorado Nursing Scholarships. Renewable awards for Colorado residents pursuing nursing education programs at Colorado state-supported institutions. Applicant must agree to practice nursing in Colorado upon graduation. Contact colleges for complete information and deadlines. *Academic/Career Areas:* Nursing. *Award:* Scholarship for use in freshman, sophomore, junior, or senior year; not renewable. *Number of awards:* 100. *Eligibility Requirements:* Applicant must be enrolled or expecting to enroll full or part-time at a two-year, four-year, or technical institution or university; resident of Colorado and studying in Colorado. *Application Requirements:* Application, financial need analysis. **Deadline:** April 1.

Contact Financial Aid Office at college/institution, Colorado Commission on Higher Education, 1380 Lawrence Street, Suite 1200, Denver, CO 80204-2059. *Web site:* www.state.co.us/cche.

Colorado Student Grant. Assists Colorado residents attending eligible public, private, or vocational institutions within the state. Application deadlines vary by institution. Renewable award for undergraduates. Contact the financial aid office at the college/institution for more information and an application. *Award:* Grant for use in freshman, sophomore, junior, or senior year; renewable. *Award amount:* $500–$5000. *Eligibility Requirements:* Applicant must be enrolled or expecting to enroll full or part-time at a two-year, four-year, or technical institution or university; resident of Colorado and studying in Colorado. *Application Requirements:* Application, financial need analysis.

Contact Financial Aid Office at college/institution, Colorado Commission on Higher Education, 1380 Lawrence Street, Suite 1200, Denver, CO 80204-2059. *Web site:* www.state.co.us/cche.

Colorado Undergraduate Merit Scholarships. Renewable awards for students attending Colorado state-supported institutions at the undergraduate level. Must demonstrate superior scholarship or talent. Contact college financial aid office for complete information and deadlines. *Award:* Scholarship for use in freshman, sophomore, junior, or senior year; renewable. *Award amount:* $1230. *Number of awards:* 10,823. *Eligibility Requirements:* Applicant must be enrolled or expecting to enroll full or part-time at a two-year, four-year, or technical institution or university; resident of Colorado and studying in Colorado. Applicant must have 3.0 GPA or higher. *Application Requirements:* Application, test scores, transcript.

Contact Financial Aid Office at college/institution, Colorado Commission on Higher Education, 1380 Lawrence Street, Suite 1200, Denver, CO 80204-2059. *Web site:* www.state.co.us/cche.

Governor's Opportunity Scholarship. Scholarship available for the most needy first-time freshmen whose parents' adjusted gross income is less than $26,000. Must be U.S. citizen for permanent legal resident. Work-study is part of the program. *Award:* Scholarship for use in freshman, sophomore, junior, or senior year; renewable. *Award amount:* $5665. *Number of awards:* up to 1052. *Eligibility Requirements:* Applicant must be high school student; planning to enroll or expecting to enroll full-time at a two-year, four-year, or technical institution or university; resident of Colorado and studying in Colorado. Available to U.S. citizens. *Application Requirements:* Application, financial need analysis, test scores, transcript. **Deadline:** continuous.

Contact Financial Aid Office at college/institution, Colorado Commission on Higher Education, 1380 Lawrence Street, Suite 1200, Denver, CO 80204-2059. *Web site:* www.state.co.us/cche.

Law Enforcement/POW/MIA Dependents Scholarship—Colorado. Aid available for dependents of Colorado law enforcement officers, fire or national guard personnel killed or disabled in the line of duty, and for dependents of prisoner-of-war or service personnel listed as missing in action. Award covers tuition and room and board. *Award:* Scholarship for use in freshman, sophomore, junior, or senior year; renewable. *Eligibility Requirements:* Applicant must be enrolled or expecting to enroll full or part-time at a two-year, four-year, or technical institution or university. Applicant must have 2.5 GPA or higher. *Application Requirements:* Application, financial need analysis, transcript. **Deadline:** continuous.

Contact Dianne Lindner, Financial Director, Colorado Commission on Higher Education, 1380 Lawrence Street, Suite 1200, Denver, CO 80204. *Phone:* 303-866-2723. *Fax:* 303-866-4266. *Web site:* www.state.co.us/cche.

Western Undergraduate Exchange Program. Residents of Alaska, Arizona, Colorado, Hawaii, Idaho, Montana, Nevada, New Mexico, North Dakota, Oregon, South Dakota, Utah, Washington and Wyoming can enroll in designated two- and four-year undergraduate programs at public institutions in participating states at reduced tuition level (resident tuition plus half). Contact Western Interstate Commission for Higher Education for list and deadlines. *Award:* Scholarship for use in freshman, sophomore, junior, or senior year; renewable. *Eligibility Requirements:* Applicant must be enrolled or expecting to enroll full or part-time at a two-year or four-year institution; resident of Alaska, Arizona, Colorado, Hawaii, Idaho, Montana, Nevada, New Mexico, North Dakota, Oregon, South Dakota, Utah, Washington, or Wyoming and studying in Alaska, Colorado, Hawaii, Idaho, Montana, Nevada, New Mexico, North Dakota, Oregon, South Dakota, Utah, or Wyoming. Available to U.S. citizens. *Application Requirements:* Application.

Contact Ms. Sandy Jackson, Program Coordinator, Western Interstate Commission for Higher Education, PO Box 9752, Boulder, CO 80301-9752. *E-mail:* info-sep@wiche.edu. *Phone:* 303-541-0214. *Fax:* 303-541-0291. *Web site:* www.wiche.edu/sep.

CONNECTICUT

Aid for Public College Students Grant Program/Connecticut. Award for students at Connecticut public college or university. Must be state residents and enrolled at least half-time. Renewable award based on financial need and academic progress. Application deadlines vary by institution. Apply at college financial aid office. *Award:* Grant for use in freshman, sophomore, junior, or senior year; renewable. *Eligibility Requirements:* Applicant must be enrolled or expecting to enroll full or part-time at a two-year or four-year institution or university; resident of Connecticut and studying in Connecticut. *Application Requirements:* Application, financial need analysis, transcript.

Contact John Siegrist, Financial Aid Office, Connecticut Department of Higher Education, 61 Woodland Street, Hartford, CT 06105-2326. *Phone:* 860-947-1855. *Fax:* 860-947-1311. *Web site:* www.ctdhe.org.

Capitol Scholarship Program. Award for Connecticut residents attending eligible institutions in Connecticut or in a state with reciprocity with Connecticut (Delaware, Maine, Massachusetts, New Hampshire, Pennsylvania, Rhode Island, Vermont), or in Washington, D.C. Must be U.S. citizen or permanent resident alien who is a high school senior or graduate with rank in top 20% of class or score at least 1200 on SAT and show financial need. *Award:* Scholarship for use in freshman, sophomore, junior, or senior year; renewable. *Award amount:* up to $2000. *Eligibility Requirements:* Applicant must be enrolled or expecting to enroll at a two-year or four-year institution or university; resident of Connecticut and studying in Connecticut, Delaware, District of Columbia, Maine, Massachusetts, New Hampshire, Pennsylvania, Rhode Island, or Vermont. Applicant must have 3.5 GPA or higher. Available to U.S. citizens. *Application Requirements:* Application, financial need analysis, test scores. **Deadline:** February 15.

Contact John Siegrist, Financial Aid Office, Connecticut Department of Higher Education, 61 Woodland Street, Hartford, CT 06105-2326. *Phone:* 860-947-1855. *Fax:* 860-947-1311. *Web site:* www.ctdhe.org.

Connecticut Army National Guard 100% Tuition Waiver. 100% Tuition Waiver Program is for any active member of the Connecticut Army National Guard in good standing. Must be a resident of Connecticut attending any Connecticut state (public) university, community-technical college or regional vocational-technical school. *Award:* Scholarship for use in freshman, sophomore, junior, or senior year; not renewable. *Award amount:* $2000–$8000. *Eligibility Requirements:* Applicant must be age 17-65; enrolled or expecting to enroll full or part-time at a two-year, four-year, or technical institution or university; resident of Connecticut and studying in Connecticut. Available to U.S. and non-U.S. citizens. Applicant must have served in the Army National Guard. *Application Requirements:* Application. **Deadline:** continuous.

Contact Education Services Officer, Connecticut Army National Guard. *E-mail:* education@ct.ngb.army.mil. *Phone:* 860-524-4816. *Web site:* www.ct.ngb.army. mil/armyguard/join/tuition.asp.

Connecticut Independent College Student Grants. Award for Connecticut residents attending an independent college or university within the state on at least a half-time basis. Renewable awards based on financial need. Application deadline varies by institution. Apply at college financial aid office. *Award:* Grant for use in freshman, sophomore, junior, or senior year; renewable. *Award amount:* up to $8600. *Eligibility Requirements:* Applicant must be enrolled or expecting to enroll full or part-time at a two-year or four-year institution or university; resident of Connecticut and studying in Connecticut. *Application Requirements:* Application, financial need analysis, transcript.

Contact John Siegrist, Financial Aid Office, Connecticut Department of Higher Education, 61 Woodland Street, Hartford, CT 06105-2326. *Phone:* 860-947-1855. *Fax:* 860-947-1311. *Web site:* www.ctdhe.org.

Connecticut Special Education Teacher Incentive Grant. Renewable award for upper-level undergraduates or graduate students in special education programs. Must be in a program at a Connecticut college or university, or be a Connecticut resident enrolled in an approved out-of-state program. Priority is placed on minority and bilingual candidates. Application deadline is October 1. Must be nominated by the education dean of institution attended. *Academic/Career Areas:* Special Education. *Award:* Grant for use in junior, senior, or graduate year; renewable. *Award amount:* $2000–$5000. *Eligibility Requirements:* Applicant must be enrolled or expecting to enroll full or part-time at a four-year institution or university. *Application Requirements:* Application. **Deadline:** October 1.

Contact John Siegrist, Financial Aid Office, Connecticut Department of Higher Education, 61 Woodland Street, Hartford, CT 06105-2326. *Phone:* 860-947-1855. *Fax:* 860-947-1311. *Web site:* www.ctdhe.org.

Connecticut Tuition Waiver for Senior Citizens. Renewable tuition waiver for a Connecticut senior citizen age 62 or older to use at an accredited two- or four-year public institution in Connecticut. Must show financial need and prove senior citizen status. Award for undergraduate study only. Must be enrolled in credit courses. *Award:* Grant for use in freshman, sophomore, junior, or senior year; renewable. *Eligibility Requirements:* Applicant must be age 62; enrolled or expecting to enroll at a two-year or four-year institution; resident of Connecticut and studying in Connecticut. *Application Requirements:* Application, financial need analysis. **Deadline:** continuous.

Contact John Siegrist, Financial Aid Office, Connecticut Department of Higher Education, 61 Woodland Street, Hartford, CT 06105-2326. *Phone:* 860-947-1855. *Fax:* 860-947-1311. *Web site:* www.ctdhe.org.

Connecticut Tuition Waiver for Veterans. Renewable tuition waiver for a Connecticut veteran to use at an accredited two-or four-year public institution in Connecticut. Military separation papers are required; see application for qualifications of service. *Award:* Grant for use in freshman, sophomore, junior, or senior year; renewable. *Eligibility Requirements:* Applicant must be enrolled or expecting to enroll at a two-year or four-year institution; resident of Connecticut and studying in Connecticut. Applicant or parent must meet one or more of the following requirements: general military experience; retired from active duty; disabled or killed as a result of military service; prisoner of war; or missing in action. *Application Requirements:* Application, financial need analysis, military discharge papers. **Deadline:** continuous.

Contact John Siegrist, Financial Aid Office, Connecticut Department of Higher Education, 61 Woodland Street, Hartford, CT 06105-2326. *Phone:* 860-947-1855. *Fax:* 860-947-1311. *Web site:* www.ctdhe.org.

Tuition Set-Aside Aid—Connecticut. Need-based program that assists Connecticut residents who are enrolled at state-supported colleges and universities in Connecticut. Award amounts are variable but do not exceed student's financial need. Deadlines vary by institution. Apply at college financial aid office. *Award:* Grant for use in freshman, sophomore, junior, or senior year; not renewable.

Eligibility Requirements: Applicant must be enrolled or expecting to enroll at a two-year or four-year institution or university; resident of Connecticut and studying in Connecticut. *Application Requirements:* Application, financial need analysis.

Contact John Siegrist, Financial Aid Office, Connecticut Department of Higher Education, 61 Woodland Street, Hartford, CT 06105-2326. *Phone:* 860-947-1855. *Fax:* 860-947-1311. *Web site:* www.ctdhe.org.

DELAWARE

Christa McAuliffe Teacher Scholarship Loan—Delaware. Award for Delaware residents who are pursuing teaching careers. Must agree to teach in Delaware public schools as repayment of loan. Minimum award is $1000 and is renewable for up to four years. Available only at Delaware colleges. Based on academic merit. Must be ranked in upper half of class, and have a score of 1050 on SAT or 25 on the ACT. *Academic/Career Areas:* Education. *Award:* Forgivable loan for use in freshman, sophomore, junior, or senior year; renewable. *Award amount:* $1000–$5000. *Number of awards:* 1–60. *Eligibility Requirements:* Applicant must be enrolled or expecting to enroll full-time at a four-year institution or university; resident of Delaware and studying in Delaware. Applicant must have 2.5 GPA or higher. Available to U.S. citizens. *Application Requirements:* Application, essay, test scores, transcript. **Deadline:** March 31.

Contact Donna Myers, Higher Education Analyst, Delaware Higher Education Commission, 820 North French Street, 5th Floor, Wilmington, DE 19711-3509. *E-mail:* dhec@doe.k12.de.us. *Phone:* 302-577-3240. *Fax:* 302-577-6765. *Web site:* www.doe.state.de.us/high-ed.

Delaware Nursing Incentive Scholarship Loan. Award for Delaware residents pursuing a nursing career. Must be repaid with nursing practice at a Delaware state-owned hospital. Based on academic merit. Must have minimum 2.5 GPA. Renewable for up to four years. *Academic/Career Areas:* Nursing. *Award:* Forgivable loan for use in freshman, sophomore, junior, or senior year; renewable. *Award amount:* $1000–$5000. *Number of awards:* 1–40. *Eligibility Requirements:* Applicant must be enrolled or expecting to enroll full-time at a two-year or four-year institution or university and resident of Delaware. Applicant must have 2.5 GPA or higher. Available to U.S. citizens. *Application Requirements:* Application, essay, test scores, transcript. **Deadline:** March 31.

Contact Donna Myers, Higher Education Analyst, Delaware Higher Education Commission, 820 North French Street, 5th Floor, Wilmington, DE 19711-3509. *E-mail:* dhec@doe.k12.de.us. *Phone:* 302-577-3240. *Fax:* 302-577-6765. *Web site:* www.doe.state.de.us/high-ed.

Delaware Solid Waste Authority Scholarship. Scholarships given to residents of Delaware who are high school seniors or freshmen or sophomores in college. Must be majoring in either environmental engineering or environmental sciences in a Delaware college. Must file the Free Application for Federal Student Aid (FAFSA). Scholarships are automatically renewed for three years if a 3.0 GPA is maintained. Deadline: March 15. *Award:* Scholarship for use in freshman or sophomore year; renewable. *Award amount:* $2000. *Eligibility Requirements:* Applicant must be enrolled or expecting to enroll full-time at a two-year or four-year institution or university; resident of Delaware and studying in Delaware. Applicant must have 3.0 GPA or higher. *Application Requirements:* Financial need analysis, FAFSA. **Deadline:** March 15.

Contact Donna Myers, Higher Education Analyst, Delaware Higher Education Commission, 820 North French Street, 5th Floor, Wilmington, DE 19711-

Profiles of State-Sponsored Programs

3509. *E-mail:* dhec@doe.k12.de.us. *Phone:* 302-577-3240. *Fax:* 302-577-6765. *Web site:* www.doe.state.de.us/high-ed.

Diamond State Scholarship. Renewable award for Delaware high school seniors enrolling full-time at an accredited college or university. Must be ranked in upper quarter of class and score 1200 on SAT or 27 on the ACT. *Award:* Scholarship for use in freshman year; renewable. *Award amount:* $1250. *Number of awards:* 50–200. *Eligibility Requirements:* Applicant must be high school student; planning to enroll or expecting to enroll full-time at a four-year institution or university and resident of Delaware. Applicant must have 3.5 GPA or higher. Available to U.S. citizens. *Application Requirements:* Application, essay, test scores, transcript. **Deadline:** March 31.

Contact Donna Myers, Higher Education Analyst, Delaware Higher Education Commission, 820 North French Street, 5th Floor, Wilmington, DE 19711-3509. *E-mail:* dhec@doe.k12.de.us. *Phone:* 302-577-3240. *Fax:* 302-577-6765. *Web site:* www.doe.state.de.us/high-ed.

Educational Benefits for Children of Deceased Military and State Police. Renewable award for Delaware residents who are children of state or military police who were killed in the line of duty. Must attend a Delaware institution unless program of study is not available. Funds cover tuition and fees at Delaware institutions. The amount varies at non-Delaware institutions. Must submit proof of service and related death. Must be ages 16-24 at time of application. Deadline is three weeks before classes begin. *Award:* Grant for use in freshman, sophomore, junior, or senior year; renewable. *Award amount:* $6255. *Number of awards:* 1–10. *Eligibility Requirements:* Applicant must be age 16-24; enrolled or expecting to enroll full-time at a two-year or four-year institution or university and resident of Delaware. Applicant or parent of applicant must have employment or volunteer experience in police/firefighting. Available to U.S. citizens. Applicant or parent must meet one or more of the following requirements: general military experience; retired from active duty; disabled or killed as a result of military service; prisoner of war; or missing in action. *Application Requirements:* Application, verification of service-related death. **Deadline:** continuous.

Contact Donna Myers, Higher Education Analyst, Delaware Higher Education Commission, 820 North French Street, 5th Floor, Wilmington, DE 19711-3509. *E-mail:* dhec@doe.k12.de.us. *Phone:* 302-577-3240. *Fax:* 302-577-6765. *Web site:* www.doe.state.de.us/high-ed.

Legislative Essay Scholarship. Must be a senior in high school and Delaware resident. Submit an essay of 500 to 2000 words on a designated historical topic (changes annually). Deadline: November 16. For more information visit: http://www.doe.state.de.us/high-ed. **Award:** Scholarship for use in freshman year; not renewable. *Award amount:* $500–$5500. *Number of awards:* 62. *Eligibility Requirements:* Applicant must be high school student; planning to enroll or expecting to enroll full or part-time at a two-year, four-year, or technical institution or university and resident of Delaware. Available to U.S. citizens. *Application Requirements:* Application, applicant must enter a contest, essay. **Deadline:** November 16.

Contact Donna Myers, Higher Education Analyst, Delaware Higher Education Commission, 820 North French Street, 5th Floor, Wilmington, DE 19711-3509. *E-mail:* dhec@doe.k12.de.us. *Phone:* 302-577-3240. *Fax:* 302-577-6765. *Web site:* www.doe.state.de.us/high-ed.

Scholarship Incentive Program-Delaware. One-time award for Delaware residents with financial need. May be used at an institution in Delaware or Pennsylvania, or at another out-of-state institution if a program is not available at a publicly-supported school in Delaware. Must have minimum 2.5 GPA. *Award:* Grant for use in freshman, sophomore, junior, or senior year; not renewable. *Award amount:* $700–$2200. *Number of awards:* 1000–1300. *Eligibility Requirements:* Applicant must be enrolled or expecting to enroll full-time at a two-year or four-year institution or university; resident of Delaware and studying in Delaware or Pennsylvania. Applicant must have 2.5 GPA or higher. Available to U.S. citizens. *Application Requirements:* Application, financial need analysis, transcript. **Deadline:** April 15.

Contact Donna Myers, Higher Education Analyst, Delaware Higher Education Commission, 820 North French Street, 5th Floor, Wilmington, DE 19711-3509. *E-mail:* dhec@doe.k12.de.us. *Phone:* 302-577-3240. *Fax:* 302-577-6765. *Web site:* www.doe.state.de.us/high-ed.

State Tuition Assistance. Award providing tuition assistance for any member of the Air or Army National Guard attending a Delaware two-year or four-year college. Awards are renewable. Applicant's minimum GPA must be 2.0. For full- or part-time study. Amount of award varies. *Award:* Scholarship for use in freshman, sophomore, junior, or senior year; renewable. *Eligibility Requirements:* Applicant must be enrolled or expecting to enroll full or part-time at a two-year or four-year institution and studying in Delaware. Available to U.S. citizens. Applicant must have served in the Air Force National Guard or Army National Guard. *Application Requirements:* **Deadline:** continuous.

Contact TSgt. Robert L. Csizmadia, State Tuition Assistance Manager, Delaware National Guard, First Regiment Road, Wilmington, DE 19808-2191. *E-mail:* robert. csizmadi@de.ngb.army.mil. *Phone:* 302-326-7012. *Fax:* 302-326-7055. *Web site:* www.delawarenationalguard/home.htm.

DISTRICT OF COLUMBIA

American Council of the Blind Scholarships. Merit-based award available to undergraduate, graduate, vocational or technical students who are legally blind in both eyes. Submit certificate of legal blindness and proof of acceptance at an accredited postsecondary institution. *Award:* Scholarship for use in freshman, sophomore, junior, senior, or graduate year; not renewable. *Award amount:* $500–$5000. *Number of awards:* 30. *Eligibility Requirements:* Applicant must be enrolled or expecting to enroll full-time at a two-year, four-year, or technical institution or university. Applicant must be visually impaired. Applicant must have 3.5 GPA or higher. *Application Requirements:* Application, autobiography, essay, references, transcript. **Deadline:** March 1.

Contact Terry Pacheco, Affiliate and Membership Services, American Council of the Blind, 1155 15th Street, NW, Suite 1004, Washington, DC 20005. *E-mail:* info@acb.org. *Phone:* 202-467-5081. *Fax:* 202-467-5085. *Web site:* www.acb.org.

DC Leveraging Educational Assistance Partnership Program (LEAP). Available to Washington, D.C. residents who have financial need. Must also apply for the Federal Pell Grant. Must attend an eligible college at least half-time. Contact financial aid office or local library for more information. Proof of residency may be required. Deadline is last Friday in June. *Award:* Scholarship for use in freshman, sophomore, junior, or senior year; not renewable. *Award amount:* $500–$1500. *Number of awards:* 1200–1500. *Eligibility Requirements:* Applicant must be enrolled or expecting to enroll full or part-time at a two-year, four-year, or technical institution or university and resident of District of Columbia. Available to U.S. citizens. *Application Requirements:* Application, financial need analysis, Student Aid Report (SAR). **Deadline:** June 28.

Contact Angela M. March, Program Manager, District of Columbia State Education Office, 441 4th Street NW, Suite 350 North, Washington, DC 20001. *E-mail:* angela.march@dc.gov. *Phone:* 202-727-6436. *Fax:* 202-727-2019. *Web site:* www.seo.dc.gov.

FLORIDA

Critical Teacher Shortage Student Loan Forgiveness Program—Florida. Eligible Florida teachers may receive up to $5,000 for repayment of undergraduate and graduate educational loans which led to certification in critical teacher shortage subject area. Must teach full-time at a Florida public school in a critical area for a minimum of ninety days to be eligible. Visit web site for further information. *Award:* Forgivable loan for use in freshman, sophomore, junior, senior, or graduate year; not renewable. *Award amount:* up to $5000. *Eligibility Requirements:* Applicant must be enrolled or expecting to enroll at a two-year or four-year institution or university; resident of Florida and studying in Florida. Applicant or parent of applicant must have employment or volunteer experience in teaching. Available to U.S. citizens. *Application Requirements:* Application. **Deadline:** July 15.

Contact Scholarship Information, Florida Department of Education, Office of Student Financial Assistance, 1940 North Monroe, Suite 70, Tallahassee, FL 32303-4759. *E-mail:* osfa@fldoe.org. *Phone:* 888-827-2004. *Web site:* www.floridastudentfinancialaid.org.

Critical Teacher Shortage Tuition Reimbursement-Florida. One-time awards for full-time Florida public school employees who are certified to teach in Florida and are teaching or preparing to teach in critical teacher shortage subject areas. Must earn minimum grade of 3.0 in approved courses. May receive tuition reimbursement up to 9 semester hours or equivalent per academic year, not to exceed $78 per semester hour, for maximum 36 hours. Must be resident of Florida. *Academic/Career Areas:* Education. *Award:* Scholarship for use in freshman, sophomore, junior, senior, or graduate year; not renewable. *Award amount:* up to $234. *Number of awards:* 1000–1200. *Eligibility Requirements:* Applicant must be enrolled or expecting to enroll part-time at a two-year or four-year institution or university; resident of Florida and studying in Florida. Applicant or parent of applicant must have employment or volunteer experience in teaching. Applicant must have 3.0 GPA or higher. Available to U.S. citizens. *Application Requirements:* Application, financial need analysis. **Deadline:** September 15.

Contact Scholarship Information, Florida Department of Education, Office of Student Financial Assistance, 1940 North Monroe, Suite 70, Tallahassee, FL 32303-4759. *E-mail:* osfa@fldoe.org. *Phone:* 888-827-2004. *Web site:* www.floridastudentfinancialaid.org.

Excellence in Service Award. This award program recognizes Florida College students who have a distinguished community service record in Florida. See web site (http://www.floridacompact.org) for application form and further requirements. *Award:* Scholarship for use in freshman, sophomore, or junior year; not renewable. *Award amount:* $1000. *Number of awards:* 3. *Eligibility Requirements:* Applicant must be enrolled or expecting to enroll full-time at a four-year institution or university; resident of Florida and studying in Florida. Available to U.S. and non-U.S. citizens. *Application Requirements:* Application, essay, photo, resume, references, transcript. **Deadline:** April 3.

Contact Saul A. Magana, Associate Director, Florida Campus Compact, 325 John Knox Road Building F, Suite 210, Tallahassee, FL 32303. *E-mail:* saul@floridacompact.org. *Phone:* 850-488-7782. *Fax:* 850-922-2928. *Web site:* www.floridacompact.org.

Florida Bright Futures Scholarship Program. Reward for Florida high school graduates who demonstrate high academic achievement, participate in community service projects and enroll in eligible Florida postsecondary institutions. There are three award levels. Each has different academic criteria and awards a different amount. Top ranked scholars from each county will receive additional $1500. Web site at http://www.firn.edu/doe contains complete information and application which must be completed and submitted to high school guidance counselor prior to graduation. **Award:** Scholarship for use in freshman, sophomore, junior, or senior year; renewable. *Eligibility Requirements:* Applicant must be high school student; planning to enroll or expecting to enroll full or part-time at a two-year, four-year, or technical institution or university; resident of Florida and studying in Florida. Available to U.S. citizens. *Application Requirements:* Application, financial need analysis, test scores, transcript.

Contact Scholarship Information, Florida Department of Education, Office of Student Financial Assistance, 1940 North Monroe, Suite 70, Tallahassee, FL 32303-4759. *E-mail:* osfa@fldoe.org. *Phone:* 888-827-2004. *Web site:* www.floridastudentfinancialaid.org.

Florida Space Research and Education Grant Program. One-time award for aerospace and technology research. Must be U.S. citizen. Grant is for research in Florida only. Submit research proposal with budget. Application deadline is March 1. *Award:* Grant for use in freshman, sophomore, junior, senior, graduate, or postgraduate years; not renewable. *Award amount:* $10,000–$30,000. *Number of awards:* 9–12. *Eligibility Requirements:* Applicant must be enrolled or expecting to enroll full or part-time at a four-year institution or university and studying in Florida. Available to U.S. citizens. *Application Requirements:* Proposal with budget. **Deadline:** March 1.

Contact Dr. Jaydeep Mukherjee, Administrator, NASA Florida Space Grant Consortium, Mail Stop: FSGC, Kennedy Space Center, FL 32899. *E-mail:* jmukherj@mail.ucf.edu. *Phone:* 321-452-4301. *Fax:* 321-449-0739. *Web site:* fsgc.engr.ucf.edu.

Jose Marti Scholarship Challenge Grant. Must apply as a senior in high school or as graduate student. Must be resident of Florida and study in Florida. Need-based, merit scholarship. Must be U.S. citizen or eligible non-citizen. Applicant must certify minimum 3.0 GPA and Hispanic origin. *Award:* Scholarship for use in freshman, sophomore, junior, senior, or graduate year; renewable. *Award amount:* $2000. *Number of awards:* 50. *Eligibility Requirements:* Applicant must be of Hispanic heritage; enrolled or expecting to enroll full-time at a two-year or four-year institution or university; resident of Florida and studying in Florida. Applicant must have 3.0 GPA or higher. Available to U.S. citizens. *Application Requirements:* Application, financial need analysis. **Deadline:** April 1.

Contact Jose Marti Scholarship Challenge Grant Fund, 1940 North Monroe Street, Suite 70, Tallahassee, FL 32303-4759. *Phone:* 888-827-2004. *Web site:* www.floridastudentfinancialaid.org.

Nursing Scholarship Program. Provides financial assistance for Florida residents who are full- or part-time nursing students enrolled in an approved nursing program in Florida. Awards are for a maximum of two years and must be repaid through full-time service. *Academic/Career Areas:* Nursing. *Award:* Scholarship for use in junior, senior, or graduate year; renewable. *Award amount:* $8000–$12,000. *Number of awards:* 15–30. *Eligibility Requirements:* Applicant must be enrolled or expecting to enroll full or part-time at a two-year or four-year institution or university; resident of Florida and studying in Florida. Available to U.S. and non-U.S. citizens. *Application Requirements:* Application. **Deadline:** continuous.

Contact Florida Department of Health, Division of EMS and Community Health Resources, 4052 Bald Cypress Way, Mail Bin C-15, Tallahassee, FL 32399-1735.

Nursing Student Loan Forgiveness Program. Forgivable loan available to LPNs, RNs, and ARNPs who are out of school and working full time at a designated facility. Program assists with repaying principal only of loans taken to subsidize nursing education. Pays $4,000 per year of outstanding debt for a maximum of four years. Contact for information. Deadlines: March 1, June 1, September 1, and December 1. *Academic/Career Areas:* Nursing. *Award:* Forgivable loan for use in freshman, sophomore, junior, or senior year; renewable. *Award amount:* up to $4000. *Eligibility Requirements:* Applicant must be enrolled or expecting to enroll at an institution or university; resident of Florida and studying in Florida. Available to U.S. and non-U.S. citizens. *Application Requirements:* Application, Nurse Diploma and Florida License (copy of each with application).

Contact Florida Department of Health, Division of EMS and Community Health Resources, 4052 Bald Cypress Way, Mail Bin C-15, Tallahassee, FL 32399-1735.

Rosewood Family Scholarship Fund. Renewable award for eligible minority students to attend a Florida public postsecondary institution on a full-time basis. Preference given to direct descendants of African-American Rosewood families affected by the incidents of January 1923. Must be Black, Hispanic, Asian, Pacific Islander, American-Indian, or Alaska Native. Free Application for Federal Student Aid (and Student Aid Report for nonresidents of Florida) must be processed by May 15. *Award:* Scholarship for use in freshman, sophomore, junior, or senior year; renewable. *Award amount:* up to $4000. *Number of awards:* up to 25. *Eligibility Requirements:* Applicant must be American Indian/Alaska Native, Asian/Pacific Islander, Black (non-Hispanic), or Hispanic; enrolled or expecting to enroll full-time at a two-year, four-year, or technical institution or university and studying in Florida. Available to U.S. citizens. *Application Requirements:* Application, financial need analysis. **Deadline:** April 1.

Contact Scholarship Information, Florida Department of Education, Office of Student Financial Assistance, 1940 North Monroe, Suite 70, Tallahassee, FL 32303-4759. *E-mail:* osfa@fldoe.org. *Phone:* 888-827-2004. *Web site:* www.floridastudentfinancialaid.org.

Scholarships for Children of Deceased or Disabled Veterans or Children of Servicemen Classified as POW or MIA. Scholarship provides full tuition assistance for children of deceased or disabled veterans or of servicemen classified as POW or MIA who are in full-time attendance at eligible public or non-public Florida institutions. Service connection must be as specified under Florida statute. Amount of payment to non-public institutions is equal to cost at public institutions at the comparable level. Must be between 16 and 22. Qualified veteran and applicant must meet residency requirements. *Award:* Scholarship for use in freshman, sophomore, junior, or senior year; renewable. *Number of awards:* 160. *Eligibility Requirements:* Applicant must be age 16-22; enrolled or expecting to enroll full-time at a two-year, four-year, or technical institution or university; resident of

Florida and studying in Florida. Available to U.S. citizens. Applicant or parent must meet one or more of the following requirements: general military experience; retired from active duty; disabled or killed as a result of military service; prisoner of war; or missing in action. *Application Requirements:* Application, financial need analysis. **Deadline:** May 1.

Contact Scholarship Information, Florida Department of Education, Office of Student Financial Assistance, 1940 North Monroe, Suite 70, Tallahassee, FL 32303-4759. *E-mail:* osfa@fldoe.org. *Phone:* 888-827-2004. *Web site:* www.floridastudentfinancialaid.org.

William L. Boyd IV Florida Resident Access Grant. Awards given to Florida residents attending an independent nonprofit college or university in Florida for undergraduate study. Cannot have previously received bachelor's degree. Must enroll minimum 12 credit hours. Deadline set by eligible postsecondary financial aid offices. Contact financial aid administrator for application information. Reapply for renewal. *Award:* Grant for use in freshman, sophomore, junior, or senior year; not renewable. *Award amount:* up to $2686. *Eligibility Requirements:* Applicant must be enrolled or expecting to enroll full-time at a four-year institution or university; resident of Florida and studying in Florida. Available to U.S. citizens. *Application Requirements:* Application.

Contact Scholarship Information, Florida Department of Education, Office of Student Financial Assistance, 1940 North Monroe, Suite 70, Tallahassee, FL 32303-4759. *E-mail:* osfa@fldoe.org. *Phone:* 888-827-2004. *Web site:* www.floridastudentfinancialaid.org.

GEORGIA

Department of Human Resources Federal Stafford Loan with the Service Cancelable Loan Option. Forgivable loans of $4000 are awarded to current Department of Human Resources employees who will be enrolled in a baccalaureate or advanced nursing degree program at an eligible participating school in Georgia. Loans are cancelled upon two calendar years of service as a registered nurse for the Georgia DHR or any Georgia county board of health. *Academic/Career Areas:* Nursing. *Award:* Forgivable loan for use in freshman, sophomore, junior, senior, or graduate year; not renewable. *Award amount:* $4000. *Eligibility Requirements:* Applicant must be enrolled or expecting to enroll full or part-time at a four-year institution or university; resident of Georgia and studying in Georgia. Available to U.S. citizens. *Application Requirements:* Application, financial need analysis. **Deadline:** continuous.

Contact Peggy Matthews, Manager/GSFA Originations, State of Georgia, 2082 East Exchange Place, Suite 230, Tucker, GA 30084-5305. *E-mail:* peggy@mail.gsfc.state.ga.us. *Phone:* 770-724-9230. *Fax:* 770-724-9263. *Web site:* www.gsfc.org.

GAE GFIE Scholarship for Aspiring Teachers. Up to ten $1000 scholarships will be awarded to graduating seniors who currently attend a fully accredited public Georgia high school and will attend a fully accredited Georgia college or university within the next 12 months. Must have a 3.0 GPA. Must submit three letters of recommendation. Must have plans to enter the teaching profession. *Academic/Career Areas:* Education. *Award:* Scholarship for use in freshman year; not renewable. *Award amount:* $1000. *Number of awards:* up to 10. *Eligibility Requirements:* Applicant must be high school student; planning to enroll or expecting to enroll at a two-year or four-year institution or university; resident of Georgia and studying in

Georgia. Applicant must have 3.0 GPA or higher. Available to U.S. citizens. *Application Requirements:* Application, transcript. **Deadline:** March 15.

Contact Sally Bennett, Professional Development Specialist, Georgia Association of Educators, 100 Crescent Centre Parkway, Suite 500, Tucker, GA 30084-7049. *E-mail:* sally.bennett@gae.org. *Phone:* 678-837-1103. *Web site:* www.gae.org.

Georgia Leveraging Educational Assistance Partnership Grant Program. Based on financial need. Recipients must be eligible for the Federal Pell Grant. Renewable award for Georgia residents enrolled in a state postsecondary institution. Must be U.S. citizen. *Award:* Grant for use in freshman, sophomore, junior, or senior year; renewable. *Award amount:* $370. *Number of awards:* 3000–3500. *Eligibility Requirements:* Applicant must be enrolled or expecting to enroll full or part-time at a two-year, four-year, or technical institution or university; resident of Georgia and studying in Georgia. Available to U.S. citizens. *Application Requirements:* Application, financial need analysis. **Deadline:** continuous.

Contact William Flook, Director of Scholarships and Grants, Georgia Student Finance Commission, 2082 East Exchange Place, Suite 100, Tucker, GA 30084. *Phone:* 770-724-9050. *Fax:* 770-724-9031. *Web site:* www.gsfc.org.

Georgia National Guard Service Cancelable Loan Program. Forgivable loans will be awarded to residents of Georgia maintaining good military standing as an eligible member of the Georgia National Guard who are enrolled at least half-time in an undergraduate degree program at an eligible college, university or technical school within the state of Georgia. *Award:* Forgivable loan for use in freshman, sophomore, junior, or senior year; not renewable. *Award amount:* $150–$1395. *Number of awards:* 200–250. *Eligibility Requirements:* Applicant must be enrolled or expecting to enroll full or part-time at a two-year, four-year, or technical institution or university; resident of Georgia and studying in Georgia. Available to U.S. citizens. Applicant must have served in the Air Force National Guard or Army National Guard. *Application Requirements:* Application, financial need analysis. **Deadline:** continuous.

Contact Peggy Matthews, Manager/GSFA Originations, State of Georgia, 2082 East Exchange Place, Suite 230, Tucker, GA 30084-5305. *E-mail:* peggy@mail.gsfc.state.ga.us. *Phone:* 770-724-9230. *Fax:* 770-724-9263. *Web site:* www.gsfc.org.

Georgia PROMISE Teacher Scholarship Program. Renewable, forgivable loans for junior undergraduates at Georgia colleges who have been accepted for enrollment into a teacher education program leading to initial certification. Minimum cumulative 3.0 GPA required. Recipient must teach at a Georgia public school for one year for each $1500 awarded. Available to seniors for renewal only. Write for deadlines. *Academic/Career Areas:* Education. *Award:* Forgivable loan for use in junior or senior year; renewable. *Award amount:* $3000–$6000. *Number of awards:* 700–1400. *Eligibility Requirements:* Applicant must be enrolled or expecting to enroll full or part-time at a four-year institution or university and studying in Georgia. Applicant must have 3.0 GPA or higher. Available to U.S. citizens. *Application Requirements:* Application, transcript. **Deadline:** continuous.

Contact Stan DeWitt, Manager of Teacher Scholarships, Georgia Student Finance Commission, 2082 East Exchange Place, Suite 100, Tucker, GA 30084. *Phone:* 770-724-9060. *Fax:* 770-724-9031. *Web site:* www.gsfc.org.

Georgia Public Safety Memorial Grant/Law Enforcement Personnel Department Grant. Award for children of Georgia law enforcement officers, prison guards, or fire fighters killed or permanently disabled in the line of duty. Must attend an accredited postsecondary Georgia school. Complete the Law Enforcement Personnel Dependents application. *Award:* Grant for use in freshman, sophomore, junior, or senior year; renewable. *Award amount:* $2000. *Number of awards:* 20–40. *Eligibility Requirements:* Applicant must be enrolled or expecting to enroll full-time at a two-year, four-year, or technical institution or university; resident of Georgia and studying in Georgia. Applicant or parent of applicant must have employment or volunteer experience in police/firefighting. Available to U.S. citizens. *Application Requirements:* Application. **Deadline:** continuous.

Contact William Flook, Director of Scholarships and Grants Division, Georgia Student Finance Commission, 2082 East Exchange Place, Suite 100, Tucker, GA 30084. *Phone:* 770-724-9050. *Fax:* 770-724-9031. *Web site:* www.gsfc.org.

Georgia Tuition Equalization Grant (GTEG). Award for Georgia residents pursuing undergraduate study at an accredited two- or four-year Georgia private institution. Complete the Georgia Student Grant Application. Award is $1045 per academic year. Deadlines vary. *Award:* Grant for use in freshman, sophomore, junior, or senior year; renewable. *Award amount:* $1045. *Number of awards:* 25,000–32,000. *Eligibility Requirements:* Applicant must be enrolled or expecting to enroll full-time at a two-year or four-year institution or university; resident of Georgia and studying in Georgia. Available to U.S. citizens. *Application Requirements:* Application. **Deadline:** continuous.

Contact William Flook, Director of Scholarships and Grants Division, Georgia Student Finance Commission, 2082 East Exchange Place, Suite 100, Tucker, GA 30084. *Phone:* 770-724-9050. *Fax:* 770-724-9031. *Web site:* www.gsfc.org.

Governor's Scholarship—Georgia. Award to assist students selected as Georgia scholars, STAR students, valedictorians, and salutatorians. For use at two- and four-year colleges and universities in Georgia. Recipients are selected as entering freshmen. Renewable award of up to $1575. Minimum 3.5 GPA required. *Award:* Scholarship for use in freshman, sophomore, junior, or senior year; renewable. *Award amount:* up to $1575. *Number of awards:* 2000–3000. *Eligibility Requirements:* Applicant must be high school student; planning to enroll or expecting to enroll full-time at a two-year or four-year institution or university; resident of Georgia and studying in Georgia. Applicant must have 3.5 GPA or higher. Available to U.S. citizens. *Application Requirements:* Application, transcript. **Deadline:** continuous.

Contact William Flook, Director of Scholarships and Grants Division, Georgia Student Finance Commission, 2082 East Exchange Place, Suite 100, Tucker, GA 30084. *Phone:* 770-724-9050. *Fax:* 770-724-9031. *Web site:* www.gsfc.org.

HOPE—Helping Outstanding Pupils Educationally. Grant program for Georgia residents who are college undergraduates to attend an accredited two- or four-year Georgia institution. Tuition and fees may be covered by the grant. Minimum 3.0 GPA required. Renewable if student maintains grades and reapplies. Write for deadlines. *Award:* Scholarship for use in freshman, sophomore, junior, or senior year; renewable. *Award amount:* $300–$3000. *Number of awards:* 140,000–170,000. *Eligibility Requirements:* Applicant must be enrolled or expecting to enroll full or part-time at a two-year or four-year institution or university; resident of Georgia and studying in Georgia. Applicant must have 3.0 GPA or higher. Available to U.S. citizens. *Application Requirements:* Application. **Deadline:** continuous.

Contact William Flook, Director of Scholarships and Grants Division, Georgia Student Finance Commission, 2082 East Exchange Place, Suite 100, Tucker, GA 30084. *Phone:* 770-724-9050. *Fax:* 770-724-9031. *Web site:* www.gsfc.org.

Intellectual Capital Partnership Program, ICAPP. Forgivable loans will be awarded to undergraduate students who are residents of Georgia studying high-tech related fields at a Georgia institution. Repayment for every $2500 that is awarded is one-year service in a high-tech field in Georgia. Can be enrolled in a certificate or degree program. *Academic/Career Areas:* Trade/Technical Specialties. *Award:* Forgivable loan for use in freshman, sophomore, junior, or senior year; not renewable. *Award amount:* $7000–$10,000. *Number of awards:* up to 328. *Eligibility Requirements:* Applicant must be enrolled or expecting to enroll full or part-time at a two-year or four-year institution or university; resident of Georgia and studying in Georgia. Available to U.S. citizens. *Application Requirements:* Application, financial need analysis. **Deadline:** continuous.

Contact Peggy Matthews, Manager/GSFA Originations, State of Georgia, 2082 East Exchange Place, Suite 230, Tucker, GA 30084-5305. *E-mail:* peggy@mail.gsfc.state.ga.us. *Phone:* 770-724-9230. *Fax:* 770-724-9263. *Web site:* www.gsfc.org.

Ladders in Nursing Career Service Cancelable Loan Program. Forgivable loans of $3,000 are awarded to students who agree to serve for one calendar year at an approved site within the state of Georgia. Eligible applicants will be residents of Georgia who are studying nursing at a Georgia institution. *Academic/Career Areas:* Nursing. *Award:* Forgivable loan for use in freshman, sophomore, junior, senior, or graduate year; not renewable. *Award amount:* $3000. *Eligibility Requirements:* Applicant must be enrolled or expecting to enroll full or part-time at a two-year, four-year, or technical institution or university; resident of Georgia and studying in Georgia. Available to U.S. citizens. *Application Requirements:* Application, financial need analysis. **Deadline:** continuous.

Contact Peggy Matthews, Manager/GSFA Originations, State of Georgia, 2082 East Exchange Place, Suite 230, Tucker, GA 30084-5305. *E-mail:* peggy@mail.gsfc.state.ga.us. *Phone:* 770-724-9230. *Fax:* 770-724-9263. *Web site:* www.gsfc.org.

Northeast Georgia Pilot Nurse Service Cancelable Loan. Up to 100 forgivable loans between $2,500 and $4,500 will be awarded to undergraduate students who are residents of Georgia studying nursing at a four-year school in Georgia. Loans can be repaid by working as a nurse in northeast Georgia. *Academic/Career Areas:* Nursing. *Award:* Forgivable loan for use in freshman, sophomore, junior, or senior year; not renewable. *Award amount:* $2500–$4500. *Number of awards:* up to 100. *Eligibility Requirements:* Applicant must be enrolled or expecting to enroll full or part-time at a four-year institution; resident of Georgia and studying in Georgia. Available to U.S. citizens. *Application Requirements:* Application, financial need analysis. **Deadline:** continuous.

Contact Peggy Matthews, Manager/GSFA Originations, State of Georgia, 2082 East Exchange Place, Suite 230, Tucker, GA 30084-5305. *E-mail:* peggy@mail.gsfc.state.ga.us. *Phone:* 770-724-9230. *Fax:* 770-724-9263. *Web site:* www.gsfc.org.

Registered Nurse Service Cancelable Loan Program. Forgivable loans will be awarded to undergraduate students who are residents of Georgia studying nursing in a two-year or four-year school in Georgia. Loans can be repaid by working as a registered nurse in the state of Georgia. *Academic/Career Areas:* Nursing. *Award:* Forgivable loan for use in freshman, sophomore, junior, or senior year; not renewable. *Award amount:* $200–$4500. *Eligibility Requirements:* Applicant must be enrolled or expecting to enroll full or part-time at a two-year or four-year institution; resident of Georgia and studying in Georgia. Available to U.S. citizens. *Application Requirements:* Application, financial need analysis. **Deadline:** continuous.

Contact Peggy Matthews, Manager/GSFA Originations, State of Georgia, 2082 East Exchange Place, Suite 230, Tucker, GA 30084-5305. *E-mail:* peggy@mail.gsfc.state.ga.us. *Phone:* 770-724-9230. *Fax:* 770-724-9263. *Web site:* www.gsfc.org.

Robert C. Byrd Honors Scholarship-Georgia. Complete the application provided by the Georgia Department of Education. Renewable awards for outstanding graduating Georgia high school seniors to be used for full-time undergraduate study at eligible U.S. institution. *Award:* Scholarship for use in freshman, sophomore, junior, or senior year; renewable. *Award amount:* $1500. *Number of awards:* 600–700. *Eligibility Requirements:* Applicant must be high school student; planning to enroll or expecting to enroll full-time at a two-year or four-year institution or university and resident of Georgia. Available to U.S. citizens. *Application Requirements:* Application, transcript. **Deadline:** April 1.

Contact William Flook, Director of Scholarships and Grants Division, Georgia Student Finance Commission, 2082 East Exchange Place, Suite 100, Tucker, GA 30084. *Phone:* 770-724-9050. *Fax:* 770-724-9031. *Web site:* www.gsfc.org.

Service-Cancelable Stafford Loan-Georgia. To assist Georgia students enrolled in critical fields of study in allied health (e.g., nursing, physical therapy). For use at GSFA-approved schools. $3500 forgivable loan for dentistry students only. Contact school financial aid officer for more details. *Academic/Career Areas:* Dental Health/Services; Health and Medical Sciences; Nursing. *Award:* Forgivable loan for use in freshman, sophomore, junior, senior, or graduate year; not renewable. *Award amount:* $2000–$4500. *Number of awards:* 500–1200. *Eligibility Requirements:* Applicant must be enrolled or expecting to enroll full or part-time at a two-year, four-year, or technical institution or university; resident of Georgia and studying in Georgia. Available to U.S. citizens. *Application Requirements:* Application, financial need analysis. **Deadline:** continuous.

Contact Peggy Matthews, Manager/GSFA Originations, State of Georgia, 2082 East Exchange Place, Suite 230, Tucker, GA 30084-5305. *E-mail:* peggy@mail.gsfc.state.ga.us. *Phone:* 770-724-9230. *Fax:* 770-724-9263. *Web site:* www.gsfc.org.

HAWAII

Hawaii State Student Incentive Grant. Grants are given to residents of Hawaii who are enrolled in a Hawaiian state school. Funds are for undergraduate tuition only. Applicants must submit a financial need analysis. *Award:* Grant for use in freshman, sophomore, junior, or senior year; renewable. *Eligibility Requirements:* Applicant must be enrolled or expecting to enroll full or part-time at a two-year or four-year institution or university; resident of Hawaii and studying in Hawaii. Available to U.S. citizens. *Application Requirements:* Financial need analysis.

Contact Jo Ann Yoshida, Financial Aid Specialist, Hawaii State Postsecondary Education Commission, University of Hawaii at Manoa, Honolulu, HI 96822. *E-mail:* iha@hawaii.edu. *Phone:* 808-956-6066. *Web site:* www.hern.hawaii.edu.

IDAHO

Education Incentive Loan Forgiveness Contract-Idaho. Renewable award assists Idaho residents enrolling in teacher education or nursing programs within state.

Must rank in top 15% of high school graduating class, have a 3.0 GPA or above, and agree to work in Idaho for two years. Deadlines vary. Contact financial aid office at institution of choice. *Academic/Career Areas:* Education; Nursing. *Award:* Forgivable loan for use in freshman, sophomore, junior, or senior year; renewable. *Number of awards:* 29. *Eligibility Requirements:* Applicant must be enrolled or expecting to enroll full-time at a four-year institution or university; resident of Idaho and studying in Idaho. Applicant must have 3.0 GPA or higher. Available to U.S. citizens. *Application Requirements:* Application, test scores, transcript.

Contact Financial Aid Office, Idaho State Board of Education. *Web site:* www.idahoboardofed.org.

Idaho Minority and "At Risk" Student Scholarship. Renewable award for Idaho residents who are disabled or members of a minority group and have financial need. Must attend one of eight postsecondary institutions in the state for undergraduate study. Deadlines vary by institution. Must be a U.S. citizen and be a graduate of an Idaho high school. Contact college financial aid office. *Award:* Scholarship for use in freshman, sophomore, junior, or senior year; renewable. *Award amount:* $3000. *Number of awards:* 38–40. *Eligibility Requirements:* Applicant must be enrolled or expecting to enroll full-time at a two-year or four-year institution or university; resident of Idaho and studying in Idaho. Available to U.S. citizens. *Application Requirements:* Application, financial need analysis.

Contact Financial Aid Office, Idaho State Board of Education. *Web site:* www.idahoboardofed.org.

Idaho Promise Category A Scholarship Program. Renewable award available to Idaho residents who are graduating high school seniors. Must attend an approved Idaho college full-time. Based on class rank (must be verified by school official), GPA, and ACT scores. Professional-technical student applicants must take COMPASS. *Award:* Scholarship for use in freshman, sophomore, junior, or senior year; renewable. *Award amount:* $3000. *Number of awards:* 25–30. *Eligibility Requirements:* Applicant must be high school student; planning to enroll or expecting to enroll full-time at a two-year, four-year, or technical institution or university; resident of Idaho and studying in Idaho. Applicant must have 3.5 GPA or higher. Available to U.S. citizens. *Application Requirements:* Application, test scores. **Deadline:** December 15.

Contact Lynn Humphrey, Scholarship Assistant, Idaho State Board of Education, PO Box 83720, Boise, ID 83720-0037. *E-mail:* lhumphre@osbe.state.id.us. *Phone:* 208-332-1574. *Fax:* 208-334-2632. *Web site:* www.idahoboardofed.org.

Idaho Promise Category B Scholarship Program. Available to Idaho residents entering college for the first time prior to the age of 22. Must have completed high school or its equivalent in Idaho and have a minimum GPA of 3.0 or an ACT score of 20 or higher. Renewable one time only. *Award:* Scholarship for use in freshman or sophomore year; renewable. *Award amount:* $500. *Eligibility Requirements:* Applicant must be age 22 or under; enrolled or expecting to enroll full-time at a two-year, four-year, or technical institution or university; resident of Idaho and studying in Idaho. Applicant must have 3.0 GPA or higher. Available to U.S. citizens. *Application Requirements:* Application. **Deadline:** continuous.

Contact Lynn Humphrey, Academic Program Coordinator, Idaho State Board of Education, PO Box 83720, Boise, ID 83720-0037. *Phone:* 208-332-1574. *Fax:* 208-334-2632. *Web site:* www.idahoboardofed.org.

Leveraging Educational Assistance State Partnership Program (LEAP). One-time award assists students attending participating Idaho colleges and universities majoring in any field except theology or divinity. Idaho residence is not required, but must be U.S. citizen or permanent resident. Must show financial need. Application deadlines vary by institution. *Award:* Grant for use in freshman, sophomore, junior, or senior year; not renewable. *Award amount:* up to $5000. *Eligibility Requirements:* Applicant must be enrolled or expecting to enroll full or part-time at a two-year or four-year institution or university and studying in Idaho. Available to U.S. citizens. *Application Requirements:* Application, financial need analysis, self-addressed stamped envelope.

Contact Lynn Humphrey, Academic Program Coordinator, Idaho State Board of Education, PO Box 83720, Boise, ID 83720-0037. *Phone:* 208-332-1574. *Fax:* 208-334-2632. *Web site:* www.idahoboardofed.org.

ILLINOIS

Golden Apple Scholars of Illinois. Between 75 and 100 forgivable loans are given to undergraduate students. Loans are $7,000 a year for 4 years. Applicants must be between 17 and 21 and carry a minimum GPA of 2.5. Eligible applicants will be residents of Illinois who are studying in Illinois. The deadline is December 1. Recipients must agree to teach in high-need Illinois schools. *Academic/Career Areas:* Education. *Award:* Forgivable loan for use in freshman, sophomore, junior, or senior year; renewable. *Award amount:* $7000. *Number of awards:* 75–100. *Eligibility Requirements:* Applicant must be age 17-21; enrolled or expecting to enroll full-time at a four-year institution or university; resident of Illinois and studying in Illinois. Applicant must have 2.5 GPA or higher. Available to U.S. citizens. *Application Requirements:* Application, autobiography, essay, interview, photo, references, test scores, transcript. **Deadline:** December 1.

Contact Pat Kilduff, Director of Recruitment and Placement, Golden Apple Foundation, 8 South Michigan Avenue, Suite 700, Chicago, IL 60603-3318. *E-mail:* patnk@goldenapple.org. *Phone:* 312-407-0006 Ext. 105. *Fax:* 312-407-0344. *Web site:* www.goldenapple.org.

Grant Program for Dependents of Police, Fire, or Correctional Officers. Award for dependents of police, fire, and corrections officers killed or disabled in line of duty. Provides for tuition and fees at approved Illinois institutions. Must be resident of Illinois. Continuous deadline. Provide proof of status. *Award:* Grant for use in freshman, sophomore, junior, senior, graduate, or postgraduate years; renewable. *Award amount:* $3000–$4000. *Number of awards:* 50–55. *Eligibility Requirements:* Applicant must be enrolled or expecting to enroll at a two-year, four-year, or technical institution or university; resident of Illinois and studying in Illinois. Applicant or parent of applicant must have employment or volunteer experience in police/firefighting. Available to U.S. and non-U.S. citizens. *Application Requirements:* Application, proof of status. **Deadline:** continuous.

Contact David Barinholtz, Client Information, Illinois Student Assistance Commission (ISAC), 1755 Lake Cook Road, Deerfield, IL 60015-5209. *E-mail:* cssupport@isac.org. *Phone:* 847-948-8500 Ext. 2385. *Web site:* www.isac-online.org.

Higher Education License Plate Program—HELP. Need-based grants for students at institutions participating in program whose funds are raised by sale of special license plates commemorating the institutions. Deadline: June 30. Must be Illinois resident. *Award:* Grant for use in freshman, sophomore, junior, or senior year; not renewable. *Award amount:* up to $2000. *Number of awards:* 175–200. *Eligibility Requirements:* Applicant must be enrolled or expecting to enroll full or part-time at a two-year or four-year institution or university; resident of Illinois and studying in Illinois. Available to U.S. and non-U.S. citizens. *Application Requirements:* Financial need analysis. **Deadline:** June 30.

Contact David Barinholtz, Client Information, Illinois Student Assistance Commission (ISAC), 1755 Lake Cook Road, Deerfield, IL 60015-5209. *E-mail:* cssupport@isac.org. *Phone:* 847-948-8500 Ext. 2385. *Web site:* www.isac-online.org.

Illinois College Savings Bond Bonus Incentive Grant Program. Program offers holders of Illinois College Savings Bonds a $20 grant for each year of bond maturity payable upon bond redemption if at least 70% of proceeds are used to attend college in Illinois. May not be used by students attending religious or divinity schools. *Award:* Grant for use in freshman, sophomore, junior, senior, graduate, or postgraduate years; not renewable. *Award amount:* $40–$220. *Number of awards:* 1200–1400. *Eligibility Requirements:* Applicant must be enrolled or expecting to enroll full or part-time at a two-year, four-year, or technical institution or university and studying in Illinois. Available to U.S. and non-U.S. citizens. *Application Requirements:* Application. **Deadline:** continuous.

Contact David Barinholtz, Client Information, Illinois Student Assistance Commission (ISAC), 1755 Lake Cook Road, Deerfield, IL 60015-5209. *E-mail:* cssupport@isac.org. *Phone:* 847-948-8500 Ext. 2385. *Web site:* www.isac-online.org.

Illinois Incentive for Access Program. Award for eligible first-time freshmen enrolling in approved Illinois institutions. One-time grant of up to $500 may be used for any educational expense. Deadline: October 1. *Award:* Grant for use in freshman year; not renewable. *Award amount:* $300–$500. *Number of awards:* 19,000–22,000. *Eligibility Requirements:* Applicant must be enrolled or expecting to enroll full or part-time at a two-year, four-year, or technical institution or university; resident of Illinois and studying in Illinois. Available to U.S. and non-U.S. citizens. *Application Requirements:* Financial need analysis. **Deadline:** October 1.

Contact David Barinholtz, Client Information, Illinois Student Assistance Commission (ISAC), 1755 Lake Cook Road, Deerfield, IL 60015-5209. *E-mail:* cssupport@isac.org. *Phone:* 847-948-8500 Ext. 2385. *Web site:* www.isac-online.org.

Illinois Monetary Award Program. Award for eligible students attending Illinois public universities, private colleges and universities, community colleges, and some proprietary institutions. Applicable only to tuition and fees. Based on financial need. Deadline: October 1. *Award:* Grant for use in freshman, sophomore, junior, or senior year; not renewable. *Award amount:* $300–$4320. *Number of awards:* 135,000–145,000. *Eligibility Requirements:* Applicant must be enrolled or expecting to enroll full or part-time at a two-year, four-year, or technical institution or university; resident of Illinois and studying in Illinois. Available to U.S. and non-U.S. citizens. *Application Requirements:* Financial need analysis. **Deadline:** October 1.

Contact David Barinholtz, Client Information, Illinois Student Assistance Commission (ISAC), 1755 Lake Cook Road, Deerfield, IL 60015-5209. *E-mail:* cssupport@isac.org. *Phone:* 847-948-8500 Ext. 2385. *Web site:* www.isac-online.org.

Illinois National Guard Grant Program. Award for qualified National Guard personnel which pays tuition and fees at Illinois public universities and community colleges. Must provide documentation of service. Deadline: September 15. *Award:* Grant for use in freshman, sophomore, junior, or senior year; renewable. *Award amount:* $1300–$1700. *Number of awards:* 2000–3000. *Eligibility Requirements:* Applicant must be enrolled or expecting to enroll full or part-time at a two-year or four-year institution or university; resident of Illinois and studying in Illinois. Available to U.S. and non-U.S. citizens. Applicant must have served in the Air Force

National Guard or Army National Guard. *Application Requirements:* Application, documentation of service. **Deadline:** September 15.

Contact David Barinholtz, Client Information, Illinois Student Assistance Commission (ISAC), 1755 Lake Cook Road, Deerfield, IL 60015-5209. *E-mail:* cssupport@isac.org. *Phone:* 847-948-8500 Ext. 2385. *Web site:* www.isac-online.org.

Illinois Student-to-Student Program of Matching Grants. Award provides matching funds for need-based grants at participating Illinois public universities and community colleges. Deadline: October 1. *Award:* Grant for use in freshman, sophomore, junior, or senior year; not renewable. *Award amount:* $300–$500. *Number of awards:* 2000–4000. *Eligibility Requirements:* Applicant must be enrolled or expecting to enroll full or part-time at a two-year or four-year institution or university; resident of Illinois and studying in Illinois. Available to U.S. and non-U.S. citizens. *Application Requirements:* Financial need analysis. **Deadline:** October 1.

Contact David Barinholtz, Client Information, Illinois Student Assistance Commission (ISAC), 1755 Lake Cook Road, Deerfield, IL 60015-5209. *E-mail:* cssupport@isac.org. *Phone:* 847-948-8500 Ext. 2385. *Web site:* www.isac-online.org.

Illinois Veteran Grant Program—IVG. Award for qualified veterans for tuition and fees at Illinois public universities and community colleges. Must provide documentation of service (DD214). Deadline is continuous. *Award:* Grant for use in freshman, sophomore, junior, or senior year; renewable. *Award amount:* $1400–$1600. *Number of awards:* 11,000–13,000. *Eligibility Requirements:* Applicant must be enrolled or expecting to enroll full or part-time at a two-year or four-year institution or university; resident of Illinois and studying in Illinois. Available to U.S. and non-U.S. citizens. Applicant must have general military experience. *Application Requirements:* Application, documentation of service. **Deadline:** continuous.

Contact David Barinholtz, Client Information, Illinois Student Assistance Commission (ISAC), 1755 Lake Cook Road, Deerfield, IL 60015-5209. *E-mail:* cssupport@isac.org. *Phone:* 847-948-8500 Ext. 2385. *Web site:* www.isac-online.org.

ITEACH Teacher Shortage Scholarship Program. Award to assist Illinois students planning to teach at an Illinois pre-school, elementary school, or high school in a teacher shortage discipline. Must agree to teach one year in teacher shortage area for each year of award assistance received. Deadline: May 1. *Academic/Career Areas:* Education; Special Education. *Award:* Forgivable loan for use in freshman, sophomore, junior, senior, or graduate year; not renewable. *Award amount:* $4000–$5000. *Number of awards:* 500–600. *Eligibility Requirements:* Applicant must be enrolled or expecting to enroll full or part-time at a two-year or four-year institution or university; resident of Illinois and studying in Illinois. Applicant must have 2.5 GPA or higher. Available to U.S. and non-U.S. citizens. *Application Requirements:* Application, transcript. **Deadline:** May 1.

Contact Dave Barinholtz, Client Information, Illinois Student Assistance Commission (ISAC), 1755 Lake Cook Road, Deerfield, IL 60015-5209. *E-mail:* cssupport@isac.org. *Phone:* 847-948-8500 Ext. 2385. *Web site:* www.isac-online.org.

Merit Recognition Scholarship (MRS) Program. Award for Illinois high school seniors graduating in the top 5% of their class and attending Illinois postsecondary institution. Deadline: June 15. Contact for application procedures. *Award:* Scholarship for use in freshman year; not renewable. *Award amount:* $900–$1000. *Number of awards:* 5000–6000. *Eligibility Requirements:* Applicant must be high school student; planning to enroll or expecting to enroll full or part-time at a two-year or four-year institution or university; resident of Illinois and studying in Illinois. Applicant must have 3.5 GPA or higher. Available to U.S. and non-U.S. citizens. *Application Requirements:* Application. **Deadline:** June 15.

Contact David Barinholtz, Client Information, Illinois Student Assistance Commission (ISAC), 1755 Lake Cook Road, Deerfield, IL 60015-5209. *E-mail:* cssupport@isac.org. *Phone:* 847-948-8500 Ext. 2385. *Web site:* www.isac-online.org.

MIA/POW Scholarships. One-time award for spouse, child, or step-child of veterans who are missing in action or were a prisoner of war. Must be enrolled at a state-supported school in Illinois. Candidate must be U.S. citizen. Must apply and be accepted before beginning of school. Also for children and spouses of veterans who are determined to be 100% disabled as established by the Veterans Administration. *Award:* Scholarship for use in freshman, sophomore, junior, senior, or graduate year; renewable. *Eligibility Requirements:* Applicant must be enrolled or expecting to enroll full or part-time at a two-year or four-year institution or university; resident of Illinois and studying in Illinois. Available to U.S. citizens. Applicant or parent must meet one or more of the following requirements: general military experience; retired from active duty; disabled or killed as a result of military service; prisoner of war; or missing in action. *Application Requirements:* Application. **Deadline:** continuous.

Contact Ms. Tracy Mahan, Grants Section, Illinois Department of Veterans' Affairs, 833 South Spring Street, Springfield, IL 62794-9432. *Phone:* 217-782-3564. *Fax:* 217-782-4161.

Minority Teachers of Illinois Scholarship Program. Award for minority students planning to teach at an approved Illinois preschool, elementary, or secondary school. Deadline: May 1. Must be Illinois resident. *Academic/Career Areas:* Education; Special Education. *Award:* Forgivable loan for use in freshman, sophomore, junior, senior, graduate, or postgraduate years; renewable. *Award amount:* $4000–$5000. *Number of awards:* 450–550. *Eligibility Requirements:* Applicant must be American Indian/Alaska Native, Asian/Pacific Islander, Black (non-Hispanic), or Hispanic; enrolled or expecting to enroll full-time at a two-year or four-year institution or university; resident of Illinois and studying in Illinois. Applicant must have 2.5 GPA or higher. Available to U.S. and non-U.S. citizens. *Application Requirements:* Application. **Deadline:** May 1.

Contact David Barinholtz, Client Information, Illinois Student Assistance Commission (ISAC), 1755 Lake Cook Road, Deerfield, IL 60015-5209. *E-mail:* cssupport@isac.org. *Phone:* 847-948-8500 Ext. 2385. *Web site:* www.isac-online.org.

Veterans' Children Educational Opportunities. Award is provided to each child age 18 or younger of a veteran who died or became totally disabled as a result of service during World War I, World War II, Korean, or Vietnam War. Must be an Illinois resident and studying in Illinois. Death must be service-connected. Disability must be rated 100% for two or more years. *Award:* Grant for use in freshman year; not renewable. *Award amount:* up to $250. *Eligibility Requirements:* Applicant must be age 10-18; enrolled or expecting to enroll at an institution or university; resident of Illinois and studying in Illinois. Available to U.S. citizens. Applicant or parent must meet one or more of the following requirements: general military experience; retired from active duty; disabled or killed as a result of military service; prisoner of war; or missing in action. *Application Requirements:* Application. **Deadline:** June 30.

Contact Ms. Tracy Mahan, Grants Section, Illinois Department of Veterans' Affairs, 833 South Spring Street, Springfield, IL 62794-9432. *Phone:* 217-782-3564. *Fax:* 217-782-4161.

INDIANA

Child of Disabled Veteran Grant or Purple Heart Recipient Grant. Free tuition at Indiana state-supported colleges or universities for children of disabled veterans or Purple Heart recipients. Must submit Form DD214 or service record. *Award:* Grant for use in freshman, sophomore, junior, or senior year; renewable. *Eligibility Requirements:* Applicant must be enrolled or expecting to enroll full or part-time at a two-year or four-year institution or university; resident of Indiana and studying in Indiana. Available to U.S. citizens. Applicant or parent must meet one or more of the following requirements: general military experience; retired from active duty; disabled or killed as a result of military service; prisoner of war; or missing in action. *Application Requirements:* Application. **Deadline:** continuous.

Contact Jon Brinkley, State Service Officer, Indiana Department of Veterans' Affairs, 302 West Washington Street, Room E-120, Indianapolis, IN 46204-2738. *E-mail:* jbrinkley@dva.state.in.us. *Phone:* 317-232-3910. *Fax:* 317-232-7721. *Web site:* www.ai.org/veteran/index.html.

Department of Veterans Affairs Free Tuition for Children of POW/MIA's in Vietnam. Renewable award for residents of Indiana who are the children of veterans declared missing in action or prisoner-of-war after January 1, 1960. Provides tuition at Indiana state-supported institutions for undergraduate study. *Award:* Grant for use in freshman, sophomore, junior, or senior year; renewable. *Eligibility Requirements:* Applicant must be enrolled or expecting to enroll at a two-year or four-year institution or university; resident of Indiana and studying in Indiana. Available to U.S. citizens. Applicant or parent must meet one or more of the following requirements: general military experience; retired from active duty; disabled or killed as a result of military service; prisoner of war; or missing in action. *Application Requirements:* Application. **Deadline:** continuous.

Contact Jon Brinkley, State Service Officer, Indiana Department of Veterans' Affairs, 302 West Washington Street, Room E-120, Indianapolis, IN 46204-2738. *E-mail:* jbrinkley@dva.state.in.us. *Phone:* 317-232-3910. *Fax:* 317-232-7721. *Web site:* www.ai.org/veteran/index.html.

Hoosier Scholar Award. The Hoosier Scholar Award is a $500 nonrenewable award. Based on the size of the senior class, one to three scholars are selected by the guidance counselor(s). The award is based on academic merit and may be used for any educational expense at an eligible Indiana institution of higher education. *Award:* Scholarship for use in freshman year; not renewable. *Award amount:* $500. *Number of awards:* 790–840. *Eligibility Requirements:* Applicant must be high school student; planning to enroll or expecting to enroll full-time at a two-year or four-year institution or university; resident of Indiana and studying in Indiana. Applicant must have 3.5 GPA or higher. Available to U.S. citizens. *Application Requirements:* **Deadline:** March 1.

Contact Ms. Ada Sparkman, Program Coordinator, State Student Assistance Commission of Indiana (SSACI), 150 West Market Street, Suite 500, Indianapolis, IN 46204-2805. *Phone:* 317-232-2350. *Fax:* 317-232-3260. *Web site:* www.ssaci.in.gov.

Indiana Freedom of Choice Grant. The Freedom of Choice Grant is a need-based, tuition-restricted program for students attending Indiana private institutions seeking a first undergraduate degree. It is awarded in addition to the Higher Education Award. Students (and parents of dependent students) who are U.S. citizens and Indiana residents must file the FAFSA yearly by the March 10 deadline. *Award:* Grant for use in freshman, sophomore, junior, or senior year; not renewable.

Award amount: $200–$3906. *Number of awards:* 10,000–11,830. *Eligibility Requirements:* Applicant must be enrolled or expecting to enroll full-time at a four-year institution or university; resident of Indiana and studying in Indiana. Available to U.S. citizens. *Application Requirements:* Application, financial need analysis, FAFSA. **Deadline:** March 10.

Contact Grant Counselor, State Student Assistance Commission of Indiana (SSACI), 150 West Market Street, Suite 500, Indianapolis, IN 46204-2805. *E-mail:* grants@ssaci.state.in.us. *Phone:* 317-232-2350. *Fax:* 317-232-3260. *Web site:* www.ssaci.in.gov.

Indiana Higher Education Award. The Higher Education Award is a need-based, tuition-restricted program for students attending Indiana public, private or proprietary institutions seeking a first undergraduate degree. Students (and parents of dependent students) who are U.S. citizens and Indiana residents must file the FAFSA yearly by the March 10 deadline. *Award:* Grant for use in freshman, sophomore, junior, or senior year; not renewable. *Award amount:* $200–$4734. *Number of awards:* 38,000–43,660. *Eligibility Requirements:* Applicant must be enrolled or expecting to enroll full-time at a two-year, four-year, or technical institution or university; resident of Indiana and studying in Indiana. Available to U.S. citizens. *Application Requirements:* Application, financial need analysis, FAFSA. **Deadline:** March 10.

Contact Grant Counselors, State Student Assistance Commission of Indiana (SSACI), 150 West Market Street, Suite 500, Indianapolis, IN 46204-2805. *E-mail:* grants@ssaci.state.in.us. *Phone:* 317-232-2350. *Fax:* 317-232-3260. *Web site:* www.ssaci.in.gov.

Indiana Minority Teacher and Special Education Services Scholarship Program. For Black or Hispanic students seeking teaching certification or for students seeking special education teaching certification or occupational or physical therapy certification. Must be a U.S. citizen and Indiana resident enrolled full-time at an eligible Indiana institution. Must teach in an Indiana-accredited elementary or secondary school after graduation. Contact institution for application and deadline. Minimum 2.0 GPA required. *Academic/Career Areas:* Education; Special Education; Therapy/Rehabilitation. *Award:* Scholarship for use in freshman, sophomore, junior, or senior year; not renewable. *Award amount:* $1000–$4000. *Number of awards:* 330–370. *Eligibility Requirements:* Applicant must be Black (non-Hispanic) or Hispanic; enrolled or expecting to enroll full-time at a four-year institution or university; resident of Indiana and studying in Indiana. Available to U.S. citizens. *Application Requirements:* Application, financial need analysis. **Deadline:** continuous.

Contact Ms. Yvonne Heflin, Director, Special Programs, State Student Assistance Commission of Indiana (SSACI), 150 West Market Street, Suite 500, Indianapolis, IN 46204-2805. *E-mail:* grants@ssaci.state.un.is. *Phone:* 317-232-2350. *Fax:* 317-232-3260. *Web site:* www.ssaci.in.gov.

Indiana National Guard Supplemental Grant. One-time award, which is a supplement to the Indiana Higher Education Grant program. Applicants must be members of the Indiana National Guard. All Guard paperwork must be completed prior to the start of each semester. The FAFSA must be received by March 10. Award covers tuition and fees at select public colleges. *Award:* Grant for use in freshman, sophomore, junior, or senior year; not renewable. *Award amount:* $200–$5314. *Number of awards:* 350–870. *Eligibility Requirements:* Applicant must be enrolled or expecting to enroll full or part-time at a two-year or four-year institution or university; resident of Indiana and studying in Indiana. Available to

U.S. citizens. Applicant must have served in the Air Force National Guard or Army National Guard. *Application Requirements:* Application, financial need analysis. **Deadline:** March 10.

Contact Grants Counselor, State Student Assistance Commission of Indiana (SSACI), 150 West Market Street, Suite 500, Indianapolis, IN 46204-2805. *E-mail:* grants@ssaci.state.in.us. *Phone:* 317-232-2350. *Fax:* 317-232-2360. *Web site:* www.ssaci.in.gov.

Indiana Nursing Scholarship Fund. Need-based tuition funding for nursing students enrolled full- or part-time at an eligible Indiana institution. Must be an Indiana resident and have a minimum 2.0 GPA or meet the minimum requirements for the nursing program. Upon graduation, recipients must practice as a nurse in an Indiana health care setting for two years. *Academic/Career Areas:* Nursing. *Award:* Scholarship for use in freshman, sophomore, junior, or senior year; not renewable. *Award amount:* $200–$5000. *Number of awards:* 510–690. *Eligibility Requirements:* Applicant must be enrolled or expecting to enroll full or part-time at a two-year or four-year institution or university; resident of Indiana and studying in Indiana. Available to U.S. citizens. *Application Requirements:* Application, financial need analysis. **Deadline:** continuous.

Contact Ms. Yvonne Heflin, Director, Special Programs, State Student Assistance Commission of Indiana (SSACI), 150 West Market Street, Suite 500, Indianapolis, IN 46204-2805. *Phone:* 317-232-2350. *Fax:* 317-232-3260. *Web site:* www.ssaci.in.gov.

Indiana Wildlife Federation Scholarship. A $1000 scholarship will be awarded to an Indiana resident accepted for the study or already enrolled for the study of resource conservation or environmental education at the undergraduate level. For more details see web site: http://www.indianawildlife.org. *Academic/Career Areas:* Natural Resources. *Award:* Scholarship for use in sophomore, junior, or senior year; not renewable. *Award amount:* $1000. *Eligibility Requirements:* Applicant must be enrolled or expecting to enroll at an institution or university and resident of Indiana. Available to U.S. citizens. *Application Requirements:* Application. **Deadline:** April 30.

Contact application available at web site, Indiana Wildlife Federation Endowment. *Web site:* indianawildlife.org.

Part-time Grant Program. Program is designed to encourage part-time undergraduates to start and complete their associate or baccalaureate degrees or certificates by subsidizing part-time tuition costs. It is a term-based award that is based on need. State residency requirements must be met and a FAFSA must be filed. Eligibility is determined at the institutional level subject to approval by SSACI. *Award:* Grant for use in freshman, sophomore, junior, or senior year; not renewable. *Award amount:* $50–$4000. *Number of awards:* 4000–6366. *Eligibility Requirements:* Applicant must be enrolled or expecting to enroll part-time at a two-year, four-year, or technical institution or university; resident of Indiana and studying in Indiana. Available to U.S. citizens. *Application Requirements:* Application, financial need analysis. **Deadline:** continuous.

Contact Grant Division, State Student Assistance Commission of Indiana (SSACI), 150 West Market Street, Suite 500, Indianapolis, IN 46204-2805. *E-mail:* grants@ssaci.state.in.us. *Phone:* 317-232-2350. *Fax:* 317-232-3260. *Web site:* www.ssaci.in.gov.

Police Corps Incentive Scholarship. Forgivable loans are available to highly qualified men and women entering the Police Corps. Up to $7500 a year can be used to cover the expenses of study toward a baccalaureate or graduate degree. For more details and an application see web site: http://www.in.gov/cji.policecorps. *Academic/Career Areas:* Criminal Justice/Criminology. *Award:* Forgivable loan for use in freshman, sophomore, junior, senior, or graduate year; renewable. *Award amount:* up to $7500. *Eligibility Requirements:* Applicant must be enrolled or expecting to enroll at an institution or university. Available to U.S. citizens. *Application Requirements:* Application, driver's license, references, transcript. **Deadline:** continuous.

Contact application available at web site, Indiana Police Corps. *Web site:* www.state.in.us/cji/policecorps.

Scholarships for Dependents of Fallen Officers. Scholarships are available to the dependents of officers who have been killed in the line of duty. For more details and an application see web site: http://www.in.gov/cji/policecorps. **Award:** Scholarship for use in freshman, sophomore, junior, or senior year; renewable. *Award amount:* up to $30,000. *Eligibility Requirements:* Applicant must be enrolled or expecting to enroll at an institution or university. Applicant or parent of applicant must have employment or volunteer experience in police/firefighting. Available to U.S. citizens. *Application Requirements:* Application. **Deadline:** continuous.

Contact application available at web site, Indiana Police Corps. *Web site:* www.state.in.us/cji/policecorps.

Twenty-first Century Scholars Award. Income-eligible 7th graders who enroll in the program fulfill a pledge of good citizenship and complete the Affirmation Form are guaranteed tuition for four years at any participating public institution. If the student attends a private institution, the state will award an amount comparable to that of a public institution. If the student attends a participating proprietary school, the state will award a tuition scholarship equal to that of Ivy Tech State College. FAFSA and affirmation form must be filed yearly by March 10. Applicant must be resident of Indiana. *Award:* Scholarship for use in freshman, sophomore, junior, or senior year; not renewable. *Award amount:* $1000–$5314. *Number of awards:* 2800–8100. *Eligibility Requirements:* Applicant must be enrolled or expecting to enroll full-time at a two-year, four-year, or technical institution or university; resident of Indiana and studying in Indiana. Applicant must have 2.5 GPA or higher. Available to U.S. citizens. *Application Requirements:* Application, financial need analysis, affirmation form. **Deadline:** March 10.

Contact Twenty-first Century Scholars Program Counselors, State Student Assistance Commission of Indiana (SSACI), 150 West Market Street, Suite 500, Indianapolis, IN 46204-2805. *Phone:* 317-233-2100. *Fax:* 317-232-3260. *Web site:* www.ssaci.in.gov.

IOWA

Governor Terry E. Branstad Iowa State Fair Scholarship. Up to four scholarships ranging from $500 to $1000 will be awarded to students graduating from an Iowa high school. Must actively participate at the Iowa State Fair. For more details see web site: http://www.iowacollegeaid.org. **Award:** Scholarship for use in freshman year; not renewable. *Award amount:* $500–$1000. *Number of awards:* up to 4. *Eligibility Requirements:* Applicant must be high school student; planning to enroll or expecting to enroll at an institution or university; resident of Iowa and studying in Iowa. Available to U.S. citizens. *Application Requirements:* Application, essay, financial need analysis, references, transcript. **Deadline:** May 1.

Contact Julie Leeper, Director, State Student Aid Programs, Iowa College Student Aid Commission, 200 10th Street, 4th Floor, Des Moines, IA 50309-3609. *E-mail:* icsac@max.state.ia.us. *Phone:* 515-242-3370. *Fax:* 515-242-3388. *Web site:* www.iowacollegeaid.org.

Iowa Foster Child Grants. Grants renewable up to four years will be awarded to students graduating from an Iowa high school who are in Iowa foster care under the care and custody of the Iowa Department of Human Service. Must have a minimum GPA of 2.25 and have applied to an accredited Iowa college or university. For more details see web site: http://www.iowacollegeaid.org. **Award:** Grant for use in freshman year; renewable. *Award amount:* $2000–$4200. *Eligibility Requirements:* Applicant must be high school student; planning to enroll or expecting to enroll at a two-year or four-year institution or university; resident of Iowa and studying in Iowa. Available to U.S. citizens. *Application Requirements:* Application. **Deadline:** April 15.

Contact Julie Leeper, Director, State Student Aid Programs, Iowa College Student Aid Commission, 200 10th Street, 4th Floor, Des Moines, IA 50309-3609. *E-mail:* icsac@max.state.ia.us. *Phone:* 515-242-3370. *Fax:* 515-242-3388. *Web site:* www.iowacollegeaid.org.

Iowa Grants. Statewide need-based program to assist high-need Iowa residents. Recipients must demonstrate a high level of financial need to receive awards ranging from $100 to $1,000. Awards are prorated for students enrolled for less than full-time. Awards must be at Iowa postsecondary institutions. *Award:* Grant for use in freshman, sophomore, junior, or senior year; not renewable. *Award amount:* $100–$1000. *Eligibility Requirements:* Applicant must be enrolled or expecting to enroll full or part-time at a two-year, four-year, or technical institution or university; resident of Iowa and studying in Iowa. Available to U.S. citizens. *Application Requirements:* Application, financial need analysis. **Deadline:** continuous.

Contact Julie Leeper, Director, State Student Aid Programs, Iowa College Student Aid Commission, 200 10th Street, 4th Floor, Des Moines, IA 50309-3609. *E-mail:* icsac@max.state.ia.us. *Phone:* 515-242-3370. *Fax:* 515-242-3388. *Web site:* www.iowacollegeaid.org.

Iowa National Guard Education Assistance Program. Program provides postsecondary tuition assistance to members of Iowa National Guard Units. Must study at a postsecondary institution in Iowa. Contact for additional information. *Award:* Grant for use in freshman, sophomore, junior, or senior year; not renewable. *Award amount:* up to $1200. *Eligibility Requirements:* Applicant must be enrolled or expecting to enroll full or part-time at a two-year, four-year, or technical institution or university; resident of Iowa and studying in Iowa. Available to U.S. citizens. Applicant must have served in the Air Force National Guard or Army National Guard. *Application Requirements:* Application. **Deadline:** continuous.

Contact Julie Leeper, Director, State Student Aid Programs, Iowa College Student Aid Commission, 200 10th Street, 4th Floor, Des Moines, IA 50309-3609. *E-mail:* icsac@max.state.ia.us. *Phone:* 515-242-3370. *Fax:* 515-242-3388. *Web site:* www.iowacollegeaid.org.

Iowa Teacher Forgivable Loan Program. Forgivable loan assists students who will teach in Iowa secondary schools. Must be an Iowa resident attending an Iowa postsecondary institution. Contact for additional information. *Academic/Career Areas:* Education. *Award:* Forgivable loan for use in freshman, sophomore, junior, or senior year; not renewable. *Award amount:* $2686. *Eligibility Requirements:* Applicant must be enrolled or expecting to enroll full or part-time at a four-year institution or university; resident of Iowa and studying in Iowa. Applicant or parent of applicant must have employment or volunteer experience in teaching. Available to U.S. citizens. *Application Requirements:* Application, financial need analysis. **Deadline:** continuous.

Contact Brenda Easter, Special Programs Administrator, Iowa College Student Aid Commission, 200 10th Street, 4th Floor, Des Moines, IA 50309-3609. *E-mail:* icsac@max.state.ia.us. *Phone:* 515-242-3380. *Fax:* 515-242-3388. *Web site:* www.iowacollegeaid.org.

Iowa Tuition Grant Program. Program assists students who attend independent postsecondary institutions in Iowa. Iowa residents currently enrolled, or planning to enroll, for at least three semester hours at one of the eligible Iowa postsecondary institutions may apply. Awards currently range from $100 to $4000. Grants may not exceed the difference between independent college and university tuition and fees and the average tuition and fees at the three public Regent universities. *Award:* Grant for use in freshman, sophomore, junior, or senior year; not renewable. *Award amount:* $100–$4000. *Eligibility Requirements:* Applicant must be enrolled or expecting to enroll full or part-time at a two-year or four-year institution; resident of Iowa and studying in Iowa. Available to U.S. citizens. *Application Requirements:* Application, financial need analysis. **Deadline:** July 1.

Contact Julie Leeper, Director, State Student Aid Programs, Iowa College Student Aid Commission, 200 10th Street, 4th Floor, Des Moines, IA 50309-3609. *E-mail:* icsac@max.state.ia.us. *Phone:* 515-242-3370. *Fax:* 515-242-3388. *Web site:* www.iowacollegeaid.org.

Iowa Vocational Rehabilitation. Provides vocational rehabilitation services to individuals with disabilities who need these services in order to maintain, retain, or obtain employment compatible with their disabilities. Must be Iowa resident. *Award:* Grant for use in freshman, sophomore, junior, senior, graduate, or postgraduate years; renewable. *Award amount:* $500–$4000. *Number of awards:* up to 5000. *Eligibility Requirements:* Applicant must be enrolled or expecting to enroll full or part-time at a two-year, four-year, or technical institution or university and resident of Iowa. Applicant must be hearing impaired, learning disabled, physically disabled, or visually impaired. Available to U.S. and non-U.S. citizens. *Application Requirements:* Application, interview. **Deadline:** continuous.

Contact Ralph Childers, Policy and Workforce Initiatives Coordinator, Iowa Division of Vocational Rehabilitation Services, Division of Vocational Rehabilitation Services, 510 East 12th Street, Des Moines, IA 50319. *E-mail:* rchilders@dvrs.state.ia.us. *Phone:* 515-281-4151. *Fax:* 515-281-4703. *Web site:* www.dvrs.state.ia.us.

Iowa Vocational-Technical Tuition Grant Program. Program provides need-based financial assistance to Iowa residents enrolled in career education (vocational-technical), and career option programs at Iowa area community colleges. Grants range from $150 to $650, depending on the length of program, financial need, and available funds. *Award:* Grant for use in freshman or sophomore year; not renewable. *Award amount:* $150–$650. *Eligibility Requirements:* Applicant must be enrolled or expecting to enroll full or part-time at a technical institution; resident of Iowa and studying in Iowa. Available to U.S. citizens. *Application Requirements:* Application, financial need analysis. **Deadline:** July 1.

Contact Julie Leeper, Director, State Student Aid Programs, Iowa College Student Aid Commission, 200 10th Street, 4th Floor, Des Moines, IA 50309-3609. *E-mail:* icsac@max.state.ia.us. *Phone:* 515-242-3370. *Fax:* 515-242-3388. *Web site:* www.iowacollegeaid.org.

State of Iowa Scholarship Program. Program provides recognition and financial honorarium to Iowa's academically talented high school seniors. Honorary scholarships are presented to all qualified candidates. Approximately 1700 top-ranking candidates are designated State of Iowa Scholars every March, from an applicant pool of nearly 5000 high school seniors. Must be used at an Iowa postsecondary institution. Minimum 3.5 GPA required. *Award:* Scholarship for use in freshman year; not renewable. *Award amount:* up to $400. *Number of awards:* up to 1700. *Eligibility Requirements:* Applicant must be high school student; planning to enroll or expecting to enroll full-time at a two-year, four-year, or technical institution or university; resident of Iowa and studying in Iowa. Applicant must have 3.5 GPA or higher. Available to U.S. citizens. *Application Requirements:* Application, test scores. **Deadline:** November 1.

Contact Julie Leeper, Director, State Student Aid Programs, Iowa College Student Aid Commission, 200 10th Street, 4th Floor, Des Moines, IA 50309-3609. *E-mail:* icsac@max.state.ia.us. *Phone:* 515-242-3370. *Fax:* 515-242-3388. *Web site:* www.iowacollegeaid.org.

KANSAS

Ethnic Minority Scholarship Program. This program is designed to assist financially needy, academically competitive students who are identified as members of the following ethnic/racial groups: African-American; American-Indian or Alaskan Native; Asian or Pacific Islander; or Hispanic. Must be resident of Kansas and attend college in Kansas. Application fee is $10. Deadline: May 1. Minimum 3.0 GPA required. Must be U.S. citizen. *Award:* Scholarship for use in freshman, sophomore, junior, or senior year; renewable. *Award amount:* $1850. *Number of awards:* 200–250. *Eligibility Requirements:* Applicant must be American Indian/Alaska Native, Asian/Pacific Islander, Black (non-Hispanic), or Hispanic; enrolled or expecting to enroll full-time at a two-year or four-year institution or university; resident of Kansas and studying in Kansas. Applicant must have 3.0 GPA or higher. Available to U.S. citizens. *Application Requirements:* Application, financial need analysis, test scores, transcript. *Fee:* $10. **Deadline:** May 1.

Contact Diane Lindeman, Director of Student Financial Assistance, Kansas Board of Regents, 1000 Southwest Jackson, Suite 520, Topeka, KS 66612-1368. *E-mail:* dlindeman@ksbor.org. *Phone:* 785-296-3517. *Fax:* 785-296-0983. *Web site:* www.kansasregents.org.

Kansas Comprehensive Grant Program. Grants available for Kansas residents attending public or private baccalaureate colleges or universities in Kansas. Based on financial need. Must file Free Application for Federal Student Aid to apply. Renewable award based on continuing eligibility. Up to $3000 for undergraduate use. Deadline: April 1. *Award:* Grant for use in freshman, sophomore, junior, or senior year; renewable. *Award amount:* $1100–$3000. *Number of awards:* 7000–8200. *Eligibility Requirements:* Applicant must be enrolled or expecting to enroll full-time at a four-year institution or university; resident of Kansas and studying in Kansas. Available to U.S. citizens. *Application Requirements:* Financial need analysis. **Deadline:** April 1.

Contact Diane Lindeman, Director of Student Financial Assistance, Kansas Board of Regents, 1000 Southwest Jackson, Suite 520, Topeka, KS 66612-1368. *E-mail:* dlindeman@ksbor.org. *Phone:* 785-296-3517. *Fax:* 785-296-0983. *Web site:* www.kansasregents.org.

Kansas Educational Benefits for Children of MIA, POW, and Deceased Veterans of the Vietnam War. Full-tuition scholarship awarded to students who are children of veterans. Must show proof of parent's status as missing in action, prisoner of war, or killed in action in the Vietnam War. Kansas residence required of veteran at time of entry to service. Must attend a state-supported postsecondary school. *Award:* Scholarship for use in freshman, sophomore, junior, or senior year; not renewable. *Eligibility Requirements:* Applicant must be enrolled or expecting to enroll at a two-year, four-year, or technical institution or university and studying in Kansas. Available to U.S. citizens. Applicant or parent must meet one or more of the following requirements: general military experience; retired from active duty; disabled or killed as a result of military service; prisoner of war; or missing in action. *Application Requirements:* Application, report of casualty, birth certificate, school acceptance letter. **Deadline:** continuous.

Contact Dave DePue, Program Director, Kansas Commission on Veterans Affairs, 700 Southwest Jackson, Jayhawk Tower, #701, Topeka, KS 66603. *E-mail:* kcva004@ink.org. *Phone:* 785-291-3422. *Fax:* 785-296-1462. *Web site:* www.kcva.org.

Kansas National Guard Educational Assistance Award Program. Service scholarship for enlisted soldiers in the Kansas National Guard. Pays up to 100% of tuition and fees based on funding. Must attend a state-supported institution. Recipients will be required to serve in the KNG for four years after the last payment of state tuition assistance. Must not have over 15 years of service at time of application. Deadlines are January 15 and August 20. Contact KNG Education Services Specialist for further information. Must be Kansas resident. *Award:* Scholarship for use in freshman, sophomore, junior, or senior year; not renewable. *Award amount:* $250–$3500. *Number of awards:* up to 400. *Eligibility Requirements:* Applicant must be enrolled or expecting to enroll full or part-time at a two-year, four-year, or technical institution or university; resident of Kansas and studying in Kansas. Available to U.S. citizens. Applicant must have served in the Air Force National Guard or Army National Guard. *Application Requirements:* Application.

Contact Steve Finch, Education Services Specialist, Kansas National Guard Educational Assistance Program, Attn: AGKS-DOP-ESO, The Adjutant General of Kansas, 2800 South West Topeka Boulevard, Topeka, KS 66611-1287. *E-mail:* steve.finch@ks.ngb.army.mil. *Phone:* 785-274-1060. *Fax:* 785-274-1617.

Kansas Nursing Service Scholarship Program. This program is designed to encourage Kansans to enroll in nursing programs and commit to practicing in Kansas. Recipients sign agreements to practice nursing at specific facilities one year for each year of support. Application fee is $10. Deadline: May 1. *Academic/Career Areas:* Nursing. *Award:* Forgivable loan for use in freshman, sophomore, junior, or senior year; renewable. *Award amount:* $2500–$3500. *Number of awards:* 100–200. *Eligibility Requirements:* Applicant must be enrolled or expecting to enroll full-time at a two-year or four-year institution or university; resident of Kansas and studying in Kansas. Available to U.S. citizens. *Application Requirements:* Application, financial need analysis, sponsor agreement form. *Fee:* $10. **Deadline:** May 1.

Contact Diane Lindeman, Director of Student Financial Assistance, Kansas Board of Regents, 1000 Southwest Jackson, Suite 520, Topeka, KS 66612-1368. *E-mail:* dlindeman@ksbor.org. *Phone:* 785-296-3517. *Fax:* 785-296-0983. *Web site:* www.kansasregents.org.

Kansas State Scholarship Program. The Kansas State Scholarship Program provides assistance to financially needy, academically outstanding students who attend Kansas postsecondary institutions. Must be Kansas resident. Minimum 3.0 GPA required for renewal. Application fee is $10. Deadline: May 1. *Award:* Scholarship for use in freshman, sophomore, junior, or senior year; renewable. *Award amount:* $1000. *Number of awards:* 1000–1500. *Eligibility Requirements:* Applicant must be enrolled or expecting to enroll full-time at a two-year or four-year institution or university; resident of Kansas and studying in Kansas. Applicant must have 3.0 GPA or higher. Available to U.S. citizens. *Application Requirements:* Application, financial need analysis, test scores, transcript. *Fee:* $10. **Deadline:** May 1.

Contact Diane Lindeman, Director of Student Financial Assistance, Kansas Board of Regents, 1000 Southwest Jackson, Suite 520, Topeka, KS 66612-1368. *E-mail:* dlindeman@ksbor.org. *Phone:* 785-296-3517. *Fax:* 785-296-0983. *Web site:* www.kansasregents.org.

Kansas Teacher Service Scholarship. Several scholarships for Kansas residents pursuing teaching careers. Must teach in a hard-to-fill discipline or underserved area of the state of Kansas for one year for each award received. Renewable award of $5000. Application fee is $10. Deadline: May 1. Must be U.S. citizen. *Academic/Career Areas:* Education. *Award:* Forgivable loan for use in freshman, sophomore, junior, or senior year; renewable. *Award amount:* $5000. *Number of awards:* 60–80. *Eligibility Requirements:* Applicant must be enrolled or expecting to enroll full-time at a two-year or four-year institution or university; resident of Kansas and studying in Kansas. Applicant must have 3.0 GPA or higher. Available to U.S. citizens. *Application Requirements:* Application, references, test scores, transcript. *Fee:* $10. **Deadline:** May 1.

Contact Diane Lindeman, Director of Student Financial Assistance, Kansas Board of Regents, 1000 Southwest Jackson, Suite 520, Topeka, KS 66612-1368. *E-mail:* dlindeman@ksbor.org. *Phone:* 785-296-3517. *Fax:* 785-296-0983. *Web site:* www.kansasregents.org.

Vocational Education Scholarship Program—Kansas. Several scholarships for Kansas residents who graduated from a Kansas accredited high school. Must be enrolled in a vocational education program at an eligible Kansas institution. Based on ability and aptitude. Deadline is July 1. Renewable award of $500. Must be U.S. citizen. *Academic/Career Areas:* Trade/Technical Specialties. *Award:* Scholarship for use in freshman or sophomore year; renewable. *Award amount:* $500. *Number of awards:* 100–200. *Eligibility Requirements:* Applicant must be enrolled or expecting to enroll full-time at a two-year or technical institution; resident of Kansas and studying in Kansas. Available to U.S. citizens. *Application Requirements:* Application, test scores. **Deadline:** July 1.

Contact Diane Lindeman, Director of Student Financial Assistance, Kansas Board of Regents, 1000 Southwest Jackson, Suite 520, Topeka, KS 66612-1368. *E-mail:* dlindeman@ksbor.org. *Phone:* 785-296-3517. *Fax:* 785-296-0983. *Web site:* www.kansasregents.org.

KENTUCKY

College Access Program (CAP) Grant. Award for U.S. citizen and Kentucky resident with no previous college degree. Provides $53 per semester hour for a minimum of six hours per semester. Applicants seeking degrees in religion are not eligible. Must demonstrate financial need and submit Free Application for Federal Student Aid. Priority deadline is March 15. *Award:* Grant for use in freshman, sophomore, junior, or senior year; not renewable. *Award amount:* up to $1260. *Number of awards:* 30,000–35,000. *Eligibility Requirements:* Applicant must be enrolled or expecting to enroll full or part-time at a two-year, four-year, or technical institution or university; resident of Kentucky and studying in Kentucky. Available to U.S. citizens. *Application Requirements:* Financial need analysis. **Deadline:** continuous.

Contact Allan Osborne, Program Coordinator, Kentucky Higher Education Assistance Authority (KHEAA), PO Box 798, Frankfort, KY 40602-0798. *E-mail:* aosborne@kheaa.com. *Phone:* 502-696-7394. *Fax:* 502-696-7373. *Web site:* www.kheaa.com.

Department of VA Tuition Waiver—KY KRS 164-515. Award provides exemption from tuition for spouse or child of permanently disabled member of the National Guard, war veteran, prisoner of war, or member of the Armed Services missing in action. Disability must have been sustained while in service; if not, time of service must have been during wartime. Applicant is eligible for 36 months of training, training until receipt of degree, or training until 23rd birthday, whichever comes first. There is no age limit for spouse. Must attend a school funded by the KY Dept. of Ed. *Award:* Scholarship for use in freshman, sophomore, junior, or senior year; renewable. *Eligibility Requirements:* Applicant must be enrolled or expecting to enroll at an institution or university; resident of Kentucky and studying in Kentucky. Available to U.S. citizens. Applicant or parent must meet one or more of the following requirements: general military experience; retired from active duty; disabled or killed as a result of military service; prisoner of war; or missing in action. *Application Requirements:* Application. **Deadline:** continuous.

Contact John Kramer, Coordinator, Kentucky Department of Veterans Affairs, 545 South Third Street, Room 123, Louisville, KY 40202-9095. *E-mail:* john.kramer@mail.state.ky.us. *Phone:* 502-595-4447. *Fax:* 502-595-4448. *Web site:* www.lrc.state.ky.us.

Department of Veterans Affairs Tuition Waiver—Kentucky KRS 164-505. Award provides exemption from matriculation or tuition fees for dependents, widows or widowers of members of the armed forces or members of the National Guard killed while in service or having died as a result of a service-connected disability incurred while serving during a wartime period. Veteran's home of record upon entry into the Armed Forces must have been KY. Applicant is eligible to get undergraduate/graduate degrees. Must attend a state-supported postsecondary institution. *Award:* Scholarship for use in freshman, sophomore, junior, senior, or graduate year; renewable. *Eligibility Requirements:* Applicant must be enrolled or expecting to enroll full or part-time at an institution or university; resident of Kentucky and studying in Kentucky. Available to U.S. citizens. Applicant or parent must meet one or more of the following requirements: general military experience; retired from active duty; disabled or killed as a result of military service; prisoner of war; or missing in action. *Application Requirements:* Application, proof of relationship. **Deadline:** continuous.

Contact John Kramer, Coordinator, Kentucky Department of Veterans Affairs, 545 South Third Street, Room 123, Louisville, KY 40202-9095. *E-mail:* john. kramer@mail.state.ky.us. *Phone:* 502-595-4447. *Fax:* 502-595-4448. *Web site:* www.lrc.state.ky.us.

Department of Veterans Affairs Tuition Waiver—KY 164-512. Award provides waiver of tuition for child of a veteran, regardless of age, who has acquired a disability as a direct result of service, as a member of the National Guard or Reserve Component. Must have served on state active duty, active duty for training, or inactive duty training or active duty with the Armed Forces. Veteran must have been a resident of Kentucky. *Award:* Scholarship for use in freshman, sophomore, junior, or senior year; renewable. *Eligibility Requirements:* Applicant must be enrolled or expecting to enroll full-time at a two-year, four-year, or technical institution or university; resident of Kentucky and studying in Kentucky. Available to U.S. citizens. Applicant or parent must meet one or more of the following requirements: general military experience; retired from active duty; disabled or killed as a result of military service; prisoner of war; or missing in action. *Application Requirements:* Application, proof of relationship. **Deadline:** continuous.

Contact John Kramer, Coordinator, Kentucky Department of Veterans Affairs, 545 South Third Street, Room 123, Louisville, KY 40202-9095. *E-mail:* john. kramer@mail.state.ky.us. *Phone:* 502-595-4447. *Fax:* 502-595-4448. *Web site:* www.lrc.state.ky.us.

Department of Veterans Affairs Tuition Waiver—KY KRS 164-507. Award provides exemption from matriculation or tuition fee for spouse or child of deceased veteran who served during wartime. Applicant is eligible for 36 months of training, or training until they receive a degree, or training until their 23rd birthday, whichever comes first. There is no age limit for spouse. Must attend a Kentucky state-supported university, junior college or vocational training institution. Must be a Kentucky resident. *Award:* Scholarship for use in freshman, sophomore, junior, or senior year; renewable. *Eligibility Requirements:* Applicant must be enrolled or expecting to enroll full or part-time at a two-year, four-year, or technical institution or university; resident of Kentucky and studying in Kentucky. Available to U.S. citizens. Applicant or parent must meet one or more of the following requirements: general military experience; retired from active duty; disabled or killed as a result of military service; prisoner of war; or missing in action. *Application Requirements:* Application. **Deadline:** continuous.

Contact John Kramer, Coordinator, Kentucky Department of Veterans Affairs, 545 South Third Street, Room 123, Louisville, KY 40202-9095. *E-mail:* john. kramer@mail.state.ky.us. *Phone:* 502-595-4447. *Fax:* 502-595-4448. *Web site:* www.lrc.state.ky.us.

Environmental Protection Scholarships. Renewable awards for college juniors, seniors, and graduate students for tuition, fees, and room and board at a Kentucky state university. Awards of $3500 to $4500 per semester for up to four semesters. Minimum 2.5 GPA required. Must agree to work full-time for the Kentucky Natural Resources and Environmental Protection Cabinet upon graduation. Interview is required. *Academic/Career Areas:* Chemical Engineering; Civil Engineering; Earth Science; Materials Science, Engineering and Metallurgy. *Award:* Forgivable loan for use in junior, senior, or graduate year; renewable. *Award amount:* $3500–$4500. *Number of awards:* 3–5. *Eligibility Requirements:* Applicant must be enrolled or expecting to enroll full-time at a four-year institution or university and studying in Kentucky. Applicant must have 2.5 GPA or higher. Available to U.S. and non-U.S.

citizens. *Application Requirements:* Application, essay, interview, references, transcript, non-U.S. citizens must have valid work permit. **Deadline:** February 15.

Contact James Kipp, Scholarship Program Coordinator, Kentucky Natural Resources and Environmental Protection Cabinet, 233 Mining/Mineral Resources Building, Lexington, KY 40506-0107. *E-mail:* kipp@uky.edu. *Phone:* 859-257-1299. *Fax:* 859-323-1049. *Web site:* www.uky.edu/waterresources.

Kentucky Department of Vocational Rehabilitation. Kentucky Department of Vocational Rehabilitation provides services necessary to secure employment. Eligible individual must possess physical or mental impairment that results in a substantial impediment to employment; benefit from vocational rehabilitation services in terms of an employment outcome; and require vocational rehabilitation services to prepare for, enter, or retain employment. *Award:* Grant for use in freshman, sophomore, junior, senior, graduate, or postgraduate years; renewable. *Eligibility Requirements:* Applicant must be enrolled or expecting to enroll full or part-time at a two-year, four-year, or technical institution or university and resident of Kentucky. Applicant must be learning disabled or physically disabled. *Application Requirements:* Application, financial need analysis, interview, test scores, transcript. **Deadline:** continuous.

Contact Ms. Marian Spencer, Program Administrator, Kentucky Department of Vocational Rehabilitation, 209 St. Clair Street, Frankfort, KY 40601. *E-mail:* marianu.spencer@mail.state.ky.us. *Phone:* 502-564-4440. *Fax:* 502-564-6745. *Web site:* www.ihdi.uky.edu/.

Kentucky Educational Excellence Scholarship (KEES). Annual award based on GPA and highest ACT or SAT score received by high school graduation. Awards are renewable if required cumulative GPA maintained at a Kentucky postsecondary school. Must be a Kentucky resident. *Award:* Scholarship for use in freshman, sophomore, junior, or senior year; renewable. *Award amount:* $125–$2000. *Number of awards:* 40,000–50,000. *Eligibility Requirements:* Applicant must be high school student; planning to enroll or expecting to enroll full or part-time at a two-year, four-year, or technical institution or university; resident of Kentucky and studying in Kentucky. Applicant must have 2.5 GPA or higher. Available to U.S. citizens. *Application Requirements:* Test scores, transcript.

Contact Tim Phelps, KEES Program Coordinator, Kentucky Higher Education Assistance Authority (KHEAA), PO Box 798, Frankfort, KY 40602-0798. *E-mail:* tphelps@kheaa.com. *Phone:* 502-696-7397. *Fax:* 502-696-7373. *Web site:* www.kheaa.com.

Kentucky National Guard Tuition Award Program. Tuition award available to all members of the Kentucky National Guard. Award is for study at state institutions. Members must be in good standing to be eligible for awards. Applications deadlines are April 1 and October 1. Completed AGO-18-7 required. Undergraduate study given priority. *Award:* Scholarship for use in freshman, sophomore, junior, or senior year; not renewable. *Eligibility Requirements:* Applicant must be enrolled or expecting to enroll full or part-time at a two-year, four-year, or technical institution or university and studying in Kentucky. Available to U.S. citizens. Applicant must have served in the Air Force National Guard or Army National Guard. *Application Requirements:* AGO-18-7.

Contact Annette Michelle Kelley, Administration Specialist, Kentucky National Guard, Education Office, 100 Minuteman Parkway, Frankfort, KY 40601. *Phone:* 502-607-1039. *Fax:* 502-607-1264. *Web site:* www.dma.state.ky.us.

Kentucky Teacher Scholarship Program. Award for Kentucky resident attending Kentucky institutions and pursuing initial teacher certification. Must teach one semester for each semester of award received. In critical shortage areas, must teach one semester for every two semesters of award received. Repayment obligation if teaching requirement not met. Submit Free Application for Federal Student Aid and Teacher Scholarship Application by May 1. *Academic/Career Areas:* Education; Special Education. *Award:* Forgivable loan for use in freshman, sophomore, junior, senior, or graduate year; not renewable. *Award amount:* $100–$5000. *Number of awards:* 600–700. *Eligibility Requirements:* Applicant must be enrolled or expecting to enroll full-time at a two-year or four-year institution or university; resident of Kentucky and studying in Kentucky. Available to U.S. citizens. *Application Requirements:* Application, financial need analysis. **Deadline:** May 1.

Contact Pam Polly, Program Coordinator, Kentucky Higher Education Assistance Authority (KHEAA), PO Box 798, Frankfort, KY 40602-0798. *E-mail:* ppolly@kheaa.com. *Phone:* 502-696-7392. *Fax:* 502-696-7373. *Web site:* www.kheaa.com.

Kentucky Transportation Cabinet Civil Engineering Scholarship Program. Scholarships are available to eligible applicants at 4 ABET-accredited universities in Kentucky. Our mission is to continually pursue statewide recruitment and retention of bright, motivated civil engineers in the Kentucky Transportation Cabinet. *Academic/Career Areas:* Civil Engineering. *Award:* Scholarship for use in freshman, sophomore, junior, senior, or graduate year; renewable. *Award amount:* $7200–$8000. *Number of awards:* 15–20. *Eligibility Requirements:* Applicant must be enrolled or expecting to enroll full-time at an institution or university; resident of Kentucky and studying in Kentucky. Available to U.S. citizens. *Application Requirements:* Application, essay, interview, references, test scores, transcript. **Deadline:** March 1.

Contact Jo Anne Tingle, Scholarship Program Manager, Kentucky Transportation Cabinet, Attn: Scholarship Coordinator, State Office Building, 501 High Street, Room 913, Frankfort, KY 40622. *E-mail:* jo.tingle@mail.state.ky.us. *Phone:* 877-273-5222. *Fax:* 502-564-6683. *Web site:* www.kytc.state.ky.us/person/ ScholarshipProgram.htm.

Kentucky Tuition Grant (KTG). Available to Kentucky residents who are full-time undergraduates at an independent college within the state. Must not be enrolled in a religion program. Based on financial need. Submit Free Application for Federal Student Aid. Priority deadline is March 15. *Award:* Grant for use in freshman, sophomore, junior, or senior year; not renewable. *Award amount:* $50–$1800. *Number of awards:* 9000–10,000. *Eligibility Requirements:* Applicant must be enrolled or expecting to enroll full-time at a two-year or four-year institution or university; resident of Kentucky and studying in Kentucky. Available to U.S. citizens. *Application Requirements:* Financial need analysis. **Deadline:** continuous.

Contact Allan Osborne, Program Coordinator, Kentucky Higher Education Assistance Authority (KHEAA), PO Box 798, Frankfort, KY 40602-0798. *E-mail:* aosborne@kheaa.com. *Phone:* 502-696-7394. *Fax:* 502-696-7373. *Web site:* www.kheaa.com.

Related Service Occupational Therapy/Physical Therapy Scholarship. Must be a Kentucky resident who is seeking related service licensure and enrolled or accepted for enrollment at a participating institution as a full-time student. Recipients who do not fulfill requirements must repay the scholarship with interest. Application deadline is in the spring. *Academic/Career Areas:* Therapy/Rehabilitation. *Award:* Scholarship for use in freshman, sophomore, junior, senior, or graduate year. *Award amount:* up to $6250. *Eligibility Requirements:* Applicant must be enrolled or expecting to enroll full-time at an institution or university; resident of Kentucky and studying in Kentucky. Available to U.S. citizens. *Application Requirements:* Application. .

Contact Mike Miller, Kentucky Department of Veterans Affairs, 500 Mero Street, Capital Plaza Tower, Frankfort, KY 40601. *Phone:* 502-564-4970. *Web site:* www.lrc.state.ky.us.

LOUISIANA

Leveraging Educational Assistance Program (LEAP). LEAP program provides federal and state funds to provide need-based grants to academically qualified students. Individual award determined by Financial Aid Office and governed by number of applicants and availability of funds. File Free Application for Federal Student aid by school deadline to apply each year. For Louisiana students attending Louisiana postsecondary institutions. *Award:* Grant for use in freshman, sophomore, junior, or senior year; not renewable. *Award amount:* $200–$2000. *Number of awards:* 3000. *Eligibility Requirements:* Applicant must be enrolled or expecting to enroll full or part-time at a two-year, four-year, or technical institution or university; resident of Louisiana and studying in Louisiana. Available to U.S. citizens. *Application Requirements:* Application, financial need analysis.

Contact Public Information, Louisiana Office of Student Financial Assistance, PO Box 91202, Baton Rouge, LA 70821-9202. *E-mail:* custserv@osfa.state.la.us. *Phone:* 800-259-5626 Ext. 1012. *Web site:* www.osfa.state.la.us.

Louisiana Department of Veterans Affairs State Aid Program. Tuition exemption at any state-supported college, university or technical institute for children of veterans that are rated 90% or above service-connected disabled by the U.S. Department of Veterans Affairs and surviving spouse and children of veterans that died on active duty, in line of duty or where death was the result of a disability incurred in or aggravated by military service. Applicant must be between the ages of 18-25. For residents of Louisiana that are attending a Louisiana institution. *Award:* Grant for use in freshman, sophomore, junior, senior, graduate, or postgraduate years; renewable. *Eligibility Requirements:* Applicant must be age 18-25; enrolled or expecting to enroll full-time at a two-year, four-year, or technical institution or university; resident of Louisiana and studying in Louisiana. Available to U.S. citizens. Applicant or parent must meet one or more of the following requirements: general military experience; retired from active duty; disabled or killed as a result of military service; prisoner of war; or missing in action. *Application Requirements:* Application. **Deadline:** continuous.

Contact Richard Blackwell, Veterans Affairs Regional Manager, Louisiana Department of Veteran Affairs, PO Box 94095, Capitol Station, Baton Rouge, LA 70804-4095. *E-mail:* rblackwell@vetaffairs.com. *Phone:* 225-922-0500 Ext. 203. *Fax:* 225-922-0511.

Louisiana National Guard State Tuition Exemption Program. Renewable award for college undergraduates to receive tuition exemption upon satisfactory performance in the Louisiana National Guard. Must attend a state-funded institution in Louisiana. Must be a resident and registered voter in Louisiana. Must meet the academic and residency requirements of the university attended. Must provide documentation of Louisiana National Guard enlistment. The exemption can be used for up to 15 semesters. Minimum 2.5 GPA required. *Award:* Scholarship for use in freshman, sophomore, junior, or senior year; renewable. *Eligibility Requirements:* Applicant must be enrolled or expecting to enroll full or part-time at a two-year, four-year, or technical institution or university; resident of Louisiana and studying in Louisiana. Applicant must have 2.5 GPA or higher. Available to U.S. citizens. Applicant must have served in the Air Force National Guard or Army National Guard. *Application Requirements:* **Deadline:** continuous.

Contact Maj. Jona M. Hughes, Education Services Officers, Louisiana National Guard—State of Louisiana, Military Department, Building 35, Jackson Barracks, DHR-MD, New Orleans, LA 70146-0330. *E-mail:* hughesj@la-arng.ngb.army.mil. *Phone:* 504-278-8531 Ext. 8304. *Fax:* 504-278-8025. *Web site:* www.la.ngb.army.mil.

Rockefeller State Wildlife Scholarship. For Louisiana residents attending a public college within the state studying wildlife, forestry, or marine sciences full-time. Renewable up to five years as an undergraduate and two years as a graduate. Must have at least a 2.5 GPA and have taken the ACT or SAT. *Academic/Career Areas:* Animal/Veterinary Sciences; Applied Sciences; Natural Resources. *Award:* Scholarship for use in freshman, sophomore, junior, senior, or graduate year; renewable. *Award amount:* $1000. *Number of awards:* 60. *Eligibility Requirements:* Applicant must be enrolled or expecting to enroll full-time at a four-year institution or university; resident of Louisiana and studying in Louisiana. Applicant must have 2.5 GPA or higher. Available to U.S. citizens. *Application Requirements:* Application, test scores, transcript. **Deadline:** July 1.

Contact Public Information, Louisiana Office of Student Financial Assistance, PO Box 91202, Baton Rouge, LA 70821-9202. *E-mail:* custserv@osfa.state.la.us. *Phone:* 800-259-5626 Ext. 1012. *Fax:* 225-922-0790. *Web site:* www.osfa.state.la.us.

TOPS Alternate Performance Award. Program awards an amount equal to tuition plus a $400 annual stipend to students attending a Louisiana public institution, or an amount equal to the weighted average public tuition plus a $400 annual stipend to students attending a LAICU private institution. Must have a minimum high school GPA of 3.0 based on TOPS core curriculum, ACT score of 24, completion of 10 honors courses graded on a 5.0 scale, and completion of a 16.5 unit core curriculum. Must be a resident of Louisiana. *Award:* Scholarship for use in freshman, sophomore, junior, or senior year; renewable. *Eligibility Requirements:* Applicant must be high school student; planning to enroll or expecting to enroll full-time at a two-year, four-year, or technical institution or university; resident of Louisiana and studying in Louisiana. Applicant must have 3.0 GPA or higher. Available to U.S. citizens. *Application Requirements:* Application, test scores. **Deadline:** July 1.

Contact Public Information Officer, Louisiana Office of Student Financial Assistance, PO Box 91202, Baton Rouge, LA 70821-9202. *E-mail:* custserv@osfa. state.la.us. *Phone:* 800-259-5626 Ext. 1012. *Fax:* 225-922-0790. *Web site:* www.osfa.state.la.us.

TOPS Honors Award. Program awards an amount equal to tuition plus an $800 per year stipend to students attending a Louisiana public institution, or an amount equal to the weighted average public tuition plus an $800 per year stipend to students attending a LAICU private institution. Must have a minimum high school GPA of 3.5 based on TOPS core curriculum, ACT score of 27, and complete a 16.5 unit core curriculum. Must be resident of Louisiana. *Award:* Scholarship for use in freshman, sophomore, junior, or senior year; renewable. *Award amount:* $1294–$3894. *Eligibility Requirements:* Applicant must be high school student; planning to enroll or expecting to enroll full-time at a two-year, four-year, or technical institution or university; resident of Louisiana and studying in Louisiana. Applicant must have 3.5 GPA or higher. Available to U.S. citizens. *Application Requirements:* Application, test scores. **Deadline:** July 1.

Contact Public Information, Louisiana Office of Student Financial Assistance, PO Box 91202, Baton Rouge, LA 70821-9202. *E-mail:* custserv@osfa.state.la.us. *Phone:* 800-259-5626 Ext. 1012. *Fax:* 225-922-0790. *Web site:* www.osfa.state.la.us.

TOPS Opportunity Award. Program awards an amount equal to tuition to students attending a Louisiana public institution, or an amount equal to the weighted average public tuition to students attending a LAICU private institution. Must have a minimum high school GPA of 2.5 based on the TOPS core curriculum, the prior year's state average ACT score, and complete a 16.5 unit core curriculum. Must be a Louisiana resident. *Award:* Scholarship for use in freshman, sophomore, junior, or senior year; renewable. *Award amount:* $494–$3094. *Eligibility Requirements:* Applicant must be high school student; planning to enroll or expecting to enroll full-time at a two-year, four-year, or technical institution or university; resident of Louisiana and studying in Louisiana. Applicant must have 2.5 GPA or higher. Available to U.S. citizens. *Application Requirements:* Application, test scores. **Deadline:** July 1.

Contact Public Information, Louisiana Office of Student Financial Assistance, PO Box 91202, Baton Rouge, LA 70821-9202. *E-mail:* custserv@osfa.state.la.us. *Phone:* 800-259-5626 Ext. 1012. *Fax:* 225-922-0790. *Web site:* www.osfa.state.la.us.

TOPS Performance Award. Program awards an amount equal to tuition plus a $400 annual stipend to students attending a Louisiana public institution, or an amount equal to the weighted average public tuition plus a $400 annual stipend to students attending a LAICU private institution. Must have a minimum high school GPA of 3.5 based on the TOPS core curriculum, an ACT score of 23 and completion of a 16.5 unit core curriculum. Must be a Louisiana resident. *Award:* Scholarship for use in freshman, sophomore, junior, or senior year; renewable. *Award amount:* $894–$3494. *Eligibility Requirements:* Applicant must be high school student; planning to enroll or expecting to enroll full-time at a two-year, four-year, or technical institution or university; resident of Louisiana and studying in Louisiana. Applicant must have 3.5 GPA or higher. Available to U.S. citizens. *Application Requirements:* Application, test scores. **Deadline:** July 1.

Contact Public Information, Louisiana Office of Student Financial Assistance, PO Box 91202, Baton Rouge, LA 70821-9202. *E-mail:* custserv@osfa.state.la.us. *Phone:* 800-259-5626 Ext. 1012. *Fax:* 225-922-0790. *Web site:* www.osfa.state.la.us.

TOPS Tech Award. Program awards an amount equal to tuition for up to two years of technical training at a Louisiana postsecondary institution that offers a vocational or technical education certificate or diploma program, or a non-academic degree program. Must have a 2.5 high school GPA based on TOPS Tech core curriculum, an ACT score of 17 and complete the TOPS-Tech core curriculum. Must be a Louisiana resident. *Award:* Scholarship for use in freshman or sophomore year; renewable. *Award amount:* $494. *Eligibility Requirements:* Applicant must be high school student; planning to enroll or expecting to enroll full-time at a technical institution; resident of Louisiana and studying in Louisiana. Applicant must have 2.5 GPA or higher. Available to U.S. citizens. *Application Requirements:* Application, test scores. **Deadline:** July 1.

Contact Public Information, Louisiana Office of Student Financial Assistance, PO Box 91202, Baton Rouge, LA 70821-9202. *E-mail:* custserv@osfa.state.la.us. *Phone:* 800-259-5626 Ext. 1012. *Fax:* 225-922-0790. *Web site:* www.osfa.state.la.us.

MAINE

Educators for Maine Program. Loans for residents of Maine who are high school seniors, college students, or college graduates with a minimum 3.0 GPA, studying or preparing to study teacher education. Loan is forgivable if student teaches in Maine upon graduation. Awards are based on merit. *Academic/Career Areas:* Education. *Award:* Forgivable loan for use in freshman, sophomore, junior, senior, or graduate year; not renewable. *Award amount:* $1500–$3000. *Eligibility Requirements:* Applicant must be enrolled or expecting to enroll full-time at a two-year or four-year institution or university and resident of Maine. Applicant must have 3.0 GPA or higher. Available to U.S. citizens. *Application Requirements:* Application, essay, test scores, transcript. **Deadline:** April 1.

Contact Trisha Malloy, Program Officer, Finance Authority of Maine, 5 Community Drive, Augusta, ME 04332-0949. *E-mail:* trisha@famemaine.com. *Phone:* 800-228-3734. *Fax:* 207-623-0095. *Web site:* www.famemaine.com.

Maine State Grant. Scholarships for residents of Maine attending an eligible school, full time, in Connecticut, Maine, Massachusetts, New Hampshire, Pennsylvania, Rhode Island, Washington, D.C., or Vermont. Award based on need. Must apply annually. Complete Free Application for Federal Student Aid to apply. One-time award of $500-$1250 for undergraduate study. *Award:* Grant for use in freshman, sophomore, junior, or senior year; not renewable. *Award amount:* $500–$1250. *Number of awards:* 8900–12,500. *Eligibility Requirements:* Applicant must be enrolled or expecting to enroll full-time at a two-year, four-year, or technical institution or university; resident of Maine and studying in Connecticut, District of Columbia, Maine, Massachusetts, New Hampshire, Pennsylvania, Rhode Island, or Vermont. *Application Requirements:* Application, financial need analysis, FAFSA. **Deadline:** May 1.

Contact Claude Roy, Program Officer, Finance Authority of Maine, 5 Community Drive, Augusta, ME 04332-0949. *E-mail:* claude@famemaine.com. *Phone:* 800-228-3734. *Fax:* 207-623-0095. *Web site:* www.famemaine.com.

Quality Child Care Program Education Scholarship Program. Open to residents of Maine who are taking a minimum of one childhood education course or are pursuing a child development associate certificate, associate's degree, baccalaureate degree or post-baccalaureate teacher certification in child care-related fields. Scholarships of up to $500 per course or $2,000 per year available. See web site for information (http://www.famemaine.com). *Academic/Career Areas:* Education. *Award:* Scholarship for use in sophomore, junior, senior, or graduate year; not renewable. *Award amount:* $500–$2000. *Eligibility Requirements:* Applicant must be enrolled or expecting to enroll at a two-year or four-year institution or university and resident of Maine. Available to U.S. citizens. *Application Requirements:* Application, financial need analysis. **Deadline:** continuous.

Contact Trisha Malloy, Program Officer, Finance Authority of Maine, 5 Community Drive, Augusta, ME 04332-0949. *E-mail:* trisha@famemaine.com. *Phone:* 800-228-3734. *Fax:* 207-623-0095. *Web site:* www.famemaine.com.

Tuition Waiver Programs. Provides tuition waivers for children and spouses of EMS personnel, firefighters, and law enforcement officers who have been killed in the line of duty and for students who were foster children under the custody of the Department of Human Services when they graduated from high school. Waivers valid at the University of Maine System, the Maine Technical College System, and Maine Maritime Academy. *Award:* Grant for use in freshman, sophomore, junior, or senior year; not renewable. *Eligibility Requirements:* Applicant must be enrolled or expecting to enroll at an institution or university; resident of Maine and studying in Maine. Applicant or parent of applicant must have employment or volunteer experience in designated career field or police/firefighting. Available to U.S. citizens. *Application Requirements:* Application. **Deadline:** continuous.

Contact Trisha Malloy, Program Officer, Finance Authority of Maine, 5 Community Drive, Augusta, ME 04332. *E-mail:* trisha@famemaine.com. *Phone:* 207-623-3263. *Fax:* 207-623-0095. *Web site:* www.famemaine.com.

Veterans Dependents Educational Benefits-Maine. Tuition waiver award for dependents or spouses of veterans who were prisoner-of-war, missing in action, or permanently disabled as a result of service. Veteran must have been Maine resident at service entry for five years preceding application. For use at Maine University system, technical colleges and Maine Maritime. Must be high school graduate. Must submit birth certificate and proof of VA disability of veteran. Award renewable for eight semesters for those under 22 years of age. *Award:* Scholarship for use in freshman, sophomore, junior, or senior year; renewable. *Eligibility Requirements:* Applicant must be age 21 or under; enrolled or expecting to enroll full or part-time at a technical institution or university; resident of Maine and studying in Maine. Available to U.S. citizens. Applicant or parent must meet one or more of the following requirements: general military experience; retired from active duty; disabled or killed as a result of military service; prisoner of war; or missing in action. *Application Requirements:* Application. **Deadline:** continuous.

Contact Roland Lapointe, Director, Maine Bureau of Veterans Services, State House Station 117, Augusta, ME 04333-0117. *E-mail:* mvs@me.ngb.army.mil. *Phone:* 207-626-4464. *Fax:* 207-626-4471. *Web site:* www.state.me.us.

MARYLAND

Child Care Provider Program-Maryland. Forgivable loan provides assistance for Maryland undergraduates attending a Maryland institution and pursuing studies in a child development program or an early childhood education program. Must serve as a professional day care provider in Maryland for one year for each year award received. Must maintain minimum 2.0 GPA. Contact for further information. *Academic/Career Areas:* Education. *Award:* Forgivable loan for use in freshman, sophomore, junior, or senior year; renewable. *Award amount:* $500–$2000. *Number of awards:* 100–150. *Eligibility Requirements:* Applicant must be enrolled or expecting to enroll full or part-time at a two-year or four-year institution or university; resident of Maryland and studying in Maryland. Available to U.S. citizens. *Application Requirements:* Application, transcript. **Deadline:** June 15.

Contact Margaret Crutchley, Office of Student Financial Assistance, Maryland Higher Education Commission, 839 Bestgate Road, Suite 400, Annapolis, MD 21401-3013. *E-mail:* ofsamail@mhec.state.md.us. *Phone:* 410-260-4545. *Fax:* 410-260-3203. *Web site:* www.mhec.state.md.us.

Delegate Scholarship Program-Maryland. Delegate scholarships help Maryland residents attending Maryland degree-granting institutions, certain career schools, or nursing diploma schools. May attend out-of-state institution if Maryland Higher Education Commission deems major to be unique and not offered at a Maryland institution. Free Application for Federal Student Aid may be required. Students interested in this program should apply by contacting their legislative district delegate. *Award:* Scholarship for use in freshman, sophomore, junior, senior, or graduate year; not renewable. *Award amount:* $200–$12,981. *Number of awards:*

up to 3500. *Eligibility Requirements:* Applicant must be enrolled or expecting to enroll full or part-time at a two-year, four-year, or technical institution or university; resident of Maryland and studying in Maryland. Available to U.S. citizens. *Application Requirements:* Application, financial need analysis. **Deadline:** continuous.

Contact Barbara Fantom, Office of Student Financial Assistance, Maryland Higher Education Commission, 839 Bestgage Road, Suite 400, Annapolis, MD 21401-3013. *E-mail:* osfamail@mhec.state.md.us. *Phone:* 410-260-4547. *Fax:* 410-260-3200. *Web site:* www.mhec.state.md.us.

Developmental Disabilities and Mental Health Workforce Tuition Assistance Program. Provides tuition assistance to students who are service employees that provide direct support or care to individuals with developmental disabilities or mental disorders. Must be a Maryland resident attending a Maryland college. Minimum 2.0 GPA. *Academic/Career Areas:* Health and Medical Sciences; Nursing; Social Services; Special Education; Therapy/Rehabilitation. *Award:* Forgivable loan for use in freshman, sophomore, junior, senior, or graduate year; renewable. *Award amount:* $500–$3000. *Number of awards:* 300–400. *Eligibility Requirements:* Applicant must be enrolled or expecting to enroll full or part-time at a two-year or four-year institution or university; resident of Maryland and studying in Maryland. Applicant or parent of applicant must have employment or volunteer experience in designated career field. Available to U.S. citizens. *Application Requirements:* Application, transcript. **Deadline:** July 1.

Contact Gerrie Rogers, Office of Student Financial Assistance, Maryland Higher Education Commission, 839 Bestgate Road, Suite 400, Annapolis, MD 21401. *E-mail:* osfamail@mhec.state.md.us. *Phone:* 410-260-4574. *Fax:* 410-260-3203. *Web site:* www.mhec.state.md.us.

Distinguished Scholar Award—Maryland. Renewable award for Maryland students enrolled full-time at Maryland institutions. National Merit Scholar Finalists automatically offered award. Others may qualify for the award in satisfying criteria of a minimum 3.7 GPA or in combination with high test scores, or for Talent in Arts competition in categories of music, drama, dance, or visual arts. Must maintain annual 3.0 GPA in college for award to be renewed. Contact for further details. *Award:* Scholarship for use in freshman, sophomore, junior, or senior year; renewable. *Award amount:* up to $3000. *Number of awards:* up to 2000. *Eligibility Requirements:* Applicant must be high school student; planning to enroll or expecting to enroll full-time at a two-year or four-year institution or university; resident of Maryland and studying in Maryland. Available to U.S. citizens. *Application Requirements:* Application, test scores, transcript. **Deadline:** March 1.

Contact Monica Tipton, Office of Student Financial Assistance, Maryland Higher Education Commission, 839 Bestgate Road, Suite 400, Annapolis, MD 21401-3013. *E-mail:* osfamail@mhec.state.md.us. *Phone:* 410-260-4568. *Fax:* 410-260-3200. *Web site:* www.mhec.state.md.us.

Distinguished Scholar-Teacher Education Awards. Up to $3,000 award for Maryland high school seniors who have received the Distinguished Scholar Award. Recipient must enroll as a full-time undergraduate in a Maryland institution and pursue a program of study leading to a Maryland teaching certificate. Must maintain annual 3.0 GPA for renewal. Must teach in a Maryland public school one year for each year award is received. *Academic/Career Areas:* Education. *Award:* Forgivable loan for use in freshman, sophomore, junior, or senior year; renewable. *Award amount:* up to $3000. *Number of awards:* 20–80. *Eligibility Requirements:* Applicant must be high school student; planning to enroll or expecting to enroll full-time at a

Profiles of State-Sponsored Programs

two-year or four-year institution or university; resident of Maryland and studying in Maryland. Applicant must have 3.0 GPA or higher. Available to U.S. citizens. *Application Requirements:* Application, test scores, transcript, must be recipient of the Distinguished Scholar Award. **Deadline:** continuous.

Contact Monica Tipton, Office of Student Financial Assistance, Maryland Higher Education Commission, 839 Bestgate Road, Suite 400, Annapolis, MD 21401-3013. *E-mail:* ofsamail@mhec.state.md.us. *Phone:* 410-260-4568. *Fax:* 410-260-3200. *Web site:* www.mhec.state.md.us.

Educational Assistance Grants—Maryland. Award for Maryland residents accepted or enrolled in a full-time undergraduate degree or certificate program at a Maryland institution or hospital nursing school. Must submit financial aid form by March 1. Must earn 2.0 GPA in college to maintain award. *Award:* Grant for use in freshman, sophomore, junior, or senior year; renewable. *Award amount:* $400–$2700. *Number of awards:* 11,000–20,000. *Eligibility Requirements:* Applicant must be enrolled or expecting to enroll full-time at a two-year or four-year institution or university; resident of Maryland and studying in Maryland. Available to U.S. citizens. *Application Requirements:* Application, financial need analysis. **Deadline:** March 1.

Contact Barbara Fantom, Office of Student Financial Assistance, Maryland Higher Education Commission, 839 Bestgate Road, Suite 400, Annapolis, MD 21401-3013. *E-mail:* osfamail@mhec.state.md.us. *Phone:* 410-260-4547. *Fax:* 410-260-3200. *Web site:* www.mhec.state.md.us.

Edward T. Conroy Memorial Scholarship Program. Scholarship for dependents of deceased or 100% disabled U.S. Armed Forces personnel, the son, daughter, or surviving spouse of a victim of the September 11, 2001, terrorist attacks who died as a result of the attacks on the World Trade Center in New York City, the attack on the Pentagon in Virginia, or the crash of United Airlines Flight 93 in Pennsylvania; a POW/MIA of the Vietnam Conflict or his/her son or daughter; the son, daughter or surviving spouse (who has not remarried),of a state or local public safety employee or volunteer who died in the line of duty; or a state or local public safety employee or volunteer who was 100% disabled in the line of duty. Must be Maryland resident at time of disability. Submit applicable VA certification. Must be at least 16 years of age and attend Maryland institution. *Award:* Scholarship for use in freshman, sophomore, junior, senior, or graduate year; renewable. *Award amount:* up to $12,981. *Number of awards:* up to 70. *Eligibility Requirements:* Applicant must be age 16-24; enrolled or expecting to enroll full or part-time at a two-year or four-year institution or university; resident of Maryland and studying in Maryland. Available to U.S. citizens. *Application Requirements:* Application, birth and death certificate, and disability papers. **Deadline:** July 30.

Contact Margaret Crutchley, Office of Student Financial Assistance, Maryland Higher Education Commission, 839 Bestgate Road, Suite 400, Annapolis, MD 21401-3013. *E-mail:* osfamail@mhec.state.md.us. *Phone:* 410-260-4545. *Fax:* 410-260-3203. *Web site:* www.mhec.state.md.us.

Firefighter, Ambulance, and Rescue Squad Member Tuition Reimbursement Program—Maryland. Award intended to reimburse members of rescue organizations serving Maryland communities for tuition costs of course work towards a degree or certificate in fire service or medical technology. Must attend a two- or four-year school in Maryland. Minimum 2.0 GPA. *Academic/Career Areas:* Fire Sciences; Health and Medical Sciences; Trade/Technical Specialties. *Award:* Scholarship for use in freshman, sophomore, junior, or senior year; not renewable. *Award* *amount:* $200–$4000. *Number of awards:* 100–300. *Eligibility Requirements:* Applicant must be enrolled or expecting to enroll full or part-time at a two-year or four-year institution or university; resident of Maryland and studying in Maryland. Applicant or parent of applicant must have employment or volunteer experience in police/firefighting. Available to U.S. citizens. *Application Requirements:* Application, transcript. **Deadline:** July 1.

Contact Gerrie Rogers, Office of Student Financial Assistance, Maryland Higher Education Commission, 839 Bestgate Road, Suite 400, Annapolis, MD 21401-3013. *E-mail:* ofsamail@mhec.state.md.us. *Phone:* 410-260-4574. *Fax:* 410-260-3203. *Web site:* www.mhec.state.md.us.

Graduate and Professional Scholarship Program—Maryland. Graduate and professional scholarships provide need-based financial assistance to students attending a Maryland school of medicine, dentistry, law, pharmacy, social work, or nursing. Funds are provided to specific Maryland colleges and universities. Students must demonstrate financial need and be Maryland residents. Contact institution financial aid office for more information. *Academic/Career Areas:* Dental Health/Services; Health and Medical Sciences; Law/Legal Services; Nursing; Social Services. *Award:* Scholarship for use in freshman, sophomore, junior, senior, graduate, or postgraduate years; renewable. *Award amount:* $1000–$5000. *Number of awards:* 40–200. *Eligibility Requirements:* Applicant must be enrolled or expecting to enroll full or part-time at a four-year institution or university; resident of Maryland and studying in Maryland. Available to U.S. citizens. *Application Requirements:* Application, financial need analysis. **Deadline:** March 1.

Contact Maryland Higher Education Commission, 839 Bestgate Road, Suite 400, Annapolis, MD 21401-3013. *Web site:* www.mhec.state.md.us.

Guaranteed Access Grant—Maryland. Award for Maryland resident enrolling full-time in an undergraduate program at a Maryland institution. Must be under 22 at time of first award and begin college within one year of completing high school in Maryland with a minimum 2.5 GPA. Must have an annual family income less than 130% of the federal poverty level guideline. *Award:* Grant for use in freshman, sophomore, junior, or senior year; renewable. *Award amount:* $400–$10,200. *Number of awards:* up to 1000. *Eligibility Requirements:* Applicant must be enrolled or expecting to enroll full-time at a two-year or four-year institution or university; resident of Maryland and studying in Maryland. Applicant must have 2.5 GPA or higher. Available to U.S. citizens. *Application Requirements:* Application, financial need analysis, transcript. **Deadline:** continuous.

Contact Theresa Lowe, Office of Student Financial Assistance, Maryland Higher Education Commission, 839 Bestgate Road, Suite 400, Annapolis, MD 21401-3013. *E-mail:* osfamail@mhec.state.md.us. *Phone:* 410-260-4555. *Fax:* 410-260-3200. *Web site:* www.mhec.state.md.us.

Hope for Nontraditional Students-Community College Transfer Scholarship Program. Award available to students who transfer with minimum 3.0 GPA and 60 credits from a Maryland two-year college to a Maryland four-year college. Annual family income limit is $95,000. Must agree to work in Maryland for up to three years. Funds are limited. *Award:* Forgivable loan for use in junior or senior year; renewable. *Award amount:* up to $3000. *Eligibility Requirements:* Applicant must be enrolled or expecting to enroll full-time at a four-year institution or university; resident of Maryland and studying in Maryland. Applicant must have 3.0 GPA or higher. Available to U.S. citizens. *Application Requirements:* Application, financial need analysis, transcript. **Deadline:** March 1.

Profiles of State-Sponsored Programs

Contact Office of Student Financial Assistance, Maryland Higher Education Commission, 839 Bestgate Road, Suite 400, Annapolis, MD 21401. *E-mail:* osfamail@mhec.state.md.us. *Phone:* 410-260-4565. *Fax:* 410-260-3202. *Web site:* www.mhec.state.md.us.

Hope Scholarship. Student must be a high school senior at the time of application and must enroll in an eligible major. Family income may not exceed $95,000 annually. Recipients must agree to work in the state of Maryland for one year for each year they accept the award. Funds are limited. *Academic/Career Areas:* Agriculture; Arts; Business/Consumer Services; Communications; Foreign Language; Health and Medical Sciences; Home Economics; Humanities; Literature/English/ Writing; Natural Resources; Political Science; Social Sciences. *Award:* Forgivable loan for use in freshman, sophomore, junior, or senior year; renewable. *Award amount:* $1000–$3000. *Eligibility Requirements:* Applicant must be high school student; planning to enroll or expecting to enroll full-time at a two-year or four-year institution or university; resident of Maryland and studying in Maryland. Applicant must have 3.0 GPA or higher. Available to U.S. citizens. *Application Requirements:* Application, financial need analysis, transcript. **Deadline:** March 1.

Contact Office of Financial Assistance, Maryland Higher Education Commission, 839 Bestgate Road, Suite 400, Annapolis, MD 21401. *E-mail:* osfamail@ mhec.state.md.us. *Phone:* 410-260-4565. *Fax:* 410-260-3202. *Web site:* www.mhec.state.md.us.

J.F. Tolbert Memorial Student Grant Program. Available to Maryland residents attending a private career school in Maryland with at least 18 clock hours per week. *Award:* Grant for use in freshman or sophomore year; not renewable. *Award amount:* up to $300. *Number of awards:* 1000. *Eligibility Requirements:* Applicant must be enrolled or expecting to enroll at a technical institution; resident of Maryland and studying in Maryland. Available to U.S. citizens. *Application Requirements:* Application, financial need analysis. **Deadline:** continuous.

Contact Carla Rich, Office of Student Financial Assistance, Maryland Higher Education Commission, 839 Bestgate Road, Suite 400, Annapolis, MD 21401-3013. *E-mail:* osfamail@mhec.state.md.us. *Phone:* 410-260-4513. *Fax:* 410-260-3200. *Web site:* www.mhec.state.md.us.

Janet L. Hoffmann Loan Assistance Repayment Program. Provides assistance for repayment of loan debt to Maryland residents working full-time in non-profit organizations and state or local governments. Must submit Employment Verification Form and Lender verification form. *Academic/Career Areas:* Education; Law/Legal Services; Nursing; Social Services; Therapy/Rehabilitation. *Award:* Grant for use in freshman, sophomore, junior, senior, or graduate year; not renewable. *Award amount:* up to $7500. *Number of awards:* up to 400. *Eligibility Requirements:* Applicant must be enrolled or expecting to enroll at an institution or university; resident of Maryland and studying in Maryland. Available to U.S. citizens. *Application Requirements:* Application, transcript, IRS 1040 form. **Deadline:** September 30.

Contact Marie Janiszewski, Office of Student Financial Assistance, Maryland Higher Education Commission, 839 Bestgate Road, Suite 400, Annapolis, MD 21401. *E-mail:* osfamail@mhec.state.md.us. *Phone:* 410-260-4569. *Fax:* 410-260-3203. *Web site:* www.mhec.state.md.us.

Maryland State Nursing Scholarship and Living Expenses Grant. Renewable grant for Maryland residents enrolled in a two-or four-year Maryland institution nursing degree program. Recipients must agree to serve as a full-time nurse in a

Maryland shortage area and must maintain a 3.0 GPA in college. Application deadline is June 30. Submit Free Application for Federal Student Aid. *Academic/Career Areas:* Nursing. *Award:* Forgivable loan for use in freshman, sophomore, junior, senior, or graduate year; renewable. *Award amount:* $200–$3000. *Number of awards:* up to 600. *Eligibility Requirements:* Applicant must be enrolled or expecting to enroll full or part-time at a two-year or four-year institution or university; resident of Maryland and studying in Maryland. Applicant must have 3.0 GPA or higher. Available to U.S. citizens. *Application Requirements:* Application, financial need analysis, transcript. **Deadline:** June 30.

Contact Marie Janiszewski, Office of Student Financial Assistance, Maryland Higher Education Commission, 839 Bestgate Road, Suite 400, Annapolis, MD 21401-3013. *E-mail:* ofsamail@mhec.state.md.us. *Phone:* 410-260-4569. *Fax:* 410-260-3203. *Web site:* www.mhec.state.md.us.

Maryland Teacher Scholarship. Available to Maryland residents attending a college in Maryland with a major in teacher education. Must be seeking initial teaching certification. Must work as public school teacher within the state of Maryland. Funds are limited. *Academic/Career Areas:* Education; Special Education. *Award:* Forgivable loan for use in freshman, sophomore, junior, senior, graduate, or postgraduate years; renewable. *Award amount:* $1000–$5000. *Eligibility Requirements:* Applicant must be enrolled or expecting to enroll full or part-time at a two-year or four-year institution or university; resident of Maryland and studying in Maryland. Applicant must have 3.0 GPA or higher. Available to U.S. citizens. *Application Requirements:* Application, transcript. **Deadline:** March 1.

Contact Scholarship Administration, Maryland Higher Education Commission, 839 Bestgate Road, Suite 400, Annapolis, MD 21401. *E-mail:* osfamail@mhec.state.md.us. *Phone:* 410-260-4565. *Fax:* 410-260-3202. *Web site:* www.mhec.state.md.us.

Part-time Grant Program-Maryland. Funds provided to Maryland colleges and universities. Eligible students must be enrolled on a part-time basis (6-11 credits) in an undergraduate degree program. Must demonstrate financial need and also be Maryland resident. Contact financial aid office at institution for more information. *Award:* Grant for use in freshman, sophomore, junior, or senior year; renewable. *Award amount:* $200–$1000. *Number of awards:* 1800–9000. *Eligibility Requirements:* Applicant must be enrolled or expecting to enroll part-time at a two-year or four-year institution or university; resident of Maryland and studying in Maryland. Available to U.S. citizens. *Application Requirements:* Application, financial need analysis. **Deadline:** March 1.

Contact Maryland Higher Education Commission, 839 Bestgate Road, Suite 400, Annapolis, MD 21401-3013. *Web site:* www.mhec.state.md.us.

Physical and Occupational Therapists and Assistants Grant Program. For Maryland residents training as physical, occupational therapists or therapy assistants at Maryland postsecondary institutions. Recipients must provide one year of service for each full, or partial, year of award. Service must be to handicapped children in a Maryland facility that has, or accommodates and provides services to, such children. Minimum 2.0 GPA. *Academic/Career Areas:* Therapy/Rehabilitation. *Award:* Forgivable loan for use in freshman, sophomore, junior, senior, or graduate year; renewable. *Award amount:* up to $2000. *Number of awards:* up to 10. *Eligibility Requirements:* Applicant must be enrolled or expecting to enroll full-time at a two-year or four-year institution or university; resident of Maryland and studying in Maryland. Available to U.S. citizens. *Application Requirements:* Application, transcript. **Deadline:** July 1.

Contact Gerrie Rogers, Office of Student Financial Assistance, Maryland Higher Education Commission, 839 Bestgate Road, Suite 400, Annapolis, MD 21401. *E-mail:* ssamail@mhec.state.md.us. *Phone:* 410-260-4574. *Fax:* 410-260-3203. *Web site:* www.mhec.state.md.us.

Science and Technology Scholarship. Provides assistance to full-time students in an academic program that will address career shortage areas in the state (computer science, engineering, biological sciences, mathematics, and physical sciences). Must be Maryland resident. Must have cumulative unweighted 3.0 GPA in grades 9-first semester of senior year if applying as a high school student. College applicants must have a cumulative average of 3.0 or greater to apply. Funds are limited. *Academic/Career Areas:* Biology; Chemical Engineering; Civil Engineering; Computer Science/Data Processing; Earth Science; Electrical Engineering/Electronics; Engineering/Technology; Engineering-Related Technologies; Fire Sciences; Physical Sciences and Math. *Award:* Forgivable loan for use in freshman, sophomore, junior, or senior year; renewable. *Award amount:* $1000–$3000. *Eligibility Requirements:* Applicant must be enrolled or expecting to enroll full-time at a two-year or four-year institution or university; resident of Maryland and studying in Maryland. Applicant must have 3.0 GPA or higher. Available to U.S. citizens. *Application Requirements:* Application, transcript. **Deadline:** March 1.

Contact Scholarship Administration, Maryland Higher Education Commission, 839 Bestgate Road, Suite 400, Annapolis, MD 21401. *E-mail:* ssamail@mhec.state.md.us. *Phone:* 410-260-4565. *Fax:* 410-260-3202. *Web site:* www.mhec.state.md.us.

Senatorial Scholarships—Maryland. Renewable award for Maryland residents attending a Maryland degree-granting institution, nursing diploma school, or certain private career schools. May be used out-of-state only if Maryland Higher Education Commission deems major to be unique and not offered at Maryland institution. *Award:* Scholarship for use in freshman, sophomore, junior, senior, or graduate year; renewable. *Award amount:* $200–$2000. *Number of awards:* up to 7000. *Eligibility Requirements:* Applicant must be enrolled or expecting to enroll full or part-time at a two-year, four-year, or technical institution or university; resident of Maryland and studying in Maryland. Available to U.S. citizens. *Application Requirements:* Financial need analysis, test scores, application to Legislative District Senator. **Deadline:** March 1.

Contact Barbara Fantom, Office of Student Financial Assistance, Maryland Higher Education Commission, 839 Bestgate Road, Suite 400, Annapolis, MD 21401-3013. *E-mail:* osfamail@mhec.state.md.us. *Phone:* 410-260-4547. *Fax:* 410-260-3202. *Web site:* www.mhec.state.md.us.

Sharon Christa McAuliffe Teacher Education—Critical Shortage Grant Program. Renewable awards for Maryland residents who are college juniors, seniors, or graduate students enrolled in a Maryland teacher education program. Must agree to enter profession in a subject designated as a critical shortage area. Must teach in Maryland for one year for each award year. Renewable for one year. *Academic/Career Areas:* Education. *Award:* Forgivable loan for use in junior, senior, or graduate year; renewable. *Award amount:* $200–$12,981. *Number of awards:* up to 137. *Eligibility Requirements:* Applicant must be enrolled or expecting to enroll full or part-time at a four-year institution or university; resident of Maryland and studying in Maryland. Applicant must have 3.0 GPA or higher. Available to U.S. citizens. *Application Requirements:* Application, essay, resume, transcript. **Deadline:** December 31.

Contact Margaret Crutchley, Office of Student Financial Assistance, Maryland Higher Education Commission, 839 Bestgate Road, Suite 400, Annapolis, MD 21401-3013. *E-mail:* ofsamail@mhec.state.md.us. *Phone:* 410-260-4545. *Fax:* 410-260-3203. *Web site:* www.mhec.state.md.us.

William Kapell International Piano Competition and Festival. Quadrennial international piano competition for ages 18-33. $80 application fee. Competition takes place at the Clarice Smith Performing Arts Center at the University of Maryland July 16-25, 2003. Next competition will be in 2007. *Academic/Career Areas:* Performing Arts. *Award:* Prize for use in freshman, sophomore, junior, senior, graduate, or postgraduate years; not renewable. *Award amount:* $1000–$20,000. *Number of awards:* up to 12. *Eligibility Requirements:* Applicant must be age 18-33; enrolled or expecting to enroll at an institution or university and must have an interest in music. Available to U.S. and non-U.S. citizens. *Application Requirements:* Application, applicant must enter a contest, autobiography, photo, portfolio, references, CD or audiocassette of performance. *Fee:* $80. **Deadline:** February 1.

Contact Dr. Christopher Patton, Coordinator, Clarice Smith Performing Arts Center at Maryland, Suite 3800, University of Maryland, College Park, MD 20742-1625. *E-mail:* kapell@deans.umd.edu. *Phone:* 301-405-8174. *Fax:* 301-405-5977. *Web site:* www.claricesmithcenter.umd.edu.

MASSACHUSETTS

Christian A. Herter Memorial Scholarship. Renewable award for Massachusetts residents who are in the 10th-11th grades and whose socio-economic backgrounds and environment may inhibit their ability to attain educational goals. Must exhibit severe personal or family-related difficulties, medical problems, or have overcome a personal obstacle. Provides up to 50% of the student's calculated need, as determined by Federal methodology, at the college of their choice within the continental U.S. *Award:* Scholarship for use in freshman, sophomore, junior, or senior year; renewable. *Number of awards:* 25. *Eligibility Requirements:* Applicant must be high school student; planning to enroll or expecting to enroll full-time at a two-year, four-year, or technical institution or university and resident of Massachusetts. Applicant must have 2.5 GPA or higher. Available to U.S. citizens. *Application Requirements:* Application, autobiography, financial need analysis, interview, references. **Deadline:** March 31.

Contact Ken Smith, Massachusetts Office of Student Financial Assistance, 454 Broadway, Suite 200, Revere, MA 02151. *E-mail:* osfa@osfa.mass.edu. *Phone:* 617-727-9420. *Fax:* 617-727-0667. *Web site:* www.osfa.mass.edu.

Higher Education Coordinating Council—Tuition Waiver Program. Renewable award is tuition exemption for up to four years. Available to active members of Air Force, Army, Navy, Marines, or Coast Guard who are residents of Massachusetts. For use at a Massachusetts college or university. Deadlines vary. Contact veterans coordinator at college. *Award:* Scholarship for use in freshman, sophomore, junior, or senior year; renewable. *Eligibility Requirements:* Applicant must be enrolled or expecting to enroll full or part-time at a two-year or four-year institution or university; resident of Massachusetts and studying in Massachusetts. Available to U.S. citizens. Applicant must have served in the Air Force, Army, Coast Guard, Marine Corp, or Navy. *Application Requirements:* Application, financial need analysis.

Contact college financial aid office, Massachusetts Office of Student Financial Assistance. *Web site:* www.osfa.mass.edu.

Massachusetts Assistance for Student Success Program. Provides need-based financial assistance to Massachusetts residents to attend undergraduate postsecondary institutions in Connecticut, Maine, Massachusetts, New Hampshire, Pennsylvania, Rhode Island, Vermont, and District of Columbia. High school seniors may apply. Timely filing of FAFSA required. *Award:* Grant for use in freshman, sophomore, junior, or senior year; not renewable. *Award amount:* $300–$2900. *Number of awards:* 32,000–35,000. *Eligibility Requirements:* Applicant must be enrolled or expecting to enroll full-time at a two-year, four-year, or technical institution or university; resident of Massachusetts and studying in Connecticut, District of Columbia, Maine, Massachusetts, New Hampshire, Pennsylvania, Rhode Island, or Vermont. Available to U.S. citizens. *Application Requirements:* Financial need analysis, FAFSA. **Deadline:** May 1.

Contact Scholarship Information, Massachusetts Office of Student Financial Assistance, 454 Broadway, Suite 200, Revere, MA 02151. *Web site:* www.osfa.mass.edu.

Massachusetts Cash Grant Program. A need-based grant to assist with mandatory fees and non-state supported tuition, this supplemental award is available to Massachusetts residents who are undergraduates at two-year colleges, four-year colleges and universities in Massachusetts. Must file FAFSA before May 1. Contact college financial aid office for information. *Award:* Grant for use in freshman, sophomore, junior, or senior year; not renewable. *Award amount:* $150–$1900. *Eligibility Requirements:* Applicant must be enrolled or expecting to enroll full-time at a two-year or four-year institution or university; resident of Massachusetts and studying in Massachusetts. Available to U.S. citizens. *Application Requirements:* Financial need analysis, FAFSA. **Deadline:** continuous.

Contact college financial aid office, Massachusetts Office of Student Financial Assistance. *Web site:* www.osfa.mass.edu.

Massachusetts Gilbert Matching Student Grant Program. Must be permanent Massachusetts resident for at least one year and attending an independent, regionally accredited Massachusetts school or school of nursing full time. File the Free Application for Federal Student Aid after January 1. Contact college financial aid office for complete details and deadlines. *Award:* Grant for use in freshman, sophomore, junior, or senior year; not renewable. *Award amount:* $200–$2500. *Eligibility Requirements:* Applicant must be enrolled or expecting to enroll full-time at a four-year institution or university; resident of Massachusetts and studying in Massachusetts. Available to U.S. citizens. *Application Requirements:* Financial need analysis, FAFSA.

Contact college financial aid office, Massachusetts Office of Student Financial Assistance. *Web site:* www.osfa.mass.edu.

Massachusetts Part-time Grant Program. Award for permanent Massachusetts resident for at least one year enrolled part-time in a state-approved postsecondary school. Recipient must not have first bachelor's degree. FAFSA must be filed before May 1. Contact college financial aid office for further information. *Award:* Grant for use in freshman, sophomore, junior, or senior year; not renewable. *Award amount:* $150–$1450. *Eligibility Requirements:* Applicant must be enrolled or expecting to enroll part-time at a two-year, four-year, or technical institution or university; resident of Massachusetts and studying in Massachusetts. Available to U.S. citizens. *Application Requirements:* Financial need analysis, FAFSA. **Deadline:** May 1.

Contact college financial aid office, Massachusetts Office of Student Financial Assistance. *Web site:* www.osfa.mass.edu.

Massachusetts Public Service Grant Program. Scholarships for children and/or spouses of deceased members of fire, police, and corrections departments who were killed in the line of duty. For Massachusetts residents attending Massachusetts institutions. *Award:* Grant for use in freshman, sophomore, junior, or senior year; not renewable. *Award amount:* $330–$2500. *Eligibility Requirements:* Applicant must be enrolled or expecting to enroll full-time at a four-year institution or university; resident of Massachusetts and studying in Massachusetts. Applicant or parent of applicant must have employment or volunteer experience in police/firefighting. Available to U.S. citizens. *Application Requirements:* FAFSA. **Deadline:** May 1.

Contact Alison Leary, Massachusetts Office of Student Financial Assistance, 454 Broadway, Suite 200, Revere, MA 02151. *E-mail:* osfa@osfa.mass.edu. *Phone:* 617-727-9420. *Fax:* 617-727-0667. *Web site:* www.osfa.mass.edu.

New England Regional Student Program (New England Board of Higher Education). For residents of Connecticut, Maine, Massachusetts, New Hampshire, Rhode Island, and Vermont. Through Regional Student Program, students pay reduced out-of-state tuition at public colleges or universities in other New England states when enrolling in certain majors not offered at public institutions in home state. *Award:* Scholarship for use in freshman, sophomore, junior, senior, or graduate year; renewable. *Eligibility Requirements:* Applicant must be enrolled or expecting to enroll full or part-time at a two-year or four-year institution or university; resident of Connecticut, Maine, Massachusetts, New Hampshire, Rhode Island, or Vermont and studying in Connecticut, Maine, Massachusetts, New Hampshire, Rhode Island, or Vermont. Available to U.S. citizens. *Application Requirements:* College application. **Deadline:** continuous.

Contact Wendy Lindsay, Director of Regional Student Program, New England Board of Higher Education, 45 Temple Place, Boston, MA 02111-1305. *E-mail:* rsp@nebhe.org. *Phone:* 617-357-9620 Ext. 111. *Fax:* 617-338-1577. *Web site:* www.nebhe.org.

Performance Bonus Grant Program. One-time award to residents of Massachusetts enrolled in a Massachusetts postsecondary institution. Minimum 3.0 GPA required. Timely filing of FAFSA required. Must be sophomore, junior or senior level undergraduate. *Award:* Grant for use in sophomore, junior, or senior year; not renewable. *Award amount:* $350–$500. *Eligibility Requirements:* Applicant must be enrolled or expecting to enroll full-time at a two-year or four-year institution or university; resident of Massachusetts and studying in Massachusetts. Applicant must have 3.0 GPA or higher. Available to U.S. citizens. *Application Requirements:* Financial need analysis, FAFSA. **Deadline:** May 1.

Contact Scholarship Information, Massachusetts Office of Student Financial Assistance, 454 Broadway, Suite 200, Revere, MA 02151. *Phone:* 617-727-9420. *Fax:* 617-727-0667. *Web site:* www.osfa.mass.edu.

Tomorrow's Teachers Scholarship Program. Tuition waver for graduating high school senior ranking in top 25% of class. Must be a resident of Massachusetts and pursue a bachelor's degree at a public college or university in the Commonwealth. Must commit to teach for four years in a Massachusetts public school. *Academic/Career Areas:* Education. *Award:* Scholarship for use in freshman, sophomore, junior, or senior year; renewable. *Eligibility Requirements:* Applicant must be high school student; planning to enroll or expecting to enroll full-time at a four-year institution or university; resident of Massachusetts and studying in Massachusetts. Applicant must have 3.5 GPA or higher. Available to U.S. citizens. *Application Requirements:* Application, essay, references, transcript. **Deadline:** February 15.

Profiles of State-Sponsored Programs

Contact Alison Leary, Massachusetts Office of Student Financial Assistance, 454 Broadway, Suite 200, Revere, MA 02151. *E-mail:* osfa@osfa.mass.edu. *Phone:* 617-727-9420. *Fax:* 617-727-0667. *Web site:* www.osfa.mass.edu.

Tuition Waiver (General)—Massachusetts. Need-based tuition waiver for full-time students. Must attend a Massachusetts public institution of higher education and be a permanent Massachusetts resident. File the Free Application for Federal Student Aid after January 1. Award is for undergraduate use. Contact school financial aid office for more information. *Award:* Scholarship for use in freshman, sophomore, junior, or senior year; renewable. *Award amount:* $175–$1300. *Eligibility Requirements:* Applicant must be enrolled or expecting to enroll full-time at a two-year or four-year institution or university; resident of Massachusetts and studying in Massachusetts. Available to U.S. citizens. *Application Requirements:* Application, financial need analysis, FAFSA. **Deadline:** May 1.

Contact college financial aid office, Massachusetts Office of Student Financial Assistance. *Web site:* www.osfa.mass.edu.

MICHIGAN

Michigan Adult Part-time Grant. Grant for part-time, needy, independent undergraduates at an approved, degree-granting Michigan college or university. Eligibility is limited to two years. Must be Michigan resident. Deadlines determined by college. *Award:* Grant for use in freshman, sophomore, junior, or senior year; not renewable. *Award amount:* up to $600. *Eligibility Requirements:* Applicant must be enrolled or expecting to enroll part-time at a two-year or four-year institution or university; resident of Michigan and studying in Michigan. Available to U.S. citizens. *Application Requirements:* Application, financial need analysis.

Contact Program Director, Michigan Bureau of Student Financial Assistance, PO Box 30466, Lansing, MI 48909-7966. *Web site:* www.michigan.gov/mistudentaid.

Michigan Competitive Scholarship. Awards limited to tuition. Must maintain a C average and meet the college's academic progress requirements. Must file Free Application for Federal Student Aid. Deadlines: February 21 and March 21. Must be Michigan resident. Renewable award of $1300 for undergraduate study at a Michigan institution. *Award:* Scholarship for use in freshman, sophomore, junior, or senior year; renewable. *Award amount:* $100–$1300. *Eligibility Requirements:* Applicant must be enrolled or expecting to enroll at a two-year or four-year institution or university; resident of Michigan and studying in Michigan. Available to U.S. citizens. *Application Requirements:* Application, financial need analysis, test scores, FAFSA.

Contact Scholarship and Grant Director, Michigan Bureau of Student Financial Assistance, PO Box 30466, Lansing, MI 48909. *Web site:* www.michigan.gov/mistudentaid.

Michigan Educational Opportunity Grant. Need-based program for Michigan residents who are at least half-time undergraduates attending public Michigan colleges. Must maintain good academic standing. Deadline determined by college. Award of up to $1000. *Award:* Grant for use in freshman, sophomore, junior, or senior year; not renewable. *Award amount:* up to $1000. *Eligibility Requirements:* Applicant must be enrolled or expecting to enroll full or part-time at a two-year or four-year institution or university; resident of Michigan and studying in Michigan. Available to U.S. citizens. *Application Requirements:* Application, financial need analysis.

Contact Program Director, Michigan Bureau of Student Financial Assistance, PO Box 30466, Lansing, MI 48909-7966. *Web site:* www.michigan.gov/mistudentaid.

Michigan Indian Tuition Waiver. Renewable award provides free tuition for Native-Americans of one-quarter or more blood degree who attend a Michigan public college or university. Must be a Michigan resident for at least one year. For more details and deadlines contact college financial aid office. *Award:* Scholarship for use in freshman, sophomore, junior, senior, graduate, or postgraduate years; renewable. *Eligibility Requirements:* Applicant must be American Indian/Alaska Native; enrolled or expecting to enroll full or part-time at a two-year or four-year institution or university; resident of Michigan and studying in Michigan. Available to U.S. and Canadian citizens. *Application Requirements:* Application, driver's license.

Contact Harriet Moran, Executive Assistant to Programs, Inter-Tribal Council of Michigan, Inc., 405 East Easterday Avenue, Sault Ste. Marie, MI 49783. *E-mail:* itchmm@yahoo.com. *Phone:* 906-632-6896. *Fax:* 906-632-1810. *Web site:* www.itcmi.org.

Michigan Tuition Grants. Need-based program. Students must attend a Michigan private, nonprofit, degree-granting college. Must file the Free Application for Federal Student Aid and meet the college's academic progress requirements. Deadlines: February 21 and March 21. Must be Michigan resident. Renewable award of $2750. *Award:* Grant for use in freshman, sophomore, junior, or senior year; renewable. *Award amount:* $100–$2750. *Eligibility Requirements:* Applicant must be enrolled or expecting to enroll at a two-year or four-year institution or university; resident of Michigan and studying in Michigan. Available to U.S. citizens. *Application Requirements:* Application, financial need analysis, FAFSA.

Contact Scholarship and Grant Director, Michigan Bureau of Student Financial Assistance, PO Box 30466, Lansing, MI 48909-7966. *Web site:* www.michigan.gov/mistudentaid.

Michigan Veterans Trust Fund Tuition Grant Program. Tuition grant of $2,800 for children of Michigan veterans who died on active duty or subsequently declared 100% disabled as the result of service-connected illness or injury. Must be 17 to 25 years old, be a Michigan resident, and attend a private or public institution in Michigan. *Award:* Grant for use in freshman, sophomore, junior, or senior year; renewable. *Award amount:* up to $2800. *Eligibility Requirements:* Applicant must be age 17-25; enrolled or expecting to enroll full-time at a two-year, four-year, or technical institution or university; resident of Michigan and studying in Michigan. Applicant or parent must meet one or more of the following requirements: general military experience; retired from active duty; disabled or killed as a result of military service; prisoner of war; or missing in action. *Application Requirements:* Application. **Deadline:** continuous.

Contact Phyllis Ochis, Department of Military and Veterans Affairs, Michigan Veterans Trust Fund, 2500 South Washington Avenue, Lansing, MI 48913. *Phone:* 517-483-5469. *Web site:* www.michigan.gov/dmva.

Tuition Incentive Program (TIP)-Michigan. Award for Michigan residents who receive or have received Medicaid for required period of time through the Family Independence Agency. Scholarship provides two years tuition towards an associate's degree at a Michigan college or university. Apply before graduating from high school or earning General Education Development diploma. *Award:* Scholarship for use in freshman or sophomore year; renewable. *Eligibility Requirements:* Applicant must be high school student; planning to enroll or expecting to enroll full or part-time at a two-year or four-year institution or university; resident of Michigan and studying in Michigan. Available to U.S. citizens. *Application Requirements:* Application, financial need analysis. **Deadline:** continuous.

Contact Program Director, Michigan Bureau of Student Financial Assistance, PO Box 30466, Lansing, MI 48909. *Web site:* www.michigan.gov/mistudentaid.

MINNESOTA

Advanced Placement/International Baccalaureate Degree Program. A non-need-based grant available for incoming Freshman who had an average score of 3 or higher on five AP courses or an average score of 4 or higher on 5 IB courses. Must be a Minnesota resident and attend a college in Minnesota. *Award:* Grant for use in freshman or sophomore year; not renewable. *Award amount:* $300–$700. *Number of awards:* 300. *Eligibility Requirements:* Applicant must be high school student; planning to enroll or expecting to enroll full or part-time at a two-year or four-year institution or university; resident of Minnesota and studying in Minnesota. Available to U.S. citizens. *Application Requirements:* Application, test scores. **Deadline:** continuous.

Contact Brenda Larter, Minnesota Higher Education Services Office, 1450 Energy Park Drive, Suite 350, St. Paul, MN 55108-5227. *E-mail:* larter@heso.state.mn.us. *Phone:* 651-642-0567 Ext. 3417. *Fax:* 651-642-0675. *Web site:* www.mheso.state.mn.us.

Leadership, Excellence and Dedicated Service Scholarship. Awarded to high school seniors who enlist in the Minnesota National Guard. The award recognizes demonstrated leadership, community services and potential for success in the Minnesota National Guard. *Award:* Scholarship for use in freshman year; not renewable. *Award amount:* $1000. *Number of awards:* 30. *Eligibility Requirements:* Applicant must be high school student and planning to enroll or expecting to enroll full or part-time at a two-year, four-year, or technical institution or university. Applicant must have served in the Air Force National Guard or Army National Guard. *Application Requirements:* Application, essay, references, transcript. **Deadline:** March 15.

Contact Barbara O'Reilly, Education Services Officer, Minnesota Department of Military Affairs, Veterans Services Building, 20 West 12th Street, St. Paul, MN 55155-2098. *E-mail:* barbara.oreilly@mn.ngb.army.mil. *Phone:* 651-282-4508. *Web site:* www.dma.state.mn.us.

Minnesota Educational Assistance for War Orphans. War orphans may qualify for $750 per year. Must have lost parent through service-related death. Children of deceased veterans may qualify for free tuition at State university, college, or vocational or technical schools, but not at University of Minnesota. Must have been resident of Minnesota for at least two years. *Award:* Grant for use in freshman, sophomore, junior, or senior year; renewable. *Award amount:* $750. *Eligibility Requirements:* Applicant must be enrolled or expecting to enroll full or part-time at a two-year, four-year, or technical institution or university; resident of Minnesota and studying in Minnesota. Available to U.S. citizens. Applicant or parent must meet one or more of the following requirements: general military experience; retired from active duty; disabled or killed as a result of military service; prisoner of war; or missing in action. *Application Requirements:* Application, financial need analysis. **Deadline:** continuous.

Contact Terrence Logan, Management Analyst IV, Minnesota Department of Veterans' Affairs, 20 West 12th Street, Second Floor, St. Paul, MN 55155-2079. *Phone:* 651-296-2652. *Fax:* 651-296-3954. *Web site:* www.state.mn.us/ebranch/mdva.

Minnesota Indian Scholarship Program. One time award for Minnesota Native-Americans Indian. Contact for deadline information. *Award:* Scholarship for use in freshman, sophomore, junior, or senior year; not renewable. *Eligibility Requirements:*

Applicant must be American Indian/Alaska Native; enrolled or expecting to enroll full or part-time at a two-year, four-year, or technical institution or university and resident of Minnesota. Available to U.S. citizens. *Application Requirements:* Application.

Contact Lea Perkins, Director, Minnesota Indian Scholarship Office, Minnesota Department of CFL 1500 Highway 36W, Roseville, MN 55113-4266. *Phone:* 800-657-3927.

Minnesota Nurses Loan Forgiveness Program. This program offers loan repayment to registered nurse and licensed practical nurse students who agree to practice in a Minnesota nursing home or an Intermediate Care Facility for persons with mental retardation for a minimum one-year service obligation after completion of training. Candidates must apply while still in school. Up to 10 selections per year contingent upon state funding. *Academic/Career Areas:* Health and Medical Sciences; Nursing. *Award:* Grant for use in senior or graduate year; not renewable. *Award amount:* up to $3000. *Number of awards:* up to 10. *Eligibility Requirements:* Applicant must be enrolled or expecting to enroll full or part-time at a two-year, four-year, or technical institution or university. Available to U.S. citizens. *Application Requirements:* Application, essay. **Deadline:** December 1.

Contact Karen Welter, Minnesota Department of Health, 121 East Seventh Place, Suite 460, PO Box 64975, St. Paul, MN 55164-0975. *E-mail:* karen.welter@health.state.mn.us. *Phone:* 651-282-6302. *Web site:* www.health.state.mn.us.

Minnesota Reciprocal Agreement. Renewable tuition waiver for Minnesota residents. Waives all or part of non-resident tuition surcharge at public institutions in Iowa, Kansas, Michigan, Missouri, Nebraska, North Dakota, South Dakota, and Wisconsin. Deadline is last day of academic term. *Award:* Scholarship for use in freshman, sophomore, junior, senior, or graduate year; renewable. *Eligibility Requirements:* Applicant must be enrolled or expecting to enroll full or part-time at a two-year or four-year institution or university; resident of Minnesota and studying in Iowa, Kansas, Michigan, Missouri, Nebraska, North Dakota, South Dakota, or Wisconsin. Available to U.S. citizens. *Application Requirements:* Application.

Contact Minnesota Higher Education Services Office, 1450 Energy Park Drive, Suite 350, St. Paul, MN 55108-5227. *Phone:* 651-642-0567 Ext. 1. *Web site:* www.mheso.state.mn.us.

Minnesota Safety Officers' Survivor Program. Grant for eligible survivors of Minnesota public safety officer killed in the line of duty. Safety officers who have been permanently or totally disabled in the line of duty are also eligible. Must be used at a Minnesota institution participating in State Grant Program. Write for details. Must submit proof of death or disability and Public Safety Officers Benefit Fund Certificate. Must apply each year. Can be renewed for four years. *Award:* Grant for use in freshman, sophomore, junior, or senior year; not renewable. *Award amount:* up to $7088. *Eligibility Requirements:* Applicant must be enrolled or expecting to enroll full or part-time at a two-year, four-year, or technical institution or university and studying in Minnesota. Applicant or parent of applicant must have employment or volunteer experience in police/firefighting. Available to U.S. citizens. *Application Requirements:* Application, proof of death/disability. **Deadline:** continuous.

Contact Minnesota Higher Education Services Office, 1450 Energy Park Drive, Suite 350, St. Paul, MN 55108-5227. *Phone:* 651-642-0567 Ext. 1. *Web site:* www.mheso.state.mn.us.

Minnesota State Grant Program. Need-based grant program available for Minnesota residents attending Minnesota colleges. Student covers 46% of cost with remainder covered by Pell Grant, parent contribution and state grant. Students apply with FAFSA and college administers the program on campus. *Award:* Grant for use in freshman, sophomore, junior, or senior year; not renewable. *Award amount:* $100–$7770. *Number of awards:* 71,000. *Eligibility Requirements:* Applicant must be age 17; enrolled or expecting to enroll full or part-time at a two-year, four-year, or technical institution or university; resident of Minnesota and studying in Minnesota. Available to U.S. citizens. *Application Requirements:* Application, financial need analysis. **Deadline:** June 30.

Contact Minnesota Higher Education Services Office, 1450 Energy Park Drive, Suite 350, St. Paul, MN 55108. *Phone:* 651-642-0567 Ext. 1. *Web site:* www.mheso.state.mn.us.

Minnesota State Veterans' Dependents Assistance Program. Tuition assistance to dependents of persons considered to be prisoner-of-war or missing in action after August 1, 1958. Must be Minnesota resident attending Minnesota two- or four-year school. *Award:* Scholarship for use in freshman, sophomore, junior, or senior year; renewable. *Eligibility Requirements:* Applicant must be enrolled or expecting to enroll at a two-year or four-year institution; resident of Minnesota and studying in Minnesota. Available to U.S. citizens. Applicant or parent must meet one or more of the following requirements: general military experience; retired from active duty; disabled or killed as a result of military service; prisoner of war; or missing in action. *Application Requirements:* Application. **Deadline:** continuous.

Contact Minnesota Higher Education Services Office, 1450 Energy Park Drive, Suite 350, St. Paul, MN 55108-5227. *Web site:* www.mheso.state.mn.us.

Minnesota VA Educational Assistance for Veterans. One-time $750 stipend given to veterans who have used up all other federal funds, yet have time remaining on their delimiting period. Applicant must be a Minnesota resident and must be attending a Minnesota college or university, but not the University of Minnesota. *Award:* Grant for use in freshman, sophomore, junior, or senior year; not renewable. *Award amount:* $750. *Eligibility Requirements:* Applicant must be enrolled or expecting to enroll full or part-time at a two-year, four-year, or technical institution or university; resident of Minnesota and studying in Minnesota. Available to U.S. citizens. Applicant must have general military experience. *Application Requirements:* Application, financial need analysis. **Deadline:** continuous.

Contact Terrence Logan, Management Analyst IV, Minnesota Department of Veterans' Affairs, 20 West 12th Street, Second Floor, St. Paul, MN 55155-2079. *Phone:* 651-296-2652. *Fax:* 651-296-3954. *Web site:* www.state.mn.us/ebranch/mdva.

Postsecondary Child Care Grant Program—Minnesota. One-time grant available for students not receiving MFIP. Based on financial need. Cannot exceed actual child care costs or maximum award chart (based on income). Must be Minnesota resident. For use at Minnesota two- or four-year school. *Award:* Grant for use in freshman, sophomore, junior, or senior year; not renewable. *Award amount:* $300–$2600. *Eligibility Requirements:* Applicant must be enrolled or expecting to enroll full or part-time at a two-year or four-year institution or university; resident of Minnesota and studying in Minnesota. Available to U.S. citizens. *Application Requirements:* Application, financial need analysis. **Deadline:** continuous.

Contact Minnesota Higher Education Services Office, 1450 Energy Park Drive, Suite 350, St. Paul, MN 55108-5227. *Phone:* 651-642-0567 Ext. 1. *Web site:* www.mheso.state.mn.us.

MISSISSIPPI

Critical Needs Teacher Loan/Scholarship. Eligible applicants will agree to employment immediately upon degree completion as a full-time classroom teacher in a public school located in a critical teacher shortage area in the state of Mississippi. Must verify the intention to pursue a first bachelor's degree in teacher education. Award covers tuition and required fees, average cost of room and meals plus a $500 allowance for books. Must be enrolled at a Mississippi college or university. *Academic/Career Areas:* Education. *Award:* Forgivable loan for use in freshman, sophomore, junior, or senior year; not renewable. *Eligibility Requirements:* Applicant must be enrolled or expecting to enroll full or part-time at a four-year institution or university and studying in Mississippi. Applicant must have 2.5 GPA or higher. Available to U.S. citizens. *Application Requirements:* Application, test scores, transcript. **Deadline:** March 31.

Contact Mississippi State Student Financial Aid, 3825 Ridgewood Road, Jackson, MS 39211-6453. *Phone:* 800-327-2980. *Web site:* www.ihl.state.ms.us.

Higher Education Legislative Plan (HELP). Eligible applicant must be resident of Mississippi and be freshmen and/or sophomore student who graduated from high school within the immediate past two years. Must demonstrate need as determined by the results of the Free Application for Federal Student Aid, documenting an average family adjusted gross income of $36,500 or less over the prior two years. Must be enrolled full-time at a Mississippi college or university, have a cumulative grade point average of 2.5 and have scored 20 on the ACT. *Award:* Scholarship for use in freshman or sophomore year; renewable. *Eligibility Requirements:* Applicant must be enrolled or expecting to enroll full-time at a four-year institution or university; resident of Mississippi and studying in Mississippi. Applicant must have 2.5 GPA or higher. Available to U.S. citizens. *Application Requirements:* Application, financial need analysis, test scores, transcript, FAFSA. **Deadline:** March 31.

Contact Mississippi State Student Financial Aid, 3825 Ridgewood Road, Jackson, MS 39211-6453. *Phone:* 800-327-2980. *Web site:* www.ihl.state.ms.us.

Mississippi Law Enforcement Officers and Firemen Scholarship Program. Award for dependents and spouses of policemen or firemen who were killed or disabled in the line of duty. Must be a Mississippi resident and attend a state-supported college or university. The award is a full tuition waiver. Contact for deadline. *Award:* Scholarship for use in freshman, sophomore, junior, or senior year; renewable. *Eligibility Requirements:* Applicant must be enrolled or expecting to enroll full-time at a two-year or four-year institution or university; resident of Mississippi and studying in Mississippi. Applicant or parent of applicant must have employment or volunteer experience in police/firefighting. Available to U.S. citizens. *Application Requirements:* Application, driver's license, references. **Deadline:** continuous.

Contact Board of Trustees, Mississippi State Student Financial Aid, 3825 Ridgewood Road, Jackson, MS 39211-6453. *Web site:* www.ihl.state.ms.us.

Mississippi Eminent Scholars Grant. Award for high-school seniors who are residents of Mississippi. Applicants must achieve a grade point average of 3.5 after a minimum of seven semesters in high school and must have scored 29 on the ACT. Must enroll full-time at an eligible Mississippi college or university. *Award:* Grant for use in freshman year; renewable. *Award amount:* up to $2500. *Eligibility Requirements:* Applicant must be high school student; planning to enroll or expecting to enroll full-time at a four-year institution or university; resident of Mississippi and studying in Mississippi. Applicant must have 3.5 GPA or higher. Available to U.S. citizens. *Application Requirements:* Application, test scores, transcript. **Deadline:** September 15.

Contact Mississippi State Student Financial Aid, 3825 Ridgewood Road, Jackson, MS 39211-6453. *Phone:* 800-327-2980. *Web site:* www.ihl.state.ms.us.

Mississippi Health Care Professions Loan/Scholarship Program. Renewable award for junior and senior undergraduates studying psychology, speech pathology or occupational therapy. Must be Mississippi residents attending four-year universities in Mississippi. Must fulfill work obligation in Mississippi or pay back as loan. Renewable award for graduate student enrolled in physical therapy. *Academic/ Career Areas:* Health and Medical Sciences; Therapy/Rehabilitation. *Award:* Forgivable loan for use in junior, senior, or graduate year; renewable. *Award amount:* $1500–$3000. *Eligibility Requirements:* Applicant must be enrolled or expecting to enroll full-time at a four-year institution or university; resident of Mississippi and studying in Mississippi. Available to U.S. citizens. *Application Requirements:* Application, driver's license, references, transcript. **Deadline:** March 31.

Contact Board of Trustees, Mississippi State Student Financial Aid, 3825 Ridgewood Road, Jackson, MS 39211-6453. *Web site:* www.ihl.state.ms.us.

Mississippi Leveraging Educational Assistance Partnership (LEAP). Award for Mississippi residents enrolled for full-time study at a Mississippi college or university. Based on financial need. Deadline varies with each institution. Contact college financial aid office. *Award:* Grant for use in freshman, sophomore, junior, or senior year; not renewable. *Award amount:* $100–$1500. *Eligibility Requirements:* Applicant must be enrolled or expecting to enroll full-time at a two-year or four-year institution or university; resident of Mississippi and studying in Mississippi. Available to U.S. citizens. *Application Requirements:* Application, financial need analysis, FAFSA. **Deadline:** continuous.

Contact Student Financial Aid Office, Mississippi State Student Financial Aid. *Web site:* www.ihl.state.ms.us.

Mississippi Resident Tuition Assistance Grant. Must be a resident of Mississippi enrolled full-time at an eligible Mississippi college or university. Must maintain a minimum 2.5 GPA each semester. MTAG awards may be up to $500 per academic year for freshmen and sophomores and $1,000 per academic year for juniors and seniors. Funds will be made available to eligible participants for eight (8) semesters or the normal time required to complete the degree program, whichever comes first. *Award:* Grant for use in freshman, sophomore, junior, or senior year; renewable. *Award amount:* $500–$1000. *Eligibility Requirements:* Applicant must be enrolled or expecting to enroll full-time at a two-year or four-year institution or university; resident of Mississippi and studying in Mississippi. Applicant must have 2.5 GPA or higher. Available to U.S. citizens. *Application Requirements:* Application, test scores, transcript. **Deadline:** September 15.

Contact Mississippi State Student Financial Aid, 3825 Ridgewood Road, Jackson, MS 39211-6453. *Phone:* 800-327-2980. *Web site:* www.ihl.state.ms.us.

Nursing Education BSN Program—Mississippi. Renewable award for Mississippi undergraduates in junior or senior year pursuing nursing programs in Mississippi in order to earn BSN degree. Include transcript and references with application. Must agree to employment in professional nursing (patient care) in Mississippi. *Academic/Career Areas:* Nursing. *Award:* Forgivable loan for use in junior or senior year; renewable. *Award amount:* up to $2000. *Eligibility Requirements:* Applicant must be enrolled or expecting to enroll full or part-time at a four-year institution or university; resident of Mississippi and studying in Mississippi. Applicant must have 2.5 GPA or higher. Available to U.S. citizens. *Application Requirements:* Application, driver's license, financial need analysis, references, transcript. **Deadline:** March 31.

Contact Board of Trustees, Mississippi State Student Financial Aid, 3825 Ridgewood road, Jackson, MS 39211-6453. *Web site:* www.ihl.state.ms.us.

William F. Winter Teacher Scholar Loan Program. Awarded to Mississippi residents pursuing a teaching career. Must be enrolled full-time in a program leading to a Class A certification and maintain a 2.5 GPA. Must agree to teach one year for each year award is received. *Academic/Career Areas:* Education. *Award:* Forgivable loan for use in freshman, sophomore, junior, or senior year; renewable. *Award amount:* $1000–$3000. *Eligibility Requirements:* Applicant must be enrolled or expecting to enroll full-time at a two-year or four-year institution or university; resident of Mississippi and studying in Mississippi. Applicant must have 2.5 GPA or higher. Available to U.S. citizens. *Application Requirements:* Application, driver's license, references, transcript. **Deadline:** March 31.

Contact Board of Trustees, Mississippi State Student Financial Aid, 3825 Ridgewood Road, Jackson, MS 39211-6453. *Web site:* www.ihl.state.ms.us.

MISSOURI

Advantage Missouri Program. Applicant must be seeking a program of instruction in a designated high demand field. High demand fields are determined each year. Borrower must work in Missouri in the high-demand field for one year for every year the loan is received to be forgiven. For Missouri residents. Must attend a postsecondary institution in Missouri. *Award:* Forgivable loan for use in freshman, sophomore, junior, or senior year; not renewable. *Award amount:* $2500. *Eligibility Requirements:* Applicant must be enrolled or expecting to enroll full-time at a two-year, four-year, or technical institution or university; resident of Missouri and studying in Missouri. Available to U.S. citizens. *Application Requirements:* Application, financial need analysis. **Deadline:** April 1.

Contact MOSTARS Information Center, Missouri Coordinating Board for Higher Education, 3515 Amazonas Drive, Jefferson City, MO 65109. *E-mail:* icweb@mocbhe.gov. *Phone:* 800-473-6757 Ext. 1. *Fax:* 573-751-6635. *Web site:* www.mostars.com.

Charles Gallagher Student Assistance Program. Available to Missouri residents attending Missouri colleges or universities full-time. Must be undergraduates with financial need. May reapply for up to a maximum of ten semesters. Free Application for Federal Student Aid (FAFSA) or a renewal must be received by the central processor by April 1 to be considered. *Award:* Grant for use in freshman, sophomore, junior, or senior year; not renewable. *Award amount:* $100–$1500. *Eligibility Requirements:* Applicant must be enrolled or expecting to enroll full-time at a two-year, four-year, or technical institution or university; resident of Missouri and studying in Missouri. Available to U.S. citizens. *Application Requirements:* Financial need analysis. **Deadline:** April 1.

Contact MOSTARS Information Center, Missouri Coordinating Board for Higher Education, 3515 Amazonas Drive, Jefferson City, MO 65109. *E-mail:* icweb@mocbhe.gov. *Phone:* 800-473-6757 Ext. 1. *Fax:* 573-751-6635. *Web site:* www.mostars.com.

John Charles Wilson Scholarship. One-time award to members in good standing of IAAI or the immediate family of a member or must be sponsored by an IAAI member. Must enroll or plan to enroll full-time in an accredited college or university that offers courses in police or fire sciences. Application available at web site. Deadline is February 15. *Academic/Career Areas:* Fire Sciences; Law Enforcement/ Police Administration. *Award:* Scholarship for use in freshman or graduate year; not renewable. *Award amount:* $500–$1000. *Number of awards:* 5. *Eligibility Requirements:* Applicant must be enrolled or expecting to enroll full-time at a two-year or four-year institution or university. Available to U.S. and non-U.S. citizens. *Application Requirements:* Application, essay, references, transcript. **Deadline:** February 15.

Contact Marsha Sipes, Office Manager, International Association of Arson Investigators Educational Foundation, Inc., 12770 Boenker Road, Bridgeton, MO 63044. *E-mail:* iaai@firearson.com. *Phone:* 314-739-4224. *Fax:* 314-739-4219. *Web site:* www.fire-investigators.org/.

Marguerite Ross Barnett Memorial Scholarship. Applicant must be employed (at least 20 hours per week) and attending school part-time. Must be Missouri resident and enrolled at a participating Missouri postsecondary school. Awards not available during summer term. Minimum age is 18. *Award:* Scholarship for use in freshman, sophomore, junior, or senior year; not renewable. *Award amount:* $849–$1557. *Eligibility Requirements:* Applicant must be age 18; enrolled or expecting to enroll part-time at a two-year or four-year institution or university; resident of Missouri and studying in Missouri. Available to U.S. citizens. *Application Requirements:* Application, financial need analysis. **Deadline:** April 1.

Contact MOSTARS Information Center, Missouri Coordinating Board for Higher Education, 3515 Amazonas Drive, Jefferson City, MO 65109. *E-mail:* icweb@ mocbhe.gov. *Phone:* 800-473-6757 Ext. 1. *Fax:* 573-751-6635. *Web site:* www.mostars.com.

Missouri College Guarantee Program. Available to Missouri residents attending Missouri colleges full-time. Minimum 2.5 GPA required. Must have participated in high school extracurricular activities. *Award:* Grant for use in freshman, sophomore, junior, or senior year; not renewable. *Award amount:* $100–$4600. *Eligibility Requirements:* Applicant must be enrolled or expecting to enroll full-time at a two-year or four-year institution or university; resident of Missouri and studying in Missouri. Applicant must have 2.5 GPA or higher. Available to U.S. citizens. *Application Requirements:* Financial need analysis, test scores. **Deadline:** April 1.

Contact MOSTARS Information Center, Missouri Coordinating Board for Higher Education, 3515 Amazonas Drive, Jefferson City, MO 65109. *E-mail:* icweb@ mocbhe.gov. *Phone:* 800-473-6757 Ext. 1. *Fax:* 573-751-6635. *Web site:* www.mostars.com.

Missouri Higher Education Academic Scholarship (Bright Flight). Awards of $2000 for Missouri high school seniors. Must be in top 3% of Missouri SAT or ACT scorers. Must attend Missouri institution as full-time undergraduate. May reapply for up to ten semesters. Must be Missouri resident and U.S. citizen. *Award:* Scholarship for use in freshman, sophomore, junior, or senior year; not renewable. *Award amount:* $2000. *Eligibility Requirements:* Applicant must be high school student; planning to enroll or expecting to enroll full-time at a two-year, four-year, or technical institution or university; resident of Missouri and studying in Missouri. Available to U.S. citizens. *Application Requirements:* Test scores. **Deadline:** July 31.

Contact MOSTARS Information Center, Missouri Coordinating Board for Higher Education, 3515 Amazonas Drive, Jefferson City, MO 65109. *E-mail:* icweb@ mocbhe.gov. *Phone:* 800-473-6757 Ext. 1. *Fax:* 573-751-6635. *Web site:* www.mostars.com.

Missouri Minority Teaching Scholarship. Award may be used any year up to four years at an approved, participating Missouri institution. Scholarship is for minority Missouri residents in teaching programs. Recipients must commit to teach for five years in a Missouri public elementary or secondary school. Graduate students must teach math or science. Otherwise, award must be repaid. *Academic/Career Areas:* Education. *Award:* Scholarship for use in freshman, sophomore, junior, senior, or graduate year; renewable. *Award amount:* $3000. *Number of awards:* 100. *Eligibility Requirements:* Applicant must be of African, Chinese, Hispanic, Indian, or Japanese heritage; American Indian/Alaska Native, Asian/Pacific Islander, or Black (non-Hispanic); enrolled or expecting to enroll full-time at a two-year or four-year institution or university; resident of Missouri and studying in Missouri. Applicant must have 3.5 GPA or higher. Available to U.S. citizens. *Application Requirements:* Application, essay, financial need analysis, references, test scores, transcript. **Deadline:** February 15.

Contact Laura Harrison, Administrative Assistant II, Missouri Department of Elementary and Secondary Education, PO Box 480, Jefferson City, MO 65102-0480. *E-mail:* lharriso@mail.dese.state.mo.us. *Phone:* 573-751-1668. *Fax:* 573-526-3580. *Web site:* www.dese.state.mo.us.

Missouri Teacher Education Scholarship (General). Nonrenewable award for Missouri high school seniors or Missouri resident college students. Must attend approved teacher training program at Missouri institution. Nonrenewable. Must rank in top 15 % of high school class on ACT/SAT. Merit-based award. *Academic/Career Areas:* Education. *Award:* Scholarship for use in freshman, sophomore, junior, or senior year; not renewable. *Award amount:* $2000. *Number of awards:* 200–240. *Eligibility Requirements:* Applicant must be enrolled or expecting to enroll full-time at a two-year or four-year institution or university; resident of Missouri and studying in Missouri. Applicant must have 3.5 GPA or higher. Available to U.S. citizens. *Application Requirements:* Application, essay, references, test scores, transcript. **Deadline:** February 15.

Contact Laura Harrison, Administrative Assistant II, Missouri Department of Elementary and Secondary Education, PO Box 480, Jefferson City, MO 65102-0480. *E-mail:* lharriso@mail.dese.state.mo.us. *Phone:* 573-751-1668. *Fax:* 573-526-3580. *Web site:* www.dese.state.mo.us.

MONTANA

High School Honor Scholarship. Scholarship provides a one-year non-renewable fee waiver of tuition and registration and is awarded to graduating high school seniors from accredited high schools in Montana. 500 scholarships are awarded each year averaging $2,000 per recipient. The value of the award varies, depending on the tuition and registration fee at each participating college. Must have a minimum 3.0 GPA, meet all college preparatory requirements and be enrolled in an accredited high school for at least three years prior to graduation. Awarded to highest-ranking student in class attending a participating school. Contact high school counselor to apply. Deadline: April 15. *Award:* Scholarship for use in freshman year; not renewable. *Award amount:* $2000. *Number of awards:* 500. *Eligibility Requirements:* Applicant must be high school student; planning to enroll or

Profiles of State-Sponsored Programs

expecting to enroll full or part-time at a two-year or four-year institution or university; resident of Montana and studying in Montana. Applicant must have 3.0 GPA or higher. Available to U.S. citizens. *Application Requirements:* Application, transcript. **Deadline:** April 15.

Contact high school counselor, Montana Guaranteed Student Loan Program, Office of Commissioner of Higher Education. *Web site:* www.mgslp.state.mt.us.

Indian Student Fee Waiver. Fee waiver awarded by the Montana University System to undergraduate and graduate students meeting the criteria. Amount varies depending upon the tuition and registration fee at each participating college. Students must provide documentation of one-fourth Indian blood or more; must be a resident of Montana for at least one year prior to enrolling in school and must demonstrate financial need. Full-or part-time study qualifies. Complete and submit the FAFSA by March 1 and a Montana Indian Fee Waiver application form. Contact the financial aid office at the college of attendance to determine eligibility. *Award:* Scholarship for use in freshman, sophomore, junior, senior, or graduate year; renewable. *Award amount:* $2000. *Number of awards:* 600. *Eligibility Requirements:* Applicant must be American Indian/Alaska Native; enrolled or expecting to enroll full or part-time at a two-year or four-year institution or university; resident of Montana and studying in Montana. Available to U.S. citizens. *Application Requirements:* Application, financial need analysis, FAFSA. **Deadline:** March 1.

Contact Sally Speer, Grants and Scholarship Coordinator, Montana Guaranteed Student Loan Program, Office of Commissioner of Higher Education, 2500 Broadway, PO Box 203101, Helena, MT 59620-3101. *E-mail:* sspeer@mgslp.state. mt.us. *Phone:* 406-444-0638. *Fax:* 406-444-1869. *Web site:* www.mgslp.state.mt.us.

Life Member Montana Federation of Garden Clubs Scholarship. Applicant must be at least a sophomore, majoring in conservation, horticulture, park or forestry, floriculture, greenhouse management, land management, or related subjects. Must be in need of assistance. Must have a potential for a successful future. Must be ranked in upper half of class or have a minimum 2.8 GPA. Must be a Montana resident and all study must be done in Montana. Deadline: May 1. *Academic/Career Areas:* Biology; Earth Science; Horticulture/Floriculture; Landscape Architecture. *Award:* Scholarship for use in sophomore, junior, or senior year; not renewable. *Award amount:* $1000. *Number of awards:* 1. *Eligibility Requirements:* Applicant must be enrolled or expecting to enroll full-time at a four-year institution or university; resident of Montana and studying in Montana. Available to U.S. citizens. *Application Requirements:* Autobiography, financial need analysis, photo, references, transcript. **Deadline:** May 1.

Contact Elizabeth Kehmeier, Life Members Scholarship Chairman, Montana Federation of Garden Clubs, 214 Wyant Lane, Hamilton, MT 59840. *Phone:* 406-363-5693.

Montana Higher Education Opportunity Grant. This grant is awarded based on need to undergraduate students attending either part-time or full-time who are residents of Montana and attending participating Montana schools. Awards are limited to the most needy students. A specific major or program of study is not required. This grant does not need to be repaid, and students may apply each year. Apply by filing a Free Application for Federal Student Aid by March 1 and contacting the financial aid office at the admitting college. *Award:* Grant for use in freshman, sophomore, junior, or senior year; not renewable. *Award amount:* $400–$600. *Number of awards:* 500. *Eligibility Requirements:* Applicant must be enrolled or expecting to enroll full or part-time at a two-year or four-year institution or university; resident of Montana and studying in Montana. Available to U.S. citizens. *Application Requirements:* Financial need analysis, FAFSA. **Deadline:** March 1.

Contact Sally Speer, Grants and Scholarship Coordinator, Montana Guaranteed Student Loan Program, Office of Commissioner of Higher Education, 2500 Broadway, PO Box 203101, Helena, MT 59620-3101. *E-mail:* sspeer@mgslp.state. mt.us. *Phone:* 406-444-0638. *Fax:* 406-444-1869. *Web site:* www.mgslp.state.mt.us.

Montana Tuition Assistance Program—Baker Grant. Need-based grant for Montana residents attending participating Montana schools who have earned at least $2,575 during the previous calendar year. Must be enrolled full time. Grant does not need to be repaid. Award covers the first undergraduate degree or certificate. Apply by filing a Free Application for Federal Student Aid by March 1 and contacting the financial aid office at the admitting college. *Award:* Grant for use in freshman, sophomore, junior, or senior year; not renewable. *Award amount:* $100–$1000. *Eligibility Requirements:* Applicant must be enrolled or expecting to enroll full-time at a two-year or four-year institution or university; resident of Montana and studying in Montana. Available to U.S. citizens. *Application Requirements:* Financial need analysis, FAFSA. **Deadline:** March 1.

Contact Sally Speer, Grants and Scholarship Coordinator, Montana Guaranteed Student Loan Program, Office of Commissioner of Higher Education, 2500 Broadway, PO Box 203101, Helena, MT 59620-3101. *E-mail:* sspeer@mgslp.state. mt.us. *Phone:* 406-444-0638. *Fax:* 406-444-1869. *Web site:* www.mgslp.state.mt.us.

NEBRASKA

Nebraska National Guard Tuition Credit. Renewable award for members of the Nebraska National Guard. Pays 75% of enlisted soldier's tuition until he or she has received a baccalaureate degree. *Award:* Scholarship for use in freshman, sophomore, junior, or senior year; renewable. *Number of awards:* up to 1200. *Eligibility Requirements:* Applicant must be enrolled or expecting to enroll full or part-time at a two-year, four-year, or technical institution or university; resident of Nebraska and studying in Nebraska. Applicant must have served in the Air Force National Guard or Army National Guard. *Application Requirements:* Application. **Deadline:** continuous.

Contact Cindy York, Administrative Assistant, Nebraska National Guard, 1300 Military Road, Lincoln, NE 68508-1090. *Phone:* 402-309-7143. *Fax:* 402-309-7128. *Web site:* www.neguard.com.

Nebraska Scholarship Assistance Program. Available to undergraduates attending a participating postsecondary institution in Nebraska. Available to Pell Grant recipients only. Nebraska residency required. Awards determined by each participating institution. Contact financial aid office at respective institution for more information. *Award:* Scholarship for use in freshman, sophomore, junior, or senior year; not renewable. *Eligibility Requirements:* Applicant must be enrolled or expecting to enroll full or part-time at a two-year, four-year, or technical institution or university; resident of Nebraska and studying in Nebraska. *Application Requirements:* Financial need analysis. **Deadline:** continuous.

Contact financial aid office at college or university, State of Nebraska Coordinating Commission for Postsecondary Education. *Web site:* www.ccpe.state.ne.us.

Nebraska State Scholarship Award Program. Available to undergraduates attending a participating postsecondary institution in Nebraska. Available to Pell Grant recipients only. Nebraska residency not required. Awards determined by each participating institution. Contact financial aid office at respective institution for more details. *Award:* Scholarship for use in freshman, sophomore, junior, or senior year; not renewable. *Eligibility Requirements:* Applicant must be enrolled or expecting to enroll full or part-time at an institution or university and studying in Nebraska. *Application Requirements:* Financial need analysis. **Deadline:** continuous.

Contact financial aid office at college or university, State of Nebraska Coordinating Commission for Postsecondary Education. *Web site:* www.ccpe.state.ne.us.

Postsecondary Education Award Program—Nebraska. Available to undergraduates attending a participating private, nonprofit postsecondary institution in Nebraska. Available to Pell Grant recipients only. Nebraska residency required. Awards determined by each participating institution. Contact financial aid office at respective institution for more information. *Award:* Scholarship for use in freshman, sophomore, junior, or senior year; not renewable. *Eligibility Requirements:* Applicant must be enrolled or expecting to enroll full or part-time at a two-year or four-year institution; resident of Nebraska and studying in Nebraska. Available to U.S. citizens. *Application Requirements:* Financial need analysis. **Deadline:** continuous.

Contact financial aid office at college or university, State of Nebraska Coordinating Commission for Postsecondary Education. *Web site:* www.ccpe.state.ne.us.

NEVADA

Nevada Student Incentive Grant. Award available to Nevada residents for use at an accredited Nevada college or university. Must show financial need. Any field of study eligible. High school students may not apply. One-time award of up to $5000. Contact financial aid office at local college. *Award:* Grant for use in freshman, sophomore, junior, or senior year; not renewable. *Award amount:* $100–$5000. *Number of awards:* 400–800. *Eligibility Requirements:* Applicant must be enrolled or expecting to enroll full or part-time at a two-year, four-year, or technical institution or university; resident of Nevada and studying in Nevada. Available to U.S. citizens. *Application Requirements:* Application, financial need analysis. **Deadline:** continuous.

Contact Financial Aid Office at local college, Nevada Department of Education, 700 East 5th Street, Carson City, NV 89701.

NEW HAMPSHIRE

Leveraged Incentive Grant Program. Award open to New Hampshire residents attending school in New Hampshire. Must be in sophomore, junior, or senior year. Award based on financial need and merit. Contact financial aid office for more information and deadline. *Award:* Grant for use in sophomore, junior, or senior year; not renewable. *Award amount:* $200–$7500. *Eligibility Requirements:* Applicant must be enrolled or expecting to enroll full-time at a two-year or four-year institution or university; resident of New Hampshire and studying in New Hampshire. Available to U.S. citizens. *Application Requirements:* Application, financial need analysis.

Contact Financial Aid Office, New Hampshire Postsecondary Education Commission. *Web site:* www.state.nh.us/postsecondary.

New Hampshire Career Incentive Program. Forgivable loans available to New Hampshire residents attending New Hampshire institutions in programs leading to certification in special education, foreign language education or licensure as an LPN, RN or an Associate, Baccalaureate or advanced nursing degree. Must work in shortage area following graduation. Deadline: June 1 for fall or December 15 for spring. Foreign language or special education students must be juniors, seniors or graduate students with a 3.0 GPA or higher. Forgivable loan is not automatically renewable. Applicant must reapply. *Academic/Career Areas:* Foreign Language; Nursing; Special Education. *Award:* Forgivable loan for use in freshman, sophomore, junior, senior, graduate, or postgraduate years; not renewable. *Award amount:* $1000–$3000. *Eligibility Requirements:* Applicant must be enrolled or expecting to enroll full-time at a two-year, four-year, or technical institution or university; resident of New Hampshire and studying in New Hampshire. Available to U.S. citizens. *Application Requirements:* Application, financial need analysis, references, transcript.

Contact Melanie K. Deshaies, Program Assistant, New Hampshire Postsecondary Education Commission, 3 Barrell Court, Suite 300, Concord, NH 03301-8512. *E-mail:* mdeshaies@pec.state.nh.us. *Phone:* 603-271-2555 Ext. 356. *Fax:* 603-271-2696. *Web site:* www.state.nh.us/postsecondary.

New Hampshire Incentive Program (NHIP). One-time grants for New Hampshire residents attending school in New Hampshire, Connecticut, Maine, Massachusetts, Rhode Island, or Vermont. Must have financial need. Deadline is May 1. Complete Free Application for Federal Student Aid. Grant is not automatically renewable. Applicant must reapply. *Award:* Grant for use in freshman, sophomore, junior, or senior year; not renewable. *Award amount:* $125–$1000. *Number of awards:* 3000–3500. *Eligibility Requirements:* Applicant must be enrolled or expecting to enroll full or part-time at a two-year, four-year, or technical institution or university; resident of New Hampshire and studying in Connecticut, Maine, Massachusetts, New Hampshire, Rhode Island, or Vermont. Available to U.S. citizens. *Application Requirements:* Application, financial need analysis. **Deadline:** May 1.

Contact Sherrie Tucker, Program Assistant, New Hampshire Postsecondary Education Commission, 3 Barrell Court, Suite 300, Concord, NH 03301-8512. *E-mail:* stucker@pec.state.nh.us. *Phone:* 603-271-2555 Ext. 355. *Fax:* 603-271-2696. *Web site:* www.state.nh.us/postsecondary.

Nursing Leveraged Scholarship Loan Program. Forgivable loan available to New Hampshire residents enrolled part- or full-time as a graduate or undergraduate in an approved nursing program at a New Hampshire institute of higher education. Must demonstrate financial need. Loan forgiven through service in New Hampshire as a nurse. Contact Financial Aid Office for deadline. *Academic/Career Areas:* Nursing. *Award:* Forgivable loan for use in freshman, sophomore, junior, senior, or graduate year; not renewable. *Award amount:* $100–$2000. *Eligibility Requirements:* Applicant must be enrolled or expecting to enroll full or part-time at a two-year, four-year, or technical institution or university; resident of New Hampshire and studying in New Hampshire. Available to U.S. citizens. *Application Requirements:* Application, financial need analysis.

Contact Financial Aid Office/HS Guidance Office, New Hampshire Postsecondary Education Commission. *Web site:* www.state.nh.us/postsecondary.

Scholarships for Orphans of Veterans—New Hampshire. Awards for New Hampshire residents whose parent died as a result of service in WWI, WWII, the Korean Conflict, or the Southeast Asian Conflict. Parent must have been a New Hampshire resident at time of death. Possible full tuition and $1000 per year with automatic renewal on reapplication. Contact department for application deadlines. Must be under 26. Must include proof of eligibility and proof of parent's death. *Award:* Grant for use in freshman, sophomore, junior, or senior year; renewable. *Award amount:* up to $1000. *Number of awards:* 1–10. *Eligibility Requirements:*

Applicant must be age 16-25; enrolled or expecting to enroll full-time at a two-year or four-year institution or university and resident of New Hampshire. Available to U.S. citizens. Applicant or parent must meet one or more of the following requirements: general military experience; retired from active duty; disabled or killed as a result of military service; prisoner of war; or missing in action. *Application Requirements:* Application, VA approval.

Contact Melanie K. Deshaies, Program Assistant, New Hampshire Postsecondary Education Commission, 3 Barrell Court, Suite 300, Concord, NH 03301-8543. *E-mail:* mdeshaies@pec.state.nh.us. *Phone:* 603-271-2555 Ext. 356. *Fax:* 603-271-2696. *Web site:* www.state.nh.us/postsecondary.

NEW JERSEY

Dana Christmas Scholarship for Heroism. One-time, non-renewable college scholarship will recognize and honor young for exceptional acts of heroism. The scholarship may be used for undergraduate or graduate higher education expenses. Must be current New Jersey resident and at time of act of heroism. *Award:* Scholarship for use in freshman, sophomore, junior, senior, or graduate year; not renewable. *Award amount:* up to $10,000. *Number of awards:* up to 5. *Eligibility Requirements:* Applicant must be age 21 or under; enrolled or expecting to enroll at a four-year institution or university and resident of New Jersey. Available to U.S. citizens. *Application Requirements:* Application. **Deadline:** October 15.

Contact New Jersey Higher Education Student Assistance Authority, PO Box 540, Trenton, NJ 08625-0540. *Phone:* 800-792-8670. *Web site:* www.hesaa.org.

Edward J. Bloustein Distinguished Scholars. Renewable scholarship for students who place in the top 10% of their classes and have a minimum combined SAT score of 1260, or are ranked first, second or third in their class as of the end of the junior year. Must be New Jersey resident. Must attend a New Jersey two-year college, four-year college or university, or approved programs at proprietary institutions. Deadline for Spring term is March 1 and for Fall term is October 1. *Award:* Scholarship for use in freshman, sophomore, junior, or senior year; renewable. *Award amount:* $1000. *Eligibility Requirements:* Applicant must be high school student; planning to enroll or expecting to enroll full-time at a two-year or four-year institution or university; resident of New Jersey and studying in New Jersey. Available to U.S. citizens. *Application Requirements:* Application, test scores.

Contact New Jersey Higher Education Student Assistance Authority, PO Box 540, Trenton, NJ 08625-0540. *Phone:* 800-792-8670. *Web site:* www.hesaa.org.

New Jersey Educational Opportunity Fund Grants. Grants up to $4150 per year. Must be a New Jersey resident for at least twelve consecutive months and attend a New Jersey institution. Must be from a disadvantaged background as defined by EOF guidelines. EOF grant applicants must also apply for financial aid. EOF recipients may qualify for the Martin Luther King Physician/Dentistry Scholarships for graduate study at a professional institution. *Academic/Career Areas:* Dental Health/Services; Health and Medical Sciences. *Award:* Grant for use in freshman, sophomore, junior, senior, or graduate year; renewable. *Award amount:* up to $4150. *Eligibility Requirements:* Applicant must be enrolled or expecting to enroll full-time at a four-year institution or university; resident of New Jersey and studying in New Jersey. Available to U.S. citizens. *Application Requirements:* Application, financial need analysis.

Contact Sandra Rollins, Associate Director of Financial Aid, University of Medicine and Dentistry of NJ School of Osteopathic Medicine, 40 East Laurel

Road, Primary Care Center 119, Stratford, NJ 08084. *E-mail:* rollins@umdnj.edu. *Phone:* 856-566-6008. *Fax:* 856-566-6015. *Web site:* www.umdnj.edu.

New Jersey War Orphans Tuition Assistance. Renewable award for New Jersey residents who are high school seniors ages 16-21 and who are children of veterans killed or disabled in duty, missing in action, or prisoner-of-war. For use at a two- or four-year college or university. Write for more information. Deadlines: October 1 for fall semester and March 1 for spring semester. *Award:* Scholarship for use in freshman, sophomore, junior, or senior year; renewable. *Award amount:* $2000–$5000. *Eligibility Requirements:* Applicant must be high school student; age 16-21; planning to enroll or expecting to enroll full-time at a two-year or four-year institution or university and resident of New Jersey. Applicant or parent must meet one or more of the following requirements: general military experience; retired from active duty; disabled or killed as a result of military service; prisoner of war; or missing in action. *Application Requirements:* Application, transcript.

Contact Patricia Richter, Grants Manager, New Jersey Department of Military and Veterans Affairs, PO Box 340, Trenton, NJ 08625-0340. *E-mail:* patricia. richter@njdmava.state.nj.us. *Phone:* 609-530-6854. *Fax:* 609-530-6970.

NJSA Scholarship Program. One-time award for legal residents of New Jersey enrolled in an accredited architecture program. Minimum 2.5 GPA required. Must show evidence of financial need, scholarship, and promise in architecture. Submit portfolio and $5 application fee. *Academic/Career Areas:* Architecture. *Award:* Scholarship for use in sophomore, junior, senior, or graduate year; not renewable. *Award amount:* $1500–$3000. *Eligibility Requirements:* Applicant must be enrolled or expecting to enroll full-time at a four-year, or technical institution or university and resident of New Jersey. Applicant must have 2.5 GPA or higher. Available to U.S. citizens. *Application Requirements:* Application, essay, financial need analysis, portfolio, references, transcript. *Fee:* $5. **Deadline:** April 25.

Contact Robert Zaccone, President, AIA New Jersey Scholarship Foundation, Inc., 212 White Avenue, Old Tappan, NJ 07675-7411. *Fax:* 201-767-5541.

Outstanding Scholar Recruitment Program. Students who meet the eligibility criteria and enroll as first-time freshmen at participating New Jersey institutions receive annual scholarship awards of up to $7500. The award amounts vary on a sliding scale depending on class rank and combined SAT scores. Must maintain a B average for renewal. Deadline March 1 for Spring term, October 1 for Fall term. *Award:* Scholarship for use in freshman, sophomore, junior, or senior year; renewable. *Award amount:* up to $7500. *Eligibility Requirements:* Applicant must be high school student; planning to enroll or expecting to enroll at an institution or university and studying in New Jersey. *Application Requirements:* Test scores.

Contact New Jersey Higher Education Student Assistance Authority, PO Box 540, Trenton, NJ 08625-0540. *Phone:* 800-792-8670. *Web site:* www.hesaa.org.

Survivor Tuition Benefits Program. Provides tuition for spouses and dependents of law enforcement officers, fire, or emergency services personnel killed in the line of duty. Recipients must be enrolled in an undergraduate degree program at a college or university in New Jersey as either half-time or full-time students. Deadline March 1 for Spring term, October 1 for Fall term *Award:* Scholarship for use in freshman, sophomore, junior, or senior year; renewable. *Eligibility Requirements:* Applicant must be enrolled or expecting to enroll full or part-time at a four-year institution or university; resident of New Jersey and studying in New Jersey. Applicant or parent of applicant must have employment or volunteer experience in police/ firefighting. Available to U.S. citizens. *Application Requirements:* Application.

Contact New Jersey Higher Education Student Assistance Authority, PO Box 540, Trenton, NJ 08625-0540. *Phone:* 800-792-8670. *Web site:* www.hesaa.org.

Tuition Assistance for Children of POW/MIAs. Assists children of military service personnel declared missing in action or prisoner-of-war after January 1, 1960. Must be a resident of New Jersey. Renewable grants provide tuition for undergraduate study in New Jersey. Apply by October 1 for fall, March 1 for spring. Must be high school senior to apply. *Award:* Scholarship for use in freshman, sophomore, junior, or senior year; renewable. *Eligibility Requirements:* Applicant must be high school student; planning to enroll or expecting to enroll full-time at a two-year or four-year institution; resident of New Jersey and studying in New Jersey. Available to U.S. citizens. Applicant or parent must meet one or more of the following requirements: general military experience; retired from active duty; disabled or killed as a result of military service; prisoner of war; or missing in action. *Application Requirements:* Application, transcript.

Contact Patricia Richter, Grants Manager, New Jersey Department of Military and Veterans Affairs, PO Box 340, Trenton, NJ 08625-0340. *E-mail:* patricia. richter@njdmava.state.nj.us. *Phone:* 609-530-6854. *Fax:* 609-530-6970.

Urban Scholars. Renewable scholarship to high achieving students attending public secondary schools in the State's urban and economically distressed areas of New Jersey. Students must rank in the top 10% of their class and have a GPA of at least 3.0 at the end of their junior year. Must be New Jersey resident. Must attend a New Jersey two-year college, four-year college or university, or approved programs at proprietary institutions. Students do not apply directly for scholarship consideration. Deadline March 1 for Spring term, October 1 for Fall term. *Award:* Scholarship for use in freshman, sophomore, junior, or senior year; renewable. *Award amount:* $1000. *Eligibility Requirements:* Applicant must be high school student; planning to enroll or expecting to enroll full-time at a two-year or four-year institution or university; resident of New Jersey and studying in New Jersey. Applicant must have 3.0 GPA or higher. Available to U.S. citizens. *Application Requirements:* Application, test scores.

Contact New Jersey Higher Education Student Assistance Authority, PO Box 540, Trenton, NJ 08625-0540. *Phone:* 800-792-8670. *Web site:* www.hesaa.org.

Veterans' Tuition Credit Program—New Jersey. Award for veterans who served in the armed forces between December 31, 1960, and May 7, 1975. Must have been a New Jersey resident at time of induction or discharge or for one year prior to application. Apply by October 1 for fall, March 1 for spring. Renewable award of $200-$400. *Award:* Scholarship for use in freshman, sophomore, junior, or senior year; renewable. *Award amount:* $200–$400. *Eligibility Requirements:* Applicant must be enrolled or expecting to enroll full or part-time at a two-year, four-year, or technical institution or university and resident of New Jersey. Available to U.S. citizens. Applicant must have general military experience. *Application Requirements:* Application.

Contact Patricia Richter, Grants Manager, New Jersey Department of Military and Veterans Affairs, PO Box 340, Trenton, NJ 08625-0340. *E-mail:* patricia. richter@njdmava.state.nj.us. *Phone:* 609-530-6854. *Fax:* 609-530-6970.

NEW MEXICO

3% Scholarship Program. Award equal to tuition and required fees for New Mexico residents who are undergraduate students attending public postsecondary institutions in New Mexico. Contact financial aid office of any public postsecondary institution in New Mexico for deadline. *Award:* Scholarship for use in freshman, sophomore, junior, senior, or graduate year; not renewable. *Eligibility Requirements:* Applicant must be enrolled or expecting to enroll full or part-time at a two-year or four-year institution or university; resident of New Mexico and studying in New Mexico. Available to U.S. citizens. *Application Requirements:* Application.

Contact Maria Barele, Financial Specialist, New Mexico Commission on Higher Education, PO Box 15910, Santa Fe, NM 87506-5910. *Phone:* 505-827-4026. *Fax:* 505-827-7392. *Web site:* www.nmche.org.

Allied Health Student Loan Program—New Mexico. Renewable loans for New Mexico residents enrolled in an undergraduate allied health program. Loans can be forgiven through service in a medically underserved area or can be repaid. Penalties apply for failure to provide service. May borrow up to $12,000 per year for four years. *Academic/Career Areas:* Dental Health/Services; Health and Medical Sciences; Nursing; Social Sciences; Therapy/Rehabilitation. *Award:* Forgivable loan for use in freshman, sophomore, junior, or senior year; renewable. *Award amount:* up to $12,000. *Number of awards:* 1–40. *Eligibility Requirements:* Applicant must be enrolled or expecting to enroll full or part-time at a two-year or four-year institution or university; resident of New Mexico and studying in New Mexico. Available to U.S. citizens. *Application Requirements:* Application, financial need analysis, transcript, FAFSA. **Deadline:** July 1.

Contact Maria Barele, Financial Specialist, New Mexico Commission on Higher Education, PO Box 15910, Santa Fe, NM 87506-5910. *Phone:* 505-827-4026. *Fax:* 505-827-7392. *Web site:* www.nmche.org.

Children of Deceased Veterans Scholarship—New Mexico. Award for New Mexico residents who are children of veterans killed or disabled as a result of service, prisoner of war, or veterans missing-in-action. Must be between ages 16 to 26. For use at New Mexico schools for undergraduate study. Submit parent's death certificate and DD form 214. *Award:* Scholarship for use in freshman, sophomore, junior, or senior year; renewable. *Award amount:* $250–$600. *Eligibility Requirements:* Applicant must be age 16-26; enrolled or expecting to enroll full or part-time at an institution or university; resident of New Mexico and studying in New Mexico. Applicant or parent must meet one or more of the following requirements: general military experience; retired from active duty; disabled or killed as a result of military service; prisoner of war; or missing in action. *Application Requirements:* Application, transcript. **Deadline:** continuous.

Contact Alan Martinez, Manager of State Benefits, New Mexico Veterans' Service Commission, PO Box 2324, Sante Fe, NM 87504. *Phone:* 505-827-6300. *Fax:* 505-827-6372. *Web site:* www.state.nm.us/veterans.

Legislative Endowment Scholarships. Awards for undergraduate students with substantial financial need who are attending public postsecondary institutions in New Mexico. Preference given to returning adult students at two-year and four-year institutions and students transferring from two-year to four-year institutions. Deadline set by each institution. Must be resident of New Mexico. Contact financial aid office of any New Mexico public postsecondary institution to apply. *Award:* Scholarship for use in freshman, sophomore, junior, or senior year; not renewable. *Award amount:* $1000–$2500. *Eligibility Requirements:* Applicant must be enrolled or expecting to enroll full or part-time at a two-year or four-year institution or university; resident of New Mexico and studying in New Mexico. Available to U.S. citizens. *Application Requirements:* Application, financial need analysis, FAFSA.

Contact Maria Barele, Financial Specialist, New Mexico Commission on Higher Education, PO Box 15910, Santa Fe, NM 87506-5910. *Phone:* 505-827-7383. *Fax:* 505-827-7392. *Web site:* www.nmche.org.

Lottery Success Scholarships. Awards equal to 100% of tuition at New Mexico public postsecondary institution. Must have New Mexico high school degree and be enrolled at New Mexico public college or university in first regular semester following high school graduation. Must obtain 2.5 GPA during this semester. May be eligible for up to eight consecutive semesters of support. Deadlines vary by institution. Apply through financial aid office of any New Mexico public postsecondary institution. *Award:* Scholarship for use in freshman, sophomore, junior, or senior year; renewable. *Eligibility Requirements:* Applicant must be enrolled or expecting to enroll full-time at a two-year or four-year institution; resident of New Mexico and studying in New Mexico. Applicant must have 2.5 GPA or higher. Available to U.S. citizens. *Application Requirements:* Application.

Contact Maria Barele, Financial Specialist, New Mexico Commission on Higher Education, PO Box 15910, Santa Fe, NM 87506-5910. *Phone:* 505-827-4026. *Fax:* 505-827-7392. *Web site:* www.nmche.org.

New Mexico Competitive Scholarship. Scholarship available to encourage out-of-state students who have demonstrated high academic achievement to enroll in public institutions of higher education in New Mexico. One-time award for undergraduate students. Deadlines set by each institution. Contact financial aid office of any New Mexico public postsecondary institution to apply. *Award:* Scholarship for use in freshman, sophomore, junior, or senior year; not renewable. *Award amount:* $100. *Eligibility Requirements:* Applicant must be enrolled or expecting to enroll full or part-time at a two-year or four-year institution or university and studying in New Mexico. Applicant must have 3.0 GPA or higher. Available to U.S. citizens. *Application Requirements:* Application, essay, references, test scores.

Contact Maria Barele, Financial Specialist, New Mexico Commission on Higher Education, PO Box 15910, Santa Fe, NM 87506-5910. *Phone:* 505-827-4026. *Fax:* 505-827-7392. *Web site:* www.nmche.org.

New Mexico Scholars' Program. Several scholarships to encourage New Mexico high school graduates to enroll in college at a public or selected private nonprofit postsecondary institution in New Mexico before their 22nd birthday. Selected private colleges are College of Santa Fe, St. John's College in Santa Fe, and College of the Southwest. Must have graduated in top 5% of their class or obtained an ACT score of 25 or SAT score of 1140. One-time scholarship for tuition, books, and fees. Contact financial aid office at college to apply. *Award:* Scholarship for use in freshman, sophomore, junior, or senior year; not renewable. *Eligibility Requirements:* Applicant must be age 22 or under; enrolled or expecting to enroll full or part-time at a two-year or four-year institution; resident of New Mexico and studying in New Mexico. Available to U.S. citizens. *Application Requirements:* Application, financial need analysis, test scores, FAFSA.

Contact Maria Barele, Financial Specialist, New Mexico Commission on Higher Education, PO Box 15910, Santa Fe, NM 87506-5910. *Phone:* 505-827-4026. *Fax:* 505-827-7392. *Web site:* www.nmche.org.

New Mexico Student Incentive Grant. Several grants available for resident undergraduate students attending public and selected private nonprofit institutions in New Mexico. Must demonstrate financial need. To apply contact financial aid office at any public or private nonprofit postsecondary institution in New Mexico. *Award:* Grant for use in freshman, sophomore, junior, or senior year; not renewable.

Award amount: $200–$2500. *Eligibility Requirements:* Applicant must be enrolled or expecting to enroll at a two-year or four-year institution or university; resident of New Mexico and studying in New Mexico. Available to U.S. citizens. *Application Requirements:* Application, financial need analysis, FAFSA.

Contact Maria Barele, Financial Specialist, New Mexico Commission on Higher Education, PO Box 15910, Santa Fe, NM 87506-5910. *Phone:* 505-827-4026. *Fax:* 505-827-7392. *Web site:* www.nmche.org.

New Mexico Vietnam Veterans' Scholarship. Renewable award for Vietnam veterans who are New Mexico residents attending state-sponsored schools. Must have been awarded the Vietnam Campaign medal. Submit DD214. Must include discharge papers. *Award:* Scholarship for use in freshman, sophomore, junior, or senior year; renewable. *Award amount:* up to $1554. *Eligibility Requirements:* Applicant must be enrolled or expecting to enroll at an institution or university; resident of New Mexico and studying in New Mexico. Available to U.S. citizens. Applicant must have general military experience. *Application Requirements:* Application. **Deadline:** continuous.

Contact Alan Martinez, Manager State Benefits, New Mexico Veterans' Service Commission, PO Box 2324, Sante Fe, NM 87504. *Phone:* 505-827-6300. *Fax:* 505-827-6372. *Web site:* www.state.nm.us/veterans.

Nursing Student Loan-for-Service Program. Award for New Mexico residents accepted or enrolled in nursing program at New Mexico public postsecondary institution. Must practice as nurse in designated health professional shortage area in New Mexico. Award dependent upon financial need but may not exceed $12,000. Deadline: July 1. *Academic/Career Areas:* Nursing. *Award:* Forgivable loan for use in freshman, sophomore, junior, or senior year; not renewable. *Award amount:* up to $12,000. *Eligibility Requirements:* Applicant must be enrolled or expecting to enroll full or part-time at a two-year or four-year institution; resident of New Mexico and studying in New Mexico. Available to U.S. citizens. *Application Requirements:* Application, financial need analysis, FAFSA. **Deadline:** July 1.

Contact Maria Barele, Financial Specialist, New Mexico Commission on Higher Education, PO Box 15910, Santa Fe, NM 87506-5910. *Phone:* 505-827-4026. *Fax:* 505-827-7392. *Web site:* www.nmche.org.

Vietnam Veterans' Scholarship Program. Award for New Mexico residents who are Vietnam veterans enrolled in undergraduate or master's-level course work at public or selected private New Mexico postsecondary institutions. Award may include tuition, required fees, and book allowance. Contact financial aid office of any public or eligible private New Mexico postsecondary institution for deadline. *Award:* Scholarship for use in freshman, sophomore, junior, senior, or graduate year; not renewable. *Eligibility Requirements:* Applicant must be enrolled or expecting to enroll full or part-time at a two-year or four-year institution; resident of New Mexico and studying in New Mexico. Available to U.S. citizens. Applicant must have general military experience. *Application Requirements:* Application, certification by the NM Veteran's commission.

Contact Maria Barele, Financial Specialist, New Mexico Commission on Higher Education, PO Box 15910, Santa Fe, NM 87506-5910. *Phone:* 505-827-4026. *Fax:* 505-827-7392. *Web site:* www.nmche.org.

NEW YORK

New York Aid for Part-time Study (APTS). Renewable scholarship provides tuition assistance to part-time students who are New York residents attending New

Profiles of State-Sponsored Programs

York-accredited institutions. Deadlines and award amounts vary. Must be U.S. citizen. *Award:* Grant for use in freshman, sophomore, junior, or senior year; renewable. *Award amount:* up to $2000. *Eligibility Requirements:* Applicant must be enrolled or expecting to enroll part-time at a two-year or four-year institution; resident of New York and studying in New York. Available to U.S. citizens. *Application Requirements:* Application.

Contact Student Information, New York State Higher Education Services Corporation, 99 Washington Avenue, Room 1320, Albany, NY 12255. *Phone:* 518-473-3887. *Fax:* 518-474-2839. *Web site:* www.hesc.com.

New York Educational Opportunity Program (EOP). Renewable award for New York resident attending New York college/university for undergraduate study. For educationally and economically disadvantaged students; includes educational assistance such as tutoring. Contact prospective college for information. *Award:* Scholarship for use in freshman, sophomore, junior, or senior year; renewable. *Eligibility Requirements:* Applicant must be enrolled or expecting to enroll full-time at a two-year or four-year institution or university; resident of New York and studying in New York. Available to U.S. citizens. *Application Requirements:* Application, financial need analysis, transcript.

Contact Student Information, New York State Higher Education Services Corporation, 99 Washington Avenue, Room 1320, Albany, NY 12255. *Web site:* www.hesc.com.

New York Lottery Leaders of Tomorrow (Lot) Scholarship. The goal of this program is to reinforce the lottery's education mission by awarding four-year scholarships, $1000 per year for up to four years. One scholarship is available to every New York high school, public or private, that awards a high school diploma. *Award:* Scholarship for use in freshman, sophomore, junior, or senior year; renewable. *Award amount:* $1000. *Eligibility Requirements:* Applicant must be high school student; planning to enroll or expecting to enroll full-time at a two-year, four-year, or technical institution or university; resident of New York and studying in New York. Applicant must have 3.0 GPA or higher. Available to U.S. citizens. *Application Requirements:* Application, essay, transcript. **Deadline:** March 19.

Contact Betsey Morgan, Program Coordinator, CASDA-LOT (Capital Area School Development Association), The University at Albany East Campus, One University Place—A-409, Rensselaer, NY 12144-3456. *E-mail:* casdalot@uamail.albany.edu. *Phone:* 518-525-2788. *Fax:* 518-525-2797. *Web site:* www.nylottery.org/lot.

New York State Aid to Native Americans. Award for enrolled members of a New York State tribe and their children who are attending or planning to attend a New York State college and who are New York State residents. Award for full-time-students up to $1550 annually; part-time awards approximately $65 per credit hour. *Award:* Scholarship for use in freshman, sophomore, junior, or senior year; not renewable. *Award amount:* up to $1550. *Eligibility Requirements:* Applicant must be American Indian/Alaska Native; enrolled or expecting to enroll full or part-time at a two-year, four-year, or technical institution or university; resident of New York and studying in New York. *Application Requirements:* Application. **Deadline:** July 15.

Contact Native American Education Unit, New York State Education Department, New York State Higher Education Services Corporation, EBA Room 374, Albany, NY 12234. *Phone:* 518-474-0537. *Web site:* www.hesc.com.

New York State Tuition Assistance Program. Award for New York state residents attending New York postsecondary institution. Must be full-time student in approved program with tuition over $200 per year. Must show financial need and not be in default in any other state program. Renewable award of $500-$5000. *Award:* Grant for use in freshman, sophomore, junior, or senior year; renewable. *Award amount:* $500-$5000. *Number of awards:* 300,000-320,000. *Eligibility Requirements:* Applicant must be enrolled or expecting to enroll full-time at a two-year or four-year institution or university; resident of New York and studying in New York. *Application Requirements:* Application, financial need analysis. **Deadline:** May 1.

Contact Student Information, New York State Higher Education Services Corporation, 99 Washington Avenue, Room 1320, Albany, NY 12255. *Web site:* www.hesc.com.

New York Vietnam Veterans Tuition Awards. Scholarship for veterans who served in Vietnam. Must be a New York resident attending a New York institution. Renewable award of $500-$1000. Deadline: May 1. Must establish eligibility by September 1. *Award:* Scholarship for use in freshman, sophomore, junior, or senior year; renewable. *Award amount:* $500-$1000. *Eligibility Requirements:* Applicant must be enrolled or expecting to enroll full or part-time at a two-year, four-year, or technical institution or university; resident of New York and studying in New York. Applicant must have served in the Air Force, Army, Marine Corp, or Navy. *Application Requirements:* Application, financial need analysis. **Deadline:** May 1.

Contact Student Information, New York State Higher Education Services Corporation, 99 Washington Avenue, Room 1320, Albany, NY 12255. *Web site:* www.hesc.com.

Regents Award for Child of Veteran. Award for students whose parent, as a result of service in U.S. Armed Forces during war or national emergency, died; suffered a 40% or more disability; or is classified as missing in action or a prisoner of war. Veteran must be current New York State resident or have been so at time of death. Must be New York resident attending, or planning to attend, college in New York State. Must establish eligibility before applying for payment. *Award:* Scholarship for use in freshman, sophomore, junior, or senior year; not renewable. *Award amount:* $450. *Eligibility Requirements:* Applicant must be enrolled or expecting to enroll full-time at a two-year or four-year institution or university; resident of New York and studying in New York. Available to U.S. citizens. Applicant or parent must meet one or more of the following requirements: general military experience; retired from active duty; disabled or killed as a result of military service; prisoner of war; or missing in action. *Application Requirements:* Application, proof of eligibility. **Deadline:** May 1.

Contact Student Information, New York State Higher Education Services Corporation, 99 Washington Avenue, Room 1320, Albany, NY 12255. *Web site:* www.hesc.com.

Regents Professional Opportunity Scholarships. Award for New York State residents pursuing career in certain licensed professions. Must attend New York State college. Priority given to economically disadvantaged members of minority group underrepresented in chosen profession and graduates of SEEK, College Discovery, EOP, and HEOP. Must work in New York State in chosen profession one year for each annual payment. *Award:* Forgivable loan for use in freshman, sophomore, junior, senior, or graduate year; not renewable. *Award amount:* $1000-$5000. *Eligibility Requirements:* Applicant must be enrolled or expecting to enroll full-time at a two-year or four-year institution or university; resident of New York and studying in New York. Available to U.S. citizens. *Application Requirements:* Application. **Deadline:** May 1.

Contact Scholarship Processing Unit-New York State Education Department, New York State Higher Education Services Corporation, EBA Room 1078, Albany, NY 12234. *Phone:* **518-486-1319.** *Web site:* www.hesc.com.

Scholarships for Academic Excellence. Renewable awards of up to $1500 for academically outstanding New York State high school graduates planning to attend an approved postsecondary institution in New York State. For full-time study only. Contact high school guidance counselor to apply. *Award:* Scholarship for use in freshman, sophomore, junior, or senior year; renewable. *Award amount:* $500–$1500. *Number of awards:* 8000. *Eligibility Requirements:* Applicant must be high school student; planning to enroll or expecting to enroll full-time at a four-year institution or university; resident of New York and studying in New York. Available to U.S. citizens. *Application Requirements:* Application.

Contact Student Information, New York State Higher Education Services Corporation, 99 Washington Avenue, Room 1320, Albany, NY 12255. *Web site:* www.hesc.com.

World Trade Center Memorial Scholarship. Renewable awards of up to the average cost of attendance at a State University of New York four-year college. Available to the families and financial dependents of victims who died or were severely and permanently disabled as a result of the Sept. 11, 2001 terrorist attacks on the U.S.A and the rescue and recovery efforts. *Award:* Scholarship for use in freshman, sophomore, junior, or senior year; renewable. *Eligibility Requirements:* Applicant must be enrolled or expecting to enroll full-time at a two-year or four-year institution or university and resident of New York. Available to U.S. citizens. *Application Requirements:* Application. **Deadline:** May 1.

Contact HESC Scholarship Unit, New York State Higher Education Services Corporation, 99 Washington Avenue, Room 1320, Albany, NY 12255. *Phone:* 518-402-6494. *Web site:* www.hesc.com.

Young Scholars Contest. The Young Scholars Contest is a research essay competition on a pre-determined theme in the humanities. New York State high school students who are legal residents of the state are eligible. Further information, guidelines and deadlines are available at web site http://www.nyhumanities.org. **Award:** Scholarship for use in freshman year; not renewable. *Award amount:* $250–$5000. *Number of awards:* 6–18. *Eligibility Requirements:* Applicant must be high school student; planning to enroll or expecting to enroll full-time at a two-year or four-year institution or university and resident of New York. Available to U.S. and non-U.S. citizens. *Application Requirements:* Applicant must enter a contest, essay.

Contact New York Council for the Humanities, 150 Broadway, Suite 1700, New York, NY 10038. *Web site:* www.nyhumanities.org.

NORTH CAROLINA

Incentive Scholarship for Native Americans. Merit-based award with a required public service component. Maximum award $3000 per academic year. Must be graduate of a North Carolina high school enrolled at North Carolina institution. Must submit tribal enrollment card. Minimum 2.5 GPA required. *Award:* Scholarship for use in freshman, sophomore, junior, or senior year; renewable. *Award amount:* up to $3000. *Number of awards:* up to 200. *Eligibility Requirements:* Applicant must be American Indian/Alaska Native; enrolled or expecting to enroll full-time at a four-year institution; resident of North Carolina and studying in North

Carolina. Applicant must have 2.5 GPA or higher. Available to U.S. citizens. *Application Requirements:* Application, financial need analysis, tribal enrollment card. **Deadline:** continuous.

Contact Ms. Mickey Locklear, Director, Education Talent Search, North Carolina Commission of Indian Affairs, 217 West Jones Street, Raleigh, NC 27603. *E-mail:* mickey.locklear@ncmail.net. *Phone:* 919-733-5998. *Fax:* 919-733-1207.

North Carolina Legislative Tuition Grant Program. Renewable aid for North Carolina residents attending approved private colleges or universities within the state. Must be enrolled full-time in an undergraduate program not leading to a religious vocation. Contact college financial aid office for deadlines. *Award:* Grant for use in freshman, sophomore, junior, or senior year; renewable. *Award amount:* $1500–$1800. *Eligibility Requirements:* Applicant must be enrolled or expecting to enroll full-time at a two-year or four-year institution or university; resident of North Carolina and studying in North Carolina. Available to U.S. citizens. *Application Requirements:* Application.

Contact Bill Carswell, Manager of Scholarship and Grant Division, North Carolina State Education Assistance Authority, PO Box 13663, Research Triangle, NC 27709-3663. *Web site:* www.cfnc.org.

North Carolina National Guard Tuition Assistance Program. For members of the North Carolina Air and Army National Guard who will remain in the service for two years following the period for which assistance is provided. Applicants must reapply for each academic period. For use at approved North Carolina institutions. Deadline: last day of late registration period set by the school. Applicant must currently be serving in the Air National Guard or Army National Guard. Annual maximum (July 1 through June 30) of $2000. Career maximum of $8000. *Award:* Grant for use in freshman, sophomore, junior, or senior year; not renewable. *Award amount:* up to $2000. *Eligibility Requirements:* Applicant must be enrolled or expecting to enroll full or part-time at a two-year, four-year, or technical institution or university and studying in North Carolina. Available to U.S. citizens. Applicant must have served in the Air Force National Guard or Army National Guard. *Application Requirements:* Application.

Contact Capt. Miriam Gray, Education Services Officer, North Carolina National Guard, 4105 Reedy Creek Road, Raleigh, NC 27607-6410. *E-mail:* miriam.gray@nc.ngb.army.mil. *Phone:* 800-621-4136 Ext. 6272. *Fax:* 919-664-6520. *Web site:* www.nc.ngb.army.mil.

North Carolina Police Corps Scholarship. Selected participants must attend a four-year institution full-time. May receive up to $10,000 per year with a maximum of $30,000. Complete 24-week training course receiving $400 per week while in residence and serve four years in selected law enforcement agency. Must have physical, background investigation, drug test, and psychological evaluation. *Award:* Scholarship for use in freshman, sophomore, junior, senior, or graduate year; renewable. *Award amount:* $7500–$10,000. *Number of awards:* 15–30. *Eligibility Requirements:* Applicant must be enrolled or expecting to enroll full-time at a four-year institution or university. Available to U.S. citizens. *Application Requirements:* Application, autobiography, essay, interview, photo, references, test scores, transcript. **Deadline:** November 15.

Contact Neil Woodcock, Director, NC Police Corps, North Carolina Police Corps, NC Department of Crime Control and Public Safety, 4710 Mail Service Center, Raleigh, NC 27699-4710. *E-mail:* nwoodcock@nccrimecontrol.org. *Phone:* 919-773-2823. *Fax:* 919-773-2845. *Web site:* www.ncpolicecorps.org.

North Carolina Sheriffs' Association Undergraduate Criminal Justice Scholarships. One-time award for full-time North Carolina resident undergraduate students majoring in criminal justice at a University of North Carolina school. Priority given to child of any North Carolina law enforcement officer. Letter of recommendation from county sheriff required. *Academic/Career Areas:* Criminal Justice/Criminology; Law Enforcement/Police Administration. *Award:* Scholarship for use in freshman, sophomore, junior, or senior year; not renewable. *Award amount:* $1000–$2000. *Number of awards:* up to 10. *Eligibility Requirements:* Applicant must be enrolled or expecting to enroll full-time at a four-year institution; resident of North Carolina and studying in North Carolina. Applicant or parent of applicant must have employment or volunteer experience in police/firefighting. Available to U.S. citizens. *Application Requirements:* Essay, financial need analysis, references, transcript. **Deadline:** continuous.

Contact Sharon Scott, Assistant, Scholarship and Grant Division, North Carolina State Education Assistance Authority, PO Box 13663, Research Triangle, NC 27709-3663. *Web site:* www.cfnc.org.

North Carolina Student Incentive Grant. Renewable award for North Carolina residents who are enrolled full-time in an undergraduate program not leading to a religious vocation at a North Carolina postsecondary institution. Must demonstrate substantial financial need. Must complete Free Application for Student Aid. Must be U.S. citizen and must maintain satisfactory academic progress. Offered by NCSEAA through College Foundation, Inc. Visit web site at http://www.cfnc.org. **Award:** Grant for use in freshman, sophomore, junior, or senior year; renewable. *Award amount:* $200–$1500. *Eligibility Requirements:* Applicant must be enrolled or expecting to enroll full-time at a two-year or four-year institution or university; resident of North Carolina and studying in North Carolina. Available to U.S. citizens. *Application Requirements:* Financial need analysis. **Deadline:** March 15.

Contact Bill Carswell, Manager of Scholarship and Grant Division, North Carolina State Education Assistance Authority, PO Box 13663, Research Triangle, NC 27709-3663. *Web site:* www.cfnc.org.

North Carolina Student Loan Program for Health, Science, and Mathematics. Renewable award for North Carolina residents studying health-related fields, or science or math education. Based on merit, need, and promise of service as a health professional or educator in an underserved area of North Carolina. Need two co-signers. Submit surety statement. *Academic/Career Areas:* Dental Health/Services; Health Administration; Health and Medical Sciences; Nursing; Physical Sciences and Math; Therapy/Rehabilitation. *Award:* Forgivable loan for use in freshman, sophomore, junior, senior, or graduate year; renewable. *Award amount:* $3000–$8500. *Eligibility Requirements:* Applicant must be enrolled or expecting to enroll full-time at a two-year or four-year institution or university; resident of North Carolina and studying in North Carolina. Available to U.S. citizens. *Application Requirements:* Application, financial need analysis, transcript. **Deadline:** June 1.

Contact Edna Williams, Manager, Selection and Origination, HSM Loan Program, North Carolina State Education Assistance Authority, PO Box 14223, Research Triangle, NC 27709-4223. *Phone:* 919-549-8614. *Web site:* www.cfnc.org.

North Carolina Teaching Fellows Scholarship Program. Renewable award for North Carolina high school seniors pursuing teaching careers. Must agree to teach in a North Carolina public or government school for four years or repay award. Must attend one of the 14 approved schools in North Carolina. Merit-based. Must interview at the local level and at the regional level as a finalist. *Academic/Career Areas:* Education. *Award:* Forgivable loan for use in freshman, sophomore, junior, or senior year; renewable. *Award amount:* $6500. *Number of awards:* up to 400. *Eligibility Requirements:* Applicant must be high school student; planning to enroll or expecting to enroll full-time at a four-year institution; resident of North Carolina and studying in North Carolina. Applicant must have 3.5 GPA or higher. Available to U.S. citizens. *Application Requirements:* Application, essay, interview, references, test scores, transcript. **Deadline:** October 31.

Contact Ms. Sherry Woodruff, Program Officer, North Carolina Teaching Fellows Commission, 3739 National Drive, Suite 210, Raleigh, NC 27612. *E-mail:* tfellows@ncforum.org. *Phone:* 919-781-6833 Ext. 103. *Fax:* 919-781-6527. *Web site:* www.teachingfellows.org.

North Carolina Veterans' Scholarships Class I. Renewable awards for children of veterans who were killed or died in wartime service or died as a result of service-connected condition incurred in wartime service as defined in the law. Parent must have been a North Carolina resident at time of entry into service. Duration of the scholarship is four academic years (8 semesters) if used within 8 years. Free tuition, a room allowance, a board allowance, and exemption from certain mandatory fees as set forth in the law in Public, Community & Technical Colleges/Institutions. Award is $4500 per nine-month academic year in Private Colleges & Junior Colleges. No limit on number awarded each year. See web site for details and where to procure an application. Deadline is May 30. *Award:* Scholarship for use in freshman, sophomore, junior, or senior year; renewable. *Award amount:* up to $4500. *Eligibility Requirements:* Applicant must be enrolled or expecting to enroll full or part-time at a two-year, four-year, or technical institution or university and studying in North Carolina. Available to U.S. citizens. Applicant or parent must meet one or more of the following requirements: general military experience; retired from active duty; disabled or killed as a result of military service; prisoner of war; or missing in action. *Application Requirements:* Application, financial need analysis, interview, transcript. **Deadline:** May 30.

Contact Charles F. Smith, Director, North Carolina Division of Veterans' Affairs, 325 North Salisbury Street, Raleigh, NC 27603. *Phone:* 919-733-3851. *Fax:* 919-733-2834.

North Carolina Veterans' Scholarships Class I-B. Renewable awards for children of veterans rated by U.S.DVA as 100% disabled due to wartime service as defined in the law, and currently or at time of death drawing compensation for such disability. Parent must have been a North Carolina resident at time of entry into service. Duration of the scholarship is four academic years (8 semesters) if used within 8 years. Free tuition and exemption from certain mandatory fees as set forth in the law in Public, Community & Technical Colleges/Institutions. See web site for details and where to procure an application. $1500 per nine month academic year in Private Colleges & Junior Colleges. No limit on number awarded each year. Deadline is May 30. *Award:* Scholarship for use in freshman, sophomore, junior, or senior year; renewable. *Award amount:* up to $1500. *Eligibility Requirements:* Applicant must be enrolled or expecting to enroll full or part-time at a two-year, four-year, or technical institution or university and studying in North Carolina. Available to U.S. citizens. Applicant or parent must meet one or more of the following requirements: general military experience; retired from active duty; disabled or killed as a result of military service; prisoner of war; or missing in action. *Application Requirements:* Application, financial need analysis, interview, transcript. **Deadline:** May 30.

Contact Charles F. Smith, Director, North Carolina Division of Veterans' Affairs, 325 North Salisbury Street, Raleigh, NC 27603. *Phone:* 919-733-3851. *Fax:* 919-733-2834.

North Carolina Veterans' Scholarships Class II. Renewable awards for children of veterans rated by U.S.DVA as much as 20% but less than 100% disabled due to wartime service as defined in the law, or was awarded Purple Heart Medal for wounds received. Parent must have been a North Carolina resident at time of entry into service. Duration of the scholarship is four academic years (8 semesters) if used within 8 years. Free tuition and exemption from certain mandatory fees as set forth in the law in Public, Community & Technical Colleges/Institutions. See web site for details and where to procure an application. $4500 per nine month academic year in Private Colleges & Junior Colleges. 100 awarded each year. Deadline is March 31. *Award:* Scholarship for use in freshman, sophomore, junior, or senior year; renewable. *Award amount:* up to $4500. *Number of awards:* 100. *Eligibility Requirements:* Applicant must be enrolled or expecting to enroll full or part-time at a two-year, four-year, or technical institution or university and studying in North Carolina. Available to U.S. citizens. Applicant or parent must meet one or more of the following requirements: general military experience; retired from active duty; disabled or killed as a result of military service; prisoner of war; or missing in action. *Application Requirements:* Application, financial need analysis, interview, transcript. **Deadline:** March 31.

Contact Charles F. Smith, Director, North Carolina Division of Veterans' Affairs, 325 North Salisbury Street, Raleigh, NC 27603. *Phone:* 919-733-3851. *Fax:* 919-733-2834.

North Carolina Veterans' Scholarships Class III. Renewable awards for children of a veteran who died or was, at time of death, drawing a pension for total and permanent disability as rated by U.S.DVA, was honorably discharged and does not a qualify for Class I, II, or IV, scholarships, or served in a combat zone or waters adjacent to a combat zone and received a campaign badge or medal and does not qualify under Class I, II, IV, or V. Parent must have been a North Carolina resident at time of entry into service. Duration of the scholarship is four academic years (8 semesters) if used within eight years. Free tuition and exemption from certain mandatory fees as set forth in the law in Public, Community & Technical Colleges/ Institutions. $4500 per nine month academic year in Private Colleges & Junior Colleges. See web site for details and where to procure an application. 100 awarded each year. Deadline is March 31. *Award:* Scholarship for use in freshman, sophomore, junior, or senior year; renewable. *Award amount:* up to $4500. *Number of awards:* 100. *Eligibility Requirements:* Applicant must be enrolled or expecting to enroll full or part-time at a two-year, four-year, or technical institution or university and studying in North Carolina. Available to U.S. citizens. Applicant or parent must meet one or more of the following requirements: general military experience; retired from active duty; disabled or killed as a result of military service; prisoner of war; or missing in action. *Application Requirements:* Application, financial need analysis, interview, transcript. **Deadline:** March 31.

Contact Charles F. Smith, Director, North Carolina Division of Veterans' Affairs, 325 North Salisbury Street, Raleigh, NC 27603. *Phone:* 919-733-3851. *Fax:* 919-733-2834.

North Carolina Veterans' Scholarships Class IV. Renewable awards for children of a veteran who was a POW or MIA. Parent must have been a North Carolina resident at time of entry into service. Duration of the scholarship is four academic years (8 semesters) if used within eight years. No limit on number awarded per year. The student receives free tuition, a room allowance, a board allowance, and exemption from certain mandatory fees as set forth in the law in public, community, and technical colleges or institutions. The scholarship is $4500 per nine-month academic year in private colleges and junior colleges. Deadline is May 30. *Award:* Scholarship for use in freshman, sophomore, junior, or senior year; renewable. *Award amount:* up to $4500. *Eligibility Requirements:* Applicant must be enrolled or expecting to enroll full or part-time at a two-year, four-year, or technical institution or university and studying in North Carolina. Available to U.S. citizens. Applicant or parent must meet one or more of the following requirements: general military experience; retired from active duty; disabled or killed as a result of military service; prisoner of war; or missing in action. *Application Requirements:* Application, financial need analysis, interview, transcript. **Deadline:** May 31.

Contact Charles F. Smith, Director, North Carolina Division of Veterans' Affairs, 325 North Salisbury Street, Raleigh, NC 27603. *Phone:* 919-733-3851. *Fax:* 919-733-2834.

State Contractual Scholarship Fund Program—North Carolina. Renewable award for North Carolina residents already attending an approved private college or university in the state in pursuit of an undergraduate degree. Must have financial need. Contact college financial aid office for deadline and information. May not be enrolled in a program leading to a religious vocation. *Award:* Scholarship for use in freshman, sophomore, junior, or senior year; renewable. *Award amount:* up to $1100. *Eligibility Requirements:* Applicant must be enrolled or expecting to enroll full or part-time at a two-year or four-year institution or university; resident of North Carolina and studying in North Carolina. Available to U.S. citizens. *Application Requirements:* Financial need analysis.

Contact Bill Carswell, Manager of Scholarship and Grant Division, North Carolina State Education Assistance Authority, PO Box 13663, Research Triangle, NC 27709-3663. *Web site:* www.cfnc.org.

NORTH DAKOTA

North Dakota Department of Transportation Engineering Grant. Educational grants for civil or construction engineering, or civil engineering technology, are awarded to students who have completed one year of course study at an institution of higher learning in North Dakota. Recipients must agree to work for the Department for a period of time at least equal to the grant period or repay the grant at 6% interest. Minimum 2.0 GPA required. *Academic/Career Areas:* Civil Engineering; Engineering/Technology. *Award:* Grant for use in sophomore, junior, or senior year; renewable. *Award amount:* $2000. *Number of awards:* 1-10. *Eligibility Requirements:* Applicant must be enrolled or expecting to enroll full-time at a four-year, or technical institution and studying in North Dakota. Available to U.S. citizens. *Application Requirements:* Application, financial need analysis, interview, transcript. **Deadline:** continuous.

Contact Lorrie Pavlicek, Human Resources Manager, North Dakota Department of Transportation, 503, 38th Street South, Fargo, ND 58103. *E-mail:* lpavlice@ state.nd.us. *Phone:* 701-239-8934. *Fax:* 701-239-8939. *Web site:* www.state.nd.us/dot/.

North Dakota Indian College Scholarship Program. Renewable award to Native-Americans residents of North Dakota. Priority given to full-time undergraduate students. Minimum 2.0 GPA required. *Award:* Scholarship for use in freshman, sophomore, junior, senior, or graduate year; renewable. *Award amount:* $700–$2000. *Number of awards:* up to 150. *Eligibility Requirements:* Applicant must be American Indian/Alaska Native; enrolled or expecting to enroll full-time at a two-year, four-year, or technical institution or university and resident of North Dakota.

Available to U.S. citizens. *Application Requirements:* Application, financial need analysis, transcript, proof of tribal enrollment. **Deadline:** July 15.

Contact Rhonda Schauer, SAA Director, North Dakota University System, 600 East Boulevard Avenue, Department 215, Bismarck, ND 58505-0230. *Phone:* 701-328-9661. *Web site:* www.ndus.nodak.edu.

North Dakota Indian Scholarship Program. Assists Native-Americans North Dakota residents in obtaining a college education. Priority given to full-time undergraduate students and those having a 3.5 GPA or higher. Certification of tribal enrollment required. For use at North Dakota institution. *Award:* Scholarship for use in freshman, sophomore, junior, senior, or graduate year; renewable. *Award amount:* $700–$2000. *Number of awards:* 120–150. *Eligibility Requirements:* Applicant must be American Indian/Alaska Native; enrolled or expecting to enroll at a two-year or four-year institution or university; resident of North Dakota and studying in North Dakota. Applicant must have 3.5 GPA or higher. *Application Requirements:* Application, financial need analysis, transcript. **Deadline:** July 15.

Contact Rhonda Schauer, Coordinator of American Indian Higher Education, State of North Dakota, 600 East Boulevard, Department 215, Bismarck, ND 58505-0230. *Phone:* 701-328-2166. *Web site:* www.ndus.nodak.edu.

North Dakota Scholars Program. Provides scholarships equal to cost of tuition at the public colleges in North Dakota for North Dakota residents. Must score at or above the 95th percentile on ACT and rank in top twenty percent of high school graduation class. Must take ACT in fall. For high school seniors with a minimum 3.5 GPA. Application deadline is October ACT test date. *Award:* Scholarship for use in freshman, sophomore, junior, or senior year; renewable. *Number of awards:* 45–50. *Eligibility Requirements:* Applicant must be high school student; planning to enroll or expecting to enroll full-time at a two-year or four-year institution or university; resident of North Dakota and studying in North Dakota. Applicant must have 3.5 GPA or higher. Available to U.S. citizens. *Application Requirements:* Application, test scores.

Contact Peggy Wipf, Director of Financial Aid, State of North Dakota, 600 East Boulevard, Department 215, Bismarck, ND 58505-0230. *Phone:* 701-328-4114. *Web site:* www.ndus.nodak.edu.

North Dakota Student Financial Assistance Grants. Aids North Dakota residents attending an approved college or university in North Dakota. Must be enrolled in a program of at least nine months in length. *Award:* Grant for use in freshman, sophomore, junior, or senior year; not renewable. *Award amount:* up to $600. *Number of awards:* 2500–2600. *Eligibility Requirements:* Applicant must be enrolled or expecting to enroll full-time at a two-year or four-year institution or university; resident of North Dakota and studying in North Dakota. Available to U.S. citizens. *Application Requirements:* Application, financial need analysis. **Deadline:** April 15.

Contact Peggy Wipf, Director of Financial Aid, State of North Dakota, 600 East Boulevard, Department 215, Bismarck, ND 58505-0230. *Phone:* 701-328-4114. *Web site:* www.ndus.nodak.edu.

OHIO

Ohio Academic Scholarship Program. Award for academically outstanding Ohio residents planning to attend an approved Ohio college. Must be a high school senior intending to enroll full-time. Award is renewable for up to four years. Must rank in upper quarter of class or have a minimum GPA of 3.5. *Award:* Scholarship for use in freshman, sophomore, junior, or senior year; renewable. *Award amount:* $2000. *Number of awards:* 1000. *Eligibility Requirements:* Applicant must be high school student; planning to enroll or expecting to enroll full-time at a two-year or four-year institution; resident of Ohio and studying in Ohio. Applicant must have 3.5 GPA or higher. Available to U.S. citizens. *Application Requirements:* Application, test scores, transcript. **Deadline:** February 23.

Contact Sarina Wilks, Program Administrator, Ohio Board of Regents, PO Box 182452, Columbus, OH 43218-2452. *E-mail:* swilks@regents.state.oh.us. *Phone:* 614-752-9528. *Fax:* 614-752-5903. *Web site:* www.regents.state.oh.us.

Ohio Instructional Grant. Award for low- and middle-income Ohio residents attending an approved college or school in Ohio or Pennsylvania. Must be enrolled full-time and have financial need. Average award is $630. May be used for any course of study except theology. *Award:* Grant for use in freshman, sophomore, junior, or senior year; renewable. *Award amount:* $210–$3750. *Eligibility Requirements:* Applicant must be enrolled or expecting to enroll full-time at a two-year or four-year institution or university; resident of Ohio and studying in Ohio or Pennsylvania. Available to U.S. citizens. *Application Requirements:* Application, financial need analysis. **Deadline:** October 1.

Contact Charles Shahid, Assistant Director, Ohio Board of Regents, PO Box 182452, Columbus, OH 43218-2452. *E-mail:* cshahid@regents.state.oh.us. *Phone:* 614-644-9595. *Fax:* 614-752-5903. *Web site:* www.regents.state.oh.us.

Ohio Missing in Action and Prisoners of War Orphans Scholarship. Renewable award aids children of Vietnam conflict servicemen who have been classified as missing in action or prisoner of war. Must be an Ohio resident, be 16-21, and be enrolled full-time at an Ohio college. Full tuition awards. *Award:* Scholarship for use in freshman, sophomore, junior, or senior year; renewable. *Number of awards:* 1-5. *Eligibility Requirements:* Applicant must be age 16-21; enrolled or expecting to enroll full-time at a two-year or four-year institution; resident of Ohio and studying in Ohio. Available to U.S. citizens. Applicant or parent must meet one or more of the following requirements: general military experience; retired from active duty; disabled or killed as a result of military service; prisoner of war; or missing in action. *Application Requirements:* Application. **Deadline:** July 1.

Contact Sue Minturn, Program Administrator, Ohio Board of Regents, PO Box 182452, Columbus, OH 43218-2452. *E-mail:* sminturn@regents.state.oh.us. *Phone:* 614-752-9536. *Fax:* 614-752-5903. *Web site:* www.regents.state.oh.us.

Ohio National Guard Scholarship Program. Scholarships are for undergraduate studies at an approved Ohio postsecondary institution. Applicants must enlist for six years of Selective Service Reserve Duty in the Ohio National Guard. Scholarship pays 100% instructional and general fees for public institutions and an average of cost of public schools is available for private schools. Must be 18 years of age or older. Award is renewable. Deadlines: July 1, November 1, February 1, April 1. *Award:* Scholarship for use in freshman, sophomore, junior, or senior year; renewable. *Award amount:* up to $3000. *Number of awards:* 3500-10,000. *Eligibility Requirements:* Applicant must be age 18; enrolled or expecting to enroll full or part-time at a two-year, four-year, or technical institution or university and studying in Ohio. Available to U.S. citizens. Applicant must have served in the Air Force National Guard or Army National Guard. *Application Requirements:* Application.

Contact Mrs. Toni Davis, Grants Administrator, Ohio National Guard, 2825 West Dublin Granville Road, Columbus, OH 43235-2789. *E-mail:* toni.davis@tagoh.org. *Phone:* 614-336-7032. *Fax:* 614-336-7318.

Ohio Safety Officers College Memorial Fund. Renewable award covering up to full tuition is available to children and surviving spouses of peace officers and fire fighters killed in the line of duty in any state. Children must be under 26 years of age. Must be an Ohio resident and enroll full-time or part-time at an Ohio college or university. *Award:* Scholarship for use in freshman, sophomore, junior, or senior year; renewable. *Number of awards:* 50–65. *Eligibility Requirements:* Applicant must be age 25 or under; enrolled or expecting to enroll full or part-time at a two-year or four-year institution or university; resident of Ohio and studying in Ohio. Applicant or parent of applicant must have employment or volunteer experience in police/firefighting. Available to U.S. citizens. *Application Requirements:* **Deadline:** continuous.

Contact Barbara Metheney, Program Administrator, Ohio Board of Regents, PO Box 182452, Columbus, OH 43218-2452. *E-mail:* bmethene@regents.state. oh.us. *Phone:* 614-752-9535. *Fax:* 614-752-5903. *Web site:* www.regents.state.oh.us.

Ohio Student Choice Grant Program. Renewable award available to Ohio residents attending private colleges within the state. Must be enrolled full time in a bachelor's degree program. Do not apply to state. Check with financial aid office of college. *Award:* Grant for use in freshman, sophomore, junior, or senior year; renewable. *Award amount:* up to $1038. *Eligibility Requirements:* Applicant must be enrolled or expecting to enroll full-time at a four-year institution; resident of Ohio and studying in Ohio. Available to U.S. citizens. *Application Requirements:* **Deadline:** continuous.

Contact Barbara Metheney, Program Administrator, Ohio Board of Regents, PO Box 182452, Columbus, OH 43218-2452. *E-mail:* bmethene@regents.state. oh.us. *Phone:* 614-752-9535. *Fax:* 614-752-5903. *Web site:* www.regents.state.oh.us.

Ohio War Orphans Scholarship. Aids Ohio residents attending an eligible college in Ohio. Must be between the ages of 16-21, the child of a disabled or deceased veteran, and enrolled full-time. Renewable up to five years. Amount of award varies. Must include Form DD214. *Award:* Scholarship for use in freshman, sophomore, junior, or senior year; renewable. *Number of awards:* 300–450. *Eligibility Requirements:* Applicant must be age 16-21; enrolled or expecting to enroll full-time at a two-year or four-year institution; resident of Ohio and studying in Ohio. Available to U.S. citizens. Applicant or parent must meet one or more of the following requirements: general military experience; retired from active duty; disabled or killed as a result of military service; prisoner of war; or missing in action. *Application Requirements:* Application. **Deadline:** July 1.

Contact Sue Minturn, Program Administrator, Ohio Board of Regents, PO Box 182452, Columbus, OH 43218-2452. *E-mail:* sminturn@regents.state.oh.us. *Phone:* 614-752-9536. *Fax:* 614-752-5903. *Web site:* www.regents.state.oh.us.

Part-time Student Instructional Grant. Renewable grants for part-time undergraduates who are Ohio residents. Award amounts vary. Must attend an Ohio institution. *Award:* Grant for use in freshman, sophomore, or junior year; renewable. *Eligibility Requirements:* Applicant must be enrolled or expecting to enroll part-time at a two-year or four-year institution or university; resident of Ohio and studying in Ohio. Available to U.S. citizens. *Application Requirements:* Application, financial need analysis. **Deadline:** continuous.

Contact Barbara Metheney, Program Administrator, Ohio Board of Regents, PO Box 182452, Columbus, OH 43218-2452. *E-mail:* bmethene@regents.state. oh.us. *Phone:* 614-752-9535. *Fax:* 614-752-5903. *Web site:* www.regents.state.oh.us.

Robert C. Byrd Honors Scholarship. Renewable award for graduating high school seniors who demonstrate outstanding academic achievement. Each Ohio high school receives applications by January of each year. School can submit one application for each 200 students in the senior class. *Award:* Scholarship for use in freshman, sophomore, junior, or senior year; renewable. *Award amount:* $1500. *Eligibility Requirements:* Applicant must be high school student; planning to enroll or expecting to enroll at a two-year or four-year institution or university and resident of Ohio. Applicant must have 3.5 GPA or higher. Available to U.S. citizens. *Application Requirements:* Application, test scores. **Deadline:** March 10.

Contact Charles Shahid, Program Coordinator, Ohio Board of Regents, PO Box 182452, Columbus, OH 43218-2452. *E-mail:* cshahid@regents.state.oh.us. *Phone:* 614-644-5959. *Fax:* 614-752-5903. *Web site:* www.regents.state.oh.us.

OKLAHOMA

Academic Scholars Program. Encourages students of high academic ability to attend institutions in Oklahoma. Renewable up to four years. ACT or SAT scores must fall between 99.5 and 100th percentiles, or be designated as a National Merit Scholar or finalist. *Award:* Scholarship for use in freshman, sophomore, junior, or senior year; renewable. *Award amount:* $3500–$5500. *Eligibility Requirements:* Applicant must be high school student; planning to enroll or expecting to enroll full-time at a two-year or four-year institution or university and studying in Oklahoma. Available to U.S. and non-U.S. citizens. *Application Requirements:* Application, test scores, transcript. **Deadline:** continuous.

Contact Oklahoma State Regents for Higher Education, PO Box 108850, Oklahoma City, OK 73101-8850. *E-mail:* studentinfo@osrhe.edu. *Phone:* 800-858-1840. *Fax:* 405-225-9230. *Web site:* www.okhighered.org.

Future Teacher Scholarship—Oklahoma. Open to outstanding Oklahoma high school graduates who agree to teach in shortage areas. Must rank in top 15% of graduating class or score above 85th percentile on ACT or similar test, or be accepted in an educational program. Students nominated by institution. Reapply to renew. Must attend college/university in Oklahoma. Contact institution's financial aid office for application deadline. *Academic/Career Areas:* Education. *Award:* Scholarship for use in freshman, sophomore, junior, senior, or graduate year; not renewable. *Award amount:* up to $1500. *Eligibility Requirements:* Applicant must be enrolled or expecting to enroll full or part-time at a two-year or four-year institution or university; resident of Oklahoma and studying in Oklahoma. Available to U.S. and non-U.S. citizens. *Application Requirements:* Application, essay, test scores, transcript.

Contact Oklahoma State Regents for Higher Education, PO Box 108850, Oklahoma City, OK 73101-8850. *Phone:* 800-858-1840. *Fax:* 405-225-9230. *Web site:* www.okhighered.org.

Oklahoma Tuition Aid Grant. Award for Oklahoma residents enrolled at an Oklahoma institution at least part-time per semester in a degree program. May be enrolled in two- or four-year or approved vocational-technical institution. Award of up to $1000 per year. Application is made through FAFSA. *Award:* Grant for use in freshman, sophomore, junior, senior, or graduate year; renewable. *Award amount:* $200–$1000. *Number of awards:* 23,000. *Eligibility Requirements:* Applicant must be enrolled or expecting to enroll full or part-time at a two-year, four-year, or technical institution or university; resident of Oklahoma and studying in Oklahoma. Available to U.S. citizens. *Application Requirements:* Application, financial need analysis, FAFSA. **Deadline:** April 30.

Contact Oklahoma State Regents for Higher Education, PO Box 3020, Oklahoma City, OK 73101-3020. *E-mail:* otaginfo@otag.org. *Phone:* 405-225-9456. *Fax:* 405-225-9392. *Web site:* www.okhighered.org.

Regional University Baccalaureate Scholarship. Renewable award for Oklahoma residents attending one of 11 participating Oklahoma public universities. Must have an ACT composite score of at least 30 or be a National Merit Semifinalist or commended student. In addition to the award amount, each recipient also will receive a resident tuition waiver from the institution. Must maintain a 3.25 GPA. Deadlines vary depending upon the institution attended. *Award:* Scholarship for use in freshman, sophomore, junior, or senior year; renewable. *Award amount:* $3000. *Eligibility Requirements:* Applicant must be enrolled or expecting to enroll full-time at an institution or university; resident of Oklahoma and studying in Oklahoma. *Application Requirements:* Application.

Contact Oklahoma State Regents for Higher Education, PO Box 108850, Oklahoma City, OK 73101-8850. *E-mail:* studentinfo@osrhe.edu. *Phone:* 800-858-1840. *Fax:* 405-225-9230. *Web site:* www.okhighered.org.

OREGON

American Ex-Prisoner of War Scholarships: Peter Connacher Memorial Scholarship. Renewable award for American prisoners-of-war and their descendants. Written proof of prisoner-of-war status and discharge papers from the U.S. Armed Forces must accompany application. Statement of relationship between applicant and former prisoner-of-war is required. See web site at http://www.osac.state.or.us for details. **Award:** Scholarship for use in freshman, sophomore, junior, or senior year; renewable. *Award amount:* $1150. *Number of awards:* 4. *Eligibility Requirements:* Applicant must be enrolled or expecting to enroll at a two-year or four-year institution and resident of Oregon. Available to U.S. citizens. Applicant or parent must meet one or more of the following requirements: general military experience; retired from active duty; disabled or killed as a result of military service; prisoner of war; or missing in action. *Application Requirements:* Application, essay, financial need analysis, transcript. **Deadline:** March 1.

Contact Director of Grant Programs, Oregon Student Assistance Commission, 1500 Valley River Drive, Suite 100, Eugene, OR 97401-7020. *E-mail:* awardinfo@mercury.osac.state.or.us. *Phone:* 800-452-8807 Ext. 7395. *Web site:* www.osac.state.or.us.

Children, Adult, and Family Services Scholarship. One-time award for graduating high school seniors, GED recipients, and college students currently or formerly in foster care or an Independent Living Program (ILP) financially supported through the Oregon State Office for Services to Children and Families. Must attend an Oregon public college. Visit web site for more details (http://www.osac.state.or.us). **Award:** Scholarship for use in freshman, sophomore, junior, senior, or graduate year; not renewable. *Eligibility Requirements:* Applicant must be enrolled or expecting to enroll at a two-year or four-year institution; resident of Oregon and studying in Oregon. Available to U.S. citizens. *Application Requirements:* Application, essay, financial need analysis, references, transcript, activity chart. **Deadline:** March 1.

Contact Director of Grant Programs, Oregon Student Assistance Commission, 1500 Valley River Drive, Suite 100, Eugene, OR 97401-7020. *E-mail:* awardinfo@mercury.osac.state.or.us. *Phone:* 800-452-8807 Ext. 7395. *Web site:* www.osac.state.or.us.

Dorothy Campbell Memorial Scholarship. Renewable award for female Oregon high school senior with a minimum 2.75 GPA. Must submit essay describing strong, continuing interest in golf and the contribution that sport has made to applicant's development. *Award:* Scholarship for use in freshman, sophomore, junior, or senior year; renewable. *Award amount:* $1500. *Number of awards:* 2. *Eligibility Requirements:* Applicant must be high school student; planning to enroll or expecting to enroll at a four-year institution; female; resident of Oregon; studying in Oregon and must have an interest in golf. Available to U.S. citizens. *Application Requirements:* Application, essay, financial need analysis, test scores, transcript, activity chart. **Deadline:** March 1.

Contact Director of Grant Programs, Oregon Student Assistance Commission, 1500 Valley River Drive, Suite 100, Eugene, OR 97401-7020. *E-mail:* awardinfo@ mercury.osac.state.or.us. *Phone:* 800-452-8807 Ext. 7395. *Web site:* www.osac.state.or.us.

Former Foster Children Scholarship. Must have been a ward of the court and in legal custody of the State Office for Services to Children and Families (now Children, Adult, and Family Services) for 12 months between ages 16 and 21. Must enroll in college within 3 years of the earlier of high school graduation (or equivalent) or removal from the care of Services to Children and Families. *Award:* Scholarship for use in freshman, sophomore, junior, or senior year; renewable. *Award amount:* $3012. *Number of awards:* 13. *Eligibility Requirements:* Applicant must be enrolled or expecting to enroll at an institution or university; resident of Oregon and studying in Oregon. *Application Requirements:* Application, essay, financial need analysis, transcript, activity chart, FAFSA. **Deadline:** March 1.

Contact Director of Grant Programs, Oregon Student Assistance Commission, 1500 Valley River Drive, Suite 100, Eugene, OR 97401-7020. *E-mail:* awardinfo@ mercury.osac.state.or.us. *Phone:* 800-452-8807 Ext. 7395. *Web site:* www.osac.state.or.us.

Glenn Jackson Scholars Scholarships (OCF). Award for graduating high school seniors who are dependents of employees or retirees of Oregon Department of Transportation or Parks and Recreation Department. Employees must have worked in their department at least three years. Award for maximum twelve undergraduate quarters or six quarters at a two-year institution. Must be U.S. citizen or permanent resident. Visit web site (http://www.osac.state.or.us) for more details. **Award:** Scholarship for use in freshman, sophomore, junior, or senior year; renewable. *Award amount:* $2500. *Number of awards:* 2. *Eligibility Requirements:* Applicant must be high school student; planning to enroll or expecting to enroll at a four-year institution and resident of Oregon. Applicant or parent of applicant must be affiliated with Oregon Department of Transportation Parks and Recreation. Applicant or parent of applicant must have employment or volunteer experience in designated career field. Available to U.S. citizens. *Application Requirements:* Application, essay, financial need analysis, references, transcript, activity chart. **Deadline:** March 1.

Contact Director of Grant Programs, Oregon Student Assistance Commission, 1500 Valley River Drive, Suite 100, Eugene, OR 97401-7020. *E-mail:* awardinfo@ mercury.osac.state.or.us. *Phone:* 800-452-8807 Ext. 7395. *Web site:* www.osac.state.or.us.

Lawrence R. Foster Memorial Scholarship. One-time award to students enrolled or planning to enroll in a public health degree program. First preference given to those working in the public health field and those pursuing a graduate degree in public health. Undergraduates entering junior or senior year health programs may apply if seeking a public health career, and not private practice. Prefer applicants from diverse cultures. Must provide 3 references. Additional essay required. Must be resident of Oregon. *Academic/Career Areas:* Health and Medical Sciences. *Award:* Scholarship for use in junior, senior, graduate, or postgraduate years; not renewable. *Award amount:* $4167. *Number of awards:* 6. *Eligibility Requirements:* Applicant must be enrolled or expecting to enroll at a four-year institution and resident of Oregon. Available to U.S. citizens. *Application Requirements:* Application, essay, financial need analysis, references, transcript, activity chart. **Deadline:** March 1.

Contact Director of Grant Programs, Oregon Student Assistance Commission, 1500 Valley River Drive, Suite 100, Eugene, OR 97401-7020. *E-mail:* awardinfo@mercury.osac.state.or.us. *Phone:* 800-452-8807 Ext. 7395. *Web site:* www.osac.state.or.us.

Oregon Occupational Safety and Health Division Workers Memorial Scholarship. Available to Oregon residents who are the dependents or spouses of an Oregon worker who was killed or permanently disabled on the job. Submit essay of 500 words or less titled "How has the injury or death of your parent or spouse affected or influenced your decision to further your education?" See web site for more details. (http://www.osac.state.or.us) **Award:** Scholarship for use in freshman, sophomore, junior, senior, or graduate year; not renewable. *Award amount:* $4786. *Number of awards:* 1. *Eligibility Requirements:* Applicant must be enrolled or expecting to enroll at a two-year or four-year institution and resident of Oregon. Applicant or parent of applicant must have employment or volunteer experience in designated career field. Available to U.S. citizens. *Application Requirements:* Application, essay, financial need analysis, test scores, transcript, workers compensation claim number. **Deadline:** March 1.

Contact Director of Grant Programs, Oregon Student Assistance Commission, 1500 Valley River Drive, Suite 100, Eugene, OR 97401-7020. *E-mail:* awardinfo@mercury.osac.state.or.us. *Phone:* 800-452-8807 Ext. 7395. *Web site:* www.osac.state.or.us.

Oregon Scholarship Fund Community College Student Award. Scholarship open to Oregon residents enrolled or planning to enroll in Oregon community college programs. May apply for one additional year. *Award:* Scholarship for use in freshman or sophomore year; not renewable. *Eligibility Requirements:* Applicant must be enrolled or expecting to enroll at a two-year institution; resident of Oregon and studying in Oregon. Available to U.S. citizens. *Application Requirements:* Application, essay, financial need analysis, transcript, activity chart. **Deadline:** March 1.

Contact Director of Grant Programs, Oregon Student Assistance Commission, 1500 Valley River Drive, Suite 100, Eugene, OR 97401-7020. *E-mail:* awardinfo@mercury.osac.state.or.us. *Phone:* 800-452-8807 Ext. 7395. *Web site:* www.osac.state.or.us.

Oregon Scholarship Fund Transfer Student Award. Award open to Oregon residents who are currently enrolled in their second year at a community college and are planning to transfer to a four-year college in Oregon. Prior recipients may apply for one additional year. *Award:* Scholarship for use in junior or senior year; not renewable. *Eligibility Requirements:* Applicant must be enrolled or expecting to enroll at a four-year institution; resident of Oregon and studying in Oregon. Available to U.S. citizens. *Application Requirements:* Application, essay, financial need analysis, transcript, activity chart. **Deadline:** March 1.

Contact Director of Grant Programs, Oregon Student Assistance Commission, 1500 Valley River Drive, Suite 100, Eugene, OR 97401-7020. *E-mail:* awardinfo@ mercury.osac.state.or.us. *Phone:* 800-452-8807 Ext. 7395. *Web site:* www.osac.state.or.us.

Oregon Student Assistance Commission Employee and Dependent Scholarship. One-time award for current permanent employee of the Oregon Student Assistance Commission or legally dependent children of employee. Also available to dependent children of an employee who retires, is permanently disabled, or deceased directly from employment at OSAC. Dependent must enroll full time. Employee may enroll part time. *Award:* Scholarship for use in freshman, sophomore, junior, or senior year; not renewable. *Award amount:* $500. *Number of awards:* 7. *Eligibility Requirements:* Applicant must be enrolled or expecting to enroll full or part-time at an institution or university and resident of Oregon. *Application Requirements:* Application, essay, financial need analysis, transcript. **Deadline:** March 1.

Contact Director of Grant Programs, Oregon Student Assistance Commission, 1500 Valley River Drive, Suite 100, Eugene, OR 97401-7020. *E-mail:* awardinfo@ mercury.osac.state.or.us. *Phone:* 800-452-8807 Ext. 7395. *Web site:* www.osac.state.or.us.

Oregon Trucking Association Scholarship. One scholarship available to a child of an Oregon Trucking Association member, or child of employee of member. Applicants must be Oregon residents who are graduating high school seniors from an Oregon high school. One-time award. *Award:* Scholarship for use in freshman year; not renewable. *Award amount:* $750. *Number of awards:* 4. *Eligibility Requirements:* Applicant must be high school student; planning to enroll or expecting to enroll at a four-year institution and resident of Oregon. Applicant or parent of applicant must have employment or volunteer experience in designated career field. Available to U.S. citizens. *Application Requirements:* Application, essay, financial need analysis, references, transcript, activity chart. **Deadline:** March 1.

Contact Director of Grant Programs, Oregon Student Assistance Commission, 1500 Valley River Drive, Suite 100, Eugene, OR 97401-7020. *E-mail:* awardinfo@ mercury.osac.state.or.us. *Phone:* 800-452-8807 Ext. 7395. *Web site:* www.osac.state.or.us.

PENNSYLVANIA

Educational Gratuity Program. This program is for eligible dependents of 100% disabled or deceased veteran whose disability was incurred during a period or war or armed conflict. Must be a Pennsylvania resident attending a Pennsylvania school. *Award:* Grant for use in freshman, sophomore, junior, or senior year; renewable. *Award amount:* up to $500. *Eligibility Requirements:* Applicant must be age 16-23; enrolled or expecting to enroll full-time at a two-year, four-year, or technical institution or university; resident of Pennsylvania and studying in Pennsylvania. Available to U.S. citizens. Applicant must have general military experience. *Application Requirements:* Application, driver's license, financial need analysis, transcript. **Deadline:** continuous.

Contact Michelle Zimmerman, Clerk Typist, Pennsylvania Bureau for Veterans Affairs, Fort Indiantown Gap, Annville, PA 17003-5002. *E-mail:* michzimmer@ state.pa.us. *Phone:* 717-861-8910. *Fax:* 717-861-8589. *Web site:* sites.state.pa.us/ PA_Exec/Military_Affairs/va/.

New Economy Technology Scholarships. Renewable award for Pennsylvania residents pursuing a degree in science or technology at a PHEAA-approved Pennsylvania school. Must maintain minimum 3.0 GPA. Must commence employment in Pennsylvania in field related to student's program within one year after completion of studies. Must work one year for each year scholarship was awarded. *Academic/Career Areas:* Science, Technology and Society. *Award:* Scholarship for use in freshman, sophomore, junior, or senior year; renewable. *Award amount:* up to $3000. *Eligibility Requirements:* Applicant must be enrolled or expecting to enroll full or part-time at a two-year, four-year, or technical institution; resident of Pennsylvania and studying in Pennsylvania. Applicant must have 3.0 GPA or higher. *Application Requirements:* Application, FAFSA. **Deadline:** December 31.

Contact PHEAA State Grant and Special Programs Division, Pennsylvania Higher Education Assistance Agency, 1200 North Seventh Street, Harrisburg, PA 17102-1444. *Phone:* 800-692-7392. *Web site:* www.pheaa.org.

Pennsylvania State Grant. Award for Pennsylvania residents attending an approved postsecondary institution as undergraduates in a program of at least two years duration. Renewable for up to eight semesters if applicants show continued need and academic progress. Submit Free Application for Federal Student Aid. *Award:* Grant for use in freshman, sophomore, junior, or senior year; renewable. *Award amount:* $300–$3300. *Number of awards:* up to 151,000. *Eligibility Requirements:* Applicant must be enrolled or expecting to enroll full or part-time at a two-year, four-year, or technical institution or university and resident of Pennsylvania. Available to U.S. and Canadian citizens. *Application Requirements:* Application, financial need analysis. **Deadline:** May 1.

Contact Keith New, Director of Communications and Press Office, Pennsylvania Higher Education Assistance Agency, 1200 North Seventh Street, Harrisburg, PA 17102-1444. *E-mail:* knew@pheaa.org. *Phone:* 717-720-2509. *Fax:* 717-720-3903. *Web site:* www.pheaa.org.

Postsecondary Education Gratuity Program. Waiver of tuition and fees for children of Pennsylvania police officers, firefighters, rescue or ambulance squad members, corrections facility employees or National Guard members who died in the line of duty after January 1, 1976. Must be a resident of Pennsylvania 25 years old or younger and enrolled full time as an undergraduate student at a Pennsylvania community college, state-owned institution or state-related institution. Award is for a maximum of 5 years. Application deadline March 31. *Award:* Grant for use in freshman, sophomore, junior, or senior year; renewable. *Eligibility Requirements:* Applicant must be age 25 or under; enrolled or expecting to enroll full-time at a two-year or four-year institution or university; resident of Pennsylvania and studying in Pennsylvania. *Application Requirements:* Application. **Deadline:** March 31.

Contact PHEAA State Grant and Special Programs Division, Pennsylvania Higher Education Assistance Agency, 1200 North Seventh Street, Harrisburg, PA 17102-1444. *Phone:* 800-692-7392. *Web site:* www.pheaa.org.

Veterans Grant—Pennsylvania. Renewable awards for Pennsylvania residents who are qualified veterans attending an approved undergraduate program full-time. Up to $3300 for in-state study or $800 for out-of-state study. Deadlines: May 1 for all renewal applicants, new applicants who plan to enroll in an undergraduate baccalaureate degree program, and those in college transfer programs at two-year public or junior colleges; August 1 for all first-time applicants who plan to enroll in a business, trade, or technical school; a hospital school of nursing; or a two-year terminal program at a community, junior, or four-year college. *Award:* Grant for use in freshman, sophomore, junior, or senior year; renewable. *Award amount:* $800–

$3300. *Eligibility Requirements:* Applicant must be enrolled or expecting to enroll full-time at a two-year, four-year, or technical institution or university and resident of Pennsylvania. Available to U.S. citizens. Applicant must have general military experience. *Application Requirements:* Application.

Contact Keith New, Director of Communications and Press Office, Pennsylvania Higher Education Assistance Agency, 1200 North Seventh Street, Harrisburg, PA 17102-1444. *E-mail:* knew@pheaa.org. *Phone:* 717-720-2509. *Fax:* 717-720-3903. *Web site:* www.pheaa.org.

PUERTO RICO

Robert C. Byrd Honor Scholarships. This grant is sponsored by the Puerto Rico Department of Education and is granted to gifted students. These are students chosen from public and private schools who graduate from high school and are admitted to an accredited university in Puerto Rico or in the United States and who show promise to complete a college career. It is granted for a period of four years if the student maintains a satisfactory academic progress. Must be a U.S. citizen and rank in the upper quarter of class or have a minimum 3.5 GPA. *Award:* Scholarship for use in freshman, sophomore, junior, or senior year; renewable. *Award amount:* $1500. *Number of awards:* 74–85. *Eligibility Requirements:* Applicant must be high school student and planning to enroll or expecting to enroll full-time at a four-year institution or university. Applicant must have 3.5 GPA or higher. Available to U.S. citizens. *Application Requirements:* Application, financial need analysis, interview, portfolio, references, test scores, transcript. **Deadline:** May 30.

Contact Eligio Hernandez, Director, Puerto Rico Department of Education, PO Box 190759, San Juan, PR 00919-0759. *E-mail:* hernandez_eli@de.gobierno.pr. *Phone:* 787-754-1015. *Fax:* 787-758-2281. *Web site:* www.de.gobierno.pr/eduportal/default.htm.

RHODE ISLAND

Rhode Island Higher Education Grant Program. Grants for residents of Rhode Island attending an approved school in the U.S., Canada, or Mexico. Based on need. Renewable for up to four years if in good academic standing. Applications accepted January 1 through March 1. Several awards of variable amounts. Must be U.S. citizen or registered alien. *Award:* Grant for use in freshman, sophomore, junior, or senior year; not renewable. *Award amount:* $250–$750. *Number of awards:* 10,000–12,000. *Eligibility Requirements:* Applicant must be enrolled or expecting to enroll full or part-time at a two-year, four-year, or technical institution or university and resident of Rhode Island. Available to U.S. citizens. *Application Requirements:* Application, financial need analysis. **Deadline:** March 1.

Contact Mary Ann Welch, Director of Program Administration, Rhode Island Higher Education Assistance Authority, 560 Jefferson Boulevard, Warwick, RI 02886. *E-mail:* mawelch@riheaa.org. *Phone:* 401-736-1170. *Fax:* 401-732-3541. *Web site:* www.riheaa.org.

SOUTH CAROLINA

Educational Assistance for Certain War Veteran's Dependents—South Carolina. Renewable aid to South Carolina Disabled Veterans' dependents under age 26. Veterans must have had wartime service in World War II, the Vietnam War, Persian Gulf or the Korean War. Must have received the Purple Heart or Medal of

Honor. Applicant must show DD214 (birth certificate and VA rating). For undergraduate study at any South Carolina state-supported college. Must be South Carolina resident. *Award:* Scholarship for use in freshman, sophomore, junior, or senior year; renewable. *Eligibility Requirements:* Applicant must be age 18-26; enrolled or expecting to enroll full or part-time at a two-year, four-year, or technical institution or university; resident of South Carolina and studying in South Carolina. Available to U.S. citizens. Applicant or parent must meet one or more of the following requirements: general military experience; retired from active duty; disabled or killed as a result of military service; prisoner of war; or missing in action. *Application Requirements:* Application. **Deadline:** continuous.

Contact Ms. Lauren Hugg, Free Tuition Assistant, South Carolina Division of Veterans Affairs, 1801 Assembly Street, Room 141, Columbia, SC 29201. *Phone:* 803-255-4317. *Fax:* 803-255-4257.

Legislative Incentives for Future Excellence Program. Scholarship for students from South Carolina to attend an institution of higher education in South Carolina. For students attending a four-year institution, two of these three criteria must be met: 1) minimum 3.0 GPA, 2) 1100 SAT or 24 ACT, or 3) graduate in the top 30% of class. Students attending a two-year or technical college must have a 3.0 GPA, SAT and class rank requirements are waived. *Award:* Scholarship for use in freshman, sophomore, junior, senior, or graduate year; renewable. *Award amount:* $3700–$5090. *Eligibility Requirements:* Applicant must be enrolled or expecting to enroll full-time at a two-year, four-year, or technical institution or university; resident of South Carolina and studying in South Carolina. Applicant must have 3.0 GPA or higher. Available to U.S. citizens. *Application Requirements:* Test scores, transcript. **Deadline:** continuous.

Contact Bichevia Green, LIFE Scholarship Coordinator, South Carolina Commission on Higher Education, 1333 Main Street, Suite 200, Columbia, SC 29201. *E-mail:* bgreen@che400.state.sc.us. *Phone:* 803-737-2280. *Fax:* 803-737-2297. *Web site:* www.che400.state.sc.us.

Palmetto Fellows Scholarship Program. Renewable award for qualified high school seniors in South Carolina to attend a four-year South Carolina institution. Must rank in top 5% of class at the end of sophomore or junior year, earn a 3.5 GPA on a 4.0 scale, and score at least 1200 on the SAT or 27 on the ACT. Submit official transcript, test scores, and application by established deadline (usually January 15th of senior year). *Award:* Scholarship for use in freshman, sophomore, junior, senior, or graduate year; renewable. *Award amount:* up to $6700. *Eligibility Requirements:* Applicant must be high school student; planning to enroll or expecting to enroll full-time at a four-year institution or university; resident of South Carolina and studying in South Carolina. Applicant must have 3.5 GPA or higher. Available to U.S. citizens. *Application Requirements:* Application, test scores, transcript. **Deadline:** January 15.

Contact Ms. Sherry Hubbard, Coordinator, South Carolina Commission on Higher Education, 1333 Main Street, Suite 200, Columbia, SC 29201. *E-mail:* shubbard@che400.state.sc.us. *Phone:* 803-737-2260. *Fax:* 803-737-2297. *Web site:* www.che400.state.sc.us.

South Carolina Hope Scholarship. One-year merit-based scholarship for eligible first-time entering freshmen attending a four-year institution. Minimum 3.0 GPA. *Award:* Scholarship for use in freshman year; not renewable. *Award amount:* $2650. *Eligibility Requirements:* Applicant must be enrolled or expecting to enroll full-time at a four-year institution or university; resident of South Carolina and studying in South Carolina. Applicant must have 3.0 GPA or higher. Available to U.S. citizens. *Application Requirements:* Transcript. **Deadline:** continuous.

Contact Bichevia Green, Life/Hope Scholarship Coordinator, South Carolina Commission on Higher Education, 1333 Main Street, Suite 200, Columbia, SC 29201. *E-mail:* bgreen@che400.state.sc.us. *Phone:* 803-737-2280. *Fax:* 803-737-2297. *Web site:* www.che400.state.sc.us.

South Carolina Need-Based Grants Program. Need-based grant awarded based on results of Free Application for Federal Student Aid. A student may receive up to $2500 annually for full-time and up to $1250 annually for part-time. The grant must be applied toward the cost of attendance at a South Carolina college for up to eight full-time equivalent terms. Student must be degree-seeking. *Award:* Grant for use in freshman, sophomore, junior, senior, or graduate year; renewable. *Award amount:* up to $2500. *Eligibility Requirements:* Applicant must be enrolled or expecting to enroll full or part-time at a two-year, four-year, or technical institution or university; resident of South Carolina and studying in South Carolina. Available to U.S. citizens. *Application Requirements:* Financial need analysis. **Deadline:** continuous.

Contact Ms. Sherry Hubbard, Coordinator, South Carolina Commission on Higher Education, 1333 Main Street, Suite 200, Columbia, SC 29201. *E-mail:* shubbard@che400.state.sc.us. *Phone:* 803-737-2260. *Fax:* 803-737-2297. *Web site:* www.che400.state.sc.us.

South Carolina Teacher Loan Program. One-time awards for South Carolina residents attending four-year postsecondary institutions in South Carolina. Recipients must teach in the South Carolina public school system in a critical-need area after graduation. 20% of loan forgiven for each year of service. Write for additional requirements. *Academic/Career Areas:* Education; Special Education. *Award:* Forgivable loan for use in freshman, sophomore, junior, senior, or graduate year; not renewable. *Award amount:* $2500–$5000. *Number of awards:* up to 1121. *Eligibility Requirements:* Applicant must be enrolled or expecting to enroll full or part-time at a four-year institution or university; resident of South Carolina and studying in South Carolina. Applicant must have 3.0 GPA or higher. *Application Requirements:* Application, test scores. **Deadline:** June 1.

Contact Jennifer Jones-Gaddy, Vice President, South Carolina Student Loan Corporation, PO Box 21487, Columbia, SC 29221. *E-mail:* jgaddy@slc.sc.edu. *Phone:* 803-798-0916. *Fax:* 803-772-9410. *Web site:* www.slc.sc.edu.

South Carolina Tuition Grants Program. Assists South Carolina residents attending one of twenty approved South Carolina Independent colleges. Freshmen must be in upper 3/4 of high school class or have SAT score of at least 900. Upper-class students must complete 24 semester hours per year to be eligible. *Award:* Grant for use in freshman, sophomore, junior, or senior year; renewable. *Award amount:* $100–$3240. *Number of awards:* up to 11,000. *Eligibility Requirements:* Applicant must be enrolled or expecting to enroll full-time at a two-year or four-year institution; resident of South Carolina and studying in South Carolina. Available to U.S. citizens. *Application Requirements:* Application, financial need analysis, test scores, transcript, FAFSA. **Deadline:** June 30.

Contact Toni Cave, Financial Aid Counselor, South Carolina Tuition Grants Commission, 101 Business Park Boulevard, Suite 2100, Columbia, SC 29203-9498. *E-mail:* toni@sctuitiongrants.org. *Phone:* 803-896-1120. *Fax:* 803-896-1126. *Web site:* www.sctuitiongrants.com.

SOUTH DAKOTA

Education Benefits for Dependents of POWs and MIAs. Children and spouses of prisoners of war, or of persons listed as missing in action, are entitled to attend a state-supported school without the payment of tuition or mandatory fees provided they are not eligible for equal or greater federal benefits. File SDDVA for E-12 available at financial aid offices. Must be a South Dakota resident intending to study in South Dakota. *Award:* Scholarship for use in freshman, sophomore, junior, or senior year; not renewable. *Eligibility Requirements:* Applicant must be enrolled or expecting to enroll at an institution or university; resident of South Dakota and studying in South Dakota. Available to U.S. citizens. Applicant or parent must meet one or more of the following requirements: general military experience; retired from active duty; disabled or killed as a result of military service; prisoner of war; or missing in action. *Application Requirements:* Application.

Contact Dr. Lesta V. Turchen, Senior Administrator, South Dakota Board of Regents, 306 East Capitol Avenue, Suite 200, Pierre, SD 57501-3159. *Phone:* 605-773-3455. *Fax:* 605-773-2422. *Web site:* www.ris.sdbor.edu.

Haines Memorial Scholarship. One-time scholarship for South Dakota public university students who are sophomores, juniors, or seniors having at least a 2.5 GPA and majoring in a teacher education program. Include resume with application. Must be South Dakota resident. *Academic/Career Areas:* Education. *Award:* Scholarship for use in sophomore, junior, or senior year; not renewable. *Award amount:* $2150. *Number of awards:* 1. *Eligibility Requirements:* Applicant must be enrolled or expecting to enroll at an institution or university; resident of South Dakota and studying in South Dakota. Applicant must have 2.5 GPA or higher. *Application Requirements:* Application, autobiography, essay, resume. **Deadline:** February 25.

Contact South Dakota Board of Regents, 306 East Capitol Avenue, Suite 200, Pierre, SD 57501-3159. *Web site:* www.ris.sdbor.edu.

South Dakota Aid to Dependents of Deceased Veterans. Program provides free tuition for children of deceased veterans who are under the age of 25, are residents of South Dakota, and whose mother or father was killed in action or died of other causes while on active duty. ("Veteran" for this purpose is as defined by South Dakota Codified Laws.) Parent must have been a bona fide resident of SD for at least six months immediately preceding entry into active service. Eligibility is for state-supported schools only. Must use SDDVA form E-12 available at financial aid offices. *Award:* Scholarship for use in freshman, sophomore, junior, or senior year; not renewable. *Eligibility Requirements:* Applicant must be age 25 or under; enrolled or expecting to enroll at a two-year or four-year institution; resident of South Dakota and studying in South Dakota. Available to U.S. citizens. Applicant or parent must meet one or more of the following requirements: general military experience; retired from active duty; disabled or killed as a result of military service; prisoner of war; or missing in action. *Application Requirements:* Application.

Contact Dr. Lesta V. Turchen, Senior Administrator, South Dakota Board of Regents, 306 East Capitol Avenue, Suite 200, Pierre, SD 57501-3159. *Phone:* 605-773-3455. *Fax:* 605-773-2422. *Web site:* www.ris.sdbor.edu.

South Dakota Board of Regents Senior Citizens Tuition Assistance. Award for tuition assistance for any postsecondary academic year of study to senior citizens age 65 and older. Write for further details. Must be a South Dakota resident and attend a school in South Dakota. *Award:* Scholarship for use in freshman, sophomore, junior, or senior year; not renewable. *Eligibility Requirements:* Applicant must be age 65; enrolled or expecting to enroll at an institution or university; resident of South Dakota and studying in South Dakota. *Application Requirements:* Application. **Deadline:** continuous.

Contact South Dakota Board of Regents, 306 East Capitol Avenue, Suite 200, Pierre, SD 57501-3159. *Web site:* www.ris.sdbor.edu.

South Dakota Board of Regents State Employee Tuition Assistance. Award for South Dakota state employees for any postsecondary academic year of study in South Dakota institution. Must be U.S. citizen. Write for requirements and other details. *Award:* Scholarship for use in freshman, sophomore, junior, or senior year; not renewable. *Eligibility Requirements:* Applicant must be enrolled or expecting to enroll at an institution or university; resident of South Dakota and studying in South Dakota. Applicant or parent of applicant must have employment or volunteer experience in designated career field. Available to U.S. citizens. *Application Requirements:* **Deadline:** continuous.

Contact South Dakota Board of Regents, 306 East Capitol Avenue, Suite 200, Pierre, SD 57501-3159. *Web site:* www.ris.sdbor.edu.

South Dakota Education Benefits for National Guard Members. Guard members who meet the requirements for admission are eligible for a 50% reduction in undergraduate tuition charges at any state-supported school for up to a maximum of four academic years. Provision also covers one program of study, approved by the State Board of Education, at any state vocational school. Must be state resident and member of the SD Army or Air Guard throughout period for which benefits are sought. Must contact financial aid office for full details and forms at time of registration. *Award:* Scholarship for use in freshman, sophomore, junior, or senior year; not renewable. *Eligibility Requirements:* Applicant must be enrolled or expecting to enroll at a two-year, four-year, or technical institution or university; resident of South Dakota and studying in South Dakota. Available to U.S. citizens. Applicant must have served in the Air Force National Guard or Army National Guard. *Application Requirements:* Application.

Contact Dr. Lesta V. Turchen, Senior Administrator, South Dakota Board of Regents, 306 East Capitol Avenue, Suite 200, Pierre, SD 57501-3159. *Phone:* 605-773-3455. *Fax:* 605-773-2422. *Web site:* www.ris.sdbor.edu.

South Dakota Education Benefits for Veterans. Certain veterans are eligible for free undergraduate tuition assistance at state-supported schools provided they are not eligible for educational payments under the GI Bill or any other federal educational program. Contact financial aid office for full details and forms. May receive one month of free tuition for each month of qualifying service (minimum one year, maximum four years). Must be resident of South Dakota. *Award:* Scholarship for use in freshman, sophomore, junior, or senior year; not renewable. *Eligibility Requirements:* Applicant must be enrolled or expecting to enroll at an institution or university; resident of South Dakota and studying in South Dakota. Available to U.S. citizens. Applicant must have general military experience. *Application Requirements:* Application, DD Form 214.

Contact Dr. Lesta V. Turchen, Senior Administrator, South Dakota Board of Regents, 306 East Capitol Avenue, Suite 200, Pierre, SD 57501-3159. *Phone:* 605-773-3455. *Fax:* 605-773-2422. *Web site:* www.ris.sdbor.edu.

TENNESSEE

Minority Teaching Fellows Program/Tennessee. Forgivable loan for minority Tennessee residents pursuing teaching careers. High school applicant minimum

2.75 GPA. Must be in the top quarter of the class or score an 18 on ACT. College applicant minimum 2.50 GPA. Submit statement of intent, test scores, and transcripts with application and two letters of recommendation. Must teach one year per year of award or repay as a loan. *Academic/Career Areas:* Education; Special Education. *Award:* Forgivable loan for use in freshman, sophomore, junior, or senior year; renewable. *Award amount:* $5000. *Number of awards:* 19–29. *Eligibility Requirements:* Applicant must be American Indian/Alaska Native, Asian/Pacific Islander, Black (non-Hispanic), or Hispanic; enrolled or expecting to enroll full-time at a two-year or four-year institution or university; resident of Tennessee and studying in Tennessee. Available to U.S. citizens. *Application Requirements:* Application, essay, references, test scores, transcript. **Deadline:** April 15.

Contact Kathy Stripling, Scholarship Coordinator, Tennessee Student Assistance Corporation, 404 James Robertson Parkway, Suite 1950, Parkway Towers, Nashville, TN 37243-0820. *E-mail:* kathy.stripling@state.tn.us. *Phone:* 615-741-1346. *Fax:* 615-741-6101. *Web site:* www.state.tn.us/tsac.

Ned McWherter Scholars Program. Assists Tennessee residents with high academic ability. Must have high school GPA of at least 3.5 and have scored in top 5% of SAT or ACT. Must attend college in Tennessee. Only high school seniors may apply. *Award:* Scholarship for use in freshman, sophomore, junior, or senior year; renewable. *Award amount:* $6000. *Number of awards:* 55. *Eligibility Requirements:* Applicant must be high school student; planning to enroll or expecting to enroll full-time at a two-year or four-year institution or university; resident of Tennessee and studying in Tennessee. Applicant must have 3.5 GPA or higher. Available to U.S. citizens. *Application Requirements:* Application, test scores, transcript. **Deadline:** February 15.

Contact Kathy Stripling, Scholarship Coordinator, Tennessee Student Assistance Corporation, Suite 1950, Parkway Towers, Nashville, TN 37243-0820. *E-mail:* kathy.stripling@state.tn.us. *Phone:* 615-741-1346. *Fax:* 615-741-6101. *Web site:* www.state.tn.us/tsac.

Tennessee Student Assistance Award Program. Assists Tennessee residents attending an approved college or university within the state. Complete a Free Application for Federal Student Aid form. Apply January 1. FAFSA must be processed by May 1 for priority consideration. *Award:* Grant for use in freshman, sophomore, junior, or senior year; renewable. *Award amount:* $100–$2130. *Number of awards:* 26,000. *Eligibility Requirements:* Applicant must be enrolled or expecting to enroll full or part-time at a two-year, four-year, or technical institution or university; resident of Tennessee and studying in Tennessee. Available to U.S. citizens. *Application Requirements:* Application, financial need analysis. **Deadline:** May 1.

Contact Naomi Derryberry, Grant and Scholarship Administrator, Tennessee Student Assistance Corporation, Suite 1950, Parkway Towers, Nashville, TN 37243-0820. *E-mail:* naomi.derryberry@state.tn.us. *Phone:* 615-741-1346. *Fax:* 615-741-6101. *Web site:* www.state.tn.us/tsac.

Tennessee Teaching Scholars Program. Forgivable loan for college juniors, seniors, and college graduates admitted to an education program in Tennessee with a minimum GPA of 2.5. Students must commit to teach in a Tennessee public school one year for each year of the award. *Academic/Career Areas:* Education. *Award:* Forgivable loan for use in junior, senior, or graduate year; not renewable. *Award amount:* $1000–$4200. *Number of awards:* 30–250. *Eligibility Requirements:* Applicant must be enrolled or expecting to enroll full or part-time at a four-year institution or university; resident of Tennessee and studying in Tennessee.

Applicant must have 2.5 GPA or higher. Available to U.S. citizens. *Application Requirements:* Application, references, test scores, transcript, letter of intent. **Deadline:** April 15.

Contact Mike McCormack, Scholarship Administrator, Tennessee Student Assistance Corporation, Suite 1950, Parkway Towers, Nashville, TN 37243-0820. *E-mail:* mike.mccormack@state.tn.us. *Phone:* 615-741-1346. *Fax:* 615-741-6101. *Web site:* www.state.tn.us/tsac.

TEXAS

Academic Common Market Waiver. For Texas residents who are students pursuing a degree in a field of study not offered in Texas. May qualify for special tuition rates. Deadlines vary by institution. Must be studying in the South. *Award:* Scholarship for use in freshman, sophomore, junior, senior, or graduate year; renewable. *Eligibility Requirements:* Applicant must be enrolled or expecting to enroll full or part-time at an institution or university; resident of Texas and studying in Alabama, Arkansas, Florida, Georgia, Kentucky, Louisiana, Mississippi, Missouri, Oklahoma, South Carolina, Tennessee, or Virginia. Available to U.S. citizens. *Application Requirements:* Application.

Contact Linda McDonough, Associate Program Director, Texas Higher Education Coordinating Board, PO Box 12788, Austin, TX 78711-2788. *E-mail:* grantinfo@thecb.state.tx.us. *Phone:* 512-427-6525. *Web site:* www.collegefortexans.com.

Border County Waiver. Award provides waiver of nonresident tuition for students of neighboring states (Louisiana, Oklahoma, Arkansas and New Mexico). Must attend a Texas public institution. Deadline varies by institution. Contact the registrar's office for details. *Award:* Scholarship for use in freshman, sophomore, junior, or senior year; not renewable. *Eligibility Requirements:* Applicant must be enrolled or expecting to enroll at a four-year institution or university; resident of Arkansas, Louisiana, New Mexico, or Oklahoma and studying in Texas. *Application Requirements:* Application.

Contact Financial Aid Office at college, Texas Higher Education Coordinating Board, PO Box 12788, Austin, TX 78711-2788. *E-mail:* grantinfo@thecb.state.tx.us. *Phone:* 512-427-6101. *Fax:* 512-427-6127. *Web site:* www.collegefortexans.com.

Conditional Grant Program. A grant that provides female minorities financial education assistance up to $6,000 per year for approved degree plans. At present, it is for civil engineering or computer science degrees. Must be a Texas resident and study in Texas. *Academic/Career Areas:* Civil Engineering; Computer Science/Data Processing. *Award:* Grant for use in freshman, sophomore, junior, or senior year; renewable. *Award amount:* up to $6000. *Number of awards:* 25. *Eligibility Requirements:* Applicant must be American Indian/Alaska Native, Asian/Pacific Islander, Black (non-Hispanic), or Hispanic; enrolled or expecting to enroll full-time at a four-year institution; female; resident of Texas and studying in Texas. Applicant must have 2.5 GPA or higher. Available to U.S. citizens. *Application Requirements:* Application, essay, interview, references, test scores, transcript. **Deadline:** March 1.

Contact Minnie Brown, Program Coordinator, Texas Department of Transportation, 125 East 11th Street, Austin, TX 78701-2483. *E-mail:* mbrown2@dot.state. tx.us. *Phone:* 512-416-4979. *Fax:* 512-416-4980. *Web site:* www.dot.state.tx.us.

Early Childhood Care Provider Student Loan Repayment. Award will repay student loans for child-care workers with a degree in Early Child Development. Must be employed at a licensed facility and work a minimum of 31 hours per week.

Must agree to provide service for two years. *Award:* Scholarship for use in freshman, sophomore, junior, or senior year; not renewable. *Award amount:* up to $3830. *Eligibility Requirements:* Applicant must be enrolled or expecting to enroll at an institution or university. Applicant or parent of applicant must have employment or volunteer experience in designated career field. Available to U.S. citizens. *Application Requirements:* Application. **Deadline:** continuous.

Contact Special Accounts, Texas Higher Education Coordinating Board, PO Box 12788, Austin, TX 78711. *E-mail:* grantinfo@thecb.state.tx.us. *Web site:* www.collegefortexans.com.

Early High School Graduation Scholarships. Award of $1000 for Texas residents who have completed the requirements for graduation from a Texas high school in no more than 36 consecutive months. Eligibility continues until full $1000 tuition award is received. Must submit high school certificate of eligibility to Coordinating Board. For more information, contact your high school counselor. *Award:* Scholarship for use in freshman year; not renewable. *Award amount:* $1000. *Eligibility Requirements:* Applicant must be high school student; planning to enroll or expecting to enroll full or part-time at a two-year, four-year, or technical institution or university; resident of Texas and studying in Texas. Available to U.S. citizens. *Application Requirements:* Application. **Deadline:** continuous.

Contact Texas Higher Education Coordinating Board, PO Box 12788, Austin, TX 78711-2788. *E-mail:* grantinfo@thecb.state.tx.us. *Phone:* 800-242-3062 Ext. 6387. *Web site:* www.collegefortexans.com.

Educational Aides Exemption. Assist certain educational aides by exempting them from payment of tuition and fees at public colleges or universities in Texas. Applicants must have worked as an educational aide in a Texas public school for at least one year and must be enrolled in courses required for teacher certification. Contact your college or university financial aid office for information on applying for this scholarship. Application cycles are as follows: Fall, June 1 through February 1; Spring, November 1 through July 1; and Summer, April 1 through October 1. *Academic/Career Areas:* Education. *Award:* Scholarship for use in freshman, sophomore, junior, or senior year; not renewable. *Award amount:* up to $605. *Eligibility Requirements:* Applicant must be enrolled or expecting to enroll at a four-year institution or university; resident of Texas and studying in Texas. *Application Requirements:* Application, financial need analysis.

Contact Financial Aid Office at college, Texas Higher Education Coordinating Board, PO Box 12788, Austin, TX 78711-2788. *E-mail:* grantinfo@thecb.state.tx.us. *Phone:* 512-427-6101. *Fax:* 512-427-6127. *Web site:* www.collegefortexans.com.

Exemption for Disabled in the Line of Duty Peace Officers. Renewable award for persons who were injured in the line of duty while serving as Peace Officers. Must be Texas resident and attend a public college or university in Texas. Submit documentation of disability from employer. For more information see registrar. *Award:* Scholarship for use in freshman, sophomore, junior, or senior year; renewable. *Eligibility Requirements:* Applicant must be enrolled or expecting to enroll at a four-year institution or university; resident of Texas and studying in Texas. Applicant or parent of applicant must have employment or volunteer experience in police/ firefighting. *Application Requirements:* Application, form letter.

Contact Texas Higher Education Coordinating Board, PO Box 12788, Austin, TX 78711. *E-mail:* grantinfo@thecb.state.tx.us. *Web site:* www.collegefortexans.com.

Fifth-year Accounting Student Scholarship Program. One-time award for students enrolled as fifth-year accounting students at a Texas institution. Must sign statement confirming intent to take the written exam for the purpose of being granted a certificate of CPA to practice in Texas. Contact college/university financial aid office for application information. *Academic/Career Areas:* Accounting. *Award:* Scholarship for use in senior or graduate year; not renewable. *Award amount:* up to $3000. *Eligibility Requirements:* Applicant must be enrolled or expecting to enroll full or part-time at a four-year institution or university and studying in Texas. Available to U.S. and non-U.S. citizens. *Application Requirements:* Application, financial need analysis, transcript, letter of intent. **Deadline:** continuous.

Contact Financial Aid Office at college, Texas Higher Education Coordinating Board, PO Box 12788, Austin, TX 78711-2788. *E-mail:* grantinfo@thecb.state.tx.us. *Phone:* 512-427-6101. *Fax:* 512-427-6127. *Web site:* www.collegefortexans.com.

Firefighter Exemption Program—Texas. One-time award assists firemen enrolled in fire science courses as part of a fire science curriculum. Award is exemption from tuition and laboratory fees at publicly supported Texas colleges. Contact the admissions/registrar's office for information on how to apply. *Academic/Career Areas:* Applied Sciences; Physical Sciences and Math; Trade/Technical Specialties. *Award:* Scholarship for use in freshman, sophomore, junior, or senior year; not renewable. *Eligibility Requirements:* Applicant must be enrolled or expecting to enroll full or part-time at a two-year, four-year, or technical institution; resident of Texas and studying in Texas. Applicant or parent of applicant must have employment or volunteer experience in fire service or police/firefighting. Available to U.S. citizens. *Application Requirements:* Application. **Deadline:** continuous.

Contact Financial Aid Office at college, Texas Higher Education Coordinating Board, PO Box 12788, Austin, TX 78711-2788. *E-mail:* grantinfo@thecb.state.tx.us. *Phone:* 512-427-6101. *Fax:* 512-427-6127. *Web site:* www.collegefortexans.com.

Good Neighbor Scholarship Waiver. Renewable aid for students residing in Texas who are citizens of another country of the Americas and intend to return to their country upon completion of the course of study. Must attend public college in Texas. Student will be exempt from tuition. *Award:* Scholarship for use in freshman, sophomore, junior, or senior year; renewable. *Eligibility Requirements:* Applicant must be Canadian or Latin American/Caribbean citizenship; enrolled or expecting to enroll full or part-time at a two-year, four-year, or technical institution or university and studying in Texas. Available to Canadian and non-U.S. citizens. *Application Requirements:* Application, test scores, transcript. **Deadline:** March 15.

Contact Texas Higher Education Coordinating Board, PO Box 12788, Austin, TX 78711-2788. *E-mail:* grantinfo@thecb.state.tx.us. *Phone:* 800-242-3062. *Web site:* www.collegefortexans.com.

Leveraging Educational Assistance Partnership Program (LEAP) (formerly SSIG). Renewable award available to residents of Texas attending public colleges or universities in Texas. Must be enrolled at least half-time and show financial need. Deadlines vary by institution. Contact the college/university financial aid office for application information. *Award:* Grant for use in freshman, sophomore, junior, or senior year; renewable. *Award amount:* up to $1250. *Eligibility Requirements:* Applicant must be enrolled or expecting to enroll full or part-time at a two-year, four-year, or technical institution or university; resident of Texas and studying in Texas. Available to U.S. citizens. *Application Requirements:* Financial need analysis, FAFSA.

Profiles of State-Sponsored Programs

Contact Financial Aid Office at college, Texas Higher Education Coordinating Board, PO Box 12788, Austin, TX 78711-2788. *E-mail:* grantinfo@thecb.state.tx.us. *Phone:* 512-427-6101. *Fax:* 512-427-6127. *Web site:* www.collegefortexans.com.

License Plate Insignia Scholarship. One-time award to Texas residents enrolled at least half-time at public or private nonprofit senior colleges and universities in Texas. Must demonstrate financial need. Contact financial aid office at college for deadlines and application. *Award:* Scholarship for use in freshman, sophomore, junior, or senior year; not renewable. *Eligibility Requirements:* Applicant must be enrolled or expecting to enroll full or part-time at a four-year institution or university; resident of Texas and studying in Texas. *Application Requirements:* Application, financial need analysis.

Contact Financial Aid Office at college, Texas Higher Education Coordinating Board, PO Box 12788, Austin, TX 78711-2788. *E-mail:* grantinfo@thecb.state.tx.us. *Phone:* 512-427-6101. *Fax:* 512-427-6127. *Web site:* www.collegefortexans.com.

Military Stationed in Texas Waiver. Award provides tuition waiver for nonresident military personnel stationed in Texas. Limited to public institutions only. Contact financial aid office at college for deadline and application. *Award:* Scholarship for use in freshman, sophomore, junior, or senior year; not renewable. *Eligibility Requirements:* Applicant must be enrolled or expecting to enroll at an institution or university and studying in Texas. Applicant must have general military experience. *Application Requirements:* Application.

Contact Financial Aid Office at college, Texas Higher Education Coordinating Board, PO Box 12788, Austin, TX 78711-2788. *E-mail:* grantinfo@thecb.state.tx.us. *Phone:* 512-427-6101. *Fax:* 512-427-6127. *Web site:* www.collegefortexans.com.

Outstanding Rural Scholar Program. Award enables rural communities to sponsor a student going into health professions. The students must agree to work in that community once they receive their degree. Must be Texas resident entering a Texas institution on a full-time basis. Must demonstrate financial need. *Academic/Career Areas:* Health and Medical Sciences. *Award:* Scholarship for use in freshman, sophomore, junior, or senior year; renewable. *Eligibility Requirements:* Applicant must be enrolled or expecting to enroll full-time at a four-year institution or university; resident of Texas and studying in Texas. Applicant must have 3.0 GPA or higher. *Application Requirements:* Application, financial need analysis, transcript, nomination.

Contact Center for Rural Health Initiatives, Texas Higher Education Coordinating Board, PO Drawer 1708, Austin, TX 78767. *E-mail:* grantinfo@thecb.state.tx. us. *Phone:* 512-479-8891. *Web site:* www.collegefortexans.com.

Physician Assistant Loan Reimbursement Program. Award will repay loans for physician assistants working in rural Texas counties. Must have worked at least 12 consecutive months in a rural Texas county designated medically underserved. Can be renewed for up to four years. *Award:* Grant for use in freshman, sophomore, junior, or senior year; renewable. *Award amount:* up to $5000. *Eligibility Requirements:* Applicant must be enrolled or expecting to enroll at an institution or university. Applicant or parent of applicant must have employment or volunteer experience in designated career field. Available to U.S. citizens. *Application Requirements:* Application.

Contact Financial Aid Office at college, Texas Higher Education Coordinating Board, PO Box 12788, Austin, TX 78711-2788. *E-mail:* grantinfo@thecb.state.tx.us. *Phone:* 512-427-6101. *Fax:* 512-427-6127. *Web site:* www.collegefortexans.com.

Professional Nurses' Student Loan Repayment. Award for licensed nurses practicing in Texas to pay off student loans. Must demonstrate financial need. *Award:* Scholarship for use in freshman, sophomore, junior, or senior year; not renewable. *Award amount:* up to $2000. *Eligibility Requirements:* Applicant must be enrolled or expecting to enroll at an institution or university. Applicant or parent of applicant must have employment or volunteer experience in designated career field. *Application Requirements:* Application, financial need analysis. **Deadline:** January 15.

Contact Grants and Special Programs Office, Texas Higher Education Coordinating Board, PO Box 12788, Austin, TX 78711. *E-mail:* grantinfo@thecb. state.tx.us. *Phone:* 800-242-3062. *Web site:* www.collegefortexans.com.

Professional Nursing Scholarships. Several awards for Texas residents enrolled at least half-time in a nursing program leading to a professional degree at a Texas institution. Contact school financial aid office for further information. *Academic/ Career Areas:* Nursing. *Award:* Scholarship for use in freshman, sophomore, junior, or senior year; not renewable. *Award amount:* up to $3000. *Eligibility Requirements:* Applicant must be enrolled or expecting to enroll full or part-time at a four-year institution or university; resident of Texas and studying in Texas. Available to U.S. citizens. *Application Requirements:* Application, financial need analysis, test scores, transcript.

Contact Student Services Division, Texas Higher Education Coordinating Board, PO Box 12788, Austin, TX 78711-2788. *E-mail:* grantinfo@thecb.state.tx. us. *Phone:* 800-242-3062. *Web site:* www.collegefortexans.com.

Teach for Texas Conditional Grant Program. This is a student loan with cancellation provisions for teaching. Prospective teachers must be enrolled in degree programs leading to certification in a teaching field designated as having a critical shortage of teachers, or agree to teach in a Texas community certified as experiencing a critical shortage of teachers. For upper division college students only. *Academic/Career Areas:* Education. *Award:* Forgivable loan for use in junior or senior year; not renewable. *Award amount:* up to $11,800. *Eligibility Requirements:* Applicant must be enrolled or expecting to enroll full or part-time at a four-year institution or university; resident of Texas and studying in Texas. Applicant must have 2.5 GPA or higher. Available to U.S. citizens. *Application Requirements:* Application, financial need analysis, references. **Deadline:** continuous.

Contact Special Accounts Servicing, Texas Higher Education Coordinating Board, PO Box 12788, Austin, TX 78711-2788. *E-mail:* grantinfo@thecb.state.tx. us. *Phone:* 800-242-3062. *Web site:* www.collegefortexans.com.

Texas National Guard Tuition Assistance Program. Provides exemption from the payment of tuition to certain members of the Texas National Guard, Texas Air Guard or the State Guard. Must be Texas resident and attend school in Texas. Visit the TNG web site at: http://www.agd.state.tx.us/education_office/state_tuition. htm. **Award:** Scholarship for use in freshman, sophomore, junior, or senior year; renewable. *Eligibility Requirements:* Applicant must be enrolled or expecting to enroll at an institution or university; resident of Texas and studying in Texas. Applicant must have served in the Air Force National Guard, Army National Guard, or Navy National Guard. *Application Requirements:* Application.

Contact State Adjutant General's Office, Texas Higher Education Coordinating Board, PO Box 5218/AGTX-PAE, Austin, TX 78763-5218. *Phone:* 512-465-5001. *Web site:* www.collegefortexans.com.

Texas Tuition Exemption for Blind/Deaf Students. Renewable award aids certain blind or deaf students by exempting them from payment of tuition and fees at public colleges or universities in Texas. Must be a resident of Texas. Deadlines vary. Must submit certificate of deafness or blindness. Contact the admissions/registrar's office for application information. *Award:* Scholarship for use in freshman, sophomore, junior, or senior year; renewable. *Eligibility Requirements:* Applicant must be enrolled or expecting to enroll full or part-time at a two-year, four-year, or technical institution or university; resident of Texas and studying in Texas. Applicant must be hearing impaired or visually impaired. Available to U.S. citizens. *Application Requirements:* Application, certificate of impairment.

Contact Financial Aid Office at college, Texas Higher Education Coordinating Board, PO Box 12788, Austin, TX 78711-2788. *E-mail:* grantinfo@thecb.state.tx.us. *Phone:* 512-427-6101. *Fax:* 512-427-6127. *Web site:* www.collegefortexans.com.

Texas Tuition Exemption for Senior Citizens-65+. Tuition exemption for Texas residents over the age of 65 at eligible Texas institutions. Pays tuition for up to six semester credit hours per semester or summer term. Nonrenewable. Awards made on a space-available basis. Contact the admissions/registrar's office for application information. *Award:* Scholarship for use in freshman, sophomore, junior, or senior year; not renewable. *Eligibility Requirements:* Applicant must be age 65; enrolled or expecting to enroll part-time at a two-year, four-year, or technical institution or university; resident of Texas and studying in Texas. Available to U.S. citizens. *Application Requirements:* Application. **Deadline:** continuous.

Contact Financial Aid Office at college, Texas Higher Education Coordinating Board, PO Box 12788, Austin, TX 78711-2788. *E-mail:* grantinfo@thecb.state.tx.us. *Phone:* 512-427-6101. *Fax:* 512-427-6127. *Web site:* www.collegefortexans.com.

Texas Tuition Exemption for Students in Foster Care or other Residential Care. Exemption from tuition and fees at Texas institution. Must have been in foster care under the conservatorship of the Department of Protection and Regulatory Services on or after 18th birthday; or on the day of the student's 14th birthday, if the student was also eligible for adoption on or after that day; or the day the student graduated from high school or completed the equivalent of a high school diploma. Must enroll as undergraduate student within three years of discharge. Must be Texas resident. Contact the admissions/registrar's office for application information. *Award:* Scholarship for use in freshman, sophomore, junior, or senior year; renewable. *Eligibility Requirements:* Applicant must be enrolled or expecting to enroll full or part-time at a two-year, four-year, or technical institution or university; resident of Texas and studying in Texas. Available to U.S. citizens. *Application Requirements:* Application. **Deadline:** continuous.

Contact Financial Aid Office at college, Texas Higher Education Coordinating Board, PO Box 12788, Austin, TX 78711-2788. *E-mail:* grantinfo@thecb.state.tx.us. *Phone:* 512-427-6101. *Fax:* 512-427-6127. *Web site:* www.collegefortexans.com.

Texas Tuition Exemption for TANF Students. Tuition and fee exemption for Texas residents who during last year of high school received financial assistance for not less than 6 months. Must enroll at Texas institution within 24 TANF months of high school graduation. Award is good for one year. Contact the admissions/registrar's office for application information. *Award:* Scholarship for use in freshman year; not renewable. *Eligibility Requirements:* Applicant must be age 21 or under; enrolled or expecting to enroll full or part-time at a two-year, four-year, or technical institution or university; single; resident of Texas and studying in Texas. *Application Requirements:* Application, financial need analysis. **Deadline:** continuous.

Contact Financial Aid Office at college, Texas Higher Education Coordinating Board, PO Box 12788, Austin, TX 78711-2788. *E-mail:* grantinfo@thecb.state.tx.us. *Phone:* 512-427-6101. *Fax:* 512-427-6127. *Web site:* www.collegefortexans.com.

Texas Tuition Exemption Program: Highest Ranking High School Graduate. Award available to Texas residents who are the top ranked seniors of their high school. Must attend a public college or university within Texas. Recipient is exempt from certain charges for first two semesters. Deadlines vary. Contact admissions/ registrar's office for application information. Must provide proof of valedictorian ranking to the registrar. *Award:* Scholarship for use in freshman year; not renewable. *Eligibility Requirements:* Applicant must be enrolled or expecting to enroll full or part-time at a two-year, four-year, or technical institution or university; resident of Texas and studying in Texas. Applicant must have 3.5 GPA or higher. Available to U.S. citizens. *Application Requirements:* Transcript.

Contact Financial Aid Office at college, Texas Higher Education Coordinating Board, PO Box 12788, Austin, TX 78711-2788. *E-mail:* grantinfo@thecb.state.tx.us. *Phone:* 512-427-6101. *Fax:* 512-427-6127. *Web site:* www.collegefortexans.com.

Texas Yes! Scholarships. Texas YES! Scholarships are awarded to women and minorities, or to applicants who have participated in the educational programs sponsored by the Texas Society of Professional Engineers: MATHCOUNTS, NEDC, TEC, TEAMS, TESC. Applicants must have a 3.0 GPA. Must major in a field of engineering, be a resident of Texas and attend a postsecondary institution in Texas. Must be a high school senior. *Academic/Career Areas:* Chemical Engineering; Civil Engineering; Electrical Engineering/Electronics; Engineering/Technology; Mechanical Engineering. *Award:* Scholarship for use in freshman year; not renewable. *Award amount:* $500–$1000. *Number of awards:* 3–5. *Eligibility Requirements:* Applicant must be high school student; planning to enroll or expecting to enroll full-time at an institution or university; resident of Texas and studying in Texas. Applicant must have 3.0 GPA or higher. Available to U.S. citizens. *Application Requirements:* Application, essay, references, transcript. **Deadline:** January 15.

Contact Kelly Melnyk, Assistant Director of Education Programs, Texas Engineering Foundation, Attn: Programs Director, 3501 Manor Road, PO Box 2145, Austin, TX 78768. *E-mail:* kellym@tspe.org. *Phone:* 512-472-9286. *Fax:* 512-472-2934. *Web site:* www.tspe.org.

Texas-Tuition Fee Exemption for Children of Disabled/Deceased Firemen, Peace Officers, Game Wardens, Employees of Correctional Institutions. Renewable award for children of paid or volunteer firemen, game wardens, peace officers, or custodial employees of the Department of Corrections disabled or deceased while serving in Texas. Must attend a Texas institution. Must apply before 21st birthday. Must provide certification of parent's disability or death. Contact institution's admissions or registrar's office for application information. *Award:* Scholarship for use in freshman, sophomore, or junior year; renewable. *Eligibility Requirements:* Applicant must be age 20 or under; enrolled or expecting to enroll full or part-time at a two-year, four-year, or technical institution or university; resident of Texas and studying in Texas. Applicant or parent of applicant must have employment or volunteer experience in designated career field, fire service, or police/firefighting. Available to U.S. citizens. *Application Requirements:* Application. **Deadline:** continuous.

Contact Financial Aid Office at college, Texas Higher Education Coordinating Board, PO Box 12788, Austin, TX 78711-2788. *E-mail:* grantinfo@thecb.state.tx.us. *Phone:* 512-427-6101. *Fax:* 512-427-6127. *Web site:* www.collegefortexans.com.

Toward Excellence, Access and Success (TEXAS Grant). Renewable aid for students enrolled in a public or private nonprofit, college or university in Texas. Based on need. Amount of award is determined by the financial aid office of each school. Deadlines vary. Contact the college/university financial aid office for application information. *Award:* Grant for use in freshman, sophomore, junior, or senior year; renewable. *Award amount:* up to $2800. *Eligibility Requirements:* Applicant must be enrolled or expecting to enroll full or part-time at a two-year, four-year, or technical institution or university; resident of Texas and studying in Texas. Applicant must have 2.5 GPA or higher. Available to U.S. citizens. *Application Requirements:* Application, financial need analysis, transcript. **Deadline:** continuous.

Contact Financial Aid Office at college, Texas Higher Education Coordinating Board, PO Box 12788, Austin, TX 78711-2788. *E-mail:* grantinfo@thecb.state.tx.us. *Phone:* 512-427-6101. *Fax:* 512-427-6127. *Web site:* www.collegefortexans.com.

Toward Excellence, Access, and Success (TEXAS) Grant II Program. Provides grant aid to financially needy students enrolled in Texas public two-year colleges. Complete FAFSA. Contact college financial aid office for additional assistance. *Award:* Grant for use in freshman or sophomore year; renewable. *Award amount:* up to $2600. *Eligibility Requirements:* Applicant must be enrolled or expecting to enroll full or part-time at a two-year or technical institution; resident of Texas and studying in Texas. Applicant must have 2.5 GPA or higher. Available to U.S. citizens. *Application Requirements:* Financial need analysis, transcript, FAFSA. **Deadline:** continuous.

Contact Financial Aid Office at college, Texas Higher Education Coordinating Board, PO Box 12788, Austin, TX 78711-2788. *E-mail:* grantinfo@thecb.state.tx.us. *Phone:* 512-427-6101. *Fax:* 512-427-6127. *Web site:* www.collegefortexans.com.

Train our Teachers Award. Awarded to employed child care workers seeking credentials or an associate degree in child development. Must agree to work 18 consecutive months in a licensed child care facility. Must attend a Texas institution. For more details and deadlines see web site: http://www.collegefortexans.com. **Award:** Scholarship for use in freshman or sophomore year; not renewable. *Award amount:* up to $1000. *Number of awards:* up to 2000. *Eligibility Requirements:* Applicant must be enrolled or expecting to enroll at an institution or university and studying in Texas. Applicant or parent of applicant must have employment or volunteer experience in designated career field. *Application Requirements:* Application.

Contact Financial Aid Office at college, Texas Higher Education Coordinating Board, PO Box 12788, Austin, TX 78711-2788. *E-mail:* grantinfo@thecb.state.tx.us. *Phone:* 512-427-6101. *Fax:* 512-427-6127. *Web site:* www.collegefortexans.com.

Tuition and Fee Exemption for Children of Prisoners of War or Persons Missing in Action-Texas. Renewable award assists children of prisoners of war or veterans classified as missing in action. Must be a Texas resident and attend a public college or university within Texas. Submit proof of service and proof of MIA/POW status. Award is exemption from tuition and fees. Must be under 21 years of age. Contact the admissions/registrar's office for application information. *Award:* Scholarship for use in freshman, sophomore, junior, or senior year; renewable. *Eligibility Requirements:* Applicant must be age 20 or under; enrolled or expecting to enroll at a two-year, four-year, or technical institution or university; resident of Texas and studying in Texas. Applicant or parent must meet one or more of the following requirements: general military experience; retired from active duty; disabled or killed as a result of military service; prisoner of war; or missing in action. *Application Requirements:* Application, proof of service and MIA/POW status. **Deadline:** continuous.

Contact Financial Aid Office at college, Texas Higher Education Coordinating Board, PO Box 12788, Austin, TX 78711-2788. *E-mail:* grantinfo@thecb.state.tx.us. *Phone:* 512-427-6101. *Fax:* 512-427-6127. *Web site:* www.collegefortexans.com.

Tuition Equalization Grant (TEG) Program. Renewable award for Texas residents enrolled at least half-time at an independent college or university within the state. Based on financial need. Deadlines vary by institution. Must not be receiving athletic scholarship. Contact college/university financial aid office for application information. *Award:* Grant for use in freshman, sophomore, junior, or senior year; renewable. *Award amount:* up to $3572. *Eligibility Requirements:* Applicant must be enrolled or expecting to enroll full or part-time at a two-year or four-year institution or university; resident of Texas and studying in Texas. Available to U.S. citizens. *Application Requirements:* Financial need analysis, FAFSA.

Contact Financial Aid Office at college, Texas Higher Education Coordinating Board, PO Box 12788, Austin, TX 78711-2788. *E-mail:* grantinfo@thecb.state.tx.us. *Phone:* 512-427-6101. *Fax:* 512-427-6127. *Web site:* www.collegefortexans.com.

Tuition Exemptions for Texas Veterans (Hazelwood Act). Renewable tuition and partial fee exemptions for Texas veterans who have been honorably discharged after at least 180 days of active duty. Must be a Texas resident at time of entry into service. Must have exhausted federal education benefits. Contact the admissions/registrar's office for information on how to apply. Must be used at a Texas public institution. *Award:* Scholarship for use in freshman, sophomore, junior, or senior year; renewable. *Award amount:* $980. *Eligibility Requirements:* Applicant must be enrolled or expecting to enroll full or part-time at a two-year, four-year, or technical institution or university; resident of Texas and studying in Texas. Available to U.S. citizens. Applicant or parent must meet one or more of the following requirements: general military experience; retired from active duty; disabled or killed as a result of military service; prisoner of war; or missing in action. *Application Requirements:* Application. **Deadline:** continuous.

Contact Financial Aid Office at college, Texas Higher Education Coordinating Board, PO Box 12788, Austin, TX 78711-2788. *E-mail:* grantinfo@thecb.state.tx.us. *Phone:* 512-427-6101. *Fax:* 512-427-6127. *Web site:* www.collegefortexans.com.

Vocational Nursing Scholarships. Scholarships for Texas residents must be enrolled in a vocational nursing program at an institution in Texas. Deadline varies. *Academic/Career Areas:* Nursing. *Award:* Scholarship for use in freshman or sophomore year; not renewable. *Award amount:* up to $1500. *Eligibility Requirements:* Applicant must be enrolled or expecting to enroll full or part-time at a four-year institution or university; resident of Texas and studying in Texas. Available to U.S. citizens. *Application Requirements:* Application, financial need analysis, test scores, transcript.

Contact Texas Higher Education Coordinating Board, PO Box 12788, Austin, TX 78711-2788. *E-mail:* grantinfo@thecb.state.tx.us. *Web site:* www.collegefortexans.com.

UTAH

Leveraging Educational Assistance Partnership (LEAP). Available to students with substantial financial need for use at participating Utah schools. Contact Financial Aid Office of specific school for application requirements and deadlines. Must be

Utah resident. *Award:* Grant for use in freshman, sophomore, junior, or senior year; renewable. *Award amount:* up to $2500. *Number of awards:* up to 3000. *Eligibility Requirements:* Applicant must be enrolled or expecting to enroll full or part-time at a two-year, four-year, or technical institution or university; resident of Utah and studying in Utah. Available to U.S. citizens. *Application Requirements:* Application, financial need analysis. **Deadline:** continuous.

Contact Financial Aid Office, Utah State Board of Regents. *Web site:* www.uheaa.org.

New Century Scholarship. Scholarship for qualified high school graduates of Utah. Must attend Utah state-operated college. Award depends on number of hours student enrolled. Please contact for further eligibility requirements. Eligible recipients receive an award equal to 75% of tuition for 60 credit hours toward the completion of a bachelor's degree. For more details see web site: http://www.utahsbr.edu. **Award:** Scholarship for use in junior or senior year; renewable. *Award amount:* $500–$1000. *Eligibility Requirements:* Applicant must be high school student; planning to enroll or expecting to enroll full or part-time at a four-year institution or university; resident of Utah and studying in Utah. Available to U.S. citizens. *Application Requirements:* Application, test scores, transcript, GPA/copy of enrollment verification from an eligible Utah 4-year institute. **Deadline:** continuous.

Contact Angie Loving, Manager for Programs/Administration, State of Utah, 3 Triad Center, Suite 500, Salt Lake City, UT 84180-1205. *E-mail:* aloving@utahsbr.edu. *Phone:* 801-321-7124. *Fax:* 801-321-7199. *Web site:* www.utahsbr.edu.

T.H. Bell Teaching Incentive Loan-Utah. Renewable awards for Utah residents who are high school seniors and wish to pursue teaching careers. Award pays for tuition and fees at a Utah institution. Must agree to teach in a Utah public school or pay back loan through monthly installments. Must be a U.S. citizen. *Academic/Career Areas:* Education; Special Education. *Award:* Forgivable loan for use in freshman, sophomore, junior, or senior year; renewable. *Number of awards:* 50. *Eligibility Requirements:* Applicant must be high school student; planning to enroll or expecting to enroll full-time at a two-year or four-year institution or university; resident of Utah and studying in Utah. Available to U.S. citizens. *Application Requirements:* Application, essay, test scores, transcript. **Deadline:** March 29.

Contact Diane DeMan, Executive Secretary, Utah State Office of Education, 250 East 500 South, Salt Lake City, UT 84111. *Phone:* 801-538-7741. *Fax:* 801-538-7973. *Web site:* www.usoe.k12.ut.us/cert/scholarships/scholars.htm.

Terrel H. Bell Teaching Incentive Loan. Designed to provide financial assistance to outstanding Utah students pursuing a degree in education. The incentive loan funds full-time tuition and general fees for eight semesters. After graduation/certification the loan may be forgiven if the recipient teaches in a Utah public school or accredited private school (K-12). Loan forgiveness is done on a year-for-year basis. For more details see web site: http://www.utahsbr.edu. *Academic/Career Areas:* Education. *Award:* Forgivable loan for use in freshman, sophomore, junior, or senior year; renewable. *Award amount:* $600–$1500. *Number of awards:* 365. *Eligibility Requirements:* Applicant must be enrolled or expecting to enroll full-time at a two-year or four-year institution or university; resident of Utah and studying in Utah. Available to U.S. citizens. *Application Requirements:* Application, essay, test scores, transcript. **Deadline:** March 31.

Contact Angie Loving, Manager for Programs and Administration, State of Utah, 3 Triad Center, Suite 550, Salt Lake City, UT 84180. *E-mail:* aloving@utahsbr.edu. *Phone:* 801-321-7124. *Fax:* 801-321-7199. *Web site:* www.utahsbr.edu.

Utah Educationally Disadvantaged Program. Renewable award for residents of Utah who are disadvantaged and attending an eligible institution in Utah. Must demonstrate need and satisfactory progress. Contact financial aid office of participating institution. *Award:* Scholarship for use in freshman, sophomore, junior, or senior year; renewable. *Eligibility Requirements:* Applicant must be enrolled or expecting to enroll at a two-year or four-year institution; resident of Utah and studying in Utah. Applicant must be hearing impaired, learning disabled, physically disabled, or visually impaired. *Application Requirements:* Application. **Deadline:** continuous.

Contact Lynda Reid, Administrative Assistant, Utah State Board of Regents, 60 South 400 West, The Board of Regents Building, The Gateway, Salt Lake City, UT 84101-1284. *Phone:* 801-321-7207. *Fax:* 801-321-7299. *Web site:* www.uheaa.org.

Utah Engineering and Computer Science Program (UECLP). A loan forgiveness program to recruit and train engineering, computer science and related technology students to assist in providing for and advancing the intellectual and economic welfare of the state. *Academic/Career Areas:* Computer Science/Data Processing; Engineering/Technology; Engineering-Related Technologies. *Award:* Forgivable loan for use in junior or senior year; renewable. *Award amount:* $1500–$5000. *Number of awards:* 90–110. *Eligibility Requirements:* Applicant must be enrolled or expecting to enroll full-time at a four-year institution or university; resident of Utah and studying in Utah. Applicant must have 3.0 GPA or higher. Available to U.S. citizens. *Application Requirements:* Application, test scores, transcript. **Deadline:** continuous.

Contact Chalmers Gail Norris, Executive Director of UHEAA of the Utah State Board of Regents, Utah State Board of Regents, 60 South 400 West, Salt Lake City, UT 84101. *Fax:* 801-321-7299. *Web site:* www.uheaa.org.

Utah Society of Professional Engineers Scholarship. One-time award for entering freshman pursuing studies in the field of engineering (civil, chemical, electrical, or engineering related technologies.) Minimum 3.0 GPA required. Must be a U.S. citizen and Utah resident attending school in Utah. Application deadline is March 27. *Academic/Career Areas:* Chemical Engineering; Civil Engineering; Economics; Electrical Engineering/Electronics; Engineering/Technology; Engineering-Related Technologies; Mechanical Engineering. *Award:* Scholarship for use in freshman year; not renewable. *Award amount:* $1000. *Number of awards:* 1. *Eligibility Requirements:* Applicant must be high school student; planning to enroll or expecting to enroll full-time at a four-year institution or university; resident of Utah and studying in Utah. Applicant must have 3.0 GPA or higher. Available to U.S. citizens. *Application Requirements:* Application, essay, resume, references, test scores, transcript, certification. **Deadline:** March 27.

Contact Tom McNamee, Scholarship Coordinator, Utah Society of Professional Engineers, 488 East Winchester Street, Suite 400, Murray, UT 84107. *E-mail:* tmcnamee@sisna.com. *Web site:* www.uspeonline.com.

Utah Tuition Waiver. Renewable awards ranging from partial to full tuition waivers at eligible Utah institutions. A limited number of waivers are available for nonresidents. Deadlines vary by institutions. Contact Financial Aid Office. *Award:* Scholarship for use in freshman, sophomore, junior, senior, or graduate year; renewable. *Eligibility Requirements:* Applicant must be enrolled or expecting to enroll full or part-time at a two-year or four-year institution and studying in Utah. Available to U.S. and non-U.S. citizens. *Application Requirements:* Application, financial need analysis, interview.

Contact Lynda Reid, Administrative Assistant, Utah State Board of Regents, 60 South 400 West, The Board of Regents Building, The Gateway, Salt Lake City, UT 84101-1284. *Phone:* 801-321-7207. *Fax:* 801-321-7299. *Web site:* www.uheaa.org.

VERMONT

Vermont Incentive Grants. Renewable grants for Vermont residents based on financial need. Must meet needs test. Must be college undergraduate or graduate student enrolled full-time at an approved postsecondary institution. Only available to U.S. citizens or permanent residents. *Award:* Grant for use in freshman, sophomore, junior, senior, or graduate year; renewable. *Award amount:* $500–$9100. *Eligibility Requirements:* Applicant must be enrolled or expecting to enroll full-time at an institution or university and resident of Vermont. Available to U.S. citizens. *Application Requirements:* Application, financial need analysis. **Deadline:** continuous.

Contact Grant Program, Vermont Student Assistance Corporation, PO Box 2000, Winooski, VT 05404-2000. *Phone:* 802-655-9602. *Fax:* 802-654-3765. *Web site:* www.vsac.org.

Vermont Non-degree Student Grant Program. Renewable grants for Vermont residents enrolled in non-degree programs at colleges, vocational centers, and high school adult courses. May receive funds for two enrollment periods per year, up to $690 per course, per semester. Award based upon financial need. *Award:* Grant for use in freshman or sophomore year; renewable. *Award amount:* up to $690. *Eligibility Requirements:* Applicant must be enrolled or expecting to enroll at an institution or university and resident of Vermont. *Application Requirements:* Application, financial need analysis. **Deadline:** continuous.

Contact Grant Program, Vermont Student Assistance Corporation, PO Box 2000, Winooski, VT 05404-2000. *Phone:* 802-655-9602. *Fax:* 802-654-3765. *Web site:* www.vsac.org.

Vermont Part-time Student Grants. For undergraduates carrying less than twelve credits per semester who have not received a bachelor's degree. Must be Vermont resident. Based on financial need. Complete Vermont Financial Aid Packet to apply. May be used at any approved postsecondary institution. *Award:* Grant for use in freshman, sophomore, junior, or senior year; renewable. *Award amount:* $250–$6830. *Eligibility Requirements:* Applicant must be enrolled or expecting to enroll part-time at an institution or university and resident of Vermont. *Application Requirements:* Application, financial need analysis. **Deadline:** continuous.

Contact Grant Program, Vermont Student Assistance Corporation, PO Box 2000, Winooski, VT 05404-2000. *Phone:* 802-655-9602. *Fax:* 802-654-3765. *Web site:* www.vsac.org.

VIRGINIA

General Mills Scholars Program/Internship. Scholarships and paid summer internships awarded to college sophomores and juniors majoring in accounting, business (sales interest), computer science, engineering, finance, human resources, information systems, information technology or marketing at a UNCF member college or university. Minimum 3.5 GPA required. Prospective applicants should complete the Student Profile found at web site: http://www.uncf.org. *Academic/Career Areas:* Accounting; Business/Consumer Services; Computer Science/Data Processing; Engineering/Technology. *Award:* Scholarship for use in sophomore or junior year; not renewable. *Award amount:* $5000. *Eligibility*

Requirements: Applicant must be Black (non-Hispanic) and enrolled or expecting to enroll full-time at a four-year institution or university. Applicant must have 3.5 GPA or higher. Available to U.S. citizens. *Application Requirements:* Application, financial need analysis, test scores. **Deadline:** February 14.

Contact Program Services Department, United Negro College Fund, 8260 Willow Oaks Corporate Drive, Fairfax, VA 22031. *Web site:* www.uncf.org.

Mary Marshall Practical Nursing Scholarships. Award for practical nursing students who are Virginia residents. Must attend a nursing program in Virginia. Recipient must agree to work in Virginia after graduation. Minimum 3.0 GPA required. Recipients may reapply up to three years for an award. *Academic/Career Areas:* Nursing. *Award:* Scholarship for use in freshman, sophomore, junior, or senior year; not renewable. *Award amount:* $150–$500. *Eligibility Requirements:* Applicant must be enrolled or expecting to enroll full or part-time at a two-year or technical institution; resident of Virginia and studying in Virginia. Applicant must have 3.0 GPA or higher. Available to U.S. citizens. *Application Requirements:* Application, financial need analysis, references, transcript. **Deadline:** June 30.

Contact Norma Marrin, Business Manager/Policy Analyst, Virginia Department of Health, Office of Health Policy and Planning, PO Box 2448, Richmond, VA 23218-2448. *E-mail:* nmarrin@vdh.state.va.us. *Phone:* 804-371-4090. *Fax:* 804-371-0116. *Web site:* www.vdh.state.va.us/primcare/index.html.

Mary Marshall Registered Nursing Program Scholarships. Award for registered nursing students who are Virginia residents. Must attend a nursing program in Virginia. Recipient must agree to work in Virginia after graduation. Minimum 3.0 GPA required. Recipient may reapply up to three years for an award. *Academic/Career Areas:* Nursing. *Award:* Scholarship for use in freshman, sophomore, junior, or senior year; not renewable. *Award amount:* $1200–$2000. *Number of awards:* 60–100. *Eligibility Requirements:* Applicant must be enrolled or expecting to enroll full or part-time at a two-year or four-year institution or university; resident of Virginia and studying in Virginia. Applicant must have 3.0 GPA or higher. Available to U.S. citizens. *Application Requirements:* Application, financial need analysis, references, transcript. **Deadline:** June 30.

Contact Norma Marrin, Business Manager/Policy Analyst, Virginia Department of Health, Office of Health Policy and Planning, PO Box 2448, Richmond, VA 23218-2448. *E-mail:* nmarrin@udh.state.va.us. *Phone:* 804-371-4090. *Fax:* 804-371-0116. *Web site:* www.vdh.state.va.us/primcare/index.html.

Virginia Tuition Assistance Grant Program (Private Institutions). Renewable awards of approximately $3,000 each for undergraduate, graduate, and first professional degree students attending an approved private, nonprofit college within Virginia. Must be a Virginia resident and be enrolled full-time. Not to be used for religious study. Preferred deadline July 31. Others are wait-listed. Contact college financial aid office. The application process is handled by the participating colleges' financial aid office. *Award:* Grant for use in freshman, sophomore, junior, senior, or graduate year; renewable. *Award amount:* $3000. *Number of awards:* 15,000. *Eligibility Requirements:* Applicant must be enrolled or expecting to enroll full-time at a four-year institution; resident of Virginia and studying in Virginia. *Application Requirements:* Application. **Deadline:** July 31.

Contact Financial Aid Office at participating institution, State Council of Higher Education for Virginia, James Monroe Building, 10th Floor, 101 North 14th Street, Richmond, VA 23219. *Web site:* www.schev.edu.

Virginia War Orphans Education Program. Scholarships for postsecondary students between ages 16 and 25 to attend Virginia state supported institutions. Must be child or surviving child of veteran who has either 1. been permanently or totally disabled due to war or other armed conflict; 2. died as a result of war or other armed conflict or 3. been listed as a POW or MIA. Parent must also meet Virginia residency requirements. Contact for application procedures and deadline. *Award:* Scholarship for use in freshman, sophomore, junior, senior, or graduate year; renewable. *Eligibility Requirements:* Applicant must be age 16-25; enrolled or expecting to enroll at a two-year, four-year, or technical institution or university and studying in Virginia. Applicant or parent must meet one or more of the following requirements: general military experience; retired from active duty; disabled or killed as a result of military service; prisoner of war; or missing in action. *Application Requirements:* Application.

Contact Beth Tonn, Administrative Assistant, Virginia Department of Veterans' Affairs, Poff Federal Building, 270 Franklin Road, S.W., Room 503, Roanoke, VA 24011-2215. *Phone:* 540-857-7104. *Fax:* 540-858-7573. *Web site:* www.vdva.vipnet.org/education_state.htm.

Virginia War Orphans Education Program. Grant is equal to tuition-free education for up to 48 months. One of the applicant's parents must have served in the armed forces of the United States and be permanently and totally disabled due to war or other armed conflict, died as a result of war or other armed conflict or be listed as a prisoner of war (POW) or missing in action (MIA). Must be a resident of Virginia studying in Virginia. *Award:* Grant for use in freshman, sophomore, junior, or senior year; renewable. *Eligibility Requirements:* Applicant must be age 16-25; enrolled or expecting to enroll at an institution or university; resident of Virginia and studying in Virginia. Available to U.S. citizens. Applicant or parent must meet one or more of the following requirements: general military experience; retired from active duty; disabled or killed as a result of military service; prisoner of war; or missing in action. *Application Requirements:* Application.

Contact Commonwealth of Virginia Department of Veterans' Affairs, 270 Franklin Road SW, Room 503, Poff Federal Building, Roanoke, VA 24011-2215.

Walter Reed Smith Scholarship. Award for full-time female undergraduate student who is a descendant of a Confederate soldier, studying nutrition, home economics, nursing, business administration, or computer science. Must carry a minimum of 12 credit hours each semester and have a minimum 3.0 GPA. Submit letter of endorsement from sponsoring chapter of the United Daughters of the Confederacy. *Academic/Career Areas:* Business/Consumer Services; Computer Science/Data Processing; Food Science/Nutrition; Home Economics; Nursing. *Award:* Scholarship for use in freshman, sophomore, junior, or senior year; renewable. *Award amount:* $800–$1000. *Number of awards:* 1–2. *Eligibility Requirements:* Applicant must be enrolled or expecting to enroll full-time at a four-year institution or university and female. Applicant or parent of applicant must be member of United Daughters of the Confederacy. Applicant must have 3.0 GPA or higher. Available to U.S. citizens. *Application Requirements:* Application, essay, financial need analysis, photo, references, self-addressed stamped envelope, transcript. **Deadline:** February 15.

Contact Second Vice President General, United Daughters of the Confederacy, 328 North Boulevard, Richmond, VA 23220-4057. *Phone:* 804-355-1636. *Web site:* www.hqudc.org.

WASHINGTON

American Indian Endowed Scholarship. Awarded to financially needy undergraduate and graduate students with close social and cultural ties to a Native-Americans community. Must be Washington resident, enrolled full-time at Washington School. Deadline is May 15. *Award:* Scholarship for use in freshman, sophomore, junior, senior, or graduate year; renewable. *Award amount:* $1000–$2000. *Number of awards:* 10–15. *Eligibility Requirements:* Applicant must be American Indian/Alaska Native; enrolled or expecting to enroll full-time at a two-year, four-year, or technical institution or university; resident of Washington and studying in Washington. Available to U.S. citizens. *Application Requirements:* Application, financial need analysis. **Deadline:** May 15.

Contact John Klacik, Washington Higher Education Coordinating Board, 917 Lakeridge Way SW, PO Box 43430 , Olympia, WA 98504-3430. *E-mail:* johnk@ hecb.wa.gov. *Phone:* 360-755-7851. *Fax:* 360-753-7808. *Web site:* www.hecb.wa.gov.

Educational Opportunity Grant. Annual grants of $2500 to encourage financially needy, placebound students to complete bachelor's degree. Must be unable to continue education due to family or work commitments, health concerns, financial needs, or similar. Must be Washington residents, live in one of 13 designated counties, and have completed two years of college. Grant only used at eligible four-year colleges in Washington. Applications accepted beginning in April and following months until funds are depleted. *Award:* Grant for use in junior or senior year; not renewable. *Award amount:* $2500. *Eligibility Requirements:* Applicant must be enrolled or expecting to enroll at a four-year institution or university; resident of Washington and studying in Washington. Available to U.S. citizens. *Application Requirements:* Application, financial need analysis.

Contact Betty Gebhardt, Washington Higher Education Coordinating Board, 917 Lakeridge Way SW, PO Box 43430, Olympia, WA 98504-3430. *E-mail:* bettyg@hecb.wa.gov. *Phone:* 360-753-7852. *Fax:* 360-753-7808. *Web site:* www.hecb.wa.gov.

State Need Grant. Grants for undergraduate students with significant financial need. Must be Washington resident and attend school in Washington. Must have family income equal or less than 55% of state median. *Award:* Grant for use in freshman, sophomore, junior, or senior year; not renewable. *Award amount:* $1900–$4000. *Eligibility Requirements:* Applicant must be enrolled or expecting to enroll full or part-time at a two-year, four-year, or technical institution or university; resident of Washington and studying in Washington. Available to U.S. citizens. *Application Requirements:* Application, financial need analysis. **Deadline:** continuous.

Contact John Klacik, Washington Higher Education Coordinating Board, 917 Lakeridge Way SW, PO Box 43430 , Olympia, WA 98504-3430. *E-mail:* johnk@ hecb.wa.gov. *Phone:* 360-753-7851. *Fax:* 360-753-7808. *Web site:* www.hecb.wa.gov.

Washington Award for Vocational Excellence. Tuition-only award for those completing a vocational education program as graduating seniors or community/technical college students who have completed first year of a two-year program. The scholarship is for 6 quarters or 4 semesters. Three are awarded in each of 49 legislative districts in the state. Must be a Washington State resident attending a postsecondary institution in Washington State. *Award:* Grant for use in freshman or sophomore year; renewable. *Award amount:* $3486–$7796. *Number of awards:* 147. *Eligibility Requirements:* Applicant must be enrolled or expecting to enroll full or part-time at a two-year, four-year, or technical institution or university;

resident of Washington and studying in Washington. Available to U.S. and non-U.S. citizens. *Application Requirements:* Application, essay, references. **Deadline:** March 1.

Contact Lee Williams, Program Administrator, Washington State Workforce Training and Education Coordinating Board, 128 Tenth Avenue SW, PO Box 43105, Olympia, WA 98504-3105. *E-mail:* lwilliams@wtb.wa.gov. *Phone:* 360-586-3321. *Fax:* 360-586-5862. *Web site:* www.wtb.wa.gov/wave-abt.html.

Washington Award for Vocational Excellence (WAVE). Award to honor three vocational students from each of the state's 49 legislative districts. Grants for up to two years of undergraduate resident tuition. Must be enrolled in Washington high school, skills center, or technical college at time of application. Complete 360 hours in single vocational program in high school or one year at technical college. Contact principal or guidance counselor for more information. *Award:* Grant for use in freshman, sophomore, junior, or senior year; renewable. *Eligibility Requirements:* Applicant must be enrolled or expecting to enroll full-time at a two-year, four-year, or technical institution or university; resident of Washington and studying in Washington. Available to U.S. citizens. *Application Requirements:* **Deadline:** continuous.

Contact John Klacik, Washington Higher Education Coordinating Board, 917 Lakeridge Way, SW, PO Box 43430 , Olympia, WA 98504-3430. *E-mail:* johnk@hecb.wa.gov. *Phone:* 360-753-7851. *Fax:* 360-753-7808. *Web site:* www.hecb.wa.gov.

Washington National Guard Scholarship Program. A state funded retention incentive/loan program for both Washington Army and Air Guard members meeting all eligibility requirements. The loans are forgiven if the soldier/airman completes their service requirements. Failure to meet/complete service obligations incurs the requirement to repay the loan plus 8% interest. Minimum 2.5 GPA required. Deadline is April 30. *Award:* Forgivable loan for use in freshman, sophomore, junior, or senior year; not renewable. *Award amount:* $200–$4000. *Number of awards:* up to 60. *Eligibility Requirements:* Applicant must be enrolled or expecting to enroll full or part-time at a two-year, four-year, or technical institution or university and resident of Washington. Applicant must have 2.5 GPA or higher. Available to U.S. and non-U.S. citizens. Applicant must have served in the Air Force National Guard or Army National Guard. *Application Requirements:* Application, transcript, enlistment/extension documents. **Deadline:** April 30.

Contact Mark M. Rhoden, Educational Services Officer, Washington National Guard, Building 15, Camp Murray, Tacoma, WA 98430-5073. *E-mail:* mark.rhoden@wa.ngb.army.mil. *Phone:* 253-512-8899. *Fax:* 253-512-8936. *Web site:* www.washingtonguard.com/education/education.htm.

Washington Promise Scholarship. College scholarships to low- and middle-income students in high school. Must either rank in top 15 percent of senior class or score a combined 1200 on SAT or 27 on ACT on first attempt. Family income cannot exceed 135% of state median family income. Must be Washington resident, attend a Washington school. School must identify applicants. Contact principal or guidance counselor for more information. *Award:* Scholarship for use in freshman or sophomore year; renewable. *Award amount:* up to $1000. *Eligibility Requirements:* Applicant must be high school student; planning to enroll or expecting to enroll full or part-time at a two-year, four-year, or technical institution or university; resident of Washington and studying in Washington. Available to U.S. citizens. *Application Requirements:* Financial need analysis. **Deadline:** continuous.

Contact John Klacik, Washington Higher Education Coordinating Board, 917 Lakeridge Way SW, PO Box 43430, Olympia, WA 98504-3430. *E-mail:* johnk@ hecb.wa.gov. *Phone:* 360-753-7851. *Fax:* 360-753-7808. *Web site:* www.hecb.wa.gov.

Washington Scholars Program. Awarded to three high school students from each of the 49 state legislative districts. Must be Washington resident and enroll in college or university in Washington. Scholarships equal up to four years of full-time resident undergraduate tuition and fees. Contact principal or guidance counselor for more information. *Award:* Grant for use in freshman, sophomore, junior, or senior year; renewable. *Eligibility Requirements:* Applicant must be high school student; planning to enroll or expecting to enroll full-time at a four-year institution or university; resident of Washington and studying in Washington. Available to U.S. citizens. *Application Requirements:* **Deadline:** continuous.

Contact John Klacik, Washington Higher Education Coordinating Board, 917 Lakeridge Way SW, PO Box 43430, Olympia, WA 98504-3430. *E-mail:* johnk@ hecb.wa.gov. *Phone:* 360-753-7851. *Fax:* 360-753-7808. *Web site:* www.hecb.wa.gov.

WEST VIRGINIA

Higher Education Adult Part-time Student Grant Program. Program to assist needy adult students to continue their education on a part-time basis. Also has a component in which 25% of the funding may be utilized for students enrolled in workforce and skill development programs. Contact institution financial aid office for more information and deadlines. *Award:* Grant for use in freshman, sophomore, junior, or senior year; not renewable. *Eligibility Requirements:* Applicant must be enrolled or expecting to enroll full or part-time at a two-year, four-year, or technical institution or university; resident of West Virginia and studying in West Virginia. Available to U.S. citizens. *Application Requirements:* Application, financial need analysis.

Contact Judy Kee, Financial Aid Manager, West Virginia Higher Education Policy Commission-Office of Financial Aid and Outreach Services, 1018 Kanawha Boulevard, East, Suite 700, Charleston, WV 25301. *E-mail:* kee@hepc.wvnet. edu. *Phone:* 304-558-4618. *Fax:* 304-558-4622. *Web site:* www.hepc.wvnet.edu.

Promise Scholarship. Renewable award for West Virginia residents. Minimum 3.0 GPA and combined ACT score of 21 or 1000 on the SAT. Provides full-tuition scholarship to a state college or university in West Virginia or an equivalent scholarship to an in-state private college. Financial resources are not a factor. *Award:* Scholarship for use in freshman, sophomore, junior, or senior year; renewable. *Award amount:* $3000. *Number of awards:* 3500. *Eligibility Requirements:* Applicant must be high school student; planning to enroll or expecting to enroll full-time at a two-year or four-year institution or university; resident of West Virginia and studying in West Virginia. Applicant must have 3.0 GPA or higher. Available to U.S. citizens. *Application Requirements:* Application, financial need analysis, test scores, transcript. **Deadline:** January 31.

Contact Robert Morgenstern, Executive Director, West Virginia Higher Education Policy Commission-Office of Financial Aid and Outreach Services, Promise Scholarship, 1018 Kanawha Boulevard, Suite 700, Charleston, WV 25301. *E-mail:* morgenstern@hepc.wvnet.edu. *Phone:* 304-558-4417. *Fax:* 304-558-3264. *Web site:* www.hepc.wvnet.edu.

Underwood-Smith Teacher Scholarship Program. For West Virginia residents at West Virginia institutions pursuing teaching careers. Must have a 3.25 GPA after completion of two years of course work. Must teach two years in West Virginia public schools for each year the award is received. Recipients will be required to sign an agreement acknowledging an understanding of the program's requirements and their willingness to repay the award if appropriate teaching service is not rendered. *Academic/Career Areas:* Education. *Award:* Scholarship for use in junior, senior, or graduate year; renewable. *Award amount:* up to $5000. *Number of awards:* 53. *Eligibility Requirements:* Applicant must be enrolled or expecting to enroll full-time at a four-year institution or university; resident of West Virginia and studying in West Virginia. Available to U.S. citizens. *Application Requirements:* Application, essay, references. **Deadline:** March 1.

Contact Michelle Wicks, Scholarship Coordinator, West Virginia Higher Education Policy Commission-Office of Financial Aid and Outreach Services, 1018 Kanawha Boulevard East, Suite 700, Charleston, WV 25301. *E-mail:* wicks@hepc.wvnet.edu. *Phone:* 304-558-4618. *Fax:* 304-558-4622. *Web site:* www.hepc.wvnet.edu.

West Virginia Division of Veterans' Affairs War Orphans Education Program. Renewable waiver of tuition award for West Virginia residents who are children of deceased veterans. Parent must have died of war-related service-connected disability. Must be ages 16-23. Minimum 2.5 GPA required. Must attend a state-supported West Virginia postsecondary institution. Deadline: July 1 and December 1. *Award:* Scholarship for use in freshman, sophomore, junior, senior, or graduate year; renewable. *Eligibility Requirements:* Applicant must be age 16-23; enrolled or expecting to enroll full or part-time at a two-year, four-year, or technical institution or university; resident of West Virginia and studying in West Virginia. Applicant must have 2.5 GPA or higher. Available to U.S. citizens. Applicant or parent must meet one or more of the following requirements: general military experience; retired from active duty; disabled or killed as a result of military service; prisoner of war; or missing in action. *Application Requirements:* Application, references.

Contact Ms. Linda Walker, Secretary, West Virginia Division of Veterans' Affairs, 1321 Plaza East, Suite 101, Charleston, WV 25301-1400. *E-mail:* wvdva@state.wv.us. *Phone:* 304-668-3661. *Fax:* 304-668-3662.

West Virginia Engineering, Science & Technology Scholarship Program. For students attending West Virginia institutions full time pursuing a career in engineering, science or technology. Must have a 3.0 GPA on a 4.0 scale. Must work in the fields of engineering, science or technology in West Virginia one year for each year the award is received. *Academic/Career Areas:* Electrical Engineering/Electronics; Engineering/Technology; Engineering-Related Technologies; Science, Technology and Society. *Award:* Scholarship for use in freshman, sophomore, junior, or senior year; renewable. *Award amount:* up to $3000. *Number of awards:* 300. *Eligibility Requirements:* Applicant must be enrolled or expecting to enroll full-time at a two-year, four-year, or technical institution or university and studying in West Virginia. Applicant must have 3.0 GPA or higher. Available to U.S. citizens. *Application Requirements:* Application, essay, test scores, transcript. **Deadline:** March 1.

Contact Michelle Wicks, Scholarship Coordinator, West Virginia Higher Education Policy Commission-Office of Financial Aid and Outreach Services, 1018 Kanawha Boulevard East, Suite 700, Charleston, WV 25301. *E-mail:* wicks@hepc.wvnet.edu. *Phone:* 304-558-4618. *Fax:* 304-558-4622. *Web site:* www.hepc.wvnet.edu.

West Virginia Higher Education Grant Program. For West Virginia residents attending an approved nonprofit degree-granting college or university in West Virginia or Pennsylvania. Must be enrolled full-time. Based on financial need and academic merit. Award covers tuition and fees. *Award:* Grant for use in freshman, sophomore, junior, or senior year; renewable. *Award amount:* $350–$2718. *Number of awards:* 10,500–10,800. *Eligibility Requirements:* Applicant must be enrolled or expecting to enroll full-time at a two-year or four-year institution or university; resident of West Virginia and studying in Pennsylvania or West Virginia. Available to U.S. citizens. *Application Requirements:* Application, financial need analysis, test scores, transcript. **Deadline:** March 1.

Contact Robert Long, Grant Program Coordinator, West Virginia Higher Education Policy Commission-Office of Financial Aid and Outreach Services, 1018 Kanawha Boulevard East, Suite 700, Charleston, WV 25301-2827. *E-mail:* long@hepc.wvnet.edu. *Phone:* 888-825-5707. *Fax:* 304-558-4622. *Web site:* www.hepc.wvnet.edu.

WISCONSIN

Handicapped Student Grant—Wisconsin. One-time awards available to residents of Wisconsin who have severe or profound hearing or visual impairment. Must be enrolled at least half-time at a nonprofit institution. If the handicap prevents the student from attending a Wisconsin school, the award may be used out-of-state in a specialized college. *Award:* Grant for use in freshman, sophomore, junior, or senior year; not renewable. *Award amount:* $250–$1800. *Eligibility Requirements:* Applicant must be enrolled or expecting to enroll full or part-time at a two-year, four-year, or technical institution or university and resident of Wisconsin. Applicant must be hearing impaired or visually impaired. Available to U.S. and non-U.S. citizens. *Application Requirements:* Application, financial need analysis. **Deadline:** continuous.

Contact Sandra Thomas, Wisconsin Higher Educational Aid Board, PO Box 7885, Madison, WI 53707-7885. *E-mail:* sandy.thomas@heab.state.wi.us. *Phone:* 608-266-0888. *Fax:* 608-267-2808. *Web site:* www.heab.state.wi.us.

Minnesota-Wisconsin Reciprocity Program. Wisconsin residents may attend a Minnesota public institution and pay the reciprocity tuition charged by Minnesota institution. All programs are eligible except doctoral programs in medicine, dentistry, and veterinary medicine. *Award:* Scholarship for use in freshman, sophomore, junior, or senior year; renewable. *Eligibility Requirements:* Applicant must be enrolled or expecting to enroll full or part-time at a two-year, four-year, or technical institution or university; resident of Wisconsin and studying in Minnesota. Available to U.S. citizens. *Application Requirements:* Application. **Deadline:** continuous.

Contact Cindy Lehrman, Wisconsin Higher Educational Aid Board, PO Box 7885, Madison, WI 53707-7885. *E-mail:* cindy.lehrman@heab.state.wi.us. *Phone:* 608-267-2209. *Fax:* 608-267-2808. *Web site:* www.heab.state.wi.us.

Minority Retention Grant-Wisconsin. Provides financial assistance to African-American, Native-Americans, Hispanic, and former citizens of Laos, Vietnam, and Cambodia, for study in Wisconsin. Must be Wisconsin resident, enrolled at least half-time in a two-year or four-year nonprofit college, and must show financial need. *Award:* Grant for use in sophomore, junior, senior, or graduate year; not renewable. *Award amount:* $250–$2500. *Eligibility Requirements:* Applicant must be American Indian/Alaska Native, Asian/Pacific Islander, Black (non-Hispanic), or Hispanic; enrolled or expecting to enroll full or part-time at a two-year, four-year, or technical institution; resident of Wisconsin and studying in Wisconsin. Available to U.S. and non-U.S. citizens. *Application Requirements:* Application, financial need analysis. **Deadline:** continuous.

Profiles of State-Sponsored Programs

Contact Mary Lou Kuzdas, Program Coordinator, Wisconsin Higher Educational Aid Board, PO Box 7885, Madison, WI 53707-7885. *E-mail:* mary.kuzdas@heab.state.wi.us. *Phone:* 608-267-2212. *Fax:* 608-267-2808. *Web site:* www.heab.state.wi.us.

Nursing Student Loan Program. Provides forgivable loans to students enrolled in a nursing program. Must be a Wisconsin resident studying in Wisconsin. Application deadline is May 3. *Academic/Career Areas:* Nursing. *Award:* Forgivable loan for use in freshman, sophomore, junior, or senior year; not renewable. *Award amount:* $250–$3000. *Eligibility Requirements:* Applicant must be enrolled or expecting to enroll full or part-time at a two-year, four-year, or technical institution or university; resident of Wisconsin and studying in Wisconsin. Available to U.S. and non-U.S. citizens. *Application Requirements:* Application, financial need analysis. **Deadline:** May 3.

Contact Alice Winters, Program Coordinator, Wisconsin Higher Educational Aid Board, PO Box 7885, Madison, WI 53707-7885. *E-mail:* alice.winters@heab.state.wi.us. *Phone:* 608-267-2213. *Fax:* 608-267-2808. *Web site:* www.heab.state.wi.us.

Talent Incentive Program—Wisconsin. Assists residents of Wisconsin who are attending a nonprofit institution in Wisconsin and have substantial financial need. Must meet income criteria, be considered economically and educationally disadvantaged and be enrolled at least half-time. *Award:* Grant for use in freshman, sophomore, junior, or senior year; renewable. *Award amount:* $600–$1800. *Eligibility Requirements:* Applicant must be enrolled or expecting to enroll full or part-time at a two-year, four-year, or technical institution or university; resident of Wisconsin and studying in Wisconsin. Available to U.S. and non-U.S. citizens. *Application Requirements:* Application, financial need analysis. **Deadline:** continuous.

Contact John Whitt, Program Coordinator, Wisconsin Higher Educational Aid Board, PO Box 7885, Madison, WI 53707-7885. *E-mail:* john.whitt@heab.state.wi.us. *Phone:* 608-266-1665. *Fax:* 608-267-2808. *Web site:* www.heab.state.wi.us.

Teacher of the Visually Impaired Loan Program. Provides forgivable loans to students who enroll in programs that lead to be certified as a teacher of the visually impaired or an orientation and mobility instructor. Must be a Wisconsin resident. For study in Wisconsin, Illinois, Iowa and Michigan. *Award:* Forgivable loan for use in freshman, sophomore, junior, senior, or postgraduate years; not renewable. *Award amount:* $250–$10,000. *Eligibility Requirements:* Applicant must be enrolled or expecting to enroll full or part-time at a two-year, four-year, or technical institution or university; resident of Wisconsin and studying in Illinois, Iowa, Michigan, or Wisconsin. Available to U.S. and non-U.S. citizens. *Application Requirements:* Application, financial need analysis. **Deadline:** continuous.

Contact John Whitt, Program Coordinator, Wisconsin Higher Educational Aid Board, PO Box 7885, Madison, WI 53707-7885. *E-mail:* john.whitt@heab.state.wi.us. *Phone:* 608-266-0888. *Fax:* 608-267-2808. *Web site:* www.heab.state.wi.us.

Tuition and Fee Reimbursement Grants. Up to 85% tuition and fee reimbursement for Wisconsin veterans who were discharged from active duty within the last 10 years. Undergraduate courses must be completed at accredited Wisconsin schools. Those attending Minnesota public colleges, universities, and technical schools that have a tuition reciprocity agreement with Wisconsin also may qualify. Must meet military service requirements. Application must be received no later than 60 days after the completion of the course. *Award:* Grant for use in freshman, sophomore, junior, or senior year; renewable. *Eligibility Requirements:* Applicant must be enrolled or expecting to enroll full-time at a two-year, four-year, or technical institution or university; resident of Wisconsin and studying in Minnesota or Wisconsin. Available to U.S. citizens. Applicant must have general military experience. *Application Requirements:* Application.

Contact Mr. Steve Olson, Public Relations Officer, Wisconsin Department of Veterans Affairs, PO Box 7843, Madison, WI 53707-7843. *Phone:* 608-266-1311. *Web site:* dva.state.wi.us.

Wisconsin Academic Excellence Scholarship. Renewable award for high school seniors with the highest GPA in graduating class. Must be a Wisconsin resident. Award covers tuition for up to four years. Must maintain 3.5 GPA for renewal. Scholarships of up to $2250 each. Must attend a nonprofit Wisconsin institution full-time. *Award:* Scholarship for use in freshman, sophomore, junior, or senior year; renewable. *Award amount:* $250–$2250. *Eligibility Requirements:* Applicant must be high school student; planning to enroll or expecting to enroll full-time at a two-year, four-year, or technical institution or university; resident of Wisconsin and studying in Wisconsin. Applicant must have 3.5 GPA or higher. Available to U.S. and non-U.S. citizens. *Application Requirements:* Transcript. **Deadline:** continuous.

Contact Alice Winters, Program Coordinator, Wisconsin Higher Educational Aid Board, PO Box 7885, Madison, WI 53707-7885. *E-mail:* alice.winters@heab.state.wi.us. *Phone:* 608-267-2213. *Fax:* 608-267-2808. *Web site:* www.heab.state.wi.us.

Wisconsin Department of Veterans Affairs Retraining Grants. Renewable award for veterans, unmarried spouses of deceased veterans, or dependents of deceased veterans. Must be resident of Wisconsin and attend an institution in Wisconsin. Veteran must be recently unemployed and show financial need. Must enroll in a vocational or technical program that can reasonably be expected to lead to employment. Course work at four-year colleges or universities does not qualify as retraining. *Award:* Grant for use in freshman or sophomore year; renewable. *Award amount:* up to $3000. *Eligibility Requirements:* Applicant must be enrolled or expecting to enroll full or part-time at a technical institution; resident of Wisconsin and studying in Wisconsin. Applicant or parent must meet one or more of the following requirements: general military experience; retired from active duty; disabled or killed as a result of military service; prisoner of war; or missing in action. *Application Requirements:* Application, financial need analysis.

Contact Mr. Steve Olson, Public Relations Officer, Wisconsin Department of Veterans Affairs, PO Box 7843, Madison, WI 53707-7843. *Phone:* 608-266-1311. *Web site:* dva.state.wi.us.

Wisconsin Higher Education Grants (WHEG). Grants for residents of Wisconsin attending a campus of the University of Wisconsin or Wisconsin Technical College. Must be enrolled at least half-time and show financial need. Renewable for up to five years. *Award:* Grant for use in freshman, sophomore, junior, or senior year; not renewable. *Award amount:* $250–$1800. *Eligibility Requirements:* Applicant must be enrolled or expecting to enroll full or part-time at a two-year, four-year, or technical institution or university; resident of Wisconsin and studying in Wisconsin. Available to U.S. and non-U.S. citizens. *Application Requirements:* Application, financial need analysis. **Deadline:** continuous.

Contact Sandra Thomas, Program Coordinator, Wisconsin Higher Educational Aid Board, PO Box 7885, Madison, WI 53707-7885. *E-mail:* sandy.thomas@heab.state.wi.us. *Phone:* 608-266-0888. *Fax:* 608-267-2808. *Web site:* www.heab.state.wi.us.

Wisconsin National Guard Tuition Grant. Renewable award for active members of the Wisconsin National Guard in good standing, who successfully complete a course of study at a qualifying school. Award covers full tuition, excluding fees, not to exceed undergraduate tuition charged by University of Wisconsin-Madison. Must have a minimum 2.0 GPA. *Award:* Grant for use in freshman, sophomore, junior, or senior year; renewable. *Award amount:* up to $1927. *Number of awards:* up to 4000. *Eligibility Requirements:* Applicant must be enrolled or expecting to enroll full or part-time at a two-year, four-year, or technical institution or university and resident of Wisconsin. Applicant must have 2.5 GPA or higher. Available to U.S. citizens. Applicant must have served in the Air Force National Guard or Army National Guard. *Application Requirements:* Application. **Deadline:** continuous.

Contact Karen Behling, Tuition Grant Administrator, Department of Military Affairs, PO Box 14587, Madison, WI 53714-0587. *E-mail:* karen.behling@dma. state.wi.us. *Phone:* 608-242-3159. *Fax:* 608-242-3154. *Web site:* wisconsinguard. com.

Wisconsin Native American Student Grant. Grants for Wisconsin residents who are at least one-quarter American-Indian. Must be attending a college or university within the state. Renewable for up to five years. Several grants of up to $1100. *Award:* Grant for use in freshman, sophomore, junior, or senior year; renewable. *Award amount:* $250–$1100. *Eligibility Requirements:* Applicant must be American Indian/Alaska Native; enrolled or expecting to enroll full or part-time at a two-year, four-year, or technical institution or university; resident of Wisconsin and studying in Wisconsin. Available to U.S. and non-U.S. citizens. *Application Requirements:* Application, financial need analysis. **Deadline:** continuous.

Contact Sandra Thomas, Program Coordinator, Wisconsin Higher Educational Aid Board, PO Box 7885, Madison, WI 53707-7885. *E-mail:* sandy.thomas@heab.state.wi.us. *Phone:* 608-266-0888. *Fax:* 608-267-2808. *Web site:* www.heab.state.wi.us.

Wisconsin Tuition Grant Program. Available to Wisconsin residents who are enrolled at least half-time in degree or certificate programs at independent, nonprofit colleges or universities in Wisconsin. Must show financial need. *Award:* Grant for use in freshman, sophomore, junior, or senior year; not renewable. *Award amount:* $250–$2350. *Eligibility Requirements:* Applicant must be enrolled or expecting to enroll full or part-time at a four-year institution or university; resident of Wisconsin and studying in Wisconsin. Available to U.S. and non-U.S. citizens. *Application Requirements:* Application, financial need analysis. **Deadline:** continuous.

Contact Mary Lou Kuzdas, Program Coordinator, Wisconsin Higher Educational Aid Board, PO Box 7885, Madison, WI 53707-7885. *E-mail:* mary.kuzdas@heab.state.wi.us. *Phone:* 608-267-2212. *Fax:* 608-267-2808. *Web site:* www.heab.state.wi.us.

Wisconsin Veterans Part-time Study Reimbursement Grant. Open only to Wisconsin veterans and dependents of deceased Wisconsin veterans. Renewable for continuing study. Contact office for more details. Application deadline is no later than sixty days after the course completion. Veterans may be reimbursed up to 85% of tuition and fees. *Award:* Grant for use in freshman, sophomore, junior, or senior year; renewable. *Award amount:* $300–$1100. *Eligibility Requirements:* Applicant must be enrolled or expecting to enroll part-time at an institution or university; resident of Wisconsin and studying in Wisconsin. Available to U.S. citizens. Applicant or parent must meet one or more of the following requirements:

general military experience; retired from active duty; disabled or killed as a result of military service; prisoner of war; or missing in action. *Application Requirements:* Application.

Contact Mr. Steve Olson, Public Relations Officer, Wisconsin Department of Veterans Affairs, PO Box 7843, Madison, WI 53707-7843. *Phone:* 608-266-1311. *Web site:* dva.state.wi.us.

WYOMING

Douvas Memorial Scholarship. Available to Wyoming residents who are first-generation Americans. Must be between 18-22 years old. Must be used at any Wyoming public institution of higher education for study freshman year. *Award:* Scholarship for use in freshman year; not renewable. *Award amount:* $500. *Number of awards:* 1. *Eligibility Requirements:* Applicant must be age 18-22; enrolled or expecting to enroll at a two-year or four-year institution or university; resident of Wyoming and studying in Wyoming. *Application Requirements:* Application. **Deadline:** April 18.

Contact Wyoming Department of Education, 2300 Capitol Avenue, Hathaway Building, 2nd Floor, Cheyenne, WY 82002-0050.

Superior Student in Education Scholarship—Wyoming. Available to Wyoming high school graduates who have demonstrated high academic achievement and plan to teach in Wyoming public schools. Award is for tuition at Wyoming institutions. Must maintain 3.0 GPA. *Academic/Career Areas:* Education. *Award:* Scholarship for use in freshman, sophomore, junior, or senior year; renewable. *Number of awards:* 16–80. *Eligibility Requirements:* Applicant must be enrolled or expecting to enroll full-time at a two-year or four-year institution or university; resident of Wyoming and studying in Wyoming. Applicant must have 3.0 GPA or higher. Available to U.S. citizens. *Application Requirements:* Application, references, test scores, transcript. **Deadline:** October 31.

Contact Joel Anne Berrigan, Assistant Director, Scholarships, State of Wyoming, administered by University of Wyoming, PO Box 3335, Laramie, WY 82071-3335. *E-mail:* finaid@uwyo.edu. *Phone:* 307-766-2117. *Fax:* 307-766-3800.

Vietnam Veterans Award/Wyoming. Available to Wyoming residents who served in the armed forces between August 5, 1964, and May 7, 1975, and received a Vietnam service medal. Award is free tuition at the University of Wyoming or a state (WY) community college. *Award:* Scholarship for use in freshman, sophomore, junior, or senior year; renewable. *Eligibility Requirements:* Applicant must be enrolled or expecting to enroll full or part-time at a two-year or four-year institution or university; resident of Wyoming and studying in Wyoming. Available to U.S. citizens. Applicant must have general military experience. *Application Requirements:* Application. **Deadline:** continuous.

Contact Joel Anne Berrigan, Assistant Director, Scholarships, State of Wyoming, administered by University of Wyoming, PO Box 3335, Laramie, WY 82071-3335. *E-mail:* finaid@uwyo.edu. *Phone:* 307-766-2117. *Fax:* 307-766-3800.

Appendix

Schools apply different COA standards for students who are living on-campus or off-campus, married or unmarried, and in-state or out-of-state.

credit, credit hours, credits—the unit of measurement of academic work successfully completed. There are several different credit systems. Under one system, a course might be worth 1 credit, while in another system the same course would be worth 3 "credit hours" or "hours," indicating the amount of time spent each week in class. Sometimes courses that are more advanced or that meet for more hours offer greater credit.

curriculum vitae (*c.v.*)—a summary account of one's life, familiarly called a *c.v.* In academe, this is a relatively lengthy document. In addition to basic biographical data, it typically covers an individual's education, employment, teaching or research positions, administrative responsibilities, ongoing research, delivered and published papers, lengthier publications, awards and honors, professional memberships and posts, and other relevant accomplishments.

demonstrated financial need—proof that one's income and assets are insufficient to cover college expenses. This is usually a formal document in which an applicant will provide required information and backup documentation concerning income and assets. This form may be supplied by the sponsor or the sponsor may rely upon a standard methodology—Federal Methodology (FM) or Institutional Methodology (IM).

dependent, dependent child—an immediate family member or spouse who lives with and receives over half of his or her support from another family member. The actual definitions of which family members may qualify and how old they can be may differ from sponsor to sponsor. Be sure to check with the sponsor to find out their particular definition of dependent status if this is a factor in your eligibility.

disability, disabilities, disabled—a limitation in one or more life functions, including sight, hearing, thinking, walking, breathing, performing manual tasks, or speaking. Some disabilities are obvious physical impediments. There is also widespread recognition of disabilities, such as learning disabilities and attention deficit disorders, that can greatly affect a student's ability to perform well academically.

entering students, entering freshmen—students who have been recently enrolled by a postsecondary institution but who may or may not have begun to attend classes.

expected family contribution (EFC)—the amount of money that a family is expected to be able to contribute to their student's education as determined by the Federal Methodology (FM). The EFC includes parent and student contributions. The EFC deducted from the Cost of Attendance (COA) is the student's financial need, which is the basis for determining any need-based financial aid.

Federal Methodology (FM)—the need analysis formula established by the federal government for analyzing the FAFSA to determine the expected family contribution (EFC).

Federal Work-Study (FWS)—a federally supported program that provides students with part-time employment during the school year. Part of the student's salary is paid by the government. Employers frequently are college or university departments or facilities. However, local businesses can and frequently do participate in the program. Eligibility for FWS is based on need. Work-Study is often one component in the financial aid package that a college offers prospective students.

fellowship—graduate and postgraduate-level awards to individuals to cover their living expenses while they take advanced courses, carry out research, or work on a project. Some fellowships include a tuition waiver.

financial aid office—college or university office that is responsible for the determination of financial need and the awarding of financial aid.

financial aid package—the complete collection of gift aid, loans, and work-study employment from all sources offered by the college or university to a student.

financial need analysis—the formula for calculating a student's financial need. This may be individual to a scholarship sponsor or be one of numerous standardized formulas, such as the Federal Methodology (FM) or the Institutional Methodology (IM). See *demonstrated financial need*, above.

forgivable loan—a form of student financial aid under which the student borrower commits to apply their training for a finite period of time in a way dictated by the lender and thereby win cancellation of the loan. Commitments may be to practicing health care in a rural or underserved area, teaching in a rural or inner-city district, or serving in a branch of the armed services. Failure to graduate or follow through on the service commitment entails repayment of the loan amount with interest.

four-year institution—a postsecondary institution or college offering one or more four-year programs of study leading to a bachelor's degree. A four-year institution may be a unit within a university or an independent college.

Free Application for Federal Student Aid (FAFSA)—the financial aid application form used to apply for all other need-based aid from the federal government, as well as the majority of aid from state governments and college-based sources. Many noninstitutional award programs that take need into account will use data that are reported on the FAFSA. In addition to the standard print version, which is available at any college financial aid office and most high school guidance offices, there are two versions available in electronic media—FAFSA Express on diskette and FAFSA on the Web that can be completed and submitted via the Internet.

freshman, freshmen—a student in the first year or with first-year standing at a college or secondary school. The term applies to both men and women.

full-time, full-time course load, full-time study—denotes a student who meets a specific minimal criterion regarding the number of credits being taken in a particular period. Colleges differ in the standards that they use to determine full-time status, and they apply different standards to different levels of study. A typical undergraduate program requires 12 credit hours or four courses each term to qualify as full-time. This standard is reduced, usually progressively, for each graduate level. You will have to check with the specific institution to find out how they define a "full-time" course load.

gift aid—financial aid which does not need to be repaid. Scholarships, grants, prizes, and fellowships are some types of gift aid.

GPA (grade point average)—a system of scoring student achievement used by many colleges and universities. A student's GPA is computed by multiplying the numerical grade received in each course by the number of credits offered for each course, then dividing by the total number of credit hours studied. Most institutions use the following grade conversion scale: A = 4, B = 3, C = 2, D = 1, and E and F = 0.

graduate student, graduate study—refers to the level of higher education that will lead to a master's degree or doctoral degree. Graduate degrees are required to enter professional careers in medicine, business, college or university teaching, and many other fields. Among other requirements, admission to a graduate program will require a bachelor's degree or its equivalent.

grant—gift aid usually awarded to support research or specific projects. Grants provide funds directly related to carrying out proposed research, but can include funds for travel and living expenses while conducting research away from a home institution. Many grant programs support doctoral dissertation research, and some can be applied to research related to a master's thesis. The term "grant" very frequently is used to refer to any form of gift aid, including scholarships and fellowships.

Hispanic—an adjective for people, regardless of race, who identify with ancestry in Mexico, Puerto Rico, Cuba, Central or South America, and other countries with Spanish cultural roots. There is ambiguity as to whether Europeans of the Iberian Peninsula, Brazilians, and American Indians with a mixed heritage of Mexican or Central or South American tribes are included in this category. If these distinctions are important to you, check with the specific award's sponsor to find out their definition.

independent student—a student who does not have over half of his or her support provided by an immediate family member.

Institutional Methodology (IM)—the need analysis formula established by CSS for analyzing the Financial Aid PROFILE used to determine the expected family contribution. Unlike the Federal Methodology (FM), the net value of the family residence is part of the consideration.

internship—a program for students to gain practical experience in their field of interest by working with and under the supervision of the professional staff of an organization. Paid internships offer a wage or fixed allowance to the student during the period of internship. Often an intern works on projects of interest to the host organization or learns specific techniques. Internships can range in length up to an entire academic year.

interview—a conversation between the candidate for an award and the individual or group that will decide who receives the award. Usually this is an actual meeting of the parties that is conducted at the sponsor's offices. The purpose is to allow the judges the opportunity to better evaluate the suitability of the candidate in accordance with the program's goals.

junior—a student in the third year or with third-year standing at a college or secondary school.

letter of recommendation—a document written and signed by an individual of professional authority or credence, typically a teacher, school administrator, or professional in a subject field, that attests to the quality of an applicant's qualifications, work, character, or abilities. The letter may be specifically addressed or written to any recipient who may be interested. Sponsors may request that the signer send the letter directly.

loan—a type of financial aid which must be repaid, with interest.

major—the academic area in which a student chooses to concentrate. Generally, major course requirements take up one quarter to one half of the student's undergraduate studies and are combined with other general education requirements.

merit-based—describes awards that are given on the basis of criteria other than financial need, including the academic field chosen, career goals, grades, test scores, athletic ability, hobbies, talents, place of residence or birth, ethnic identity, religious affiliation, one's or one's parents' military or public safety service, disability, union memberships, employment history, community service, or club affiliations.

minority—a group of people with a coherent identity that historically has been frustrated in achieving parity with an antithetical group that comprises the "majority." In the U.S., the traditional and most common usage of the term is in reference to racial or ethnic populations, specifically African Americans, Hispanics, and Native Americans. In higher education, the "minority" label has been claimed by or attached to other kinds of groups, such as women, homosexuals, and people with disabilities, that have experienced bias or relative lack of economic opportunity or progress.

Native American—denotes identity with one of the aboriginal tribal populations of the Americas, excluding Inuit or Eskimo people. American Indian is a widely used alternative term. If this is used as a criterion for a scholarship award, proof of tribal membership usually will be required.

need, needy, needy student—in the jargon of student financial aid, the difference between the cost of attendance (COA) and the expected family contribution (EFC). The financial aid package is based on the amount of financial need. Needy describes student need in this context and does not connote that the student or family is in poverty.

nominated, nomination—describes the action of having one's eligibility for an award brought to the consideration of a sponsor by a third party or organization. Usually the nominator must be in a position of professional authority or high reputation, be unrelated to the candidate, and be familiar with the candidate's academic achievements, community service record, talents, or character.

nonrenewable—description of awards that will not be awarded more than once to the same recipient.

one-time award—description of awards that have a term limit of coverage. Check with the sponsor to find out if reapplication for a new award is allowed when the current award period ceases.

postsecondary—description of any organized education above grade 12 of the secondary (high school or preparatory school) level.

prize—gift aid given for outstanding achievement or winning a competition.

professional degree—a degree in a field such as law, education, medicine, pharmacy, or dentistry. Many fields that require advanced or specialized educational degrees are also referred to as professions, and a sponsor may be referring to a profession other than one of these specifically cited. It is advisable to check with a scholarship's sponsor if this distinction may be important to you.

PROFILE—the financial aid application form distributed through the College Scholarship Service (CSS) that is used by about 300 private colleges and universities as the basis for awarding college-based aid. The FAFSA also must be filed to receive aid from these colleges. There is an application fee with the PROFILE form.

quarter—a division of a college or university's academic year if the institution divides its year into four terms (quarters).

reapplication, reapply—indicates that a new application is required to secure renewal of an award. Frequently in a reapplication you have no intrinsic advantage over other applicants for the award.

recommendation—see *letter of recommendation*, above.

registration fee—a fee charged by certain sponsors to consider your application.

renewable—describes awards that may be for a length of study beyond a single year. Some renewable scholarships will require the student to reapply for the scholarship each year; others will just require a report on the student's progress to a degree.

resident—a reference to having one's primary residence within a place for a specified length of time. Many awards require that recipients be residents of a particular state. Each state of the United States sets its own criteria for what conditions must be met to be considered a "legal" resident. A "permanent resident" of the U.S. is a non-U.S. citizen who has been granted this official status by the U.S. Immigration and Naturalization Service. A "permanent resident" can be considered to be a legal resident of one of the United States if he or she otherwise can meet that specific state's residence criteria.

résumé—a summary account of one's life, education, and experience. Typically this is shorter than a *curriculum vitae,* usually between one and two pages in length. In addition to basic biographical data, it typically covers an individual's education, employment, teaching or research positions, responsibilities, and other relevant information.

SASE—a stamped, self-addressed envelope to be included with inquiry or application material to ensure a response.

SAT—a standardized test, offered by the College Board through the Educational Testing Service, required for admission to many colleges.

scholarship—precisely defined, gift aid to cover tuition and fees for undergraduate study. Usually a scholarship can be applied to tuition and fees, but rarely to room and board. Scholarship programs occasionally cover room and board, but this is rare. However, scholarship is frequently used generically to describe all forms of gift aid, including fellowships and grants. You will need to read the full description of a scholarship award program in order to ascertain to what level of study it may apply.

school—a general term used to refer to any institution of secondary or higher education. This includes high schools, colleges, universities, and graduate or professional institutions.

self-help aid—financial aid in the form of loans and student employment. Many college and university financial aid packages automatically include a minimum amount of self-help aid before any gift aid is granted.

semester—a division of a college or university's academic year if the institution divides its year into two terms (semesters).

seminar—an advanced or graduate-level class or course of study on a particular subject in which each student does original research under the guidance of a faculty member.

seminary—a professional school or other institution of higher education for training in religion, usually as preparation for priesthood, ministry, or rabbinate.

senior—a student in the fourth year or with fourth-year standing at a college or secondary school.

sophomore—a student in the second year or with second-year standing at a college or secondary school.

Student Aid Report (SAR)—an official document based on the FAFSA that goes to the Financial Aid Office and describes the amount of any possible Pell Grant funds, and the expected family contribution (EFC). The SAR usually arrives one to two months after the FAFSA is filed. This is the basis for the individual college's student financial aid decisions. It should be reviewed carefully to ensure that there are no errors.

Test of English as a Foreign Language (TOEFL)—test of a student's ability to communicate in and understand English that most colleges and universities require international students to take as part of their application.

transcript—the record of one's academic work. Many award programs will require the submission of an official copy, translated into English, of your secondary school transcript.

trimester—a division of a college or university's academic year if the institution divides its year into three terms (trimesters).

tuition—fees that pay for instruction in an academic institution. Other expenses, such as those for room and board (lodging and meals), health insurance, activities, and transportation, are not included in tuition figures.

two-year institution—a postsecondary institution at which the associate degree is the highest credential awarded. A typical course of study is two years. Credits earned at an accredited two-year institution generally will be transferable for study at a four-year college or university.

undergraduate—an associate or bachelor's degree candidate or a description of such candidate's courses. Once students have earned a bachelor's degree, they are eligible for entry to graduate programs at the master's and doctoral levels.

university—a large educational institution comprising a number of divisions, including graduate and professional schools. Academic offerings are usually more comprehensive than at colleges. A few universities have no professional schools or offer no doctoral programs.

veteran—a former member of the U.S. armed forces. Awards to veterans usually require active service duty in one of the U.S. armed service branches (Army, Air Force, Coast Guard, Navy, Marines) and an honorable discharge.

vocational-technical schools—institutions of postsecondary education that offer certificates or diplomas requiring fewer than two years of study. Programs of study usually are directly related to preparation for specific careers.

Indexes

Note: The number reference found in the Indexes is the sequence number of the award, not the number of the page on which it is found.

AWARD NAME INDEX

SPONSOR INDEX

Sponsor Index

Family, Career and Community Leaders of America-Texas Association • 115
Finance Authority of Maine • 310
Financial Service Centers of America, Inc. • 463
First Catholic Slovak Ladies Association • 251
Florida Association of Postsecondary Schools and Colleges • 404
Florida Department of Education • 81, 249, 252, 322, 323
Florida Department of Health • 136
Florida Leader Magazine/College Student of the Year, Inc. • 328
Florida Police Corps • 452
Fond Du Lac Reservation • 245
Foundation of the National Student Nurses' Association • 128
Fraternal Order of Eagles • 162
Freedom Forum • 116
General Board of Global Ministries • 268
Georgia Student Finance Commission • 75, 324, 336, 337, 338, 400
Gina Bachauer International Piano Foundation • 138
Golden Apple Foundation • 78
Golden Key International Honour Society • 148
Grand Lodge of Iowa, AF and AM • 372
Greater Bridgeport Area Foundation • 395
Greater Kanawha Valley Foundation • 121, 285
Guardian Life Insurance Company of America • 459
GUIDEPOSTS Magazine • 453
Health Professions Education Foundation • 60, 105, 108, 123, 125, 126, 127
Hebrew Immigrant Aid Society • 149
Hellenic Times Scholarship Fund • 218
Henry Sachs Foundation • 244
Herbert Hoover Presidential Library Association • 401
Herschel C. Price Educational Foundation • 484
Hispanic College Fund, Inc. • 5, 9, 10, 17, 39
Hispanic Engineer National Achievement Awards Corporation (HENAAC) • 27
Hispanic Heritage Foundation Awards • 230, 235, 236, 237, 238, 246
Hispanic Scholarship Fund • 45, 259
Hopi Tribe • 221, 223, 224
Horatio Alger Association of Distinguished Americans • 491
Hugh Fulton Byas Memorial Funds, Inc. • 114
Humana Foundation • 165
Idaho State Board of Education • 291, 292, 293
Illinois Restaurant Association Educational Foundation • 98
Illinois Student Assistance Commission (ISAC) • 83, 87, 184, 197, 209, 332, 334, 349, 350, 352, 358, 359
Independent Colleges of Washington • 397
Indian Health Services, United States Department of Health and Human Services • 266
Institute of Food Technologists • 94
Institute of International Education • 499
International Association of Culinary Professionals Foundation (IACPF) • 95
International Association of Fire Chiefs Foundation • 450
International Facility Management Association Foundation • 23
International Society for Optical Engineering-SPIE • 16
Internationaler Musikwettbewerb • 119
Iowa College Student Aid Commission • 388, 407
Iowa Division of Vocational Rehabilitation Services • 189
Italian Catholic Federation, Inc. • 274
J. Wood Platt Caddie Scholarship Trust • 185
J.D. Archbold Memorial Hospital • 112

Pueblo of Isleta, Department of Education • 240
Puerto Rico Department of Education • 469
R.O.S.E. Fund • 282
Red River Valley Association, Inc. • 210
Rhode Island Higher Education Assistance Authority • 312, 402
Roothbert Fund, Inc. • 468
Rotary Foundation of Rotary International • 100, 434, 438
SACHS Foundation • 255
Salvadoran American Leadership and Educational Fund • 239
San Antonio International Piano Competition • 424
Science Service, Inc. • 423, 441
Seabee Memorial Scholarship Association, Inc. • 212
ShopKo Stores, Inc. • 277
Sid Richardson Memorial Fund • 179
Sociedad Honoraria Hispánica • 101
Society for Advancement of Chicanos and Native Americans in Science
    (SACNAS) • 233
Society of Physics Students • 141
Society of Plastics Engineers (SPE) Foundation • 46
Sons of Italy Foundation • 256
South Carolina Department of Education • 421
South Carolina Police Corps • 118
South Carolina Student Loan Corporation • 82
South Carolina Tuition Grants Commission • 297
South Dakota Department of Education and Cultural Affairs • 308
Southern Scholarship Foundation, Inc. • 415
State Council of Higher Education for Virginia • 304
State of Georgia • 61, 135, 147, 193
State of North Dakota • 254, 373
State of Utah • 77
State Student Assistance Commission of Indiana (SSACI) • 71, 131, 195, 315,
    316, 317, 331, 335, 383
Stephen Phillips Memorial Scholarship Fund • 462
Submarine Officers' Wives Club • 181
Sunshine Lady Foundation, Inc. • 446
Swiss Benevolent Society of New York • 247
Talbots Charitable Foundation • 473
Tau Beta Pi Association • 91
Tennessee Student Assistance Corporation • 74, 79, 286, 295, 318
Terry Fox Humanitarian Award Program • 216
Texas 4-H Youth Development Foundation • 399
Texas Department of Transportation • 53
Texas Higher Education Coordinating Board • 177
Third Wave Foundation • 475
Thurgood Marshall Scholarship Fund • 493
Triangle Community Foundation • 390
Trimmer Education Foundation • 55
Tuition Exchange, Inc. • 178
Two/Ten International Footwear Foundation • 173
Union Plus Scholarship Program • 157
United Federation of Teachers • 346
United Methodist Church • 142, 231, 257
United Negro College Fund • 32, 38, 40
United States Department of Health and Human Services • 35
United States Environmental Protection Agency • 120
United States Junior Chamber of Commerce • 496

ACADEMIC/CAREER AREAS INDEX

National Association of Minority Engineering Program Administrators National Scholarship Fund • 29
National Hispanic Explorers Scholarship Program • 17
Society of Plastics Engineers Scholarship Program • 46
SPIE Educational Scholarships in Optical Science and Engineering • 16
University and Community College System of Nevada NASA Space Grant and Fellowship Program • 28

Civil Engineering

AeA Technology Scholarship Program • 52
AGC Education and Research Foundation Undergraduate Scholarships • 56
Barry M. Goldwater Scholarship and Excellence in Education Program • 14
Conditional Grant Program • 53
Hispanic Engineer National Achievement Awards Corporation Scholarship Program • 27
HSF/General Motors Scholarship • 45
Kentucky Transportation Cabinet Civil Engineering Scholarship Program • 54
National Association of Minority Engineering Program Administrators National Scholarship Fund • 29
National Hispanic Explorers Scholarship Program • 17
NAWIC Undergraduate Scholarships • 19
Society of Plastics Engineers Scholarship Program • 46
Trimmer Scholarships • 55

Communications

College Fund/Coca Cola Corporate Intern Program • 40
Denny's/Hispanic College Fund Scholarship • 5
First in My Family Scholarship Program • 10
Hispanic College Fund Scholarship Program • 9
Hispanic College Fund/INROADS/Sprint Scholarship Program • 39
John Bayliss Broadcast Radio Scholarship • 57
Mas Family Scholarships • 37
National Hispanic Explorers Scholarship Program • 17

Computer Science/Data Processing

AeA Technology Scholarship Program • 52
Astronaut Scholarship Foundation • 18
Barry M. Goldwater Scholarship and Excellence in Education Program • 14
BPW Career Advancement Scholarship Program for Women • 33
College Fund/Coca Cola Corporate Intern Program • 40
Conditional Grant Program • 53
Denny's/Hispanic College Fund Scholarship • 5
Eaton Corporation Multicultural Scholars Program • 59
First in My Family Scholarship Program • 10
Hispanic College Fund Scholarship Program • 9
Hispanic College Fund/INROADS/Sprint Scholarship Program • 39
Hispanic Engineer National Achievement Awards Corporation Scholarship Program • 27
Household International Corporate Scholars • 38
Lucent Global Science Scholars Program • 15
Maryland Association of Private Career Schools Scholarship • 49
Math, Engineering, Science, Business, Education, Computers Scholarships • 43
Micron Science and Technology Scholars • 51
National Association of Minority Engineering Program Administrators National Scholarship Fund • 29
National Hispanic Explorers Scholarship Program • 17
University and Community College System of Nevada NASA Space Grant and Fellowship Program • 28

Electrical Engineering/Electronics

Engineering-Related Technologies

Engineering/Technology

Fashion Design

Filmmaking

Fire Sciences

Food Science/Nutrition

Food Service/Hospitality

Meteorology/Atmospheric Science

Music

Natural Resources

Natural Sciences

Nuclear Science

Nursing

Math, Engineering, Science, Business, Education, Computers Scholarships • 43

Social Services
Developmental Disabilities and Mental Health Workforce Tuition Assistance Program • 107
Graduate and Professional Scholarship Program-Maryland • 62
Janet L. Hoffmann Loan Assistance Repayment Program • 76
Kaiser Permanente Allied Healthcare Scholarship • 108
Ordean Loan Program • 2

Special Education
Developmental Disabilities and Mental Health Workforce Tuition Assistance Program • 107
Emergency Secondary Education Loan Program • 30
Indiana Minority Teacher and Special Education Services Scholarship Program • 71
ITEACH Teacher Shortage Scholarship Program • 87
Kentucky Teacher Scholarship Program • 88
Minority Teachers of Illinois Scholarship Program • 83
Minority Teaching Fellows Program/Tennessee • 74
South Carolina Teacher Loan Program • 82

Sports-related
National Athletic Trainer's Association Research and Education Foundation Scholarship Program • 145

Surveying; Surveying Technology, Cartography, or Geographic Information Science
Budweiser Conservation Scholarship Program • 31

Therapy/Rehabilitation
Alberta Heritage Scholarship Fund Aboriginal Health Careers Bursary • 34
Alice M. and Samuel Yarnold Scholarship • 109
Allied Health Student Loan Program-New Mexico • 63
AMBUCS Scholars-Scholarships for Therapists • 106
Developmental Disabilities and Mental Health Workforce Tuition Assistance Program • 107
Indiana Minority Teacher and Special Education Services Scholarship Program • 71
Janet L. Hoffmann Loan Assistance Repayment Program • 76
Kaiser Permanente Allied Healthcare Scholarship • 108

Trade/Technical Specialties
AGC Education and Research Foundation Undergraduate Scholarships • 56
American Welding Society District Scholarship Program • 90
Firefighter, Ambulance, and Rescue Squad Member Tuition Reimbursement Program-Maryland • 93
Intellectual Capital Partnership Program, ICAPP • 147
Marion D. and Eva S. Peeples Scholarships • 72
Maryland Association of Private Career Schools Scholarship • 49
NAWIC Undergraduate Scholarships • 19
Society of Plastics Engineers Scholarship Program • 46
Vocational Education Scholarship Program-Kansas • 146

TV/Radio Broadcasting
John Bayliss Broadcast Radio Scholarship • 57
Maryland Association of Private Career Schools Scholarship • 49

ASSOCIATION AFFILIATION INDEX

Other Student Academic Clubs

Young American Bowling Alliance

CORPORATE AFFILIATION INDEX

EMPLOYMENT EXPERIENCE INDEX

Employment Experience Index

U.S. government foreign service
American Foreign Service Association (AFSA) Financial Aid Award Program
  • 156

IMPAIRMENT INDEX

MILITARY SERVICE INDEX

Air Force
General Henry H. Arnold Education Grant Program • 191

Air Force National Guard
General Henry H. Arnold Education Grant Program • 191
Georgia National Guard Service Cancelable Loan Program • 193
Illinois National Guard Grant Program • 197
Indiana National Guard Supplemental Grant • 195
Kansas National Guard Educational Assistance Award Program • 194
Ohio National Guard Scholarship Program • 196
Washington National Guard Scholarship Program • 192
Wisconsin National Guard Tuition Grant • 198

Army
Army ROTC Historically Black Colleges and Universities Program • 201
Army ROTC Two-Year, Three-Year and Four-Year Scholarships for Active Duty
    Army Enlisted Personnel • 202
Four-Year and Three-Year Advance Designees Scholarship • 200
Two- and Three-Year Campus-Based Scholarships • 199

Army National Guard
Army ROTC Historically Black Colleges and Universities Program • 201
Army ROTC Two-Year, Three-Year and Four-Year Scholarships for Active Duty
    Army Enlisted Personnel • 202
Dedicated Military Junior College Program • 203
Four-Year and Three-Year Advance Designees Scholarship • 200
Georgia National Guard Service Cancelable Loan Program • 193
Illinois National Guard Grant Program • 197
Indiana National Guard Supplemental Grant • 195
Kansas National Guard Educational Assistance Award Program • 194
Ohio National Guard Scholarship Program • 196
Two- and Three-Year Campus-Based Scholarships • 199
Two-Year Reserve Forces Duty Scholarships • 204
Washington National Guard Scholarship Program • 192
Wisconsin National Guard Tuition Grant • 198

General
American Legion Department of Alabama Scholarship Program • 205
Explosive Ordnance Disposal Scholarship • 176
Illinois Veteran Grant Program—IVG • 209
MOAA Base/Post Scholarship • 208
North Carolina Veterans' Scholarships Class II • 207
North Carolina Veterans' Scholarships Class III • 206
Red River Valley Association Scholarship Grant Program • 210

Marine Corp
Marine Corps Scholarship Foundation • 211

Navy
Bowfin Memorial Scholarship • 181
Dolphin Scholarships • 213
Seabee Memorial Association Scholarship • 212

NATIONALITY OR ETHNIC HERITAGE INDEX

Asian/Pacific Islander

Black, non-Hispanic

Canadian

RELIGIOUS AFFILIATION INDEX

Christian
Mary E. Bivins Religious Scholarship • 143

Methodist
Ernest and Eurice Miller Bass Scholarship Fund • 142
National Leadership Development Grants • 268
United Methodist Church Ethnic Scholarship • 231
United Methodist Church Hispanic, Asian, and Native American Scholarship
    • 257

Presbyterian
Appalachian Scholarships • 273
National Presbyterian College Scholarship • 272
Student Opportunity Scholarship-Presbyterian Church (U.S.A.) • 258

Protestant
Ed E. and Gladys Hurley Foundation Scholarship • 144

Roman Catholic
Catholic Aid Association College Tuition Scholarship • 275
First Catholic Slovak Ladies Association Fraternal Scholarship Award for College
    and Graduate Study • 251
Fourth Degree Pro Deo and Pro Patria Scholarships • 160
ICF College Scholarships to High School Seniors • 274

STATE OF RESIDENCE INDEX

Colorado
Boettcher Foundation Scholarships • 345
Colorado Leveraging Educational Assistance Partnership (CLEAP) and SLEAP • 329
Colorado Undergraduate Merit Scholarships • 330
Cooperative Studies Scholarships • 11
Governor's Opportunity Scholarship • 283
Henry Sachs Foundation Grants • 244
Micron Science and Technology Scholars • 51
SACHS Foundation Scholarships • 255
ShopKo Scholars Program • 277

Connecticut
Big Y Scholarships • 379
James Z. Naurison Scholarship • 409
NBFAA/Security Dealer Youth Scholarship Program • 174
Pellegrini Scholarship Grants • 247
Regional and Restricted Scholarship Award Program • 276
Scholarship Award Program • 395

Delaware
Christa McAuliffe Teacher Scholarship Loan-Delaware • 65
Delaware Nursing Incentive Scholarship Loan • 134
Diamond State Scholarship • 348
Legislative Essay Scholarship • 363
Long & Foster Scholarship Program • 382
Pellegrini Scholarship Grants • 247
Robert C. Byrd Honors Scholarship-Delaware • 306
Scholarship Incentive Program-Delaware • 301

District of Columbia
DC Leveraging Educational Assistance Partnership • 278
DC Leveraging Educational Assistance Partnership Program (LEAP) • 302
DC Tuition Assistance Grant Program • 406
Long & Foster Scholarship Program • 382

Florida
American Cancer Society, Florida Division College Scholarship Program • 371
Archbold Scholarship Program • 112
Critical Teacher Shortage Tuition Reimbursement-Florida • 81
Florida Association of Postsecondary Schools and Colleges Scholarship Program • 404
Jose Marti Scholarship Challenge Grant • 214
Jose Marti Scholarship Challenge Grant Fund • 252
Mary McLeod Bethune Scholarship • 322
Nursing Scholarship Program • 136
Robert C. Byrd Honors Scholarship Program-Florida • 323
Selby Scholar Program • 368

Georgia
Appalachian Scholarships • 273
Archbold Scholarship Program • 112
Georgia Leveraging Educational Assistance Partnership Grant Program • 400
Georgia National Guard Service Cancelable Loan Program • 193
Georgia Tuition Equalization Grant (GTEG) • 324
Governor's Scholarship-Georgia • 337
HOPE—Helping Outstanding Pupils Educationally • 336
Intellectual Capital Partnership Program, ICAPP • 147

TALENT INDEX

Art
Elizabeth Greenshields Award/Grant • 24
Scholastic Art and Writing Awards-Art Section • 25

Athletics/sports
Jimmie Condon Athletic Scholarships • 270
Travel and Training Fund • 436

Bowling
Pepsi-Cola Youth Bowling Championships • 151

Designated field specified by sponsor
Discovery Channel Young Scientist Challenge • 441
Executive Women International Scholarship Program • 426
Intel Science Talent Search • 423
Lucent Global Science Scholars Program • 15
Print and Graphics Scholarships • 103
United States Senate Youth Program • 442
Washington Crossing Foundation Scholarship • 443

Foreign language
Rotary Foundation Academic-Year Ambassadorial Scholarships • 434
Rotary Multi-Year Ambassadorial Scholarships • 438

French language
Teaching Assistantship in France • 428

Golf
J. Wood Platt Caddie Scholarship Trust • 185
Women's Western Golf Foundation Scholarship • 425

Leadership
American Institute for Foreign Study International Scholarships • 429
American Institute for Foreign Study Minority Scholarships • 267
California Junior Miss Scholarship Program • 376
Coca-Cola Scholars Program • 440
Coca-Cola Two-Year Colleges Scholarship • 433
Florida College Student of the Year Award • 328
Harry A. Applegate Scholarship • 42
Mas Family Scholarships • 37
Micron Science and Technology Scholars • 51
Principal's Leadership Award • 435
Ron Brown Scholar Program • 232
Rotary Foundation Cultural Ambassadorial Scholarship • 100

Music
Chaffer Scholarship Trust • 102
National Solo Competition • 437
William Kapell International Piano Competition and Festival • 140

Music/singing
ASCAP Foundation Morton Gould Young Composer Awards • 137
Gina Bachauer International Artists Piano Competition Award • 138
Liederkranz Foundation Scholarship Award for Voice • 431
San Antonio International Piano Competition • 424
YMF Scholarship Program • 139

548

Portuguese language
Joseph S. Adams Scholarship • 101

Public speaking
American Legion Department of New York State High School Oratorical Contest
• 320
American Legion National Headquarters National High School Oratorical Contest
• 422

Spanish language
Joseph S. Adams Scholarship • 101

Writing
Atlas Shrugged Essay Competition • 439
Ayn Rand Institute College Scholarship Essay Contest Based on Ayn Rand's
Novelette, "Anthem" • 432
Fountainhead College Scholarship Essay Contest • 427
Lee-Jackson Foundation Scholarship • 410
Scholastic Art and Writing Awards-Writing Section Scholarship • 26
Writer's Digest Annual Writing Competition • 430

NOTES

NOTES

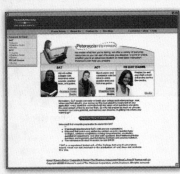